4/16

5

010

D1.

DYNASTY 32

The Fallen Kings

Also in the Dynasty series:

DYNASTY

32

The Fallen Kings

Cynthia Harrod-Eagles

sphere

SPHERE

First published in Great Britain in 2009 by Sphere

Copyright © Cynthia Harrod-Eagles 2009

The moral right of the author has been asserted.

All characters and events in this publication, other than those
clearly in the public domain, are fictitious and any resemblance
to real persons, living or dead, is purely coincidental.

All rights reserved.
No part of this publication may be reproduced,
stored in a retrieval system, or transmitted, in any
form or by any means, without the prior
permission in writing of the publisher, nor be
otherwise circulated in any form of binding or
cover other than that in which it is published and
without a similar condition including this
condition being imposed on the subsequent purchaser.

A CIP catalogue record for this book
is available from the British Library.

ISBN 978-1-84744-115-7

Typeset in Plantin by
Palimpsest Book Production Limited, Grangemouth, Stirlingshire
Printed and bound in Great Britain by Clays Ltd, St Ives plc

Papers used by Sphere are natural, renewable and recyclable
products sourced from well-managed forests and certified
in accordance with the rules of the Forest Stewardship Council.

Mixed Sources
Product group from well-managed
forests and other controlled sources
www.fsc.org Cert no. SGS-COC-004081
© 1996 Forest Stewardship Council
FSC

Sphere
An imprint of
Little, Brown Book Group
100 Victoria Embankment
London EC4Y 0DY

An Hachette UK Company
www.hachette.co.uk

www.littlebrown.co.uk

To the memory of those who fell in the Great War, with gratitude for the freedom they bequeathed us

THE MORLANDS OF MORLAND PLACE

James

Benedict
1812–1870
m. (1) Rosalind
Fleetham

m. (2) Sibella
Mayhew

Lucy

THE LONDON MORLANDS (qv)

George
1849–1885

TEDDY
b. 1850

HENRIETTA
b. 1853
m. (2) Jerome
Compton

m. (1) Edgar
Fortescue

Regina
1857–1907
m. Sir Peregrine
Parke, Bt

BERTIE
b. 1876
m. 1909
Maud
Puddephat

RICHARD
1912–1917

NED
1885–1915
m. 1911
Jessie
Compton

m. (1)
Charlotte Byng

m. (2)
Alice Meynell

POLLY
b. 1900

JAMES
b. 1910

LIZZIE
b. 1872
m. 1897
Ashley
Morland

JACK
b. 1886
m. 1915
Helen
Ormerod

ROBERT
b. 1887
m. 1909
Ethel
Cornleigh

FRANK
1889–1916
m. 1916
Maria
Stanhope

JESSIE
b. 1890
m. 1911
Ned Morland

MARTIAL
b. 1898

RUPERT
b. 1899

ROSE
b. 1909

BASIL
b. 1916

BARBARA
b. 1917

ROBERTA
b. 1911

JEREMY
b. 1912

HARRIET
b. 1915

JOHN
b. 1916

MARTIN
b. 1916

THE LONDON MORLANDS

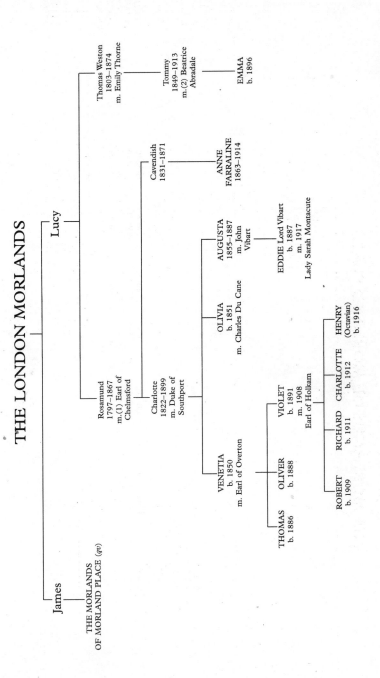

James

Lucy

THE MORLANDS
OF MORLAND PLACE (*qv*)

Rosamund
1797–1867
m.(1) Earl of
Chelmsford

Charlotte
1822–1899
m. Duke of
Southport

Thomas Weston
1803–1874
m. Emily Thorne

Tommy
1849–1913
m.(2) Beatrice
Abradale

EMMA
b. 1896

Cavendish
1831–1871

ANNE
FARRALINE
1863–1914

VENETIA
b. 1850
m. Earl of Overton

OLIVIA
b. 1851
m. Charles Du Cane

AUGUSTA
1855–1887
m. John
Vibart

EDDIE Lord Vibart
b. 1887
m. 1917
Lady Sarah Montacute

THOMAS
b. 1886

OLIVER
b. 1888

VIOLET
b. 1891
m. 1908
Earl of Holkam

ROBERT
b. 1909

RICHARD
b. 1911

CHARLOTTE
b. 1912

HENRY
(Octavian)
b. 1916

THE LAST PHASE · July to November 1918

0   Miles   50

BOOK ONE

Journeys

Across the miles between us
I send you sigh for sigh.
Good-night, sweet friend, good-night:
Till life and all take flight,
Never good-bye.

A Wink from Hesper, W. E. Henley

CHAPTER ONE

January 1918

It had been grindingly cold all day, and now in the afternoon a fine snow had begun to fall. It gathered on the shoulders of the King's greatcoat and the crown of his uniform cap as he came along the line, his breath clouding as he spoke a few words to each man. Coming face to face with him, Bertie could see specks of snow glistening in the royal beard, and thought of the jewels worn in the beards of certain tribal leaders he had known in his Indian days. But the tip of the royal nose was unromantically crimson, and the small blue eyes were watering. Hazebrouck was not where anyone would have much wanted to be that day.

The aide at the King's shoulder murmured Bertie's name and handed him the medal. The King slipped it onto the hook ready in Bertie's lapel, offered a leather-gloved hand and said, 'Good show. Jolly good show.'

The handshaking went on rather longer than was natural, for the King kept glancing sideways at the official cinematographer, bobbing about adjusting his focus, to see if he had finished with the 'shot' – as they were all learning to call it in these publicity-conscious days. The man finally straightened up and said, 'Thank you, sir,' and the King let go of Bertie's hand with an appearance of relief. Then, seeming to feel he had been ungracious, he smiled at Bertie and said again, but with emphasis this time, '*Jolly* good show,' before hurrying indoors with his suite behind him.

The room in the town hall, prepared for the reception, was rather shabby, but at least it was warm, with a big wood fire under the vast marble fireplace. A couple of oil stoves, placed unobtrusively in corners, were adding their distinctive smell to the principal odour of wet wool and cigarettes. Bertie was glad to note there were refreshments: a heartening profusion of sandwiches, and coffee, which, though weak, was made from real coffee beans and not the mysterious *ersatz* they had been consuming in the trenches (rumour said it was made from ground roasted acorns). The King was at once surrounded by various dignitaries, civilian and military, and Bertie hurried to secure some of the bounty before the official mingling should begin. If the war had taught him nothing else, it was to grab food when you had the chance.

The other guests – a mixture of men from the two services, who had all come to receive their decorations and be photographed for the public benefit – had had the same idea, and there was a certain amount of grimly polite jostling at the buffet tables, and a potentially embarrassing emptying of the rest of the room. Bertie found himself elbow to elbow with an airman, a short, fair, jolly-looking youngster, who grinned at him and said, 'Haven't been in a scrum like this since Winchester. But you don't see sandwiches like this every day. My God!' His tone became reverent. 'Is that real ham? I don't think I've had anything but bully in a sandwich since I got in.'

'Grab me one while you're at it,' Bertie urged. The ham sandwiches were just beyond his reach.

The airman slapped a couple onto Bertie's plate and yielded his place to the hungry behind him. Backing into an open space, the young man found himself more or less at eye level with Bertie's new decoration, the rather modest-looking bronze cross on its claret ribbon, which lay next to the prettier white enamel cross of the DSO on Bertie's chest. He raised his eyes and said reverently, 'The VC? My God, you're Major Parke!

I've heard all about your stunt, sir – taking a trench from the Hun single-handed. *Jolly* good show! It's an honour to meet you, sir.'

Bertie found his hand being shaken with a vigour that made him feel rather old and tired. 'You've done pretty well yourself,' he said, nodding towards the youngster's Military Cross.

The lad looked down at it with enormous, almost astonished pride, but said in the accustomed throwaway manner, 'Oh, it's nothing, really. They have to give 'em to someone, y'know.' He grinned up at Bertie. 'The chaps in my squadron say I got it for flying with my tongue stuck out. I do that when I'm concentrating – ever since school days.' He demonstrated the frown of purpose with the tip of the tongue just protruding. 'They say it's bloody brave of me because I'm bound to bite it off one day.'

Some others who had managed to load their plates drifted up and there was an interval of pleasant, professional chat between the munching, before the approach of the royal party broke it up. A steward nipped in and relieved Bertie of his crockery just as the King reached him, ungloved and coatless now, and with Bertie's CO, Colonel Scott-Walter (the men called him Hot Water), among the figures at his elbow.

'This is something more like, eh, what?' the King said genially. 'Damned cold out there. Sorry about that palaver outside, but the publicity wallahs say the public like to see medals being given out of doors. Reminds 'em what it's all about.'

'Quite, sir,' Bertie said, since some response seemed to be required of him.

The King looked at him quizzically. 'Hard to sound sincere when you know there's a camera pointed at you. So I just want to say again, *jolly* good show! The Queen and I read about what you did, and we're full of admiration. Absolutely splendid – best traditions, and so forth. You're an example to us all.'

'Thank you, sir,' Bertie managed to say, while longing for decent obscurity or, failing that, a sack to put over his head. His natural modesty was whimpering in the pit of his stomach.

The King extended his hand again, and Bertie shook it – small, dry and surprisingly hard, it was – and bowed.

'Congratulations, Colonel,' said the King.

Bertie straightened, feeling the crosses on his breast thump back into place. A significant nod and slight cough from Scott-Walter warned him that it had not simply been a lapse of memory on the King's part.

'Sir?' Bertie said.

The King was smiling through his beard, his eyes twinkling as he enjoyed Bertie's moment of surprise, but it was Scott-Walter who elucidated. 'You've been promoted to lieutenant-colonel, Parke.'

'And not a moment too soon, from what I hear,' the King interjected.

'You're to take over the battalion,' Scott-Walter went on. 'I'm going up to Brigade.'

'The poor man's bewildered,' the King said, chuckling.

Bertie found his tongue at last. 'Thank you, sir.'

'Don't thank me,' the King said. 'There are tough times ahead, and we need the best men for the job. Sir Douglas said to me that he wished he had a hundred of you. They're going to put that in the newspaper report.'

Praise from Haig, from the C-in-C himself? Embarrassment could go no further. It was fortunate that the party moved on just then, leaving Bertie with Scott-Walter and a red face.

'Don't look like that,' Scott-Walter said. 'It's good for the regiment, this sort of thing. And for the battalion's morale. The men are exhausted, but stunts like this keep their spirits up, however much you may dislike it.'

'I'm not cut out to be anyone's hero,' Bertie said. He felt a fraud, because the mad dash under fire that had brought him this distinction had been carried out in the conviction that he would not survive, so he had felt no fear – and in his book, if you felt no fear you could not, by definition, be said to have displayed courage. Courage was being afraid and *still* doing whatever it was, as he had seen his men do over and over. They were the brave ones.

'Well, we're all proud of you,' said Scott-Walter, 'so you'll just have to find a way to live with it.'

Bertie smiled at that. 'But congratulations to you, sir, on getting the brigade.'

'Buggins's turn,' Scott-Walter said, with a shrug. 'Pat Cordwainer's gone up to Corps to replace Darcy, and I'm next in line.'

Now he was a colonel, Bertie noted, these high-ranking officers had become unadorned surnames in conversation. 'What's happened to General Darcy?' he asked.

'Gone back to Blighty. Heart condition.'

'So everyone moves up one seat?'

'Not in your case,' Scott-Walter said sharply. 'Your promotion is more than deserved – and long overdue. If you hadn't insisted on keeping a company command, you'd have been a colonel long before now. But you can't play with the soldiers any more, Parke. We need good men at the top – good *soldiers*, what's more. We've lost all too many of 'em.'

'I know,' Bertie said bleakly. His dearest friend Fenniman, with whom he had served since the war began, had been killed last year.

Scott-Walter laid a hand on his shoulder. 'We all miss Fen. He was a damned fine soldier – and a good egg. He kept us all in spirits at Battalion HQ.'

The last words he had written to Bertie had been a joke. It seemed that with Fenniman's death, laughter had gone out of his life – and it was laughter that had always enabled them to get through the war, with all its ghastliness.

Conversation ceased as the King took his departure, and when he was gone, there was a general movement towards reclaiming caps and greatcoats and getting back to units – except for a small hard core of cheerful younger officers who felt unable to abandon the buffet tables while there was anything left on them. Bertie and Scott-Walter walked out together to wait their turn in the porch until the CO's car arrived. Dusk had come and the weather had closed in while they were inside: the snow was falling thickly now.

Scott-Walter sniffed. 'Smells a bit warmer to me. What do you think?'

'The wind's gone round,' Bertie confirmed. 'But this snow looks like settling in.'

'It's lying, too. There'll be six inches by tomorrow if it keeps up.'

They were glad to get into the car, and Scott-Walter was not too much of a warrior to scorn a rug over their knees.

'So what next, sir?' Bertie asked.

'For you, a spot of leave,' the CO said. 'Comes with the decoration. You can go straight off tonight if you like. I'm staying with the battalion for a couple of weeks more, just to tidy up some things, so you're not needed.'

'Thank you, sir,' Bertie said. 'And when I come back, what then?'

'It'll be retraining for the battalion – the reinforcements should have arrived by then so they'll need bedding in.'

'Do you know how many we're getting?'

'Not the foggiest. Not enough, I'd be willing to bet. Why in God's name we keep six hundred thousand trained men in England instead of having them sent here I can't imagine. The last I heard, the prime minister agreed on ninety thousand being sent out for the entire BEF.'

'But—' Bertie protested. It was a ridiculously small number, far less than was needed.

'I know, I know. I'll fight for our fair share, you can depend on that, but how we're supposed to do the job if we're starved of men . . .' He shrugged. 'One good thing – I'm told we're getting a fresh batch of Pioneers out. Mostly coolies, I understand, but who cares as long as they know how to dig a hole?'

'We're going to be doing a lot of digging, then, I take it?'

It was well known all through the army, though it hadn't been officially announced yet, that the government had agreed to take over another section of the line from the French. Their defences were always badly maintained, and taking over from them meant a great deal of hard work to bring them up to scratch. But more seriously, without adequate reinforcements from home, it meant more of the line would be held by the same number of men, thinning out the army and weakening the cover.

Scott-Walter offered cigarettes – 'Turkish. The memsahib sent them out. God knows where she found 'em. A bit stale, but it makes a change from gaspers' – and they both lit up. 'It's going to be a different sort of war for the next few months,' he continued. 'We know the Germans are going to attack. They've got all the extra men coming down from the Eastern Front, now the Russkies have collapsed, and they're going to want to make a big push before the Americans come in. *We're* not in a position to attack *them*. But if three years of trench war have taught us anything, it's that it's easier to defend than attack, so the idea is to hold on and let 'em wear 'emselves out. Then, when the Yanks are ready, we counter-attack and roll 'em up.' He took a deep draw on his cigarette. 'That's the theory, anyway.'

There were plenty of things wrong with it, but such matters were not in the hands of lowly colonels. 'Do we know when Fritz is coming?'

'Haig says March, around the fifteenth. The French think the Boche'll move earlier. But they can hardly start anything before March, given the weather and the state of the ground. And the Americans won't be ready until May or June. Which reminds me – when you get back, after battalion training there'll be brigade training. We're going to have a battalion of Doughboys brigaded with us, to give them experience.

The officers particularly.' He shook his head and sighed. 'If only Pershing had agreed to let us use his men as re-inforcements, we could have given the Boche a damn good hiding last year. As it is, Gerry's been let off the hook.'

Bertie nodded. It had been a grave disappointment to everyone that the Americans had insisted they would only fight as a discrete army, under their own officers. You could train a civilian to be an adequate soldier in a matter of months – and the American volunteers were strong, healthy and hugely enthusiastic – but to train an officer took much, much longer. The first Doughboys could have been in the line last summer if they had been seeded around the Allied units. The deter-mination to keep themselves separate came from the top, from the President and the Commander-in-Chief. Many young Americans, eager for the fray, had sidestepped the whole issue by enlisting in the Canadian Army, and many more had become airmen and were serving with the RFC and RNAS.

'If we're going to hold to a defensive role for the next few months,' Bertie said, 'I take it a lot of the training will be in defensive techniques?'

Scott-Walter tapped the ash precisely off his cigarette into the ashtray. 'You've put your finger on the flaw, of course. In three years of trench war we've always been the aggres-sors. It will be a whole new trick to learn – and we won't have very long to learn it. But you can put all that out of your head for now. You've got two weeks of leave ahead of you, and you might as well enjoy it. God knows when you'll get away again. Any idea what you'll do?'

Scott-Walter had heard some rumour that Parke had had trouble at home, though naturally he would not wish to pry into that. Parke's little boy – only son, he believed – had been killed in an air-raid last year, shocking thing; and hadn't there been something about the madam doing a bolt after-wards? Probably awful rubbish – these rumours usually were – but there might be something in it. It was a fact that Parke had not seemed quite so merry and bright lately.

'Oh, I'll go home,' Bertie said vaguely. 'See to a few things.'

Scott-Walter nodded, and looked out of the window at the lowering sky and whirling snow. 'Pity about the weather. Not much hope of enjoying yourself out of doors. Trouble with the army – they always want you to be fighting when the weather's good. I haven't had a club in my hand since – oh, must have been the autumn of 'fifteen. Play golf at all?'

'No, sir,' said Bertie. 'The closest I ever got to it was polo.'

And suddenly he had a vision, like a lightning flash in the mind, of his old place in India, up in the north, with the Himalayas an eternal backdrop; of the dazzlingly clear air and the crystal sunshine, which made the blue of the sky and the green of the foliage seem almost unnaturally intense. He remembered his bungalow, and the rough little curly-tailed dog that had adopted him, and how it used to hunt crickets in the grass, and lie at his feet on the verandah of an evening when the servant brought his sundowner. He remembered the polo ground in Darjeeling, the *thwock* of mallet on ball, the lithe, muscular body of the pony beneath him twisting after it, and the polite clapping of the shantung-clad ladies in the shade of the members' pavilion. For a moment his mind stood bewildered by the contrast with the scene beyond the car window. How in God's name had he got from there to here?

Scott-Walter had been talking, and now stopped as he realised Bertie wasn't with him. 'I say, you look as though you've seen a ghost,' he said mildly. 'What were you thinking about?'

Bertie turned to him with an effort. 'Oh, just life in general.'

'Tricky chap, Life,' said Scott-Walter, wisely. 'Just when you think you've got a grip on him, you find yourself flat on your face with a bloody nose.'

★　★　★

11

Bertie's wife Maud had bloodied his nose pretty effectively last year when, after their son had been killed by a Gotha air-raid, she had told him she blamed him for the boy's death, and went away to live with relatives in Ireland. Even then he had supposed she would come back eventually, perhaps when the war was over, but a few months later she had written to say that she wanted to marry someone else, and asked him for a divorce.

It was hard to accept that the man she now preferred to him was John Manvers, a fellow horse-breeder he had known in India, a business colleague of her father. Bertie had liked and trusted Manvers so much he had felt glad that he would be 'keeping an eye on' Maud while he, Bertie, was away at the Front. He had been pleased, when Maud went to Ireland, to know that Manvers, who had recently quit India and bought an estate in County Wicklow, would be on hand if she needed help or comfort. Well, comfort it seemed Manvers had offered. Now Maud wanted Bertie to do the decent thing and allow her to divorce him; and he supposed he would have to go along with it. Nothing was to be gained by trying to keep an unwilling wife, and certainly no gentleman could be so ungallant as to divorce his wife, no matter how culpable she was.

But he discovered that what he really wanted to know was how culpable Maud had actually been and, even more than that, *why* it was she preferred Manvers. And why Manvers, whom he had always thought one of those happily donnish individuals content to live their lives without womenfolk, had succumbed to Maud and to no-one else. So it seemed, now he had his leave, that to Ireland he would have to go, inclement weather and wartime railways notwithstanding.

The journey was tedious, the trains dirty, the Irish Sea inhospitable. Bertie felt himself cut off as much from the indomitably cheerful soldiers all around him, who were going home on leave, as from the civilians – mostly poor-looking and either elderly or accompanying young children – whose purposes he could not guess. But at least as he travelled westwards it grew warmer, and Ireland was snow-free. It was as he remembered it, intensely green but very wet, and with a particularly Irish wind that seemed to be able to drive the cold rain into your face whichever way you were facing. In Dublin he was overtaken by the longing for a large fire, a hot bath and a comforting dinner, and he abandoned the last part of the journey. Cold and weary, he took refuge for the night in the club that was affiliated with his own in London, and excused himself from ploughing on to Wicklow by sending a couple of telegrams announcing his intention of visiting on the morrow.

The club dining-room was crowded, and the waitress asked him if he would share his table with another member, a request he was not churlish enough to refuse; but his involuntary companion turned out to be a very pleasant artillery officer on his way home to Clonmel. They got on so well over dinner that they ended by repairing to the drawing-room to drink a couple of large whiskeys and blow a cloud together. They had a very satisfying talk that started, inevitably, with the situation in France, passed via field guns to field sports, and settled at last on horses, where it kept them happily occupied until the witching hour. Major Callan also very usefully knew of a place where Bertie could hire a motor-car, which would make the journey to Rathdrum much less of a trial. They parted with hearty handshakes and the usual promise to look each other up after the war, and Bertie went to bed feeling much warmer in all senses, and better primed to face the next day.

The Carnews, Maud's cousins, lived on the outskirts of the village in a large, modern house with all the appurtenances of middle-class comfort: stone gateposts, a gravel sweep, extensive shrubberies, and a large glass conservatory on what would be the sunny side of the house if it ever stopped raining. At the back there was a tennis lawn, stables, and a coach house converted to a garage. The Carnews were a cheerful, hospitable family. Carnew *père* – by name Harold – was a shipping agent with an office in Wicklow. There were two energetic, tennis-playing daughters of marriageable age, another of around twelve who lived for horses, and a boy of eight, as well as a grown son, the subject of great pride, who had just joined the army and was hoping for a transfer to the RFC when he had finished his basic training.

Into this ménage Maud had inserted herself without difficulty: she had stayed with them before, and Bertie knew they would have been brimming with practical sympathy over the loss of her son. What he didn't know was what his reception would be – whether Maud had told them that Richard's death was his fault (which it wasn't) or that she wanted a divorce; and if she had told them the latter, whether she would have portrayed *that* as his fault as well.

But the door was opened to him by the bouncing seventeen-year-old (Jean? No, Joyce), who beamed and shook his hand and used it to pull him eagerly into the house. 'Come in, come on in! You're lovely and early, Cousin Bertie. We didn't think you'd manage to get here before luncheon, what with the trains the way they are. Ma! He's here! But is that your motor? No wonder you're early, then. Is it yours? It's not an army car. Did you drive yourself?'

A servant arrived in the hall, belatedly and indignant – 'Don't be opening the door like that, Miss Joyce, before I've the chance to get there. Haven't I told you before? What will people think of us?' – followed by Carnew *mère*, a plump, smiling, bespectacled little woman, who grasped Bertie's hand, just released by her daughter, and cried, 'Bertie, *there* you are!' as if she'd been looking for him everywhere.

'Hello, Annie.. How are you?' Bertie said, kissing the offered cheek. Obviously Maud had not said anything to make him unwelcome, which was a relief.

'He came in a *motor*,' Joyce informed her. 'That's how he got here so quick.'

'We asked the station master at Wicklow to let us know when you got in, and put you in a taxi,' Annie explained. 'We'd have sent our motor for you, but Harold has it and he's over to Waterford today, and there's not another thing in the village, if you believe me, what with the war and everything.'

'Everything got requisitioned,' Joyce said. 'I'll ring Mr Hook, Ma, and tell him he can stop looking out.' And she bounced away.

Annie, who had been helping Bertie out of his coat, handed it to the servant and said, 'But where's your bag? Is it in the motor?'

'I'm afraid I can't stay,' Bertie said.

'What – all this way, and not stay?' Annie cried, in great consternation. 'Not even one night?'

'I have to get back,' Bertie said, apologetically but firmly. If he stayed, they would expect him to share Maud's room.

'Oh, it's a shame. Maud will be so disappointed. This wretched war! Well, if it has to be . . . Mary, tell Cook that he's here for luncheon after all, and to have it ready as soon as possible.'

'I know, I know,' the maid grumbled, brushing the rain off Bertie's coat with irritable movements, 'and I suppose you'll want the sherry sent in right away? Anyone'd think I have five pairs of hands.'

She went away, and Annie, who had started for the sitting-room, turned back and took Bertie's hand again. 'Ah, Bertie, it's good to see you, and I'm as sorry as I can be about your poor little boy. What a terrible, wicked thing! Those Germans ought to be made to pay for what they've done.'

'How is Maud?' Bertie took the opportunity to ask.

'Poor soul, she's doing as well as can be expected. Indeed, she's remarkably cheerful most of the time – but, then, she always was one to keep her feelings to herself. I think it all came over her last night when your telegram arrived, though – she looked quite shocked and white for a minute. But she'll be glad to see you. Come on in the sitting-room, everyone's there.'

'Everyone' consisted of the nineteen-year-old Margaret, tall, curly-haired and bonny; twelve-year-old Phyllis, with large round glasses and long plaits down to her waist; eight year-old Benedict, who was far too angelic-looking to be other than a holy terror; an elderly half-sister of Harold's known as Aunt Sarah, who lived with them permanently; and a Labrador, a foxhound puppy and two terriers.

And Maud. She stood up as Bertie came in and, through the clamour of greetings, questions and explanations that poured over and around him, she regarded him in still silence, like a rock in a torrent. He had not seen her since May. She looked different – thinner and paler, though that might have been simply the contrast with the robust and rosy cousins, and somehow prettier. She had been a hand-some girl and had grown up into a polished, enamelled kind of beauty, but now he found that it seemed to have soft-ened into a more conventional attractiveness. She was dressing her hair differently, he decided, trying to puzzle it out; and her clothes were less formal. Instead of one of her severely cut, fashionable costumes she was wearing a lavender silk blouse and a dark brown tweed skirt. He had never seen her in simple skirt and blouse before. It was as if she had dressed down for the country, but she never did that – or never had in the past. The looser style suited her. It made him think for some reason of a tight rosebud unfurling its petals into flower.

She met his eyes quizzically, but though she did not smile, he got the impression of happiness from her – or contentment at least.

'Bertie,' she said, and her voice came to him clearly through the babble. 'It's good to see you.'

He stepped across to her, avoiding underfoot dogs,

Benedict and Aunt Sarah's knitting wool, which had rolled off her lap and across the carpet, and when she held out both hands, he took them and stooped to kiss her. He felt her lips tremble against his cheek, and took the opportunity to whisper into her ear, 'I take it you haven't told them anything?'

'Of course not,' she whispered back.

He was glad not to find himself pariah. It made it possible to get through the family gathering, the sherry, and the noisy luncheon that followed before Annie said, with elephantine tact, 'Now, Maud, why don't you take Bertie into the conservatory to look at the orchids?' and prevented any of the children from offering to accompany them. As the dining-room door closed behind them, Bertie heard Phyllis wail, 'But I wanted to show him the stables. I bet he'd rather see horses than those dull old orchids!' and Annie's reply, 'They want to talk privately, for goodness' sake, child! And don't you dare go past the window, either . . .'

Bertie felt like laughing at the mere thought of the glacial Maud living with these warm, impulsive people, but she led the way down the tiled passage to the conservatory calmly, as though this was the way life had always been. The conservatory was warm and smelled of damp moss. There were big ferns and palms in pots, with seats hidden away among them, and bright-coloured tropical plants in the windows. It was rather a pleasant contrast to the drear green and grey outside, while the rain on the glass roof made a steady pattering sound, soothing like running water.

Maud sat down on a wrought-iron bench and invited him by a look to join her.

'I can't get over seeing you with all these people around you,' he said.

'They're dears,' Maud said calmly.

'But rather noisy?'

'It's not usually like this. They're excited because you're here. They love visitors.'

17

'I've told them I'm not staying.'

'Ah.'

'I thought it would be difficult, if you hadn't told them. Why didn't you tell them?'

She blushed. 'How could I have? They'd have been shocked. I couldn't have stayed here if I had, and it's so convenient – Laragh's only a few miles down the road. It would be awkward to have to move just now.'

'Yes, I can see that,' Bertie said, but without sympathy. She was, in effect, duping these kind people so as to take advantage of their hospitality. 'Do they know Manvers at all?' he asked.

'They've met him several times. The whole neighbour-hood's talking about how he's going to restore Laragh Castle and the estate.'

'But do they know you know him?'

'Of course they do. I'd talked about him when I was here before, anyway; and he calls on me. He fetches me in his motor to go and see the place and what he's been doing to it.'

'So you've been to his house?'

She blushed again. 'Bertie, I give you my word there's been nothing improper between us. And nor will there be. Why do you think I'*m* here and not at Laragh? I won't go to him until I'm decently married to him.'

'You won't be able to keep it a secret from the Carnews, once the divorce business starts,' he pointed out, wondering at her thought processes.

'I know that. I'll have to tell them some time, and then I'll have to go somewhere else. They won't want me to stay once it all comes out, even if—'

'Even if you tell them *I'm* the guilty party?'

She looked away from him. 'I won't do that. I won't talk about it with anyone.'

But others would, that was for sure, he thought.

She regained her composure and returned her gaze to him,

18

flat and emotionless, though he guessed now that it was a defence on her part. 'We have to talk about the divorce.'

'Go ahead, then,' he said. He pulled out his cigarette case and, with a gesture, asked her permission to smoke.

She made an impatient movement. 'Bertie, I've done my part. I've retained a solicitor in Dublin – this is the name and address.' She handed him a piece of paper from her pocket. 'But you have to do yours. When are you going to get on with it? It's been months now. You aren't holding back because you think I'll change my mind, are you?'

'No, I don't think you'll change your mind,' he said. He blew the smoke up through the fronds of a parlour-palm. 'It's a matter of opportunity. I've been rather busy.'

'Fighting the war, I know,' she said, as though it were an inconvenient hobby of his. 'But you're here *now*, which means you do get away sometimes.'

He raised a hand. 'I'll get on with it, I promise.'

'Soon.'

'As soon as I can. What else?'

'There's the question of money. The allowance you're paying me won't be enough if I have to leave here and set up in a place of my own.'

'I'll arrange with the bank to let you draw whatever you want.'

'That's – very kind of you,' she said. She seemed to have expected him to be difficult on that point. 'And there'll have to be a settlement,' she went on, with a hint of defiance. 'Given the size of my dowry when I came to you, it'll need to be a substantial one.'

'Maud, you can have whatever you want,' he said wearily.

'I only want what's fair,' she protested.

'I'll speak to your solicitor about it.'

'Oh, there's no need. I trust you,' Maud said. 'All that can be agreed later. The important thing is for you to get on with the – you know, the practical business of it.'

Bertie nodded neutrally. 'Anything else?' he asked.

She looked at him a long moment. 'Only to say – I'm sorry.'

'Are you?'

'Sorry that you'll be all alone. And I'm sorry I said what I said – about Richard. It wasn't really your fault. You couldn't have known the bombers would come. Though you should have respected my judgement about what was right for my own child,' she added, with a return of spirit.

It seemed as close to an apology as he was likely to get. 'I'm sorry too,' he said.

'What for?' she asked, with a hint of suspicion.

'For everything,' he said, waving his cigarette to indicate the wide range of his regrets.

She frowned. 'Why will you never be serious?'

He sat up. 'All right, I'll ask you a serious question, if you'll give me a serious answer.'

'What, then?' She eyed him a touch nervously.

'Are you happy? Do you love him?'

'Yes, I'm happy,' she said.

'But do you love him? What is it about him? Why him and not me?'

'You were never there to *be* loved,' she said, and the hint of anger in her voice convinced him he would be hearing the truth. 'After Father died, I was so alone. I don't think you have any idea of how I felt. First my mother died, then my brother. But I had Father, and he was always *there*, advising me, caring for me. Then he was gone and you were at the war and I had no-one. John makes me feel safe. I know he will always look after me.'

Bertie nodded slowly, drawing on his cigarette to avoid having to reply. Yes, he saw it now. It made perfect sense. Manvers had been her father's business associate. He was quite a bit older than Maud, and she wanted someone to take her father's place. For a long time it had been just the two of them, Maud and her father, and they must have grown very close. She had been his hostess and kept house for him, and after she had married Bertie, Richard Puddephat had continued to live with them. He had made a much bigger hole in Maud's life by dying than ever Bertie could by going away to war.

There was nothing left now for Bertie to do but to bow out gracefully and let her have what she wanted. But he hoped it would answer. He still did not understand the other side of it, Manvers's side. He needed to be sure of that before the final act.

He stood up. 'I'll say goodbye, then, Maud,' he said.

She stood too, disconcerted at the suddenness. 'It's no use being angry about it. You asked me for the truth.'

'I'm not angry about it. But I have things to do and very little time to do them in, so I must go now.'

'But *where* are you going?'

'To see Manvers,' he said.

The next evening he was back in London, having had plenty of time on the tedious return journey to reflect on his interviews with his wife and, later, with Lord Manvers. The estate was indeed conveniently nearby, just a few miles along the road from Rathdrum, between Laragh and Glendalough, a lush place with the green background of the Wicklow Mountains in every view. The estate was extensive, though run down, and the castle turned out to be entirely, amusingly bogus. What remained of the original was confined to a few bits of wall that had been incorporated into the 1880s structure: all the turrets, crenellations, pointed windows, ribbed ceilings and other Gothic extravagances were Arthurian fantasies realised in solid Victorian engineering. He wondered whether Maud, who had a weakness for the romantic, knew that, or whether she thought she was to be chatelaine of a real Camelot.

He had found Manvers, forewarned by his telegram, at home. He was living comfortably in the one wing he had so far restored, with modern central heating to augment the log fires in the vast inglenooks, bathrooms installed in the vaulted dressing-rooms, and even electricity, run from a huge generator in the cellar. It was odd to meet this man, whom he had always liked and considered straightforward and businesslike, surrounded by so much decorative bogosity; to see an Irish pallor replacing the Indian tan of his complexion; to find that his firm stance and level gaze had given way to a hesitant and guilty look, like a dog caught with feathers round its mouth.

The interview was much more embarrassing for Manvers than for Bertie, who, having faced Maud, was almost euphoric with relief, and approached his rival with the detached interest of a zoological explorer. He just wanted to know *why*. What he came away with was an impression of bewilderment. Manvers seemed as surprised by the whole thing as Bertie had been. He gallantly defended the position and his beloved, and staunchly held by the marriage plans, while miserably deploring the trouble Bertie would be put to, and evidently feeling it was utterly caddish to expect a man so to denigrate himself in the interests of enabling another man to make off with his wife. His confusion was evident to Bertie; and the closest he could get to an answer to the question of why a man who had never had any need of women before should get himself into these straits was that it was what Maud had wanted. Manvers, he felt, had been dazzled and flattered by her desire for him. He had always been fond of her, as his business friend's pretty daughter; and leaving India had rocked him off balance and left him feeling rather isolated, if not actually lonely. It was enough to make him vulnerable to a determined woman's pursuit – especially as Maud's would have been so subtle and feminine as to make him feel like the hunter rather than the hunted. And now, having given his word to her, he could not get out of it. He was regularly for it, like it or not. So, being at heart a gentleman, he had to make himself like it, because the alternative was insulting to Maud.

Yes, it all made sense; and as Bertie sat out the train journey in the usual wartime spirit of endurance, the principal feeling he brought back with him was sadness for them both. He was sorry for them. He hoped it would work, but he was sure that, if it didn't, neither of them would ever admit it.

It wasn't until the train reached the grimy outskirts of London, made grimmer by a heavy sky, yellow-grey like an old bruise, and the usual pall of smoke, that he began to feel a little sorry for *himself*. He went to his club, and could not help remembering as he pushed in through the revolving door how often he had done that with Fenniman close behind him and a cheery evening for the two of them in prospect. But West, the senior porter, was at the porter's desk, and greeted him with a broad smile and a 'Good evening, Colonel!' – proving yet again that, by some mysterious alchemy, club servants always knew everything.

He shed his coat and bag, engaged a room, spoke for a table for dinner, and made his way into the bar. There were several members he knew, many of them the usual ancient fossils who never seemed to leave the premises, but also a couple of younger ones, officers home from the Front, whiling away the hour before dinner. So he was able to enjoy a couple of stiff whiskies along with some male and soldierly conversation, which restored the balance of his mind. Someone else came in and joined them, bringing an evening newspaper in which there was a photograph of Bertie receiving his VC from the King, together with a report of his exploit and Haig's flattering opinion, which caused much comment and congratulation and a fresh round of drinks.

The newspaper did not mention his promotion, which reminded him again of West. The commonplace that club servants knew everything had put a fresh idea into his mind. He excused himself and slipped out for a private word, which, along with the transfer of a couple of half-crowns, elicited the promise that information would be provided as soon as possible, and Bertie went in to dine with his colleagues in an easier frame of mind.

West caught his eye as he was coming out of the dining-room a couple of hours later, and he peeled away from the company to go over to him.

'Just goin' off duty, sir,' West said, 'but I thought you'd like to know toot sweet rather'n wait till tomorrow. Made a couple o' telephone calls, sir, an' I think this is what you'll be wanting.' He slipped a folded piece of paper towards Bertie, concealing it, like a card-sharp, between his fingers. 'Very discreet and respectable, my friend says. They'll see you all right, sir.'

'Thanks, West,' Bertie said, pocketing the paper, and producing another five bob, money well spent. 'This is between you and me, of course. It won't go any further?'

'What won't go any further, sir?' West said with broad innocence, making the coins disappear. 'Well, goodnight, then, sir.'

The next morning Bertie went to the solicitor's address on the square of paper, and found it was an office above a shop in Victoria Street. The door was between an ironmongery and a greengrocer's, and the shabbiness of the entrance rather depressed him. But the office was clean and the furniture, if shabby, was well polished; and the solicitor himself, by the name of Paterson, was not a seedy old wreck or a drunkard, as he had feared, but a youngish man with a brisk air, clear eyes and neatly cropped hair.

'I was given your name by a friend,' Bertie began hesitantly.

'Yes, most people are,' Paterson said, with a sympathetic air. 'Won't you sit down and tell me how I can help you?'

Bertie felt there was nothing for it but to plunge in. 'My wife wants to divorce me,' he said. 'She wants to marry someone else. And I—' Bertie couldn't think how to phrase it.

Paterson offered a cigarette box. 'And you want to do the

gentlemanly thing and oblige her? Yes, I see.' He lit Bertie's cigarette and then his own before continuing. 'Now, I should assure you first of all that client privilege prevents my mentioning anything that passes between us to any other person.'

'Thank you,' said Bertie.

'And, second, I should warn you that for *you* to mention anything that passes between us to anyone else might result in the process I suspect you are interested in being aborted. The King's Proctor does not take kindly to conspiracy. You have a family solicitor, I imagine?' Bertie named them. Paterson nodded. 'Old-fashioned firm. Fatal to mention anything of this to them. What about your wife? Is she represented?'

Bertie told him about the solicitors in Dublin. 'But I don't know them,' he said.

'Nor do I,' said Paterson, 'but that's just as well. Any hint of collusion would ruin our case. Do I take it that you wish to provide your wife with grounds for divorce, and that you wish me to arrange it for you?'

Bertie nodded dumbly. Briskness notwithstanding, he had come to the tawdry part of the business.

Paterson smiled suddenly. 'Don't worry. It can all be done quite discreetly. I have some very good, genteel girls who know just what's expected of them, and several hotels nearby where the servants are accustomed to giving evidence. The area is very well off for small hotels, and I assure you this sort of thing is arranged all the time, so everyone will be very tactful.'

'Thank you.'

'I can set it up for you whenever you like, at twenty-four hours' notice.'

Bertie cleared his throat awkwardly. 'And after that?'

'After that it's rather up to your wife's solicitor. We provide a copy of the hotel servants' evidence, and he serves us with the process.'

25

'And how long does it all take?'

'It depends whether it comes on this term. If the other solicitor works quickly and we can get in before the recess, with luck it will all be over by July.'

'Six months?' he said.

'Is the timing important?'

'Not particularly,' Bertie said. 'I shall be going back to the Front in a few days.' He hesitated. 'It had occurred to me that the action there might solve my wife's problem for her without the need for divorce.'

Paterson seemed to find this assessment chilling. 'Oh – dear me! I'm sure—' He cleared his throat and rearranged some papers on his desk. 'Would you like me to go ahead and arrange the first part of the business for you? As you are in London, perhaps it might be wise to strike while the iron is hot.'

Bertie stubbed out his cigarette. All of a sudden he felt very tired, and rather soiled. He needed restoration before he could face any more of this. He rose to his feet. 'You're very kind, but I would like to think about what you've told me for a day or two.'

'Just as you please,' said Paterson. 'I shall be ready to take your instruction at any time that suits you.'

Bertie went back to the club, and while he packed his bag he asked Neeson, the porter on duty, to look up a train for Salisbury for him. There was a good one a few minutes before noon, and he just had time to send off a telegram to Downsview House before the taxi arrived to take him to the station.

CHAPTER TWO

In Wiltshire it was very cold, and the recent snow lay unmelted in thick billows over the slumbering curves of the downs; but the sky had cleared and was a startling, improbable blue, the only colour in a world of monochrome. The air was so still that Jessie could hear the clamour of sheep folded at a farm several miles away. The snow had been expected, so farmers had had time to fetch in their flocks, but she knew how the cost in hay and turnips would be anxiously counted. At home, at Morland Place in Yorkshire, she had heard that the snow was not so deep. The sheep would still be out, but her horses would be in and eating their heads off. Fortunately the hay harvest last year had been abundant . . .

Thus she occupied her thoughts as she tramped along, in her heavy coat and boots, keeping within sight of the house. Downsview was the home of her brother Jack, who was in France with the Royal Flying Corps, and sister-in-law Helen. It had been a farmhouse once, but the land had been sold off separately. It stood, a rather unprepossessing red-brick box, at the end of a lane that led nowhere else. Beyond it there was nothing but Wilsford Down and the endless wild vista of Salisbury Plain. They had bought it for the view. Helen said she loved the peace, and perhaps normally Jessie would have agreed with her, but just now the quietness added to the troubles of her

27

mind, making her feel isolated, swept down a backwater and forgotten.

She missed the war. Insane though it sounded, she was lonely for it. For two years she had been a military nurse, for the last seven months serving in France. The khaki world had been her world, its language and priorities and discipline hers. The urgent, fierce needs of the wounded soldiers had filled her life. Here, the only reminder that the war was still going on was the occasional aeroplane, far away over at Netheravon, where the flying school and Royal Aircraft Factory were sited. When the wind was in the right direction, you could hear the minuscule buzzing of their engines as the trainee pilots did their 'circuits and bumps'.

Helen had a job. She had learned to fly before the war, and now delivered new aeroplanes from the factory to the various military units. From time to time she was absent from the household for a day or two, returning refreshed and invigorated from her contact with the real world outside. But Jessie was a nurse no longer, sent home in disgrace, pregnant without a husband. Her record was blackened for ever. If the war went on ten years, she would never be allowed to nurse again. All the skills and cool-headed capability she had developed in the fiery furnace of Étaples were now wasted.

So she walked and made herself think about farming, crops, horses – anything but her situation. Helen watched her with anxious eyes, too tactful to press her to tell her story. She had rescued Jessie from Morland Place where, if she had stayed, the family would inevitably have learned about her disgrace. Jessie could not bear that they should be ashamed of her, and suffer social stigma for her fault. She was grateful to Helen for providing her with a hiding place, and for letting her keep her silence. She was four months pregnant now, and the bump was visible. Helen's servants believed her husband was away at the war, and treated the pregnancy as a normal and therefore joyful thing – coals of fire to Jessie. They found her

28

distracted state of mind understandable enough: a woman expecting a child, and her husband at the Front? Who wouldn't be nervous and unhappy? Mrs Binny and Aggie discussed it cosily in the kitchen over endless pots of strong tea, giving themselves the comfortable horrors by imagining how Mrs Morland would react if that telegram came to say her husband was dead, never having seen his child.

Every woman with a man at the Front – husband, father, brother, son – lived in dread of 'the telegram'. There had been telegrams for Jessie's husband Ned, missing at Loos, and for her brilliant brother Frank at the Somme, cut off in all his promise. So when a distant cry alerted her and she turned to see Helen hurrying towards her from the house with something in her hand, she felt her heart contract painfully. She started back. Helen was calling something, but she could not distinguish the words. Jessie's lips felt numb. There was Jack, and her other brother Robbie, and Cousin Lennie, all serving in different parts of the world. Most of all, there was—

'It's not bad news!' She could hear Helen's words now. Helen of all people would know what would immediately jump to Jessie's mind. 'It's not bad news!' She was tramping as fast as she could and the words were breathless with her effort. Jessie lifted a hand in acknowledgement, and Helen stopped, waiting for her to come, a ginger-brown cut-out from the endlessly white background, in Jack's old pre-war greatcoat, her dark head bare.

'It's all right,' she said, in a normal voice, as Jessie reached her. 'It *is* a telegram, but it's not bad news. It gave me such a start when the boy brought it, but it's just from Bertie, to say he's coming to see us. Well, you, principally, I should think, because you're much closer to him than I am – Jessie! What is it? Are you all right?'

Jessie had whitened at Bertie's name, and now she swayed. Helen's hard, strong hand clasped her arm, and the keen eyes searched Jessie's face.

Jessie's lips moved, and after a silent rehearsal she managed to say, 'He's not hurt?'

Helen, still surveying her questioningly, said, 'No – at least, he doesn't say so. And, after all, if he's travelling down from London on the train, he can't be, can he? It's probably just leave. Perhaps he got it for his promotion.'

Jessie nodded distractedly, the colour coming back into her face. Helen, keeping hold of her arm, turned towards the house. 'You'd better come in and sit down. I was trying *not* to give you a shock, but I didn't make a very good job of it.'

'I'm all right now,' Jessie said, in an almost normal voice.

'You've probably walked too long and worn yourself out. Come and sit down and I'll get Mrs Binny to make some cocoa.'

Jessie said no more, thinking of how often cocoa had kept them going at Étaples: the universal elixir when strength ran out or spirits were battered. When that lowest point of night-duty came at around three o'clock – the hour when the borderline cases gave up and died, when a nurse's legs and head felt like solid lead – how often had she and her best friend Beta Wallace brewed up cocoa on the Beatrice to keep them going until dawn? Beta was still in France. She had turned her face away from Jessie and said they could not be friends any more, so there would not be any letters. Jessie missed Beta as much as she missed the war.

In the house, in the sitting-room with the wide windows that looked out at that staggering view, Helen divested Jessie of her outer clothes like a brisk nanny, instructed Mrs Binny on the cocoa front, then sat down beside her still silent sister-in-law. After a moment, when Jessie looked at her – rather apprehensively, it seemed – she said, 'It *is* Bertie, isn't it?' Jessie didn't answer at once, but there was no surprise in her expression, and Helen knew she had guessed right. 'It is Bertie whom you love?' she said, seeking a gentle phrasing.

Jessie nodded slowly. And then she blurted, 'Oh, Helen, don't hate me! I can't regret it. I would do it again. I love him so much.'

'I don't hate you,' Helen said. 'I'm only wondering at my own stupidity. I ought to have guessed. It's been going on a long time?'

'Since I was a little girl. I fell off trying to ride my father's stallion, and Bertie was there and took care of me, got me home, and came and visited me every day. I suppose it was a little girl's crush at first. He was my kind grown-up cousin. He wrote to me all through the South African war, but then he went to India, and he was away for years.'

'Yes, I've heard the story,' Helen said.

'When he came back, I knew the moment I saw him that I loved him, that I could never love anyone else. But he had married Maud. So I married Ned. It seemed the best thing to do.'

'And Bertie? How did he feel about you?'

'The same. We confessed it one day to each other. But we were both married, so we swore only to be cousins after that, and we kept to it, though it was – hard,' she finished inadequately.

'I can imagine,' Helen said. She thought of Jack. 'But Jessie – this.' She made a vague gesture with her free hand to indicate not just the pregnancy but the situation that went with it. 'How did it happen?'

'When his little boy was killed, Maud blamed him and said she couldn't live with him any more. Then she wrote to say she loved someone else and wanted to divorce him. He told me about it one day in France. He was so sad, because he said that Maud leaving him would have meant he and I could have been together after the war.'

'*Could* have?' Helen queried.

'He's been in it since the beginning, since August 1914. Almost everyone who joined with him is dead now. His best friend, Fenniman, was killed last year.'

'Oh, Jessie,' said Helen.

'He said a soldier's luck runs out in the end.' She drew breath. 'So I said—'

'I understand.' Helen could hardly bear to hear the words.

'I said we should take our time together, right then. Just once, to pay for all.'

She stopped, and they sat in silence a moment. War did these things to people, Helen thought. What would she have done in those circumstances? Probably the same. Women ought not to love men in time of war – it hurt too much. You lived from day to day, dreading the telegram, longing for the letter. New pilots, they said, had a life expectancy of two weeks, and if they survived long enough to learn the skills they needed, the two weeks became six months. Jack had been out there almost a year.

There were so many ways for a pilot to die: they crashed, or were blown up, or riddled with bullets, or went down in flames. Fire was feared the most. Some jumped from their burning aircraft: the government would not allow them to have parachutes, and they chose to fall a moment, through the kindly air that had always cherished them, to a different death, rather than feel themselves turn to charcoal. Jack, her love, father of her children, whose body and mind and spirit she delighted in – would he survive the war? The odds were against it. Women shouldn't love in war time. It hurt too much.

She said gently, 'Does he know?'

'About the baby? No. I didn't tell him. I was afraid it would make things worse for him – harder to bear. And besides,' her hand tightened involuntarily on Helen's, 'I've been pregnant before, twice, and I lost both babies. If I told him, and then lost it—'

'Yes, I understand,' Helen said. 'But, Jessie—'

Aggie came in at that moment, carrying a tray on which were two cups of cocoa and a plate of shortcakes, Mrs Binny having divined that the call for cocoa meant there had been a shock and that something sweet would be required. She had primed Aggie to find out what had happened, but Aggie was not secret-agent material, and the best she could manage was to ask straight out, 'Is everything all right, mum?'

'Yes, quite all right,' Helen said briskly. 'Thank you, Aggie. Go away now.'

The maid retreated, baffled, and Helen turned again to her sister-in-law. 'But, Jessie, Bertie is coming here, today, and he'll know when he sees you.'

'He might not,' Jessie said feebly.

'Unless you cover yourself up with a rug the whole time, and he might think that rather odd.'

The tears spilled over at that moment, and Helen saw it was from a strange kind of relief. 'I've wanted to tell him,' Jessie said through them. 'I want to marry Bertie and be *normal* at last, but if I can't have that, I want the baby.'

Helen took her in her arms and they held on to each other until the tears were done. Then Helen said, 'Let's have the cocoa before it gets cold. It's a sin to waste it. And eat a biscuit. You have to keep your strength up.'

Jessie wiped her face and blew her nose, and took a sip of comforting cocoa, and felt instantly better. Bertie was coming! She would see him again!

'You two will have a lot to talk about,' Helen said, 'so I shall keep out of the way. And you must ask him to stay, if he doesn't have to go straight back.'

'Really?' Jessie had not expected so much generosity.

'We'd better let the servants think he's your absent husband. They may not be the brightest people in the world,' she said wryly, 'but they're sure to notice the way you look at him. He can have the bed in the study, where Jack used to sleep when his ankle wouldn't heal and he couldn't climb the stairs. I'll tell Mrs Binny to make it up, and say that he doesn't sleep well since being at the Front. That will trigger her motherly feelings towards him, so she won't think it strange. But he can stay as long as he likes.'

'You're so good to me, Helen.'

'You saw the piece about him in the newspaper. Nothing's too good for our heroes! Now finish your cocoa, and then you can go and look for something pretty to wear, while I instruct Mrs Binny about dinner and get Aggie to air some sheets.'

Jessie smiled. 'I think I'm rather beyond wearing something pretty for him, given the circumstances.'

'Nonsense. He deserves to have the woman he loves make *some* effort for him, and frankly, darling, that skirt and blouse look better suited to farm work.'

'I thought they concealed the bump better,' Jessie said, looking down.

'Well, they don't, not from this angle, so you might as well dress nicely and be proud of it, and give poor Bertie a bit of pleasure.'

When Bertie arrived in the ancient, creaking taxi – all that had been available at the station – it was almost dark. He climbed out and stood staring at the ugly, isolated little house with surprise. 'Is this it?' he asked the cabman.

'That's it, all right,' the man said. 'Used to be Spakeley's Farm, before the airman bought it. No mistake, sir.'

He paid the man off and retrieved his bag, and when he turned to the house again the front door was open and a woman was standing in the doorway. He would have known her anywhere, in any light. He walked up the path towards her. When he was close enough to read her expression, he saw it was one of unexpected shynesss. Words did not come easily to either of them just then, and for a measure of seconds they could only gaze at each other in silence.

And then he noticed. Everything became suddenly clear – why she had left France, why she had come here, why she had kept it a secret. He was staggered by her courage.

'Oh, Jessie,' was all he could say. Then she was in his

arms, and he was cradling her head to his chest, feeling her arms tight round him.

Aggie, who had craned her head out from the kitchen door to goggle, was jerked back inside by an invisible hand. Helen had forbidden anyone to interrupt the first moments of reunion on pain of savage punishments, and Jessie's maid Tomlinson (who had chosen to share her exile) was making sure the order was obeyed.

Jessie lifted her head, and he looked down into her loved face. 'Should we go inside?' he said tenderly. 'We don't want the little mother to catch cold.'

Despite the narrowness of the entrance, they managed somehow to go in without letting go of each other.

'But, you know, this changes things,' Bertie said, when they were having another private conversation, after dinner. Helen had tactfully extracted herself on some excuse. He explained to Jessie what he had done about setting the divorce in train. 'I felt there was no particular urgency about it, given the war, but now there's a real need to hurry it along. I wish you'd told me sooner.'

'I didn't want to raise your hopes. You know I lost my other babies.'

He squeezed her hand. 'This time it will be all right. I know it.'

'Bertie, I was a nurse. You don't have to give me sugar-pills.'

'It's not a sugar-pill. Those other babies weren't meant to be, but this one is.' She looked at him. He smiled. 'Hold on to that thought. I'm sure you'll find it very comforting.'

She shook her head at his foolishness. He had lost his only child, and she knew how important it was to him. He would have to go back soon and face death again. Her body was the cradle for perhaps the only issue he would leave behind on earth.

He returned to the subject of the divorce. 'How quickly it gets through depends on Maud. I don't know whether she will feel any urgency about it. She's not a hurrier by nature.'

'No,' said Jessie, remembering the glacially calm Maud of old. 'But perhaps now that she has an object . . . ? Doesn't she want to marry Lord Manvers? If she loves him, she won't want to wait.'

'*He's* not in uniform,' Bertie said. 'And I don't know if she does love him, in the way we love each other. Though she did seem – changed. I can't quite put my finger on it, but there was something.'

'She doesn't know about us?'

'No, and I really don't want to tell her. I hope you don't think that dishonest of me, but I feel that what's between us is our business and no-one else's.'

'No, I don't want you to tell her,' Jessie said. 'But . . .'

He took the point. 'If I don't tell her about the baby, I can't give her a reason for hurrying.'

'And if you *do* tell her about the baby, it might give her a reason for *not* hurrying.'

Bertie couldn't deny it. 'But the lawyer chappie said that even if I got on with it at my end it could take six months. That would make it July.'

'And the baby's due in June.'

'And if Maud doesn't get a move on at her end, it could drag on into next year. Oh, Jessie, I'm sorry!'

'It's not your fault.'

'It is.'

'It was my idea, if I remember rightly. And I don't regret it.' She put a hand up to touch his cheek. 'I love you, and I'm carrying your child. How could I regret any of that?'

He caught the hand and kissed it, too full for words.

After a while she said, 'So it looks as though we won't be able to get married before the baby comes.'

'No, it doesn't look likely.'

It was something they both had to face. There was nothing to be done about it. The child would be born outside wedlock, with all the implications and consequences of that. And if Bertie did not survive, the child would never have a name, and Jessie would never have a husband or a place in society.

He stayed three days, and they were the happiest days Jessie had ever spent. The weather closed down again, and they were confined to the house for much of the time, but they could not have enough of just being together and talking. They had hardly ever had so many hours together, and there was a backlog of conversation that could never be got through. They did manage to get out of doors once or twice, well wrapped up, to walk, leaning together like two trees that had grown that way. Helen gave them plenty of time alone, but they made it clear that they enjoyed her company too; and Bertie, who loved children, was delighted to play with her son Basil, whose second birthday was approaching, and hold the baby, Barbara, with the skill and tenderness of a man who had been a father.

When Jessie was out of the room once, Bertie thanked Helen for helping her. 'I suppose you must think me every kind of a cad,' he said.

'What I think is neither here nor there,' Helen said. 'You don't have to answer to me.'

'If I could make things right, I would. But I think it's impossible to get married in time, now. And I will almost certainly be in France when the baby's born.'

'That seems likely,' said Helen.

'It's wrong to put it all on you,' Bertie said wretchedly.

'You don't. I took it on myself when I gave Jessie a home. Don't worry, I'll take care of her.'

'I'm going to make arrangements with the bank. There'll be money for whatever is necessary. She should have the best care – the best doctor – anything she needs.'

'She will.' Jessie had money of her own, but Helen knew he wanted to pay, since he could do nothing else.

'And if – if I don't come back,' Bertie said awkwardly, for it was not his taste to sound melodramatic, but it was a situation that had to be faced, 'the baby will need to be taken care of. I'll see the solicitor about that, but—'

'Jessie will have a home with me as long as she wants it,' Helen said. 'And I know Jack will feel the same. She was always his favourite.'

Bertie closed his eyes a second in relief. 'Thank you,' he said. And then, in a low voice, 'I want so much to live.'

Helen felt her throat close. There was something about men's courage that moved her almost to tears. Bertie and Jack both knew that the odds were against their coming back, but still they did their duty, left all they loved willingly behind, because this was what they had to do to protect them. Basil and Barbara, as well as Jessie's child – if it came to be born – might grow up fatherless. It was the price that had to be paid.

Bertie might have stayed longer, but now there was business to conduct. He had to see Paterson and perform the squalid little deed that would release Maud; and he had to see his solicitor and the bank about money for both women. So he had to tear himself away. They had talked little about the war, but in their last hour together he explained to her the situation.

'The Germans have to attack before the Americans come in in force. Our intelligence chaps think they'll move some time in March, when the ground starts to dry out. And as it's their last chance, the attack is likely to be a furious one.'

'So, March, then,' she said, as if to herself. That was when she would have to brace herself. 'But you're a colonel now,' she added hopefully. 'Battalion CO.'

He knew she wanted to hope that made it safer for him. But he could not lie to her. 'Darling, we all face the same

38

dangers. Even generals get killed.' At Loos, a third of divisional commanders had been lost. 'But the end is in sight now,' he went on. 'We just have to hold them back for a few more months. Then, when the Americans are ready, we can counter-attack, and with the numbers we'll have to call on, the enemy won't stand a chance. Everyone thinks we'll beat them next year. The war will be over some time in 1919.'

She tried to make it easy for him to go, to be calm and matter-of-fact, but when the taxi was at the door and she was in his arms for the last time, she pressed herself against him and whispered, 'Come back to me. Come back to me!'

He held her close and kissed the crown of her head. 'Take care of yourself,' he said.

And then he was gone.

The business in London was not as bad as he had feared. Paterson suggested that, to make sure of the outcome, Bertie should engage a detective, rather than relying solely on the hotel servants' testimony. 'Some judges can be a little difficult, especially if the hotel name is familiar to them from other cases, and we don't know at this stage what judge we'll get. Of course, it *is* an extra expense . . .'

Bertie waved that away. 'Whatever is necessary.'

'Well, I have a very good man, Jeaks, available. He'll be able to advise you on the spot, in case anything should arise. Everything must look quite natural, you understand.'

As Paterson had promised, the girl – her name was Mary Pearson – was 'genteel'. She was neatly dressed in a grey flannel two-piece over a white blouse which, while cheap, were clean and pressed; and her shoes, though worn, were well polished. She was small and thin, and wore a pinched look that Bertie guessed came from money worries – why else would she be doing this, indeed? Had she been less poor, she would have been quite pretty; probably she once had been. But she had put on *maquillage*, and sported a bright smile. Jeaks, the detective, was a large, prosperous-looking man with a marked limp, which explained why he was not in uniform. He was there when Bertie met the girl at Victoria station (though he studiously and professionally ignored them, as though he hadn't already met Bertie at Paterson's office) and followed them as they walked arm-in-arm (Paterson's instructions) to the St Ermine Hotel in Warwick Square, Pimlico.

Paterson had reserved the room for them, and Bertie registered and wrote 'Sir Perceval and Lady Parke' in the visitors' book. As they were shown towards the elevator, he saw Jeaks signing himself in on the line below. The book, Bertie had been told, would be part of the evidence. The room was the best one in the hotel, with an adjoining sitting-room and a bathroom just next door – Paterson had thought it would not look natural for Sir Bertie Parke to be 'roughing it' too much. Here they changed for dinner, which had to be taken in the hotel's dining-room for evidential purposes.

Since it was his way to make the best of what was to hand, Bertie tried to put Mary Pearson – 'Everyone calls me May' – at her ease. She had changed into a low-cut evening-dress of artificial silk suitable to a fallen woman, with a string of false pearls round her neck and false pearl earrings. Though she was smiling brightly at him, he thought she was all too aware of the presence of Jeaks, who had been shown to the table just behind and to the left of Bertie, where May, facing him, could hardly avoid looking at him. To help things along, Bertie ordered champagne, and commented on the rather pretty cameo brooch she was wearing at the point of her décolletage, which looked genuine in contrast to the rest of her toilette.

She warmed at the question, and said it had been her grandmother's. Her mother had died when she was three and her father had abandoned them, so her grandmother had pretty much brought her up. May spoke of her with great affection. She had left her several pretty things when she died – of TB, she answered Bertie's question – but May had had to sell most of them. There was only this brooch, and a queer little ring with a plait of hair in it, which her grandmother had always worn. It was too small for May's fingers, but she would never part with it.

To Bertie's patient questioning the rest of the story came out. It was probably quite a common one. May had been engaged to a decent lad, a mechanic, but he had volunteered at the beginning of the war. When he came home on leave, they had anticipated the wedding, and she became pregnant. Before he could get home to retrieve the situation by marrying her, he had been killed – at Neuve Chapelle in March 1915. The baby had been born, and then her grandmother had died, and now May had to make a living however she could to support herself and the child. She worked as a waitress at a café in Hoxton, where she rented a room, but the pay was not enough, especially with clothes and shoes to buy for a growing child. She couldn't get a better job because people wouldn't take on a girl with a baby. Then she had seen an advertisement for smart-looking girls to do occasional evening work. She had been afraid it might be prostitution, and she would never do that, but Mr Paterson had turned out to be really nice, and there was never any funny stuff. She hadn't liked it at first, and thought it a bit queer and not quite respectable, but it paid really well, and mostly the gentlemen were kind to her. She only wished Mr Paterson wanted her more often, but he said he had to change the girls around so the judges didn't start to recognise them. Mr Paterson had said she was one of his best because she came across so respectable in court, and gave her evidence just right.

Bertie made sure she got outside of a good meal, and afterwards lingered downstairs and smoked a cigarette while she went up to the room, so that she could undress and get into bed in privacy. He lingered so long that eventually Jeaks, who was drinking at the bar and keeping an eye on him,

41

felt obliged by winks and gestures to send him upstairs, where he found May fast asleep with the covers pulled up tightly round her neck. He looked sadly at the thin, blue-white face on the pillow, and wondered who was taking care of her child while she earned the money to clothe him. He dozed in the armchair in the sitting-room for the rest of the night, until it was time to get into bed beside her to be 'seen' by the hotel servants bringing their breakfast on trays. One of them gave Bertie a complicit wink to assure him they were in on the plot, a rare moment of humanity in an otherwise seamlessly professional performance on all sides.

After that it was just a matter of dressing, taking coffee in the hotel lounge, with Jeaks in a nearby chair to witness their 'affectionate behaviour', and paying the bill. Outside, Bertie parted from his companion with a handshake and grave thanks. She looked so thin in the harsh morning air that he gave her five pounds, on top of what she would get from Paterson, 'for the baby'. She thanked him almost tearfully, and walked off and out of his life, towards the bus stop on Warwick Way, while he went in the other direction to find a taxi on Belgrave Road. Jeaks was still inside obtaining a copy of the receipt, so Bertie didn't see him leave. He would have liked to slip him something, too, but reflected afterwards it was probably not etiquette. He was not supposed, after all, to know him; and Jeaks seemed in mortal fear of the King's Proctor and 'conspiracy'.

Emma Weston had been recruited into the First Aid Nursing Yeomanry by Vera Polk. Emma guessed, though it was not so stated, that Vera had also helped to shorten her probation time so as to get her out to France as soon as possible. She was grateful, so when Vera invited her to come and stay for a few days before she embarked, Emma was glad to accept.

Vera lived in a house on Paultons Square, just off the King's Road. 'I let out some of the rooms to help pay the rent,' she said. 'They're all women, and very nice types, so it's quite comfortable.'

Emma, who was very rich, had never lived in a lodging-house before, and was quite intrigued at the thought. Already the FANY training had provided new experiences for her, living cheek-by-jowl with other women and without servants, polishing her own shoes and pressing her own clothes, taking turns with cooking and cleaning. Some of them had told her eagerly about the fun of summer camp, where they lived under canvas and had games and competitions and demonstrations, but Emma had joined too late for that, and would be in France by next summer. She had learned a lot about the lore of the FANY, which was based on an intense loyalty to the corps and each other. FANYs were recruited very much from the educated and moneyed classes, and exhibited the independence of mind that came with privilege. They rejected stale thinking and pointless protocol, taking pride in adapting to whatever might be thrown at them. 'I cope' was their motto – and Emma learned that the FANY had been coping with a great variety of jobs and situations out in the war zone.

Absorbing the *esprit de corps* might have been the most important part of the training course, but she learned a great many practical things as well, such as how to put up a tent, dig a latrine, pump a Primus stove, cook a stew, and light a fire with damp wood, as well as first aid, bandaging, and how to lift and move a stretcher. She took courses in cavalry drill with a Guards instructor at Hounslow Barracks (that was great fun) and in Morse and semaphore with a Signals corporal (more difficult for the unstudious Emma). She already knew how to drive, but she took the BMA test to get the required certificate, and then she received intensive training on vehicle repair and maintenance, which was to be her 'speciality', and the reason she would be getting out to France sooner than usual.

There had been a strange satisfaction in investigating

vehicular entrails and bringing dead motors back to life. It was like first aid for the inanimate, she thought; and she got fond, in an odd way, of the cantankerous lorries and vans that were provided as patients, rather as one could grow fond of an awkward but lovable horse. Now she was impatient to get to France and put her new skills into action, to do her part in winning the war, to help the men out there who were fighting with such terrible courage to free the world from tyranny. It was all she could do now, to honour Fenniman, her fiancé, killed at Ypres, and it was something to put into the emptiness inside. Sometimes, when grimed to her elbows in oil solving the problem of a malfunctioning cylinder, or lying under a lorry struggling with a spanner and a frozen nut to free a broken camshaft, she would find she had stopped thinking about him just for a bit. Of course, the pain returned, but even temporary relief was welcome.

Vera had been very helpful in advising her on what to pack for France, but Emma gathered that space in Vera's house was limited and so took only a small bag to Paultons Square, leaving her trunk in the left-luggage office at Victoria station.

The house, like others in the area, had once been quite smart but was now grown shabby. The narrow hall had black and white marble tiles on the floor, but the paintwork was scuffed and the windows needed cleaning. The kitchen was in the semi-basement down a flight of stairs, and there was a drawing-room and dining-room, divided by folding doors. The drawing-room was a revelation to Emma, being furnished in a very odd style that she supposed to herself, after a first surprised look, must be 'Bohemian'. Her cousin Violet, with whom she had been living, had had a brush with the Bohemian set two years ago when she had begun her tragic affair with the artist Octavian Laidislaw. But that had been a wealthy and aristocratic sort of Bohemia; this was obviously at the other end of the movement.

Three of the room's walls were painted dark red and

44

the fourth, startlingly, was black. In one alcove there was a parlour-palm planted in an elephant's foot; in the other a dressmaker's dummy wearing a papier-mâché reproduction of David's head and swathed with ivy growing from a brass pot. There was a sagging sofa covered with crimson chenille, and instead of chairs a large number of cushions on the floor. There was a low table of intricately carved Indian wood and another of Benares brass, a leather footstool in the shape of a pig, and what looked like an inlaid brass hookah. Over the mantelpiece there was a huge, unframed oil painting of a Venus de Rokeby entirely made of barley-sugar and liquorice allsorts, while other walls were decorated with posters, fixed with drawing-pins. The air was heavy with a mixture of turpentine and an aromatic, smoky smell that Emma could not identify. She felt enormously cheered by the strange surroundings, so different from the staid drawing-rooms she had grown up in. With convention thrown aside like this, she felt anything might happen, and probably would. It suited her new, daring persona as a FANY.

As the days passed, Emma met the other residents. Two ballet girls, Millie and Agnes, shared a room on the top floor, and were often found practising in the dining-room using the chair backs as a *barre*. The other top-floor room housed Freda, the painter of the barley-sugar Venus, a heavy-built woman in her thirties with a foghorn voice, who smoked like a chimney and was always spattered with paint, and whose other works were equally modern, inscrutable and violently coloured. On the first floor two middle-aged sisters shared a room, one a singing-teacher and the other a writer of sensation stories. In a second room was a female of independent means who was devoted to some cause for preventing girls from becoming prostitutes; and in the third room was Vera, with whom Emma was to share for her visit.

The evenings were lively, with much use of Vera's gramophone, the drinking of bottled beer and endless tea, and a great deal of smoking, both of the hookah and cigarettes. Emma had not much been around women who smoked, though Vera told her lots of the FANY out in France did. Emma found it rather shocking at first, and later rather annoying, as the fug built up in the small rooms. But she enjoyed the conversation, which was always wide-ranging and thought-provoking. The inmates cooked in turn on a rota with varying success, and the deficiencies were made up with suppers of toast or sausages burned before the fire, or late-night sorties to the fish-and-chip shop at World's End. Sometimes, sitting on a cushion in the noisy, smoky room, eating a sausage with her bare fingers and listening to someone talking about Kant and Schopenhauer, Freud and Charcot, Lentulov and Cézanne, she could hardly have been more amazed at finding herself there than she was at the things she heard.

Here were people casting out the old and embracing the new, searching out fresh ways of thinking about the world and its problems. They were doing away with the conventions, which were universally held to be 'stifling'; tradition was 'oppressive'; morality was 'bourgeois' – which Emma quickly understood was a pejorative term. Art, in particular, had to be 'freed' from the 'chains' of bourgeois convention and allowed to express what the artist really felt. There was talk of something called 'free love', which puzzled her as she couldn't think what the alternative was. But she was to understand that all of their parents had got pretty much everything wrong in the past, and that after the war things would have to change completely. It would be a new world. Emma found it much more interesting than the usual drawing-room conversations about shopping and theatres and what other people one knew had been doing.

Apart from the residents, there were friends dropping in, so that there seemed to be a party atmosphere every night. She enjoyed Freda's friends – other painters, sculptors and modellers – who were always loud and opinionated but liked to laugh a lot. The singing-teacher's friends were music-hall artists, small-part actresses and hard-worn musicians, who amused Emma with their practical and down-to-earth comments on the sometimes far-flung philosophies that were aired in those rooms. Millie and Agnes brought other dancers, often foreigners, including pale Russian boys who had fled the military conscription and were among the few male visitors. When they had drunk and smoked enough they sometimes sang sorrowful songs about Mother Russia in close harmony, and ended hanging limply on each other's shoulders and sobbing.

Vera's friends were very political and impatient of anyone who wasn't. They made a lot of cryptic utterances, which tended to exclude everyone else, which Emma thought impolite in company. And one or two spoke disparagingly of men, which seemed disloyal when the men were fighting and dying at the Front. But they could be amusing on other subjects, and they liked word-games, and dressing-up and playing charades, which they were very good at. One could even do conjuring tricks, which she attempted to teach Emma, saying it would be 'useful at the Front', though she did not explain why.

All in all it was an exciting and mentally challenging visit, and when she was lying in bed composing herself for sleep, Emma compared it with what now seemed the dull and predictable social life she had previously known. She felt she had been jolted out of her old self and into a new world of possibility. Apart from anything else, she felt that the company of women with no men present (she hardly counted the mournful Russian boys) was somehow much jollier and more vivacious, though she couldn't think why that should be.

The one person she could not fathom was Vera, who remained an enigma – briskly practical, sometimes engaging in frighteningly obscure conversations with her political friends, offering good advice but never really revealing anything about herself. When she had asked Emma if she minded sharing, Emma thought that being in such confined quarters with Vera, and sharing her bed, they would inevitably become closer; but Vera spoke less than ever when they were alone.

Only on Emma's last night, when she was lying in bed analysing the visit and the company, and thought her companion was long asleep, did Vera suddenly say, 'So, have you enjoyed yourself these last few days?'

'Oh, yes,' Emma said. 'You all have so much to say for yourselves. I've been wondering why women's conversations are so different when there are men present.'

'Because women have to try to "catch" husbands, and men don't care for women with brains. Silent adoration is what they look for.'

'Not always,' Emma said. 'It was one of the things I loved most about my fiancé, that we had such wonderful conversations. He loved me to talk.'

'It wouldn't have lasted. Once you were married he'd have reverted to type – rattling the newspaper and saying, "*Must* you insist on chattering when I'm trying to read?"' She put on a gruff and testy voice, uncannily like someone's father at the breakfast table.

'The older generation might be like that, but he wasn't,' Emma protested.

'All men are like that,' Vera said flatly. 'You had a lucky escape.'

Emma was so hurt she could not answer.

After a while, Vera said, 'Don't cry. I didn't mean to upset you.'

'You didn't know him,' Emma said angrily.

'Of course *you* thought he was different. Perhaps he was. But men are men underneath, and there's not many of them worth the room they take up.'

'Why do you hate men so?' Emma demanded.

'Oh, I don't hate them,' Vera said. 'I just don't think much

48

of them. I've known too many takers, and charlatans, and opinionated asses. Where would men be without the women to support them? But they never acknowledge that. It's all *them* – as if a man could be a minister or a judge or a banker without the army of wives and servants and secretaries to clean and cook and sew and write letters and keep house, and give them the time and leisure to be important.'

'I suppose that's true,' Emma said doubtfully.

'Women could do the men's jobs just as well, if not better, but that would mean the men would have to do their own cooking and cleaning, and they won't stand for it. Much easier to keep a female slave, and tell her that's all she's fit for.'

'Slave?' Emma queried.

'Slave, wife, it's the same thing. Give her a different title, stuff her head with rubbish about "love" and a woman's nature and the holiness of motherhood, and she connives at her own enslavement. And, of course, the damnable thing is that it's easier to give in than go on fighting, so most women do.'

Emma thought this an extreme view. Probably Vera had never been in love as she and Fenniman had. 'It doesn't seem like that when it's happening,' she said kindly.

'Of course not. That's the trickery. They charm you and flatter you and drug you with the love-nonsense, and you sleep your life away while they run the world the way they want it. But *you* have a chance now, Emma. You can wake up and live *your* way – find out what *you* want, and get it by your own efforts. Going to France with the FANY is the best opportunity you could have. That's why I said you had a lucky escape when your fiancé was killed. I know you loved him and you're sorry he's dead, but try to look on it as an opportunity rather than a tragedy.'

The words stung Emma. 'How can you say that? How can you be so cruel?'

'Perhaps I should have said, "Try to see it as an opportunity

49

as well as a tragedy." I just want to put you on your guard before you go to France and find yourself surrounded by officers, all being charming, entirely for their own ends. Promise me you won't be taken in.'

Emma didn't answer, struggling with tears. How could Vera think she would even notice any other man? She missed Fenniman so much. She couldn't bear it that she would *never* see him again – the knowledge hit her with a fresh shock every time it came to her. He had filled her life with hope and happiness, and now there was just emptiness. She tried to cry quietly, but in the end she couldn't help letting out a sob.

Vera said, 'Oh, come here, poor Emma, poor thing.' And she reached out and took Emma in her arms, and held her, stroking her head while she cried. Emma resisted at first, still angry at Vera's tactlessness; but there was a kind of comfort in it, as in any act of kindness, and Emma had never had a mother. Gradually her tears subsided and she began to feel drowsy and warm. She was still on Vera's shoulder when she fell asleep.

CHAPTER THREE

At Morland Place, Polly was exercising her cousin Jessie's horse Hotspur, her mind on other things. It was safe to do that with Hotspur, who was well schooled and polite. Polly liked riding him, but she preferred the challenge of her own wilful mare Vesper, who never walked if she could dance, and whose response to inattention was to dump her rider on the cold hard earth if at all possible.

It was what Jessie always used to call 'an iron day': dry and cold, with a blank grey sky. The snow had mostly worn away, though pockets remained in corners where the sun did not reach, and white furrows lay along path and field edges. In the black tracery of trees against the mute sky you could see the clumps of rooks' nests, like balls of mistletoe; but the birds were all out in the fields, following the plough and the harrow.

Polly was thinking about the letter she had received yesterday from Cousin Lennie, who was serving in Salonika, much to his disgust. Having been out of the war for a year because of a serious injury taken at Gommecourt, he had hoped to be sent back to France. Instead, he had been relegated to one of the 'side-shows'.

You know I meant to serve the whole war as a private soldier, but the fellows I joined up with are dead now, and when the colonel asked me if I would take a commission, it seemed foolish to hold out any longer. I am now a 'one-pipper', otherwise 2nd Lt Manning. I hope you will not think I have 'caved in'. But there is very little to do out here, and I am much busier as an officer than ever I was as a private. I have to go on courses, and attend lectures on map-reading, weapons and communications. I'm at base at present, which is in the town, and a nasty, dirty place Salonika is. Dangerous, too. Almost every week some Tommy is offered a lift on a Greek lorry, then robbed and dumped somewhere outside the walls. I'm reminded of the old saw, beware Greeks bearing gifts! I'm hopeful of being sent somewhere up-country when my training is done, though there's little chance of action. Apart from sending over the occasional shell, the Bulgs don't seem at all interested in trying our defences. I feel so wasted here when the real war is going on in France. I am due some leave soon but it is too far to come home for it. There is a safe village on the coast where officers go. A bunch of us will head up there, so I may get some fishing. What I long for most is something new to read. I have read my few books to bits, and there's not much to borrow as my fellow subs seem indifferent to reading, though three of them have gramophones! I would love to have a letter from home to take with me on leave, as that is something I can read over and over. Could you find it in your heart to oblige,

Your loving cousin,
Lennie Manning

Polly was glad Lennie had accepted the commission – it seemed silly to her to refuse agreeable things on a principle – and she planned to write and tell him so as soon as she had a moment. She was more interested in the leave plans of Lieutenant David Holford, who was in France and there-fore easily close enough to come home. Would he come to

Yorkshire? The answer to that question would go some way to solving the riddle of how much he liked her – something his behaviour while he was in York last year had made maddeningly difficult to tell. She was fond of Lennie, but France was infinitely more dangerous than Salonika, which added considerably to Holford's glamour.

Her thought-train was broken by the raucous braying of a mule. She felt Hotspur's sides brace as he answered with a long, loud whinny. Coming round a curve of the track, she saw the source away to her right, halfway up the gentle slope of a half-ploughed field – one of the outlying pastures of Woodhouse Farm.

It was one of Ezra Banks's mules, of course. They were famous in the neighbourhood. Old Ezra had been distraught when the army had requisitioned his beloved plough horses. He had threatened to shoot the requisitioning officer who came to take them away, and Jessie had had to go over and calm him down. Ezra had poured scorn on the army's offer of mules in exchange, saying that mules were 'an abomination before the Lord'. His beautiful horses, which he had bred and raised by hand and were like children to him, were not to be spoken of in the same breath as those freaks of nature.

But a pair of mules had been delivered, and he'd had no choice but to work with them. The animals were young and strong and intelligent, and as he trained them to his ways, they slowly won his heart. Now, much to everyone's amusement, he loved them even more than his horses, and defended them, whiskery chin jutting, against the wicked prejudices of the world. He groomed them lovingly before work, plaiting their manes with ribbons, and quite often after dinner (according to his daughter-in-law Willa) he took his pipe into their stable and stayed chatting with them until bedtime. The greatest proof of his surrender was that he had given them traditional plough-horse names: Ezra's mules were called Boxer and Beauty.

Polly had to admit that there was something beguiling about them. They had a way of looking at you that was somehow humorous and knowing; and they certainly repaid Ezra's care with affection. She was riding on when the mule bellowed again, and she drew rein, realising that something was not right about the tableau in the field. The old hand-plough Ezra always used was there, but there was no sign of Ezra. Moreover, the mule that had been braying was standing up, but the other was lying down – not flat out, but folded comfortably on its shoulder, as horses do to rest. She could not think of any reason the old man would leave his team alone in the middle of a field. With a reluctant sigh – because she had been heading home for luncheon – she went to investigate.

When she was halfway across the field she finally saw Ezra, lying behind the recumbent mule on the cold, stony ground. He must be hurt – and it could not be good for a man of his age to lie there. Though tough as weathered oak, Ezra was all of eighty-four. The standing mule, Boxer, was watching her with bright, expressive eyes, long ears cocked forward, lips trembling on the verge of another salute. Hotspur was snorting to him as he picked his way through the stony plough. This field had always been left as pasture because of the poor nature of the soil, but crops had to be grown wherever possible these days.

Slipping down from Hotspur's back, Polly saw that the mules were uncoupled from the plough. The rope that had attached Beauty to the yoke had broken, and the yoke hung down from Boxer's side. Beauty pointed his ears as Polly approached, but did not move. He was lying close up against Ezra, and now Polly saw that Ezra's eyes were open.

'Eh, Miss Polly,' he said, in a thread of a voice.

She hurried to his side. The plough's blade was buried deep in a hole, and Ezra's booted foot was down there too, the ankle bent at an unnatural angle. 'What on earth happened?' she asked, kneeling beside him. His face and

54

hands were cold, but he was not shivering, courtesy, she saw, of Beauty's big warm body, which was resting along the length of his.

In weak sentences he told the story. The plough had gone down a hole and stuck, and he could not shift it. He had unhitched the mules, meaning to try to drag it out backwards, but his foot had slipped on the crumbling edge of the hole and gone down. Now it was trapped under something, and because of the angle he could not pull it out. The mules could have wandered off, but they'd stayed by him, and Beauty had pulled away from Boxer, breaking the yoke-rope, and lain down beside him. Ezra had hitched himself close to the mule and waited. No-one would miss him for the day, as he had his dinner with him, and precious few people passed this way. He'd thought he was stuck here till dark, until he'd seen Hotspur's ears over the hedge. He'd tried to shout out, but his voice was gone with the cold and all. And then old Boxer had let out a bellow fit to wake the dead.

Polly had been examining the situation while he talked. 'Does it hurt a lot?'

'Gone numb now,' Ezra said. 'Hurt like the Dickens to begin with.' For him to acknowledge it proved how bad it was, for Ezra was of the stoical school. 'Try if you can get it out.'

'I – can't – shift it,' she said, after a moment. She sat back on her heels. Despite the cold there was sweat on Ezra's lip, and his face was pale under the mahogany tan of a lifetime. 'I need to make the hole bigger. I'd better go and get help.'

'Nay, miss,' Ezra said, holding out a feeble hand to stop her. He didn't want to be left. 'In ma satchel, under the hedge ower theer. Ma big knife. Try that.'

Polly ran, clumsy in her riding boots, and brought back the satchel. In it there was Ezra's dinner – wedge of cheese, an onion, a lump of apple tart hard as a brick, and a bottle of cold tea. There were some odds and ends – a short length of rope, sundry nails, a stub of indelible pencil, a hoof-pick, a small dark bottle of some animal salve – and a large clasp-knife in a leather sheath. She pulled it out, and then, before she began operations, handed Ezra the bottle. 'You must be thirsty.'

While he took a pull she got down on her knees and, with the big blade, began working at the hard earth to enlarge the hole, scraping out what she loosened with her hands, glad she was wearing leather gloves. Now and then the point grated with a horrible sound on what she could now see was a rock, a big one, not far under the surface. The ploughshare was down one side of it, and Ezra's foot down the other. Finally the hole was large enough for her to see that the toe of the boot was rammed right in under the rock, but she thought it ought to be possible to get Ezra's foot out of the boot. She only prayed that nothing was broken. She loosened the laces as far as they would go, worked the thick, stiff leather open, and pulled back the tongue.

'I'm going to try to get you out now,' she said.

'Ay, Miss Polly,' Ezra croaked.

Polly clasped her hands round his ankle and pulled. She heard him gasp in pain, but he didn't beg her to stop. At last the foot in its thick woollen sock came slithering loose. Ezra gave a bitten-off cry. He didn't seem able to move his legs – probably a mixture of the cold and their having 'gone dead'. She carefully straightened them, examined the leg that had been trapped and saw that the ankle was grossly swollen and blackening with bruise. Despite the first-aid classes she had attended since the war began, she couldn't be sure whether it was broken or not.

'Eh, miss,' Ezra said weakly, and with a tremor in his voice. It was as close as he would come to complaint.

She urged another gulp of tea on him, and wished she had a hunting flask with her. 'Now I'm going to get help,' she said firmly. He didn't argue this time. He couldn't walk, and she couldn't possibly carry him on her own. She struggled out of her riding coat and, despite his protests, made him put it on – it wouldn't do up, but at least it was something between him and the cold earth. 'You'd better keep close to Beauty.'

Ezra looked up at her. 'Ay, miss. Awd Beauty saved ma life. He knew Ah needed t' be kept warm.' And his frail hand reached out and tremblingly stroked the mule's flank. The animal flicked its ears back and forth, but did not otherwise move.

Polly caught Hotspur, who had wandered a little way in search of grazing (Vesper would have been halfway across the county by now), and led him to the gate to mount. As she rode full pelt for Woodhouse Farm, she thought of how Boxer and Beauty had stayed with him. It would certainly do nothing to make Ezra think less of his 'abominations', and it would be a grand tale to tell at home.

When Polly reached Woodhouse farmyard, she found no menfolk. Ezra's son Eli and Eli's son Jeb were out building folds for the lambing that would start any day. The other men were muck-carting elsewhere. Willa, Eli's wife, was there – she was seldom anywhere but in the house and the immediate farmyard, cooking the vast meals and doing all the thousand jobs farmers' wives came in for. So were Jeb's wife Ivy, and Willa's sixteen-year-old daughter Rosie, who had long since finished school and now helped on the farm, while secretly dreaming of joining the Women's Auxiliary Army Corps when she was old enough.

Willa briskly took charge. 'Rosie and me'll coom, miss,' she said. 'Ivy can stay and mind things.' Ivy had two small babies to watch over, but Willa sternly reminded her to stir the stew as well while they were gone. 'Else nobody'll get no dinner. We can easy lift Granddad between three of us. His boots weigh more than he doos. Is the ankle brokken, d'you think, Miss Polly?'

'I don't *think* so,' Polly said cautiously.

'How are you going to carry him?' Ivy asked. 'Won't you need a stretcher?'

'The trestle top out o' the dairy, Ma?' Rosie suggested.

'Too heavy. We'd better just link hands and carry him between us. You'll coom and help us, miss, won't you? You see how we're fixed. Rosie, get a blanket off Granddad's bed. I dare say he's frozen stiff. He'll have pewmony before you know it – oh, he's such a trial to me!'

Polly volunteered to ride on ahead with the blanket and a nip of homemade parsnip wine – the farmhouse had no brandy but 'Dad's parsnip is stronger, if truth be told.' It took the women time to walk up there, and Polly, having wrapped Ezra in the blanket and administered the parsnip wine, sat close and talked to him, and was glad to see him recover noticeably. He had been frightened by his helplessness, which had oppressed his spirits more than the pain. Now rescue was at hand, and all he wanted was to talk about the wonder of his mules.

When the women arrived, it proved unnecessary to carry him – which, though he weighed so little, would have been hard going over rough ground – for his strength had returned enough for him to sit up. Polly freed Boxer from the yoke and between the three of them they lifted Ezra astride the mule's back. Willa and Rosie got up on Beauty, Polly remounted Hotspur, and they rode one on either side to make sure Ezra didn't fall off (though he grumbled loudly and continuously that it was not necessary, they needn't treat him like an invalid, he wasn't in his dotage yet, thank you very much . . .).

By the time they got back to the farm, Polly had missed Morland Place luncheon, and Willa begged her to stay and eat with them. Polly gladly accepted. Willa bathed and examined Ezra's foot, decided nothing was broken, and dressed it with salve and bandages. He wanted to get up and tend the mules, but Willa could be formidable when

58

roused, and told him not to be such an old fool. They were safe in their stable and Rosie would give them an armful of hay and see to them after dinner. The men could be heard in the yard, washing at the tap, and dinner had to be put on the table right away.

Two of the four men were from the Labour Corps, soldiers who had sustained injuries that meant they could no longer serve at the Front, and had been detailed for farm work. It was a blessing for farms like Woodhouse, where all the pre-war labour had been called up. The Tommies didn't mind it at all. It beat being shot at, they said. Eli and Jeb, like Ezra, had taken their dinner to the top fields with them, so at the table, apart from the Tommies and the two labourers, there was only a shy boy of sixteen, big of body and slow of speech, whom Rosie treated with robust scorn, in case anyone should think she was interested in him. Ezra was helped to his place, and mutton stew and potatoes were served.

Polly and the old man were obliged to tell the whole story again in detail for the new company. One of the Tommies, a cheerful Cockney, could not get enough of it, and marvelled at the mules' intelligence. 'And I fought they was just dumb beasts! Cor, animals'll surprise you every now and then, wunt they? Reminds me of a parrot I knew once, back 'ome. Belonged to this old man down our street what used to be a sailor. Knowing old bird, it was, and I'll tell you what it useter do . . .'

Ezra would much rather have talked about the mules, but his voice was hoarse after his exposure in the field, while the Cockney's was young and strong, so the conversation got away from him.

When Polly arrived home at last, it was mid-afternoon. The hall was pleasantly warm after the cold air outside, and a blanket of dogs was toasting beside the fire in the great fire-place. Her hound, Bell, did at least detach himself, stand up, stretch fore and aft with a massive yawn, and click across the black and white marble floor to apologise half-heartedly for having abandoned her a mere fifteen minutes into the ride. His glance back at the fire said as clearly as words, 'But you see how it was?' None of the other dogs so much as stirred at her entrance. So much for guarding the house, she thought.

Sawry, the butler, came into the hall on his way somewhere and started at the sight of her. 'Oh, Miss Polly! I didn't hear you come in.' He hurried towards her to take her hat.

'My coat needs brushing,' she said. 'It's a bit muddy.'

'I'll see to it, miss.' He took it from her. 'You didn't take a fall, Miss Polly?'

'From Hotspur? I should think not. I've been good-Samaritaning, that's why I'm late.'

'You must be hungry. Shall I have Mrs Stark prepare you something?'

'No, it's all right, I had luncheon at Woodhouse Farm.'

'Tea won't be long, Miss Polly. The mistress has a meeting of ladies in the drawing-room, and I'll be taking tea in to them any time.'

'I'd forgotten the meeting. What's it for, again?'

'About opening a "national kitchen" in York to provide cheap meals to the poor,' Sawry said.

'Oh, yes, I remember now. Daddy was saying something about it – it'll be like the canteen he set up to feed his factory workers.'

'Yes, miss, except that the government will pay a bit towards it, and people will have to hand in their food tickets, once the rationing starts next month. Coupons, I think they're calling them – though why we should have to use a French word when there's a perfectly good English one I don't know.'

He was having to do too much, now all the footmen had gone, and was entitled to grumble now and then.

Polly smiled and patted his hand. 'Don't worry, we won't be bothered with rationing here. It's only things you have to buy, not things you produce yourself.' She glanced at the clock. 'How long have they been talking?'

'An hour and a half, miss,' Sawry said.

'Oh, then they'll be ready for an interruption, and I've such a good story to tell.'

Sawry smiled. 'I'll bring the tea in, Miss Polly. Mrs Stark's made Fat Rascals and parkin.'

'Wonderful,' said Polly, who was partial to both. 'But won't the ladies want something more delicate?'

'There'll be thin bread and butter for them as are too dainty for good Yorkshire baking,' Sawry said, 'but I don't anticipate there'll be many.' And he went away with what was very close to a wink.

In the drawing-room Polly found her aunt Henrietta presiding over a meeting that had obviously degenerated into general conversation. Polly's stepmother Alice was there, with her friends Mrs Winnington and Mrs Spindlow, Mrs Cornleigh, and one or two of York's second rank of important ladies – Mrs Portwaine, Mrs Enderby, Mrs Cowey of Beverley House, and Mrs Upton-Hayes of Clifton Grange. A gathering, Polly thought, of the eminent, the charitable – and the bored.

As Polly came in, Henrietta looked towards the door with an expression of relief that said, *If Polly comes, can tea be far behind?* It was impossible to get charitable ladies to commit themselves without an injection of tea and cake at the critical moment. She had put the idea before them at the beginning, and had been meeting objections until her throat was dry.

Mrs Upton-Hayes was the worst. She saw herself as the leader of York's philanthropic society, which meant that nothing benevolent ought to happen if she had not insti-gated it. She wanted the proposed national kitchen to be sited at her house, and had not liked Henrietta's pointing out that it would be a long walk for the poor people to get there. She hadn't approved of the title 'national kitchen', either. It ought to be called 'The York Ladies' Benevolent Committee's Christian Refectory for the Poor and Needy'.

'But it's a government scheme,' Henrietta said helplessly. 'That's why it's called a *national* kitchen. The government will pay money towards the cost of it, Mrs Upton-Hayes. It isn't a soup-kitchen, it's to provide cheaper meals for the working classes. Of course, we'll have to get up subscriptions as well—'

'There's no difficulty about subscriptions, Mrs Compton,' said Mrs Cowey complacently. 'I flatter myself we have raised as much money for good causes as any neighbourhood in England. But is this the best thing to spend the money *on*? Aren't there more pressing needs? The wounded, for instance, and widows and orphans?'

'They are already being taken care of,' Henrietta said. 'This is a new need because of the terrible food shortages. And food is surely the most pressing need of all.'

'But,' said Mrs Upton-Hayes, 'to be giving out free food without any requirement for moral improvement—'

'It's not free food, it's cheaper food. So many of the poor people don't have proper facilities for cooking. And, of course, there's the benefit of cooking in quantity – making Irish stew on a large scale brings it within the reach of—'

'The Irish above all,' Mrs Upton-Hayes overrode her, 'know the value of prayer when combined with philanthropy – though, of course, then you come up against the problem of Catholicism,' she short-circuited herself with a frown.

'I don't see why the Irish should get free food and no-one else,' Mrs Portwaine complained. 'All we hear about is the Irish, and after that shocking business in Dublin—'

'It isn't for the Irish,' Henrietta unravelled patiently, 'it's for all the working people, so that they get enough nourishment to do their jobs properly. Some of the girls at the munitions factory, for instance—'

'Oh, I can't agree with girls working in factories,' Mrs Cowey interrupted. 'What are we supposed to do for servants? It's all but impossible to get a decent housemaid, these days.'

'I so agree, Mrs Cowey, dear,' Mrs Enderby cried. 'I had a girl last month – I had to let her go, of course – but can you guess what the impudent hussy did? Why, she'd no sooner arrived than . . .'

And so it went. Henrietta knew that she'd get the thing done at last, but it was a long process, and when Polly appeared at the door she was glad of the interruption and longing for a good, strong cup of tea.

Judging by the eagerness of the greeting Polly received, everyone else had had enough of philanthropy for the time being, too. She greeted everyone, allowed herself to be petted, then told a rapt audience the story of Ezra and the mules, which lasted until Sawry came in with the maids and the loaded tea-trays. As well as the Fat Rascals and the squares of parkin, there was a beautiful Madeira cake – Mrs Stark's speciality – jam tarts, and lots of brown and white bread and butter. The sight was greeted with bright eyes and glad cries of pleasure.

'Oh, Mrs Compton, you always put on a good tea!'

'Your Mrs Stark is worth her weight in gold.'

'I must say my throat is dry with all this talking.'

'Tea already? Goodness, I wasn't looking for it for ages yet!'

Polly obeyed a look from Henrietta and eased herself in beside her. 'Poor Ezra. How bad is it, Polly dear?' Henrietta asked.

'Willa Banks doesn't think it's broken,' Polly said, 'but it's very swollen and he won't be able to walk for days.'

'I'll drive over tomorrow and see him myself,' Henrietta said. 'It's a great nuisance for them all – and the field only half ploughed, you say?'

'A bit less than half. It's a wonder to me he got so far,

if it was all like the bit where he stopped. It was a massive stone, and only just under the surface.'

Henrietta frowned in sudden thought. 'Wait, I know that field. There used to be a cottage in it when I was a girl. An old woman lived there – what was her name? Dykes? Dacres?'

'There's no cottage now,' Polly pointed out, through the melting deliciousness of Mrs Stark's Fat Rascal.

'No, it was taken down long ago, and the stones used for other buildings. But I'm willing to bet that what Ezra got stuck on was the footings,' Henrietta said.

'Gosh, yes, that's probably it,' Polly said.

'Don't say "gosh", dear. Your father wouldn't like it. If it is the footings, it'll be impossible to plough over them.'

'What about Daddy's tractor? Couldn't that do it?'

'Prospect has got it for the next couple of weeks, for fleet-ploughing, and then White House want it. Besides, it couldn't plough through foundations any more than a hand-plough. And no-one at Woodhouse knows how to drive it.'

'I bet the Tommies do,' Polly said. 'The London one, Auden, was so funny, Aunty—'

Henrietta smiled. 'I think his name's Horden, dear.'

Polly thought. 'Oh, yes, I see! Anyway, he told everyone a story about a parrot, and then he went on to stories about ferrets and goldfish and someone's pet goat and a dog that could count up to ten, and poor old Ezra was simply bursting to talk about his mules, but he couldn't get a word in edge-wise. And then when the meal was over and the Tommies got up to go back to work, Auden – Horden – dropped me such a wink! I'm sure he was doing it deliberately to tease Ezra. I suppose they've heard a lot about those mules at mealtimes, one way and another.'

Henrietta laughed, but she said, 'Ezra is a difficult old man sometimes, but I don't know what the Bankses would do without him. He does a tremendous amount around the farm. If he's laid up for any length of time—'

'Gosh, yes,' Polly said, 'and that was something else I

64

meant to tell you, Aunty. Willa Banks says Jeb's been called up.'

Henrietta was shocked. 'Jeb? But who's going to do the work if he goes?'

'That's what Willa said, but he's within the age limit, and apparently they think Eli and Ezra ought to be enough.' Eli, at sixty, was too old for conscription. 'She's awfully worried, Aunty.'

'Yes, she must be.'

'I think I'll ask Daddy about it when he comes home,' Polly said. Teddy was in Liverpool, where he had gone to sort out a shipping problem, concerning some goods from one of his factories that had been held up. While there, he usually stayed with the chief recruiting officer for Liverpool, Major Benjamin Finch, who was an old friend, so his visits tended to extend themselves pleasantly. 'Perhaps he could speak to someone and get Jeb let off. I know everyone has to do their bit, but surely Jeb is more useful on the land than in the army.'

Henrietta shook her head. 'I don't know, dear. If he passes the physical examination, I don't think there'll be anything your father can do.'

Tea was coming to an end, so Polly took herself off to wash and change, leaving Henrietta to battle the meeting to its conclusion.

Later that week as Polly was crossing the staircase hall, Maria, Frank's widow, came out of the steward's room where she worked as Teddy's secretary, keeping his personal correspondence and the estate accounts. She had been accustomed to earning her living before she married Frank, and working helped her get through the days without him.

She paused when she saw Polly and said, 'Oh, Polly, I've got something for you. Wait there a moment.' She went back into the steward's room and emerged with an envelope in her hand. 'This came for you by the second post.' Her eyes scanned Polly's face and observed her expression as she looked at the envelope and recognised Holford's small, difficult hand. 'It's none of my business,' she said, 'but if it's something your father wouldn't approve of, you know he'll probably find out in the end.'

Polly looked up. 'You won't tell him? It's only a *letter*. There's nothing wrong with that, only Daddy's so old-fashioned. But oughtn't we to write to the men at the Front, to keep their spirits up?'

Maria turned away. 'You argue it out with yourself any way you want. As I said, it's none of my business.'

So she wouldn't tell, Polly thought, with satisfaction, and ran up the stairs to her room, where she could read the letter in privacy.

When Henrietta finally found time to tell Teddy about Jeb Banks being called up, he shook his head. 'I know it's hard, but there's nothing I can do. Even *miners* are being taken now, and you know they were always exempt. There's going to be a big push this year and they'll need everyone they can get.'

'There's always a big push,' Henrietta said sadly. 'Another one every year.'

Teddy did not try to explain to her why this one would be different. He was not convinced himself that it would be. He offered her a counter-irritant. 'I hear from Pike over at Eastfield Farm that their Jack has had his call-up.'

'Oh, Teddy, no! Not Jack Eastfield as well! They've already taken Jimmy and Mike. What on earth will the Pikes do?'

'Well, they have that land-girl, and she seems a decent sort,' Teddy said. 'And, of course, the school children help when they can.' As a member of the Schools Board he knew how high truanting rates were among boys, and why. No-one on the board was much inclined to enforce school attendance once the boys reached eleven or twelve, given how much they were needed elsewhere.

'But they can't do all the jobs,' Henrietta said. 'Sometimes it needs a man's strength.'

'Yes, I know,' Teddy said, 'and there is a solution, but I'm not sure how the neighbourhood would take to it.'

'What do you mean?'

'It happens that I mentioned the labour shortage at dinner at Major Finch's, and he said the government wants to use German prisoners of war on the land. A large number of them were farm workers originally, you know. And yesterday when I talked to our Colonel Barrisford at Fulford, he said they're already planning to set up a labour camp here.'

'Oh, Teddy, no!' Henrietta said, looking shocked.

Teddy noted her look with interest, for it was an indication of how everyone else would react. Of course the Germans were the hated enemy, and since the beginning of the war the newspapers had been full of stories of their 'frightfulness', portraying them as sub-human beasts capable of any atrocity. But times were changing, and men had to change with them.

'Well, you know,' he said apologetically, 'some of these prisoners are only lads, eighteen or nineteen years old, and they never wanted to go to war. They were called up, just like our lads, and had no choice about it. Barrisford says a lot of them were glad to be captured, so they didn't have to go on fighting.'

'You want me to feel sorry for them?' Henrietta said. The enemy had taken his son Ned and her son Frank.

'It's the Kaiser and the German government and the generals, the fellows at the top, that we ought to hate,' Teddy said. 'A lot of these boys don't even know what it's all about. They were dragged away from their farms, had a rifle pushed into their hands, and were marched off to the trenches. All they want is to go back home.'

'When we've beaten them, they can go back home,' Henrietta said.

'Of course,' said Teddy. 'But meanwhile we have all these

fit young fellows on our hands, and none of our own to tend our fields. There's a big PoW camp on the Isle of Man, and Finch said they want to move some of them out to make room for a new intake when the campaigning starts again. Now, doesn't it make more sense to have them work for their living, rather than keeping them idle, eating their heads off at our expense and giving nothing in return?'

Henrietta shook her head doubtfully, trying to imagine it. Hun soldiers with English blood on their hands let loose across Yorkshire fields? 'How could we trust them?' she said. 'What's to stop them escaping? What's to stop them murdering us in our beds?'

'The ones they send out on labour details will be the ones they can trust, the ones who'd sooner be doing honest work out in the fields than rotting behind barbed wire. They'll be grateful for the chance, and won't do anything to spoil it.'

Henrietta looked resentful. 'I can see you've already made up your mind.'

'I'm just telling you what Finch told me. The government's keen to get some of the expense of them laid off, and we need the labour if we're to feed the nation this year. We don't want a repeat of last year's shortages. You might even find you like them once you get to know them,' he added mischievously.

'Never!' Henrietta cried.

Holford's letter, even when read for the third time, was not as satisfying as Polly had hoped it would be. There was a lot about him and not very much about her in it. She didn't mind hearing about his experiences in France, and what the CO had said to him, but she would have preferred to read what Holford thought about her, and how much he missed her.

He did mention his forthcoming leave, but that was disappointing too. He was going to spend it at home with his parents, which meant London and Surrey, and there wouldn't be time for a trip to Yorkshire. Polly conceded reluctantly that a fellow had to visit his parents, but in his position she felt she might have made *some* kind of excuse – he had friends in York and his parents must know it.

With a sigh, she put the letter away in her drawer and wandered discontentedly downstairs. Hearing voices in the steward's room she turned that way. It was her father, talking to her aunt, and as she came in, she caught the end of an interesting-sounding exchange.

'You might even find you like them once you get to know them,' her father said.

And Aunt Henrietta said vehemently, 'Never!'

Polly looked from one to the other. 'Get to like who, Aunty?'

'It's a private conversation, Polly,' Henrietta said, with unusual sharpness, for she was still ruffled by the whole idea.

'We didn't close the door,' Teddy said reasonably, 'and she'll have to know sooner or later.'

'Not if nothing comes of it,' Henrietta said.

'Comes of what, Daddy?'

'Getting German prisoners of war up here to work on the farms.'

Polly's eyes grew round, and she drew a breath of surprise. 'Germans? Here?' For years her father had been drilling the household and tenants in home defence and what to do if they were invaded, which included, in Polly's case, using one of her father's sporting guns to kill as many of them as she could before they killed her. 'Daddy, you can't mean it!'

Teddy proceeded to explain the situation to his darling daughter at some length. She, too, had always heard the Germans talked about in the most pejorative terms, but she was ready to have her mind changed, and this was her father, after all. He must know what he was talking about. His words mingled with the canon of literature she had been exposed to, photographs and illustrations in books and the papers, and created in her mind an intriguing picture of a dozen tall, muscular Fritzes (the 'good' ones) scything and tedding and digging in her very own father's fields, marching home into the sunset with their tools across their shoulders, singing German songs in close harmony.

Adding herself into the picture, which at seventeen was pretty much automatic, she saw herself bringing them water in the noonday heat, showing her magnanimity towards the defeated – 'Even a German is entitled to quench his thirst.' She saw their looks of humble admiration for her as they eased their dusty throats. It was a more interesting attitude than the usual blind condemnation, and Polly liked to be different.

And the excitement of it! Tamed murderers, defeated in war, bowing their necks, trying to make amends – and she, the young lady of the house, lording it over them. The thrill of wondering whether they were completely tamed! The frisson of their indescribable wickedness! And if they did prove treacherous, she saw herself holding the door of Morland Place, one of her father's Purdeys in her hands, shooting them down one by one with magnificent marksmanship, while the servants cowered behind her. She would be given a medal – she saw the King pinning the VC to her breast, saying in awed tones, 'Twenty Germans shot single-handed? You are a national heroine, Miss Morland!'

'Oh, Daddy,' she said, 'I definitely think we ought to have them.'

He looked surprised and pleased to have won her over. But Aunt Hen was still very much against, and the discussion prolonged itself, with Polly joining in enthusiastically. Holford's letter – Holford himself – had vanished for the moment from her mind. After all, it was no use crying over what couldn't be helped. She had inherited a great deal of her father's practicality. The determination to make the best of what was to hand frequently warred with her desire for drama and romance but, to her credit, most often won.

CHAPTER FOUR

It was a beast of a day when Emma sailed to Calais: forbidding sky, troubled grey sea and driving sleet. She was not the only female on board: there was a draft of WAACs, chattering like starlings in their excitement at going abroad for the first time, and two rather aloof VAD nurses, going back off leave, she supposed. The weather soon drove them below, but despite the cold, Emma remained on deck, clinging to the rail as the sea heaved the steamer about under her feet, staring blindly at the murk that had replaced any semblance of a view. She thought of how often Fenniman had done this same trip, going back after leave. She imagined him in his greatcoat and cap leaning on the rail beside her, watching the white cliffs disappear, the cloud of his breath mingling with hers. The tears felt warm on her cold cheek. *But I'm coming to do my part*, she told his shade. She thought he would be glad.

Her old life was ending, and she sensed that the new one, which would begin when she set foot on French soil again, would be very different. Fenniman belonged in her old life, and in this hiatus between the two she clung to him, the sad ghost at her side, knowing their time was almost up. The salt on her lips was like the taste of sorrow. When the ship eased into dock, he would slip away into the shadows. He was one of The Dead now. He did not belong in the busy precincts of the living world. But in this place between worlds she felt his presence, and she stayed, longing and lost, alone on the deck, caught between the grey sky and the grey sea, like a ghost herself.

Disembarking at seething Calais ousted every thought from her mind but the problem of getting through the official checks while keeping all her luggage together. When the Customs shed finally spewed her onto the slippery wet cobbles of the dock, in a renewed spat of wind-driven sleet, she found herself the only female in a mass of purposeful, indifferent men, and felt the first qualm. The nurses had disappeared, huddled arm in arm, and the WAACs had been marched off in crocodile towards the town. Only she was left ungarnered, not knowing where to go.

But just as she was considering seeking some form of official help, she saw a small, elderly box lorry with a red cross on its canvas side coming towards her. It stopped a few feet away and an odd-looking figure jumped down: short and wide, wearing a very hairy fur coat, skewbald in colour, with a woollen scarf tied round the head over the top of a cap. The vision was plastered to waist-level with crystals of sleet. These it proceeded to beat off with a leather-gloved hand, which it then extended to Emma.

'Hello! Sorry I'm a bit late,' said a cheery, female voice, with the unmistakable, crisp accent of the *ton*. 'I meant to be here before you, but Megan objected to rather a large puddle, and then she wouldn't start again. Forty-eight swings it took, and she *always* starts on thirteen!'

'Megan?' Emma queried, mystified.

'This old girl, here.' She patted the lorry's bonnet as one might pat the neck of a horse. 'I had a Welsh pony called Megan when I was seven. Exhibited many of the same traits – couldn't get her across water for nuts. I say, you are Weston, aren't you? Of course you are,' she answered herself. 'You're the only FANY waiting. I'm Foxton. Everyone calls me Foxy. I've been sent to collect you and take you back to Unit Three, but we've got to pick up some supplies for Camp Nieulay first. I hope you don't mind.'

'Of course not,' Emma said. She had located a round, crimson face with a blue nose in the encircling wool, and saw now that the cap under the scarf was a soft FANY beret like her own. The bulkiness of the figure was apparently due to the many layers of clothing under the strange hairy coat, which, as Foxton was not tall, made her look even wider. The crimson-ness and the crusting of sleet were explained by the fact that the lorry had no windscreen. 'Can't you get the windscreen mended?' she asked.

'It's not broken, it's been removed. The reflection from a windscreen gives the German flyers a target so we don't use 'em.' She grinned cheerfully. 'Welcome to Calais Convoy! Just the first of the little treats waiting for you! Plastered with snow in winter, plastered with dust and insects in summer, and soaked with rain at every point in between. You'll soon get used to it. Is that all your luggage? Let's stow it in the back, then.'

Either Foxton was much stronger than she looked or she had learned a knack in handling heavy objects, for she made nothing of Emma's trunk – Emma felt more of a hindrance than a help on the other end of it. When her bags were stowed she climbed clumsily up into the lorry, while Foxton clambered up the other side as nimbly as a monkey, and perched herself on a cushion on the box. She looked absurdly small to be in charge of even this under-sized lorry, but as the engine had been left running, she had only to put it into gear and drive off.

She cast several sideways glances at Emma, and then said, 'I say, I really admire your coat. It looks splendidly warm.'

'It is,' Emma said. It was a FANY greatcoat in navy blue with red piping, but it was fur-lined, and with a fur collar big enough to act as a hood if needed. 'The collar detaches – I wasn't sure if I'd be allowed to wear it. They said you weren't strict about uniform, but then I got a letter from the secretary telling me *exactly* what I had to wear.'

'Oh, gosh, yes! She wrote an article in the *Gazette*, too. They have a spasm every now and then of trying to trim our nails, but we're rather an independent-minded bunch, so it doesn't stick. As you can see from this noisome object.' She gestured to her own coat.

'I was wondering what it was,' Emma confessed.

'Ponyskin. Ghastly, isn't it? But jolly practical. Some of the others have goatskin coats. Biddy said it was disloyal of me to wear a horse, since we *are* a yeomanry, but I said the horse didn't want it any more. Of course, it wasn't an *English* pony.'

'Who's Biddy?' Emma asked, remembering that she had been told they didn't use Christian names in the corps.

'Joan Biddeford, one of ours. There are twenty-two of us – twenty-three counting you – plus two chaps, mechanics who also act as dressers when needed. Our commandant is Lilian Franklin – we just call her Boss. Our section leader used to be Muriel Thompson. Have you heard of her?'

'No, sorry, I haven't.'

'She was a racing-driver before the war. Isn't that splendid? Bit of a come-down for her, with nothing but these old wrecks to drive.' She patted the dashboard as she said it, as though she might have hurt Megan's feelings. Then she stopped speaking to concentrate: the quayside was very narrow and another ambulance was coming towards them. Emma was conscious that the edge of the harbour wall and the dark, heaving sea were very close to their outside wheels. When they were past Foxton said, 'It seems like a good moment to tell you that the rule here is that empties take the seaward side – for obvious reasons. The quay's horribly narrow and it gets beastly slippery when it freezes, like today.'

'Has anyone ever . . . ?' Emma began nervously.

'Just once. She got out, luckily. They even managed to winch the ambulance out later. But if anyone's to go in, they don't want it to be the wounded, so when you're empty you drive on this side. Ah, that's better – free and clear. Now we've got to find Shed Twenty-eight. Picking up something for one of our local Geraniums – that's what we call the top brass. Vital supplies, I was told, but I've no idea what they are or how big. That's why I came on Megan. I hope it'll all fit in. You don't mind helping me shift it, do you? Might take a while if there's a lot of it. I know you're not officially on duty until tomorrow, but—'

'Of course I'll help,' Emma said, proud to have a chance so soon to 'muck in'. A FANY always coped, and she was a FANY now.

It turned out that there was not a great deal of mucking in to be done, for when they found the right shed and enquired for the vital supplies, they discovered it was a case of Scotch whisky and two crates from Fortnum and Mason's, presumably packed with edible delicacies.

'But you can't get much more vital than that,' Foxton asserted. 'Grab that one, will you? I can manage the others.' She chuckled as they heaved and slid the boxes into the back of the lorry. 'I'll bet it's for Colonel Hunter. Poor thing, he's just not used to roughing it.'

Outside the dockyard, they drove through the narrow, crowded streets of Calais, Foxton handling the lumbering lorry with a careless skill that Emma vowed silently to replicate. 'Watch out for the trams,' she told Emma. 'Now the French've seen us in action – us FANYs, I mean – they've started to use women tram drivers and, of course, the poor dears have no experience. It's like going for a hack with a beginner on an unschooled horse. Don't assume they'll ever stop for you, even when you have right of way.'

'I suppose you have to drive through Calais often?'

'Every day, pretty much. We have to meet the ambulance trains and barges, and transport the wounded to the various hospitals, or take them to the ship if they're going home to Blighty. And we transfer the wounded from one

76

hospital to another, and pick them up from the camps. That's the main part of our duties. But we also collect rations and other supplies and deliver them to various places, and sometimes people, too. We've always ferried the sisters between the hospitals and the dock when they go on leave or come back, and that seems to have set a precedent: since we had the telephone put in, we get all sorts of requests now, especially from the outlying camps. People take advantage, you know,' she said, with unusual severity. 'We don't mind a reasonable request during a quiet spell but, as Boss says, many people seem to forget that an ambulance convoy is not a cab rank. She's had to be quite firm about it.' She smiled suddenly. 'She's a dear. Don't be put off by her fierce demeanour, will you? She has to be tough to fight our corner, but underneath she's an absolute trump.'

'I'll try to remember that,' Emma said. 'What else do you do?' The sleet was gathering on her face and chest, but the warmth of Foxton's character was making the journey tolerable.

'Oh, let me see. Well, the worst thing is doing corpses – collecting dead bodies and taking them to the morgue.'

Emma was taken aback. 'Oh! Do we have to do that as well?'

'Yes. Of course, it's rather upsetting. Sometimes they're pretty ripe, poor things, and cleaning out the ambulance afterwards isn't very nice. But we cope. If the call comes in near a mealtime, the thing to do is wait and have the meal first, because you won't feel like it afterwards. And, after all, the dead don't mind hanging around.' She glanced sideways at Emma. 'Have I upset you?'

'Oh – no! Not really. It just takes some – adjustment of mind.'

'That's the spirit! We were all "nice young ladies" once – and I suppose we will be again when all this is over. In the meantime,' she looked mischievous, 'you can comfort yourself with the thought that you might get a turn on James.'

'James?'

'Our motor-bath. He's got ten collapsible canvas baths, a huge water-tank heated by Primus, and a disinfecting cupboard. He can give two hundred and fifty baths a day and disinfect all the lice-ridden clothes at the same time. The Tommies love him, but he's rather a challenge to drive, with two gear levers, a most peculiar hand-brake and no accelerator – that's if you can get him started in the first place! Believe me, however much driving you've done up to now, you've never met anyone like James.'

'I believe you,' Emma said, laughing. 'I can see I've got a lot to learn.' She was beginning to feel rather light-headed, though whether that was the effect of the blood leaving her frozen face, or the strange thoughts of transporting corpses and giving baths to lice-ridden male strangers, she wasn't sure.

They left the town and drove out into the surrounding country, unwelcoming in the bleak winter half-light. The wind seemed to increase as they left the shelter of the buildings, but now it was coming from the direction of the sea and hitting the lorry side-on, rocking it with the fury of its onslaught and making the canvas crack like gunfire. It meant at least that it was not driving full into their faces, though it now came in through the side window and crusted their laps. But it was not far to Camp Nieulay, where they stopped to make their delivery of vital supplies. Even so, by then Emma was frozen, and was ashamed to find her teeth chattering.

'We'll take this stuff to the orderly room,' Foxton said, 'and then I ought to introduce you to some of the chaps. You'll be seeing quite a bit of them, I expect, in the course of duty.'

They unloaded the cases, Emma taking the whisky and Foxton the two boxes, which she said were quite light, and walked towards the orderly room. Foxton said, 'I don't know if I ought to mention the protocol regarding chaps. Pursuitors, we call them, because they do like to pursue, bless the dear fellows. There's something about young women driving big ambulances that makes us uniquely fascinating! We don't have many rules because it's assumed that our own good breeding will keep us out of trouble. We're all on our honour not to let the corps down, and there's never been the slightest breath of scandal about a FANY. Just about the only rule is that when we dine out with a chap – we're allowed to once a week when it's quiet – we have to go in pairs and be back by ten.'

Emma said, rather more abruptly than she meant to, 'My fiancé was killed at Ypres last year.'

Foxton stopped and looked at her over the top of the boxes, her eyes round with distress. 'Oh, golly, I'm so sorry! How absolutely ghastly for you – and here am I babbling on about chaps. Please forgive me. I'm so dreadfully sorry for you. None of us in Unit Three has lost a fiancé, but two of us have lost brothers, and it's devastating.'

There was no doubting her companion's genuine sympathy, and Emma managed a bleak smile and said, 'It's all right. I just thought I ought to mention it now, rather than—'

'Of course, of course,' Foxton rushed on, 'and I'll tell the others so you won't have to go through my tactlessness all over again. Perhaps we won't call on the chaps just now. We're all invited to a camp entertainment next week, so you can perfectly well meet them then.'

It was a relief to get in out of the cold, into the fug of a wooden hut heated by an oil stove. The odour of paraffin and cigarettes was so thick, after the biting freshness of the air outside, that Emma felt you might have sliced it. There was an officer with the orderly clerk, the latter seated at his desk, the former leaning over his shoulder to examine a sheaf of documents he was holding.

The officer straightened up as they came in, and said, 'Foxy! To what do we owe the pleasure?'

'Emergency supplies. Probably for the CO,' Foxton said. 'To be applied internally, by the look of them.'

'Must be the goodies for our mess beano. Good old FANY! You never disappoint.'

'I'd remind you,' Foxton said, with mock severity, 'that we are not the grocer's boy.'

'Ah, but you'll get the benefit next week,' he said beguilingly. 'We couldn't entertain you ladies on bully and biscuit, now could we? Dickens!'

The corporal hardly needed prompting to go round the desk and take Foxton's two boxes, and the officer moved the other way and came to relieve Emma of her burden. He was a slim young man, taller than Emma but not as tall as Fenniman had been; dark, like him, though, with a lean face and eyes of an unusual light brown that was almost golden. They lit with a pleasant, welcoming smile as they examined her face. He was much younger than Fenniman – not much older than Emma herself, probably – but he was no boy: the maturity of war was in the kind but capable lines of his face. He was a man, her instant judgement suggested, who would always manage to get things done.

'A new face,' he said. 'I'm sorry, I didn't immediately realise – though I should have known I didn't recognise that coat. I can tell Foxy even at a distance by her unique pelt. Yours is splendid, by the by! But we haven't been introduced. Foxy, won't you do the honours? I'm babbling like an idiot, here.'

Foxton, who had been using her newly freed hands to scrape the ice off her seaward side, looked up and said, 'Oh, sorry – remiss of me. Weston, this is Captain Wentworth of the Thirty-seventh – who, among other incarnations, is the entertainments officer here, and excels at amateur dramatics. So he's a man of parts, literally and figuratively. Captain Wentworth, this is our new recruit, Trooper Weston, just arrived from Blighty. I picked her up from Calais when I was collecting the colonel's medicine.'

'Miss Weston, I'm delighted to meet you,' Wentworth said, shaking her hand, and scanning her face with a hint of a question. 'Forgive me, but haven't we met? Your face seems familiar.'

'I don't think so,' Emma said. 'I'm sure I'd remember you.' With his dark colouring and those hazel eyes, his was not a forgettable face. She meant no more than that, but he looked pleased.

'How kind of you to say so. Perhaps I've seen your photograph somewhere, then?'

He obviously meant it as a question, so she said, 'It has been in the illustrated papers occasionally. My father was Thomas Weston, the MP.'

'MP and philanthropist – of course.' His face lit with recollection, and he went on, 'And last year in the *Illustrated London*—' A further memory intruded, and stopped him dead.

Emma could read his mind. He had seen the lavish articles and photographs that had accompanied the announcement of her engagement; and now he had remembered the report of Fenniman's death. She felt as if she were carrying visible open wounds.

Impulsively he took her hand again. 'I'm so sorry. I'm an idiot for insisting on bringing it up.'

'Not at all,' she said politely. 'You weren't to know.'

'I knew Major Fenniman slightly,' he said. 'May I be permitted to say he was a great loss, and I can only imagine your sadness?'

'Thank you,' Emma said.

He released her hand and said, 'I won't mention it again, I promise,' and such was the kindness and understanding in his voice and his look, she found herself feeling oddly comforted. Perhaps this was what it would have been like, she thought, to have a brother.

Foxton intervened. 'We'd better be getting back,' she said. 'Who knows how many emergencies have arisen in our absence? They could be crying out for Megan in a dozen places while we stand here chatting.'

'Yes, I'm sure there's a transport major somewhere with a dinner-date whose car won't start,' said Wentworth.

'I shall make you regret those words, Wentworth,' Foxton said severely, 'when I've had time to think of a suitable method. Say goodbye nicely.'

'Goodbye nicely,' Wentworth repeated obediently.

'And to Weston.'

'Goodbye nicely,' he said, smiling at Emma, though his eyes still questioned whether he had offended her. 'You will come to our entertainment next week, won't you?'

'We're all coming,' Foxton answered for her. 'And Weston will be as ready for a diversion as anyone by the time she's been here a week. Well, toodle-oo. Goodbye, Dickens.'

Outside, it seemed to have got even colder, and the sleet was now falling as enormous wet flakes of snow. 'I hope he didn't tread on your toes,' Foxton said as they went back to the lorry. 'He doesn't mean any harm. He's like a big, clumsy puppy. Which reminds me. I dare say you'll find everyone calling you Westie before long. I hope you don't mind. Do you like dogs? We have two at the camp, but we've never had a Westie. Waddell had a dear little fox-terrier, a tremendous mouser called Tuppence, but he disappeared. I dare say he wandered off and got run over, poor little beast. He was always one for wandering, and the roads hereabouts aren't safe for drivers, never mind four-footed pedestrians.'

She chattered on, and Emma guessed she was trying to distract her, in case the talk of Fenniman had upset her. But she didn't feel upset – nor that Wentworth had been clumsy. He had been the soul of kindness, she thought. And that he had actually known Fenniman, even if only slightly, made her feel that, out here, she really was entering Fenniman's world, the army world with all its idiosyncrasies.

82

Before, it had been the place he went away to, away from her, where she could not follow. Now she had come to be part of it, and that made her feel closer to him.

There was no doubt that Jack was shocked, angry and hurt, in that order, when he came home on leave and Helen told him the truth about Jessie. With Helen's connivance Jessie made sure she was not present when he arrived. She went for a long walk on the downs, a walk that extended itself as she found she couldn't face seeing her favourite brother's disappointment in her.

So it was Helen who bore the brunt of it.

'My sister, so far to forget herself!'

'I don't think it was really a case of forgetting,' Helen said mildly.

'And Bertie! I can't believe it. *Bertie!*'

'Darling, do try to understand. They've been secretly in love for years and years, and behaved very honourably all that time—'

'Well, why couldn't they go *on* behaving honourably?' he cried in wounded tones.

'Because they knew it might be their only chance to – to be together. They both know the odds of his surviving the war.' It was a hard thing to say aloud, and she hated the sound of it on the air. It stopped Jack's next words before they were uttered, and he met her eyes in a moment of stillness. Knowledge, fear and love passed between them. He took her hand and pressed it in acknowledgement of all they had not said on that subject.

But he said, 'It still doesn't make it right.'

'I know it doesn't. But you don't know all yet. Maud has left Bertie and wants a divorce.'

'Because of this?'

'No, no, she left him before this. She wants to marry Lord Manvers.'

'Ah,' said Jack, and turned away a moment to stare out

83

of the window. Long ago, in his youth, he had courted Maud, had been in love with her, had asked her to marry him. She had turned him down – not good enough for her, was how he had always interpreted the rejection. He was then just an engineer with nothing but his salary, and she had married Bertie instead, who was rich and had a title. 'So she's swapping a baronet for a baron,' he said. 'Perhaps her ambition will be satisfied now.'

'Darling!' Helen protested, and he turned back to see her smiling wryly. 'If Maud hadn't turned you down, you wouldn't have met *me*.'

'True,' he said, kissing her in apology. 'But, oh, Helen, what a Dickens of a mess! What's to be done about Jessie?'

'I've told her she can stay here as long as she needs to. Was I right? You won't cast her out into the snow?'

He shook his head, but she could see it was in sadness and wonder at the situation, not denial. 'This will be very bad for them at home. And they're bound to find out.'

'What about the child?' Helen said, feeling that was the more important consideration. 'Bertie wrote to Jessie that he's put things in motion, but I gather there's little chance of the divorce coming through before it's born. Poor little thing. Its whole life will be affected.'

'She should have thought of that beforehand,' he said with a last spasm of severity. And then, 'We must do everything we can to support her. She's my sister.'

'True,' Helen said, seeing with relief that he had got all his anger out. 'And the child will be your nephew or niece.'

'Poor Jessie,' Jack said. 'Where is she, by the way? Hiding?'

Hunger was driving Jessie inexorably back to the house. She was always ravenous now. And she was beginning to feel she had played an ignoble part in *not* facing Jack, though Helen had said it was better if she broke the news to him alone. All the same, Jessie had always been one to take her lumps, and the thought that he might be even more disappointed in her for running away made her brace her shoulders and start trudging back. Near the house she was accosted with much energy by Jack's disreputable-looking mongrel, Rug, who had been let out into the garden when Jack first arrived, and had soon found it too small for his ambitions. Jessie knelt on one knee to accommodate his frenzy of greeting, and resumed her walk with him frisking delightedly about her.

She shed her boots and outerwear in the back hall, and went into the sitting room, as nervous, shy and embarrassed as if she were eleven again, feeling her cheeks burn with shame and hoping it would be attributed to the cold air outside. Her eyes flew straight to Jack, and she saw his drop from her face to the bulge below. Her hands went to it in a gesture automatically defensive, and there was something about the movement that both broke Jack's heart, and brought him finally and completely onto her side.

'Oh, Jessie,' he said, and held out his arms.

She went to him, and her own heart surged with the complexity of love, regret and fear that she knew all too well now, but would never have known if it were not for the war. The same truth held for him as for Bertie: every time she saw him might be the last.

Jack felt her tears on his neck, and it touched him more than he could bear. 'Don't cry, Jess,' he said. 'I – I understand.'

She put herself a little back from him to study his face. '*Do* you? I'm sorry for how this will hurt people, but I'm not sorry I did it. I'd do it again, if I could go back. Can you understand that, Jackie, and not hate me for it?'

'I don't think that's important now. We're past all that. We have you and the child to take care of, until Bertie can do it for himself.' He had thought it would be hard to say Bertie's name to her, but it slipped out without his noticing. 'That's the important thing. You know, the more I think about it, the more I think you ought to go home. They have to know sooner or later,' he stemmed her immediate denial, 'and the longer you leave it, the more hurt they'll be that you didn't tell them.'

'I don't agree. I think the sight of me like this will hurt them far more than my turning up one day with a child. It's more – more *personal*.'

'Bertie intends to marry you?'

'Of course.' The question hurt her. 'And the best thing of all would be not to tell them about the child until after I'm married.'

As a statement it begged so many questions: would she carry to term, would it be a live birth, would Bertie get his divorce, would he live long enough to marry her? And such a marriage! A second marriage after a divorce was not something anyone could feel wholeheartedly glad about. But these questions were known to them all, and there was no point in airing them again.

'If I can stay here until then . . . ?' she concluded.

Jack sighed. 'As far as I'm concerned, my home is yours and always will be. But I don't like deceiving Mother and Uncle Teddy, and I still think you'll make things worse the longer you leave them.'

'But you won't tell?' Her face was tense with the urgency of the plea.

Rug put his paws up on Jack's leg, pushing his rough head under his hand, disturbed by the atmosphere. Jack caressed his ears automatically, and said, 'I won't tell, if you don't want me to.'

'Thank you.'

And after all, Jack reflected, the situation might resolve itself without the need to tell them anything at home. Jessie had a history of miscarriage, and if she should lose the child, the family would have been upset for no good reason by being told about it. In fact, it would probably be the best thing all round if she did lose the child; but he was surprised by how little satisfaction the thought gave him.

★ ★ ★

The camp of FANY Unit 3 was set up on a slight hill among the sand dunes, halfway between Calais and the Casino, which had been taken over by the British Red Cross and was now a hospital. In the summer, it might have been a pleasant spot, overlooking the Channel, but now in winter the sea seemed always bad-tempered, and the biting wind came romping in unchecked to test the deficiencies of their shelters. These consisted of a series of wooden huts, which, made of unseasoned wood, had warped quite badly in the extremes of weather and seemed to let in as much damp and cold as they kept out.

Each FANY had her own cubicle off a central corridor, fitted with a bed and shelves, and such other furniture as they scrounged or manufactured for themselves. There was a bathhouse, supplied with hot water by a boiler and furnace, and a mess hut: together, these provided their chief comforts. Cooking was done on Primus stoves in a corrugated-iron shed under the shelter of some trees, and in case of air-raids there was a dugout in the side of the hill – a long tunnel with wooden benches on either side and a hurricane lamp.

And then there were the vehicles: the ambulances, which were mostly converted motor-cars, a large and a small lorry, a motor-bicycle, and James, the mobile bath unit. They were a motley collection, all of different makes, mostly old, all erratic and prone as much as any motor vehicle to mechanical breakdown, punctures and mysterious losses of function. The cleaning, greasing, repairing and general upkeep of these cantankerous beasts kept the FANYs busy when they weren't driving.

Emma was amused to see how the girls treated them like the horses they had grown up with, giving them names, and generally using horseman's language to talk about them. They spoke of being 'on' a certain vehicle, rather than 'in' it, talked about them 'baulking at water' and 'galloping well today'. An undiagnosed engine trouble might well be described as 'colic'; an ambulance with a puncture was 'lame in her off-fore'.

'Boss' Franklin turned out not to be at all daunting, a small, compact woman with dark wavy hair, piercing dark eyes and a brisk manner. But in between answering calls from the telephone, which seemed hardly ever silent, she was nothing but kindness to Emma, said how delighted they were to have her, and told her she would have to do a few days in the motor repair shop, getting to know the vehicles. 'They all have their strange little ways, as no doubt the others will tell you. You can accompany someone on a call or two, to see how things are done, and learn your way around. Then we'll see about giving you an ambulance of your own. In general our drivers stick to the same one. They're all such beasts to drive, and need understanding – and, of course, you have to be able to do running repairs when it breaks down in the middle of nowhere.'

'When do you think that will be, ma'am? When will I get my own ambulance?'

Franklin smiled. 'Don't call me "ma'am". "Boss" is quite enough. I think if what I hear about you from home is right, you should have your own ambulance by next week. I hope you're prepared for the challenge. It's a great deal of hard work even in quiet times like this, and that could change in an instant.'

'I'm looking forward to it,' Emma said, with truth.

'Good. Off you go, then, and get settled in. And, by the way, you don't need to salute me again. We have one salute first thing in the morning, and we find that's quite enough for the day.'

Emma was secretly relieved not to be going on calls straight away, for she did feel out of her depth in this strange environment, but the other women did everything they could to make her feel at home. As Foxy had predicted, she was 'Westie' by the end of the second day, and was introduced to every new person who came to the camp (and there seemed to be comings and goings all day) as 'one of ours'. There was no doubting the warmth and mutual affection within the unit, and that she was accepted unquestioningly into it was very heartening.

She enjoyed putting on her breeches and blue smock to go and toil in the motor workshop, and started to learn her way around the elderly vehicles and their heavy, coughing engines. The mechanics, Sparkes and Gibbs, were friendly lads, and helped her all they could. One of the difficulties in the camp was the shortage of water, which made cleaning the ambulances difficult. As the insides had to be cleaned, the outsides tended to be neglected until time could be spared to take them into a depot in Calais to be thoroughly hosed down. On her second day, Emma took one, following Sparkes in another, to have this done, and had her first experience of driving on the terrible roads around Calais: muddy, slippery, snowy, and pocked with shell holes. Some holes had been partly filled but, as Sparkes told her, you needed to know which were packed hard and could be driven across, and which were traps of soft mud where you would only dig yourself in. Each ambulance carried two planks to lay over the worst holes when necessary – not so much on the route into Calais, but when going out to the camps or up towards the line, where no maintenance had been done. At night, he told her, it was vital to know the roads for they were not allowed to use headlights, because of enemy action, and the small oil sidelights gave only the dimmest illumination.

Night duty was not something Emma was looking forward to, for despite the ambulance bonnets being covered with blankets and tarpaulins (which the FANYs called 'rugging up'), the engines would freeze in this weather if left standing all night. The drivers on night duty had to stumble out into the icy darkness every hour, hand-crank the motors and run them for a few minutes to warm them up. Cranking was immensely hard and strenuous work, and a certain knack

89

was needed if the crank handle was not to recoil and break a finger. Doing it in the dark in the middle of the night, with frozen hands and a head heavy for sleep, was doubly difficult.

In addition to working on the vehicles, Emma had to take her share of camp fatigues, such as general cleaning and tidying, helping in the cookhouse, chopping wood and stoking the furnace. And before the end of the week she was introduced to another regular task. The night before there had been a call from one of the outlying camps where there had been enemy shelling, and three ambulances had been dispatched. In the morning, one of the drivers, Pomeroy, always known as 'Pom', came up to Emma and said, almost apologetically, 'Boss wants you to help me clean out my bus. Show you how it's done.'

Pom was a quiet, dark-haired girl with an eager face, never talking much in the mess at night, but always listening avidly as if she had an inner secretary taking everything down.

Emma got up at once to go with her, and as they walked out, Pom said, 'It won't be very nice. Thought I'd warn you.'

The air was keen and cold that morning, still coming in off the sea, with a smell of iodine and snow on it, and a tang of woodsmoke from the furnace. Perhaps that made the contrast all the more pointed when Pom opened the rear doors of her ambulance and the stench assailed Emma's unprepared nostrils. She had heard of smells being bad enough to knock you down, but this was the first time she had encountered one in real life. In automatic reaction, she whipped her head away from it so hard that she ricked her neck and lost her balance. If Pom had not caught her elbow with a small, hard hand, she might have sat down in the mud. It was not just the blood, with its coppery reek, it was the pools of vomit. It had not occurred to her that men wounded and in pain might be sick, but Pom told her later it was often the case. Pain and fear also had the effect of loosening the bowels, and in absence of any other facility, the men had used a corner. That also, said Pom, was quite usual. And as a bass note to the other smells, there was the stink of unwashed bodies, dirty feet, and the mud that was a feature of the Front by this stage of the war. This foul, grey slime had nothing in common with the ordinary mud at home, but was a nightmare substance compounded with blood and detritus, rotting flesh, lyddite and bodily fluids.

Pom said, 'You have to get used to it. No-one likes the job, but it has to be done. And at least they were fresh wounds last night. It's worse when there's gangrene – I can't seem to get that smell out of my nose for days.'

Emma looked at her dumbly for a moment, thinking, *Why did I want to do this? Why did I lie about my age to get here?*

And Pom smiled a little and said, as if she had heard the thought, 'It's only one part of the job. And think of the poor wretches who *made* this mess. Think what they're going through.'

'You're quite right,' Emma said faintly. 'It was just the surprise. I shan't make a fool of myself again.'

'Oh, I expect you will,' Pom said cheerfully, handing her a bucket. 'We all do, all the time. It's what keeps us human.'

The work was physically hard on Emma, who had never been accustomed to it before, and at the end of each day she was exhausted. But a bath restored her a great deal – she had never before in her pampered life so appreciated the therapeutic value of hot water – and then there was supper and the evening in the mess to look forward to. The company of the other women, the conversation and laughter and sense of comradeship, made every difficulty worthwhile. She had never in her rather lonely life known what it could be to be surrounded by 'sisters', joined together in hard work and a common purpose. It was as stimulating as the conversation at Vera's, but more warming, because the subjects meant something to her, and she was part of the sisterhood now.

91

Each of them brought her own unique personality and talents to the communal fun. There were many who sang, one who played the violin, one who performed comic monologues, one with a perfect gift for stories, another who could manufacture jokes out of the most meagre material. They talked of their experiences during the day, their lives back home, of their childhoods, their brothers and sweethearts and odd characters they had met, of adored pets and favourite horses, quirky governesses and beloved teachers. And soon Emma was drawn in, and added her own strand to the tapestry they wove anew every evening. The two dogs, and Hutchinson's tabby cat, Pussica, dozed by the stove. Cocoa was brewed, and the women wrapped calloused, oil-stained hands that had once been soft and magnolia-white round the tin mugs, and held conversations of which their mothers – not to mention the governesses and teachers – would not have understood one word in three.

Exhausted Emma might be, and her hands would probably never look the same again, but she was content. She wrote to Vera to say that she understood now what she had meant about opportunity, was glad she had come, was ready to do her part. She felt she had found a family. And though she still thought of Fenniman every night when she got into bed, she no longer wept before she fell into a heavy, dreamless sleep.

CHAPTER FIVE

It had been hard enough for Henrietta to have Jessie go off to nurse, to be without her support when things were so difficult at home. Still, in wartime everyone had to make sacrifices. But Jessie's sudden return from France, and her departure for Wiltshire after only a few days at home, worried her. She felt instinctively that Jessie was in some kind of trouble. She hoped it was not that she was ashamed of having given up the nursing. Everyone had their limits, and Jessie had done her bit.

She missed Jessie every day. There was always so much to do, and the war seemed to add more all the time. There was the duty of calling on local families whose sons and husbands had been killed, which always took a great deal out of her: Jessie would have helped her with that. And she'd have been so useful in entertaining the soldiers from their 'own' camp – the officers to dinner and the men to tea-parties. The men often brought their little problems up to the 'big house', and Henrietta was glad to help them, read their letters, advise them on matters practical and heartfelt, but it all took time. Now there was the national kitchen to get under way, too. And if Teddy's idea of bringing in German prisoners came to anything, she knew it was she who would have to deal with the flood of complaints and anxieties that would spring up in the neighbourhood.

The low undercurrent of worry about Jessie did nothing

to lighten her burden. She worried about her boys, too –
Jack in the RFC and Robbie, who was with Allenby's troops
in Jerusalem. He had written to say he was due for leave:
they were being released in turn to rest after their exertions
in December when, after successfully driving the Turks out
of the Holy City, they had had to deal with a counter-attack
and fierce fighting to secure the road to Jaffa. Rob had
written proudly of his part in the fighting, and his wife Ethel
thought him the greatest hero on earth, and wearied everyone
with reading aloud passages from his letter, which they all
knew by heart now.

Ethel's pride gave way to annoyance when he wrote that
he would not be able to come home for his leave, as it
was too far. She seemed to think the army was keeping
him away deliberately to vex her. And then a letter arrived
early in February from his commanding officer to say that
Robbie had been taken sick on the evening before his
leave fell due.

'He has PUO?' Henrietta said. 'What on earth is PUO?'

'I've never heard of it,' Ethel said. 'I thought you might
know. Oh, I wish he'd never gone to Palestine!' she wailed.
'All these foreign countries are full of disease and flies and
bad water. My poor children! What will we do if he dies?'

'He's not going to die,' Henrietta said automatically,
though the initials worried her more than if it had been
something she had heard of, like typhoid or dysentery. Initials
might hide a multitude of sins. Why couldn't his CO have
written it out in plain language? But she went on, 'Pull yourself together, Ethel, and don't make such a noise. Robbie
can't be very ill, or I'm sure the colonel would have said
so. It's bound to be something quite mild and he'll be better
in no time.'

'But he says Robbie's in hospital! And if it was something
mild, he would have written himself.' She was working herself
up into a panic. 'I want to go out there and nurse him,' she
cried. 'I *ought* to be there. A wife ought to nurse her husband.

94

It's my right, isn't it? I'm going to ask Uncle to send me out there. I know he'll get better if I can be with him.'

'Please don't talk in that foolish way,' Henrietta said, exasperated. Ethel had never had much common sense. Henrietta had not been wholly in favour of Rob's marrying her in the first place, but then he didn't have much common sense either, as she had to admit, though he was her son. In that respect they suited each other; and there was no doubt it had been a happy marriage. 'In the first place you can't possibly go into a war-zone. And Robbie wouldn't want you to, what with U-boats and mines and Zeppelins on the journey, and shells and gunfire when you got there. And in the second place, by the time you arrived he'd already be well again. And, anyway, the army has trained nurses who will look after him much better than you could.'

'No-one is a better nurse than a loving wife,' Ethel insisted stubbornly. It was the kind of thing she had heard said and liked to repeat. It saved the effort of original thinking.

'I'm sure it can't be anything serious,' Henrietta said firmly. 'And it would be better to find out what it is before panicking.'

'I can't help it if I'm worried for him. I'm his *wife*. What if it's typhus? What if he gets malaria?'

If only Jessie were here, Henrietta thought, *she'd* know what PUO was. Just for a moment, she toyed with the idea of ringing Jessie up on the telephone. Downsview House had had one put in when Jack first went there. But to use the telephone was a major undertaking for Henrietta, who still mistrusted the thing.

Then she had a better idea. 'Father Palgrave was in the trenches for two years – he's bound to have heard of it. I'll go and ask him.'

Denis Palgrave had served with the Green Howards until the end of 1916 when, following a shell explosion, he had been buried under rubble for several hours before he was found. His physical injuries had not been grave but his nerves had been affected, and he had been invalided out of the army with what was now being called 'shell-shock'. He had been recommended by Teddy's friend Colonel 'Hound' Bassett for the position of domestic chaplain and tutor to the household's children. He had been with them a year now, and already it was hard to imagine Morland Place without him.

At that time of day he was conducting lessons in the schoolroom for Ethel's older children and Teddy's son James. A knock and a polite, enquiring face at the door were enough to have him come through to the day nursery to listen to Henrietta's question.

His answer was prompt and reassuring. 'PUO? Oh, yes, it stands for "Pyrexia of Unknown Origin". It's just trench fever.'

'Trench fever? I've heard of that, but none of mine has ever had it before. Is it bad?' Henrietta asked.

'Well, it's not pleasant, but it isn't dangerous. I visited lots of fellows in hospital in France who had it. It's something like an influenza, except that there's no running nose or sore throat, just a very high temperature. It comes with pains like rheumatism in the muscles and bones, but the temperature goes down after two or three days. He should be back on his feet in a couple of weeks.' Henrietta was scanning his face for truth, and he added, 'It's never fatal.'

Palgrave had made light of it, for it was true that it was not a dangerous disease, but the muscle pains were accompanied by great weakness and exhaustion, violent headaches, and a boring, gnawing pain in the skin, which was sometimes so violent the patient could not even bear the touch of bedclothes. It was certainly not a pleasant thing to endure, and was very debilitating. He also did not mention that in some cases the disease could recur at irregular intervals over a long period. He pitied Robbie from his heart, but there was no sense in upsetting his family with the details.

Henrietta could see he was not telling her everything. 'What is it?' she asked. 'Don't spare me.'

He searched for something to distract her from the scent. 'Some army doctors I've spoken to think that the disease may be borne by lice.'

'Lice?'

'Or possibly their excrement. It's very light, you see, and breaks down into a sort of dust which is easily blown into the air, and may settle into an abrasion on the skin, or even be breathed in.'

She made an expression of distaste. 'I don't think we'll tell Ethel any of that,' she said hastily. 'Lice! Poor Robbie. Of course, one knows that there are such things in the trenches, but it brings it home when it's your own child. What do you suppose will happen to him now?'

'I expect he'll stay at the base hospital until the acute phase is over,' Palgrave said, 'and then be moved somewhere else to convalesce.'

'He may come home?'

Palgrave shook his head. 'Unlikely. It isn't considered a Blighty touch. But he'll have a couple of weeks in some pleasant place. Out there the hospitals are often attached to a monastery or convent, with lovely gardens for the convalescents to sit out in, green and shady with orange trees and splashing fountains. He might enjoy it very much.'

'Oh, I do hope so! He was just about to go on leave when he fell ill, poor boy. Thank you, Father. I'd better go and reassure Ethel that Robbie isn't going to die. But not a word about lice, remember.'

'As you wish. Should I tell the children anything about it?'

'Oh, you can tell them he has an influenza, perhaps,' Henrietta said, 'and have them pray for his speedy recovery – without alarming them, of course.'

'I will pray with them,' Palgrave said. 'And don't worry – it really isn't serious.'

★   ★   ★

Henrietta wrote of Robbie's illness to Jessie in her regular letter, not needing to add any details, since Jessie would know what PUO was as well as Father Palgrave. She couldn't forbear, however, from adding at the end of the letter in a wistful coda that she wished Jessie would come home. 'I miss your level head, particularly at times like this. Cannot Helen manage without you?'

But Helen couldn't. The day before Henrietta's letter arrived, a telegram had come from Helen's brother Freddie to say that their father had died. He had been suffering with a weak heart for some time and it wasn't completely unexpected, but it was still a shock.

'I remember when my father died,' Jessie said, trying to comfort Helen as she sat beside her on the sofa that evening. 'He'd been bedridden for years, and we'd always known it was only a matter of time, but still I couldn't believe it when it finally happened. I'm so sorry, Helen.'

Helen wiped her eyes and blew her nose. 'I oughtn't to cry for him,' she said. 'He'd been feeling wretched for months, Mother said, and he hated to be ill. Now he's free of it. It's just the shock. One's parents are always *there*, you know.'

'I know.'

But the event necessitated Helen's departure from Downsview. Her sister Molly was working for the Ministry of Munitions and could not be there in the daytime to support their mother. 'And Mother will need supporting,' Helen said. 'She always depended on Daddy for everything. She won't have the first idea what to do. I must go.' She looked at Jessie apologetically. 'And I ought to go straight away – tomorrow. I hate to leave you, but—'

'Of course you must go,' Jessie said. 'Don't worry about me. I shall be perfectly all right.' Helen was still studying her doubtfully, and she said, 'Isn't this exactly why I'm supposed to be here, to help you with the children? If I weren't here to be left, you'd have to take them with you.'

Helen's eyes widened. 'Goodness, yes. I hadn't even thought about that. Where are my wits wandering? I'd entirely forgotten the children.'

'Tomlinson and I will take care of them – and she'll take care of me. Go and start your packing, and I'll look up a train for you.'

Helen jumped up, back to her normal brisk practicality. 'Yes, and I'd better get a telegram off to Mother at once, to tell her I'm coming, so that Molly doesn't worry. And one to Freddie. I suppose I'll have to stay until after the funeral – and then there may be papers to clear up, financial matters, the Will and so on. Freddie ought to do all that, really, but he has his own business to run and, frankly, he isn't the most tactful person. It would bother Mother to have him around her, and he'd get impatient with her when she didn't understand things.'

'Stay as long as you need to. Really, Tomlinson and I can cope perfectly well.'

So, when Henrietta's letter arrived, Jessie was able to reply with a clear conscience that Helen needed her at Downsview and, in relaying the news of Helen's father's death, gave an unassailable excuse for not coming home.

All the same, when she had waved Helen and her luggage off in a taxi and turned back into the house, it seemed horribly empty, and she knew she would miss her dreadfully. There would be no-one, now, to distract her from worrying about Bertie, Jack and Robbie. And what if something happened? What if she had a miscarriage while Helen was away? Mary Tomlinson would cope, of course, but it wouldn't be fair on her to expect her to. Without Helen to lean on, Jessie felt suddenly exposed and lonely. In her absence, she longed anew for her mother.

By the end of her second week, Emma had been assigned her own ambulance, a Siddeley-Deasy, whose various awkwardnesses had prompted its previous driver to dub it the 'Considerably Beastly'. Pom said it was a compliment to her work in the motor-shop that Boss had given it to her instead of the Napier, which was the other spare and much less temperamental. 'Anyone might have to drive the spare, if their own bus goes sick, so it's better that it's the Napier. But she obviously thinks you have the skills to keep the Beastly going.'

Emma thought the name too long for convenience and rechristened it Dorcas, for no particular reason except that she thought it suited it. She had done two solo runs, one to a hospital at Wimereux to collect eight nurses going on leave and take them to Calais docks; and one to the railway depot to collect a load of supplies and take them to an outlying camp. And then, at last, she had been to meet her first hospital train.

It had been dark when they set out, but at least driving in convoy was not so worrying, despite the feeble illumination of the sidelights and the pitted, slippery roads, for she only had to follow the big, dark shape in front of her. It was a moonless night, but the sky had cleared after sunset and there was no rain, only the smell of salt and damp earth coming in on the slight, cold breeze. The canvas tops of the ambulances were cut out against the starry sky; and in the glow-worm glimmer of her sidelights she could see the marram grass waving on the top of the dunes, bowing as she passed, like a court reception. In the dark distance the occasional small light twinkled, but the lack of any perspective made it impossible to tell how far away it was. It brought home to her very clearly how much any light stood out on a night like this: an aeroplane would spot it from miles away. Fortunately, bombers needed a moon to find their way – starlight was not enough.

When they reached the sidings, the train had not yet arrived. Thompson, who was leading the convoy, went to make enquiries at the transport office and came back to tell them that it had been delayed and was still a couple of hours away.

It was an intensely cold night, with no cloud cover, but a canteen was open at the depot, so the drivers left their vehicles and crowded into the steamy warmth, to be served Camp coffee and Marlborough buns by two cheerful WAACs. Lyttleton – inevitably nicknamed 'Lofty' – who was always hungry, had just decided to essay a bully-beef sandwich when an orderly stuck his head round the door to say the train had just passed the last signals and would be arriving in five minutes. They buttoned up their various outer layers, resumed their caps and went out again into the bitter cold.

The headlight of the locomotive was already visible in the depthless dark, seeming not to grow any larger or nearer until quite suddenly it was upon them, the great black hissing shape, clanking over the endless sets of points and coming at last to rest in a cloud of steam. Instantly the scene burst into action. Light fell out onto the yard as carriage doors were opened; orderlies ran up and dressers jumped down, and the 'sitters' – the less badly wounded – were helped off. Then it was the FANYs' turn. They backed their ambulances up to the doors, and the stretchers were slid out onto the runners inside the ambulances. Like bakers sliding bread into the oven, Emma thought, and, like bread, the bundles on the stretchers were brown: hunched figures wrapped in brown blankets, each with a small brown pillow. Four of them, Dorcas could take, two above and two below. Emma had a sudden hollowed-out moment of panic so intense she thought she would be sick. She was now officially responsible for these four wounded men – and who knew what conditions, what horrors those blankets concealed, what agony they were bearing? She was terrified to move in case anything she did made it worse for them. If she jolted them, they might haemorrhage, they might die!

'Number nine BRC,' a sister said to her briskly, making a mark on a list she was holding. Emma stared at her wildly. The nurse was a QA, an army sister – a middle-aged woman with tired eyes and a scrap of grizzled hair escaping from the brow of her cap. She repeated the command impatiently. 'These four are for the number nine British Red Cross hospital.'

The orderly closing Dorcas's doors nudged Emma helpfully and said, with an air of talking out of the side of his mouth, 'Jus' foller that'n in front. She's goin' to the number nine. Most of these'll be.'

Emma flung him a look of desperate thanks and scuttled for the driving seat to get away before the other ambulance – it was Lofty's Crossley, Jenny, she realised – should be out of sight. In her haste to get moving she forgot how difficult the gear-box was, made a terrible clashing noise, and Dorcas jumped like a horse hit with a switch. One of the stretchered forms behind her moaned pitifully. 'Sorry!' she cried, feeling her face flame. She took a deep breath, remembered what she had learned this past week, and eased Dorcas carefully into motion.

The journey was a nightmare – even following Jenny, and even though Jenny was going very slowly – for every uneven movement caused the men to moan, and there were inevitably a great many of them. Emma drove as carefully as she could, trying to pick the smoothest piece of the road. Her heart was in her mouth when she had to cross the tram lines. She eased Dorcas as slowly as she dared – too slow, and she would stall, and what if she stopped right on the lines and a tram came? – but even so there was a jolt as the off-hind went down on the other side of the far rail where the road had been worn away, and one of the men let out a piercing cry that cut into Emma like a knife. As they trundled on, the same man – he had looked only eighteen or nineteen when they had loaded him, his head and one side of his face bulging with bandages – began crying for his mother. 'I'm so sorry, I'm so sorry,' was all Emma could think of to say.

One of the others said feebly, 'Don't you mind, miss. You're doing grand. 'E's been like this all the way from the Front. 'E don't know what 'e's saying.'

'I'm afraid the bumping is making it worse for him.'

'It ain't your fault. You just get us there, miss.'

Following Jenny into the hospital yard at last, Emma thought she had never been so glad to get any journey over. A single orderly came up as she jumped down. Others were already unloading Jenny and another ambulance beyond her.

'Top or bottom?' he asked her briskly.

'I – beg your pardon?'

He eyed her consideringly. 'New, aren't you? You'd better stand down here and I'll pass 'em out to you.' He jumped up nimbly into the back and began to slide the first stretcher along its rails. 'Grab the handles – no, the other way. That's it. Now walk backwards slowly. Ready to take the strain? Here we go.' With his help she remembered the stretcher drill she had taken part in a thousand years ago in England. She felt her biceps muscles cracking with the effort and remembered, with a spare part of her mind, how the girls had talked of 'stretcher face' – an ugly grimace, eyes screwed up and teeth gritted – whenever they had to move heavy objects. Foxy had said she was afraid it would stick one day and she'd look like that for ever.

They had carried two of the stretchers inside and put them down on the floor before a second orderly ran up and relieved her of the task. As she was closing her doors again, Lofty came over and said, 'Need to follow me, or can you find your own way back?'

'Can I follow you, please? I'm not quite sure of the way yet.'

'You will be by the end of tonight,' said Lofty. 'Come on, then.'

The return journey was quite different from the outward one: with no wounded to nurse over the bumps, Lofty put her foot down and Jenny took every obstacle at a gallop. Emma had the greatest difficulty in keeping up with her for she was still nervous about holes and ditches. She had not grown up in the country and had only ever been hunting once or twice in her life, and she did not have the same blithe trust in her 'mount' as the other, horsy, FANYs.

The hospital train held about two hundred and fifty cases, and it took several hours to empty it. 'This is a quiet time,' Thompson said, when the last stretcher was accounted for. 'You wait until we have a big push on. Then there'll be four hundred, four fifty on board.'

'And as soon as we've emptied one train,' Foxy added, 'another comes in. Sometimes we don't stand down for a week.'

Thompson straightened her cap and peered at Emma through the dark. 'Well, it's back to camp now. How are you feeling?'

Emma's arms and back were aching and her head hurt from trying to see where she was going without enough light, and she thought she had never been so tired. But she had helped – she didn't know how many – soldiers. She had done a real, important job of work. She straightened her shoulders. 'Terrific!' she said.

Camp Nieulay was so close to Unit 3's camp that it was felt everyone could go to the entertainment, leaving only a skeleton night shift on duty to keep the engines turned over. No action was expected, but if there should be an unforeseen emergency, the drivers could be driven back to camp in a matter of minutes.

Emma felt she ought to offer to stay behind, though it was not her turn on the rota, because she was the new girl and hadn't 'earned' the treat yet. 'Besides, you all know the chaps and I don't,' she said to Foxy. 'They're your friends.'

'Oh, rot,' Foxy said. 'Everyone deserves a little fun and relaxation, you as much as anyone. The first weeks are the hardest, until you get used to it. Anyway,' she forestalled further argument, 'Boss won't hear of it. The rota's sacrosanct, you know. That way everyone gets their fair share of the rotten jobs – and the cushy ones.'

104

Emma smiled. 'And this is one of the cushy ones? I didn't realise it was a job at all.'

Foxy opened her eyes wide. 'Of course. Cheering up our brave lads? Boosting military morale? It's war work. Couldn't be more important – so, best bib and tucker, Westie, my girl. The full soup and fish tonight.'

Emma felt tired, and not in the mood for the outing, but there seemed no getting out of it, so she told herself it was a duty and made the best of it. Camp Nieulay sent a Crossley transport for them, and when they climbed aboard, she could feel the excitement in the others. Their eager chatter and frequent laughter at first made her feel left out, alone in not anticipating pleasure from the evening; but as they left the unit behind she found her spirits rising with theirs. Roberts – 'Bobby' – and Lofty lit cigarettes. It was forbidden for a FANY to smoke in public, but many of them privately smoked like chimneys, and Lofty argued that this did not count as a public place.

At the camp they were received at first in the officers' mess, and Emma could see that Foxy had only partly been joking that it was war work. The eager pleasure of the officers, all in their mess 'blues', showed how important it was to them. The colonel himself led the reception, beaming with hospitable delight. It was clear the others knew the 'chaps' very well, but all had to be introduced to Emma, and there followed a stream of faces and names, each attached to a hearty shake of the hand, which left her bemused. She'd never remember any of them.

Fortunately the last face was familiar. The colonel said, 'And Captain Wentworth I think you know?' and she shook his hand with a relief that showed in her smile.

'Bit overwhelming?' he said, with a conspiratorial grin. 'Don't worry – I'll stick to you this evening and see you through.'

A steward came up with a tray of sherry, the colonel turned to attend to Boss, and general conversation broke out.

'Now,' said Wentworth, 'let me reintroduce Captain Ward and Lieutenant Curzon, because I'm sure they got lost in the general throng, but they're splendid chaps, quite worthy of your attention.'

Emma shook their hands again and tried to fix the names and faces in her mind, something she did quite easily in social situations at home – but, then, she had never been so tired and disoriented at home.

'Don't worry,' Ward said, as if he had perceived her difficulty. 'I know we all look alike in uniform. After all, that's the purpose of it, really.'

Emma smiled and made an effort. 'But at parties before the war all the men were in evening dress, which is a uniform of sorts.'

'True,' said Wentworth. 'I never thought about that before. No wonder the young ladies back home were always mislaying my name! It was because my tails and shirt-front were just like everyone else's.'

'No, Wentworth,' said Ward, kindly, 'it was because you're so dull.'

'It was easier in Scotland,' Emma said. 'At least the kilts were in different tartans. I never learned which was which, but I could tell they weren't the same.'

'Have you been much in Scotland, Miss Weston?' Curzon asked eagerly, and she noted that he had a slight Scottish accent.

'I had a Season in Edinburgh last winter,' Emma said. A discussion ensued and it emerged that Emma and Curzon had an acquaintance in common in Lord Knoydart, who had been a suitor of hers during her Season. Angus Knoydart was a distant cousin of Curzon's, and he had visited his estate on the Sound of Sleat for the shooting and stalking.

The mention of these sports alerted Ward, who had been waiting impatiently for a chance to move the conversation southwards. 'Do you hunt, Miss Weston?'

'I haven't hunted much, but I do like to ride,' Emma said.

Wentworth snatched the baton smoothly from Ward, saying, 'There are some rather nice gallops hereabouts, along the shore and in the dunes. When you have your day off, perhaps you'd enjoy getting out for a ride?'

'That would be lovely,' Emma said, 'but I don't have a horse.'

Wentworth smiled. 'Nothing could be easier than to borrow one for you. This is the army, and where the army is, there will horses be also. I know that in the FANY you ride across, which removes the only possible difficulty, because I doubt if we'd find a side-saddle anywhere this side of the Channel.'

'The weather isn't the best for pleasure outings,' Ward said.

'We ride in worse conditions in Scotland.' Curzon had put in a bid for attention. 'We're hardier folk, perhaps, than you southerners.'

'Don't talk to me about hardiness, Curzon, my boy,' Ward said. 'After two years of this war, I've endured everything the weather-gods can throw at me. I don't know how it is, but each year seems to have four winters in it.'

They were interrupted by Foxy walking up with another officer, and the conversation changed to local affairs, which Emma could not follow; but it lasted only a few minutes, until the colonel caught everyone's attention and said the entertainment was due to start and they should repair to the theatre.

Wentworth bowed to Emma. 'I've been assigned to look after you. Will you take my arm?' Emma hesitated only fractionally, but Wentworth was sensitive enough to notice it. 'I know you don't anticipate any pleasure from this evening,' he said quietly, 'but please believe that just the sight of women's faces and the sound of women's voices do us all the greatest good. It's easy out here, living this life, to forget what it is we're fighting for. Your fiancé was a soldier: I swear to you he would agree with me, and approve

107

of your being here. I'll keep anyone from pressing unwanted attentions on you.'

There was nothing but kindness in his face, and his smile was brotherly. Emma thought, *War work*, and was ashamed of holding back. She took his arm, and, feeling the rough serge of the sleeve under her fingers, felt a huge pang, which was a combination of missing Fenniman desperately and, oddly, being comforted by the protecting presence of a man. It was good, she thought, that he knew of her circumstances. He would not flirt with her, and would make sure no-one else did, without her having to go through the painful process of explaining.

The 'theatre' was an enormous marquee, with a proper stage built at one end, and rows of wooden chairs, which gave way to benches after the first three. There was electric light – run from a generator, Wentworth explained – and a small orchestra established between the stage and a wall of straw-bales covered with black cloth, which constituted the pit.

The FANY were escorted to seats in the second row, behind the senior officers, and military and local dignitaries. More officers filled the third row, and the men piled in behind and shuffled themselves along the benches, bringing with them a smell of hair oil and trampled grass. The noise level rose, and with so many bodies under one canvas roof, it became quite pleasantly warm despite the cold outside.

The show was extremely good, surprising Emma with its polish. She asked Wentworth in a whisper, but was assured they were 'our own men, from this camp', and not profes-sional troupers. The entertainment began with a rousing chorus of a song from a show currently popular back home, but with new words suitable to the occasion, poking fun at army life and Camp Nieulay in particular. There were roars of laughter at what were evidently esoteric jokes among the men. Wentworth whispered that there was another version of this song, but they only did it at entertainments when no ladies were present.

The rest of the show included many musical numbers, some traditional songs, some comic, some popular croonings of the intensely sentimental sort beloved of Tommies, about girls left behind, silver-haired mothers, cottages with roses round the door, sunsets, faithful dogs and green hills. There were comic monologues; there was a short and utterly ridiculous melodrama of a betrayed maiden, a villain with huge mustachios and a noble hero who rescued her, made more ridiculous by the fact that the maiden was played by an enormous soldier and the hero by a very small one. There was a juggler, a man who recited poems, a pair of acrobats who did balancing tricks, and a Tommy with a small white dog that walked on its hind legs, balanced things on its nose, jumped through hoops, and answered questions by barking once for yes and twice for no.

The funniest act was a ventriloquist, played by one of the officers, whose 'dummy' was another officer who sat on his knee, moved his arms and turned his head jerkily, and managed to talk while making his mouth open and shut in a convincingly wooden way. The dialogue between them was so amusing that Emma found herself laughing out loud; the Tommies behind her were roaring, and the shoulders of the officers in front were shaking.

The final act was a violin solo by a Lieutenant Linzer, a slight, dark young man, who seemed transported by the music, oblivious of his surroundings, to wake with a start at the storm of applause at the end of the beautiful 'Romance' he had chosen. The applause went on and on, with stamping and calls for an encore. He obliged, grinning and fully present this time, with an Irish jig, which he played faster and faster at each repeat until the bow was a blur and Emma thought his fingers must catch fire from the friction.

Then the CO got up on the stage, thanked everyone who had taken part, led the singing of 'God Save the King', and it was all over.

'I enjoyed that so much,' Emma said, as she and

Wentworth made their way with the other officers and FANYs back to the mess. The Tommies were having their own celebration supper, with beer, in their own mess. 'I never thought there could be so much fun out here.'

'They are good, aren't they?' Wentworth said. 'Of course, we've all seen most of the acts before, at previous camp shows, but they polish them a bit more each time, and add new things. In any case, any diversion is welcome in army life.'

'The violinist – Linzer, wasn't it? He was especially good,' Emma said.

'Yes, poor Linzer. He was going to be a soloist. He studied under Kreisler, you know, but he had to hurry home when the war broke out. Now he frets that he's not improving, and that his skills will have atrophied by the time the war ends. He lives for music. I do think the war is especially hard on chaps like him. I wouldn't be surprised if one day the name Max Linzer wasn't as famous as Fritz Kreisler.'

In the mess there were more drinks, and a delicious supper brought round on trays by stewards in white jackets, delicacies like foie-gras sandwiches and anchovies on toast, all cut into small portions so they could be eaten without cutlery or crockery.

'What a good idea,' Emma said.

'It's the colonel's. It means everyone can go on talking to everyone else,' Wentworth said. 'Let me introduce Linzer to you. He'll take it kindly if you tell him how good he is.'

She said it with such obvious sincerity that the young man flushed and looked pleased, but quickly changed the subject. 'Modest,' Wentworth mouthed to her. They were joined by Ward, with Foxy at his side, and it became apparent that they were more than casually interested in each other. It turned out that Foxy's mother knew Linzer's mother. The conversation turned homewards, to concerts and then other London entertainments, and Emma was able to contribute the shows she had seen last year, until it reminded her abruptly that she had seen some of them with Fenniman and, on the instant, the pleasure of the occasion shut down for her. She was silent for the rest of the evening, and was glad when Boss signalled that it was time to go. She felt headachy and low, and impatient with the business of taking leave, which seemed to go on much too long.

True to his promise, Wentworth had stayed at her side. Now, as he escorted her to the door, he said, 'I wonder if I might ask you a favour.'

She looked wearily at him, wondering what was coming, but there was no flirting in his face. He seemed quite serious and steady. 'What is it?'

'I expect you know that Foxy and Ward are, well, interested in each other. Ward wants to take Foxy out to dinner next week, and as your FANY rule is that you must go in pairs, he's asked me to go with him, and I would be very grateful if you would make the fourth.' As she hesitated, he went on, 'It would be doing me the greatest kindness, because the last time I helped them out, Ward and Foxy had eyes for no-one else, and the young lady who accompanied Foxy was not much of a conversationalist.'

'Who was it?' Emma asked.

'Oh, no-one you know. She's gone home now – in fact, I think you are her replacement. A nice girl, but with nothing to say for herself. Lovers are the worst company in the world: in a situation like that you need a friend to get you through. So would you, in a friendly way, be my dinner-guest?'

'In a friendly way,' Emma repeated, and it sounded like a stipulation.

He gave her a frank look. 'I know your circumstances. I promise I would never embarrass or upset you.'

'Very well, then,' Emma said, not wishing to seem churlish.

He smiled. 'Thank you. At least I can promise you a decent dinner for your pains.' The smile disappeared. 'And we'd better enjoy our leisure while we can. The war's going to start up again next month, and who knows then where the winds will blow us?'

'You'll be leaving here?' Emma said.

'This is just a training camp. We'll be going up to the Front when the campaign reopens, but we won't know which part of the Front until the order comes.'

She thought of what the campaign reopening would mean – she had heard enough from the others about 'rushes' to make a guess at it. 'I hope . . .' she began, but that was not a sentence she could finish. *I hope you'll be all right* was the same as *I hope you don't get killed like Fenniman*. It wasn't something you could say to a soldier.

Wentworth seemed to know what was in her mind. He shrugged lightly. 'It's the war,' he said, which meant nothing and everything.

In the Crossley going back to camp, Foxy sat beside Emma and said, 'Did Wentworth ask you? I hope you don't mind, but I really wanted to go with someone he'd get on with, and I saw he liked you.'

'Foxy, you know I'm not interested in anything like that.'

Foxy's eyes widened. 'That's exactly the point. You'll be able to spend the evening talking to him in a purely friendly way. He's such a nice boy, he gets taken advantage of, and it isn't fair. I don't suppose he told you about the last time, because he's too much of a gentleman, but I went with Johnson – she's gone home now, so there's no harm in my telling you – and she hardly said a word, simply made cow's eyes at him all evening, which was embarrassing for him, as well as boring, poor chap. *Do* be a chum, and say you'll do it. Wentworth has three sisters at home, and he misses them.'

'I've already said I'll come,' Emma told her.

'Thanks,' Foxy said, with a smile. 'I promise you it'll be all right.'

It was all right. The men collected them in a motor-car

and drove into Calais, where they had booked a table at the Hôtel Lion d'Or. Contrary to what Emma had expected from Wentworth's words, Foxy and Ward did not concentrate on each other to the exclusion of their companions. In fact, there was nothing to suggest to any outsider that they were two couples: rather, they were like four old friends, and the conversation flowed pleasantly and equally between them. They talked about the camps and the area, the war, and things back home, discussed their favourite books and shows they had been to, talked about food – it seemed impossible for any conversation between serving people not to touch on food at some point – and horses and dogs they had owned, and from horses Foxy turned to ambulances and told amusing stories about the vagaries of the various vehicles they had to struggle with.

The only complaint Emma had about the evening was that it seemed too short, for by FANY rules they had to be back by ten. The men drove them back to camp, and they parted with thanks and handshakes all round. When Emma settled into her flea-bag to sleep soon afterwards, she felt a satisfaction that men and women could be friends, even in difficult circumstances like this; and had a last, sleepy thought that she wished Vera could have been an invisible witness to that dinner, and see that men could enjoy women's conversation, and be sensible, and treat them as equals. She wondered how it was that Vera had never come across the right sort of man when she was in France, but the soft billows of sleep overcame her before she could finish the thought.

CHAPTER SIX

A letter came at last for Ethel from Robbie, but it did nothing to reassure her. The writing hardly looked like his. It was begun in ink and finished in pencil, and the letters grew larger and shakier as it went on.

'I expect he changed to pencil because the ink was running so badly,' Henrietta said, doing her best in the face of Ethel's alarm. 'You can see the paper must have been damp.'

'Yes, but *why* was it damp?' Ethel cried. 'Because his hands were sweating. Because he's in a fever.'

'Dear, it's very hot out there,' said Henrietta. 'Look, he says he's feeling better.'

'Temp. has gone down,' Robbie had written, 'though will probably go up again. This is typical and nothing to worry about. I'm not feeling too rotten at the moment. The medicos are moving me to fever hosp. in Malta. I'm glad as it will be cooler there. Very hot here and beastly flies everywhere. Will write again from Malta when I'm up to it.'

Ethel was especially worried about their sending him to a fever hospital, which meant he must need special care. In vain Maria reminded her how pleasant Malta was – Frank had been there a year before he was sent to France, and had written about it. In vain Henrietta extolled the relief of a sea-voyage and the therapeutic value of sea-breezes. In vain Teddy pointed out that it was only common sense for the army to keep all fever cases together: 'Everything spreads like wildfire when you've got a lot of men together in close quarters, especially in those hot, dirty places like Egypt.'

Nothing soothed Ethel. She begged to be allowed to go out to Malta and nurse Rob herself. Teddy said, 'It's not in my power, even if I thought it was a good idea. These army nurses are the best in the world, m'dear. He's in the right place, believe me, and he's getting the best of care. He'll be as sound as a trivet in a week or two, you'll see.'

'And then they'll send him back to that dirty place to get sick again,' she said bitterly.

Henrietta wished she was quicker-witted and could think of the right things to say, for the sake of peace in the house. But the fact of the matter was that if he did not get sent back to 'that dirty place', he would probably be sent to France. There was no safe place for a mother's son in a war; except underground, like Frank. *If these poor limbs die, safest of all.*

'We must pray for his recovery and his return home when the war's over. That's all any of us can do,' she told Ethel, as firmly as she could.

Ethel's mouth trembled, but she spoke quietly. 'Do you really think he'll get better?'

'Father Palgrave says PUO is not dangerous,' Henrietta said. 'Now, why don't you come with me to the national-kitchen meeting this morning? It will do you good to think about something else. It's a woman's duty to keep cheerful in wartime.'

To her credit, Ethel did make an effort after that. Teddy insisted that everyone in the house attend daily prayer, but hitherto Ethel had been inclined to use the time in the chapel to plan her day. Now she really prayed instead of seeming to, and she found it helped. She wrote a long letter to Rob, and took comfort from planning and dispatching a parcel of such useful items as new hand-kerchiefs, good soap, writing-paper, lavender water, a jar of calf's-foot jelly, ditto of Morland Place honey, and the usual cigarettes and chocolate.

115

She longed most of all for a letter from Robbie in return. He was not mankind's best correspondent, but just a line or two would reassure her that he was able to hold a pencil, and therefore not at death's door. She looked up eagerly every morning when Maria brought in the post, and tried to seem indifferent to the small shake of the head that was all she received. She was much annoyed, though conversely comforted, when she overheard one of the servants saying that Mr Robert was probably having too good a time in Malta to be bothered to write.

It was two weeks before a letter came from Malta; and it was beaten to the post, by one day, by an official letter in a buff envelope. It was one of those printed forms, with spaces for details to be filled in by hand, which began, 'It is my painful duty to inform you that a report has this day been received from the War Office notifying the death of . . .' Robbie's name was here; and on the line under 'The cause of death was' someone had written in a careful hand, 'cardiac and renal failure consequent upon typhoid fever'.

Ethel's cry as she read these words was heard throughout the house, and never forgotten.

The letter that came the next day was from the commanding officer on the island, and did something to dispel the utter bewilderment in the house, though it could do nothing to ease the pain.

The chief medical officer tells me that he believes your husband was suffering not from PUO but from Undulant Fever, which is endemic in many parts of the Mediterranean where goat's milk is a staple of diet, goats being commonly affected, though rarely showing symptoms of the disease. The CMO further believes that the Undulant Fever was 'masking', as he phrases it, the typhoid, the latter infection probably contracted as a result of the weakness caused by the former. None of this, I know, can be of any comfort to you in your

116

sad loss, but be assured that your husband received the best of care and attention at all times. There being no treatment for any of the three conditions except careful nursing, the CMO assures me that a different diagnosis could not have made any difference to the tragic outcome.

Sorrow and mourning descended on the house. Ethel collapsed entirely and had to be helped to bed; Dr Hasty was sent for, and prescribed her a mild sedative. The black bands were got out again. Teddy sent a notice to the newspaper. Henrietta, helped by Maria and Polly, began writing the letters. There were calls of sympathy, which Henrietta received in person as far as she could, for they were often from people who had lost a son themselves, and she knew from her own visits how much effort it took to make them. Sympathy for the family was profound and sincere in the neighbourhood. Morland Place had given two sons already; that the third had been taken by disease rather than by shot or shell in no way diminished the sacrifice.

Palgrave conducted a special service, for which Ethel rose from her bed and was helped downstairs, a pitiful figure, fainting and tear-ravaged. To her it mattered deeply and painfully that Robbie had not died a hero's death in battle. In that she might have found some slight comfort for all that his loss would mean to her. It seemed a shocking, hateful waste that he had died of typhoid, as though the army had thrown his life away. What had he been doing out there, in that 'hot, dirty place'? What had capturing Jerusalem to do with beating the Germans? When she flung this question angrily at Father Palgrave or Uncle Teddy they tried to explain, but it never made any sense to her. Jerusalem to her was the place the Lord had entered on a donkey, familiar from illustrations in childhood books: white walls, green palms, bright-coloured crowd, a little grey donkey, and the Christ in shining white robes with a golden halo over his

117

head. It was a place that existed only in Bible stories. Why had the army sent Robbie there to die of sickness, instead of to France to kill Germans, where the sacrifice might have meant something?

Ethel's mother, Mrs Cornleigh, had a long talk with Henrietta after the special service, as a result of which she begged Ethel to come home for a spell and be looked after by her own mother. Henrietta thought a change of scene would be beneficial to her; Mrs Cornleigh thought Henrietta looked worn to death and could do with at least one of her troubles being taken off her shoulders. After some tactful persuading, Ethel agreed to go, and was transported, well wrapped up, in Teddy's big blue and silver Benz, along with her two youngest children, Harriet and John, to the Cornleigh villa at Clifton.

Having Ethel out of the house eased things a little for Henrietta, and allowed her to spend some time with Rob's eldest child, Roberta, who, at nearly seven, was well able to understand what had happened and to feel bewildered and unhappy. Her brother, six-year-old Jeremy, seemed to accept the news quietly, but then had a series of nightmares, which caused broken nights for everyone.

And as a result, perhaps, of the heightened emotional temperature of the house, Denis Palgrave had a relapse and began again the sleep-walking episodes they all thought he had left behind him.

Henrietta felt she hardly had time to come to terms with her own loss, which perhaps was as well, for keeping busy, as she knew, was the best way to get through things. But she did find the odd few minutes every day to go to the chapel and pray, or just to sit and let her thoughts expand in quietness. She remembered Rob as a baby, staggering after Jack with a beaming smile and a sticky starfish hand extended in an offering of pure love. Later, he and Jack had been the ones to leave little Frank behind: with only a year between them, they had been close until Jack went away to engineering school and their lives had diverged.

118

Two sons, taken in their prime. The pain was terrible. Parents ought not to outlive their children. She thought of her husband, Jerome, the great love of her life, long departed but still missed, now more than ever. She hoped the boys were with him. She saw them standing together, Jerome in the middle with his arms around their shoulders; and for the first time in years she saw his face clearly, not as a recollection of a photograph but as he had been in life. He smiled at her – young again, and well, and free from pain – and though he did not speak, she heard the words clearly in her mind: *Be at peace. All is well.* Even as she heard the words, the vividness of his face began to fade. She tried desperately to cling to the moment, but it was instantly gone, and when she tried to think of him again, all she saw was the face in the photographs.

Loss settled on her as she came back to her present surroundings. She was sitting, as she always did on these private occasions, before the statue of the Lady; and as the day was dark outside, she had lit a candle on the Lady's altar. She took out her handkerchief to dry her eyes and cheeks, and as she did so, she looked up at the Lady's face. A small draught was moving the cold air of the chapel and making the candle flames waver, and as the yellow light shifted on the golden face, she thought she saw something shine, something small and moving and reflective, like tiny diamonds.

The Lady was weeping.

Henrietta stiffened; her heart turned cold and heavy, making it hard to breathe. She clasped her hands together without knowing it, her nails digging into her palms. *The Lady was weeping.* Suddenly she felt the house around her, an ancient, brooding presence, the composite of all the lives that had ever animated it; the joys and fears and sorrows of the family sunk into its stones and down into its foundations. Below the chapel floor was the crypt where the Morlands through the ages had been buried. (Her sons, she thought, with a fresh spike of agony, would not lie there.) She had never minded those bones. They were a comfort, a reminder that the family, like the house, went on, no matter what happened to each individual. But now, suddenly, she was afraid. The Lady wept when something bad was coming to the house. Were all those bones not sacrifice enough? Was more required?

Is it me? she asked in her mind. So many of those she loved were in places of danger. She was old, her life had been rich. *Take me, if it has to be*, she thought. *Is it me?* But there was no answer. The moment had passed. The face of the Lady was serene, no tears to be seen. The house had settled again into its ancient sleep. She no longer felt it watching her.

All is well, Jerome had said. And the thought came to her, cleansing her of fear, that the Lady had been weeping for Robbie.

So much to do. She got to her feet, squared her shoulders, and went out to meet the demands of the day.

The sight of a girl doing anything to a lorry seemed irresistibly fascinating to the British soldier. Whenever Emma was forced to stop on the road – which was often – to make running repairs, change a tyre, restart Dorcas after a stall, every eye would be turned towards her, every passing male in khaki would slow and gawp. When military necessity allowed, a little knot would gather round to watch her perform and – to do them justice – offer help. Sometimes she accepted and sometimes she didn't, depending on whether she was loaded or empty and what the weather was doing. Sometimes – she admitted it to herself – she just liked showing off, making them marvel that a young and pretty girl (without vanity, she knew she was) could service a great mechanical beast like Dorcas.

It was just like the general perversity of life, however, that when Dorcas skidded on black ice and put her off-fore down a ditch – a situation from which Emma could not rescue her alone – no-one was in sight. The engine coughed and stalled, and there was silence all around, apart from the soughing of the wind and the sullen flapping of the canvas sides. Fortunately, Emma had been running empty, on her way back from delivering a load of medical supplies to a casualty clearing station up near the line. After a period of milder weather, accompanied by constant rain, it had turned cold again, with iron-grey skies and occasional flurries of fine snow. She had been looking out for ice but, of course, the thing about black ice was that you couldn't see it. She had nothing to blame herself for, but she felt a fool all the same, and asked herself severely what would have happened if she had had wounded men in the back.

There was nothing to be done but wait for help to come along – and at least that couldn't be long in this part of the world. It was only a surprise that she was alone on this road at all. She jumped down from the driver's seat and walked round, inspecting the damage – nothing seemed to be broken, fortunately, though Dorcas was leaning at a nasty angle. But even if she could get a plank under that wheel, there was no possibility of reversing out under her own power: the ditch was too deep.

It was bitterly cold again, but Emma had adjusted to the climate by now, and didn't feel it so much. Besides, taking the lead from the other girls, she had added more layers to her clothes, and now under the fur-lined coat her body was quite warm. It was hands and feet that suffered, for there was a limit to how many layers you could wear on them. She stamped about a bit and beat her hands together to get the blood going, and pulled up the big fur collar to keep the cold wind off her neck.

It was not long – though it was long enough for her to realise she was hungry and would have given five pounds for a hot cup of tea – before she heard the sound of an engine approaching, and pretty soon over the brow of the hill came a Crossley transport with a corporal driving and an officer beside him. She stood away from the shelter of her ambulance so they would see her, and at once the vehicle slowed and came to a stop. Down from the passenger side jumped the officer in greatcoat and cap, and the polite smile of entreaty she had prepared broke into a wide one of welcome as she saw it was Captain Wentworth.

'Well, if it isn't my friend Westie!' he exclaimed.

'If it isn't my friend Wentie,' she responded in kind.

'It is, I assure you. In the flesh. I thought I recognised Dorcas as soon as we came over the hill, but there was no mistaking that coat. What are you doing here?'

'If you need to ask that, I'm afraid your brain must be softening.'

'My dear girl, I can see you are down a ditch, but I assume that was not your purpose in coming out to this spot.'

'I'm on my way back from a delivery, but I hardly see that matters.' She pointed twice. 'Black ice. Ditch. *Voilà le situation*. What are you doing here, if it comes to that?'

'On our way back after road-repairing duties. The important thing is that I have a fatigue party in the back, which means I'm in a position to offer you help.'

'Jolly good! Please do so, then, without further ado. I'm freezing here, not to say starving.'

It did not particularly surprise her that it was Wentworth who had come along. In the weeks she had been working on the convoy, she had passed him often on the road, bumped into him in various places, had been several times on deliveries or collections to his camp; and from time to time he had called at the FANY camp on military business. She knew a great many of the officers from the local units by now, and most of the medical officers in the various hospitals. There was a great deal of interaction between officers and FANY, and it made for a pleasant, family feeling. It helped to mitigate the strenuous and grim nature of much of the work.

There was social interaction, too. After the entertainment at Camp Nieulay, Unit 3 had reciprocated with a dance, not on such a grand scale, but an agreeable diversion nonetheless, with a small band provided by Nieulay and two dozen officers from there and other local camps.

In the course of things her friendship with Wentworth had flourished, to the extent that they were now completely comfortable together, and teased each other lightly. On this occasion she took him on a circuit of Dorcas to inspect the problem, while he shook his head and said, 'While you were about it, couldn't you have put the rear wheel down as well? The ditch is big enough. Surprising you didn't see it, really.'

'Oh, I saw it all right. I guessed you'd be along and thought you might like a challenge to relieve the tedium of your life.'

'It isn't too much of a challenge,' he said. 'There's no way of driving out, so we shall have to tow you out backwards. A simpleton could tell you that.'

'I thought one just did,' she said innocently.

'*Touché*, Trooper Weston. Now stand back and let the men get to work. I always said you little girlies oughtn't to be trusted with great big lorries.'

She spread her hands. 'I shall keep out of the way, and observe and wonder, O mighty paradigm of your sex.'

Wentworth jumped his grinning men down from the back of the Crossley, got out a coil of rope, and went about organising things. She knew he was putting on an act of being ostentatiously brisk and efficient, and it made her laugh inwardly, though she stood back with her hands stuffed in her pockets and assumed an exaggeratedly admiring expression. The rope was attached to Dorcas's rear axle, the men were stationed around her front and lower side and, with the Crossley pulling and them pushing, she was dragged ignominiously backwards onto the road again.

'I'd better see if she'll start,' Emma said, and reached in under the driver's seat for the crank handle.

Wentworth took it from her with a lordly air. 'Cranking's

not the work for dainty white hands,' he said. He held it out to one of his men. 'Unger, start her up, will you?'

The men were much amused by this pantomime, and Unger looked as sheepish as a boy being asked to recite for the grown-ups at Christmas. He went round to the front, inserted the crank, and started to swing. It added greatly to the hilarity of the occasion that he could not get a peep out of Dorcas. After a dozen swings, Emma went and pushed him gently out of the way. 'She's just a bit temperamental. There's a knack to it. She usually comes up all right on the thirtieth turn.'

Because Dorcas was still warmish, she consented to start at twenty, and there was a cheer and applause from the audience before Wentworth ordered them to get back in the Crossley.

'Thank you all very much!' Emma called to them, and they smirked and shuffled modestly in response.

Wentworth came and stood close, shielding her from the wind. 'I can't offer you a cigarette, I know,' he said. 'It's a pity you don't smoke. It makes a nice little social ritual at moments like this.'

'Haven't you anything else in your pockets? Chocolate, for instance? I'm absolutely famished.'

He patted himself down. 'Nothing, I'm sorry to say. I shall make it a point from now on never to leave camp without some. Oh, wait, I've found a cough-drop. You're welcome to that. It's paregoric.'

'Better than nothing. Thanks,' she said, and popped it into her mouth. 'Fluff,' she explained a moment later, daintily extracting it.

'It's been in there rather a long time.'

'Now he tells me.' She shoved her hands back into her pockets. 'I'm glad you came along.'

'I'm glad I did too. There's something uniquely invigorating about the sight of a woman swinging on a starting handle.'

'No, but really, thank you very much for rescuing me.'

'It was a pleasure,' he said, cocking an enquiring eye at her. 'Anyone passing would have done the same, you know.'

'Yes, but you made me laugh while you were doing it, and didn't make me feel foolish for being in the ditch in the first place.'

'All part of the service.' He bowed. 'We'd both better get going before we embarrass each other. Are you going back to camp? You might as well follow me, then – in case you find another hole you can't resist inspecting.'

She laughed. 'Now you've gone and spoilt it! All that chivalry wasted. You go on and don't wait for me. I'll curb my archaeological urges for the rest of the day.'

'As you please. I'll pop over later this evening and make sure you're all right – haven't caught a cold or anything.'

The Crossley drove off, and Emma took her time about following, not relishing pootling along behind it with all those Tommies grinning at her. She caught it up just as it was turning into the Nieulay camp gates, and thought that someone would undoubtedly tell Wentworth they had seen her so he would know she had got back safely. Then she drove on to Unit 3, a good hot wash and, best of all, supper.

Wentworth did come over later that evening, and was received cheerfully in the mess, for he was a universal favourite. Conversation was general, and he did not speak privately to Emma until he got up to go, and she saw him out. They stepped outside into the darkness and closed the door, cutting off the yellow light and the warmth. Instantly their breath smoked on the chill air. The sky was still lowering and there was no moon or starlight, just a faint glow from the covered mess window. Wentworth got a torch out of his pocket and pointed it politely downwards, and she could just see the paler shape of his face between the cap and coat. Then he reached into another pocket and took out something, which he offered to her.

'What's that?' she asked.

'The chocolate I should have had for you earlier.'

'Foolish,' she laughed.

'No, take it. Really. It's for you.'

'All right, then. Thank you. I'll have it later, if you don't mind. And thanks again for rescuing me,' she said.

'It was nothing. No ill effects?'

'None. I'd only been waiting a few minutes before you came along.'

'Glad to have been on the spot. When's your day off?'

The FANY had one day off per month, except in busy times when it had to be deferred. 'Next week – Wednesday,' she said.

'If I can wangle it, would you like to go riding? You know we talked about it, and I'd love to have a gallop along the strand, if you're up to it.'

'I'd love it, too. It's ages since I was on a horse. But can you get off at the same time? And what about horses?'

'I'll have to wangle a duty with someone, but I'm pretty sure I can. And I know where I can lay my hands on two polo ponies – a fellow I know with the Eighty-first brought them out with him, and they don't get enough exercise. Is it a date, then?'

'Yes, thank you,' Emma said gladly. 'I can't think of anything I'd rather do with my day off.'

'I'll send over a note, then, to confirm it when I've sorted everything out.'

She gave him her hand to shake, and it seemed perfectly natural when he supplemented it with a brief, brotherly peck on the cheek, simultaneously pushing her towards the door and saying, 'Go on in, now. You'll catch cold.'

Jessie had never felt so alone as at that time, when she was mourning the loss of another brother. She had never been as close to Robbie as to Jack, but with all his faults he was her brother, and they had grown up together, played the same games and shared the same memories. She wanted very badly to go home, to be with her mother and family at such a time.

126

The exile forced upon her by her condition only made her suffering worse. Helen was still away, looking after her mother, but from Henrietta's perspective Jessie could have brought the children with her. There was no hint of reproach in her letters to her daughter, but Jessie provided it for herself.

Her only comfort came in letters from Jack and Bertie. Jack, deeply affected, referred to the leave last summer when he and Robbie had been home at the same time. They had worked together at the haysel, and it had been like a return to their boyhood:

I'm so glad I had that time with him, to remember how it used to be when we were young. I little thought when I saw him off at the station that it would be the last time. One ought to be prepared in wartime, but somehow one never is – I still can't believe Frank's gone. I wish to God this war was over and we could come home. We are busier than ever in my squadron, doing two or three stunts a day. At least it leaves no time for thinking. Take care of yourself, little sister. I hope you are staying well. A thing like this puts other matters into perspective. In the end, the only thing that counts is life.

She understood what he meant – that his anger and dis-appointment with her were over. If only it could be like that with the rest of the family. But Jack was a young man, and in the thick of it. Jessie knew that her mother and Uncle Teddy would not be able to accept her sin in that spirit.

Bertie wrote a long letter, full of his sympathy, wishing he could be with her, begging her to take care of herself and the baby.

I have written again to Maud, asking her to expedite matters, because it seems her solicitor has not put forward any papers, though Paterson assures me the necessary documents were with them a fortnight ago.

It can't be that she has changed her mind, because her last letter was still talking about Manvers in the same terms. I think it must be that she is simply not accustomed to business of any sort and expects things to happen without any action on her part. I hope my urging will have some effect. If she mentions the letter to Manvers he may make her see that she has to do something if she wants the divorce. Oh, my darling, I wish all this were not necessary. I hate having even to write the word 'divorce' in a letter to you. The moment it is through I will come home by hook or crook and marry you. And if it cannot be before the child is born, I swear to you he will not suffer by that if anything I can do will protect him.

We are going back up to the line tomorrow, which at least will make a change from digging. It's quiet at the moment, so don't be afraid for me. In fact it's so quiet that we are leaving units in the line for longer than usual, so as not to disrupt the work in the rear by frequent changes. So I shall be up there for twelve days, but should still be able to write to you. When you write, tell me how you are – not just 'I am well' but every twinge and ache. I know you must long to go back to Morland Place, and I feel wretched to be the cause of your having to stay away. A lifetime will not be enough to make it up to you, but if I'm spared, I swear I'll do my best.

If I'm spared. It was the uncertainty of everything in her life that made Jessie suffer most. The newspapers were now openly discussing the probability of a German offensive, and when it came, Bertie and Jack would be in the thick of it. And though she was feeling well at the moment, so she had in her other pregnancies but she had still lost the babies. There was nothing concrete to cling to.

'The only thing that counts is life,' Jack had written. New

life within her, and the lives of those she loved at the Front, and the lives of those who had been taken, Ned and Frank and Robbie. She saw the war as a giant chiaroscuro of harsh shapes and jagged outlines, stretching across Europe: black and white, life and death.

Emma was coming out of the Casino hospital, on her way back to Dorcas, when she was hailed by an officer crossing the courtyard.

'Miss Weston! I say – Miss Weston, is that you?'

She paused and turned, not recognising the voice, and since only one of the people passing through the yard was standing still and staring, she took a step towards him, and then recognised him under his cap. It was Lord Knoydart.

They shook hands. 'Imagine its being you,' she said, with a smile.

'Imagine its being *you*,' he countered. 'I heard that you had come out and were serving with a FANY unit, but I never thought to be lucky enough to bump into you.'

'Oh, they say you meet everyone you know if you hang around this part of the world for long enough,' Emma replied. Knoydart looked very well, she thought. He had always been a handsome young man, but military service had given his face the firmness and decision it had lacked. He had been an uncomfortably shy suitor back in Edinburgh, but this Knoydart was looking directly at her without blushing, and seemed disposed to chat.

She wondered for a painful moment what he thought of her now, for she did not suppose she was in her best looks. Though the weather had turned milder and she had shed some of the layers under her coat, she must still look bulky and shapeless, and there was nothing feminine or attractive about the khaki uniform, though she thought the FANY cap quite becoming. And since she had had trouble with Dorcas on the way over, there would undoubtedly be oil marks on her face. She never managed to do anything oily without at some point dabbing it on her nose, cheeks or brow.

This feminine concern passed only fleetingly through her head, aroused by the fact that Knoydart's previous context was the social round in Edinburgh, where they had seen each other evening-clad and exquisitely burnished.

'I've met someone recently who knows you,' she remembered. 'An officer called Curzon – says he's a distant cousin and used to shoot with you on your estate.'

'Oh, yes, of course, Jimmy Curzon. Nice chap. I haven't bumped into him yet.'

'He's at Camp Nieulay, just down the road from us. Where are you based?'

'We're just passing through,' Knoydart said. 'We're on our way up to the line, but one of my chaps had a bit of an accident and ended up here.' He nodded towards the Casino. 'So I'm just popping in to see him before we go.'

'Nothing serious, I hope.'

'Not too bad. I expect he'll catch up with us later.'

Emma smiled. 'In that case, I may have the pleasure of delivering him to you. We do a lot of that sort of thing.'

'I hear the FANY are doing fine work. Are you enjoying the life?'

She thought he seemed puzzled by the idea, and was nettled. 'Very much. It's good to be doing something important, instead of frittering away one's life dancing and going to parties. But perhaps you're surprised women can do anything useful?'

Now Knoydart blushed and looked confused – much more like the young man she remembered. 'Goodness, no! I wasn't thinking that. I always thought Miss Weston was capable of doing anything she set her mind to. It was just . . .' He hesitated.

'Yes?'

'This is so different from the places I remember you in, that's all.'

She smiled then. 'I was just thinking the same thing about you.'

'It's a funny old world, isn't it,' he said. He looked at her keenly. 'Your loss – Major Fenniman – it must have been so dreadful. I hope being here helps you, in some way, to come to terms with it.'

'I'm not sure I'll ever come to terms with it,' she said. 'But, yes, it helps, being here. I understand a lot more. His death doesn't seem so – so random and unconnected.'

Knoydart nodded. 'Perhaps that's all one can hope for.' He offered his hand again. 'It's been good to see you. I hope we'll meet again – after the war, if not before.'

'Yes. They say it might be over next year. Good luck, Knoydart.'

They clasped hands for an instant, and went their separate ways.

The following afternoon, Emma was underneath the Napier, working on a worn bearing on the connecting rod, when a pair of officer's boots came up alongside her and a familiar voice said, 'Dr Livingstone, I presume?'

Emma wriggled out, and took the offered grasp to help her up. 'What are you doing here, Stanley?'

Wentworth inspected his palm. 'That's what I get for being chivalrous.'

Emma pulled a rag from her pocket and belatedly wiped her hands. 'And it never comes off,' she informed him solemnly. 'Never, ever.'

'Shall I treasure each smudge in remembrance of you,' he said, 'or may I borrow your rag?' She handed it to him. He nodded towards the Napier. 'What's the problem?'

'Bearings. Got to keep 'em oiled, you know.'

'I didn't, but I do now. My expertise in motor-cars extends only as far as driving them to some agreeable little place, preferably by the river, where they do a roast duck and green peas, and keep a good cellar.'

'Oh, don't,' Emma groaned. 'There's something unfair about talk of food in wartime. Are you here for a reason, or is it just to stop me working?'

'A reason. I want to ask you a favour.'

'Ask away.'

'You have to come to the car,' he said. He had driven himself over in one of the battalion's motors. She followed him to where it was parked, and watched in silence as he opened the door, reached inside, and turned back to her with a dog in his arms.

'Oh, how sweet!' she said, putting out a hand. The dog wriggled in Wentworth's arms, trying to reach her to lick her face. It was a mongrel, though it obviously had a great deal of wire-haired fox-terrier in it – the right size and shape, and with a tightly curly coat and splendid eyebrows and moustache. But the coat was grizzled grey, and the ears were upstanding and pointed like an Alsatian's, while the tail had evidently been borrowed from a passing collie and ought to have been given back. 'Is it yours?'

'Not entirely,' Wentworth said. He took a piece of string from his pocket, slipped it through the dog's collar and put it down on the ground. The dog waved its reprehensible tail and thrust itself under Emma's hand for caressing. 'He was hanging around the camp, begging, when we moved in, and the officers' mess sort of adopted him because he was such a nice friendly fellow. We called him Benson, after a famous RSM back home, who had a similar moustache. The thing is, I was wondering whether you would allow me to give him to you.'

'To me?' Emma looked up in surprise. 'But why?'

He returned the look apologetically. 'We're moving out tomorrow – going up to the line. We won't be back, and I don't like just to leave the little fellow, which was what the previous unit obviously did. When we found him he was pretty thin and dirty – hadn't been having much of a time of it. I'd really rather know he was being taken care

132

of properly. So I thought perhaps you'd take him on – as a favour.'

'Why can't you take him with you?' Emma asked.

'It's too dangerous up there. He'd just be in the way, and if he wandered off – well, apart from unexploded shells, they say the Germans like to use anything that moves as target practice. And once the big offensive starts . . .' He shrugged. 'It seems to have fallen on my shoulders, as mess president, to find him a home, so I naturally thought of you. He could ride along beside you when you go out on Dorcas. I'd like to think of you having a protector. And he'd help to keep my memory green.'

'Don't be silly,' she said. 'I don't need a dog for that.'

'But will you take him? I feel awfully responsible for the little tyke. And I know you FANYs are allowed to have dogs, because there are two in the camp already.'

Emma squatted down and caught the dog's face between her hands. 'Would you like to come and live with me, Benson? Would you like that?' Benson expressed himself ecstatically on the subject, attempting to climb up into her lap while licking any part of her he could reach.

'I think we could take that as a "yes",' Wentworth urged, smiling down at them.

Emma stood up and took the string from his hand. 'The first thing is to buy him a proper lead. I do hope he won't fight with the other dogs.'

'Thank you,' Wentworth said warmly. 'You've taken such a weight off my mind.'

'Thank *you*,' Emma said. 'I've never had a dog of my own before. I think he's lovely. It's the best present I've ever had.' They smiled at each other for a moment, and then she said, 'But you're going away. Going to the Front.'

The smiles faded.

'Yes, tomorrow, first thing. I'm sorry I couldn't give you more notice, but we were only told this morning. They like to keep these things secret to make sure the Germans don't hear.'

133

'It will be dangerous up there,' Emma said.

'Not at first,' he reassured her. 'Not until the offensive starts.'

'They're saying the middle of March for that.'

'That's what we hear. It will be a novelty, at any rate, to be defending rather than attacking.' He was speaking lightly, for her sake, but she had been there long enough now to know what was what, and to guess what a major offensive would mean. Even in these quiet times there were wounded coming back, and the wounds were not pretty.

She said, in a low voice, as if it was forced out of her, 'I shall miss you.'

He seemed to receive the words with relief, as if he had not been sure she would. 'I shall miss you, too. We've been good friends, haven't we?' She nodded. 'Can I write to you?' he asked. 'Just to find out how Benson's going on?'

She managed a smile. 'Just for that, of course. I'll get him to reply.'

'And if we're ever in the same area again, can I call on you?'

'Just to see Benson.'

'He'd be offended if he knew I was around and hadn't called.'

She tried to laugh and in the middle of it tears surprised her. She forced them back and hid her face for a moment by blowing her nose. She had forgotten it was the oily rag she was holding, not a handkerchief, and she emerged much smeared and with a coal-black nose-tip.

Wentworth smiled, feeling a surge of tenderness, and was not disposed to tell her about the smudges. 'Chin up,' he said. 'The war won't last for ever. And when it does end, well, Benson gives me a perfect excuse for calling on you back home.'

He offered his hand, shook and held hers a moment, and said, 'I'll say toodle-oo, then. I shan't be able to call again before we go. Cheerio, Benson, take care of the missus now. Goodbye, Westie. Keep those beastings oiled.'

'Bearings, you idiot!' she said, and couldn't help grinning. He got into the car, backed up and turned, and stuck his hand out of the window to wave as he drove away. 'Take care of yourself,' she said, but too quietly for him to have heard her.

Benson watched him go, waving at one end but with a puzzled cock of the head at the other, and a faint enquiring whine. Emma bent to scratch his head. 'It's you and me now, Benson, old chap.' He licked her hand equably, and Emma supposed he had had too many masters in his short life to mind too much changing one for another.

That night he slept on top of her flea-bag, and she found the weight of his small, hot body against her feet extremely comforting. A dog was a good thing for a FANY to have, someone to love without putting too much of one's heart at risk. She thought about Fenniman, and the same old ache rose up, with the hollow emptiness behind it of death, the thing that could never be put right. If she lived another sixty years to be an old, old woman, he would never be alive again, he would never come back.

She didn't want to think about Wentworth going into the line, or the coming offensive. She thought instead about Benson, imagining how he would fit in with her duties, what it would be like to have him beside her on journeys. She thought about the dog so as *not* to think about the man who had given him to her, which was perhaps not what Wentworth had intended, but was as close to it as he was going to get.

CHAPTER SEVEN

At her first free moment, Emma went into Calais and, in a small back-street shop, bought Benson a new collar – the one he had on was worn almost through – and a proper lead. She didn't think it would often be needed: he was almost embarrassingly devoted to her, and followed her like her shadow. Perhaps because he had had so many masters, none of whom had cared very much about him, he seemed determined to show her what canine faithfulness could be. Even when she took a bath, he pressed himself to the closed door, tail wagging hopefully, quivering nose applied from time to time to the gap under the door to make sure she was still in there.

The only time he had voluntarily left her side was when a large rat shot out from behind the cookhouse almost under his nose. In fairness, no-one could ask a self-respecting terrier to ignore that. He raced after the rat, across the dunes and into the gorse bushes, and returned twenty minutes later, much dishevelled and bethorned, but with his jaws clamped round the dead rat, which he proudly laid at Emma's feet in tribute.

On the cajoling of the shopkeeper, who had a wife and family to support, she also purchased an identity disc for his collar, on which she had engraved:

My name is
BENSON
I belong to
Trpr E. Weston
F.A.N.Y.

Benson came with her in Dorcas whenever she went out, sitting up on the seat next to her. The weather had turned fine and dry, and he seemed positively to relish the wind blowing in his face, but she thought that if they were both still there next winter, she ought to arrange some sort of cape for him to keep the snow and rain off. She enjoyed his presence and his company, and he was already a familiar sight to the soldiers. They would come up to pat him when she stopped for any reason; and she thought interest in him provided a distraction from pain for some of the wounded.

One morning at the beginning of March Boss sent for her, such an unusually formal proceeding that she entered the office with faint trepidation. Behind the desk, Boss gave a small, tight smile. 'Don't worry, it isn't a wigging. I've had a request from Muriel Thompson of Unit Eight at St Omer. She needs an extra person, and though there's a new FANY coming out from England, she particularly needs someone who's good with maintenance and repairs. You've done wonders with Dorcas, and the mechanics tell me you show a real flair with the other vehicles. So I thought if you cared for it, we could have the new girl here, and you could go to St Omer. What do you think? You'll be a little further up towards the line, and the work may be different. You may find it more interesting.'

'I've found it interesting here,' Emma protested.

Again, Boss read her thoughts. 'Don't think I'm not satisfied with your performance. This is meant as a compliment to you. Also, having been here only a short time, you ought to find it easy to adjust to a new unit. But if you don't want to go, you don't have to.'

Emma thought about it. 'No, I think I'd like to. Thank you.' A change was always welcome, and being nearer the line might be a challenge – and Calais was lacking something now her particular friend Wentworth was gone. Probably the others felt much more attached to Unit 3 than she did, so it was partly a case of 'last in, first out'.

'Very well, I'll make the arrangements,' said Boss.

Venetia, Lady Overton, had been involved with the women's movement since the 1870s when, struggling to qualify as a doctor, she had naturally come into contact with those striving to get the vote for women. She had been registered in 1878, and in the forty years since then, there had been many times when the vote had seemed almost within reach, only to be snatched away. The peaks and troughs of hope and despair had been enough to make one seasick, and as recently as 1912 she had been convinced that the goal would never be reached.

But then suddenly last year the measure was once again before the House, this time with government support, riding on the back of the Soldiers' Vote. Resistance seemed to be melting away – not because the MPs really welcomed the idea, but because they couldn't any longer see how to prevent it. As a government bill, it was passed in the Commons in June 1917 with an overwhelming majority; but, of course, that was only the Lower House. The real struggle would be in the Lords.

The measure had come on in the Upper House on the 8th of January, 1918, and Venetia, with her old friend and fellow campaigner Millicent Fawcett, had sat through every minute of the three-day debate. Much of it was weary work, as the old arguments were brought up all over again: women were not intellectual; women were emotional, irrational, unreliable; they would be at the mercy of charlatans; they would cast their votes not for the good of the country but on a whim, swayed by a handsome moustache; women were delicate creatures, unfitted for the rough-and-tumble of politics; a woman's place was in the home – this above all – and exposure to the world of men would unfit them for their proper feminine duties.

All this was sickeningly familiar to the two friends listening in tense silence in the gallery above. The one thing that was different about the debate from the many others they had attended was its seriousness. There was no ribaldry or mockery. The views were expressed on either side with passion, but with gravity. And Venetia noticed, with a rising sense of hope, that the younger men in the chamber seemed to be on the women's side.

On the third day Lord Curzon stood up to close the debate with his summary. He was the arch enemy, the president of the Anti-Suffrage League, implacably opposed to the emancipation of women. And as leader of the house, he had great influence. The enthusiasm of the younger peers for the measure could be swept away like straws if he made a good, thundering speech against it. Venetia had her handkerchief twisted up in her hands; she saw Mrs Fawcett lean forward slightly as Curzon rose, her hands gripping the rail so tightly her knuckles were white.

But as Curzon spoke, Venetia's painfully held breath was gradually released, Mrs Fawcett's fingers relaxed, and they glanced at each other with astonished, fearful joy. Curzon was not for the measure – nothing, not even the war, would create such a revolution in his thinking – but he was urging the House not to vote against it. Giving women the vote would be a disaster for the country, he said, would destroy the sacred traditions of home and marriage, but it was now plainly inevitable. His argument was political: the Lords could not emerge with credit from a struggle with the Lower House when it had voted so determinedly in favour of the measure. The only thing he could do, he said, and the only thing he could urge his peers to do, was to abstain from voting altogether.

Venetia's eye picked out various lords she knew to be on their side, and saw them relax, and nod to each other, and she knew from their reaction that they believed they were home and dry. She looked at Mrs Fawcett, and saw her smile. 'It's over,' Mrs Fawcett whispered. Venetia nodded. She knew it too, in her bones.

They waited for the result, which came after a mere ten minutes. The majority in favour of women's suffrage was sixty-three. Venetia closed her eyes. It really was over. Fifty years of struggle! They had been abused, reviled, insulted verbally and physically; they had been manhandled, imprisoned, tortured, and some had died – all to prevent this small, simple, equitable step from being taken. Venetia felt, oddly, rather sick, as though with vertigo, as if she had fallen suddenly from a great height. She longed for her husband, who would have understood: he would have been so glad for them all. She thought of her cousin, Anne Farraline, and wished she could have been here to witness this moment; but Anne was dead and, given the circumstances of her death, it was fair to say she had given her life to the Cause.

She opened her eyes again, and saw Mrs Fawcett looking at her oddly. 'This is the greatest moment of our lives,' she said, 'but you don't look happy.'

'I *know* I am,' Venetia said. 'It will take a while for me to *feel* that I am.' And then suddenly she laughed. 'Milly, do you realise? Next time there's a general election, we shall be able to vote!'

And Mrs Fawcett laughed too, giving her her hands. 'I can't believe it! For you and me to vote! For the first time in our lives! It's too strange!' They stood, hands linked, gazing at each other. 'From today – from this moment – we are beginning a whole new world.'

Together they went out into the lobby, and thence to the yard outside, where the suffragists had been waiting for news, and there were scenes of great rejoicing. Peers who had been in favour came to shake the hands of the two great ladies of the Cause; photographers took pictures; reporters hovered, hoping for a comment. MPs came from the Commons to join in the happy moment, and even the policemen seemed to be beaming with satisfaction, making Venetia remember the savagery with which they had once arrested her and her colleagues simply for daring to be there, in the sacred male precincts of Parliament.

But it was over, there was no going back, and it was important for the future that such things be forgotten. There must be no resentment, no bitterness, to sour the great victory, or the relationship they must have with the male half of humankind.

Later, when a reporter had asked her how she felt about the ups and downs of the struggle, she told him firmly, and to his obvious surprise, that there had been no downs. 'Movement over the last fifty years has sometimes been miserably slow, but it has always been in the same direction – towards the removal of the intolerable grievances and disabilities of women. With each gain we have been passing slowly and gradually from subjection to independence. There is still further to go, but we are moving, as we always were, in the right direction.'

That had been in January; now in March there was to be a celebration. Everyone in the various suffrage movements felt that, the war notwithstanding, it was absolutely necessary to have just one great public thanksgiving. It took place in the Queen's Hall, and was a glorious occasion, with the banners under which they had so often marched hung around the hall like the triumphant colours of any great regiment. A sea of joyful faces filled the body of the hall. There was wonderful music – the *Leonora* Overture, and the suffrage hymn, Blake's 'Jerusalem', set to glorious new music by Sir Hubert Parry, who had been one of the staunchest of supporters. Outside the hall, the grim reminders of war might be all around – dimmed streetlights, Zeppelin warnings, ration books, food queues, the telegrams that brought death to the hearts of so many families – but inside, for that one evening, there was nothing but gladness.

To a tumult of acclaim, Venetia processed through the hall with Mrs Fawcett, smiling and nodding to either side, but when they reached the steps to the platform, Venetia held back, shaking her head. 'This is your moment, Milly,' she said. 'It's you they want.' She stepped to one side and joined in the applause; and Mrs Fawcett mounted the steps alone, to receive an ovation that might well have lifted the roof off.

Nothing could blunt the joy of that occasion, but it stood out from a bleak background of war work and worry. March was a time of particular tension for Venetia, for it brought to London the Norwegian businessman Jonas Lied, who arrived on the 3rd of March at the invitation of the British government. It was a visit of the utmost secrecy, arranged through Colonel Browning of MI 1C, the foreign-operations branch of the Secret Service, which was not even acknowledged to exist. Browning installed Lied in a suite he had reserved for him at the Savoy, and called in to see Venetia on his way to other urgent meetings.

Venetia already knew from Browning that Lied was coming. It was movement at last on a plan that had first been discussed the previous December, after Venetia had provided MI 1C with a map of the house where the Romanovs – the former Russian emperor and his family – were being held in Tobolsk.

It had been drawn by her son, Thomas, who had been a military attaché to the court of St Petersburg, protégé of the ex-Tsar and practically one of the family. When the Romanovs had been taken prisoner by the revolutionary government, Thomas had remained with them. His presence was invaluable to the British diplomatic service, but it was the cause of Venetia's deepest heartache. The Romanovs were now being held in the ice-bound depths of Siberia, at the mercy not only of dictator Lenin's government, but of the local soviet – and everyone knew that the further from the centre, the more extreme and violent the Reds became. Lenin was statesman enough not to hurt a hair on the head of a serving British officer, but if the local revolutionaries decided to kill Nicholas, they might easily kill all those around him, regardless of nationality.

So when Browning was shown into her drawing-room that day in March and greeted Venetia excitedly with the cryptic words, 'He's here!' she caught his meaning at once, and replied, 'Thank God!'

They sat down, and she asked, 'How is he?'

'He ought to be seasick, considering the journey he's just had, across the North Sea to Aberdeen,' Browning said, settling his tails, 'but, of course, he's a consummate seaman. I dare say he's more at home on the deck of a ship than on dry land.'

'But what sort of a man is he?' Venetia pursued.

'He seems sensible, level-headed. A man of business. He has a keen mind, and asked me penetrating questions. Speaks perfect English, which will be a relief all round. All he was told was that we wanted to discuss an expedition to Siberia, but given his close connection with Nicholas, I don't suppose he can be in any doubt as to what we're talking about.'

'So will he *do*, do you think?' Venetia asked anxiously.

'Yet to be determined. There will have to be meetings, of course, and a lot of people will have to assess him before we can go any further. Arthur Balfour. Lord Robert Cecil. Sir Reginald Hall.'

Balfour was foreign secretary, Cecil the Foreign Office man who had been dealing personally with royal enquiries about the Romanovs. And Hall was the Director of Naval Intelligence, a man of formidable reputation for efficiency and ruthlessness, and with wide connections. It would be his duty to arrange the British end of any possible rescue by sea.

'We must be sure he's sound before we go any further.'

'But will he do it, Colonel?'

'It's too early to say, but my personal belief is that he will. He seems the sort of man who likes to get on with things, and his personal gratitude to Nicholas is well documented. He hinted as much to me almost as soon as we had shaken hands.'

'I must see him,' Venetia said decidedly.

'And you shall,' said Browning, 'but a little further down the line. If nothing comes of this, I don't want to jeopardise your son's position by having your name linked with Lied's. He's too valuable to us where he is. When we've talked with Lied some more, we'll have to present him to the King, and I think at that point it will be appropriate for you to meet him.' He looked thoughtful and added, 'Going by past experience, the King may need some persuading, and it could be that you would be the person for that.'

'I will certainly do everything I can,' said Venetia. 'You know that.'

'Yes,' said Browning, 'but it will be more effective, I fancy, coming from you than from a politician or a diplomat. The King has his – shall we say? – sentimental side, and that may be what we need to appeal to.' He rose to go. 'I must get back to the ministry and report to my chief.'

Venetia rose too, rang, and shook his hand. 'You'll keep me informed of what's going on?'

'Of course,' said Browning. 'You are at the heart of the whole thing.'

By the time Venetia finally met Jonas Lied, the plan had taken on some flesh. The Vickers company had been brought in – the arms and shipbuilding firm had made millions supplying both Britain and imperial Russia, and had excellent connections in that country. It was to lend a fast armed boat, which was to be sent to Lied's sawmill depot at the mouth of the Yenisey river. Lied was to bring the Romanovs down-river in one of his cargo vessels, transfer them, and the armed boat was to escape on a northerly course into the Arctic through Novaya Zemlya, in the hope of foxing any possible Russian pursuit.

The first meeting between Lied, Venetia and the King was held in secret, using the house of her nephew Eddie, now Lord Vibart, in Piccadilly, as a neutral site. The venue had been suggested by the Prince of Wales, to whom Eddie was equerry, and who had already met Lied. Eddie's wife was down in the country, staying with her parents, the Marquess and Marchioness of Talybont, so did not need to be brought into the matter, and nothing was more natural than that Eddie should entertain the Prince and a few gentlemen at his house, or that the King should drop in on them.

Venetia took to Lied at once – a rather abrupt man, the sort, she guessed, who would suffer fools badly, but with a quickness of perception she found encouraging. His level blue eyes seemed faded by long staring at horizons, his hair and stiff sandy moustache were grizzled, his face deeply tanned and lined by exposure to the weather. His handshake was as hard as a plank, but there was sympathy in the look he gave Venetia when he was introduced, and he said, 'You are worried about your son. There's much to arrange, but the plan is sound. I believe it can work.'

Much to arrange, she thought, was an understatement by some length, but they had two full months before the thaw in which to get everything in place. Until the rivers ran again, nothing could be done.

It had been anticipated that one of the obstacles to overcome would be the attitude of the King, who last year had set his mind against offering the Romanovs asylum, fearing that Nicholas's unpopularity would cause unrest and threaten his own throne. But when the King arrived, Venetia found she had no persuading to do: he was already eager to have Lied presented, and showed himself at once in favour of the plan.

Later Venetia spoke privately to Eddie for a moment and expressed her surprise at the King's change of heart. 'Last year when Lloyd George could have brought them here without difficulty, it was the King who vetoed it.'

'I know, Aunty,' Eddie said, 'but I don't think he really understood then how dangerous the situation was. The Prince thinks he was sure some other country would take them all right. And in any case, he didn't really think the Reds would do anything – you know – *violent*. Not to an emperor. But he sees the danger is real now.'

Venetia frowned. 'As long as he doesn't change his mind again.'

'I don't *think* he will,' Eddie said. 'It was one thing not to want the Emperor here, but quite another to allow him to be – well – *killed*.'

Venetia took the point. One king could not condone the regicide of another. And Nicky was not only a monarch but a cousin, a childhood friend, someone who had stayed in one's house and gone out shooting with one. As Browning had said, there was a sentimental side to the argument, and it was time for it to come to the fore.

When the King took his leave later, after much serious conversation – which revealed to Venetia how much there still was to discuss, not least the tricky business of how to get the Romanovs from the house in Tobolsk down to Lied's boat on the river – he shook hands with Venetia and said with a directness and kindness she had not experienced before, 'I know you are worried about your son, but without his help we couldn't begin to form a plan. I think – I'm sure – this fellow Lied can be trusted. And our Secret Service is the best in the world. We'll get them all out somehow, don't worry.'

When he had gone, Venetia said to Browning, 'Get them out, yes. And then what? Where will they go?'

It was a question Browning did not want to answer. 'Let's not get ahead of ourselves,' he said.

Emma was ferried from the station at St Omer to her new unit on an army transport, driven by a very friendly RASC private who was fascinated by the whole idea of a FANY, especially one who knew about things mechanical, and was beautiful *and* well bred *and* had a little dog with her. He offered her cigarettes and plied her with sweets and had so many questions he hardly had time to listen to the answers, especially as he also wanted to tell her all about himself. It emerged that he came from York, and when she said she knew the city, all she had to do from then on was to smile and nod as he told her about the little terraced house on Emerald Street where he had grown up, his school in Lowther Street, the bend of the Ouse at Fulford Ings where he used to fish when playing hookey from said school, the Blossom Street tram he drove when he'd left school, the girl he'd started walking out with, and how he'd taken her to the Electric Cinema in Fossgate to see the moving picture of the battle of the Somme, and couldn't wait to be old enough to join up. 'I've been out here three months now,' he concluded.

'Is it the way you expected?' Emma asked.

'Pretty much, miss,' he agreed. 'It's a bit of a lark, really, but I can't wait for the big push to start. Mostly I wish I could have a chance to kill a German. Bertha – that's my girl – well, I don't think she'll respect me if I don't.'

Emma thought of a young Tommy she had transported in Dorcas the week before, no older than this boy. 'I'm sure she'll be glad just to get you back safely,' she said, but she could see it didn't convince.

''Ere y'are, miss. This is you,' he said, pulling up.

She and Benson jumped out, and he passed down her luggage. 'Thanks for the lift. And good luck.'

'Mebbe see you driving around,' he said, with a cheerful, gappy grin, plugged a Wild Woodbine in his mouth, and drove off.

The new camp was right beside the main road to Arques, rather an exposed spot. It was flat and did not drain very well. Emma could see at first glance it was extremely muddy,

147

with pools of standing water glinting in the light from the further side. The camp consisted of a series of Nissen huts forming three sides of a square, with a large parade-ground across the road, which formed the park for the thirty ambulances and other vehicles, and also held a large workshop.

Each FANY – and the VADs who were attached to the unit and worked with them – had a cubicle screened off in one of the four sleeping-huts, so it was not as private or as comfortable as at Unit 3, but there was a large mess hut with a good stove, and kitchen, office, bath and lavatories beyond. The new 'boss' was Muriel Thompson, and her second in command was Beryl Hutchinson, both old Calais hands. For the rest, Emma found a warm welcome among just such young women as Calais had been full of, energetic, independent, high-spirited, capable, and undaunted by anything the war wanted to throw at them.

There was work to be done immediately.

'There's a small lorry that's been abandoned in a ditch not far from here,' Thompson told her, almost as soon as they had shaken hands, 'and no-one seems to want it. If we can get it out and running, it could be very useful to us.'

'Even if it can't be got running,' Emma suggested, 'it might be good for spare parts.'

'Exactly. That's the right spirit. Would you like to dump your things and go with Armstrong and Bullock in the Vulcan to see if you can get it out?'

Emma did like, and went off with two new friends, some rope and chain, in the big Vulcan on the scavenging exercise. Armstrong was a tall, quiet, fair young woman with a rather sardonic sense of humour, Bullock a small, bubbly dark girl, round and bouncy as an india-rubber ball. Within ten minutes Emma felt as if she had known them all her life. On the drive out, Armstrong said she had been in Unit 3 too – Bullock had come straight out to St Omer from England – and asked after various old friends, both FANY and army.

'And our old friends the Thirty-seventh, who used to be at Nieulay, came through here the other week. They're up near Armentières, which is only about twenty miles away, so I dare say we shall see something of them,' she mentioned.

'Really?' Emma said eagerly.

'Oh yes. The men and officers come down to St Omer for rest now and then, and of course they're always back and forth to the railway station and various headquarters. Did you . . . ?' She hesitated delicately. 'Was there someone in particular . . . ?'

'Oh, it's nothing like that,' Emma said, feeling herself blush, to her annoyance. 'I was friendly with Captain Wentworth, and he gave me Benson. I thought he'd be glad to know how he was – how Benson was, that is.'

'Oh, yes, Wentworth,' Armstrong said, with a glance at Bullock.

'Nice chap,' Bullock said. 'Always friendly.'

Emma was sure they were getting hold of the wrong end of the stick, and felt the need to change the subject. 'What do you do in your time off?' she asked. 'Is there anything going on?'

'Well, if you like riding,' Bullock said, 'there's a French cavalry riding school in St Omer, and they let us borrow their horses. And there's a mobile cinema with a new programme each week. And, of course, restaurants and so on. We do all right.'

It was quite a job getting the lorry out of the ditch. It proved impossible to start it where it stood so they had to tow it back to camp where Emma, after a quick meal and a change into her smock, got to work on it with relish. Benson found a sheltered spot nearby and went to sleep, whiskery nose on paws and one ear pricked in her direction so he would know the moment she had finished and was ready to pay him attention again.

Emma wrote to Wentworth to say where she was, and he wrote back, saying that he was in the line but hoped to be able to come and see her as soon as they were relieved:

St Omer is not quite Calais, but I'm sure there must be a restaurant of some sort there, so perhaps when I am next at leisure you will allow me to buy you and one of your new colleagues dinner. I hope Trooper Benson is behaving himself and proving his worth, as a companion, perhaps, since I don't have much faith in him as a watch dog. Altogether too friendly – though he might lick a burglar to death! But you FANYs always cope, so I wouldn't care to be the villain who set myself against you. We are having a quiet time of it at present. The CO was even able to entertain our brigade commander to dinner at Bttn HQ the day before yesterday and invited captains-and-above, so we got a decent meal out of it. Linzer played his fiddle after-wards, a piece I hadn't heard before – a Caprice by his old master, Kreisler. Very jolly. I wish you had been there to hear it. We need all the high art we can get in these barbaric times!

It was quiet along the front in the second and third weeks of March – too quiet, Bertie thought. There was an air of tension, as everyone believed an attack was coming. Letters *to* the Front were not censored, so the men were hearing from home that the newspapers were openly discussing the likelihood of a big German offensive. Besides, all the digging and training they had been doing for the last two months told them the same thing. Bertie was glad to see that spirits were high, and the men did not seem troubled by the prospect of action. The newcomers were, typically, eager for the fray, while old hands were intrigued at the thought of being defenders rather than attackers.

There was no sense of urgency about the anticipation, for everyone knew that a German attack would be preceded by a bombardment lasting several days, and there was nothing like that going on at present. There was some shelling on both sides, and as always the danger of snipers, but otherwise the days in the trenches passed quietly. The weather was warm and pleasant, green shoots were appearing, the men smoked, played cards and had sing-songs, while settling into the eternal rhythm of duties and fatigues, fetching water and rations, digging out and reinforcing trenches, cleaning their equipment, running messages, and now and then going out on patrols.

The main purpose of these patrols was to take German prisoners for interrogation, but it proved very difficult to find any. As soon as a raiding-party was detected the enemy retreated, leaving the first line empty, and from the safety of the second line opened fire with mortar, shell and machine-gun. This was the main cause of casualties during the early part of March. Bertie offered twenty-four hours' leave to anyone who took a German prisoner, but no-one managed it, and though several Germans deserted to the British line, they turned out to be Bavarians who had only just been put in to hold the line, and swore they did not know anything about an offensive: they had been expecting the British to attack.

But the Royal Flying Corps had been busy with reconnaissance, and it was known that the German back areas were full of troops, that those in the forward areas were hard at work carrying ammunition, and that there were a great many ammunition dumps and field guns close to the German front line. By the morning of the 19th, British Intelligence concluded that there would be an attack on the British Third and Fifth Armies on the 20th or 21st, after a short bombardment.

Everyone stood-to as usual before dawn on the 20th, but nothing happened, and the day that followed was exceptionally quiet, with little German activity of any sort. After stand-down, the men relaxed, went about their usual tasks, and Bertie overheard several conversations supposing the whole thing to be a severe case of 'wind-up' among the senior officers. During the morning Bertie's headquarters received a visit from the corps commander, who said that the battle, when it came, would be a very serious and important one. 'The general has said that he expects us to hold the position to the last man and the last round of ammunition. If we have to die here, he expects us to do that.'

'What about reinforcements, sir?' Bertie asked. He knew how thinly held this part of the line was. If estimates of German numbers were accurate, they would roll right over them. 'The GHQ reserve divisions?'

The commander looked uncomfortable. 'There's no question of weakening the northern sector of the Front,' he said. 'Haig holds that vital, as you well know. GHQ believes we should be able to manage with what we have.'

'I see, sir,' Bertie said. What the corps commander had not said was as revealing as what he had.

'Our reserves are being moved up closer to the line as we speak,' he went on. 'We fight the Germans in our own battle zone for as long as we can hold them here, and if we have to fall back, we fight every inch of the way.'

Bertie spent the rest of the day visiting his companies, checking that all was in readiness. It was warm, sunny and quiet, and the men not on duty were dozing on the firing steps and along the side trenches. The only activity was when a German spotter aeroplane came over at about five hundred feet – a 'Nosy Parker', the men called these low-flyers. Bertie ordered it to be fired on, but it turned away as soon as they opened fire and was out of range before the gunner had got the right elevation.

Bertie went back to Battalion Headquarters and his dugout and wrote a brief letter to Jessie.

Everyone seems calm and confident. Everything is ready, and all we can do now is wait for them to come.

152

I'm sure it will begin tomorrow. Whatever happens, you must take care of yourself and our child. You, and he, are why we are all here. You are the important ones now. What we love and value must survive, or it is all for nothing. No more time, except to say I love you, love you, love you. That seems to be the only thing that matters at this exposed edge of life.

As soon as it was dark, there was a feeling of activity from behind the German lines. There was little sound, but experienced men could sense the unrest and movement, and the night was clear and cold and starry, the best sort for listening. But there was no gunfire at all from the German side, and unusually they were not sending up any of the flares they were so fond of. Presumably, then, they had something to hide. Bertie sent out several patrols into no man's land, but they returned to say all was quiet, although they had found some gaps in the German barbed wire.

At one in the morning, a patrol came back to say they had heard the sounds of wheels and occasional voices coming from the other side. Bertie sent out no more, but by three o'clock such sounds could be heard from the firing step at several places in the line. By then all his preparations had been made, but he could not rest. He went over everything again in his mind, as nervous as a dog smelling thunder.

The morning fog had rolled in. In the darkness it was the dank smell that identified it. Then at four forty exactly a white rocket flare shot up from behind the German lines, its edges fuzzy in the mist. Immediately afterwards their heavy guns roared out in near unison, in an explosion that ripped the early morning apart. Along fifty miles of the front line the brazen mouths spoke with one voice. It was not possible to hear any individual gun fire: it was a continual thunder that made conversation impossible, almost made thought impossible. The ground shook with the concussion, the very air trembled.

When the first volley went off, the thrust of air knocked the unwary men on the firing steps in the nearest trenches off their feet. The darkness was ripped with flame, while the smell of the exhaust fumes and burned cordite began to creep down on the foggy air, for there was hardly any wind. And the shells began crashing down, blasting the earth into fountains of soil and stones. The shrill, intolerable sound of them was like ten thousand giant glasshouses all cracking to pieces at the same moment.

There was nothing to be done under such a bombardment but to seek what shelter was possible, in the dugouts, in the funk holes, hard against the parapet or flat on the floor of the trench; to crouch down, cover one's ears and wait it out.

Bertie was being shaved by Cooper when the guns started. He had expected the bombardment to begin either earlier or later, and when three thirty and then four passed without incident, he had agreed to coffee, breakfast, and a wash and shave. The coffee had been most welcome – he had got cold poring over maps and standing outside in the fog listening for movement – and he had washed and sat down to be shaved, looking forward to the porage and bacon Cooper had promised him. Cooper's porage was somehow more heartening than other people's. He said he made it to 'an old Scotch recipe' a Highlander had given him. Bertie suspected he put a slug of whisky in it to give it body.

At the first crash of the guns he tried to leap from the chair, and was pressed back by Cooper's large hand. 'Nearly finished, sir.'

'Damn you, let me up!'

'Three more strokes, sir. Can't go out there half shaved. Two more. Think of morale, sir. Keep *still*, sir – don't want to lose your nose, do you? One more stroke. And just here. There, sir. You're done.'

Bertie grabbed the towel from him, wiping his face as he raced for the steps. Then, mindful of appearances, he curbed himself and walked briskly but without running. As he stepped outside a concussion like an earthquake almost knocked him off his feet, and he smelled the bitter cordite in the fog. He could hear the shells whistling just overhead and exploding behind him, between here and Brigade Headquarters, and the thunder of the guns was continuous. This was it, then, he thought, *der Tag*. Those who had murmured that the 21st would be the chosen day, because it was an important date to the Boche – the anniversary of the opening of the first Reichstag of the German Empire in 1871 – had been right.

It was only a few steps to the telephone pit where the signals officer, hunched over his equipment, looked up at him with a hunted expression. He was only a youngster and had never been under fire before.

'Steady, lad,' Bertie said. 'They're not firing at us. All this lot's going overhead. Get me each of the companies in turn, starting with C Company.'

The boy steadied and did as he was told, but all his plugging in and whirring was useless. 'Everything's dead, sir,' he said.

'Impossible!' Bertie exclaimed. As part of the preparation for this battle, the telephone lines had been buried six feet deep – veterans like him remembered how in the early stages of battles like Loos and Neuve Chapelle the lines, laid on the surface, had been cut by shells and left everyone fighting blind.

But it was true. Every line was dead, cut by the sheer weight of the massive bombardment. No information could get in or out, except by the old-fashioned method of runners, and with shells falling both in front of and behind their position, it was no place to send them out. A few of the units had wireless transmitters, but not in Bertie's section, and with the thick fog making the darkness impenetrable, they were completely cut off. Bertie went outside again, bumping into Cooper who had brought him his tin hat. '*If you please, sir*,' Cooper said, in a voice that brooked no refusal. Bertie put it on with a distracted air. 'I can't hear our guns,' he said. 'For God's sake, is no-one firing back?'

His staff was gathering out of the gloom, looking to him for guidance. There was a tremendous explosion over to the north-west, which seemed to make the ground lift under their feet, and despite the fog, the sky bloomed in a hideous red and orange glow that increased rather than faded as the seconds passed. 'That must be the Engineers' petrol dump,' said the adjutant, Wellby, in the detached voice of shock. 'Orders, sir?'

'Let's get inside first,' Bertie said. As he turned towards his dugout again, the immediate bombardment stopped for a moment – though he could hear it going on everywhere up and down the line – and in the momentary bliss of its cessation he didn't think what it might mean.

'Hello!' said Major Weekes. They all stopped and looked round.

'Sir!' said Cooper, urgently.

Bertie met his eyes and read the old soldier's message. 'They're changing aim,' he said. 'Get inside!'

The guns spoke again, and this time the screaming of the shell had a different pitch. It struck thirty yards away, flinging Bertie off his feet, and he heard the lethal whick-whick of a piece of shrapnel spinning past above him like a horizontal guillotine. Cooper had fallen to his knees, and was up now and grabbing Bertie's arm to help haul him to his feet. Wellby and Weekes, the battalion signals officer and young Forest, the staff lieutenant, had all reached the dugout and were scampering down the steps. Bertie heard the other shell coming but did not hear it explode – it was sometimes that way when it was too close. He had just got to his feet and was flung off them again, upwards and side-ways this time, flying through the air, feeling Cooper's fingers biting his arm and then release him, feeling the

156

ground come up to smack him while his ears and head rang with the silent cacophony of explosion. Light and then heavy objects pattered and thumped down around him, some hitting his back and legs as he rolled with the fall. Something heavy and soft hit him jarringly in the small of the back. He stopped rolling, lying on his back facing upwards, saw something huge fall towards him and stop miraculously in mid-air.

Cooper was there, thrown with him, scrabbling alongside him on his belly. 'Stay down, sir,' he said, as Bertie tried to get up. 'They're shelling us, the bastards. We're all right here.'

Bertie shook his head, wiped the dirt out of his eyes and got his bearings. He saw that that falling thing was a huge sheet of corrugated iron, and that it had been arrested on its way to earth by a series of blasted tree-trunks to the side of the open space in front of his dugout. With one end on the ground and the other on the stumps it had formed a sort of lean-to, under which he and Cooper were sheltered, and onto which earth and stones were still crashing as another shell exploded nearby.

'Are you all right?' he said to Cooper. His voice rang strangely inside his head, while other sounds seemed too far away – the effect of being temporarily deafened by the explosion. Cooper turned a drawn face to him. There was blood across it from a cut at his hairline, and Bertie saw him wipe it, and say, 'I'm all right.' His focus changed, and he looked with distaste at something just beyond Bertie's head. It was the soft, heavy thing that had hit him in the back. Bertie rolled over and reached for it, then pulled his hand back. It was an arm, still in its sleeve, with the shoulder tab still attached at the ruined end. The tab had two lieutenant's pips on it. Forest, as junior, would have gone down the steps last.

Cooper was looking out of their shelter towards the camp. 'Oh, blimey,' he said. 'Oh, bloody 'ell.'

Bertie wriggled up beside him. There was a crater where the dugout had been. He felt sick. The dugout had not been a permanent, concrete-lined structure like those at Brigade HQ – or, indeed, like the Germans had in their trenches, built for long occupation – but something that had been dug in the last few weeks as the battalion had taken over this section, a hole in the ground supported with wood, secure enough against anything but a direct hit.

Cooper, beside him, was breathing harshly. 'They might be all right,' he said. 'We got to see.' He started to wriggle out, but another shell screamed down, everything heaved about under them, and the debris rattled against their roof. It was a perilous enough kind of shelter, but better than being out in the open.

'Stay put,' Bertie said. 'Wait until it moves on again.'

'They could've made it,' Cooper said, but Bertie could hear from his voice that he didn't believe it. It was simply guilt speaking, the guilt you always felt, however briefly, when the man next to you copped a packet and you survived.

Bertie's eyes had measured the extent of that crater, and he knew it was no good. A direct hit – a big shell, too. You couldn't even see where the steps had been. The dugout and everything in it – including his officers – had been blown to nothing. Forest's arm was all that was left.

When the shelling eased, he must find out who was left of his staff and send them back to Brigade Headquarters with the information. For himself, he was going in the other direction. His men were in the trenches to the front of him, cut off by telephone and fogged in, left to the leadership of the company commanders, and when the bombardment stopped, the Germans would attack. He didn't know how many were still alive, but he had to find out, and either lead them out, or organise their last stand, as circumstances dictated. His place was with them. He'd never left his men yet and, battalion command notwithstanding, he couldn't do it now.

BOOK TWO

Offensives

Oh! we, who have known shame, we have found release
   there,
Where there's no ill, no grief, but sleep has mending,
Naught broken save this body, lost but breath;
Nothing to shake the laughing heart's long peace there
But only agony, and that has ending;
And the worst friend and enemy is but Death.

Peace, Rupert Brooke

CHAPTER EIGHT

B Company was in reserve, and he found them in good shape. The shelling had mostly passed over them, and there had been only about a dozen casualties, most of them light, though the company commander had a nasty cut to his face. But they were shocked and subdued by the bombardment. These were his least experienced men and, apart from the 'salting' of old hands he had put in to stiffen them, they had never been under shellfire before. The noise was something you never got used to, but you learned to endure it. For newcomers, it was a mental and physical assault that left them numb and bewildered. Though he was desperate to get forward, he walked among them, cheering and reassuring them, preparing them for the real work to be done when the German infantry advanced. He saw them brace themselves for his sake, then went to see how the captain, Evans, was.

'That looks as if it needs stitches,' he said. The wad of cotton his batman had pressed over it had reddened through at once.

'I'll do well enough, sir,' Evans said. 'It's not as bad as it looks. Faces always bleed like the Dickens.' His voice was a little shaky, but his eyes were steady enough. Bertie gestured to Cooper with a flick of his head to go and help. Between them they got enough bandage on to stop the blood coming through, though Evans's head was grotesquely bulky and white.

'I'm going forward to the other trenches,' Bertie told him. 'Major Weekes and the adjutant are dead, and I'm sending the rest of the staff back, so you'll be the senior officer here. If we have to fall back, I want you here to fall back to. Do you understand?'

'Absolutely, sir. We shan't move,' Evans said. He seemed terribly young.

Bertie laid a hand on his shoulder, and felt him vibrating like a tapped drumskin. 'You'll be all right,' he said quietly. 'If we fall back, we'll be here ahead of the Germans. Just don't shoot us by mistake.'

Evans managed a grin. 'I can imagine what you'd say if we pooped off at you, sir.'

'I hope you can't, Evans,' Bertie said. Across the lad's shoulder he caught the eye of the sergeant. He had given B Company his most experienced sergeant, 'Reliable Jack' Richards, to counterbalance the general newness. Richards gave him an infinitesimal nod and, with a last squeeze of Evans's shoulder, Bertie left them.

A and D Companies were in the support trenches. Bertie and Cooper, with two runners taken from B Company, made their way forward through the hell of the barrage, falling flat whenever a shell passed over close. In the normal course of things it should have been getting light now, but with the fog, mingling with the smoke from the German guns, it was still dark as Hades, except for the occasional flashes from explosions. The noise and darkness were confusing to already battered senses, and it would have been easy to wander in circles. Bertie navigated by his compass and the general direction of the firing.

The support trenches were more solidly built, with decent dugouts and funk holes, and the officers, quite rightly, had sent everyone down possible, leaving only a handful to man the firing steps and give the alarm. There had been several shell hits, and in places the parapets were blown out, while at one end, where the earth was wetter and softer, the whole wall had come down in a mud-slide, blocking a side trench. But because the men were in shelter, there had been few casualties, only three dead and one seriously injured. Bertie did a quick round, encouraged the men, steadied the officers, and went on.

The German bombardment had not only been concentrated on the front lines: it had also deliberately targeted the areas to the rear, where the headquarters and command posts were. Their spotting beforehand must have been extremely good for, despite the fog, the shelling was unnervingly accurate. Some headquarters were well dug in and did not take much damage, but others, more recently set up, were mostly above ground and in huts, and proved very vulnerable. While strikes on headquarters did not result in heavy casualties, it interrupted the chain of command. Along with the loss of telephone lines, this hampered communication between the front and the rear.

As well as headquarters, other targets behind the lines were now being blasted: the billets of reserve battalions, petrol and ammunition dumps, stores, lorry parks, tankodromes, railheads, road junctions. The German long-range guns were reaching so far that they were hitting medical units, railway stations and airfields eleven miles behind the line. It all helped to sow confusion. Reserve troops moving up to their forward positions had to pass through this area of shelling, and many battalions suffered serious casualties in the process.

It was no great distance from the West Herts support line to the front-line trenches, but the shells were falling heavily, the fog and smoke thick. Progress was frequently a scuttle from one shell hole to the next. Tommies believed that shells never fell in the same place twice, and Bertie found this thought wandering in an inconsequential way round his brain as they worked their way forward.

The trenches, when they finally dropped into them, were in a bad way. In some places there was nothing but a ruin of craters and rubble, and there were dead men and pieces of dead men everywhere. In other places the trenches had been damaged but not destroyed, and here the men were huddled right up under the parapet for shelter. There were no dugouts: the defences here had been placed before open approaches so as to have a good field of fire. In normal daylight the Germans would be seen coming from some distance, and the purpose of the forward unit was to kill as many as possible and break the impetus of the attack. The Tommies sometimes called them 'sacrifice units'. Today, however, there was no clear field of fire. The fog, if anything, seemed to be growing thicker. It should have been full daylight by now, Bertie realised, glancing at his watch.

He set about assessing the situation and re-forming the defences. There were about thirty men left, one or two slightly injured but all capable of firing; and as they had done no firing yet, they had plenty of ammunition. There was a Lewis-gun team, a Vickers, and a good supply of pineapple and stick grenades. On the negative side, it was cold, dank and foggy. The men had not slept, they had had no breakfast, and the four-hour bombardment they had endured had left them numb and stupefied. And their officers were dead: the most senior men left were two corporals, whose relief on seeing Bertie far outweighed their nervousness of his high rank.

The first thing he had to do was shake them up, for in their dazed state they were more likely to surrender than fight. He reorganised the survivors, spread them out more evenly, and made one in two sit down on the trench floor and eat some rations. It was only cold biscuit with a swig of water, but it put some strength into them. Then he swapped them over so the rest could eat. He wished he could have got someone brewing up – hot tea would have done more for them than five-star brandy – but there was no possibility of that under the present bombardment. The weakest part of the defences was where the whole trench had been reduced to a series of craters, and he sent the Lewis team there, to set up in a shell hole just a little in front of the line.

He knew he was right to have come. They were calmed and heartened just by seeing him. Before, with their officers dead, they had felt themselves alone and abandoned in the fog, and he guessed some would have been slipping away had the shells not been falling behind as well as in front. C Company had contained the highest proportion of his experienced men, and he resented and regretted every one of them who had died in the bombardment. But there were a good few left, and there was a difference in the way they looked at him from the way the boys did. They had been through a lot together, and knew 'what was what'.

Just after half past nine the barrage suddenly – and one would have thought impossibly – intensified. What had been a nightmare became a hell as the Germans poured out a hurricane of high explosive, hitting the line with everything they had. The youngsters crouched, hands over their ears, some of them whimpering like puppies. But Bertie and the veterans knew what this was: there was always a five-minute increase in shelling before the advance. He sent the runners and Cooper crawling along to warn everyone, and went himself to shake up the boys in the most vulnerable places.

And at nine forty the shelling stopped. The silence was so reverberant and the ears so distressed that, for a moment, it seemed some other clamour was going on, some insane change-ringing from the church towers of hell. Bertie climbed onto the nearest firing step and eased himself upwards. Nothing before him but grey fog, though it was daylight enough to see it swirling a little. The senior corporal was beside him.

'They'll be coming now,' Bertie said, 'and with this fog we won't see them until the last minute. Tell the men to be ready. Quickly, now. They won't wait long.'

They appeared quite suddenly, hard to see against the fog, grey on grey, a uniform blanket of men advancing in silence. They had been ordered not to yell, so as to take advantage of the conditions. Bertie thought they must have crept quite far out into no man's land during the barrage to have got so far so quickly.

He didn't need to order the men to fire. They all opened up at more or less the same moment. The Lewis started to rattle from its crater, and the men he had chosen as bombers hurled stick grenades. Germans seemed to be falling in great numbers, though it was possible some were just going to ground.

His runner was beside him, round-eyed. 'I've never seen a Gerry before, only at the cinema,' he said. 'Not a real live one.'

Bertie turned on him sternly. 'Go and tell the men with the grenades to save them for groups – not to waste them on single men. Run!'

The Germans had reached the wire now, most of it miraculously intact despite the long bombardment. There was a cheering interval when it held them up, and they were cut down by British fire. Bertie could see wire-cutters, but there were only a few – perhaps one to twenty men. Bertie ordered the best shots to pick them off. He saw them fall, saw others take up the cutters and carry on. Some were getting through now, but the Lewis, tracking back and forth, was seeing to them. The men were firing steadily, elated beyond personal fear by the fact of having something to do, instead of suffering helplessly under the artillery fire.

Speaking of which, he realised that it had resumed and was falling to his rear: the German gunners had raised their elevation. In poor visibility, there was always a risk of the creeping barrage hitting its own men, and he hoped the enemy was suffering elsewhere in the line. It didn't seem to be happening here. They were still coming on, like a colony of ants – always more than you thought could possibly exist, and however many you killed, more and more would boil up out of the ground. They were firing as they came, and his men were being hit. The boy next to him fell back without a cry, shot through the throat. Bertie took his rifle and climbed up the parados onto the rear of the trench, lay down and took aim. They were holding them, but only just, and only because the wire was still slowing them.

One of those who had got through hurled a stick grenade into the crater where the Lewis team was still in business. Bertie's heart leaped to his throat, but one of the team was quick enough to throw it back out before it exploded. It went off in the air, and two Germans fell, one to either side, symmetrically, as though something invisible holding them together had been neatly sliced.

But the Lewis crater was a target, and other grenades followed. There were several explosions and the gun fell silent. The Vickers was still spraying out bullets, and the men were still firing; but without the Lewis their position was hopeless, and more of his men were being hit. A German shell, falling short, landed among the advancing enemy and blew a hole in the attack; but the next landed on the trench twenty yards from Bertie and blew the defence and the defenders into oblivion.

Cooper was beside him. 'One o' the corporals gone,' he said. There was a question in his eyes. *Fall back?*

'We wouldn't get five yards,' Bertie said. He shoved the rifle he was holding into Cooper's hands, while he took out his pistol. 'Keep firing,' he said.

And after that it was over quite suddenly. The Germans were on the parapet; what remained of Bertie's guns fell raggedly silent. A German sergeant moved his rifle back and forth and shouted, 'De hants up! Up! Climb up!'

With the German sergeant only a handful of his men had halted. The others were jumping over the trench and disappearing into the fog to the rear. Bertie guessed their orders had been to advance as quickly as possible and not to stop for anything. Besides, there was little enough left of C Company to delay anyone. His heart swooped sickeningly as he realised he was going to be taken prisoner. A prisoner of war! He would be caged until the war ended, and his spirit cried out at the thought. Almost he jumped up to attack the sergeant – better death than imprisonment.

But Cooper's hand was on his arm, digging in savagely as he read Bertie's thought. His other hand grabbed the pistol from him and dropped it on the ground. 'We need you, sir,' he muttered fiercely. 'Don't do it.'

Together they climbed onto the firing step and pulled themselves up. The sergeant gave them no more than a glance, probably not taking in Bertie's rank. His eyes scanned up and down the trench, reckoning the numbers. Bertie looked, too, and saw only seven or eight of his men, including the remaining corporal, their hands raised – all that was left. Oh, dear God!

The sergeant gestured impatiently with his rifle. 'You are prisoners. Go now to de rear. Keep de hants up or you be shot. Go!'

A shove from Cooper got Bertie stumbling forward, and his men followed him. The German sergeant was already gone, and the men he had with him. For a few moments Bertie's small band was passed by a flood of men in grey, hurrying forward, no-one paying them any attention. It was a moment of utter unreality. The German attackers didn't want to be burdened with prisoners: undoubtedly their orders were to make haste, and they were relying on the second wave to deal with little groups like Bertie's – or perhaps they didn't really care if anyone dealt with them or not. The fog swirled around them. The ground trembled with explosions.

There was a large shell hole just to his right, and no-one was looking at him. He shoved Cooper hard, shouted, 'Come on!' to his men, and dived for it.

It was an inelegant movement, and the shell hole was not

a nice place to land in face down, but he wanted anyone who happened to be looking to think he had been shot. He slid to the bottom and lay still, his skin crawling at the thought of a German pausing at the rim of the hole and shooting him in the back to 'make sure'. But nothing happened. He dared to open his eyes. Cooper was there, and three of his men. He lifted his head. Another two were on the far side of the hole. There were no more grey men passing at the top. He wriggled cautiously up to the rim and looked out into a field of fog unbroken by human forms, except for the dead German who was hanging on the wire just to the front of him.

'It's clear,' he said. 'Let's go.'

One of the boys sat up and looked at him like a beaten dog. 'Where, sir?'

He still thought they were going to give themselves up. Bertie almost laughed. 'Back to our own lines,' he said. 'We're not done for yet.'

The boy's face lit with relief. The others scrambled up and they climbed out of the hole. A frightened face was looking out of another ten yards away, and the missing three men climbed out too, to Bertie's relief. One was clutching an arm to his chest, and his sleeve was reddened through. 'Took one in the arm, sir, back there. I'm all right, sir,' he answered Bertie's questioning glance.

Bertie nodded. 'Let's get out of here before the next wave comes.'

As they crossed their own trench again, he ordered them to grab rifles. There wasn't time to look for his pistol, so he grabbed one too, and they climbed up the parados – someone had to boost the wounded man from behind – and set off in the wake of the Germans towards their own rear. 'We live to fight again, Cooper,' he said, in momentary elation: sooner *anything* than be a prisoner.

'We ain't dead yet,' Cooper conceded gloomily, 'but we ain't out of the woods, neether.'

★   ★   ★

The fog had prevented the Royal Flying Corps from making any effective reconnaissance, and the senior officers, fifteen miles to the rear, had to rely on reports filtering through from the forward areas. Since most of the telephone lines had been cut in the massive bombardment, this meant whatever could be got through by carrier pigeon or runner, or the witness of a wounded officer who managed to get back.

What surprised them first was the overpowering weight of the bombardment and, second, its extent. An attack on twenty miles of front, or two separate attacks on seven, ten, twelve miles would be understandable. But fifty miles! The whole of General Gough's Fifth Army and a large part of Byng's Third were under bombardment simultaneously. Gough had taken over the extended line from the French only eight weeks ago. He had been undermanned to begin with, his forces already covering too great a stretch of front. Having all of it under attack at once meant there was no possibility of 'thinning out' a safe sector to reinforce his line elsewhere. His meagre reserves were already used up. There remained only the two GHQ divisions in the rear and the French on his right.

But Haig was determined not to endanger the north and centre of the Front, even if it risked losing the south. In the south of the British sector, the line was seventy miles from the sea, which left a lot of room for strategic retreat. In the north, a breakthrough by the Germans could mean losing the Channel ports. As for the French, though they knew of the heavy fighting on their left flank, there was no likelihood they would send reinforcements. They had never done so before, and throughout the war, generals had learned the folly of relying on help from that quarter. Instead, Gough did what he could to scrape together a fighting force from the 'odds and sods': administrative personnel, the noncombatants of the various headquarters and other units in the rear.

★ ★ ★

The fog was Bertie's friend, hiding him and his small band from the Germans, but by the same token it hid the Germans from him. They had to move carefully, straining their eyes and ears to interpret the confusing sounds and deceiving shadows. In the fog he lost the boy with the injured arm. He had been bleeding heavily, and Bertie guessed he had fainted or simply fallen down in his weakness. At any rate, he was there one minute, lagging behind but struggling on, and gone the next. The rearmost soldier called, 'Sir, Chalky's gone! I looked round and he wasn't there.'

There was nothing to be done. Bertie said, 'The Germans coming behind will take care of the wounded. He'll be all right. We must make sure we aren't taken.' But privately he thought Chalky – his name must be White – had been bleeding to death and was a 'goner'.

He was worried that they might be shot by their own men when they approached the support trenches, but there was no need. The parapets had been badly battered by shell fire, and there were a great many dead men, but everyone else had gone. Had their officers ordered them to fall back? He hoped it was that, and not that they had run away – not *his* men.

He expected to find at least some of his missing men in the reserve line, where he had told Captain Evans to hold fast no matter what. There was a lot more evidence of a fight, a large number of dead, Germans as well as his own; but it was plain from the numbers that the main body of his men must have gone. Either they had retired or been taken prisoner. Given the speed and overwhelming numbers of the enemy, he could hardly blame them for not standing to the last man and bullet, but he wished fervently and bitterly he had been with them, and wondered how he would answer the questions that were bound to be asked. He still felt he had done the right thing in going forward, and if things had been otherwise he could have fallen C Company back. Without the fog, he'd have consolidated his position and might have held the support trench for hours and died a hero's death. Between a successful officer and a court-martial there often lay only the fine dividing line of circumstance.

In one of the dugouts they discovered a young and terrified soldier attending to a dozen men too badly wounded to be moved. He screamed when the first of them appeared at the top of the steps, probably expecting a German hand grenade or a bayonet through the guts, but when he saw the khaki he scrambled up, babbling with relief. Cooper grabbed him and shook him a bit until he calmed down, and then they were able to get his story. It was simple enough. First there had been the shelling, then the sounds of firing from up ahead. No-one knew what was happening. Captain Evans had told them to hold their fire, because it might be A and D Companies retiring. And it was. They had plunged into the trenches, and some of them had plunged straight out the other side. Captain Evans had managed to stop most of them, and they had manned the firing steps. But the Germans had appeared so suddenly – and there were so many of them! – and the captain was shot through the head right off, and Lieutenant Gibbs right after, and the Germans had got in further up the trench and started shooting round the traverses, so some of the men had decided to scarper while they could.

Once they started to go back it would be harder for the rest to stand steady, Bertie saw that, especially when their officers were dead.

'Sergeant Richardson, sir, he told me to come down here and look after the wounded,' the boy said. 'They was bringing 'em down here out the way, sir. An' I could hear him, sir, up top, shouting and swearing something awful, and there was shooting, sir, lots of shooting, and voices an' all, shouting an' that. And then it went quiet. After a bit I peeped out but they was all gone, the Gerries too, sir, barring the dead 'uns. There was some more wounded, too, and I helped 'em crawl down here. But I didn't know what to do,' he concluded miserably. 'They've been dying, sir, and I don't know how to help 'em, and I thought more Germans'd be coming.'

Bertie's heart was wrung for the pathetic creature, but he could not help him. A quick round of the wounded showed that four were dead, two more near death, and the rest were too badly hurt to be moved. 'You've been doing very well, Connor,' he said. 'I'm going to leave you in charge. Give them water, try to stop their bleeding. When I get to our Red Line I'll send help back. But if the Germans get here first, don't be afraid. They won't hurt you. They'll take care of the wounded along with their own. Be steady, lad. All these men are depending on you.'

Connor's legs trembled and he gulped visibly, but there was good stuff in him. He nodded and managed to whisper, 'Yes, sir,' and Bertie was confident he would not run.

The fate of Richardson was discovered when they climbed out of the trench. The big sergeant was lying dead a little way from the parados, half his face gone and a torn-open wound in his chest. He was lying face up, his remaining eye open, his feet pointing towards the trench, a rifle in his hands – shot as he stood defying the oncoming enemy. Bertie felt bad about leaving him. Reliable Jack was a great loss to the regiment – and he had a wife and five children back home.

Since they had been involved in creating them, most soldiers at the Front knew how the defences against the expected attack were arranged. First of all there was the Forward Zone, the very front line against the enemy. It was intended more as a sort of shock-absorber, to blunt the attack and delay it as long as possible. In many places the line was only lightly manned, a few strong points or machine-gun emplacements linked by shallow trenches, while the main body of the forward defenders were in support and reserve trenches a hundred and two hundred yards to the rear.

Behind the Forward Zone was the Battle Zone, the main defensive structure. It consisted of the Red Line, a strong, continuous conventional trench with thick barbed wire and a clear area of fire, with heavy machine-gun, trench-mortar and field-gun positions behind it. About two thousand yards behind the Red Line was the Brown Line, another conventional trench, and the last serious barrier between the Germans and the sea. It had been intended to create a third line, the Green Line, but it had hardly been begun, and even the Brown Line was far from complete in the Fifth Army's sector, owing to the shortage of manpower and the concentration of defences in the north.

But the Forward Zone had scarcely delayed the German advance at all. The phenomenal weight of the bombardment had smashed the defensive structures, and the sheer speed of the advance when the bombardment stopped, helped by the fact that the enemy was able to creep well forward in the fog, had taken the defenders by surprise. Often it was only a matter of two or three minutes between the guns falling silent and the Germans arriving, and the British were caught still under cover, waiting to be sure it really had stopped before emerging. Those caught in the dugouts had no choice but to surrender: refusal meant grenades would be tossed down the steps, the conventional response in those circumstances.

The Germans moved with unprecedented speed, pushing on fast towards the Battle Zone, not staying to consolidate the positions, often not even bothering to secure prisoners but sending them back without escort. This first wave were the 'storm-troops' that the papers back home had been writing about, and their mission was to storm the positions and move on at once, while the conventional troops followed in the second wave. Sometimes they moved so quickly they outstripped their own side's creeping barrage and fell victim to their own guns. But speed of movement, aided by the fog, allowed them to roll over the Forward Zone almost as if it were not there.

Other survivors from the front line were wandering in the fog, in the area between the Forward Zone and the Battle Zone. Twice Bertie's band was fired on by Tommies they surprised. Fortunately a nervous man's aim tends not to be accurate, and the shots went wide. Mostly the survivors were doing what Bertie was doing, trying to get back. Having hidden until they were sure who was coming, they came out and joined him, relieved to have an officer to take responsibility from them. By the time the group came to a road, a narrow country track, which the map in Bertie's head suggested would take them in the right direction, their numbers had risen to twenty. All but one of the newcomers were from other regiments. One or two had lost their rifles, and when they came across a dead man, he insisted they took his rifle and searched his pockets and pack for ammunition. With such a force, properly armed, they had some chance, he felt, of fighting their way through if they should encounter resistance.

And there were plenty of dead to donate weapons, just as there were plenty of shell holes, and shrapnel everywhere, like a weird, metallic autumn fall, crunching underfoot. Fortunately, the creeping barrage had moved forward, and they were not now being shelled, but there were still shots and other sounds in the murk to alarm them. They followed the road, keeping to one side of it, ready to drop if the enemy came up behind them. The fog, Bertie thought, seemed to be thinning: the day certainly seemed lighter, though still gloomy enough, considering it was ten in the morning. The front part of his mind was preoccupied with their situation, with navigating and looking out for danger, but there was enough spare capacity for him to be gnawed with anxiety about the rest of his battalion.

The mist was definitely thinning as they came to a side

track that led down to a small wireless station, set in a dip. 'It's just possible it might still be functional,' Bertie said to Cooper. 'Then we could get a message back to Brigade, and find out what's happening.'

'Best we all go, sir,' Cooper said. 'Case someone else's been before us.'

'I wasn't thinking of abandoning you,' Bertie assured him, and beckoned to his little band. With their rifles at their hips in the ready position, they walked down the chalky track, approaching with caution, ready to fall flat if anyone should open fire. But all that happened was that out of a window came a white handkerchief on the end of a rifle muzzle, which was wagged solemnly from side to side. Bertie raised his hand to halt his men, and shouted, 'Come on out! We won't shoot.'

The door opened, and three German soldiers walked out with their hands raised defensively, palms out, to shoulder height. One held a pistol, which he threw to the ground in front of him in token of surrender. Bertie lowered his rifle and walked forward. The German advanced too, his eyes lighting up as he saw Bertie's rank. 'I am Leutnant Reine of the First Bavarian Regiment. These are Seiffert and Gruber. I surrender to you, sir,' he called. 'I am very glad to surrender. I do not wish to fight any more. I like very much your country. I was there before the war and everyone was very kind to me. I was a student at Oxford University. Our countries should be friends. I don't like war.'

The other two, while less voluble, seemed no less eager to surrender. Bertie saw they were young, and looked scrawny and underfed; their boots were worn, and their coats thin. There was a further surprise, however, when five more men came out behind the Germans, these wearing khaki – the original Signal Company team, who had been manning the wireless station and had been captured earlier by the Germans.

Their leader came eagerly up to Bertie. A frown warned

him to salute and report in form, and he identified himself as Sapper Hooper, and explained what had happened.

'Well, sir, we could hear a lot of noise and we thought there was voices, so Hayes here,' he indicated a very young sapper, whose spots flared with a blush as he became the object of attention, 'went up the top to see, and he come back to say our lot must have took a lot of prisoners because there was a lot of Gerries marching along the road. Well, sir, Hayes here, he's a bit green, if you get my meaning, so I goes up with him meself to 'ave a butcher's, and I sees 'em, must've been fifty of 'em, marching down the road, and all these Gerries, sir, is carrying bayonets! Well, sir, so we come back down pretty sharpish and tell the others. We talked about getting out, but it was too late. They must've seen Hayes and me and follered us, 'cause about twenty of 'em come marching up, and we had to surrender, sir.' He looked appealingly at Bertie, who nodded slightly. Outnumbered like that, there had been no choice. Hooper looked relieved and went on. 'So then the Gerries takes our arms and go off again, heading for our lines, but they leave these three here. Freeman, Hardy an' Willis, we been calling 'em, sir. O' course, we didn't know any of 'em spoke English,' he added, with a reproachful look at Reine.

'Very well, Hooper,' Bertie said. 'You can join my men now. We're making our way back to the lines. But, first, can we get a message through from your station?'

The sappers exchanged a regretful look, and Hooper said, 'Well, sir, no, sir. Sorry, sir. Y'see, when we knew they wasn't prisoners coming up the road, we sent out the "forced to dismantle" signal, and went about busting up the instruments with our rifle butts. That's standard procedure, sir, what we was taught in training. That's what delayed us so we couldn't get away before Freeman – before these 'ere three turned up. It's NBG now, sir. *Fini kaput* – pardon my French.'

Damn, Bertie thought. But there was no help for it. 'All

right, Hooper. Get your things and come with us. We'll fin
you rifles on the way.'

'Yessir,' Hooper said, and as the others turned away, h
lingered a moment to add, in a lowered voice, 'Funny thin
about them Gerries, sir. You'd think they was half starvec
All they been doing, sir, till you come along, was scoffin
our hard tack, goin' at it like it was roast turkey an' Christma
pud! You never seen the like, sir.'

With their numbers thus further increased, they set o
again. The German prisoners were a decided nuisance t
Bertie, and he would have been glad to do what the German
had done to him and send them off unescorted. But, c
course, they were all travelling in the same direction nov
and the Germans seemed determined not to be left. Rein
was disposed to chatter to Bertie, and had to be shushe
peremptorily. The other two spoke English less well, bu
enough to make themselves agreeable. They offered cigar
ettes, and seemed quite relaxed as they marched along wit
their captors. They had evidently filled their pockets in th
wireless station as a precaution, for now and then one woul
pull out another army biscuit and nibble it as he walkec
Reine, having had his overtures of friendship rebuffed, dre
out from the cuff of his greatcoat a map and offered it t
Bertie. It was depressingly accurate, various places marke
with rings. Bertie asked what they were. Reine said the
were their objectives: it had been drummed into them tha
not to reach them would be a serious disciplinary matte
Bertie was surprised and unnerved to see that the first day
objective was a village thirteen miles from the front line.

By eleven o'clock the mist was nearly gone, and aerc
planes were buzzing about overhead again: RFC observer
which were cheering to see, but German scouts too, whic
meant taking cover if they came too close. Strafing of groun
troops from the air was a custom now on either side, bu
it was only dangerous if you were caught in the open. Mor
dangerous, at least in the trenches, was that the aeroplane

178

also dropped bombs, but they were unlikely to waste one on a small group on the move.

As they neared the Red Line, there was shelling, too, and the sound of firing from all sides. Several times Bertie had to lead his group in a sudden change of direction as they spotted the field grey of German infantrymen in the distance. He worried at first that the prisoners might try to give them away, but they seemed as determined to avoid notice as their captors, and were perfectly willing to lie down in a ditch or crouch behind a bush, or run down a hollow into a lingering pocket of fog.

The result of these diversionary movements was that Bertie was no longer in his own territory. He knew the sector pretty well on paper, and had travelled over much of it before the battle, but outside the area his battalion was defending, he did not know every ridge and furrow, wood and track. He did not know how far off course he was, or which battalion he would be approaching, and the presence of the three Germans might give a nervous sentry the wrong idea and get them all shot. So he took what cover he could find, getting forward by increments, and was glad to come across a sunken lane that led in more or less the right direction. He had just got his men into it, with the prisoners to the rear (he still half hoped they might slope off if no-one watched them), when he heard a shout and spotted a company of German infantry making their way in the same direction as him, along the top of a wooded ridge to the north of the lane.

The Germans had seen them, halted and, after a brief pause, presumably for discussion, they swung out of their way and started to come down the slope, rifles ready at their hips.

'We've got company, lads,' Bertie said to his men. The wreck of a farm cart was quietly rotting away just ahead, and they quickly hauled the larger parts of it up against the hedge to give them more cover. Bertie made the Germans lie face down with their hands linked behind their heads, and his own men took their positions. They seemed calm and ready – even poor young Hayes took his place with a grim look of determination, though his hands shook as he raised his rifle.

'Don't waste your shots,' Bertie shouted. 'Make 'em tell.'

And then the firing started. At times like these, it always seemed that time stopped working normally, with patches when it seemed to move like a glacier, and others when it rushed like a torrent. At the beginning of the war, before the trenches, in the war of movement, he had been in many situations like this – at Mons and St Quentin and all the way to the Aisne and back. What there had never been was time to be afraid. You were too busy aiming and firing, firing as fast as you could, and feeling only faint relief when a grey shape fell, swinging aim to the next one. Vaguely he was aware that some of his men had been hit, but the Germans had stopped coming, were lying or crouching and firing from that position.

They were holding them. No, except for a small group who were trying to outflank them, rising and scuttling a few feet and dropping again, then a few feet more, not firing but concentrating on getting forward and sideways, evidently meaning to jump into the lane further up and enfilade them.

Bertie called to the man nearest him – it was the corporal, 'Windy' Gayle, one of his veterans – pointed out the danger and beckoned him to follow. He stumbled on one of the Germans and cursed automatically. The two of them took up position on the group's flank, and stood up like snipers when the outflankers stood, trying to pick them off, and failing. The first three jumped down into the lane, firing as they did. It was wild firing and went nowhere, and they were exposed. Bertie and Gayle, kneeling to make a smaller target, shot them. More followed; then a third lot, jumping down behind these, were shielded by them and able to take proper aim. Bertie and Gayle fired steadily, but they were being fired at now, and not accounting for all of them. Once there were enough, they would rush them and it would be over.

Suddenly Cooper was on Bertie's other side, on one knee and firing. In the mad fluctuations of time, Bertie had a moment to wonder whether he had ever seen Cooper fire a rifle before. He did it well enough. Now, with three of them, they were keeping the numbers down just enough.

Then there was a shot with a different sound, and Gayle said, 'Shit!' and fell sideways, clutching his arm, his rifle falling from his hands. Bertie had no time to look, but out of the corner of his eye he could see Gayle writhing like a snake, heard him letting loose a stream of profanity. Not a mortal shot, then, if he could still swear. But it would make no difference in a moment or two. They were outnumbered and would be killed or captured. He kept on firing, making himself aim properly.

But something was happening. The Germans up on the slope had stopped firing, were looking round uncertainly. Those in the lane were scrambling frantically up through the hedge. Bertie stood up to fire after them as they ran up the slope. They were all running, all that were left, leaving a surprising number of still grey shapes on the hillside. And now a sound infiltrated the fog of Bertie's brain, which explained it all. It was an aeroplane. He squinted up and saw the RFC roundel, cheeringly red and blue, under the wings, heard the whine of its engine and then the brattle of its machine-guns as it strafed the fleeing Germans, catching two or three, who flung their arms out and dived forward as though going into water. Others had reached the trees, and after firing a few more rounds at the stragglers, the aeroplane banked and came back round over them. Bertie heard his men cheering, and glancing round, saw them capering and waving in elation. The pilot leaned out – he was so low that Bertie could see his goggled face above a garish red-and-yellow striped scarf – and gave the thumbs-up, turned again, skimming the hedge, and climbed away, wagging his wings in farewell.

'Go on, you split-arsing bastard!' someone shouted. 'I could kiss yer!'

Bertie regrouped. Two of his men were dead, one of them Hayes, who had taken a round in the head – one eye was a red cave, but the other looked surprised in death, as well he might, poor little beast. Three were injured, one with the top of his ear missing, one shot in the shoulder, and Gayle, whose upper arm Bertie guessed to be broken. They bound up the wounds with field packs as best they could.

And one of the Germans, Gruber, was dead. A bullet from the outflankers had struck him in the thigh, severed an artery and he had bled out in seconds. A wild shot it must have been, Bertie reflected; and an irony to be killed by one's own side after taking such pains to escape the war. He felt sorry for the man.

'Three cheers for 'Yde Park!' someone shouted – one of his own West Herts, obviously, since he had used Bertie's nickname. The men cheered, and Bertie silenced them, frowning, though it was only release of tension, as he knew. But Reine and Seiffert, the surviving Germans, were bending over their fallen comrade in shock.

Reine looked up and caught Bertie's eye. 'I knew him since a child. We went to school together. My mother and his mother are friends,' he said helplessly.

Bertie did not say, 'I'm sorry,' but he gave a little shrug of sympathy.

'I hate the war,' Reine said, standing up slowly, grimacing with anger and grief. 'Four years! Four long years, in a ragged coat, fed worse than a Chinese coolie, marched from one battlefield to the next, and this is the end for him. Poor Ernst. May I take his tag? And his wallet, to send to his mother?'

'Hurry up,' Bertie said. 'We have to move on – they may be back.'

'Not them,' said Reine, with a shake of the head. He knelt beside his comrade and felt inside his coat. It was indeed ragged, Bertie saw now – the hem was torn and the sleeves were frayed at the cuff.

'We're leaving,' Bertie said. Reine was still kneeling. 'You can stay with him if you like. Give yourself up later.'

'No. We come with you,' Reine said, standing. 'We are your prisoners. This war is over for us.'

I wish to God it were for me, Bertie thought, wearily gathering his little band. The Germans, not being encumbered with weapons, voluntarily took the job of supporting the two worst-wounded men and, after the first recoil of surprise, the men allowed it. A few more moments down the lane, it didn't even seem strange.

They reached the line ten minutes later and were able to get across and into a trench without being shot.

'Who are you?' was Bertie's first question.

'Leicesters, sir,' they said, their eyes on stalks. 'Captain Foreman's our officer.'

'Take me to him.'

Foreman nobly withheld the thousand questions he must have wanted to ask. Unsurprisingly, he had no idea where the West Herts were. 'There's been fighting further up the line, sir, but we haven't seen any here, only the shelling, of course, and a few parties of Germans in the distance.'

'You'll get your turn,' Bertie said. 'They'll be coming. But I must find my men.'

'P'raps if you went to Brigade HQ, sir,' Foreman suggested. 'They've moved since this morning. All the head-quarters and support units have been falling back since the fighting got closer. But I know where I can get my hands on a lorry, sir, if you want to take your men with you.'

He sounded wistful, though perhaps it was only because he would have liked to hear the full tale of how this lieutenant-colonel and his rag-tag-and-bobtail had got there. Bertie took the offer of the lorry, and by one thirty he was at Brigade's new headquarters, having his hand wrung by Scott-Walter, who said, 'By God, we thought we'd lost you! It's good to see you, by God! What the Dickens were you doing out there? Another VC stunt I'll be bound. I begin to think you have a charmed life, Parke, by God! Come in and have something to eat while you report.'

The remnants of the battalion, those who had fought and fallen back or, like Bertie, had been captured but not escorted and had taken the opportunity to escape, were still scattered, filtering in across the line, being gathered up and directed to a rendezvous like other lost soldiers of that action. They would come in in dribs and drabs all day, and at some point Bertie would be reunited with them. In the mean time there was a great deal of information to be imparted and reported further up the chain of command. Having eaten – a piece of game pie and a glass of wine from Scott-Walter's own basket – and cleaned up a little, he was taken to Corps Headquarters to report and confer. The relief of being out of the fighting for a time was countered by his anxiety for his battalion, and he could not take any pleasure in the lovely spring day outside or the knowledge that he would be certain to get a proper meal tonight.

But at least he had managed to shed his two German prisoners, scraping them off unashamedly on the hapless Captain Foreman, whose problem they now were.

CHAPTER NINE

When darkness came on the 21st of March – at around half past seven – the action was mostly over, except for one or two isolated counter-attacks. In the north of the battle area, two dents had been punched in the Third Army's lines, and during the night the adjacent units had to fall back to avoid being left 'in the air'. But the Flesquières Salient, which General Byng had been determined not to yield, had been held.

To the south, the Fifth Army had taken the brunt of the massive assault. But though the Forward Zone had everywhere ceased to exist, only one section had been pushed to the rear of its Battle Zone. Elsewhere, the Germans had been held up, either inside the Battle Zone or at its front-line defences. The German gains of territory, though on an unprecedentedly wide front, were shallow: in all but one small section, less than a mile.

The difference between the north and the south was that General Byng still had plenty of reserves in hand, while General Gough, who had been short-numbered to begin with, had none. And his losses in manpower were grave. Whole battalions had virtually ceased to exist, though it was unknown whether the missing were dead, taken prisoner, wounded, or still working their way back from the old front line. Because of the speed of the German advance, most of the British wounded had been overtaken by the enemy, so the low numbers actually being treated at British aid posts were no help in calculating the total. Prisoner numbers would not be known for months, and the dead, lying in what was now German territory, might never be counted.

The fact remained that Gough would have nothing to fall back on when the Germans resumed the attack. Back in January, the British had taken over the line between St Quentin and La Fère from the French Third Army on condition of French support should the area be attacked. But even if help were forthcoming, it would be days before French divisions could be marched up from further south. So with no reserves of his own, Gough requested permission from Haig to withdraw to the west of the Crozat Canal, some five miles from the old front line. It was a large yield of territory, but would shorten the line considerably, allowing the remaining troops to be consolidated, and the canal would provide a defensive barrier against the next onslaught.

As Bertie had learned from Leutnant Reine, the German infantry had been given ambitious goals for the day, and they had outnumbered the British by a huge factor – intelligence had estimated that more than sixty German divisions were facing the twelve of the Fifth Army and the six of the Third. So Bertie thought they had done pretty well to hold off the attack.

One of the things that had slowed down the Germans was the opportunity to loot. German prisoners told of the desperately short rations in the German trenches: they had been kept in good heart by being told that the Tommies were even worse off, so when they found ample supplies of biscuit, jam and bully in the British trenches – some of them had not tasted meat for weeks – it was a severe blow to their morale. Even the ration tins of Maconochie, a sort of thin vegetable stew regarded by Tommies as inedible unless heated, were eagerly plundered.

The large food dumps they came across gave the lie to their belief that the British Army was being starved into submission by the submarine blockade. The Tommies' rum ration was even more of a setback, both to morale and performance; to say nothing of officers' supplies, with bottles of wine and even champagne, tinned dainties, cheeses, cake. Hungry soldiers stopping to gorge themselves and fill their pockets, and to swap their worn boots for good British ones, made it impossible for the momentum to be kept up.

Still, the fact remained that the Germans had gained ground and the British had fallen back for the first time since the trench war had begun. The news would not go down well back in Blighty. The public had been brought up on the idea that the British Army never retreated; and the concept of strategic withdrawal was beyond most civilians' understanding. And if the newspapers didn't like it, someone would have to be found to take the blame.

Bertie's own concerns were more immediate. The night was cold and frosty, foggy, but with a moon, and the darkness was invested with the rumbling of wheels, the jingling of harness and the soft thump and shuffle of feet as thousands of soldiers were fallen back to new positions. Bertie spent the night travelling to and fro behind the lines, gathering his lost men from the various places they had fetched up. Given what had happened to C Company, it was not as bad as he had feared, but his battalion had been below capacity anyway, with a rifle strength of around five hundred, and more than half of them were now missing.

In the early hours he was at Brigade Headquarters again, summoned by Scott-Walter.

'I'm sorry about this, Parke,' the brigadier said, 'because I know your chaps must be pretty worn out, but you'll have to go back into the line. You know the situation we're in. We've no reserves to speak of and the enemy is right on our heels. Someone's got to be there come daylight, and I'm afraid your fellows will have to stand up.'

'I understand, sir,' Bertie said. It was no more than he had expected.

'I'll put you as far back as I can, but God knows what Fritz is going to throw at us today, so I can't give you any guarantee as to when you'll be relieved.'

'We'll manage, sir,' Bertie said. 'But my numbers are pretty low. So far I've found about two hundred fit to answer roll call.'

'I know. Quite a few battalions have suffered. The Notts Foresters are down to a hundred and fifty. But I'm going to give you some odds and sods from around the brigade to make you up to a fighting force.'

It was what had been called in the old days a 'half battalion': orphaned units too small to stand alone banded into a single force. Bertie had been part of one before. It usually went by the name of its commanding officer.

'I've got a hundred and fifty light cavalry who've been fighting on foot that you can have,' Scott-Walter went on, 'and a hundred survivors from a service battalion. That will give you four hundred and fifty, and I might scrape up a few cooks and bottle-washers from around the back of HQ as well. We'll call you Parke's Force for now.'

'Yes, sir. Thank you. Which service battalion is it?' Bertie asked.

'They're from your part of the world, as a matter of fact,' Scott-Walter said. 'One of the old "Pals" units – what's left of the Fifteenth North Yorks.'

Bertie could not help smiling. They had lost their name in the reorganisations of 1916, but among themselves they still used it, and no doubt there would be one or two left from the original intake. It would be something to write home about, in the popular phrase, that he was about to find himself commanding Uncle Teddy's York Commercials!

At dawn on the 22nd, the Germans resumed their attack.

When news of the action began to filter back to St Omer, Emma had been glad to remember that the 37th had been sent into the line at Armentières. In the present circumstances, that meant safety, for there was no regular fighting anywhere north of the Third Army. Indeed, Armentières had had a relatively quiet war, and was looked upon as a cushy billet. It had been occupied briefly in 1914 but soon recaptured, and though the shelling over the last three and a half years had left it the worse for wear, it was far from being a shattered ruin like Ypres.

The news from the fighting Front was alarming: the German hordes, released from the Eastern Front by the ceasefire of February, were smashing the Allies with everything they had. And the British were falling back! As the first wounded started to come in, and the FANYs began meeting ambulance trains, they felt a tension, a nervousness there had never been before. For the first time the shattered Tommies, exhausted, blood-sodden, were subdued. The tremendous spirit with which they had always made light of their suffering had been dented. They were silent in the back of Emma's new lorry, and often when she was holding one end of a stretcher the occupant would look at her with desperate appeal and say, 'There was thousands of 'em, and only a handful of us. We couldn't hold 'em.' To their shame and pain was added the first whisper of fear, never before felt, that it might be possible to lose the war.

Benson proved his worth in these days by going among the wounded and cheering them up. He gave them something to think about apart from their own predicament, and often a silent, suffering quartet would fall to discussing dogs of their own back home.

'I had a little terrier when I was a lad . . .'

'Me dad had this big old lurcher . . .'

'I left our Towser with the missus an' kids. He'll look after 'em.'

'Prince of a dog, he was.'

'Best ratter in the village.'

Benson would put his paws up on the edge of the stretcher, tail wagging, with a look that demanded his head be scratched. Eyes would follow him as he went from man to man; his every movement was fascinating as it drew them out of the lonely place of their suffering.

'Look at 'im! 'E's a knowing 'un.'

'See 'im scratch 'isself! I 'ad a dog shut 'is eyes just like that when 'e scratched.'

And he seemed to have an instinct for who was the worst wounded, and would push his nose under their cold hands and lick them lovingly. Emma felt sure there were Tommies brought back from the brink that way, for he was the connection to the simple animal life in every human, the spark that wanted to live but could be quenched by loss of heart.

Except in the few seconds before she fell asleep each night, she was too busy to think about the fact that she had not had a reply to her last letter to Captain Wentworth; but she was glad in a faintly guilty way that he was out of it. Then one day when she backed her ambulance up to a hospital train she found herself looking down at a face that was faintly familiar. It was unshaven, and lined with pain, which made it difficult to place it. 'I know you,' she said. 'I'm sure I've seen you before.'

The man met her eyes, and attempted a smile. 'Yes, miss,' he said. 'I know where. I seen you in the audience when we done that show at Camp Nieulay. Couldn't forget a pretty face like yourn,' he added gallantly.

She had it now. 'You did a comic monologue,' she said. 'About an undertaker – it was very good.'

'That's right, miss,' he said, and quoted, '"Pratt's Funeral Parlour, the Pride of Nuneaton, for tasteful interments we cannot be beaten."'

'It was very funny,' Emma smiled. 'You ought to be on the stage.' Only then did it occur to her. 'But you're in the Thirty-seventh – you were in Armentières. What are you doing on this train?'

'We got moved, miss. Just before the balloon went up.

Quite a few units got moved down at the last minute. Reinforcements. Ours got sent to Bapaume.'

She didn't know how to ask the next question. 'Was it – bad? You were in the fighting? Did – were there— Have many of you been hurt?'

'I got caught by shrapnel, miss, early on. In the bombardment. I dunno what's happened to the rest of 'em.'

Emma said, 'I'm very sorry. I hope it's not too bad.'

'I hope it's a Blighty 'un, miss,' the man replied. 'I've not seen my missus in a year.' She loaded him, and as she was leaving him, he said, 'Don't worry, miss. It'll be all right.'

They were meaningless words, but she felt comforted all the same, though it didn't last long. The 37th in the fighting! All day as she drove back and forth and loaded and unloaded stretchers with their freight of pain, her mind kept slipping back to the thought. They were in the fighting after all.

Helen had also comforted herself with the knowledge that Jack's squadron was attached to the support of the Second Army near Ypres, which at that point in its tortured history was relatively quiet, with nothing but routine activities going on. There were always dangers, even in routine patrolling, but an experienced pilot had a good chance of keeping out of trouble in those circumstances.

So she was dismayed to receive a letter from him dated the 21st of March, obviously hastily scribbled, which said, 'Last-minute change of plan. Our squad off to parts south. Cannot tell you more, but we are flying down to join the fun, so don't be alarmed if you hear nothing for a while. My guess is that we'll be busy! Kiss the babies for me, love to Jessie, and my most precious love to you, Jack.'

Helen held the piece of paper until the words became mere shapes and lost their meaning. He had gone into the big battle, about which they were beginning to read reports in the newspapers: an unprecedented bombardment, fierce fighting, Germans advancing in overwhelming numbers.

A 'readjustment' of the front line. By this stage she knew that the newspapers, for purposes of morale, emphasised every success and made little of any setback, so a 're-adjustment' meant the army had fallen back, which in turn suggested heavy losses.

She stared at the letter, knowing the look of Jack's writing so well that, now she was not reading the sense of the words, it was like looking at him – a part of him, bearing his like-ness as a photograph did. And she knew what that letter was, and almost hated it for it – if it were possible to hate anything that came from him. He had had to take the oppor-tunity of writing to her what might be his last words. *My most precious love to you.* It might be the last thing she ever heard from him. He had not had time to think it out and compose it carefully, to select from millions the exact words that expressed his thoughts. She saw him sitting on the edge of his bed, already in his flying jacket, while his batman packed his things, and Rug sat looking up at him ques-tioningly. In the hurry of leaving, with the sound of running feet in the corridor and aeroplane propellors already being swung outside, he had seized what words came to mind. *My most precious love to you.* His warm hand had held the pencil that had scribbled those words. And then he had grabbed his helmet and goggles, and said, 'See that gets posted, Corrie,' and hurried out to lead his flight. It would have taken no more than half an hour to fly down from Steenvoorde to the battle area. He might have been dead before Corrie even finished his packing

Jessie came in. 'Helen? Are you all right?'

Slowly Helen refocused. Jessie's face was pinched with worry, in contrast with the burgeoning of her body. So far, her pregnancy was progressing normally, and she was past those danger spots, the third and the fifth month. But nothing was sure until it was sure. And Bertie was in the fighting. Helen had no words for her. Silently she held out the letter.

Jessie read it, and looked up. 'Oh, Helen, I'm sorry,' she said.

On a mutual impulse they took hold of each other. Jack was Jessie's favourite brother, the one to whom she had always been closest, and her other two brothers were dead. Helen felt it should be she who did the comforting. 'He'll be all right,' she said at last. But she had a bad feeling about this letter. *My most precious love to you.* She didn't want to be in the position of having to treasure those words, or the scrap of paper they were written on.

It was, in the soldiers' phrase, a picnic, which meant it was as far as it could be from anything resembling a picnic. Jack had never seen a German bombardment like that first day's. His first stunt had been early, while it was still going on. The mist was beginning to clear by then, but it was still horribly cold in the dank air. There was not much to be seen, however, as he couldn't go in very low because of the shells. He was able to observe something of the mass of men behind the German front line before he was driven off by some Pfalz scouts.

By the time he went up again, mid-morning, the mist had gone and they were flying in bright sunshine, which was more pleasant and made observation easy but, by the same token, made them easier to spot too. The action below was no longer static, and he saw how already the concept of lines had been lost. It was really a mass of small battles taking place out of sight of each other. He spotted a huge fire – a petrol dump, he guessed, with a column of smoke rising fifteen hundred feet. There seemed to be many abandoned British field-gun positions now, but also many gun crews moving westwards at the trot, which was more encouraging.

The pilots had been given bombs to carry this time, which required flying in at around five hundred feet and dropping them where there was to be a good target – a trench full of soldiers, a railhead, a transport movement, a field-gun position. 'Low work', as it was called, also meant machine-gunning ground positions and German troops on the move; and they had to prevent German aeroplanes from attacking the British troops with low work of their own. But they were finding out how different this was in a war of movement, compared with the static trench warfare of old. Scouts and fighters could appear from any point of the compass and some brisk dogfights took place. Jack accounted for one Fokker triplane, which went down spouting smoke, and an Albatros that went into a spin and was last seen at five thousand feet going sideways on its back, completely out of control. With other enemy aircraft still coming at him he couldn't follow up either to see what became of them. There would be no 'kill' to claim. That was another luxury of trench warfare that seemed to have gone. He remembered once taking a transport from his airfield to pick up a German pilot he had shot down, to make him a guest of his mess for the night. At this point, he didn't even have a mess . . .

In the afternoon he went up again, detached this time to drop message bags at various HQs and two batteries. On his way back he saw a lone enemy aircraft below him at fifteen hundred feet and, dropping behind it, fired fifty rounds from short range. It dived steeply and he thought he had not damaged it, but as he followed it down it suddenly showed flames from the portside engine, so he knew it was a 'kill'. He started to turn away and climb when he heard a tremendous shriek and felt a violent shock, and at once his machine began to falter. Bits of canvas whirled away and the singing of the wires changed pitch. A shell had passed right through the fuselage. In retrospect he remembered the flash from somewhere down below and on his left, which must have been the gun firing it. He was lucky it had not exploded; but it had severed some control wires. He made a few cautious movements and hoped he had enough control to get home, but he dared not get into another fight. He climbed away to give himself some room to manoeuvre, and began to nurse his way back, keeping a sharp lookout for enemy aircraft.

It was an extremely nervous flight, but at least it did not last long. In ten minutes he was coming in over the airfield he had left a couple of hours ago. The aeroplane was behaving very erratically by then – the air coming in underneath from the holes in the fuselage was disrupting the normal flow over the planes – and it was not one of his better landings. But he was down and safe, and as soon as he came to a halt he was out and examining the damage with the mechanics. Then he set off for the wooden hut doing service as squadron office to make his report.

'Damn,' said the squadron leader, frowning, when Jack described the damage. 'That rather puts you out of it for the moment. I haven't got a single spare crate or I'd send you on another message drop. Oh, well, you'd better go and get some rest. I'll need you at dawn tomorrow, if your bus is fixed by then.'

'I think it will be, sir,' Jack said. 'I'll give the mechanics a hand when I've got my kit off.'

Rug was at the door of the mess hut, almost wagging his rear end off the ground in his delight at seeing his master. Corrie had brought him by road with the other servants and the squadron's belongings. 'He's been whining ever since we saw you coming in,' Corrie said. 'How he knows it's you I can't fathom.'

Jack was stooping to rub the ecstatic dog's head. 'Where are we sleeping tonight? Break it to me gently.'

'Tents, sir,' said Corrie, gloomily.

'Oh. Well, I probably won't get much sleep anyway. I've got to work on my bus. Any news of the others?'

'Mr Healey, Mr Barndale and Mr Richards is back, sir. They're in the showers. Mr Healey brought down a Rumpler. Nothing about the others yet.'

Corrie helped him off with his outer gear, and insisted

195

he must sit down in an armchair in the mess – he would bring him a cup of tea and a round of corned-beef sandwiches – before he went off to the sheds to work on his Camel. When he had eaten and drunk, Rug jumped up onto his knee, so he thought he'd give the dog five minutes of attention before he got up; but the chair was comfortable, and the next thing he knew he was being woken by the rest of his flight coming in. Still, he reflected afterwards, it had only been half an hour, and the sleep had done him good. Probably would have dropped off in the sheds otherwise, and shamed himself.

When Maud came into the Carnew sitting-room, her cheeks bright from the open air, only Mrs Carnew – Annie – was present, sitting by the fire with her knitting. Women everywhere seemed wedded to their knitting, these days. The Labrador was lying spread out on the rug, belly to the flames, snoring gently.

Annie looked up and said, 'Did you have a nice drive, dear?'

'Yes, thank you,' said Maud. She sniffed delicately. The old dog always added his distinctive savour to the atmosphere, but lying so close to the fire he was adding another: the aroma of scorching hair.

'Will you take tea?' Annie continued.

'No, thank you. I had some with Lord Manvers at the castle,' said Maud.

Annie put down her knitting. 'Maud, dear, sit down. I have to talk to you.' Her cheeks were rather pink, but there was something of determination about the set of her small mouth. Maud sat opposite her, looking calm and unconcerned though inside she was wondering what was coming. 'Maud, dear,' Annie resumed, 'I'm wondering whether it's quite right of you to be visiting Lord Manvers at the castle alone. Now, don't take offence,' she said quickly, before Maud could say anything, 'I know you wouldn't do anything

– well – unseemly, but you know, you are seeing an awful lot of him.'

'He's an old friend of my father's,' Maud said.

'Oh, I know that, but he's a single man, dear, and you're seen driving about everywhere in his motor-car, and with your husband away at the Front, well, there's already whispers.'

'Whispers? From whom?' Maud demanded icily.

Annie blushed even more. 'It's just idle gossip, I know that, but you know how people talk. And, Maud dear,' she concluded, with some courage in the face of Maud's cold look, 'I have to think of the girls. Riding in his motor-car's bad enough, but if it's known you go and visit him alone in his house . . . *I'm* not saying you're doing anything wrong, dear, but it's how it *looks*. That sort of thing matters, you know, in a small community like this. Maggie and Joyce have their lives before them, and it'll be hard enough on them, getting married, with all the men away at the Front. And Phyllis is at an impressionable age.'

'What is it you want me to do?' Maud asked.

Annie looked uncomfortable. 'Don't see so much of him. I know, with him being your father's friend, you want to be polite, and I'm happy to invite him here to dinner and such-like, but going out driving alone with him – it's kind of him to offer, but you should say no. What with that, and going to the castle, well, it doesn't look right.'

Maud took a decision. 'I think I ought to tell you,' she said, 'because you'll have to know sooner or later, but I have an understanding with Lord Manvers.'

Annie looked blankly puzzled. 'An understanding? What *can* you mean?'

'I intend to marry him. Bertie and I are going to be divorced.'

Annie made a small shocked cry at the sound of that word, and her hand flew to her mouth. Her eyes were wide, and for a moment she could not summon anything to say.

Maud watched her impassively. It was always going to be difficult, telling them, she thought. She had not wanted to do it so soon, but perhaps it was as well after all.

'You—' Annie stopped, clasped her hands together in a little knot of anxiety at her breast, and said, 'Maud, dear, you can't mean it. Not a—' She couldn't even say the word 'divorce'. 'Not you and Bertie?' she pleaded.

'I'm sorry it shocks you, Annie, but I'm afraid it's all settled. Bertie and I can't live together any more. That's partly why I came to Ireland, so that we could be separate. And once I was here, and Manvers was so kind to me, I realised that he was the right man for me. So I'm going to divorce Bertie and marry him.'

Annie gave a little moan. 'Oh, don't say it! Don't say that! You can't, Maud, you really can't! Think about it. There's never been such a thing in our family, never! The disgrace! I'm sure you and Bertie could be happy together if you just put your minds to it. But even if you can't – well, people do just put up with it, you know. Hundreds and hundreds do. Whatever you might think,' she concluded, with a burst of pink-faced determination, 'a divorce *just isn't right!*'

Maud stood up. 'I'm sorry, Annie, but my mind's made up. And now I think I'll go up to my room. I've some letters to write.'

She was not quite as calm as she seemed, and in her room she sat in the chair by the window for some time before she stopped shaking. She didn't like to hurt Annie's feelings when she had been so kind; and it was horrid to be the object of gossip and unpleasant thoughts.

She heard the motor-car come back and saw, from the clock on her mantelpiece, that it was before Harold's usual time. Annie must have telephoned him. Maud straightened her back defiantly, anticipating that there would be unpleasantness to face. Ten minutes later a maid came in with the wherewithal to make up her fire, and said pleasantly, 'The master would like to see you, mam, in the libery – right away, if you've a minute.'

So Maud went down to get it over with.

Harold was alone, and looked as embarrassed and determined as Annie had. 'Ah, Maud, sit down, won't you?' Maud sat, giving him no help. He walked about a bit, cleared his throat, rubbed his hands together. It was a nasty, raw, foggy afternoon, just getting dark, and the fire was the one bright spot in the room.

'You must know what I have to talk to you about,' he began at last, probably more abruptly than he had meant to. 'This business – a divorce – it won't do, you know.'

'I'm afraid there's no choice,' Maud said. 'Manvers and I wish to be married.'

'I know you're fond of him – but a *divorce*? In our family? And you've been staying in our house – it's bound to reflect on us. I have to think of Annie and my girls, Maud. We can't have a disgrace of that sort associated with us.'

'If you want me to leave, I'm prepared to do so,' Maud said. 'I anticipated that it might be necessary.'

Harold looked angry. 'Oh, you did, did you? And what had you intended to do in that case?'

'I should take a house somewhere until things were settled. You weren't thinking that I would move into the castle, were you?' Harold's face suggested he had thought just that. 'Nothing improper has passed between Manvers and me, and nor will it until we are married. You have my word on that.'

Her word did not seem to placate him. 'You'd set up in a house on your own – and still go on seeing Lord Manvers, I suppose. Why – can't you see that would be even worse? At least while you live here there's a shred of decency about it.'

Maud stood up. 'I think this conversation should end, and that I should pack my bags.'

'Whatever you do, it's going to reflect on us, don't you

see that? And if – when – you do marry Manvers, you'll be our neighbour and our cousin and everyone will know there was a divorce to bring it about. You can't do this, Maud.'

Maud's eyes flashed. 'I shall do whatever I think fit,' she said, in the closest thing to a snap she was capable of.

She turned to walk out, but Harold held out a hand. 'Now wait – Maud – please. Sit down again and listen to me. You owe me that, at least, given you've been living here all this time and never mentioned a word of your plans before now. Will you just listen to me?'

Maud stared a moment, then sat on the sofa, composing her hands in her lap. 'Very well,' she said. 'What do you have to say?'

He walked about a bit more, thinking, then came and sat beside her, turning to face her so that their knees were almost touching. He looked anxious and tired rather than angry: a father with too many cares, and Maud his wayward daughter busy putting thorns in his crown.

'You and Bertie, can't you be reconciled?' he asked gently. 'Have you actually done anything about a divorce?'

'I have the papers,' Maud said, 'but I haven't done anything with them yet. I've been putting it off.'

Harold brightened. 'Bertie's a good man,' he suggested. 'We always liked him.'

Maud had not been putting it off because she had any doubts about the matter, but because affairs of business were foreign to her. They did not fit into the landscape of her mind. First her father and then Bertie had always taken care of such things for her. A deep reluctance came over her every time she thought about reading the papers through. Even less did she wish to go into Dublin and interview the solicitor. But it was the process she was averse to, not the purpose. She quickly doused Harold's little spark of hope.

'It's all over between Bertie and me. Even if John Manvers didn't exist, I could never live with him again.'

Harold searched her face, sighed, and said, 'Very well,

then. But why a divorce? It's so extreme. All right, I understand you want to marry Manvers, but what sort of a marriage
is that? Not a proper kind of marriage at all, not one decent
people will recognise. You'd have folk the rest of your life
whispering about you, and cutting you. And us drawn into
it, too, and our girls made part of it. Now wait,' he said,
seeing her about to expostulate. 'Wait till you've heard my
suggestion.'

'If you're suggesting I forget about Manvers—'

'I wish you would, but no. I know that once women have
their minds set on something . . . Maud, why not wait a bit?
That's all I'm asking. There's no great hurry, is there?'

'I suppose not,' Maud frowned. 'But wait for what?'

He reddened, and his eyes slid away from hers. 'Bertie's
at the Front,' he said. 'There's the big action we're reading
about in the papers. I'm not saying it, and I'm not wishing
anything on him, because he's a fine chap and a brave soldier
– but these things happen. I mean, it wouldn't be so very
strange if – if—' He met Maud's eyes again with a desperate
courage. 'What I'm saying is, a divorce might not turn out
to be necessary in the end. D'ye see? That's all I mean. It
might turn out, if you wait a while, that . . .

'I understand,' Maud said, in a toneless voice.

'They say the war will end next year. By then, you'll know
one way or the other. Just wait until then, that's all I'm
asking. You can do that, can't you? And if – well, you know
– if it happens, you can marry Manvers, after the proper
period, and there'll be no shame on anyone. And if it doesn't
happen, you'll be no worse off than you are now.'

He thought, though he didn't say it, that when the men
came back from the Front at the end of the war, there would
be such an upheaval, and so many marriages, and so many
disappointed hopes, that Maud's liaison with Lord Manvers
might pass, if not *un*noticed, at least *less* noticed.

'Very well,' Maud said, after a moment's thought. 'I'll do
as you say.'

Harold's relief was almost palpable. 'That's the girl! And you'll be a bit more careful – on the lines Annie mentioned? Don't go to the castle. Don't be seen with him so much. You can meet him here, you know. We'll invite him as often as you like.'

Maud assented, and went away. There was, after all, she reflected, no hurry, nothing to rush for, no reason to get things done this year rather than next. It couldn't matter to Bertie when it happened – and it occurred to her that when he came home after the war (she did not wish him to be killed, nor believe he would be) he might mind it a lot less, in the general euphoria, than he would at the moment. She was going to be happy with Manvers, and wished Bertie no more pain than was necessary.

Parke's Force started the day, on the 22nd of March, in the reserve line near a village called Monchy. It was chilly before dawn, and most of the men had had little sleep, but hot tea was on the brew, and a ration of biscuit and bacon had been delivered, which the men heated in their canteens. Bertie had a bit of bacon, with biscuit crumbs fried in the fat, which was cheering, and the inscrutable ways of Cooper produced a cup of coffee to go with it. Cooper was wearing a strip of bandage around his brow. It had long ceased to be white, and his face was so weather-beaten it never lost its colour. Bertie told him he only needed a feather sticking up at the back to look like a Red Indian. Cooper treated him to an old-fashioned look. 'Anything that amuses you, sir. Shall I go and look for a chicken?'

It was as well to begin with a little humour, for there was precious little after that. The Germans attacked at dawn, and within an hour Parke's Force was ordered up to the front line. Bertie could see at once that they were hopelessly outnumbered: there must have been a whole German division opposite them, and even with Parke's Force they made up less than two full battalions. They held on for as long as they could, but by eleven o'clock there was no choice but to fall back.

Bertie had done this before, and it was as well that he had experience in the art of retiring and fighting in the open, because none of the other officers had. Under his orders they dropped back by sections, leapfrogging each other to prevent the Germans overrunning them. Fortunately, the amazing speed of the previous day's advance was not repeated: the Germans came on quickly, but they were not so sure of what was in front of them, and checked frequently, trying to maintain a line, which gave Bertie's men just enough advantage to keep going. By nightfall they had fallen back between four and five miles. The Germans halted as darkness fell, and their artillery stopped firing. Parke's Force had reached Brie, just short of the Somme Canal. There seemed to be a great deal of British activity, the presence of support units, and several temporary headquarters, which suggested this was the new line.

Bertie found his own Brigade Headquarters in a barn just on the edge of the village. Scott-Walter was looking rather the worse for wear, no less neat in person than ever – a senior officer had to keep up standards – but with a ragged look to his face and deep circles under his eyes. 'Glad you made it,' he said tersely. 'How are the men?'

'Holding up. We've lost about ten dead and twenty wounded, but morale is good.' He managed a brief smile. 'I think the novelty of the situation stimulates them.'

'Thank God for that,' Scott-Walter said. 'The resilience of the Tommy, eh?'

'They're pretty tired, though – and we're all hungry,' Bertie mentioned.

'I'm afraid you'll have to go on a bit further before you can sleep,' Scott-Walter said. 'The REs are mining the bridges, so you'll have to get across the river tonight. That ought to slow the Boche down a bit, give us time to dig in tomorrow morning. You'd better go on right away. Send back a runner when you're settled and we'll make sure some rations get to you. We're pretty well found here, but God knows what we'll find on the other side, so we'd best see the men get a good meal tonight.'

Bertie went back to his men, waiting for him in a field outside the village, and passed the order down. Most had fallen asleep where they sat, and had to be prodded awake, and there was a good deal of grumbling, but they were up quickly enough, and he was able to march them smartly over the bridge and a short way down the road. There was a large, shallow chalk pit off to one side, which seemed a good enough spot, so he settled them in there, posted sentries, and sent a runner back to Headquarters to let the brigadier know where they were.

About an hour later a ration lorry found them, and the men were woken again, this time to a good meal of bully stew and floaters – suet dumplings – followed by cold rice pudding with jam. The jam was gooseberry-and-rhubarb, rather a suspect mixture, but it made a change, at least, from plum-and-apple, and the men liked anything sweet. The food put heart into them, and they began to chatter over the tea that followed – though not for long. Very soon they were all asleep again. Bertie was delighted to receive, along with the food, thirty more of his missing men, including some of his old HQ staff, who had been mistakenly directed by the redcaps to a rendezvous at Péronne during the night of the 21st, and had been transported from pillar to post ever since. Once Brigade HQ had been located at Brie they had been taken there by lorry, and Scott-Walter had sent them on to Bertie. He was glad to find one of his communications officers, Gerard, among them – a bright lad, and under-promoted because of his important expertise. In the absence of any wireless for him to be expert with, Bertie made him his second in command.

At dawn on the 23rd the Germans came on again in massed formation. The canal held them for a time, and considerable losses were inflicted on them, by rifle, machine-gun and from above by the RFC, but the outnumbered British soon had to fall back. The process went on all day. By nightfall they were at Barleux, and when the Germans stopped, they stopped too. Parke's Force slept in an open field, and this time no food came up. Presumably the support units were somewhere behind them, but it was hard to locate specific units in conditions like these. The men had had nothing since breakfast, and the day had been one of strenuous activity. Few were still carrying their 'last hope', as they called the iron rations. What there was was shared round, and Bertie ordered Cooper to break out a tin of five hundred cigarettes from his own stores and pass them out. Many of the men had finished theirs, and without a smoke, a Tommy's morale soon went downhill.

They slept like the dead in the open field, but at four in the morning the Germans stirred so they had to move, and Bertie marched them about five miles along the road to Fay. Here there was an ammunition dump, and they were put on fatigues loading ammunition onto limbers. It was a change from fighting, and the men took to it philosophically, especially as where there was an ammo dump there were rations. Bertie personally went in search of cigarettes and chocolate, and made sure a sufficiency was sent down with the food that evening. They spent the night at Foucaucourt, again in an open field.

Several groups of survivors from other units had come in during the night, and Bertie had taken them into Parke's Force. He questioned them before sending them off to sleep, and the main worry that emerged was that of being surrounded. The Germans were still coming on and no-one knew any more exactly where all of them were. The retreating British were unable to keep any sort of line, breaking up into separate groups at the dictates of the terrain or the action, so any unit might find itself in the air as its neighbours fell back at different speeds. Bertie called his officers together and emphasised to them the importance of maintaining order as they fell back. He was determined not to end the war as a prisoner.

The following morning, the 25th, began very cold, with a thick, dank fog. He had the men roused while it was still dark, so that before they were forced to move again they could have a chance to brew up, and to eat the breakfast ration they had brought from Fay. Cooper managed enough hot water either for coffee or a shave, and Bertie chose the coffee; he shaved painfully in cold water, half wishing he'd thought of joining the navy. As it grew light, the fog lifted, to reveal a cold, dripping dawn, and the unwelcome fact that the Germans had come up in the darkness and were on the high ground to the left. As soon as it was light, they opened fire. The men took what cover they could and began firing back and lobbing bombs. Fortunately, the day at the ammunition dump had left them well provided. But it was hard going, and they had little cover. Shells, machine-gun fire and shrapnel exploding everywhere were cutting them down.

And there was another danger. Through his field glasses, Bertie noted that the ridge the Germans were holding ran on a slight curve towards Rainecourt, a village that was ahead of them on the long, straight road to Villers-Bretonneux. It was clear to him that if the Germans reached Rainecourt before them, they would be cut off from their retreat, surrounded and done for. They had to get out – must move quickly – and someone must cover the retreat, to hold the Germans up and stop them winning the race to Rainecourt.

He held a quick meeting with his company commanders, and gave them their orders. 'The men must be got out in good order, and there must be no running. Once they start running it'll be hard to stop them. I shall stay behind with the rearguard.'

'No, sir!' Knyvett protested. Knyvett and Cheeseman

were the two officers who had come to him with the cavalry unit.

Bertie gave him a crooked smile. '"No, sir"?'

Knyvett flushed, and Cheeseman stepped in. 'Begging your pardon, sir, but shouldn't the CO stay out of it?' Duncan and Firman, the other two – Duncan a lieutenant from his own former A Company, and Firman a lean, educated man he had chosen from the York Commercials – murmured agreement.

And Gerard, his second in command, said quickly, 'I'll stay behind, sir. If anything happened to you, what would we do without you?'

Bertie looked round at them, his heart warming to them. They were all new in their present responsibility, all young, untried, three of them strangers to him. But he knew instinctively what kind of men they were. 'A fine attempt at flattery,' he said, 'but the fact of the matter is that I have experience of fighting my way out over open ground, and none of you has. Your business is to get the men away down that road and stay ahead of the Germans. I'll join you later. Don't worry, I have no intention of getting myself killed or captured.' Gerard was still looking doubtful, and Bertie, guessing he felt there was some kind of criticism involved in his not being allowed to take the rearguard, said, 'I'm entrusting my precious battalion to you, Gerard. Keep it safe for me.'

There was no time to waste. Already they were suffering high casualties, and the Germans might get going at any moment. The officers went back to their companies, and within minutes had begun to move out. Bertie kept C Company back for the rearguard, for no other reason than that C had been his own when he first joined the West Herts. As soon as the others started to move off, he ordered the rearguard to open rapid fire, while a small bomb party threw stick bombs as fast as they could – anything to keep the Germans occupied for those essential first minutes.

It was a hateful business, seeing his men falling on every side, but there was little time to think. As soon as the rest were clear, he gave the order to the rearguard to withdraw, and led the way across the route he had chosen earlier with the field glasses. He had the bomb party stay until last, throwing until the supply of bombs ran out, and as they got moving, he saw the Germans moving too, beginning to work their way along the ridge. He had picked out a sort of gully as the place to take a stand, which would give them some cover, and put him between the Germans and his retreating battalion. C Company was down to about fifty men, but he had machine-guns and ammunition for them, and he felt he ought to be able to keep the enemy at bay for half an hour, with luck. After that they would probably have to run and fight, moving from cover to cover, and he was the only person with any experience of that, so the only one who could hope to bring any of the rearguard out safely.

There was a sort of comfort, once they were settled into the gully, in being in a trench-like environment again; and since they were now under a modicum of cover and the Germans were in the open, there was a cheering period where their own injuries were few and the Germans fell in number. But C Company was shrinking, and the Germans were making ground. Soon he would have to decide whether to try to get out before it was too late, or fight there to the last man. He had a few more minutes, though – just until that group of Germans reached that stand of trees, after which they would be outflanking him and escape would be almost impossible.

But just as the men he was watching reached the trees and he was about to give the order, something changed, and he put the field glasses to his eyes again. Instead of coming down towards them, the Germans at the trees had gone the other way, over the other side of the ridge and out of sight; and as he watched, the rest of the force began turning too, heading away from them, over the crest, and disappearing northwards.

The last of them stopped firing and hurried after their companions, almost running as shots from Bertie's force chased them up.

His men stopped firing, and a ragged cheer ran along the gully, the survivors standing up and waving their arms in jubilation, even capering, despite their weariness, and shouting that they had beat ole Fritz and put him on the run. Bertie let them express their feelings for a moment or two before calling for silence and giving the order to move out. He was no less relieved and glad than his men that the Germans had gone, but he did not flatter himself it was their resistance that had effected the miracle. Obviously there must be something important going on over the ridge to the north, and the order had come down to the Germans to go and join it.

But never mind – it was a miracle none the less, and Bertie felt a lightness of heart as he led the remains of C Company out of the gully and towards the rest of the battalion. They were far from being 'out of the woods' yet, but they had got out of one tight situation; and in this sort of warfare, you couldn't look too far ahead. You simply had to survive from tight place to tight place, and take your luck where you found it.

CHAPTER TEN

The Fifth Army continued to retreat, but fought every inch of the way, slowing the German advance and inflicting significant loss on them. To their left, the Third Army had managed to hold on, but was forced to fall back, though more slowly, to keep in touch. After the 25th, there was no semblance of a Front: the battle was broken down into local actions, each unit holding on and retreating as circumstance dictated, forming a section of line, holding it for a time, retiring again.

Supplying these disparate forces was a problem, and many of them were obliged to forage for themselves as they went. The ground over which they were fighting had been inhabited until now, but with the word that the Germans were coming the population had fled, and the roads along which the British soldiers had to pass were frequently clogged by refugees loaded with burdens and babies, some dragging trolleys or handcarts with their more precious possessions piled on them, the family dog on a lead and bewildered children stumbling along beside them.

The homes they left provided food and shelter for the soldiers. The pretty villages were untouched so far by the war, and as they emptied of life, seemed like so many *Mary Celeste*s. When the inhabitants fled, by custom they left their front doors open, and all the evidence of their normal daily lives was on display inside. The tired and hungry soldiers might find breakfast laid on the table, a pot of coffee unconsumed in the haste of departure, or a sewing-machine with pieces of work laid ready beside it. But there was bread to be found, cheese, dried garlic sausage, sacks of potatoes and onions, sometimes a whole ham, precious eggs, bottled fruit. In the larger houses they might find tea, coffee, sugar, even chocolate and cigarettes. The domestic animals had been left behind, too, and the soldiers milked the unhappy, bellowing cows, giving them relief in the process, and killed and cooked backyard chickens and rabbits.

Looting had always been expressly forbidden in the British Army, and the officers kept it sternly in check. Bertie allowed his men to take the food, and sometimes sanctioned the removal of a barrel of beer or cider for issue to the men, but nothing else was to be touched, and wanton damage was severely punished. He knew, from his experience of the early days of the war in the long retreat to the Aisne, that the Germans following them would not show such restraint, that the houses would be looted of everything that could be carried, and probably smashed up in the process, but there was nothing he could do to prevent that. It would not be his men, at any rate, who so insulted the natives.

So, as the month of March drew towards its end, they fought and retreated from St Quentin towards Amiens, growing always fewer but learning new skills in the process; and the fear of the first few days – that the war might be lost – dissolved. 'Elasticity' was the new word: they might bend, but they would never break.

At home the news caused consternation, as the days passed and names familiar from other years reappeared in the news-papers. Péronne fell on the 23rd, Bapaume – so fiercely and expensively fought for in 1916 – on the 24th; Albert, famous for its 'hanging Virgin' – the golden statue on top of the basilica that a German shell had left dangling at right angles over the square below – was lost on the 26th. The specula-tion now was whether Amiens, the capital of Picardy, would fall, and whether, if it did, anything could stop the Germans reaching the sea. Would the whole BEF have to be evacuated from France?

In the face of so much concern in the newspapers, Lloyd George and the government had to do something. The first essential was a scapegoat. On the 28th of March, General Gough was relieved of his command of the Fifth Army and sent home; General Sir Henry Rawlinson took over, and the Fifth Army was renamed the Fourth (Rawlinson's own previous army, and at present an empty title).

Second, it became obvious that, however little the prime minister liked it, reinforcements must now be sent: 170,000 of the troops ready at home were released, two divisions were called back from Palestine and one from Italy; and Lennie wrote jubilantly to Morland Place that he was going back to France at last, as his battalion in Salonika was replaced by a new draft from England. As a further measure, the age of conscription was expanded, and now ran from seventeen and a half to fifty-five. With the realisation that old England's back was to the wall, there was a surge of patriotism that had young men, stirred by the images in the newspapers and on cinema screens, turning up at the recruitment offices even before they were called.

But the German advance was slowing from those first shocking days, partly through sheer weariness, but also because of the increasing problem of looting. The rich pickings proved too much temptation for soldiers who had been on short rations for years, and whose families back home wrote of desperate privation. The British policy was to carry away all they could of their own food dumps when they fell back, but often the transport was not available, and sometimes they had to move too quickly. As well as food dumps there were the numerous canteens, comforts clubs and officers' dining-rooms that had grown up over the years to the rear of a static front line. These yielded beer, rum, cider and quantities of wine: the German soldiers drank themselves to insensibility. And when their officers did get them to move on, they were encumbered by looted goods – plate, jewellery, perfume, clothes, boxes of cigars, even things like clocks and statuettes – which did nothing to add to their soldierly qualities.

By the 30th of March, Easter Saturday, when Bertie's force finally reached Villers-Bretonneux, a fine town some ten miles east of Amiens, it looked as though that was going to become the new front line. The Germans had all but halted, and were beginning to shell the town, while on the British side headquarters units had felt it worthwhile to set up there. Parke's Force spent the night under cover in various buildings in the town, ate the best meal they had had in ten days, and enjoyed the cheering novelty of having their mail catch up with them. Bertie received a welcome letter from Jessie, and an unsettling one from Maud, saying she felt there was no real urgency about the divorce and that it could wait until the war ended. What had changed her mind? And how could he change it back? That was a problem to set aside until he came out of the line and had time to worry about it.

He had no leisure that night, barely managing to snatch an hour's sleep, for there was too much reporting, planning and briefing to get through. He did manage to get outside of a fine stew of pork and beans with mashed potato, bottled pears and half a bottle of claret while he caught up on some essential reading. There was no time even to write to Jessie, only to dash off another field postcard to her, for in the hour before dawn they were on the move again, ordered to march about three miles towards Bertaucourt, to the south-west of Villers-Bretonneux, there to dig in against the expected onslaught from the Germans.

Here, Bertie thought, they must make their stand. His men, like the rest of the former Fifth Army, were dead weary and in need of a long rest; but at least now their supply units knew where they were. In this respect they were better off than the Germans who, according to rumour, had outrun both their supplies and much of their artillery.

Jessie had heard nothing from Bertie since the field postcard he had managed to get away to her during the night of the 21st, with all the printed phrases crossed out except 'I am quite well' and 'Letter follows at first opportunity'. She knew he was in the fighting and, following the reports in the newspapers with the help of Helen's atlas, that he was in the thick of it. You would have thought, she told herself, that after three and a half years of war one would get used to this helpless waiting It was no comfort to her to know that Helen was just as worried about Jack. But at least Helen had a job. Jessie, not one of nature's needlewomen, had even taken up sewing and knitting in desperation for something to do. Helen forbade her any housework, and Tomlinson had decreed she was not to be bothered by the children (Jessie suspected she was enjoying her new job as nanny too much to want to share it). But sewing and knitting left the mind free to brood.

She hated her uselessness. She couldn't help remembering her time in the hospital at Étaples, and imagining the scenes there now. When there was a rush on, convoys would come in at any hour; they would work fourteen-hour days and be called again in the middle of the night. The operating theatres would be going non-stop, the wounded arriving not just on trains and ambulances but in anything that would carry them – troop lorry, supply lorry, farm wagon, cattle truck. And in the wards the nurses would wage an unending battle to restore order from chaos. Stretchers everywhere on the floor, for there were never enough beds; muddy boots and stinking socks, mud- and blood-streaked khaki; brown blankets and filthy bandages.

And everywhere the soldiers in their hideous suffering, smashed limbs and torn flesh, ripped abdomens, missing ears and noses, broken jaws, exposed bone and raw, cavernous wounds, looking and smelling of the butcher's shop: everything that brute metal could do to the frail poetry of the human form. You closed your mind to that aspect, or you could not do your job; the sheer volume of the work, and the speed at which you had to perform it, kept you going. Strip them, wash them, change the dressings, prepare them for the theatre or for onward dispatch to England or, hastily laid out, to the morgue. Forceps, tourniquets, splints, gauze, peroxide, Lysol; each man removed replaced at once by another; no end to the work, the ward never tidy, the floor never cleaned, the smell of blood never absent. It was exhausting, hateful – exhilarating, at least afterwards, when you could look back on what you had done, and how you had not failed in the face of impossible demands.

Jessie thought of Beta, missed her, and felt useless and guilty. At night she dreamed of Red Cross ambulances rolling up, hundreds of them, and no orderlies to fetch the wounded in, only her to do it all. But when she tried to get the ambulance doors open, they were stuck fast. She could hear the wounded inside, but could not get to them. Behind her the other nurses stood silent, ghostly in white aprons and caps, and when she called for them to help her they did not move. *Help me!* she would cry. *Help me!* But they only stared at her, silent, motionless – accusing. She would wake from the dream shuddering, sometimes with tears on her cheeks. Helen would look with concern at her hollow eyes across the breakfast table, but Jessie kept her problems to herself, knowing Helen had enough to worry about. Jack had not written since the 23rd.

As the Germans advanced and the British fell back, so the RFC had to fall back too, and find new airfields on which to base themselves. Jack had been out at the beginning of the war, and remembered the days of the retreat from Mons when, going up in the morning, you had no idea where your unit might be in the evening. Sometimes you had to fly around looking for somewhere to land, and ask if anyone knew where it was. It was not that bad this time. The army was retreating over its own territory, and there had been plenty of airfields in the rear, with communication between them. But it was still a gypsy life. Corrie took his kit and Rug by lorry each day, along with the ground crew and their equipment, but at night all except immediate requirements would stay packed for speed of departure in the morning. And in the morning there would be a hurried pilots' conference, with orders for the day, a rendezvous for the evening, and a poring over maps to pick out places to land in the interval, should they be needed.

There were rarely, in these days, explicit orders, for no-one knew what might be found out there. Rather, it was a general mission to 'annoy the Boche', as the major put it, by strafing any columns or emplacements they saw, helping any British units that were being pinned down or harassed, and taking note of any large movements that might be significant. Each machine was armed with four twenty-five-pound bombs, and they were to drop them if they saw a worthwhile target, such as an artillery position, a supply train, or a large body of troops. They also, of course, had to do all they could to harass the enemy air force, prevent their scouts from scouting and fighters from strafing, and bring down as many as they could in combat.

But on the morning of the 24th, Jack's flight was given a particular mission. The Germans were thought to be bringing up reinforcements in large numbers on the far side of the Somme canal, between Brie and Ham. They were to investigate, estimate the numbers, and do what they could to disrupt the process before reporting back. The rendezvous was a temporary airfield near Moreuil. Jack divided his flight into groups of three – for low-level work it was impossible to fly in a larger formation – and told them to look out for each other. He took for himself the two newest and youngest, Healey and Barndale, hoping to keep them out of trouble. They looked so young to him, rosy-cheeked and wide-eyed, that he felt positively fatherly towards them.

'I'm not even sure they're shaving yet,' he said to his old friend Harmison, as they walked across the field towards the aeroplanes.

'You've been out here too long,' Harmison replied, fastening his flying-helmet. An explosion some way off shook the air. 'Christ, listen to 'em! It's barely light yet. This is not a civilised time to get up.'

'Men in a hurry,' Jack said. 'They know if they don't win now they never will.'

'I'll tell you what,' Harmison sniffed, 'they're letting a lot of riff-raff into the war, these days. Gentlemen don't shoot at each other before nine in the morning.'

Their banter was making the boys smile, which was partly the point. Jack stopped by the canvas hangars and said to them, 'When you're over the German line, if the fire gets too heavy, remember to keep low. That's the safest place. The Archie will be aimed higher and it takes time to change the elevation. But watch out for machine-gunners.'

Healey grinned. 'Yes, sir. We'll be all right, sir.'

'I did my teeth and I've got a clean hankie,' Barndale added cheekily.

'I'm glad you haven't got the wind up, anyway,' Jack said.

'Going up with you, sir? It's safer than being on the ground,' said Barndale.

Nothing like freedom from responsibility, Jack thought wryly. He bent to stroke Rug's rough head just once in farewell and received a lick on his wrist in return. Corrie took the little dog up and carried him out of the way, putting him down beside one of the mechanic's tool kits. Rug folded his tail under him and sat on it, as though determined to be sure of one thing in his life.

Jack's Camel was waiting for him, and the sight of it was reassuring, like the sight of one's own house at the end of the road. 'Don't forget once we're up to test your guns,' he said to his boys. 'But don't shoot each other – or me!' And they grinned at the old jibe.

Once they were airborne he took them up immediately to around fifteen hundred to assess the general situation. It was not like looking down on the battlefield over a trench line. There the land was ravaged, barren and pockmarked for a couple of miles on either side, and the trenches and the various strongholds stood out clearly. Here, the land was still unruined and green, and the battle had spread out over a wide and deep area. But where the grey-silver line of the canal ran, roughly south-east from Péronne to Ham, there was still something like a German front, though no trenches, and a great deal of activity in the rear.

The mass of grey there was, he supposed, the rumoured reinforcements. Jack had never liked the idea of strafing soldiers on the ground, even Germans: it had seemed somehow unsporting, like shooting sitting ducks, though it always helped if they shot at him first – which, obligingly, they always did. But his attitude had hardened as the war went on and the Germans showed that no holds were barred on their side. He remembered his captured German flyer, von Liebeswald, and how, when they had parted after a convivial night in his mess, the man had said seriously, 'If I meet you again I will try to kill you.'

There was artillery beyond the canal, too, and they were already shelling long-distance. Jack thought it a hazardous exercise when they must have a limited idea of where their own troops were. But there were a lot of German aircraft around: perhaps they were reporting back on how far their infantry had progressed.

It was a strange thing, Jack thought, that you could fly over a battlefield in the middle of a battle and not hear a thing. The roar of the engine and the singing of the wind in the wires blotted out everything. It was strange to look down and suddenly see a great gout of earth and stones leap upwards, as if of its own accord, because you had not heard the explosion of the shell that caused it. The aircraft noise was so familiar it became unheeded, so that it would seem to be in a kind of silence that a building would collapse eerily into rubble, like a sandcastle on a beach being washed away by the incoming tide. The occasional flash of light, and the bumpiness of the air, like driving over heavy potholes, were the only evidence up here of the explosions going on down below.

Time to go in closer. Every soldier killed was one fewer to kill a Tommy. He checked that the other two were on his wings, gave them the signal and dived in. There didn't seem to be any anti-aircraft guns set up here, but below fifteen hundred they were vulnerable to machine-guns as well, so they had to go in fast and pull out as quickly as possible not to give the gunners an easy target. Because of the tendency of infantry to drop to the ground as soon as an aeroplane came over them, it was not possible to tell if they were hitting anyone, or if the strafing was having much effect, other than annoying and frightening the Germans – but that was an object in itself, he supposed.

Two passes, he thought, and then they'd get out, climb and have a look further in. But after the second pass, Healey signalled to him that his guns had jammed. This was all too common a fault, and there was nothing for it but to go home. He told Healey as much in dumb show, and the lad gave a shrug of regret, made the sign of understanding, and peeled away.

With Barndale on his port wing, Jack climbed and circled, passing over Ham and turning towards St Quentin. A column of men in grey was coming down the main road marching briskly, with transports in the rear – half a battalion at least, he estimated. The other half would be behind them, he supposed, leaving a gap for safety's sake. He'd do what he could to break this lot up, then fly on to St Quentin and see what was what. He rocked his wings and pointed downwards, and saw Barndale stick his thumb up. He half rolled and dived, opened fire, saw the white circles of faces turn upwards. The men scattered and some fell, whether hit or just lying down for safety he couldn't tell. Some scrambled into a ditch and he pulled up, turned and came back for another pass. Those in the ditch had their rifles to their shoulders and he presumed, from the little jerks, that they were firing, though the chances of hitting an aeroplane with a rifle were negligible. But at the end of the first section an enterprising NCO had got a machine-gun set up, and he saw it swing towards him as he approached. He couldn't hear it, but he felt something strike the fuselage as he passed. Barndale was behind him, and two of the men at the gun reeled away and fell to the ground. That was good shooting.

He climbed again, and circled to indicate 'well done'; Barndale grinned at him. And then with horrible suddenness, an Albatros D.III dropped out of the air and hurtled down behind Barndale. They had been lucky so far not to meet any enemy aircraft, but it was inevitable that they'd find them sooner or later. There was a burst of fire and Jack saw bits of debris fly as the bullets struck the frame. Barndale's mouth was a startled O beneath his goggles, and he went at once, instinctively, into a half-roll to get away. Never had Jack been so glad of the Camel's tight torque. He opened the throttle and turned the opposite way, whipping round so fast that he was behind the Albatros before it even knew he was coming. He fired and fired again, emptying fifty rounds into it. The Albatros twisted and turned to get away from him, forgetting its own quarry. Out of the corner of his eye, Jack saw Barndale, black smoke streaming from his engine, turn away, heading home while he still had power.

Jack was on the Albatros's tail, and since he could turn more quickly, it could not shake him off. He kept after it, firing bursts until at last he saw one of the interplane struts fly to pieces, and the upper plane partly collapsed. At once the Albatros went into a dive, spinning as it fell like a badly made paper bird. He climbed and turned back to see it hit the ground and break up. One down, he thought; how many to come? Where there was one, there were bound to be others. He was very exposed here, and he gave up the idea of flying over St Quentin. Better to disrupt the German line where he could. He still had his bombs.

He turned back, relieved to be operating alone again. It was how he had got used to fighting the war, and formation flying could be rather restricting. As he came back over Ham, he saw the dark specks of an enemy flight in the distance coming his way. He had better get a move on, pick a target while he could and get out.

Down below on the edge of the town he saw a large wooden structure like a barn, surrounded by other, smaller sheds, and a large number of German troops, busily loading something or other onto lorries. It was a scene of purpose, with a chance of knocking out some transports as well as the men, and destroying whatever was in the barn. He swooped in, saw white faces turn up towards him as he came, pulled the bomb-release handle, dropped the first bomb, heard the dull echo of explosion behind and underneath him as he pulled up and circled. He had hit one of the smaller sheds – he saw black smoke – but missed the barn. The fighters were closer now. Just time for one more pass, he thought, and went in again. The little figures were kneeling down and aiming their rifles at him now. He concentrated on that barn, hand on the bomb-release, judging the distance. Nearly . . . nearly . . . Now! Two bombs away.

There was a huge explosion, which flung his Camel up into the air as if it were a piece of paper, kicking the tail upwards so that it almost turned over. Even as he was being tossed about, his mind told him it was not his own bombs that had caused such an explosion: there must have been something in the hut, fuel or ammunition. That was what they had been loading onto the lorries. Well, he'd got it, anyway. Good job!

But there was no time for speculation. He struggled to

get control again, feeling, rather than hearing or seeing, that the fighters were after him and firing at him. The Camel put her nose down; the stick was heavy; the ground was howling up to meet him. He knew then, with a blank absence of any feeling about it, that he was going to die. The canal flashed by underneath him, just glimpsed, and ahead there were trees, horribly close. Bullets smacked off the dashboard in front of him and the glass of his altimeter smashed as the pursuing fighters fired at him. He had a vague feeling that there were more buses around than just them – perhaps some of his own side? – but he had no leisure to look. He couldn't get her nose up. There was a terrible sound of smashing and splintering, and everything shuddered and jolted as the undercarriage was ripped off by the treetops below.

He was past the trees, but there were more woods ahead. He would not reach them, he saw. Going down fast, going to crash right now. Then, at the moment when the angle of descent should have meant that the machine's nose ploughed fatally into the earth, the ground fell away. He had come to the edge of a ridge. The slope was not great, not a scarp or anything of that sort, but just enough of a downhill angle so that the nose came up a few feet, and the wounded aeroplane still lived. She crashed down the hill, glancing it, lifting and striking again. He tried desperately to get her into the air again, but the stick was a dead thing in his hand and the rudder was jammed. All he could do was hold on, the safety harness cutting into him, as she smashed her way headlong through whatever was in her way, until the slope gave out to level ground, she planted her nose in the mud and flipped tail over head with the last of her momentum.

Jack was upside down, hanging by the safety-belt. Then one of the wings hit something with a ghastly noise, ripping it off, flinging the machine over again, but sideways this time. It hit something, which stopped it short with a violent jolt and more rending sounds. He was jerked out of the cockpit, the safety-belt breaking, and flew briefly, feeling things cutting at his face. Then he struck something hard, and everything went dark.

Jessie came in from her walk, heading towards the back door as Helen's motor-car pulled up at the front so she walked round to meet her. 'Any news?' she asked.

Helen drew off her gloves and blew on her fingers. It was a raw day, not at all spring-like. 'Yes, I've got another job. They want me to deliver an aeroplane to the Lympne park tomorrow. I thought I might go up to London afterwards and see if I can find some lengths of cloth in the Army and Navy for the children's clothes, and then, if you didn't mind, have supper with Molly and stay the night. I haven't seen her for such ages.'

'Of course I don't mind,' Jessie said. 'It sounds like a good plan. You might look for buttons, too, while you're in the Army and Navy. I don't know where they all go. I think Basil must eat them.'

'Don't joke about it. He probably does. You're sure you won't be lonely on your own?'

'I shan't *be* on my own,' Jessie said, 'with a house full of people.'

'Servants and children aren't the same thing,' Helen said, as they walked towards the front door.

'Why are you suddenly asking me?' Jessie countered. 'You've been away dozens of times and you haven't worried about it before.' She knew why, of course: the larger Jessie got, the more Helen worried that she might start labour while she was away. 'I'll be all right,' she said. 'You deserve a little pleasure.'

Jessie, who was in front, opened the door and stepped in, and Helen came behind her, reaching past to put her gloves on the hallstand. At the same instant they saw the buff telegram envelope. Helen dropped the gloves nervelessly on the floor.

Jessie stared at the thing as though it were a poisonous snake. *Which one of them?* her mind cried. *Which one?*

Helen said, 'Is it for you or for me?' Her voice sounded most peculiar. And Jessie looked at her, and thought of Helen and Jack and their children, and something tight and fierce inside her gave up and lay down. *Let it be for me, then,* she thought. *I'll be hurt either way, but Helen has more to lose.*

Aggie looked out from the kitchen door. 'Oh, mam,' she said, her face creasing with anxiety, 'that come just a few minutes ago. Oh, mam, I hope it's not the master!' *She shouldn't have said that,* Jessie thought. But it was absurd to worry about words when—

Helen picked it up. Jessie saw how much courage that took. She stepped closer, trying to offer support with her nearness. *It's Jack,* she thought. *Oh, God, it's Jack.*

Helen opened the envelope and unfolded the slip inside, and turned a little so that Jessie could read it at the same time.

REGRET INFORM YOU CAPT J COMPTON SHOT DOWN BEHIND ENEMY LINES STOP LETTER FOLLOWS STOP MAJ E GATES

Helen folded the telegram, pushed it into her coat pocket, a blind look on her face, and walked past Jessie without a word. Aggie opened her mouth to ask questions but Jessie stopped her, shaking her head and pinching Aggie's arm to reinforce the prohibition. The difference between the moment before knowing and the moment after impressed itself on her bitterly. She had stepped closer to Helen, instinctively to offer support. But what support or comfort could she offer, when the blow fell on her, too?

The letter came two days later – a strange two days of numbness, when Jessie was unable to think at all, could only walk until she was dog weary. Helen had gone to do her delivery job anyway, saying there was nothing to be learned by staying at home, but she had put off her evening in London with Molly to come straight back on the train the same day, in case any further news arrived. During that night Jessie heard her get up and move around the house, and debated whether to get up too, whether Helen would want to see her or not. In the end she decided not. There was nothing new to be said about the situation, and nothing else to be spoken of.

But when the letter came, it did nothing to ease the state of mind of either woman. It was kind, it was courteous, it was sympathetic, but though they read every detail of the circumstances greedily, it could not tell them what they wanted to know.

Another section of his flight, which was following on the same mission, saw his aeroplane, apparently badly damaged, being pursued and fired on by three enemy aircraft. The section turned and engaged the EA and succeeded in driving them off, but Capt. Compton's Camel had sustained visible heavy damage to the tailplane and rudder. It went down in scattered wood-land to the south-east of Ham. As this area was then, and still is, behind enemy lines, it was impossible to get to the crash site. Lt Kay reports that as far as he can tell the Camel did not catch fire. Please be assured that all possible enquiries will be made, but in the present volatile situation I cannot hold out any hope that they will be speedily answered. Until further infor-mation is forthcoming, Capt. Compton has been posted as missing in action.

Missing, Jessie thought with a sick feeling. Her own husband, Ned, had been posted missing after the battle of Loos. He had never been found, and eventually, after months of enquiries, the army had altered the 'missing' to 'missing believed killed'. But no-one would ever know for sure what had happened to him. Uncle Teddy still did not believe it, and continued to search for him by letter and enquiry. The army and the law had declared Jessie a widow, and she accepted that Ned was dead, but that evil, insidious word always left a trail, like a bad taste in the mouth that would not go away.

And now Jack was 'missing': crashed behind enemy lines, with the battle rolling over him, lost and never to be found again. The only tiny grain of comfort in the letter was that the aeroplane had not caught on fire. She did not need to imagine, in the ghastly emptiness of night, her brother hurt but still alive, struggling to release himself as the flames consumed him.

'Well,' Helen said at last, when they had read and reread the letter in silence; but the word did not seem to lead anywhere. What was there, after all, to say? They looked at each other, and then looked away. Jessie saw a grimness come to the line of Helen's pleasant mouth, which she guessed would never leave it now. 'I shan't tell the children,' she said. 'Not yet.' Jessie wondered if that meant she harboured hope that Jack had survived. A crash in woodland was the worst sort – surely she must know that? But Helen finished flatly, 'I couldn't bear to at the moment.' She looked at the letter blankly as though it was written in Chinese. 'Someone must tell them at Morland Place.'

'I'll do it,' Jessie said automatically. Then the implications came home. Oh, God, her mother! All three sons gone. Pain came to her at last. Her brothers, all gone. She was the only one left now. Frank, Rob, Jack – the whole of their shared lives – her family torn up like waste paper. She drew a shaky breath. She must hold on, for Helen's sake. But how could she tell her mother? And Uncle Teddy? They would want her to come home – and she wanted to go home to her mother – but how could she? She could not add more pain to what they would already be suffering. And Helen needed her. As never before, she was grateful to Helen for giving

226

her a refuge. Helen and Jack. Oh, God, Jack! Her thoughts circled, trying to escape the pain, but the pain just followed.

On Easter Sunday, the 31st, they all went to church, Helen driving them crammed into the motor, the three servants in the back with the children on their knees. Helen had insisted they go. Jessie had not been since she discovered she was pregnant. But Helen had said, 'You needn't go up to the altar. But it would do you good.' And she was right. She needed to talk to God, and surely even the prayers of a sinner like her, added to such a weight of them from good people, might be acceptable. She didn't know what to pray for, when she had lowered herself with some difficulty onto her knees, she could get no further than 'Oh, God, please,' but she thought afterwards, as they drove back through thin sunshine, with the first primroses on the hedge banks seeming like something in another world, seen through thick glass, that God could probably work it out for Himself.

On the Tuesday, the 2nd of April, a field postcard came from Bertie, dated the 30th of March, 9 p.m., with everything crossed out except 'I am quite well' and 'Letter follows'. He was alive! Thank God.

But Jack – oh, Jack . . .

At Morland Place, Henrietta went down in the middle of the night to the chapel, a dressing-gown over her nightdress, her hair in its night plait hanging down her back. There was a candle on a shelf just inside the chapel door, and she took it and walked down to the Lady chapel, where she lit the two candles on the altar. The ancient statue of the Lady came softly into being, flowing with the gentle, yellow light, rounded against the shadows, as if she had been made from them. She seemed so old, so permanent, that Henrietta felt, as she always did, the transitory nature of her own sorrows. The Lady had lost her Son, too, sacrificed in the greater battle against sin and death itself: she had known the same

227

grief. Who better would understand Henrietta's heart? She lowered herself to her knees, and thought of her children.

She did not pray for long, these days, thinking it too much like nagging when so many millions must be sending up their prayers too. She got up (how stiff she was – kneeling was getting harder) and sat, her hands in her lap. It was peaceful here, with the thick walls keeping out the sounds of night, and that sense of stillness that always lives at the heart of a chapel that is used daily. The sanctuary lamp glowed red, unwavering, and she thought of it as a faithful watchdog, keeping guard over her. Perhaps she dozed a little, for she came to suddenly with her heart beating hard. There had been a sound, or a movement – yes, there was something moving down there, coming towards her. The thought of the house ghosts came to her, and though she knew a ghost could not harm her, she felt a moment of white terror. And then the thing moved into the far edge of the light of her candles, and she knew it was the priest.

He was in a dressing-gown over a nightshirt. He must have come down the priest's stair into the vestry. He stood beside her, looking down, and she said, 'I couldn't sleep.'

'I couldn't sleep either,' he said. 'Did you have another nightmare?'

'The same one. I see Jack falling through the air. I wake before I see – the end.'

He said nothing, but sat beside her, reached out and took her hand. It was cold, but warmed in his grasp – light, with the bones too close to the surface, it reminded him of a bird's claw.

'The Lady weeps when something bad's going to happen to the house,' she said. 'When I saw it – a month ago – I thought it was for Robbie.'

Palgrave looked at it: an old wooden figure with gold-painted hands and face, worn soft with age. Henrietta had told him that, in the old days, it had always been dressed in fine silk robes, with a crown of gold and pearls. Unacceptably

228

close to idolatry now. But the statue was so old there was something almost uncanny about it. And the chapel itself – it was as if the prayers had tempered it over the generations: it had a patina, like old wood, a sort of richness of Christian thoughts and feelings. If ever one had doubts, this place would dissolve them, he thought.

But he had his duty. 'There were no tears,' he said. 'It was a trick of the light. Just the candles flickering, the reflection of light moving.' She turned her face towards him, the light like points of glee in her tired dark eyes. 'These superstitions are not Christian,' he went on gently. 'As a good Christian, you should not believe in such things.'

She nodded, to please him; but she was a Morland, and her ancestors for five hundred years had been born and died here, and their lives had sunk into the stones of the house like smoke. Their bones lay in the crypt beneath her feet, and they spoke directly to her heart. Palgrave was a newcomer, and his voice was as light as the patter of rat's feet in comparison, and had no substance, no conviction. *The Lady knows. She always knows*, she thought.

She looked at the worn golden face, and prayed just once more. *My boys are with you now. Take care of them for me – all my boys.*

The Lady's face was inscrutable. Whatever was God's will would be. It had taken her a lifetime to learn that. She could feel in the priest beside her that there was a struggle still. Well, that was natural – he was young and vigorous and a man, and men were never as close to things as women. It was in their nature to fight, and she supposed God had made them that way for His own purpose. But you couldn't hold out for ever. She felt the great weight of her grief inside her like a separate thing, a consuming agony eating her human heart, but it didn't touch the quietness that was the soul's trust.

The candles flickered. Far off in the Great Hall the clock struck, just audible. Henrietta sighed. Such rarefied moments never lasted long. She felt her age and her sorrow settle round her like unbearably heavy clothes that she had to wear for the rest of her life.

Palgrave looked at her. 'What are you thinking?' he asked softly. She turned to him, and he almost quailed before her humanity.

'Now I have no-one left to worry about,' she said.

CHAPTER ELEVEN

When Jack came to, he was being pulled out of the wreckage by strong, rough hands. His face felt wet and he could taste blood. His first terror was for his leg, the one he had smashed before, but the sharp, splintering agony was not there. In fact, at first he could feel no pain at all. Was he numb, then? Paralysed? Broken back? Then he became aware of stinging in his face where something had whipped at him as he crashed. And as he was bumped clear of the wreckage he felt his bruises. He had feeling, at least. But could he move?

Someone was speaking to him. He was lying on the ground – the grass was damp under his hands. The speaker repeated the question but he didn't understand it. He couldn't see properly. He tried to lift a hand towards his eyes, but there was no power in it. A second attempt brought it up, weak and trembling, but he could not raise it far enough. The man who was talking to him made a sound like '*Ach!*' and then he was wiping Jack's eyes with a rag of some sort. It came away red. There had been blood in his eyes, he thought, as reason slowly sank back into his shaken brain: that was why he couldn't see.

Someone said, '*Es gibt so viel Blut!*' and he realised at last that the other speaker had been asking his question in German. That was why he hadn't understood.

Weakly, he lifted his head a little. The shattered remains of his Camel were nearby. There were torn trees and bushes.

231

He had plunged into a sort of copse. Probably it was twigs that had cut his face, and a tree-trunk that had finally halted her. There were three German soldiers, the two who had dragged him out, and the third, who had spoken of the blood. Now a fourth came into his range of vision, very young, rather gawky, tall and lean and fair. One of the older ones squatted down and said, in a heavily accented English, 'Are you all right? Did you hurt anysing bad?'

'I don't know,' Jack muttered. 'I feel dizzy.' He saw the word wasn't understood, and twirled his finger to illustrate. 'Dizzy.'

'*Schwindlig*,' the man nodded, understanding. 'Better you lying down go.'

Jack had come to that conclusion too. Even lying down, black wings swept about his head. He felt nauseous, and closed his eyes. The men talked among themselves, but he couldn't catch more than a word or two, which told him nothing. Beyond them, his Camel lay: a write-off, he could see that. In a compartment in the cockpit there was a flare, with which they were supposed to set the machine on fire in a situation like this. But he couldn't get to it now.

He was a prisoner. Despair at the realisation sank into him. He thought of Helen and the children. He thought of years in a German prison, shut in, grounded, while the war went on without him. He closed his eyes. His whole body was bellowing pain now, but a cautious flexing suggested nothing was broken. He tried minute movements of each part, and there was no paralysis, no sharp agony. Bruising and shock, then. A miracle. He thought back over the crash. The explosion must have damaged his tailplane and rudder – that was why he had had no control. If it hadn't been for the slope of the hill he'd have crashed headlong and he'd be dead now. Whatever the prospect of prison, he had much to be grateful for.

The Germans were arguing. He opened his eyes a slit. Three of them were telling the other, the thin and weedy one – a natural victim, Jack thought – to do something he didn't like. Finally, sulkily, he agreed.

The one who spoke English crouched by him again. 'Pilot, can you walk?' he asked.

'No,' Jack said. 'Can't move.'

'We leave you here – send help. *Verstehen Sie?* Medic come, later some time.'

'Understand,' Jack said, hope dawning. '*Verstehe.*'

'Volman will stay with you.' Hope sank again. 'He does not speak English. But waiting not be long.'

Volman was the reluctant one, and he was even more reluctant as his companions swung their rifles over their shoulders and left him. He argued some more, following them a short way until they disappeared into the trees, then came back, muttering to himself. Suddenly his anger overcame him and he aimed a frustrated kick at Jack, fortunately only connecting with his booted leg, which did not hurt too much. Jack decided to feign unconsciousness, feeling it was the safest option, least likely to provoke. Volman muttered some more. Then there was the scratch of a match and the smell of burning tobacco.

Jack felt the movement as Volman sat down beside him, and risked a slit of a glance. The man sat staring, discontented, at the broken aeroplane, smoking, his rifle on the ground beside him. Jack thought about the rifle, but it was on the far side of the German from him, and even if he got to it first, he doubted he could wrestle it, in his shaken-up state, out of the hands of an uninjured young man.

When the cigarette was finished and the stub ground out in the mud, Volman got to his feet, stretched, took a step away, turned back for his rifle, stared at Jack and prodded him with a foot, then walked across to look at the Camel. He started muttering to himself again. He walked back and forth, peered through the trees, sighed and muttered again. Jack watched him under his eyelashes. Evidently Volman thought this whole business was stupid. He wanted to rejoin his companions and, from his expression, he was beginning to think his companions had abandoned him and that no-one was coming. The day was advancing. Volman came back and stood over Jack, and Jack had to close his eyes properly for fear of being found out. He was prodded again, first in the leg, then in the mid-section. A movement of air, and Volman was crouching down and looking right into his face – Jack could feel his breath, and smell it: stale tobacco and the sweet, rotten odour of bad teeth. '*So viel Blut,*' Volman said again. He wiped a finger in it. '*Sind Sie tot, Englisch?*' He stood up and kicked Jack again, harder this time, so that Jack had difficulty in not reacting. '*Verdammung!*' Volman said. '*Warum bin ich hier? Es ist dumm. Die anderen kommen nicht zurück.*'

He walked about again, muttering, and Jack risked a glimpse. He was over by the Camel. Then he turned and looked at Jack, and seemed to come to a decision. He swung his rifle off his shoulder, and a sick coldness griped Jack's stomach. He was all that was keeping Volman here. If Volman shot him, he could leave and go after his colleagues. Shot him or bayoneted him. Jack tensed himself. Could he roll out of the way? Could he jump up and get to Volman before he fired? His body was still clamouring with pain and he wasn't sure he could move at all. But he could not simply lie here and be killed.

Volman untwisted the strap on his rifle, and swung it onto his other shoulder. He said, '*Sie sterben bald, sowieso.*' He shrugged, painstakingly lit another cigarette, and stamped away through the trees.

Sweat, of relief, broke out all over Jack's body. He lay still for a long time, suspecting a trick, watching the trees, straining his ears to hear Volman's return. The jangling pain in his body was loosening up, moving about, focusing on certain places with additional stabs like electric shocks. At last, with infinite caution, he sat up. Nothing happened – no German leaped out of the bushes with a triumphant cry

– but the dizziness struck again, so that he felt as if he were swinging back and forth like a bell in a church tower. His head hurt, and he felt sick. Probably he had a concussion, he thought. But he could not stay here. For one thing, more Germans might come. For another, Volman's friends might return. He could imagine Volman telling them that the Englishman was dead so he had left him. But they might not believe him – he looked the type the others would consider a fool. They might come back with him to see. And if Volman came alone, he would make sure he was dead.

He tried to stand, but could not manage it at first. He got over onto his hands and knees and crawled towards the broken aeroplane. He must burn it – that was his duty, but it might also help if any other German patrols appeared. They might think he had perished in the crash and therefore not go looking for him – probably they would not approach too closely. Then he must find somewhere to hide. He didn't know where he was, except that he had been going south-east from Ham – probably more south than east – when he had crossed the canal. At any rate, he was a long way from home. The chances of making it back to some place held by the British without being either shot or recaptured were pretty thin but, by God, he was going to try! If he could find somewhere to hide, he could lie up until dark, and by then he might feel better, and could make his way back under cover of darkness. Was that a good plan? If only his head would stop whirling, he'd be able to think better.

Jack woke with the sense that it was dark, but to begin with he could not open his eyes to make sure. He was not lying in bed, that was for certain. He could smell damp grass and earth, and he was lying on something so hard it aroused a symphony of aches and pains in every part of his body. For a moment he thought of the retreat from Mons, when he had had more than once to sleep under a hedge. But no

– that was a long time ago. He searched the clouded recesses of his brain. The name St Quentin occurred. Ah, yes, the German advance. They had to keep moving out, ahead of the enemy. But why no bed? Were they sleeping in fields again?

And then, with a roll and a thump, memory arrived in his brain. The crash. The discontented Volman. Setting light to his dear old Camel. And then a period of struggling and stumbling and sometimes crawling as he tried to hurry away from the burning wreckage, and make some progress towards the British lines, wherever they might be. In the end, the agonising clamour in his head had driven him to seek refuge. Knowing he must sleep or simply pass out, he had dragged himself under a clump of bushes, wriggled as far in as he could, and let go.

How long ago was that? He had a sense that hours had passed, but he had slept like the dead with no dreams and no awareness of his surroundings or any noises. It was quiet now. And why couldn't he open his eyes? He reached up and felt them, and discovered that they were crusted with blood. A moment's panic was superseded by the memory of Volman saying *so much blood*, and his fingers, creeping upwards, encountered the crusty lips of a scalp wound. The blood must have run down from that and glued his eyes together. He fumbled in his pocket for his handkerchief, wet a corner with saliva, and went to work.

At first when he was able to open his eyes it was just as dark as it had been when they were shut; but, then, he was at the heart of a clump of bushes. Pausing to listen for a moment, and hearing nothing at all, he rolled onto his front and, using his elbows and toecaps, wriggled his way out. Sitting up, he saw trees around him and a path, much trampled and rutted. Above, through the trees, the dark night sky was pitted with stars. No sounds at all. The night was unnaturally quiet. There was no firing anywhere, no voices or sounds of movement, feet or wheels; not even the normal rustlings, no bird, owl or barking dog. He might have been alone in the universe. He wished he was.

Tilting his arm to the starlight he squinted at his watch. It was a fine new one he had been sent as a gift by the Rolex Company when he had won his DSO the year before. Several organisations had sent him commemorative gifts, but the watch had been the most useful of them – not a pocket watch, but fixed onto a leather strap so that it could be worn on the wrist where it was more easily consulted. Trench watches, they were sometimes called, because some army officers now wore them – though trench watches generally had a metal grille over the face to protect the crystal. As he looked now, he wished, with dismay, that his had been so endowed. The crystal had been shattered – only a small portion still adhered to the face – and the hour hand was missing. He held it to his ear and it was not ticking. He shook it, to try to make it go, and the other hand fell off. Disappointed, he took it off and shoved it into his pocket, wondering if it could be mended, then forced his mind to come to grips with the situation. It seemed to want to wander away, and he could not afford that.

Night it definitely was, though how much of it was left he could not now tell. The quietness suggested the enemy was sleeping, but they would be on the move again before dawn. He must make some distance while he could, and find somewhere to hide – somewhere he could lie up all day if necessary. He could not think what sort of place that might be. His head still ached, and when he tried to think hard, there was a slipping, vertiginous feeling that made his eyes hurt. He must still have a concussion. Nevertheless, he could not stay here – he must move.

It was hard getting to his feet. Every bit of his body protested. The front of his legs – his shins – were particularly painful, and he guessed he had bruised them on something in the crash; and his neck and shoulders hurt so much he could not turn his head. He remembered the bus turning over with him hanging by the harness. Wrenched his muscles, no doubt. He had started to stumble along the path, but stopped, realising that, for one thing, he had no idea which direction he was heading, and for another, paths were likely to be used by Germans.

He stopped and tried to think again. Something from the depths of his childhood surfaced, from the days when he and Robbie and Frank had run wild about the Morland estate. One of the farmer's children had told them that you could always tell north in a wood because trees grew moss on the north face of their trunks. He went to examine the nearest trees. Some seemed to have moss all round them; those nearest the path none at all. Perhaps the sun shone through the gap above it, preventing moss from growing. He tried the trees further into the wood. Ah, yes, now there was a definite greenness on one side. That must be north. For a moment he stood, head hanging slightly, not knowing what to do with the information. North side of the tree? What now? He made himself grapple with it. England was to the west, Germany to the east. The British were retreating westwards, towards home. He must go west. Sooner or later he would find the army, or the sea. West meant home. Now, if this was the north side of the tree . . . west must be that way. The path led roughly east and west, so he must follow it, but not on it, in case someone came along. Pity – it would have been much easier going. He pushed further into the wood, then realigned himself by the mossy side of the trees. He must go west, always west. West was home.

It wasn't easy. Without a path, he was wandering almost blindly. He staggered on, his aching head hanging, drifting into a state of semi-consciousness from which he startled himself awake every so often, making himself check the direction again by the trees. The conviction came upon him that he was going in circles. But how could he, if he kept going west? Were the trees telling the truth? He suddenly found himself thinking of Rug. Dogs always knew the way home. If only Rug were here, he would guide him. He missed the little fellow sharply, saw in his mind's eye the way he jumped up, wagging his whole hind quarters in ecstasy when Jack got back from a stunt. Poor Rug, he'd be waiting in vain at – wherever the unit had fetched up, sitting by some hut waiting to hear the old bus coming in. Corrie said he always knew the sound of Jack's aeroplane, though it was one Camel among many. He would break his heart, poor old Rug. Jack felt a surge of determination. He must get home, for Rug's sake. You couldn't explain to a dog. West was home. Suddenly it was as if he could see Rug trotting ahead of him. All he had to do was to follow the dog . . .

And quite abruptly he came out of the woods. It was still dark, but he fancied he could smell dawn coming, and dawn spelled danger, though he couldn't for the moment think why. Rug sat and looked up at him. What now? When the sun comes up, I'll definitely know which way is west, he told him. But it would be light, and light meant – it meant— Yes, it meant he could be seen. He mustn't be seen. We have to find somewhere to hide, Rug old man. He could see a hedge across some open ground in front of him, and went towards it, crossing a tussocky field that smelled of cows. The hedge was tall and thick, and he walked along for a bit in its shelter, though he had a suspicion it wasn't going in the right direction. At the field's corner there was a gate, and on the other side another field with a hedge that went off almost at right angles. That seemed good to him. He climbed over the gate at the third attempt, and stumbled along beside the new hedge.

It was definitely growing lighter. He must find somewhere to hide. If he could lie up by day and walk by night he could do it: he could get back to freedom, to Helen and the children, to home. West was home. Yes, there was a lighter patch in the sky, a lemony shade to the greyness. The hedge was leading him too far south. At the end of it another gateway, without a gate, led into another field, sloping downwards, and at the foot of it, cut out dark against the fading stars, the shape of a group of buildings, barns and a farmhouse most likely. What decided him was that they were directly to the west, and west meant home. He looked around for Rug, but Rug was not there. He frowned. No, of course, Rug was with Corrie. He must have been dreaming. He stumbled down the hill, longing now to lie down, greedy for sleep like a schoolboy for cream buns. He lusted after a pile of hay and oblivion as he had never longed for anything else in his life. Coming closer he saw that one of the buildings, standing separate from the rest, was definitely a barn. He would get in there, burrow into a pile of hay and sleep until nightfall. Nothing else, not even his terrible thirst, mattered.

The stars had gone and it seemed darker now, except for the lemony patch, but there was a sense of things stirring that made him hurry, nervously. Somewhere not far off a cockerel greeted the dawn stridently. Foolish bird, he thought, to make a noise: someone would be sure to kill and eat it. He reached the barn, touched the rough warmth of its wooden side with gratitude, felt his way along it, found the door, closed but not fastened. There was a wooden bar that fitted into slots on either side, but it was lying on the ground. His bruised and thumping brain made nothing of that. He eased the door open just enough to slide through, let it shut behind him and stood, trying to see in the darkness.

Something was wrong. It smelled wrong. It sounded wrong. There was a sound in the darkness where there should be none, a sound like composite breathing. Were there animals in the barn? But that rough little sound, that was a snore. Cows didn't snore. And it didn't smell like cattle.

Someone spoke, and the hair stood up on his head. He felt behind him for the door again as he heard the distinctive sound of a match scratching on a boot sole, and a crocus of light bloomed in the darkness.

'*Ver ist das?*' said the voice. A man, sitting up just in front of him, held up the light so as to see him. He was wearing a grey uniform; and the small light touched, all around him, the sleeping but now stirring shapes of twenty or thirty other men in grey uniforms. He had not been the only person to see the beauty of a barn for sleeping in. He pushed at the barn door behind him, though knowing deep in his soul that there was nowhere for him to run, and the man with the match scrambled to his feet and grabbed at something lying beside him. Jack knew what that was.

'*Hände hoch!*' said the voice, high with fear and excitement, and the rifle made a jabbing motion towards him.

Slowly, his heart breaking, Jack raised his hands.

After the British troops evacuated Albert, they subjected it to heavy battery fire, with the object of bringing down the basilica's tower. The given reason was to deny the advancing Germans its use as an observation post, but the Tommies believed there was a different motive. The legend had long circulated that the war would not end until the golden Virgin fell. It eased some of the sting of losing Albert to know that the end of the war was thus brought nearer.

The Germans were shelling Paris. The firing was in fact, as the RFC had reported, coming from very long distance, thrown by a giant German gun (similar to the 'Fat Bertha' that had shelled Verdun), which was believed to be at least seventy miles from the capital. But the Parisians believed that the Germans were much closer than that. They had spent the war so far ignoring any possibility of occupation and making as much money out of the British soldiers – and latterly the much-better-endowed Americans – as possible. Now they fell into a panic, and many started to evacuate, adding to the general flight that was clogging the roads.

Emma's unit was busy, although as the action was much further south, the great rush of wounded did not come through St Omer. But they had more to do than usual, and it was good to be kept busy. At one time she and Armstrong were asked to take over a mobile canteen at Hazebrouck, and for two days they served endless tea and sandwiches to troops passing through. They seemed to be some of the 170,000 reinforcements sent from Blighty; many were very young and all rather bewildered, not knowing where they were going or what was ahead of them. She was quite glad when the canteen was taken over by some WAACs, and she and Armstrong could get back to their ambulances.

It worried her considerably when she heard that Péronne had fallen, but there was nothing in the world she could do about it. Sad news came, however, from the chief medical officer at the Casino in Calais, via 'Boss' and Muriel Thompson, that Lieutenant Max Linzer had been received there as a casualty with a serious head wound. Emma thought of his divine, lyrical playing, and was desperately sorry. Hutchinson let it slip later, though Thompson hadn't given it out, that there was some doubt that he would survive, and if he did he was almost certain to be blind. What kind of world was it, Emma wondered, that allowed such things to happen? Men with such talent ought to be cherished, no matter who fought with whom. At night she lay in her flea-bag with Benson's sturdy weight against her feet, and wondered whether Wentworth was all right. And she thought of Fenniman, his warmth and humour, and the sensitive side of him, which he had shown only to her, and his smile, which had made her feel life was full of possibilities; how it had all been there one moment and gone the next, snuffed out as easily as a candle flame. Human life ought not to be that easy to end.

On the 2nd of April she heard from Wentworth at last. The 37th was out of the line and at rest in Doullens.

We took rather a pasting [he wrote], but we gave Mr Fritz one in return. We had him on our heels no

242

more than a mile behind and had no sleep for four nights, keeping ahead of him. The Bttn has lost heavily, but I would not have missed these days for anything in the world. The men fought like heroes, and nothing can equal the way they threw themselves at the enemy. It somehow makes one feel tremendously uplifted, to know that nothing matters but duty and helping each other, and I feel the joy and vigour of life as never before. I don't know if you have heard that poor Linzer caught a packet. I don't know what happened to him, except that he was carried off – we have not heard any more. But I am awfully well and fit, so don't worry about me. If there is any chance of a transport to St Omer be sure I will call in and see you. How is my little friend Benson? I imagine you have been busy too, but if you have time, do write and say how you all are.

On the same day the news filtered down that a tremendous battle had begun at Villers-Bretonneux in defence of Amiens, and Emma was glad to know that Wentworth and her other friends were out of it. She could put them to the back of her mind now, knowing they were safe at Doullens. They heard also that Linzer had been sent back to Blighty, but what his condition was, no-one seemed to know. And she heard from Molly, her regular correspondent, that Jack had been shot down and was missing. It made her glad to be kept busy.

The fierce battle for Amiens went on at Villers-Bretonneux from the 2nd to the 5th of April, with the Australians and the French coming to the aid of the beleaguered remnants of the Fifth, now Fourth, Army, and taking the brunt of the last German efforts to break through. On the morning of the 6th all was quiet. The German commander Ludendorff had called off the offensive. They had pushed the British back forty miles, and occupied a thousand square miles of ground, but they had not taken Amiens, and they were still fifty miles from the sea. They had not taken Paris, either, and further north on the line, Arras was still in British hands. The losses on either side had still to be calculated, and certainly on the British side they had been heavy. But the fact remained that the enemy had thrown everything they had at them and they had not broken. The exhausted men coming out of the line in the week after Easter had their tails up, the alarms of the 21st and 22nd forgotten. The Gerries had not beaten them, and they never would!

As the most junior and most expendable of the men in command during the March offensive, General Gough took whatever blame was going to be handed out back home. There was a debate in Parliament in which Lloyd George was pressed about having kept the BEF fatally short of men, but by counting in the Italian, South African and Chinese natives he had sent out as labourers, he was able to quote statistics refuting this; and by praising General Byng, whose line had held, he was able to suggest that the whole thing was Gough's fault and that, as he had already been brought home, the canker had been cut out.

Bertie's brigade went out to rest on the 7th of April. Of Parke's Force, which had fought under that name to the end of the battle of Villers-Bretonneux, just under three hundred of the four hundred and fifty were left – an achievement in the circumstances. Scott-Walter told Bertie that, when they had rested, a new draft of men would be coming out to bring them up to strength. The cavalrymen and the York Commercials would be leaving them to be reunited with their own kind, and Bertie's remnants would become part of a new battalion in the West Herts regiment.

Bertie would have a couple of weeks after rest to absorb the new men and train the battalion together – 'assuming no great emergency arises, that is. Of course, we don't know what Fritz is going to do now, but I doubt he's quite ready to give up yet. Haig still thinks there'll be an attack in the north of the line, and that could come at any minute. If reserves are needed you'll have to go. But I'll give you a month of training if I can. Anyway, get your men settled, and take some leave yourself. They'll be at rest for a fortnight, I promise you that absolutely.'

'Thank you, sir,' Bertie said, and his mind leaped eagerly to Jessie, and then with rather less relish to Maud. He would have to do something about the problem of Maud. Perhaps he ought to tell her the truth: he would have done so before except for the residual fear that it would set her back up and make her refuse to divorce him at all. But would she be so vindictive? It occurred to him that, despite all those years of marriage, he really didn't know her very well. Jessie thought that Maud did not like her, and if that were true, it might well incense her to discover the truth. It was hard, though, to associate Maud with any emotion so violent as being incensed. Even her passion for John Manvers seemed cool and polite enough to be put off until after the war.

He dragged his mind back from these thoughts as he realised that Scott-Walter had not finished talking, and he had missed the last part of what he had said. 'I beg your pardon, sir,' he said.

The brigadier looked at him quizzically. 'Wool-gathering? Now I know you're tired! Either that, or it's disinterest taken to an abnormal degree.'

'I'm sorry, sir,' Bertie confessed. 'I really didn't hear what you said.'

Scott-Walter smiled. 'Only that I'm putting you in for a bar to your DSO, for your actions between the twenty-first and the twenty-fifth. It was a superb show. I doubt if any other man could have brought as many men through as you did, in the circumstances.' He offered his hand and Bertie shook it, feeling rather dazed. 'They'll be running out of medals to award you, at this rate. Now go off and have a jolly good rest. You damn well deserve it.'

When Bertie got back to Battalion Headquarters his staff

had had the news and were already packing. Gerard came to him to say that they had received notice they were to go back to billets in a village near Abbeville. 'It'll be good to be near a town that hasn't been beaten up,' he remarked.

'All you officers will get leave in turn,' Bertie told him, 'and we should see about leave for the men at the top of the list, too.'

'Well, sir, of course we don't have lists, being Parke's Force and full of orphans,' Gerard said.

'Quite so. We'd better start compiling them again. Get the warrant officers in each unit on to it, and make sure the first twenty men go straight away. We're being re-formed with a new draft from England, and I'd like as many as possible of the present force to get leave before we're called into action again.'

Cooper came up to him. 'Post, sir. Personal.'

Bertie took a sheaf of letters from him, and sorted through them quickly. There was one from Ireland, in a hand unknown to him. He turned it over, and saw on the reverse that the return direction was 'Carnew, Rathdrum Lodge'. A sense of foreboding struck him. Now what? Had the Carnews discovered All and decided to cast Maud off? Were they writing to expostulate with him? He shoved the other letters back at Cooper to hold while he slit this one open.

Dear Cousin Bertie,
    No doubt our telegram has prepared you to some degree –

'Telegram?' Bertie said, 'Cooper, was there a telegram from the Carnews in Ireland?'

Cooper looked as though it was an insulting question. 'No telegram, sir. Must've got lost somewhere. I'd've given it you, else.'

'Lost?' Bertie said sternly. The British post for men at the Front didn't get lost.

'Or follerin' us about, sir,' Cooper said, 'seeing the number of places we've been in in the past two weeks, and the different names we've had . . .'

'I suppose so,' Bertie admitted, and continued to read.

– but I still find myself grasping after words to tell you the <u>terrible news</u>. I suppose you have been taken up with the fighting we've been reading about and that's why you did not come after the telegram, but to ease your mind I have to tell you that you would not have been in time even if you had. The accident I mentioned was as follows. On Easter Saturday, Maud was out driving with Lord Manvers in his motor, and I had gone along myself and was in the back seat because, Bertie, I didn't think it <u>quite right</u> for her to be jaunting about in public with him on her own so much, though I knew she would <u>never</u> cross the line, don't mistake me, but it was the way it <u>looked</u>, do you see? But anyhow, it was this way. We had had <u>very stormy</u> weather in the week before, and the roads were slippery, and coming down the hill towards Glendalough, there is a place where it is quite narrow and there is a sharp bend. Somehow or other the motor-car skidded on the bend and went across the road and hit a tree. Well, we were not going so very fast, as Lord M is a <u>very careful</u> driver. But with the high winds in the storms the week before a big branch must have got weakened, for when the motor hit the trunk of the tree, this big branch fell down and hit Maud in the head. Oh, Bertie, it was such a shock! Lord M had a blow to his shoulder and I had some slight scratches from the twigs, but Maud took the worst of it and was knocked unconscious. We hurried her home and had the doctor in at once. He did <u>everything</u> he could. I assure you Dr Farlane is the <u>best</u> doctor in the world and I would trust him with my life so you must not think anything was not done as it ought. But poor Maud never regained consciousness and the next afternoon she passed away. Oh, Bertie, I'm so sorry. It was quite peaceful at the end, and Dr Farlane says she didn't suffer, but she was so young, and such a tragic way to go! Oh, Bertie, I tremble to write these words as we all loved her, and I know that you did too. I knew about her Plan, to get the d—e I mean (I can't bring myself to write that word). She told me all about it, but I'm sure that in time she would have thought better of it, and when you came back after the war you would have been reconciled and got back together, which is God's will for those who once marry, whom no man should put asunder. Only now it's too late and you never will, and I am racked inside for thinking what a state of mind she might have been in at the end. It was so sudden, you see. We are all in a state of shock and grief. Not knowing where you were or when you might be able to get back, Harold felt we should not delay the funeral for your instructions on that account, so we held it on Tuesday, at the church here in Rathdrum. She was laid away in the churchyard, where our family graves are, and it was all done as beautifully as could be. When you come back you can see the grave, and make any arrangements you wish for the headstone. I am so sorry to be the one to write you this news. I know how it will shock you for I know you loved her and you are far from home fighting for King and Country. I wish there had been some way to spare you. We put white lilacs on the coffin in your name with the message 'From a loving Husband' and 'Rest in Peace'. I hope we did right. Please write soon and say if there's anything you want done, and when you will visit, for there are her things to sort out. Oh dear, I can't believe she's gone. I keep going into her room and thinking that maybe I dreamed it all. It's a horrible shock. Bertie, write and let us know that we

248

did the right things. It all happened so <u>fast</u>, and you never sent a telegram or telephoned, so we just had to do our best. Harold sends his deepest condolences.

Your affec cousin,

A. Carnew.

PS Lord Manvers has behaved <u>impeccably</u> throughout, not putting himself forward at all but ready to help in any way. No-one could be more sorry than he is. I don't know if you will mind me mentioning his name to you in the circumstances, but I ought to say <u>in justice</u> that it wasn't his fault, being a <u>pure accident</u> that no-one could help, and Maud being the one to <u>insist</u> on going out that day. He sent white iris and narcissus to the funeral and we put them with the rest on the grave. I hope you think we did right. We didn't think it right to put them on the coffin, of course. There was just yours and ours on the coffin. It looked lovely.

Bertie came back from the reading of this long, rambling letter – much underlined, and blotted pathetically where tears had dropped and made the ink run – to discover an unusual silence around him. His expression must have given away something of its contents. Cooper was looking at him curiously, and the staff officers were equally curiously *not* looking at him, though their minds were evidently out on stalks.

'Bad news, sir?' Cooper said, using the privilege of the old servant.

Bertie might have damned his impertinence, but he was just too tired. Anyway, Cooper would know soon enough. 'My wife,' he said. 'There's been an accident. I shall have to go home. Gerard, can you take charge of getting the men back to Abbeville?'

'Of course, sir,' Gerard said, his nice face creased with concern. 'I hope it's not too serious, sir?'

Bertie preferred not to answer that. There was a hollow-ness of shock inside him, but apart from that he could not say that he felt anything yet. That was probably down to sheer exhaustion. He hoped it was. Poor Maud was a week in her grave. The thought bewildered him – he didn't know what to do with it. He must go back at once and see to things, and it was fortunate that he was at liberty to do so, for with the men going out to rest there was no need for him to be there. Normally he'd have seen them settled, but Gerard and the others could cope perfectly well. He must telephone the brigadier and let him know. Perhaps Scott-Walter would send someone down from his staff to help out, as they were short of officers.

'Cooper, pack my things, and find out when the next train is. Gerard, see the transport officer for me and get me a warrant as far as London. Smith, get me the brigadier on the blower.' They were all staring at him, and he frayed a little. 'Clear out, will you, and give me some privacy?'

They cleared.

A man must always tackle his least pleasant duty first, so after a single day in London – necessary to perform some pieces of business, seeing solicitors and so on, and sending telegrams – he set off for Ireland. The journey was worse than last time, for though it was warmer in England and didn't rain quite so much, the Irish Sea was still in its March mood and threw everything it had at ships impertinent enough to venture out on it. Bertie thought for a short time that he might actually be going to join Maud, which would have been ironic after surviving the Boche onslaught. But they steamed at last into Queenstown, and he tottered with the rest to the train, where a more level mode of progression and two large brandies restored him to equilibrium.

But he was very tired when he reached Rathdrum, and perhaps that was useful in blunting what he might otherwise have felt. It was desperately sad to stand by the newly turned earth of Maud's grave. His wife of nine years, mother of the son he had loved so much, little Richard, blown to pieces by a German bomb dropped on Folkestone. Maud was a victim of the Germans too, in a way, for she would not have been in Ireland to be killed by the falling branch had Richard not died. She had always done her duty to him as a wife until that time, and would no doubt have gone on doing it. It was not her fault that he and she were not suited, and he had never wished her anything but happy. If they had divorced he would have been glad for her to have the life she wanted with Manvers – and who knew but that it would have answered? Perhaps Manvers really had been the man for her. But they would never know now. Her life had been cut short. He was full of sorrow, as he stood with his head bowed in the icy April rain at her graveside, that she had died without reaching the place of comfort she had envisaged.

In the Carnews' house he sat patiently and listened while they told him all over again every detail of the accident and what had followed, and while Annie Carnew went back over what she and Maud had discussed and what she felt about it, and forward over what she thought might have happened in the future had the accident not occurred. He listened gravely, and thanked them over and again, reassured them that they had done exactly right. It was the least he could do in all courtesy and kindness, for they had been good to Maud and cared for her, and in the shock of what had happened they needed to talk it through to see if they could be to blame in any way. He did what he could to assuage the guilt they felt, as people always do in such circumstances. Every sudden death seemed to leave the immediate survivors feeling uncomfortable for still being alive.

He discussed the style and wording of a headstone, which they kindly offered to order for him, and a memorial on the wall in the church, and gave them a draft on his bank to cover both, and all incidental expenses, including the doctor's fee, the funeral costs, and a gift to the church. He went up to Maud's room and pretended to look over her things, but gave the servant five shillings to pack them up, and asked the Carnews to have them shipped to him at his London club – not because he wanted them, but because they wanted him to want them. He offered Annie Maud's fur coat – a very fine sable – as a sort of gesture of thanks, and she refused with a shocked look, which made him feel awkward; but later she retracted and said she would like it, and thanked him for thinking of it. The only thing of Maud's he took with him was a photograph of her with Richard on her knee that she had kept on the mantelpiece in her room. He slipped it out of the frame and put into his wallet.

And then he could go, feeling more tired than ever, sad and weary and with a sense of helplessness: whatever man might do and whatever dispositions he might make, God in the end could bring them all to nothing. He had wanted to be released from Maud, but not like this. Not like this.

He did not go to see Manvers. He bore the man no ill-will – would have been glad to see him happy with Maud – but he saw no good reason to put himself through that.

And then, feeling like something that had been put through the wringer, he made his way to Wiltshire. He fell asleep on the train, so completely and heavily that had the ticket-collector not been an alert man and remembered him, he would have missed his stop. He felt no lifting of his heart as he sat in the ancient taxi rattling its way towards the woman he loved – it was too damned exhausted to lift – but he did feel, after the cold misery of Ireland and Maud's fate, a sense of residual comfort, as of going home.

His telegram had prepared them, and they were expecting him. They did not talk about it to begin with. He was welcomed in, his coat removed, tea provided immediately. The children were still up, excited to see a visitor, and had to be played with, and his heart, which he had thought to be safely frozen, woke to painful life as he wrestled with Basil and played all the father's tricks he had learned on Richard, and heard his giggles that were just like every boy's;

252

while Barbara, soft and pretty and already unignorably feminine, wanted to climb on his knee and flirt with him.

Jessie watched him with them as though it were painful for her, too; and he looked at her with longing and love, and wondered if that rather unflattering smock she was wearing concealed a son or a daughter.

When the children had been taken away, the women wanted to hear about the action, and talk about Jack. It was the first he had heard about Jack being missing. He was able to put what they knew into some context for them, though he was unable, of course, to tell them what they most needed to know. But he said, 'Pilots can survive the most worrying-looking crashes. I've seen them climb out of what looks like a pile of matchwood and walk away. There's a good chance he survived, you know. I wouldn't give up hope yet.'

Helen's dark eyes remained troubled. 'I don't know whether it would be worse to hope and then be disappointed, or not to hope and get it over with. And supposing we never know? Never hear anything?'

He knew they were thinking of Ned, and said, 'It's different in this case. To begin with, the area wasn't being heavily shelled, as it was at Loos. And there were large numbers of German infantry moving through. Someone is bound to have found him. If he was injured, they'll take care of him. And if he was dead, or taken prisoner, you'll hear eventually. It takes time to get the information back, but one pilot, when so few are lost, is a very different prospect from one infantry officer among so many. I'm sorry, Jessie.'

She waved the apology away.

'So you really think there's hope?' Helen asked painfully.

'There's hope that you will know, one way or the other, in time. But I don't want to buoy you up too much. He may be dead. You have to face that, too.'

'I know,' Helen said. 'Don't you think I know that?'

The discussion lasted through dinner, which tasted superb

to Bertie's deprived taste organ: he found himself eating the way he did in France, and had to check himself. And then, when the pudding was cleared, they came to the other subject.

'We should get married as soon as possible,' he said abruptly, to Jessie.

Helen half stood. 'Would you like me to leave you alone?'

'No,' Bertie said, surprised. 'Of course not. I know,' he addressed Jessie again, 'that it seems callous—'

Jessie looked down. 'You've only been a widower for two weeks. It looks like indecent haste.'

'It isn't the way I would have wanted it,' Bertie said. 'I'd have wanted a proper mourning period, out of respect for you as well as her. I don't want this hurried, rushed thing any more than you do.'

Helen spoke. 'But you have to be practical.'

'Thank you,' Bertie said. 'We have to be practical. There's more than just our feelings – or even the family's – to think about. There's our child. And I don't know when I may be able to come again. The baby's due in June. This may be our only chance to do the right thing.'

'The right thing?' Jessie questioned dolefully. 'It's almost macabre.'

'But it can't be helped,' Bertie said. 'Don't you want to marry me?'

She turned her face to him, and all her love and longing was in her eyes. 'Can you doubt it?'

He took her hand across the table. 'Then the sooner the better,' he said. 'I got hold of a special licence while I was in London. We can go into Salisbury tomorrow. Will you come with us, Helen?'

'Of course. But don't you need your birth certificates too?'

'I got copies of those as well at Somerset House.' He smiled tenderly at Jessie. 'I'd forgotten, if I ever knew, that you were christened Jessamine. You've always just been Jessie to me.'

'I think my father liked it,' she said.

'I'm sorry it won't be a wonderful wedding in a church. I'd marry you in Westminster Abbey if I could. Or York Minster.'

'Or the chapel at Morland Place?' Jessie said, but her eyes were teasing.

'But I'm afraid it will just have to be a register office.'

'That was all I would have had if you had been a divorcé,' Jessie said; and she thought, Poor Maud! In dying she had saved them that. They were properly free to marry each other. 'Anyway, this will be a wartime wedding,' she went on. 'It's quite common nowadays. We won't be the only ones by any means.'

CHAPTER TWELVE

The April weather turned kind for Jessie's wedding day, with a light breeze from the west that blew the clouds through too quickly for showers, and intermittent spring sunshine, pale, but with a definite warmth to it. There seemed to be lambs everywhere on the downs, and on the banks and field edges the stiff little wild daffodils stood up on their short stems, looking as if their petals were being blown backwards like a dog's ears.

Helen did her best for Jessie, despite having only a few hours, adapting a navy serge suit of her own by inserting a length of broad elastic into the waistband. The skirt was full, with a wide, waving hem eight inches above the ground, so there was plenty of material in it, and the jacket was longish with a deep peplum, which hid her rather hasty handiwork. Jessie had a nice pair of long buttoned boots, which looked smart with it, and Helen lent her a hat, a new one she hadn't worn yet. It was wide-brimmed and flat-crowned, much more fashionable than anything owned by Jessie, who had spent the previous two years in uniform.

'There. You look very smart,' Helen said, pushing in the final jet-headed hat-pin.

'But not very bridal?' Jessie queried.

'As long as you *feel* bridal,' Helen said, 'that's all that matters.'

What Helen felt was largely relief that the outcome was

not going to be worse, but she kept that to herself and kissed her sister-in-law affectionately. In wartime, you just had to do the best you could.

The servants had sponged and pressed Bertie's uniform for him and polished his boots. They could not be told about the wedding, since they believed Jessie already married to him, but there was nothing unusual in the request to buff up his uniform, since he had come without his servant. But Jessie had told Tomlinson, of course, and when they were ready to leave, she pressed Jessie's hands, with tears in her eyes, and whispered that she hoped she'd be always happy. 'God bless you, Miss Jessie,' she said. 'This is for you, from me, with love.' She gave her a small package wrapped in tissue paper.

Jessie opened it. Inside was a little brooch, a round stone of lapis lazuli, in a twisted circle of silver.

'It was my mother's.'

'Oh, Mary, it's beautiful!' Jessie said. 'But you shouldn't give it to me. It's too much.'

'I want to,' Tomlinson said firmly. 'And you ought to have something blue, for good luck.'

Jessie kissed her, and there were tears in her eyes too, as she stood for Tomlinson to pin it onto her. Her boots were old, the hat was new, and the suit was borrowed, so the brooch was the final element. She hadn't thought about the old rhyme before, too preoccupied with everything that had been going on; now she really did feel bridal.

They set off in Helen's motor, and when they entered Salisbury, Bertie suddenly asked Helen to stop for a moment. He jumped out, and returned a moment later with a bunch of white violets he had bought from a flower-seller he had spotted on the street as they passed.

'A bride ought to have flowers,' he said and, a little awkwardly, for it was not something he had ever done before, he pinned them to Jessie's hat with one of the jet-headed pins.

'Thank you,' she said. Helen drove on. Out of sight, between them on the back seat, their hands were clasped together now.

The registrar, a very elderly gentleman who had come out of retirement when the war stripped out all the young ones, seemed rather resigned to hurried marriages between serving officers on leave from the Front and females who – an experienced and rather grim single glance suggested to him – had definite need of his services before it was too late. He seemed not at all placated by the relatively advanced age and steadiness of the protagonists, and conducted the business with a faint air of reproach. This might have made for gloom, but fortunately it tickled Helen's unruly sense of humour. Jessie met her eyes and saw the suppressed amusement in them, and guilty feelings fled away. She was marrying the man she loved, at last, and against all expectations, and there should and could be nothing but gladness in her about that. The mood communicated itself to Bertie, overcoming his physical tiredness, and to the clerk, who had been called in from another office in the building to be the second witness. The clerk was glad anyway to have this unexpected break from work, and she liked the look of the couple, and was pleased they really seemed so much in love. Mr Crampthorne oughtn't to spoil people's weddings, the miserable old beast, she thought, and she looked from face to face of the other three and positively grinned.

The ceremony didn't take long. It rather threw them off balance to be back outside so soon, with no crowds of well-wishers, flowers, bells – not even a photographer in sight!

'What now?' Helen asked. 'We can't very well have a wedding breakfast at home.'

'Nor shall we,' Bertie said. 'What's the biggest and best hotel in Salisbury? We'll go and have lunch there, with champagne if they have it. And afterwards I thought perhaps we could find a photographer's shop and have our portrait taken

– the three of us. We ought to have *one* wedding photograph to show our grandchildren.'

Jessie looked at him with love and gratitude, and Helen thought what a nice person he was, to understand that even such a wedding day as this must be something to be looked back on by the bride with pleasure in years to come. They had all put aside their misery and anxiety about Jack for the occasion; a celebratory lunch would help to keep it that way.

'Excellent idea,' she said. 'I think the White Hart opposite the cathedral ought to fit the bill. It's only a step from here.'

Bertie offered each of them an arm, and escorted his two companions to lunch.

That night, after the servants had gone to bed, Bertie climbed the stairs to Jessie's room, feeling absurdly conspiratorial, which in turn made him feel absurdly young. Perhaps a little element of daring and excitement was not out of place at the very beginning of a marriage. But along with huge joy and anticipation, he felt a sense of overwhelming relief, of coming home. Perhaps it would be like this when the war ended, if he survived – perhaps he would feel the same deep sigh in his bones and his soul then as he felt now when he slipped under the blankets and into Jessie's waiting arms.

'My darling,' he whispered to her in the darkness. 'My wife.'

'It's been so long,' she said. 'Sometimes I thought—'

He kissed her hair, laid his lips to her ear and murmured, 'No more of that. We're together now.' He moved his mouth to find hers, so ready for him, and kissed her, his wife in truth now, as she had always been in his heart. And gently, carefully because of the baby, they made love.

The old, old habit of the trenches made him wake an hour before dawn, and for a moment he didn't know where he was.

Stand to! Where was Cooper with his coffee? What bed was this? Too soft, too clean. Why was it so quiet? Outside in the darkness a blackbird spoke questioningly, lifting its head from the warmth of its back feathers, sensing the morning approaching. It repeated the question, alone in the blackness, and somewhere a little further off a robin answered with a long, trilling call, ending in the sweet upward lilt of his spring song. Bertie remembered, and breathed deeply of clean sheets and furniture wax and the indoor smell of carpets, then rolled over to immerse himself in the soft, fragrant warmth of his wife – his wife! Utter joy overcame him and he lay still and let it have its way with him, putting away all other thoughts that might try to intrude, the questions, fears or worries that would have to be faced some time, and soon – but not now. Would she wake? He didn't want to disturb her, but he very much wanted her to be awake. They had so little time together. Very, very gently he kissed her brow, and it was as if he had touched the catch on a secret compartment. She seemed to unfold and unfurl, lips rising to his, arms opening to him, her sleepy warmth curling into and around him.

'Bertie,' she whispered, against his lips.

'I love you,' he said.

Afterwards she turned over on her side facing the window – she always left the curtains open, except on the coldest nights, so that she could see the morning coming. He put his arms round her from behind, and they seemed to fold together easily and naturally like spoons in a drawer. The sound of birdsong became a riot, and the greyness came, and then began to be suffused with pale golden light.

'It's going to be a fine day,' she murmured. The baby stirred and stretched – she could feel its feet pushing against her abdomen and imagined it arching its back in that contented way she had seen babies do in their cradles. She took Bertie's hands and laid them over it, and said, 'Feel.'

It was something he had never experienced before. Maud

260

would never have done such a thing. Indeed, her pregnancy with Richard had always been something to be concealed, certainly never spoken about, far less drawn attention to in this way. Almost unmanned with wonder, he felt the surgings and ripplings of his child inside her body. She guided his fingers until he actually, for a fleeting moment, took hold of a tiny foot, the outline pressing through her flesh. It was too much – it was almost agony. His love – his wife – his child – he so wanted to live! To be with them, to share this most natural but – it had always seemed – unattainable of graces! He didn't want to go back to the war. He didn't want to die. He pressed his face into the back of her neck, trying to hold back the torrent of his feelings.

She felt the change in him. 'What is it?' she asked.

He couldn't answer for a moment or two. When he had control again, he said, almost abruptly, 'You must go back.'

She understood him. To Morland Place, he meant – and she had thought about it herself, of course, on and off ever since he had come back to marry her. She was married to Bertie, and her child would not be illegitimate. So far so good. But it would not quell all the other talk, would not alter the fact that she had conceived out of wedlock, that they had committed adultery, that they had married a bare two weeks after Maud's death. It would still hurt and shock them back home, and she didn't want to do that to them, to her mother and Uncle Teddy particularly, when they were already in such trouble, mourning Robbie and Jack.

'I don't want to face them,' she said at last.

'I know. But you will have to sooner or later. And better to do it when I can be there with you. I can stand beside you and hold your hand and be part of it, take my share of the blame. You shouldn't have to do it on your own.'

'I could stay here,' she said, in a small voice that said she knew it was not a possibility.

'They need you,' he said. 'And you need them.'

Yes, she thought. She wanted her mother. She had wanted

her very badly when the news about Rob came, and even more when Jack went missing. And how could she leave her mother comfortless in the face of all this sorrow? She ought to be there with her.

'I'd feel happier about you if I knew you were at Morland Place being taken care of,' he said, much as Jack had said to Helen before Barbara was born.

'What about Helen?' Jessie said, on the back of this thought.

'I suppose she may have to go too,' Bertie said.

'Poor Helen, ordered about from pillar to post to suit my convenience.'

'Hardly that. I dare say she'd be glad of the support, until the news comes about Jack.'

It was true, Jessie thought, that Helen had not entirely wanted to take the children away from Morland Place, where Basil had enjoyed being in a large nursery with his cousins, and Barbara had had a dedicated entourage of besotted nurses to cater to her every need. She had done it for Jessie's sake.

'And she may be glad not to have to be responsible for you,' Bertie added, 'when she's away from home so much. But if she doesn't want to go, you could always leave Tomlinson here with the children.'

Jessie thought of facing childbirth without Bertie and also without Helen and Mary Tomlinson. She would have her mother, and Nanny Emma, of course, and she mustn't be selfish. 'We should ask her,' she said, 'and let her decide for herself.'

'Of course,' Bertie said. 'But you will go home? I really think you ought to.'

'Yes,' Jessie said, with not much of a sigh. 'As you say, better to do it while I can have you by me.'

'We'll face it together,' he said, kissing her.

Helen saw the logic of it, of course. 'And I'd be happy for the children to go back. It is rather isolated for them here, and who knows how long the war is going to go on? And I dare say Tomlinson will want to be with you anyway.' She thought for a bit. 'Let's do it this way. It will take me a little while to get things settled here. You and Bertie do what you have to do. Tomlinson can stay here with me for a week or two until I've made my arrangements. Then she and I can bring the children down, and I'll go back to my gypsy life, staying here when I need to and at Morland Place when I want to see the children.'

Jessie looked anxious. 'I seem to be imposing a way of life on you—'

'It was my choice to bring you here,' Helen said. 'Mine and Jack's.' The sound of his name was like a full stop on the air, and she went on quickly – she didn't want him to become a taboo, something never spoken about. 'Jack wanted what was best for you, and I believe he'd think it was best for you to go home now.'

'I think so too,' said Bertie.

Jessie nodded, unable to speak for a moment. Then she reached across the space between them and took his hand. 'Then we'd better do it soon,' she said, 'before you get called back to France.'

He smiled at her courage. 'We could have a day or two more of honeymoon – don't you think, Helen?'

'Tomorrow's Sunday,' Helen said. 'You won't want to travel on a Sunday. Send a telegram on Monday, and go on Tuesday.'

Jessie smiled her thanks at such generosity. Two whole days, and the rest of this one, to be at peace with Bertie before facing the storm. It seemed a great blessing.

Life at Morland Place went on, even in the face of great sorrow and anxiety. It was what you had to do, and it was even more important in wartime. Hundreds of local families had lost sons, husbands, brothers. The Morlands were looked up to for an example. There must be no extravagant mourning, no loss of spirit, no wavering. The war effort must be given everything, just as if one's heart were not breaking.

So Henrietta continued to do her twice-weekly stint at the national kitchen, to host her weekly tea-parties for selected Tommies from the army camp up by the Monument, and her monthly dinners for selected officers. She continued to sit on her various committees, to visit estate pensioners and the sick, and the bereaved families who had now been added to her list. The widow's pension was often not enough to live on, especially if there were young children, and baskets of food and cast-off clothing as well as advice were offered and, what was sometimes wanted most, a sympathetic ear. In between she continued to run the house – a task she was well used to, but which was complicated, these days, by the rapid arrival and departure of servants – and keep up her correspondence; in her spare moments she knitted socks and balaclava helmets for soldiers.

It was good to have every waking moment taken up with work, and to go to bed so exhausted that sleep came almost before thought could start. But she still dreamed of Jack, the same dream, in which she saw him falling through the air. But now the dream came to her without any sense of urgency: he fell slowly, like a feather, turning a little, as though the fall would go on for ever, quite peacefully, without ever coming to a dangerous end. She supposed that must mean he really was dead, and she folded her memories of him away with those of Frank and Robbie, put them tidily with her memories of Jerome, to be taken out one day, when there was leisure, and pored over.

For now there was the war, and there were Bertie and Lennie in France; and dear little Emma not entirely outside danger, for one FANY had been quite seriously hurt when her ambulance got stuck on a railway track; and now there was her grandson Martial too, eldest son of her daughter by her first husband, Lizzie. He had written to her to say he had arrived in France from America with his two cousins, Aubrey and Anderson Flint, and was looking forward tremendously to the scrap, though it was not known yet exactly when they would be joining the fray, since the good old US government and the US Army seemed to think they needed a great deal of training before they could be allowed to kill Germans.

And just last week there had been a telegram from Bertie in London (she supposed he was on leave) saying that poor Maud had been killed in a motoring accident in Ireland. The news shocked her – she had known Maud since she was a young woman of Polly's age. Oh, this was a terrible war! And Bertie had paid as highly as any of them, with first his only son and now his wife. Bertie, who'd been like an extra son to her since his turbulent youth – how badly she felt for him.

If she ever had any spare worrying capacity, there was always Lieutenant Holford, also in France, on whom Polly seemed to have developed a crush. He had seemed a nice sort of young man, on the occasions when Henrietta had met him, but Polly was too young to be thinking seriously about marriage. It was true she would be eighteen in May, and that was a lot more grown-up now than it had been in her day. Henrietta had been just less than eighteen when she married the first time, but she had been still completely a child. Polly was a very self-confident young woman, and already showing a serious interest in her father's business, especially the drapery side of it, which would come to her when he died. But Teddy would certainly not permit her to marry before she was twenty-one. Even after that, it was hard to see who would be good enough for her in his eyes. David Holford's father might be what was called these days a 'millionaire' (so hard to imagine any one person having a million pounds: she always thought of it, for some reason, in a big basket, like a picnic hamper, all in banknotes – so worrying if someone were careless with a match!) but he lived in London and Surrey and they had never met him, so Holford could hardly be counted as a serious suitor, whatever Polly thought of him.

Worrying about Jessie was hard for Henrietta to do, since she did not know what was wrong with her, though she was sure there was something. But now, with Jack missing, there was less chance than ever that she would come home: Helen would need her, and Henrietta could not be so selfish as to rank her own loss with Helen's, or to want to deprive her of Jessie's support.

So when the telegram arrived from Jessie saying that she would be coming home, and to expect her on Tuesday evening, it gave Henrietta almost more surprise than pleasure.

'She doesn't mention Helen,' she said to Teddy. 'Surely she wouldn't leave Helen alone with the children. Don't you think they must be coming too?'

'I don't know, my dear,' Teddy said, trying to get through the newspaper before he had to leave for a meeting in York. 'Have Helen's old room made up for her just in case. There's always space in the nursery for the children.'

'That's the trouble with telegrams,' Henrietta said. 'They leave out too many words. Just "arriving Tuesday evening", not "we are arriving" or "I am arriving".'

Teddy looked up good-naturedly. 'Would you like me to telephone Downsview House and find out?'

Henrietta recoiled. There was no need for anything as drastic as using the telephone. 'No, thank you. I'll make up both beds, as you suggest. And I'll tell Mrs Stark to make a ragout with that salt pork she's been soaking. Helen's very fond of her ragout of pork. And an apricot pudding. Jessie loves apricots, and we've plenty in bottle.'

Teddy caught the tremor of anticipation in his sister's voice. He smiled at her. Hen worked so hard, and there was little enough of pleasure in her life, these days, but having Jessie back would make up for a lot. He only hoped she would stay this time. It would be hard on Hen if she was going back to nursing and this was just a stop on the way. 'Should we have some guests to meet them?' he asked. 'If you're planning a big dinner, perhaps we should have some officers from the camp to share it, or some friends from York.'

Henrietta considered for a moment or two, but then said, 'No, let's just have a family dinner the first evening. We can invite other people when they've settled in.'

She thought about that afterwards – how close they had come to having guests that evening. There were several possible trains Jessie might be arriving by, so they hadn't been sure exactly when she would reach Morland Place. Henrietta sat in the drawing-room with one ear cocked to hear the sounds of arrival, the other turned to Alice's gentle murmur of conversation, with the sound of the fire crackling in the background, the soft click of ivory and ebony as Teddy and Father Palgrave played chess, and the scratch of pen on paper as Polly wrote in her diary. Ethel was still staying with her mother; Maria was reading.

But for all Henrietta's restless alertness – she hadn't knitted a row in the past half-hour – it was Teddy's old spaniel, Muffy, who heard it first, waking from the depths of a dream beside the fire to raise his head with a quiet *wuff!* as the taxi-cab came into the yard. Henrietta looked enquiringly at the dog, straining her ears, but he was sure of himself, struggled to his feet and ran to the door, shaking his stump of tail eagerly. Then she heard the house-door opening and voices in the hall, and jumped up too, to hurry out and meet her daughter, with Muffy scampering past, slithering on the marble tiles of the hall floor.

Sawry was already there – he must have been listening for the taxi, too – with one of the maids, Peggy; and the dogs that had been sleeping by the hall fire were surging about, with Muffy shoving his way in among them. But Henrietta's eyes leaped straight to the figure of her daughter, muffled up in an all-enveloping greatcoat, just taking off her hat to give to Peggy, and to her face, rosy with cold, but looking so much better than when she had last seen her, at Christmas, not tired and drawn but positively healthy. Relief surged through her.

But Jessie was not alone. Henrietta now took in the other figure, tall, a dark cut-out against the pale plaster of the wall, not Helen or Mary Tomlinson, not a woman at all, but a man, a man in an officer's greatcoat, a man turning to look at her as she appeared in the archway, looking at her with a troubled smile – and, good God, it was Bertie!

'Bertie!' she cried in happiness, going towards them. 'Jessie, darling! It's so good to see you! But, Bertie, how do you come to be here? Did you meet on the train? Why didn't you say you were coming?'

But she stopped before she reached them. Jessie had turned her back to Sawry so that he could help her off with her coat, and now when she turned again towards her mother, her eyes held a warning and an appeal, and Henrietta saw the unmistakable shape of her pregnancy. In a split second she had taken in how advanced it was, had realised that Jessie must have known about it at Christmas, and that this was why she had gone away.

'Jessie,' she said falteringly. 'You – but—'

Sawry, good servant that he was, took charge. He thrust Jessie's coat into Peggy's arms and dismissed her with a fierce look, stepped round to help Bertie out of his great-coat and, before Bertie could speak, said, 'If you would care to go into the drawing-room, sir, I will bring sherry in a few moments.'

And then he disappeared with Bertie's coat, leaving the three of them alone but for the milling, happy dogs.

Jessie sought her mother's face. 'Don't be angry, Mother. I had to go away. But it's all right now. We're married.'

Henrietta's mind was still reeling. 'You're married? But who to? I don't understand.'

Bertie closed the one step that separated him from Jessie, and took her hand into the crook of his arm. '*We*'re married, Aunt Hen. Jessie and I. It's a long story, and we both need your forgiveness. We've come to tell you everything.'

Henrietta stared at him, and her first thought was that he had known about it – the reason Jessie had left home – and had sacrificed himself to save her reputation, at a time when he must have been deep in mourning. Maud had only been dead a little over two weeks! It was like his kindness – and he had always been fond of Jessie. 'But you didn't have to do that,' she said.

Bertie saw her confusion and read her thought. 'I am the father of the child, Aunty,' he said gently. 'Let's go and sit down somewhere, and I'll explain.'

It was as well, Henrietta thought afterwards, that Ethel wasn't at home for she was the one person who would have made a noise about it. As it was, they went into the drawing-room, where Henrietta's look of shock and the sombre expressions of the other two checked the exuberance of greeting, and in a moment were sitting down, and told the story to a circle of attentive and absolutely silent faces. Jessie was scarlet with embarrassment and mortification, but she made herself sit straight and meet her mother's and uncle's eyes. And there was no doubt that both Henrietta and Teddy were profoundly shocked. Teddy was so taken aback by the whole thing that he forgot to send Polly out of the room, and she made herself invisible behind Maria, fading into the background at the far end of the drawing-room so as to be sure of hearing everything.

Father Palgrave also effaced himself, slipping back to sit with Maria, his eyes bent on the floor between his knees where his quiet hands were clasped. Maria watched the faces of the main protagonists, feeling pity for the pain of all of them. She did not blame Jessie, despite the fact that Bertie had been a married man. She had loved Frank, and remembered what it was like to believe that she and he were separated for ever by social rules. If she had been tempted as Jessie had been, she was not sure she could have held out. She could not throw the first stone. She wondered what Denis Palgrave thought, and what he would say if appealed to for judgement. She hoped he would not be. A priest might condemn or forgive – both were in his remit. She hoped – oh, how she hoped – that if he did speak, he would not disappoint her.

It was not possible, then as ever, to tell what Alice was thinking. She continued with her embroidery as she listened, her face impassive, her eyes on her stitches. Only once did she look up, when Jessie said she had not told Bertie at first that she was pregnant because she believed she might lose the baby anyway. Alice had lost a child, and could never have another. She had sat by Jessie's bed after one of her miscarriages, offering silent sympathy. And now, as Jessie told that part of the story, Alice's mouth quirked a moment in pain, before she returned her gaze to her work.

The reaction to the story, as Jessie had always known it would, came from her mother and uncle. Teddy was shocked at his niece's moral turpitude; angry with Bertie for having betrayed both Jessie and Maud by his actions (it was no excuse that Maud had left him for another man); angry with Jessie for having concealed the truth for so long, adding deceit to her sins and putting her mother through so much anxiety; shocked with Bertie for having contracted a marriage in such indecent haste when his wife was hardly cold in her grave.

Henrietta had been looking miserable throughout the interview, her eyes going from one speaker to the other but saying nothing herself – as if (Jessie thought) it was all so bad it was as beyond speech as it was beyond forgiveness. But when Teddy expressed himself on that last point, she suddenly stirred and spoke: 'No, Teddy. What would you have had them do? There's the baby to think of.'

'I'm trying *not* to think about the baby,' Teddy said angrily. 'There should never have *been* a baby.'

'I know,' Henrietta said, 'but there's nothing to be done about that now. We can't change the past. The child has done nothing wrong. Bertie and Jessie have done great wrong, and they know it, but this last thing was the one thing they did right. The baby won't be born out of wedlock, and that's something we ought to be glad about.'

'People will talk,' Teddy said. 'They'll find out – they always do. Married only a fortnight after his wife died? The baby born only two months after the wedding? We'll never live it down.'

Suddenly Henrietta felt serene. The shock was slipping away. Instead, a warmth was stealing over her – like that feeling after a long day's hunting when one was sitting by the fire having tea, a sense of perils past and hardships endured and strenuous goals attained. Jessie, her beloved, was home, and she was all right. Better than that, she was happy. And Bertie, her dear 'extra son', was Jessie's husband, and they loved each other and had done for years, and they were happy together. If the war spared him, they might have the sort of loving union she had always wanted for Jessie, the sort she had had with Jerome.

And there was a baby coming, a new grandchild for her, a baby for Jessie, who had none. Beside that, concerns about wrongdoing and scandalous behaviour and things in the past that no-one could change now, let alone what the neighbours might think and say, seemed as unimportant as chaff in the wind.

'Of course we'll live it down,' she said. She reached out a hand to rest it on Teddy's arm, because she knew he was hurting. He was the family's head and had to worry about it; and Ned was gone, and Ned and Jessie's babies had died. 'We're the Morlands,' she said. 'We can get through anything. People may talk a bit, but they'll forget. What's a bit of haste in marrying beside the fact that Bertie's a hero, with a VC as well as a DSO? And Jessie went to France to nurse. Who knows how many lives she saved? She isn't the first girl to get into trouble, and she won't be the last. These things happen in wartime. If we face the gossips down, and show how glad we are that they're married, it will all blow over, just like everything else. We're the Morlands of Morland Place, Teddy. We have plenty to be proud of. We've given four sons to the war. The neighbourhood can allow us our little eccentricities.'

Maria almost clapped as Henrietta paused, and only just managed to restrain herself. Behind her, Polly hugged herself, feeling wonderfully, warmly Morlandish. Maria looked cautiously at Father Palgrave, and was relieved to see on his half-hidden face a smile of approval. He was not going to condemn!

And Teddy thought suddenly, painfully, of how *he* had once been the focus of the neighbourhood's gossip, to the point at which people had actually cut him, and he was asked to resign from his clubs. He had been vilified in the newspapers for having survived the *Titanic* disaster. What had been written about him had been lies, but still he had felt guilty, though he had done what he thought was right at the time. But all that was forgotten now. Hardly anyone remembered the old story, and if they did, they kept their doubts to themselves, and he was once again accepted as a leader of York society. Perhaps they *could* live this down. His own sense of disappointment in Jessie, of shame in her moral laxity, of sadness at how she had let them all down, he would have to bear in private. Henrietta was right. They must face down their critics, not cringe and hide.

'It doesn't make a wrong into a right,' he said. 'The fact that Bertie and Jessie have behaved bravely in the war doesn't excuse what they did.' He met their grave eyes. 'But you're right, we must think of the child. We must show a united front to the world, and make sure that Jessie's child is never made to feel ashamed. Are we all agreed on that?' Alice and Henrietta nodded.

Bertie said, 'Thank you, Uncle. It's Jessie and the child I'm thinking about now. I will have to go back very soon. I have no home I can take her to, and I would feel much happier about leaving her if I knew she was here and being looked after properly.'

Teddy's head lifted in surprise. It had never occurred to him that Jessie might live anywhere but Morland Place. Even in the middle of his shock and anger over the whole business, he had been assuming that she had come home to stay. The notion that Bertie might have had a home elsewhere that he was entitled to take her to was what, in the slang of his youth, he would have called 'a facer'.

'Of course she stays here,' he said, almost indignantly. 'Did you think I would cast my own niece out? This is Jessie's home – yours too – so don't talk nonsense. You can go back to the war with a clear mind. We'll take care of her, and the baby. And if anyone dares to look down their noses at her, they'll have me to answer to.'

That night Jessie slept in her own old bed in her own old room, where everything was almost unbearably familiar, and the only astonishing thing was that her husband was lying in it with her. They lay spoonwise, the only comfortable way to hold each other at this stage of her pregnancy, and watched the firelight wander about the room, touching things.

'I can't believe you still have those shells we picked up on the beach last year,' he said after a long, contented silence.

'You'd be surprised at the things I've kept over the years,' she said. 'I'll show you one day. All your letters from South Africa. The photograph of you with the little pony you were so fond of . . .'

'Good God, yes, Dolly! I'd forgotten her. The bravest little horse in the veld. Did you really keep the photo? I'd like to see it again.'

'I kept everything of yours. Even a piece of string you

273

once showed me how to tie knots with. I have a little box in my bureau where I keep them. They're my treasure.'

He folded his hands over the baby. 'Now there's another treasure. Keep it safe for me.'

'It feels so strange lying here with you,' she said, after a moment. 'Strange but nice.'

'To me it feels so natural, it's as if we've been doing it all our lives.'

'Oh, yes, that too,' she said. 'Oh, Bertie, we're so lucky!'

It seemed a strange summing-up to their turbulent history, especially given the cataclysm they had survived today. But he understood. There were storms outside, but they had found a haven for a little while. And they might never have had this time at all. Thousands, millions never knew what it was to love like this, and to be together in utter, blissful communion. However short their time was, whatever happened in the future, they were as happy right now as it was possible for humankind to be.

'Yes,' he said, kissing the rim of her ear where the firelight touched it. 'We're very lucky.'

Helen did not really have much to do in the way of arrangements. She could have completed them in a couple of days; but she was in no hurry to leave. She wanted to stay a bit longer in the house that she and Jack had chosen together, which had been their home. She had an odd, nervous feeling that if she left he would not know where to find her. If he was dead – and she thought that he must be, for otherwise wouldn't she have heard by now? – she hoped that he would haunt her. She could imagine him in these rooms, and out there walking on those downs, and there was comfort in it. But if his ghost came back and found the children gone and her hardly ever there . . . It was foolishness, she knew, but she couldn't help it.

So she lingered on at Downsview House, playing with the children, taking long walks, aware of Tomlinson's curious gaze on her as she waited for instructions to pack up. The children hadn't been told yet that they were to go back to Morland Place. Helen had said she didn't want them to be over-excited by the idea, and Tomlinson had agreed. They had accepted Jessie's departure philosophically. Since she had grown large with child, she hadn't been able to play with them much, so she wasn't missed as she might have been, and with spring coming the allure of the world outdoors filled any gaps.

So she was still there a week later when Aggie came into the sitting-room one afternoon, where Helen was writing letters and Mary Tomlinson was attempting to teach Basil his letters while Barbara took her afternoon sleep, and said. 'There's a motor just pulling up outside, mam. I think I saw a gentleman in it.'

'I wasn't expecting anyone,' Helen said. 'Probably someone who's got lost, stopping to ask directions.' It happened from time to time. The road to the house didn't lead anywhere else, but at the other end it looked as though it was going to. She got up. 'I'll come and see to it,' she said. Aggie always got ridiculously excited about any kind of visitor, even an inadvertent one, which made her incoherent about directions.

When she opened the front door, she saw at once that the 'motor' was nothing more than the station cab. 'You foolish girl,' she said to Aggie. 'Don't you know Mr Beales's taxi by now?'

But Mr Beales wouldn't have brought anyone here by mistake. It must be someone for her. She stepped out onto the path just as the door of the taxi opened and a tall man in khaki got out. Her breath caught and her heart leaped. She caught a glimpse of wings on the breast of the tunic. The RFC had become the RAF on the first of April, but airmen would be using up the old uniforms for a long time yet. A pilot – he was a pilot! All the blood seemed to flee from her head, and she swayed unsteadily.

A small, hard body shoved past her from behind, and Basil ran out, his voice lifting in a glad cry, '*Daddy!*'

Helen took a step forward too, her hand going out to catch him, but the man, who had been about to get something out of the back seat of the taxi, turned at the sound of Basil's voice, stooped to receive him as he cannoned into his legs, and looked up across the boy's head at Helen. It was not Jack. It was a stranger. An airman she had never seen before.

'Hello,' she said, and was amazed to hear her own voice, for she had not thought herself capable of speaking.

'I'm sorry,' he said. It seemed to cover a great deal.

Basil detached himself and stared up at the man with a frown of affront, as if he had been deliberately imposed upon. But out of the corner of his eye he could see Tomlinson coming to retrieve him, and a visitor was a visitor and, at all events, better than learning letters. 'I have a model aeroplane,' he said, with dignity. 'Would you like to see it?'

The man didn't answer. He was still looking at Helen. Then he turned and opened the back door of the taxi, took out a kit-bag, which he dropped on the ground, then reached in for something else. He emerged with something small and rough-coated in his arms.

The creature, which had been lying docile, almost limp, suddenly started wriggling violently. It burst out of the man's grasp like a missile, hit the ground with a scrabble of paws, and raced to where Helen was standing to fling itself passionately at her.

'Rug!' she cried. 'Dear old Rug!'

She squatted down to receive the dog's frantic embraces, wondering where his bark was – he had always been vocal on these occasions – and ran her hands over his body. She looked up at the airman. 'He's nothing but skin and bones.'

'He's been pining,' the man said. 'We couldn't get him to eat, so as I was coming on leave, I volunteered to bring him to you because we were afraid he'd die otherwise. I've brought Compton's kit, too,' he added apologetically, with a gesture towards the bag. 'There's a trunk as well, but they're sending that separately. My name's Hipkiss, by the way. I'm a flight commander in Compton's squadron. I'm most awfully sorry. We all liked him tremendously.'

Helen stood up. 'There's no more news, then,' she managed to say.

'Nothing, I'm afraid. The Boche are all over that sector now, so we can't get in there, and there's nothing to see from the air. It's a wooded area. We haven't even been able to spot any wreckage.'

'Tell me truthfully,' Helen said, picking up Rug to keep him from clawing her stockings, 'do you think he could have made it?'

'There's always hope,' Hipkiss said awkwardly.

'I can see you think there isn't.'

'Oh – no – well, I don't mean—'

'Please, tell me the truth.'

He met her eyes unwillingly. 'I really mean it, there is always hope. We've all had awful crashes and walked away from them. But – the thing is – in a wooded area . . . Well, if you have to crash-land, you want a nice open spot. Crashing into trees is not frightfully good for the health.' He stopped, and looked at her almost appealingly, as if to be told he had done the right thing in saying it.

'Thank you,' Helen said faintly, her eyes distant. Rug licked her face, and settled his head on her shoulder with a sigh, as though ready to sleep at last now that he was safe. She roused herself. 'Won't you come in, Captain Hipkiss? It was very kind of you to bring me Rug. Let me get you some refreshments.'

'Oh, thanks awfully, but I won't, if you'll forgive me.' He bit his lip, and she thought he did not want to have to talk to her about Jack. But he said, 'I don't have much leave, and I'd really like to get home tonight if I can, to

277

see my wife. She's having a baby, you see, and if I miss the next local train, there isn't another that connects.'

'I understand,' Helen said. 'Please don't let me delay you, in that case. I do understand – and I'm grateful to you for bringing Jack's things.' Still he hesitated, and she made herself smile. 'Go on now. You'll miss that train.'

When he had gone, Tomlinson picked up the kit-bag with one hand and took hold of Basil with the other, and they went back inside, Helen still carrying Rug. She stopped at the kitchen and ordered a plate of scraps for the dog, and held him on her lap and fed him by hand, since that seemed to be the only way she could get him to eat. When he had finished, he fell heavily asleep, as though for the first time in weeks.

Tomlinson had taken Jack's bag away, and Helen was glad. She didn't think she could face seeing it just yet, let alone unpacking it. Her heart was sore. Having Rug back seemed to make Jack's absence more solid and permanent. And that nice young Hipkiss had said that landing in trees was hard to survive. From her own experience as a pilot she knew that was true, and the very fact that he had said it when he would clearly have preferred not to showed that Jack's colleagues thought he was dead. Her marriage was over. She was a widow. Jack was never coming back. She knew it, but she could not feel it yet. She wondered if other women felt as she did, or if it was just because she had not had the official confirmation. There were thousands of women, of course, whose husbands' bodies were never found, who never knew for sure – except that when the man did not come back, that was assurance enough.

Rug grunted and twitched in his sleep, his body, in its absolute relaxation, amazingly heavy on her lap for such a small, skinny creature. Poor little dog! He'd been so devoted to Jack.

Tomlinson came in and said, 'I'm going to make you a cup of tea.'

'Where's Basil?' Helen asked automatically.

'He's playing with his aeroplane in the bedroom.'

'He was so disappointed it wasn't his daddy.'

'He'll get over it,' Tomlinson said shortly, and held out something she had been carrying. 'The bag came open when I put it down, and this was on the top. I thought you might like to see it.'

It was a framed photograph of Jack's flight, formally posed in two rows. Jack was in the middle of the back row, and beside him – sitting on top of a stepladder so that he was at the same level – was Rug, in his flying helmet, with his goggles slung round his neck. Everyone was grinning happily, but Rug's was the biggest grin of all.

'It's a good picture,' Helen said at last. The mount had a foot at the back, and she pulled it out and set the photograph on the side table where she could see it.

Later, when Barbara woke up, and Tomlinson brought both children down, Basil saw the photograph and spotted his father in it, and reverted to his indignation over the airman who had visited who was *not* Daddy. He was so cross about it that, for the sake of peace, Helen decided to distract him by telling him that they were going to go back and live at Morland Place again. 'With the cousins. And Nanny Emma. You'll like that, won't you?'

Basil was ecstatic. 'And can I play with the toy soldiers? And ride on the rocking horse?'

'Yes, of course, but you'll have to take your turn with the others.'

'I *like* Morland Place,' Basil said, with great satisfaction.

The ruse had done its trick, for he was so excited at the idea, and so busy reminding Barbara of all the wonderful things there were to do there, that he quite forgot about the airman and his disappointing non-daddy-ness.

But, of course, the thing was that now they really did have to go. Helen deposited the slumbering Rug in the corner of the sofa, and went to start packing.

CHAPTER THIRTEEN

Tobolsk was still locked in the breathtaking, cruel beauty of the Siberian winter, the ice-bound river silent. In the Governor's House the ex-Tsar and his family were enduring a confinement that was gradually becoming more irksome.

The season had not been without its pleasures: there was something exhilarating about such extreme cold, and the children had enjoyed snowball fights, and sliding down an ice-mountain they had built in the yard with the help of the soldiers, who had been considerate, even friendly at first. But in March Russia signed the humiliating treaty of Brest-Litovsk with Germany. In return for being left alone by the German Imperial Army, Russia gave away a huge tract of her best territory, losing a third of her agricultural land, a third of her population, half of her heavy industry and nine tenths of her coal mines. The ex-Tsar was as angry about the treaty as anyone in the country, but it brought resentment towards the family from their keepers.

First their ice-mountain was destroyed, and their harmless fun curtailed; then they were told that their budget was to be severely cut. They were to be allowed to draw only six hundred roubles a month each from their personal capital. Half of the household would have to be sent away. Furthermore, the family was to be put on plain soldier's rations: no more luxuries, no little comforts; no coffee or butter, only half a pound of sugar per month between them.

Lunch was to be soup and one dish; dinner, two dishes, no soup.

A fortnight after the rationing started, there was a more ominous change. The regular army detachment that had been stationed in the town was removed in the middle of March, its place taken by a detachment of Red Guard. The guard on the family was doubled, and a machine-gun was set up at the corner of the street. The members of the household who were living in a separate building, the Kornilov House across the street, were told they must move in with the family or be dismissed, so everyone had to squash in together in the Governor's House. At the end of the month it was decreed that no-one in the house was allowed out into the town. Before, those living in the Kornilov House had been considered at liberty; now they were under arrest like the family, and like them had to take their exercise and fresh air in the yard.

It meant that Venetia's son Thomas, still in the Kornilov House, was now the only one in regular contact with the outside world. Perhaps the commissars would have liked to lock him up, too, but they could not do that to a serving British officer. He wondered anxiously what the changes portended. Certainly a hardening of attitude towards the Romanovs: they had always known that Russia's dropping out of the war would change things, but it had been impossible to guess in what way. Revolutions were, by their very nature, volatile and unpredictable.

The family's miseries were increased by the fact that the tsarevitch, Alexei, was ill. He had had a serious internal haemorrhage and was confined to bed, with intermittent fever and severe pains in the groin and legs. Forced to lie flat and immobile, the child was miserable and bored, and had no appetite. He ate almost nothing, grew thin and yellow, and his cries of pain in the night kept everyone wakeful.

Then, in the third week of April, a special plenipotentiary from Moscow arrived with a guard of a hundred and fifty horsemen, showed his papers of accreditation to Colonel Kobylinsky, who was in nominal charge of the Romanovs, and took up residence in the Kornilov House.

The news of his arrival caused consternation in the Governor's House, where nerves were already stretched by long confinement, overcrowding, lack of solid news and a surfeit of rumour. The very title 'special commissar' seemed ominous; the suddenness of his arrival, with letters from the Central Committee in Moscow, seemed like a portent of doom, especially as the letters gave him power of summary execution over anyone who defied his authority.

Thomas was as puzzled as the family: he knew nothing about Vassily Yakovlev, and had not been expecting him. The plot he had been involved in all winter, to get the family out secretly by boat via the Tobol and the Yenisey to the Kara Sea, seemed to be running into sand. While all the private individuals involved were still ready and eager, only waiting for the May thaw to put the plot into action, the prime minister, Lloyd George, now seemed to be having second thoughts about it. Thomas exchanged regular letters and coded messages with his mother, and she told him that, because the Bolsheviks seemed to be forming a stable regime, Lloyd George was hoping it might be possible to regularise relations between the two governments. He was therefore stalling on the river-escape plan.

'He doesn't want to upset the Reds now, and he's never liked N personally, so he doesn't care if time is running out,' Venetia wrote. 'I do what I can to advance matters but I have no influence with LG. The King can't move without him.'

Time was indeed of the essence. The imperial family's fortunes already hung by a thread, for jurisdiction over them was being hotly disputed by two rival soviets, that of Omsk in western Siberia, and of Ekaterinburg in the Urals. Both soviets had sent representatives to Tobolsk to argue their case for supremacy, but while the Omsk delegation was relatively moderate, the Ekaterinburg deputies had come with their own detachment of Red Guard, and wanted to see the Romanov family thrown into a real prison and stripped of all remaining comforts. If that happened, Thomas felt sure they would never be heard of again: murder or summary execution were but small steps from there. At this delicate moment, the arrival of a special commissar from Moscow was bound to complicate his position.

His first sight of Yakovlev was reassuring. He was no boot-faced, piggy-eyed committee thug, but a tall, thin, energetic man in his thirties, with a mass of unruly black hair, an intelligent face and bright, quick eyes. He was dressed in naval uniform, which suggested an independence of mind, and when Thomas first met him, in the hall of the Kornilov House, he found himself subjected to a swift and comprehensive inspection, which was followed by a firm handshake, and a greeting in good English. 'We must talk together. Have luncheon with me later.'

'Gladly,' was all Thomas had time for before the man ran up the stairs two at a time. He did everything as quickly. Before the morning was out he had addressed the soldiers' committee, and convened a meeting of the rival soviet delegates, at which he deftly turned the moderates from Omsk against the extremists from Ekaterinburg, until the latter were booed and hissed for spreading false alarms about escape plots. He had paid a visit to the Governor's House (where he arrived so early Alexandra was not yet dressed), made himself smilingly known to Nicholas and asked him if he was being well treated, rapidly inspected every room, and looked in on Alexei in his sick-bed. He had a meeting with Kobylinsky, another with the guard committee, returned to the Governor's House to meet Alexandra, then visited Alexei again, this time taking the regimental doctor with him to assess the boy's condition.

When Thomas was shown into his room for luncheon, he was standing by the window, reading a document, and looked up with a quick smile. 'Thomas Winchmore, Lord Overton – the English earl. Also Colonel Lord Overton of His Britannic Majesty's Horse Guards – "the Blues", I think you are called? I have heard much of you. I am glad to meet you at last. How do you do?'

Thomas shook the offered hand, wondering cautiously *what* the man had heard of him. Had the plot been discovered? Was Yakovlev a spy, sent here to trap him? 'You speak English very well,' he said neutrally.

'Also French and German. I travelled widely in my youth – but I suppose such is the privilege of the sailor. And you, I understand, speak Russian very well, after your long service here. That is good. Colonel Kobylinsky will be joining us and it will be more convenient then to speak Russian.'

For a few moments they chatted politely, and even as Thomas did his best to discover what Yakovlev was, he was aware that he was being equally curiously probed. Yakovlev was evidently an educated and well-travelled man with cosmopolitan tastes. Could he really be a Bolshevik spy sent by Moscow? He did not seem at all the type. His face and manner, while firm and authoritative, were open, and Thomas felt nothing but goodwill coming from him.

Kobylinsky arrived, and the food was brought in at the same moment by two soldier servants, who laid a small table by the window. Yakovlev waved them abruptly away, saying they would serve themselves. The food was simple, a tureen of potato soup, and a platter of bread and meat. Yakovlev ladled out the soup, and without further conversation began to eat, spoon in one hand and a piece of bread in the other. He ate as rapidly as he did everything else: neatly, like a gentleman, but with a dispatch that suggested his meals were often interrupted by calls of duty. Kobylinsky tried at first to make polite conversation, but seeing that eating was the order of the day he desisted and stolidly made sure of his share of the provisions.

Yakovlev pushed aside his plate, wiped his lips on his

napkin, and said, 'I believe you must know by now that I have come from Moscow. My authority comes from the very highest source.'

'You have papers signed by Comrade Sverdlov,' Kobylinsky said, as though that was an answer. Sverdlov was the chairman of the Soviet Central Executive Committee, the highest authority in the new order.

'My authority comes from the *very highest source,*' Yakovlev now said again, as though Kobylinsky's had *not* been the answer. 'Do you understand me?' This seemed to be addressed more to Thomas than Kobylinsky, and a small flame of hope sprang up in him. He must mean Lenin himself. 'I have come to take His Majesty to Moscow.'

Kobylinsky paled. 'To put him on trial? I know how these things go. An empty show trial to give a veneer of respectability to what is effectively murder.'

But Thomas had not missed the fact that Yakovlev had said, 'His Majesty', as no real Bolshevik would do. 'That's not it, is it?'

'There will be no trial,' Yakovlev said. 'But there are those around us who would be better left to think there will be. I will let you into my confidence, but it must go no further. I have quietened our brothers from the Urals for the time being, but hyenas do not make reliable domestic pets. It is better to placate them by tossing them the meat they like.'

'You can rely absolutely on my discretion,' Thomas said.

'Mine too,' Kobylinsky agreed, with dawning hope.

'Then this is the situation. Once in Moscow, the Tsar is to be taken to Petrograd, and thence to Finland where a ship will be waiting to transport him to Sweden. There he will be safe, and the question of his final destination can be discussed at greater leisure.'

'His final destination is not fixed, then?' Thomas asked.

Yakovlev shook his head. 'You will perhaps have heard rumours that there was a clause inserted by the German imperium into the treaty of Brest-Litovsk, to the effect that the Tsar and his family must be handed over to them unharmed?'

'I had heard such a rumour,' said Kobylinsky. 'I did not know whether it was true or not. Their Majesties discussed it, and both agreed that they would sooner die in Russia than live in Germany. The enemy, you see – they can't forgive . . .'

'Yes, and that is why the final destination is in question. Our highest authority has given his word to release them, but at present the Germans are not insisting on taking delivery. They have their own troubles, to which the presence of the Tsar and Tsaritsa would only add. It is hoped it may still be possible to negotiate an asylum in England.' He looked at Thomas. 'Your government blows hot and cold, but I dare say they will be glad to have the imperial family conveyed to safety, at any rate. Wherever safety may lie.'

'Yes,' said Thomas. 'That is the most important thing.'

'Very well. For now, Sweden is the immediate destination, and you may allow the family to believe as strongly in England as seems appropriate to you. But we must move quickly. I do not trust our comrades from Ekaterinburg. These petty local dictators do not always respect the authority of the centre as they ought – which is why, of course, Russia will always be an impossible country to rule.'

'When do you plan to leave?' Thomas asked.

'Tomorrow morning, at four o'clock.'

'So soon!' Kobylinsky gasped.

'With luck we will take them all by surprise. They will think that as I have only just got here, I will be taking my ease for a few days. That is what *they* would do. I will see Their Majesties this afternoon, and you will help them pack what they wish to take.'

Thomas said anxiously, 'You speak of Their Majesties – but what of the children?'

'I mean to take them all, of course,' Yakovlev said, sounding a little surprised.

'Thank God for that,' Thomas murmured.

'But the Tsar *must* be got away,' Yakovlev went on. 'That is the essential point. As long as he is out of their hands, they will not care so much about the others.'

Thomas nodded, but he was indulging in a brief but potent daydream. Safety in Sweden, and then – England! Olga, free from danger, and Nicholas, in exile, perhaps not finding an English earl an unworthy mate for his eldest daughter.

Nicholas eyed the newcomer with suspicion, too tense and anxious to take Yakovlev's smiles and gentle demeanour at their face value. He and Alexandra had long suspected that they might be taken to Moscow for the sort of show trial they had heard of, which would not only end their lives – something they were almost resigned to now – but blacken their names and pervert history. It was a prospect to terrify. The very word 'Moscow' now blanked everything else from Nicholas's mind.

'I refuse to go,' he said, and Thomas saw his jaw set at its most mulish angle, while a nerve at his temple jumped with tension.

'I'm afraid I have my orders, Your Majesty,' Yakovlev said. 'Please be calm. I am responsible with my life for your safety.' And then, seeing that Nicholas was too agitated to accept any reassurance, he tried a different tack. 'If I do not take you, I will have to resign my commission, and in that case the Central Committee will probably send a far less scrupulous man to replace me, the sort of man you would not care to have to deal with. You will come to no harm with me, I swear it.'

'I suppose there is no point in protesting,' Nicholas said bitterly. 'But what of my family?'

'Anyone who wishes to accompany you may do so. There will be no objection.'

'But my son is ill, too ill to travel. I cannot leave him.'

'Your Majesty, you and I *will* leave tomorrow,' Yakovlev said. 'Who else comes I leave up to you. But anyone left behind I will come back for, and you will see them again in a week or two. I imagine the round trip will take ten or eleven days.'

Yakovlev left them, with a swift, hard look at Thomas that said, *Now it's up to you.* Nicholas went to speak with his wife, and a little while later they called in Thomas and Kobylinsky to discuss it. The Tsaritsa was wringing her hands with anxiety; Nicholas, standing by the fire, had his hands clasped behind him, his chin sunk on his chest, frowning with the weight of the decision.

Everything was gone through again, several times. 'But do you trust him?' Alexandra asked.

'I believe he is telling the truth, Majesty,' said Kobylinsky.

Thomas answered, 'If you'll forgive me, Your Majesty, in a way it hardly matters. He will leave tomorrow morning and His Majesty will go with him. That is certain.'

'It is a trial, a show trial, I'm sure of it,' she said. 'I cannot let him go alone. We must face it together.'

'My dear,' Nicholas began, but she shot him a look.

'No! You know what they will do. If we are separated they will work on you by threatening us. We must all go.' The other half of the dilemma gripped her. 'But Alexei cannot possibly be moved. If he stays, I must stay. I cannot leave him! What if some emergency arose? But I *must* go with you, Nicky. Oh, God, what shall I do? Where does duty lie?'

'Yakovlev says it is not a trial,' Thomas said patiently, not for the first time. 'After Moscow it will be Finland and freedom.'

'But do you *trust* him?'

Did he? His own life was not, perhaps, in danger, but the lives of the family he had served, whom he had sworn to protect, and the life of the woman he loved, would be in Yakovlev's hands. Nicholas would have to go, but the others might stay, and if they stayed, the original plan to get them

288

away might still come off – if the Urals soviet did not seize them first. What would he want for Olga? To stay here or to go with Yakovlev? If Yakovlev's orders really were from Lenin himself, surely that must be the better option. These outlying soviets were too unstable, and went from bad to worse. Anything was better than being in their hands.

'I trust him, Your Majesty,' he said. 'I believe he is telling the truth, and that he intends to take you to safety.' He sought for words to convince her. 'I believe he is a man of honour.'

She nodded slowly, and he saw some of the tension leaving her. 'Then we must decide who is to go and who is to stay.' Suddenly she seemed quite calm. 'I have decided. I must go with the emperor. Alexei must stay here until he is well enough to travel, and the girls shall stay with him.'

'You should perhaps have one of your daughters with you, Your Majesty,' Kobylinsky said, 'to attend you, and for company, now that you have no ladies-in-waiting.'

Thomas's heart leaped. 'Yes, Your Majesty, that would be a good idea. Perhaps Grand Duchess Olga would be best. She has a level head in an emergency.'

But the Tsaritsa dismissed the idea without a thought. She did not care much for Olga. 'No, Olga must stay with Alexei. That's clear. And Tatiana had better stay, to help her. I will take Marie.'

'I must have Dolgorukov with me,' Nicholas said. 'And you will need Dr Botkin, my love. Your maid and my man, and a footman to handle the baggage.'

'I will stay with the family, sir, if you wish,' Thomas said, but even as he said it, he knew it was impossible.

Nicholas said at once, 'No, no, you must come with us. You are our chief ally, and the only one who can communicate with England. We cannot do without you. Who knows what political situation we may encounter? You must come.'

'Yes, Thomas Ivanovich, we must have you in Moscow,' said Alexandra. 'Olga will look after everyone until we are reunited. You do *believe*,' she added, with sudden suspicion, 'that we will be reunited?'

'I trust Yakovlev,' Thomas said, but it wasn't quite an answer. Two weeks was a long time in Russia, and who knew what might happen? Once separated from Olga . . . And yet he was a soldier. It was his duty to go with the Tsar, and he must do his duty. But his heart ached at the thought of leaving her.

It was hard on all of them. Since the Tsar had returned to Tsarskoye Selo after the abdication, being together had been their one source of comfort. The family spent the whole afternoon in Alexei's room, and then those who were to go went to pack. They were not to take a great deal: the main bulk of their belongings could be brought later when Yakovlev came back for the rest of them. The family dined alone, but Thomas went across at about ten o'clock to take tea with them, and found a melancholy calm prevailing, though the eyes of the girls were swollen with tears. One by one the servants and household came in to say goodbye. Thomas sat beside Olga on a sofa, as close to her as he could get. He hardly cared now whether anyone noticed. She was trying to be brave for Anastasia's sake, but she had thrown Thomas a look, not exactly of reproach but of dismay and apprehension, when it was announced that he would be going with her parents.

When the tea-things came in, she got up automatically and went to pour, which had always been her job, and Thomas went with her. There, by the tea-tray, with their backs to the room, and speaking in low voices, they had all the privacy they were likely to get.

'I have to go. It is my duty,' he said. 'But you know that if I could I would stay.'

'You must do your duty, of course,' she said stiffly. Then, with a little melting movement of her hands, 'Oh, Thomas, I'm so afraid! Are they really taking Mama and Papa to Sweden? It's not a trick?'

'It's not a trick. Your parents, and you too – all of you. To Sweden, and then, please God, to England.'

'England!' It was a rapturous indrawn breath. 'Little green fields and brown cows, cricket matches, tea on the lawn . . . The magic of it all! It hardly seems real to me. *Will* I see England with you, Thomas?'

'If I don't see it with you, I will never see it again,' he said fiercely.

Her hand shook a little, the perfect arc of tea from the spout touched the edge of the cup and broke, and a drop fell onto the traycloth. 'You will come back for me? Promise that when Yakovlev comes back for us, you will come with him?'

It was agony. How could he promise what he could not be sure of fulfilling? 'If I can, I will come back. You know that. Nothing that I can help will keep me from you.'

She raised her eyes to his face, steady, cool grey eyes in a pale face, framed with soft gold-brown hair. She was not really pretty, but she was beautiful. She read his face, and nodded gravely. 'I understand. I ought not to ask you when it is not in your power to promise. But, oh Thomas, I wish we weren't to be parted. I'm so afraid that if we part, we may never meet again.'

'We shall,' he said. 'I believe it, and you must believe it too. In this, the heart *must* rule the head, or how can we survive?'

She smiled then, no more than a small quirk of the lips, but he was moved by her courage. 'I must take the tea round. People will wonder. But I'll say goodbye now, Thomas. Later there will be people listening. This is our real goodbye – do you understand?'

'I understand. Goodbye, Princess.'

'Say my name.'

'Goodbye, Olga Nicholayevna. Goodbye, Olishka.'

'Goodbye, my Thomas. I love you.'

The last was so quiet a whisper he hardly heard it, but she

looked into his eyes at the same moment and her heart was in the look. He took the cup she was holding out to him, and under cover of the movement laid his other hand a moment on hers, resting on the table. Her cold fingers closed round his for a fleeting second.

'I love you, too,' he whispered back. 'Always, always.'

By two in the morning the courtyard was full of horses, voices, movement. A number of carriages had been acquired, and some of Yakovlev's own guard brought down the luggage and saw it roped on, with an air of great haste. Thomas came out to speak to Yakovlev, who said that he was afraid the Ekaterinburg delegates had already been wiring their committee at home, suspicious about the move. 'We must get them away at once. Go in and hurry them up, will you?'

Soon the Tsaritsa and her daughter came out, wrapped in furs, followed by Nicholas, with the others who were to go behind them. It was bitterly cold, with that dead, black cold of the middle of the night that makes you feel as though life is ending. Yakovlev came up to the Tsar and said, with concern, 'What? You're only wearing an overcoat?'

'It's all I ever wear,' said Nicholas.

'No, that's out of the question,' Yakovlev said, and ordered one of his men to bring another coat to put round the Tsar's shoulders.

The carriages were far from grand, nothing but crude wooden tarantasses with straw on the floor. The Tsar climbed into the first, and the Tsaritsa would have followed him, but Yakovlev intervened. 'No, I must travel with His Majesty,' he said firmly, and escorted her to the second carriage, where he redeemed himself a little in her eyes by ordering one of his men to bring a mattress to pad the wooden seat for her. She suffered dreadfully from arthritis, and walked with a stick; when it was bad, she had to use a wheeled chair. Marie climbed up beside her; Thomas, Dolgorukov and the doctor got into the third carriage, the servants into a fourth, and at a little before four, the procession rattled out of the yard, with eight rifles of the household guard riding in front and ten of Yakovlev's men behind. Thomas craned out as the carriage lurched forward to see if there might be a glimpse of Olga. But the three girls had given way to tears, and had gone on their parents' request straight to Alexei's room, which had no window on this side. They must be there still, he thought, all sobbing together.

The journey begun in darkness had the flavour of a bad dream in its hurried departure; and even after the sulky sun finally rose, swollen and red, turning the snow to blush, the conditions of the roads prolonged the nightmare. Frozen ground, mud, pockets of snow, sheets of thin ice concealing puddles so deep the horses went in to their bellies; great rocks rolled down by the weight of snow and revealed – or half revealed, which was worse – by its melting; great ruts where expanding ice-water had split the earth during the freezing. It was ground over which to crawl with extreme caution, if one had to travel at all, but Yakovlev had them driven as though the hounds of hell were behind them; and Thomas, thinking of the suspicious Ekaterinburg delegates, supposed he was not wrong. The poor horses lurched and struggled and the wretched passengers were flung from side to side and jounced up and down on the hard wooden seats as the wheels hit ruts and rocks. Thomas thought of the Tsaritsa's arthritis and pitied her from his heart.

They changed horses at eight o'clock, and again at twelve in a tiny village, where they stopped to allow the passengers to stretch their legs for a few minutes, and hot tea was brought to them from the post tavern to go with the cold luncheon of bread and meat they had brought with them. Then it was on again, changing horses every four hours. In the middle of the afternoon a wheel broke, and Yakovlev had to requisition another carriage. It was more primitive even than the crude vehicle it replaced, so the servants went into it and everyone else moved up one. At eight o'clock the procession reached a slightly larger village, and Yakovlev ordered a halt for the night.

'I wish we could keep going,' he confided to Thomas. 'I would ride right through the night, but sixteen hours of such hell in a tarantass is all one can subject the passengers to. God knows how Her Majesty endures it.'

'Early training,' Thomas said. For all her faults, Alexandra had courage, and was steeped in the English attitude, learned in Queen Victoria's court, that a lady never complained of personal discomfort.

The largest house in the village had been the village shop at one time, and Yakovlev requisitioned it. Nicholas and Alexandra had a bed, and Marie a mattress. The rest of them had to sleep on the floor. Thomas, aching all over and with a headache caused by the jolting, thought he would not be able to sleep, but exhaustion overcame him, though he woke every half-hour or so from the pain of lying on floorboards.

The next morning dawned bright, and it was much warmer; and as they travelled closer to the town, the roads improved, though it was still very muddy in the woods where the sun had not had a chance to dry out the ground. The passengers did not get much benefit from the improvement, for their bodies were aching from the abuse of the previous day. They reached Tyumen – the town with the nearest railhead to Tobolsk – that night, under a clear, bright full moon, and a detachment of mounted soldiers at once surrounded them. Thomas felt a moment of panic, but it seemed this was part of Yakovlev's arrangements, for they escorted the party directly to a siding where a train was waiting with steam up. Everyone quitted the carriages with relief, and climbed aboard the train. Inside the accommodation was primitive and not very clean, and there was no water for washing, but there were no complaints. Nicholas, Alexandra and Marie were dirty and dishevelled from the journey, but they paused only to drink some tea and eat some bread and cheese before climbing stiffly into the bunks, covering themselves with the stale-smelling blankets, and falling into exhausted sleep.

Yakovlev, however, was apprehensive. The train had been ready to depart when they arrived, but he said to Thomas, 'I'm worried about Ekaterinburg. I have a feeling we've been followed. And even if we haven't, the railway takes us right through the town.'

Ekaterinburg was on the direct rail route from Tyumen to Moscow. Thomas saw the point. He imagined a barrier across the track and a hostile soviet, backed by the usual rabble of Red Guard, ordering the Tsar and Tsaritsa to dismount, salivating at the thought of getting their hands on them.

'What will you do?' he asked.

'I must consult,' Yakovlev said, frowning with thought. 'There is a telegraph office in town. Do you know how to work a Hughes telegraph? I'd rather not trust the clerk.'

Thomas almost smiled. 'Sadly, that has not been something it came in my way to learn. I wish it had.'

'No matter,' said Yakovlev. 'I'll use my own man. I *think* I can trust him.'

He was away several hours. Thomas had no inclination to get into his bunk, though he ached all over and yearned for proper sleep. The situation seemed too perilous. He thought of the Ekaterinburg delegates shadowing them, like wolves waiting for the fire to die down. He thought of the town up ahead. He thought of Olga, far behind them now. Kobylinsky alone stood between her and the locals. He was twitchy with exhaustion and there seemed menace everywhere, which he could do nothing to avert. Helplessness was the worst aspect of danger.

Yakovlev returned just before five, and Thomas went at once to meet him. 'Well?'

He was grave and preoccupied. 'The danger is real enough.

It's at times like this I wish Russia were not such a big country. A thousand miles to Moscow! Too much opportunity on the way. However,' he shook himself, 'we must do our best, that's all. It is thought wise not to go through Ekaterinburg. We go to Omsk.'

'Omsk?' Thomas said. That was in the wrong direction for Moscow, five hundred miles further east than Ekaterinburg.

'There is another railway line there that will take us to Moscow – rather an indirect route but at least we know the Omsk soviet wishes us no harm. And with luck we can throw our enemies off the scent and lose ourselves in the vastness of Russia – about which I complained a moment before. Get aboard, Colonel. We must waste no more time.'

Yakovlev had the train start off towards Ekaterinburg, because there were, doubtless, many eyes watching them from Tyumen, but after a short distance he ordered all the lights to be extinguished and the train went back the way it had come, passed through Tyumen in darkness and picked up speed, rattling towards Omsk.

When the Romanovs woke in the morning, they soon realised, from the names of the stations they passed through and the position of the sun, that they were heading eastwards. Thomas heard them debating what the change meant. Nicholas thought perhaps they were being taken to Vladivostok instead of Moscow. Well, Vladivostok was a port. Perhaps that would be a safer route than through the heart of Russia. From Vladivostok they might easily go to neutral Japan, or perhaps to Hong Kong, where a British ship could meet them. The conversation and speculation passed the time and cheered them, so Thomas saw no reason to disabuse them.

But the telegraph travels faster than a steam engine, however it may race. The following night they were still some distance from Omsk when they stopped to take on water. Yakovlev got down to stretch his legs and Thomas went with him. They were strolling beside the track, smoking, when a nervous-looking railway worker, a short, thickset man in stained overalls and an oily cap, sidled up to them with the air of one who had secrets to impart. Yakovlev offered the man a cigarette, and this gesture of solidarity was enough to have him unburden himself.

'I thought I ought to warn you,' he said, looking round furtively. 'They're on to you, sir. 'Katrinburg telegraphed to Omsk, saying you was a traitor to the revolution and an outlaw – begging your pardon, sir. They said you was to be stopped and sent back to 'Katrinburg, and the Omsk soviet reckons you must be a renegade, 'cos of going the wrong way for Moscow, so they're going to do it.'

'My orders are from the very top, to take the ex-Tsar to Moscow,' Yakovlev said. 'I was travelling via Omsk because I thought it safer.'

'Bless you, sir, *I* don't care,' the workman said. 'I don't like that lot in 'Katrinburg. Too big for their boots. What do they want with the Little Father anyway? He ought to be sent away somewhere safe, to my mind. I don't hold with harming him. Anyway, I just thought you ought to know.'

'Thank you,' said Yakovlev. 'You're a good fellow.' He slipped a coin to the man, who pocketed it and eased away into the darkness.

'Do you think it's true?' Thomas asked. That was the worst of treachery, that you never knew where it ended. But he couldn't think what sinister motive the man could have had for saying what he had said.

Yakovlev sighed. 'I'm afraid it is. It was always on the cards that Ekaterinburg would try to stop us. The only chance now is to try to persuade Omsk on to our side. I had better go ahead on my own, explain to them why I'm heading east instead of west. I turned them against Ekaterinburg once before, so perhaps I can do it again. You had better stay with the family, Colonel. Your presence is their best surety, in case anyone thinks of attacking.'

Yakovlev had the engine uncoupled from the train, and went on to Omsk to try to reason with the local committee and to use the telegraph again. But he was back before daylight, his face grim.

'It's no good. They won't believe me. I showed them my orders – I even showed them the printed tapes of my telegraph conversations with Moscow. It didn't make any difference. I think the moderates are tired of the whole thing and want to be rid of us, while the more extreme elements of their own committee are turning against them. They're ready to believe Ekaterinburg rather than me. I began to get a distinctly chilly feeling about the neck that they were thinking of clapping me in jail right there and then. I had to promise to take the train back to Ekaterinburg.'

Thomas could see that there was no alternative. Trains could not go across country. If Omsk would not let them through, there was nowhere else to go – and he could see that Yakovlev now knew himself to be in danger. A traitor to the revolution not only could but should be shot. If he could not re-establish his credentials with the revolutionaries, his life was likely to be a short one.

The next morning Nicholas, of course, saw that they were retracing their steps, and called Thomas to ask him what was going on. 'They did not want us to pass through Omsk, sir,' he said. 'We are going back to Ekaterinburg.'

'I see,' Nicholas said. He studied Thomas's face for a moment, and abruptly seemed to decide he did not want to know anything more. A blankness came over his expression, and he dismissed Thomas, and went back to playing bezique with the Tsaritsa, something they did for hours on end to pass the time. The loneliness and boredom of being a prisoner added greatly to the burden of it.

The train was stopped at one point by a barrier across the track, and an excited group of commissars from a local soviet came to meet it, backed by the usual ruffians, some in soldiers' uniform and carrying rifles – probably deserters

– and others armed with sticks and pitchforks. They had heard who the train was carrying and wanted to take them prisoner. What a coup it would be for their obscure little town! The Tsar and Tsaritsa in their own town gaol! Yakovlev had to get down and, at his grandest, argue his way out of a very tight spot. Whatever awaited them in Ekaterinburg, it was better than this mob. He was magnificent, scornful, authoritative, standing square with his hand on his pistol butt, talking and talking, for words were a better weapon against the ignorant than force – which, in any case, the ignorant had more of. Eventually, the locals let them go on, and Thomas was almost amused by their baffled expressions, foiled of their prey and not really understanding how it had happened. But in truth there was nothing to laugh about.

They arrived at last in Ekaterinburg at about half past eight and the train was directed to a goods siding. There, the regional commissar, Beloborodov, arrived in a motor car, and demanded that Yakovlev hand over the Tsar and Tsaritsa to him at once. 'We have a house prepared for them,' he said. 'I will take them in my motor. The rest of them will be sent for later.'

'I will go with them' Yakovlev said.

'You, Colonel,' said Beloborodov harshly, 'will remain where you are until sent for. You will be going before the committee to explain yourself. You have very serious questions to answer. I hope for your sake that you can give satisfactory reasons for your actions, but I cannot imagine what they may be.' The hard eyes slid over Thomas, who felt a chill down his spine, in spite of himself. 'Who is this?'

'Colonel Overton, of the British Army,' Yakovlev said, tactfully leaving out the 'lord'. 'He was the liaison officer at the former imperial court, and has remained with the family ever since, at the behest of the British government.'

There was calculation in the cold examination, but after a moment Beloborodov said, 'I have no jurisdiction over officers of the British Army. You had better report yourself to the British consulate in the town, Colonel Overton. The consul's name is Sir Thomas Preston. No doubt he will have fresh orders for you.'

Nicholas and Alexandra climbed down from the train and were helped into Beloborodov's motor, and driven away. After a time, another motor came for Yakovlev. He shook Thomas's hand, gave him a meaningful look, then stepped into the car and was driven away without a backward glance. Thomas wondered what would happen to him, and hoped hard that he would be able to talk his way out of trouble. He was too good a man to be wasted.

Eventually other motors arrived, the rest of the household and the luggage were loaded, and they drove off through the wide, empty streets. Ekaterinburg was an important town, capital of the Urals and formerly the site of the Imperial Mint, set in the centre of a mineral- and gold-mining area. Gold and fur trading had made the local merchants rich, and there were many large houses in the town. That to which the Romanovs were taken had belonged to a merchant called Ipatiev. It was near the centre, in the wide Voznesensky Avenue, a two-storey house of white stucco, with a semi-basement because it was set into a slight slope. It was imposing in its way, and might have been pleasant enough when it was a private residence, but a tall wooden palisade had been built round it, close up to the façade, and now it looked what indeed it was: a prison.

The motors drew up outside, and some guards came at once to unload the trunks, to take them away to be searched. The servants were passed inside, and Dr Botkin followed, but when Prince Dolgorukov tried to enter, the commissar, Goloshchokin, who had been talking to the guards' captain, turned and said, 'You will oblige me by getting back into the motor, Citizen Dolgorukov. We have other accommodation for you.' Dolgorukov did not at once obey, and the commissar jerked his head to the captain, who stepped

300

forward and laid a hand on Dolgorukov's arm. 'If you please, citizen,' Goloshchokin repeated.

Dolgorukov had no choice but to allow himself to be escorted by the two of them back to the car. As he passed Thomas, he gave him an urgent look, and whispered in French, 'Stay with them!'

While the attention was on the prince Thomas tried, with an air of insouciance, to walk into the house, hoping that once he was inside, they would assume he was meant to be there and allow him to stay. But the commissar had eyes in the back of his head. As he reached the sentry, the commissar said, 'Not you, Colonel.' The guard stepped into Thomas's path.

Thomas turned to face Goloshchokin, who gave him a grim but not unhumorous look. 'There is no accommodation for you, Colonel. You must find a billet elsewhere. And if I were you, I should stay there. The Romanovs are no concern of yours any more. There's nothing here for you to do now. Why don't you go home, while you still can?'

'I am a soldier, sir,' Thomas said. 'I don't choose when I go home.'

Goloshchokin shrugged, and walked past him into the house. The motor with the prince inside it roared away, the door in the palisade was slammed shut, and Thomas was left alone in the empty street. The Tsar and Tsaritsa were now prisoners indeed.

CHAPTER FOURTEEN

On the 7th of April, Captain Wentworth managed to get a transport from Doullens to St Omer, in the company of his friend Captain Ward. From there he scrounged a lift out to Unit 8, and he was waiting, leaning against a hut wall in the vehicle park, hands stuffed in his pockets, when Emma came in on her ambulance. Benson knew him at once, and sprang out of the cab in a flying leap that would have done credit to a gazelle before Emma could stop and get down.

'He remembers me,' Wentworth said, by way of greeting.

'He'd have been an ungrateful wretch if he hadn't,' Emma said. She felt suddenly shy and could not look directly at Wentworth, so bent instead to join in the stroking of the dog. 'How do you think he seems?'

'Much better than when he lived with us. I believe you must be spoiling him. And what a smart new collar!' His caressing hand bumped into Emma's, and she snatched hers away as if stung. Their eyes met, and he was intrigued and not displeased to see the blush spread across her face, though this time she made herself hold his gaze.

'I wanted to make sure someone would bring him back if he got lost,' she said, 'but he never goes very far from me.'

'Wise dog,' Wentworth said, and then was sorry he had, because her blush intensified and she lowered her eyes again. 'How are you all?' he asked heartily. 'Have you been busy?'

'Yes, very,' she said, relieved at the new tack. 'We've been out every day since the offensive started, though of course it's not as bad here as further south. I believe they've been absolutely swamped at Étaples. How's everyone in the Thirty-seventh?'

'Well, we took some heavy hits,' he said. 'We lost about fifty, killed and wounded. And poor Linzer, of course, I told you about.'

'Yes, that was awful. We heard from the Casino that he's been shipped back to England. They think he'll live, but they don't know what damage has been caused.'

'It's a wretched business,' Wentworth said, glad that she was looking at him again. 'Look here, I came down with Ward, and we have to go back tomorrow, but we thought it would be nice for us, and a species of charity on your part, if you and a couple of chums would have dinner with us tonight in St Omer. Apart from Ward and me there's a very decent RAMC officer we've met, who fortunately has a motor-car, so we could come down and pick you up, and bring you back afterwards.'

'It's very kind of you—' Emma began, and he interrupted with a comical look.

'No, no, you don't understand. The kindness will be on your part, because we're all going mad for want of civilised dining, which requires female company, so this is purely a charitable act on your part, and the enjoyment will be on ours. I'm afraid it doesn't make it sound like a very attractive proposition, put that way, but I find it's always best to be honest on these occasions.'

She laughed. 'You're such a fool, Wentworth!'

'Ah, but you can't resist me, can you? Have you two kind-hearted, short-sighted friends you can call on?'

'Why short-sighted?'

'We shouldn't like them to be put off by the deficiencies of our toilet, so it's best if they are well-meaning but myopic. However, failing that, any two ladies willing to put up with us will do.'

'I think I can manage that,' Emma said, still laughing.

'Excellent. Then shall we collect you at six o'clock? Can you be ready by then? We can have a drink first at the officers' club. Since you have to be back in by ten, we need to start earlyish.'

'I shan't let you down,' she assured him.

Armstrong knew Wentworth and Ward from her Calais days, and she and Bullock were delighted at the idea of an evening out and dinner with masculine conversation.

'Wouldn't it be heaven to put on an evening dress again?' Bullock sighed. 'Sometimes I get very tired of khaki – although it does cover a multitude of sins. I must have put on half a stone since I came to France. I can't think how, when the food is so ghastly.'

'It's because there's nothing else to do but eat,' said Armstrong.

'I suppose so. One must take comfort where one finds it. But I shan't be able to get into anything after the war. I'll have to have a whole new wardrobe.'

'I'm sure that will give you great pain,' Armstrong said gravely.

Emma smiled, but said, 'Can you imagine going into shops again, and having new clothes – *and* somewhere to wear them?'

'Too much of a stretch,' said Bullock. 'Do you think it's possible that we'll go on fighting the Germans for ever?'

'No, it will all be over once the Americans join in,' said Armstrong.

'Oh, the Yanks. I'm not sure I believe in them. I've never seen one. Do they actually exist?'

The men arrived right on time, and there were introductions all round. The RAMC officer was a nice, gently spoken man, a little older than the others, perhaps in his mid-thirties, a tall man with a lean face, dark hair and quick, noticing eyes. He seemed to take an instant liking to Armstrong, and she responded to him, Emma noticed.

She had told Emma on a previous occasion that she did not like to be taller than the man she was being escorted by, and that as she was herself tall, it limited her choice. Captain Savile overtopped her by half a head, and she liked his gentle demeanour. Ward was very happy to offer his arm to the bubbly Bullock, and they were soon chatting together like old friends, which left Wentworth free to concentrate on Emma.

They had drinks at the officers' club, where Ward made a point of indicating several American officers in the room to Bullock, who had evidently expressed her doubts to him on the way over in the motor. He even offered to go and catch one and bring him back for inspection. Bullock giggled and denied she could see the men he was pointing to, upon which he actually left the group and went to accost a tall stranger on the other side of the room and, after an earnest conversation, brought him back.

'Major Schulz, US Artillery,' he presented the stranger. 'Major, may I make you known to Trooper Bullock of the First Aid Nursing Yeomanry, who believes that America does not exist – and also that the earth is flat and the sun revolves around it?'

Bullock was laughing, but tried to look outraged. 'How can you be so rude? Please forgive Captain Ward, Major. He was dropped on his head as a baby.'

The major bowed charmingly, and said, 'There's no need to apologise, ma'am. I have to confess that until I came out here a week ago, I hardly believed that Europe existed. Actually to find myself here in France – I have to keep pinching myself to make sure I'm not dreaming! And I've never yet been to England, so I only have other people's word for it that it's there.'

'Now, isn't that exactly what I said about America?' Bullock pronounced, with great satisfaction. 'You see, Ward? How do you find France now you're here, Major?'

'Most beautiful, ma'am, only rather too full of Dutchmen

– but we mean to do something about that.' He bowed again. 'I'd better get back to my party, but it's been an honour to meet you, and do my bit to convince you we're real.'

When he was gone, Bullock said, 'What did he mean about Dutchmen?'

'A lot of the Americans I've met here call the Germans Dutchmen or Dutch,' Savile said. 'I think it's from the word "*Deutsch*" – *Deutsch*-men, you see. Of course,' he added, 'it's always possible they don't know there's a difference. America is a very long way away, and only someone who knew would associate the word Dutch with Holland, after all.'

'Yes, why *are* Holland people called Dutch?' Bullock said.

'Why are Americans called Yanks, come to that?' said Ward, and the conversation wandered off on those lines, ending with the revelation that the small Portuguese contingent was known to the Tommies as Pork-and-beans, while the officers tended to refer to them as the Goose.

'We had them on our right when we were at Armentières,' Wentworth said. 'I can't say it was a happy experience. Shocking soldiers – no sentries set, sleep all night with their boots off, rusty rifles. It's a good job Armentières is a quiet sector.'

'They shouldn't be here at all, poor things,' Savile said. 'They've no interest in the war to begin with, they're not properly trained, and they haven't any trench expertise. That's why they've put them on the Lys plain. It doesn't dry out until May, so there's no chance of an attack there before that, and they'll rotate them out by the end of the month.'

'I hope they rotate us back in,' said Wentworth. 'Ah, Armentières of fond memory! Would I had never left you!'

They decamped shortly after that to the restaurant Fleur-de-lys, where a table was waiting for them, and they dined on excellent onion soup, some rather tough beef with fried potatoes, and a blue cheese served with dried figs and dates, all washed down with a hearty wine from the southern regions of France. Savile had visited Settes quite frequently before the war and described some of the famous places down there, such as Avignon, Narbonne and Nîmes; while Wentworth mentioned the Camargue region, where he had been taken by his parents as a child. Emma listened, enthralled, to his description of the white horses, black bulls and pink flamingos. It seemed quite another sort of France from the shabby restaurant in St Omer, and the army-trampled areas she was familiar with.

'It's a pity,' he said, when she mentioned the thought, 'that for a whole generation of us, this is what France will mean to us. When the war's over, we ought to make a point of visiting the parts the war hasn't touched.'

He was looking at Emma as he said it, and for a moment she thought of going on a tour with him, and how wonderful that would be. And then she recollected herself, and dragged her eyes away, and said, 'I don't suppose, after the war, that any of us will *want* to come back.'

'Yes, too many memories,' said Bullock. 'Poor old France – tarred with a horrid brush.'

'Nonsense,' said Armstrong. 'I'd come back. My parents used to take my sister and me on holiday in Brittany years ago. There's the most wonderful beach at a place called St Malo where I used to make sandcastles.'

'I know it,' said Wentworth. 'Very like Bournemouth, I thought – except for the plumbing.'

So it ended in laughter.

The evening was over too soon, and their ten o'clock curfew seemed an imposition.

'But no doubt we'll be busy again tomorrow,' Armstrong said, 'so we ought to get some sleep.'

'And we'll have to be off very early, too,' Ward said. 'The lift we've arranged to take us back leaves at five o'clock, or some such ungodly hour.'

'When will you be able to get away again?' Emma asked Wentworth quietly. They were squashed together on the back seat, and she rather liked the warmth of his male body so close to her, although she didn't allow herself to think in those terms. He was a friend, nothing more; but definitely a male friend. One needed male friends as well as female, didn't one?

'I'm not sure. We ought to be on rest for a fortnight, so I might be able to come down again next week. But then we'll be going back into the line, and I'm not due any leave until July. Still,' he said, brightening, 'you never know what may happen. One can be sent on special courses, or to take messages – all sorts of reasons one might find oneself in the area.'

'Well,' Emma said gravely, 'you know my address. I shall instruct the servant to say I am at home, should you call.'

'I didn't know you'd taught Benson to talk,' he replied, equally gravely.

At the camp, they all got out to shake hands and make their goodbyes, and Emma heard Armstrong and Captain Savile agreeing to meet again, and thought that it was nice for her that Savile was stationed so handily at St Omer.

Emma gave Wentworth her hand, and he took it in both of his for a moment. 'Thank you for this evening,' he said.

'I've enjoyed it,' she said.

'Me too. I wish – oh, well, there's no sense in that sort of talk. Will you write to me?'

'If you'll write back.'

He nodded, and let go of her hand rather abruptly. 'Take care of yourself, Trooper,' he said. 'Come on, you fellows. We must let the ladies go in before they get into trouble.'

In her cubicle, reassuring the frantic Benson that she had never meant to abandon him *permanently*, she wondered whether Wentworth was developing feelings for her beyond friendship, and whether that was why he had left so suddenly. Perhaps, if that was the case, she ought not to write to him. It would be unfair to encourage him. But then, she told herself, he knew what the situation was, he knew about her and Fenniman, and he proceeded at his own hazard.

Lennie was in the line near Sailly, just south of Armentières, from which the river Lys ran through Estaires and Merville, and in canalised form down to St Omer. He could have told anyone who asked that, contrary to previous experience, the Lys plain had dried out by the time he got there in late March. However, no-one was expecting an attack, and while some were congratulating themselves on being in a quiet part of the line when the action was going on to the south around St Quentin, Lennie was quite disappointed about it. Having been out of the war for months with an injury and then sent to Salonika, he had been hoping for another chance to shoot some Germans, because the sooner the Boche were defeated, the sooner he could get back to Morland Place and court Polly. She had been damnably taken up with that smooth wretch Holford last summer, and all the time he was away he was imagining him, or some other plausible rogue, hanging around her and stealing her heart.

So he was as surprised as anyone, but less immediately upset, when, just after four a.m. on the 9th of April, the Germans began an intense bombardment to the south of them, towards Laventie. The earth of the dugout he was sharing with the other officers of his company trembled continuously with the weight of the gunfire. His captain, Crozier, was out of his cot in a second.

'That's more than just routine hate. I'll lay any money the Germans are going to attack. I'm going to telephone HQ. Manning, you come with me. The rest of you, get to your posts.'

They scrambled along the communication trenches to the telephone pit, with the sky lit as if by a bonfire. Crozier had a terse conversation with the colonel at Battalion HQ, then turned to Lennie.

'The CO says he can't raise the Portuguese on our right. It seems the lines are cut already, and that's where the heaviest of the shelling is, so it looks as if the Boche mean to attack the Goose and try to break through there. The CO wants me to go to Goose HQ right away and find out what's happening. You'd better come with me.'

It was about a quarter to five when they set out by motor on the main road that ran past Sailly to Estaires. Though it was still officially dark, the light from the bombardment over to the south lit the way eerily, so the driver hardly needed the slit of light through his painted-over headlamps. After a few moments, the driver remarked, 'We're goin' into it, sir.' And when they reached the outskirts of Estaires, it was being heavily shelled. The very air vibrated with the explosions, and the noise of the shells screaming overhead was worse than anything Lennie had experienced before. He discovered his long absence from the Western Front had softened him: he didn't like it at all.

Portuguese Headquarters was at Lestrem, beyond and to the south of Estaires, and the main road crossed the Lys in a northerly direction, ran through Estaires, then crossed the river again going south. 'I don't like the idea of going through that,' Crozier shouted, to be heard above the noise. 'Batty, is there another road? Can we avoid Estaires?'

'Dunno, sir,' Batty shouted back. 'But I reckon there must be. There's another village, La George, this side of the river. Must be a road through that, though I dunno if it joins the main road after.'

'Let's try it,' Crozier said, and added to Lennie, 'That's La Gorgue. I remember it on the map.'

When they came to the bridge, Batty swung the car southwards on the Lens road, and sure enough there was a turning almost immediately to the right, signposted for La Gorgue. It was a rough country road, and the car bounced and jolted as they hit ruts, before they reached the cobbles of the village outskirts. But even avoiding going through Estaires did not mean a quiet passage. The shells were shrieking overhead and explosions were coming from all sides of them now. As they ran through the centre of the village, a shell hit the house they were just passing and blew the back part away with an explosion that made Lennie's ears ring and his teeth jam together; then – almost slowly, it seemed – the front of the house and the one next to it collapsed gracefully into the street. Crozier screamed something incoherent at Batty, but the driver needed no prompting. He slammed his foot on the accelerator and the car shot forward as bricks and stones rained down on them, bouncing off the metalwork and their helmets, and small shards of hard, ancient mortar shot past them like shrapnel, followed by a cloud of plaster dust. Lennie's cheek was cut, his head rang from a ding on his helmet, and they were all coughing from the plaster cloud, as Batty hurled the motor through the right-angled turns of the typical village street, and more houses exploded behind them.

They were out at last into the comparative quiet of the open country beyond.

'By God, that was a close one,' Crozier said. 'Closer than I like. But I'm forgetting – you were on the Somme in 'sixteen, weren't you? I suppose that was pretty hot?'

'Can't remember much about it, to be honest, sir,' Lennie said, as one did.

'Makes me feel quite a new boy, thinking of what you've seen already,' Crozier said. 'That must be Lestrem up ahead. Oh, good God, they're shelling that now!'

The German gunlayers must have raised their elevation, for now shells were falling not only on Lestrem but away towards Merville. As they neared the chateau where Portuguese Headquarters was sited, a huge explosion lifted the motor off the road for a second, and almost blinded them with its brilliance. Moments later they pulled into the courtyard, and saw that the chateau had taken a direct hit.

Half the roof was gone, and on that side the three storeys were reduced to one.

They scrambled out and headed for the main entrance. Inside, the hall was undamaged, though the air was full of dust. There were desks and telephone equipment, maps and papers, so this had evidently been the main operations room. There was no-one there, however, except for three British officers, one of whom was attending to the needs of an elderly gentleman sitting on a hard chair by the fireplace.

'Hello,' said one of the officers, a major. 'What are you bods doing here?'

Crozier introduced them. 'Our CO couldn't raise the Goose – I beg pardon – the Portuguese unit to our right, where the shelling was heaviest. He told us to come to Portuguese HQ.' He looked round hopefully.

The major smiled cynically. 'This is it. I mean, we are it. The Goose has flown – all except the general there, bless him, who was just coming out of his bedroom when the first shell came down and almost blew his epaulettes off. Oh, don't worry, he doesn't speak much English, and he's quite deaf – even deafer since the shell exploded, poor old dear.'

Lennie looked across at the general – elderly and white-haired, with large white moustaches and eyebrows, like four blanched prawns in his pale face, but sitting very upright, and still dignified in his full uniform, despite the dust and plaster on its shoulders.

'We're giving him a brandy or two, prior to telling him he's on his own – but I think he's beginning to realise that.'

'His staff is all gone?' Crozier asked.

'Every bird of it. Flew away as soon as the bombardment began. *We* couldn't stop 'em. We're British Liaison, and we'd like to know what's going on at the Front as much as anyone, but the lines are down and we can't raise anyone. If the experience here is anything to go by, I should think our oldest ally is in full retreat. Your unit's on their left, then?'

'Yes, sir.'

At that moment another British officer burst in, a very irate captain, beating dust off his shoulders as he spoke. 'What the devil's going on? Where's Goose HQ?'

The major, who seemed almost to be enjoying his position as doomsayer, answered languidly, 'This is the Goose's nest, but you're too late. The bird has flown.'

'Dammit! I beg your pardon, sir, but we're being heavily attacked at Laventie, and the Portuguese on our left are gone. We've been trying to raise their HQ, but – nothing!'

'Attacked? You mean the Germans are moving?'

'They are, and even if we hold 'em, with the Portuguese gone we'll be outflanked. Who are you?' he asked abruptly, turning on Lennie.

Crozier answered. 'Crozier, Fourth Yorks. We're at Sailly.'

'Well, you may not be much longer,' said the captain, grimly. 'They're shelling Sailly now, and all the way to Croix-du-Bac. That's where your headquarters are, isn't it?'

'Yes,' said Crozier. 'They're shelling us now? There was nothing coming over when we left.'

'It's my belief the Boche knew exactly who was in the line in front of them. They attacked the Goose first, knowing they'd fold, and now they're extending the attack up and down the line. If I were you—'

'You're right,' Crozier anticipated. 'We must get back. Come on, Manning.'

Outside, it was clear that the battle had spread, and that getting back would be a great deal more difficult than coming here had been. The bombardment had been extended, and the fact that it was hitting places further behind the line suggested that the infantry advance had started.

'Look here,' Crozier said, 'if anything happens to me, you've got to get back and let them know what we know. Don't stop for anything – understand?'

It took them four hours to get back to Croix-du-Bac, where the outward journey had taken three-quarters of an hour. By then they were very dirty, very thirsty and very hungry. But there was no time to waste on frivolities like eating. As soon as they had reported, they hurried back to their company, which was already engaged with the enemy. Lennie rejoined his platoon, and was almost relieved to have something to do, rather than passively enduring the bombardment as he had been all morning. There was fierce fighting, and they managed to hold the position until around noon, for a reserve battalion of the 40th had moved in and partially plugged the gap left by the Portuguese, but the Germans had taken too good a hold there, and eventually the order came to fall back.

There began for Lennie a period of the sort of warfare Bertie could have described to him, had they been able to meet, of falling back and fighting in the open, finding cover and being driven out of it, holding the line for a time with oddments of other units gathering together at some defensible point, of no sleep, and living off the land. It was exhausting, it was frightening, but in a way Lennie felt more alive than he had at any time in his life. His past experience now made him an invaluable officer, and as casualties mounted he found himself, willy-nilly, commanding an ever-increasing band of survivors. But he had no time to think of that. Staying alive was the order of the day; staying alive and preventing the Hun from passing.

The situation in April was more serious than it had been in March, for the attack around St Quentin had happened a long way from the sea, and there was room to fall back, plenty of open countryside to absorb the force of the German advance. But the attack on the Lys, which quickly spread northwards all the way to Ypres, was too close to the coast for comfort. If the Germans broke through, there was a real danger that they might reach the sea and take the Channel ports, and then the game would be up.

Now, back home, the public was again hearing the names

314

of famous places being taken by the enemy: Armentières, Estaires, Sailly, Merville, the Messines Ridge – the Passchendaele Ridge, which had been fought for with such blood and pain only the year before. By the 16th, the Second Army was once again defending a tight semi-circle around Ypres, and vowing, like the French at Verdun, that 'they will not pass'.

The seriousness of the situation was proved on the 11th of April: the Commander-in-Chief, Field Marshal Sir Douglas Haig, issued a Special Order, addressed to 'All Ranks of the British Army in France and Flanders':

Three weeks ago today the enemy began his terrific attacks against us on a fifty-mile front. His objects are to separate us from the French, to take the Channel Ports and destroy the British Army.

In spite of throwing already 106 Divisions into the battle and enduring the most reckless sacrifice of human life, he has as yet made little progress towards his goals. We owe this to the determined fighting and self-sacrifice of our troops. Words fail me to express the admiration which I feel for the splendid resistance offered by all ranks of our Army under the most trying circumstances.

Many amongst us are now tired. To those I would say that Victory will belong to the side which holds out the longest. The French Army is moving rapidly and in great force to our support. There is no course open to us but to fight it out. Every position must be held to the last man: there must be no retirement. With our backs to the wall and believing in the justice of our cause each one of us must fight on to the end. The safety of our homes and the Freedom of mankind alike depend upon the conduct of each one of us at this critical moment.

That their dour and reserved commander, famed for his clipped delivery, suppressed emotions and economy with words, should think fit to send out such an eloquent appeal to every soldier in the army, especially when he had never done anything like it before in nearly four years of war, impressed everyone with the gravity of the crisis. But the Special Order itself had a mixed reception. At home, the newspapers printed it with admiration and acclaim. In the field, many, particularly the newcomers, felt braced by it, and inspired to a new determination. The veterans, though, didn't heed it too much, feeling they didn't need to be told to fight on to the last man, since that was what they did anyway. Many, fighting it out in open country, never even heard that there had been such an address; others had it read aloud to them by their officer and, on being told their backs were to the wall, looked around them at the bits of battered hedge that were their only shelter and muttered, 'What f—g wall?'

The collapse of the Portuguese let the Germans through, and the army on either side of the gap had to retire to avoid being outflanked, until there was a salient about six miles deep centred on Armentières. And as this country had been quite densely populated with farmers and villagers, a stream of panic-stricken civilians was soon complicating the issue.

For Emma and the others at Unit 8, there now began a period so busy and fraught with anxiety and effort that anything they had witnessed before paled into insignificance. For the fighting, unlike that of March, was now on their doorstep. All the hospitals in the area were evacuated, which meant that for forty-eight hours they worked non-stop, running a shuttle service taking the occupants from the hospitals to the station. Meanwhile, ambulance trains still came in bearing wounded from the Front, and soon casualties were so heavy that the troop trains were pressed into service as well. Called Temporary Ambulance Trains, or TATs, they took reinforcements up, and came down loaded with wounded, whose condition was often exacerbated by having to sit with severe wounds in ordinary compartments.

The casualty clearing stations fell back as the Germans advanced, and provided the immediate treatment before the wounded were loaded onto trains and barges for the next stage of their journey.

Various headquarters had to fall back, too, and soon the town was full of them, and of exhausted troops sent for a few days' respite before returning to the Front. The crowded streets were full of refugees, and out on the main road they stumbled along between the masses of military traffic, so utterly bewildered and miserable it tore at the girls' hearts to have to pass them by. Some came in on the few trains that civilians were allowed to ride, and were turned out in the town because their places were needed from there on for the wounded. Others got lifts on lorries, squeezed in by some sympathetic driver, but most came on foot, with what they had managed to salvage tied to a cart or piled into the baby's pram. The women were often in their best clothes – the only way to save them was to wear them – which somehow made it all the more pathetic. They were so dazed by their flight they were in danger of being run down, as they hardly heeded the lorries and artillery thundering past them.

And still the wounded came, in trains, in lorries, in barges, in cattle trucks, on handcarts, on their own feet, supported by a 'mate' – a seemingly unstaunchable flood. Men in torn, bloody uniforms, blood-soaked bandages, men grimed with smoke, or white with blood-loss, all looking so utterly dead-beat it added to the sense of peril. The ambulances were always sticky with drips and pools of blood. The men were coming in straight from the fighting now, in uniforms stained from the country they had fought over, often with the wound not even bandaged. Some were glued to the canvas of the stretcher by their own congealing blood. Many were going to die, and some were dead already. Every morning several ambulances had to ferry the previous night's dead to the mortuary, an unhappy task since there was no time now to lay them out or even cover them, and the bodies

317

were often a terrible sight, covered with more blood than it was possible to imagine, one with a missing foot, one with half of its skull gone, one with the inside of the mouth horribly visible where the cheek was torn away, one with the bone of the leg sticking out of the flesh in three places . . .

Exhaustion numbed the shock somewhat, but they lived in a nightmare world, like a mediaeval painting of hell. There was no off-duty, no time to rest; often the only sleep they could snatch was by lying on a stretcher in the ambulance while they waited for a train to come in. One evening Emma and Armstrong cut each other's hair short, for it was impossible to find time or water to wash it, and they couldn't bear it as it was any longer. Neither was very good with the scissors, but it was a relief to be rid of it, and the FANY cap hid the ragged results. At least they did not go hungry. Their own cookhouse staff set up an extra buffet in the station yard so that they could get something to eat while waiting for the train, and often the cooks would send the drivers off with a bacon sandwich to carry with them in case of emergencies.

Once Emma was sent to pick up a headquarters staff and take them to a new safe place on the other side of St Omer. She became aware, for the first time in days, of how badly the ambulance needed cleaning from the way the first few officers sniffed as they got in, and put their hands over their noses. When the colonel finally appeared, he stared at her in amazement. 'Good God, a woman!' he exclaimed. He seemed quite young to her for a colonel, but his face was so careworn it was plain he would soon shed what youth he had. 'You shouldn't be here,' he said, almost angrily.

'I was told to pick you up, sir,' Emma said patiently, too tired to object to his rudeness, 'and take you to Nordausques.'

'No, I mean you shouldn't be *here*, so near the fighting. It isn't safe. It isn't decent. As for driving ambulances – it's man's work.'

'There aren't enough men to go round,' she said, putting the ambulance into gear and edging out into the traffic.

'You'll have to move out. Dammit, we're not fighting this war to expose our women to this sort of thing. You'll all have to evacuate.'

'I'm sorry, sir, we're just too busy to leave at the moment. Maybe when the rush dies down.'

'I shall speak to the divisional commander about this,' he said. His anger seemed to buoy him. The others were sitting limply, too tired even to smoke.

Emma didn't answer his last remark. There seemed nothing to say. She just wanted to get to Nordausques as quickly as possible and get rid of them so that she could rejoin the convoy. She resented, now, being taken off ferrying the wounded to drive men with the use of their own legs.

Small pieces of news broke through the haze of exhaustion. On the evening of the 16th of April, the story came back that during the afternoon when Albert, which was occupied by the Germans, was being shelled by the British, there was a direct hit on the damaged tower of the basilica and the Hanging Virgin had finally crashed down into the square. Emma heard some wounded Tommies discussing it, and arguing about what the legend actually *had* said. One, gloomily, believed that the side who finally brought her down were doomed to lose the war; others said it was only that the war couldn't end until she did fall; and one ingenious lad said *he* had heard that the side in occupation of Albert at the time of the fall would be the ones to lose.

On the 21st, it was heard that Baron Manfred von Richthofen, the German air ace famed as the Red Baron, because his Albatros was painted red and his whole flight had some bit of red about their aeroplanes, had been shot down and killed in the Somme region. He had been attempting to claim his eighty-first victim. No-one seemed to know which British pilot had accounted for him at last, but there was, curiously, a little melancholy in the pride and

319

satisfaction with which the story was told. Though he had been on the wrong side, he had been a sort of hero.

And on the 23rd of April – St George's Day – the Royal Navy attacked the German-occupied Belgian ports of Zeebrugge and Ostende, with the intention of sinking block-ships in the mouths of the harbours to stop the Germans using them as U-boat pens. The operation, against heavy resistance, was counted a success, and there was great celebration in the country at large and the navy in particular: stirring sea-stories had been few in this war. It cheered everybody up to think of Nelson's navy bearding the Germans in their den.

But still the fighting went on, the Germans crept nearer, the wounded poured into St Omer, and the FANY drivers toiled back and forth. Towards the end of the month the fighting reached Hazebrouck, only twelve or fifteen miles away. They could hear and feel the shelling now, and sometimes German aeroplanes came over in night raids and bombed the roads and the various camps. Now the girls of Unit 8 felt they were really in the front line, but they were too busy even to think about evacuating. 'When we have time to take a bath,' Thompson said, 'we'll have time to think about that.' Emma disliked the shelling much more than she worried about the bombing. She felt sure that it was extremely unlikely a bomb would find a small target like her; but if the Germans got any nearer and started shelling St Omer, she felt she would start to worry – on Benson's account, if not her own. In her dreamlike state of exhaustion, she thought that death would mean she would see Fenniman again, but she wasn't sure (she sometimes debated it to herself in a mad sort of way as she drove the heavy ambulance through the crowded streets) whether dogs had an after-life. And she hated to think of Benson's being left alone, and made Armstrong and Bullock promise to look after him if she was killed.

She hadn't heard anything from Wentworth since he had

gone up to the line and, of course there was fighting now from Ypres all the way down to Amiens: Villers-Bretonneux was taken by the Germans on the 24th, though it was recaptured the next day in splendid style by a joint attack of British and Australian troops, at heavy cost. The line at Amiens stabilised there: and in what was now being called the Lys offensive, the Germans were again running out of steam.

On the morning of the 26th, Emma was driving an ambulance-load of corpses to the mortuary when someone in a motor standing at the side of the road hailed her. Looking across she saw it was Lord Knoydart. She pulled the ambulance off the road, jumped down, and walked back to meet him halfway between the vehicles. His left arm and shoulder were heavily swathed in grubby bandages, one of which formed a sling to immobilise the arm against the chest.

'Knoydart, you're wounded,' she said.

'Oh, it's just a scratch,' he said automatically.

'I can see that it isn't. Tell me the truth. What happened?'

'I was careless enough to get caught by a shell,' he said lightly. 'Piece of shrapnel took a chunk out of my shoulder. Stupid, really. So I've had to leave the chaps. But how are you? I'm amazed to find you here. I've been thinking of you safely tucked away in Calais, and here you are in the thick of it.'

She told him how she had changed units.

'But surely you shouldn't still be here,' he said anxiously. 'They've been evacuating all the non-combatant units.'

'I know,' she said, with grim humour. 'I keep having to ferry headquarters staff to places of safety. But our unit is simply too busy to go. Someone must drive the wounded.'

'Speaking of which,' he said, with a guilty look at her ambulance.

'Oh, no, don't worry about them. They're beyond complaint now. I'm on my way to the mortuary.'

She was half sorry for speaking so lightly, for he looked

really distressed. But it seemed to be on her account rather than her passengers'. 'You shouldn't have to do things like that,' he said; and then, before she could speak, gave her a rueful smile. 'I'm sorry, I shouldn't have said that. You tore me off a strip last time for saying something like it.'

'Oh, hardly,' she protested.

'Let me say instead that I think you're perfectly splendid for doing what you do, and all of us in the army ought to be eternally grateful to you FANYs.'

'Never mind that,' Emma said. 'Where are you off to? To have that shoulder looked at, I hope.'

'Yes. We'd just stopped so that the driver could – um – relieve himself. The poor fellow has a problem. He's taking me to the station, where he should be picking up some fresh subalterns come out from England – poor blighters. What a point to be pitched into it!'

'But you're out of the game now?'

'I'm afraid so. The arm's quite useless at the moment, so I suppose they'll send me home to Blighty for a week or two.'

'Don't sound so regretful. Most people I drive would be delighted.'

'Would they? But I hate to leave the chaps. They've been so splendid. You can't imagine how they've fought – like tigers.'

'I'm sure,' Emma said, rather touched at his enthusiasm.

'But it can't last much longer,' he went on. 'This phase, at any rate.'

'Really? You think the advance is being halted?'

'I'm sure of it. We're holding the Germans now. My unit was in front of a wood just beyond Hazebrouck, and we thought the Germans were going to come storming out, but they didn't. The attack has run out of steam, and I can tell you why. Half the Hun troops are dead drunk, and the other half are unfit for combat. There's a huge depot of wine and spirits that we passed as we were falling back, and I'll lay any money they got into it.'

'We heard that was happening last month in the advance from St Quentin.'

'Well, it's happening again. They guzzle it like lemonade when they find it. We've seen them in the distance, walking along with their rifles slung over their shoulders and each man carrying a whisky bottle and drinking from it.' He smiled suddenly. 'You might say that if the offensive is stalling it's not from a lack of German spirit but from an excess of Scottish spirit!' Emma laughed. 'At any rate, we're holding them, and I don't think they're going to get any further.'

'I'm glad to hear it.' She shuddered. 'I hate the sound of the shelling. I don't want them to be shelling me.'

'God forbid,' Knoydart said. He swayed a little, and Emma noticed that he was very pale, and there was a little sweat on his brow.

'You shouldn't be standing here talking to me,' she said sternly. 'You must go and get seen to. I can see you're quite knocked up.'

'I'm sorry,' he said. 'I think I shall have to go and sit down. Feel a bit woozy. Silly thing.'

'Not silly at all. Go on back to your car. I'm glad to have seen you, Knoydart. I wish you well, and a speedy recovery.'

'I wish I weren't going home and could take you out to dinner,' he said. 'But as it is . . .'

'Next time,' Emma said, giving him a little push.

'Really?'

'Really. When you're back in France. Good luck!'

'Take care of yourself,' he said, and turned away. She watched him climb back into the motor, and a moment later waved to him as he was driven past her. Then she went back to her ambulance and the eager greetings of Benson, who had been watching carefully to see she didn't stray too far from him.

An attack in the Ypres area on the 29th proved the last thrust of the Lys offensive. As Knoydart had said, the

Germans had run out of steam again, at least partly because of the stocks of wine and spirits they came upon, to which they were totally unused and over which their officers seemed to have no control. The line stabilised again, with a salient of about ten miles' depth centred on Armentières. But for Emma and the others at Unit 8, the work hardly slackened. The fighting went on on the new line, and the wounded kept coming down; and as April turned into May, the air-raids increased. To the wounded from the line were added the victims of bombings; and as the weather warmed up, the work had to be done in conditions of unpleasant stickiness. The war, Emma was reminded daily, was not over yet by a long chalk.

CHAPTER FIFTEEN

Venetia found the latest coded letter from Thomas waiting for her when she returned from operating a list at the New Hospital. Though she was hot and tired and longing for a bath and perhaps a glass of sherry before dinner, she took it straight to her office to decipher it. The news that the Romanovs were prisoners in the hands of an extreme soviet was bad indeed, and though she allowed herself one instant of hope that Thomas would now decide there was nothing more he could do and come home, she knew that he would not leave them.

Consul has been very kind and taken me into his home, but I spend little time there. We have another house across the road from Ipatiev where we can come and go unobserved. I spend most of my time in a small attic whose window looks over the palisade into the garden. We can signal to N when he walks there. We have conversations through a third party with guards. They say the Rs may have only 1 hour exercise a day to make it seem more like a prison regime. Also this morning they whitewashed over the windows so they cannot see out. We hear the rest of the family is to leave Tobolsk on the 7th. I don't know whether to be glad or not. Of course they wish to be together but I can't see how we shall get them out. But there are agents here, one of ours and at least two German. Secret offers have been made to N who refuses to be rescued by Germans. However agents now plan to kidnap him for his own safety. Denmark the destination. Recommend you say nothing of this. I do not trust LG, and King may let something out.

Venetia had already heard from diplomatic sources that Berlin had been making representations to the Bolsheviks along the lines that, while the fate of the Tsar was a matter for the Russian people, they would take it very badly if the Tsaritsa, a German princess by birth, should be harmed. This was a legitimate position, and probably Lenin would be glad enough to be rid of Alexandra and the children, provided Nicholas remained his to send to trial. But Alexandra would refuse to go without Nicholas, and Venetia could imagine Nicholas indignantly refusing to be rescued by the Germans, whom he regarded now as his mortal enemies. A secret plot to extract them all, while publicly making the correct noises about Alexandra through the diplomatic route, made sense for both sides. Thomas's request that she say nothing to the King made sense too. She knew that the King was increasingly anxious about his cousins, and increasingly impatient with the prime minister, who at the moment had other fish to fry, as the saying was. The situation in Russia was increasingly volatile. If they were to be got out, it would have to be soon.

She went downstairs, deep in thought, to find her other son, Oliver, still sitting by the window in the drawing-room, as she had left him to go upstairs. Oliver was an RAMC doctor and had served in France, but was now attached to the new plastics unit in Sidcup, which allowed him to live at home most of the time. He was occupied with some drawings, but looked up as she came in, and said, 'How is my illustrious brother?'

Venetia started, then realised he must know from her

odd behaviour that the letter was from Thomas. 'He's well,' she said, and realised there was nothing else she could divulge.

'But not coming home – I can tell from your face,' Oliver said. 'What is he *doing* out there? You never let me in on the secret.'

Venetia sighed. 'I can't. I'm sorry.'

'You don't trust me,' he said, in wounded tones.

'Darling, it isn't that. It isn't my secret to tell. And, really, it's better if you don't know.'

'There you are, you see. You *don't* trust me.'

'Oh, Oliver!'

'It's all right, Mum. I'm teasing you. You're quite right. A secret gets weaker and leakier the more people who know it. Papa would have approved of you. He was a great one for not telling us things.'

'I can't think of anything your father didn't tell me,' Venetia said.

'Exactly,' said Oliver.

Venetia had to laugh. 'Oh you are an impossible boy!' She sat down by him. 'How are your patients?'

'My zoo?'

'Oh, don't call them that!'

'It's what they call themselves. When you look like that, you have to develop a specialised kind of humour. And they are a bit of a zoo – elephants, camels, several tapirs . . .'

She looked at his drawings, and he pushed them over and explained them to her. The men had all suffered severe disfigurement as a result of the war, and now the St Mary's unit was rebuilding their faces using transplants of flesh and bone from other parts of their bodies. One of the techniques was to raise a pedicle of flesh, from the arm or shoulder or forehead, and when it was long enough, sew it into place while still attached at source, not severing it until the blood supply had developed in the new position. Sketching the various stages of the rebuilding, and the proposed results, was an important part of the process, and Oliver had always been talented with the pencil.

Venetia studied the drawings with professional interest. Here was a patient with no nose, and a pedicle like a small trunk growing out of his forehead – the elephant, she supposed. And this man, whose entire cheek was missing, had had a pedicle raised from his upper arm to his jaw, so his arm was now attached to his face and had to be supported by a frame in the raised position. This strip of flesh would be only the first of many, she knew. The reconstruction might take years.

'It's remarkable work,' she said. 'I can see why it fascinates you.'

'They're remarkable men,' Oliver said. 'I've never met anyone so brave, in that dogged, unostentatious way. It can't be easy knowing ordinary people would run screaming from you if they saw you. That's why it's so good to keep them all together – at least they don't flinch from each other. But they get awfully bored, poor dears. Most of them aren't ill in the ordinary way so you can't keep them in bed, but they can't do anything strenuous, and walks outside the grounds are out of the question. They read a lot, of course, and play draughts and cards and do jigsaws, but it's bland fare for red-blooded males.'

'And to have endured what they endured, they must be extremely red-blooded,' Venetia said. 'What about moving pictures?'

'Can't take them to a cinema,' Oliver said bluntly. 'It's the running-and-screaming thing all over again.'

'But what about buying a cinematic apparatus for the hospital? I don't know what it's called, but it must be possible to purchase it and hire the films, given how many new cinemas seem to open up all the time.'

Oliver looked his interest. 'It's a genius of an idea, Mummy darling, but with one teensy weensy problem.'

She laughed. 'Oh, Oliver, of course I can find the money!

What with the war and everything, I'm living extremely frugally here, saving money hand over fist. Find out how much you would need for it, talk to the hospital, and let me know.'

'You're a very wonderful person,' Oliver said. He had no money of his own, beyond his army wages, but living here 'at home' – as one always tended to call the house of one's parents – meant he could enjoy comfort while staying within his means, despite his liking for West End shows and restaurants. But his mother never let him feel in any way dependent or ashamed of being a mere penniless army officer. And her bounty was as subtle as it was boundless. She seemed to know by some uncanny instinct when he was running short. Then, when one of the servants took his clothes away to sponge and brush them, he would find a folded banknote in one of the pockets on their return that he had quite forgotten he had.

'There's one other thing I know they'd like even more than a cinema,' he said now, 'but it's harder to arrange.'

'What's that? If there's anything I can do . . .'

'I'm not sure if you can. But they would love to meet some women.'

'Ah.'

'I don't mean for romantic purposes. Just meet them and chat to them, share a cigarette or a drink, tell them a joke and see them laugh, as normal men do. They *are* normal underneath. They can't help looking like that. But, of course, any normal girl would fall into a dead faint. I did think of perhaps hiring some prostitutes and *paying* them not to faint, but these are all decent boys, and it's not what they want.'

'As you say, it may be harder to arrange,' Venetia said. 'Well, suppose, just for a start, I come and visit them. I may not be young and attractive, but I am a woman.'

'Would you?' Oliver said eagerly. 'I know they'd like it. I've talked about you a lot so they feel they know you. They often ask me what you're doing.'

'I've wanted to come for a long time – I'm so interested in your work – but we've both been so busy. Once I've seen them, I can give some thought to how to find girls willing to help. One mustn't let them think anyone is visiting them out of charity. That would hurt their feelings.' She frowned in thought, and then said, 'Why don't I bring Violet along? The sight of her would cheer up any man.'

Oliver brightened. His sister was one of the most beautiful women in London. 'Do you think she'd come?'

'She will if I talk to her. And if you can leave me drawings of the men, I can make her look at them and get her used to the sight before we come.'

'That's a splendid idea,' Oliver said. 'She's such a good-hearted creature, she's bound to say yes. I don't know why I didn't think of it. I suppose it's because I haven't seen much of her lately. Though it's all to the good that she's seeing so much of Cousin Eddie's crowd.'

Eddie, Lord Vibart, was in Italy at that moment with the Prince of Wales, to whom he was equerry, but his wife, who had been Lady Sarah Montacute, daughter of the Marquess of Talybont, entertained frequently in their house at 143 Piccadilly, and all the best people went there.

'It's better,' Oliver went on, 'than that Bohemian set she got mixed up with.'

'Oh, Oliver, "Bohemian set" indeed,' Venetia said. 'The Verneys are perfectly respectable. I knew Laura Verney's mother – she was at Court with your aunt Olivia. It's only because they're intellectual that they're considered at all odd. And, in fact, it's really only Laura who's clever. George Verney is a perfectly nice ordinary man.'

'Nevertheless, they weren't a good influence on Violet,' Oliver said.

Through the Verneys, Violet had met the artist, Laidislaw, with whom she had had a shocking and torrid *affaire*, with all the consequences of scandal, shame and sorrow that followed. Oliver loved his sister, and was glad all that social turmoil seemed to be over: Laidislaw had died on the Western Front, and Violet's husband, Lord Holkam, had acknowledged her last child, so that seemed to be that. Violet was very far from being intellectual, and the Vibart set ought to suit her much better. It was a little of a surprise to him that she still saw the Verneys.

'Do you know,' Venetia said thoughtfully, 'I think Laura Verney would be someone you could ask to visit your poor boys. She's clever enough to do it tactfully, and she's beautiful too. I wonder if she has any war work? You might do worse than to ask her.'

'Let's just start with you and Violet, and see how it goes,' Oliver said.

Jessie had a letter from Bertie.

My dearest, dear Jessie, my wife,
How I love to know I can call you that at last! Thank you for your splendidly regular letters. I need to know most of all that you are well, and I can't hear it too often! My battered and refurbished battalion has been moved to the quietest sector of the line, what we call the Sanatorium, along with several other units who suffered heavily in the March and April offensives. The idea is to rest us and give us time to retrain. The countryside here is beautiful, a series of pastel ridges receding into the hazy distance, neat stone villages snugged down against their ancient churches and chateaux, rolling green pastures and lush woodland, tidy vineyards and fields of growing corn. It is a balm to the eye and to the heart to see so much verdant growth and untouched beauty, after the spoiled lands of the north. This sector has only been fought over once and those scars have been covered over by long grass and wild flowers. Even a burned-out tank can look attractive when mantled in wild clematis! Our Bttn HQ is in a pretty village full

331

of white and purple lilac trees in full bloom, and the scent in the afternoons is delicious. Even no man's land is comfortably wide here, in places 800 yards, so the enemy is almost out of sight and – for the men – definitely out of mind! We are out of the line at the moment, and it really is rather like a rest camp. Our facilities are excellent, the weather is fine and warm, the birds are in full song. Despite fatigues, the men are perfectly happy. The only drawback is that we are under French command here, but no action is expected so it probably doesn't matter. You may think of me as being as safe as it's possible to be in this war. The food is good, and we indulge ourselves in half a bottle of champagne each before dinner, and have a few rubbers of bridge after it. And there was a nightingale singing in the little wood behind our HQ last night. My bedroom window was open so I could hear him perfectly.

I pray you are as comfortable, and long inexpressibly to see you, in lieu of which I send you all the love of

Your devoted husband,

Bertie.

It was such luxury to Jessie to have a letter from Bertie. She took it out into the rose garden, Rug pattering behind her – when Helen was away he attached himself to her, and she was glad of his company. She had missed having a dog at her heels since her old Brach died. She settled in her favourite sunny seat, with Rug basking on the hot stones at her feet, and read it several times over, making the pleasure last.

In spite of everything, she was happy. She was home again. Tomlinson had come with the children, and Basil and Barbara were now reunited with their cousins in the nursery, while Tomlinson, shocked at how tired Henrietta seemed, had firmly taken over the running of the house, leaving her free for her war work – which was ample occupation. Jessie had persuaded her mother to regularise the situation by making Tomlinson housekeeper, so she was now Mrs Tomlinson, in possession of the basket of keys and the small room off the kitchen passage where the good china was kept. In private, Jessie still called her Mary; and as Mary, she generally managed to be there when Jessie went to bed, to 'maid' her, and have the comfortable chat they both enjoyed.

Tomlinson did what she could to suppress gossip in the servants' hall, but it was inevitable that Jessie's sudden marriage and not-so-sudden pregnancy should be discussed. And it was inevitable, too, that the story should eventually escape the servants' hall into the community at large. Jessie did not go out anywhere, and if anyone called at the house she kept out of sight, so she managed to avoid cold looks and impertinent questions. Even when Ethel, still living with her parents, appeared to express her anger and outrage – for Mrs Cornleigh, who visited and was visited widely, had not been spared the comments of the neighbourhood – the family kept her from expressing them to Jessie face to face.

The physical tiredness of late pregnancy, and the weariness of war, were cushioning her from the sorrows of losing Robbie and her darling Jack, blunting her feelings. Back home, she felt almost like a child again. She yielded up her sadness, along with responsibility, to her mother, and let herself drift along almost in a dream, waiting for birth. After the baby was born, she would feel it all as it really was.

She was not afraid now. She had carried the baby normally and without alarms for eight of the nine months. Surely all would be well. And she was married to Bertie. If he survived the war, they would have the life together that she had never allowed herself to dream of. They would be together every day and sleep together every night and raise their children and be normal and happy.

It was good – especially good for the baby – that Bertie had been sent to a quiet sector. Uncle Teddy said that the Sanatorium was the Champagne country, which accounted for the nightly half-bottle, she realised. It had always been a French sector, and last year there had been a disastrous offensive that had led to the French mutiny, but apart from that it had seen no action since the beginning of the war when, she dimly remembered, there had been fighting on the Aisne that Bertie had been involved in. Under the new closer liaison between the Allies, several exhausted divisions from the British Army had been swapped for fresh French divisions. Bertie's battalion would be part of the French Sixth Army, Teddy told her, while they recovered from their ordeals.

Jessie enjoyed chatting about the war with Uncle Teddy in the steward's room. Maria was away from home at present. Her mother had written to say she was ill and needed Maria to come and look after her. Uncle Teddy had urged her to fetch Mrs Stanhope to Morland Place instead, arguing that the fresh air, good food and peace-and-quiet of Yorkshire would do her much more good than having Maria care for her in a dark flat in Hammersmith. It would also be an opportunity to see her grandson.

But Mrs Stanhope would not come. She was not even really ill: she just wanted Maria to pay her some attention. Since her husband had died she had been living with her cousin Mrs Wilberforce. They had been childhood friends and were comfortable together. But things were so hard, what with rationing, blackouts, the servant problem, the fear of Zeppelins. There had been a terrible air-raid on London on the night of the 19th of May, with forty-nine people killed and 177 injured, and although Hammersmith itself had not been hit, the bombers had got as close as Maida Vale. Who knew when the next raid would come?

And the news in the papers was all bad, with U-boats sinking ships all over the place, and the Germans breaking through on the Western Front. Some people were saying they were nearly at the Channel, so it was no wonder her nerves were in shreds. It was only a step from there to fancying herself ill. Maria was her only daughter, and her place was at her mother's side.

As for her grandson, she had practically forgotten such a creature existed. Maria's marriage to Frank had been so short it had faded from Sadie Stanhope's memory. Much of the time she thought of Maria as being away working somewhere, and *surely* she could spare *some* time from her job for her own *mother*.

So Maria went. In her absence, Jessie took on a small part of her work, looking after Uncle Teddy's correspondence, or at least sorting it into categories and trying to see that it did not pile up too much for when Maria returned. It gave her something to do when Helen was away: she missed having her to talk to. It was a sadness to her to discover, while going through some of the files, that Uncle Teddy was still trying to find out what had happened to Ned, her first husband. She had thought he had accepted it by now, but here, more than two years later, there was evidence that he could not let the matter rest. With Maria's help he was still trying to trace anyone who had been in Ned's company, or in any other unit fighting in the area at the time, hoping for information.

She put the files away, feeling the baby turn and kick inside her, and for a moment the softening veil of gauze between her and reality was torn aside, and she saw in stark detail all the misery the war had brought to the house, the loss of Ned, of Frank, of Rob, and now of Jack, her favourite brother. The sorrow was like a great lump in her chest, preventing her from breathing, and she had to sit down and bow her head, holding onto the edge of the desk until the wave of grief passed. It was not only her dear ones: there was Fenniman, too, and Maud and little Richard, and Cousin Venetia's husband, kind Lord Overton. And beyond them, in the nation at large, countless thousands more, leaving behind them a void that could not be filled. Just for a moment she was every widow, parent, sibling, and all loss was one. People carried on as if nothing had happened, faced forward and got on with things because the war had to be won; but they would not be the same when it was over. They would be marked people. Life would never be the same and, for a moment, that seemed almost the saddest thing of all.

Violet did not *want* to visit Oliver's hospital, but Venetia was right to think she would agree to it. Her mother hardly ever asked anything of her, and when she did, Violet submitted. The only time she had ever rebelled against her parents was when they had begged her to give up Laidislaw. Well, that was over. Love was over for her. Now there was duty. She had her war-work, like every fashionable lady, but she did not feel particularly engaged by it. She supposed it was useful, rather than felt it so. Venetia made her look at Oliver's sketches of the poor mutilated men, and it was horrible. It was some time before she could even look directly at them, and she knew that the reality would be a great deal worse. But her mother had asked, in that firm, never-shy-from-duty way she had, and so on the appointed day she called at Manchester Square in her motor-car to pick up her mother and drive down to Sidcup.

At Oliver's request that she look her best, she had dressed in a silk crêpe dress and jacket of harebell blue, a colour that suited her dusky curls and violet-blue eyes particularly well, with a wide-brimmed hat of navy glazed straw.

Venetia looked at her with appreciation. 'I don't know how I ever managed to have a daughter so beautiful,' she said. 'You are quite, quite lovely. Of course, your father was very handsome – that must be it. He wasn't called "Beauty" Winchmore for nothing.'

She climbed into the motor and was greeted by the little dogs, Violet's blond Pekingeses, Lapsang and Souchong. Oliver had asked her to bring them – the men would enjoy seeing them.

'Have you heard from Thomas?' Violet asked, as they started off.

'Yes,' Venetia admitted. 'Last week.'

'How is he?'

'He's well,' Venetia said, after a pause. There was really so little she could tell Violet. Her daughter looked at her with faint reproach. Thomas had been gone so long now that he was like a character out of a story, but they had been very fond of each other in her childhood. She had been closer really to Thomas than to Oliver, who had always been a tease, too mercurial for gentle, simple Violet. Thomas, the brave, manly boy, prefect, head of his house, cricket captain, adored and looked up to by the younger boys and kind to his fag, had been Violet's hero, while Oliver had been as annoying as a wasp at a picnic.

'Is he ever going to come home?' she asked, in a small voice.

'Darling, I wish I could tell you more, but I can't. He's well, and he's not in any danger at the moment, but he's doing important secret work that no-one must know about, not even you. As soon as I can tell you, I will.'

Violet sighed and turned away. 'I don't believe he ever will come back,' she said quietly. 'He would have by now, if he could have. Why does he care so much about those horrid Romanovs? The Tsar was a bloody tyrant. He deserves whatever happens to him.'

'But the children – you wouldn't have them suffer? They couldn't help what their father did.'

'Oh—!' said Violet, with a shrug, and left it at that.

The sights that met her at the special unit were worse even than she had imagined. She could hardly bring herself to look at the men, and felt her face grow hot and her head light with the shock of it. But she had been brought up to behave properly in public and to people of all ranks and conditions, so she concealed her shock and distaste better than she imagined. She was ashamed of her feelings of revulsion, and shook

337

hands and smiled gallantly and did her best to think of things to say that would spark a conversation.

The men were equally gallant and, seeing that she was doing her best, refused to be offended. She was *there*, that was the point, and not running away; and, by God, she was lovely! Men in uniform often felt starved of female company. However much they enjoyed the harsh rough-and-tumble of the communal life, they missed the softness of women, the sight and sound and smell of them. And, despite what might have been thought by outsiders, their terrible ugliness craved beauty. She satisfied the aesthetic sense that all human creatures carry.

They crowded round her and Venetia, chatted, asked questions, told their stories, admired the dogs; and as Violet got past the shock and grew used to the way they looked, she found she was able to forget about it, to look directly at them, and enjoy their company. As she warmed, so did they, until a good time was being had by all. They even began to flirt a little – very gently and respectfully – as they would have done had they been normal-looking.

Oliver was delighted with his experiment. The men had been distracted from their pain and distress, their spirits had been raised enormously, and they had been given material for conversation for days afterwards. Violet's beauty and Venetia's intelligence alike had stimulated them. And Violet, as she drove away with her mother afterwards, thought what nice boys they were, and how interesting to talk to, as well as so tremendously brave it made her want to cry now she was away from them.

'Well, darling,' Venetia said, after a silence, 'I thought that was well done. I'm glad we went.'

'So am I,' Violet said. 'I'd like to go again. And, Mother, I think it would be awfully good if we could find some other ladies to go as well. They'll soon use up all my conversation – and it was hard to pay attention to so many at once. Wouldn't it be good if, say, half a dozen of us went?'

338

'I think it would be very good,' Venetia said, secretly pleased that Violet was showing so much character. 'I'm afraid I can't go with you on a regular basis. I have too much to do as it is. Why don't you make it *your* scheme? Find your ladies and take them down and make the arrangements. The chaps would prefer young things like you, anyway, I'm sure, to bony old horses like me.'

'You're not a bony old horse,' Violet said, with a surprise that was more flattering than indignation would have been. 'I've always thought you beautiful. And they enjoyed talking to you just as much as to me – more, really, because you have more to say.'

'Thank you, darling,' Venetia said. 'I'll come when I can. But I'm sure they'll be even more pleased to have a flock of young ladies to flirt with.'

'I'll do it, then. I can start calling on people tomorrow. I wonder if Sarah Vibart would come. I think Ravenna would. And Angela Draycott. It's important to get the right sort of person. I'll come over and talk to Oliver about it tonight.'

'Come to dinner, then,' Venetia said. 'I'm so pleased you've taken to the idea. It's just the right sort of war work for you.'

Violet was glad to have her mother's approval in this, for she doubted she would approve of something else she was involved in. She had never discussed it with her, but she felt instinctively that Venetia would not approve of spiritualism.

She had got into it through the Verneys, who were always interested in new movements. Modern art, modern music, modern philosophy – even new scientific theory, tougher intellectual meat though it was – all were welcome in the Verney salon, and were set about with the vigour of healthy, enquiring minds.

So they could not be expected to ignore the upsurge in interest in spiritualism, which was giving birth to new societies every week. Thousands of people had lost men to the war, and the normal means of mourning were denied to them. It was considered unpatriotic to wear weeds, weep publicly, shut up the house or make the sort of demonstrations that had helped previous generations to come to terms with loss. Death in battle came so suddenly and inexplicably, and there weren't even any funerals, for the fallen were buried abroad by the army. There was no grave to visit. Private memorials and monuments were specifically banned by the government. And the Church did not have any form of prayers for the dead, while its attitude to the war had to be one of brisk determination.

It was not surprising that, given no traditional means to express their grief, many people turned elsewhere. Spiritualism, frowned on in Christian teaching, had generally been regarded as faintly disreputable, but lately Sir Arthur Conan Doyle, respected author and a prominent lay member of the Established Church, had done much to change that view. In an extensive public tour, he had lectured that spiritualism and Christianity were complementary, not antipathetic, ideas, and claimed to have positive knowledge of life after death. Further, a leading scientist, Sir Oliver Lodge, whose son had been killed in 1915, had been attending seances, which had convinced him of their validity, and he published a book on the subject in 1916. He said, 'There is no real breach of community between the dead and the living, and methods of intercommunication across what has seemed to be a gulf can be set going in response to the urgent demand of affection.'

For many who had lost the person dearest to them, without even the chance to say goodbye, the hope of contacting them beyond the grave was irresistible. Mediums offering seances sprang up everywhere, and every town had its spiritualist society – London, of course, had dozens. The Verneys went into it in a spirit of intellectual curiosity, but there was certainly a thrill to be had out of the whole paraphernalia of dimmed lights, exotic costumes, planchettes, rocking tables and ghostly voices. Of course, there were plenty of charlatans around, and the Verneys were just as keen to expose them as to discover the real thing, if it existed. This gave a veneer of respectability to their interest, and the seances they held in their drawing-room were well attended; so well, they had to limit numbers. But in any case, all the mediums agreed that it was not possible to hold a successful session with more than a small number. The atmosphere was all-important.

Violet, invited by Laura Verney, had gone along doubt-fully at first, and with a feeling of guilt. The Church disapproved of spiritualism, and she was sure her mother would too. But the Verneys emphasised the importance of keeping an open mind about everything.

'Just because something is intangible doesn't mean it doesn't exist. Think of wireless waves. Think of bacteria: your own mother, Violet, was vilified for believing disease was caused by invisible organisms when everyone else thought it was caused by noxious smells. Science would never advance if we didn't look into things. We mustn't condemn something without testing it.'

So Violet settled her conscience along those lines, and quickly fell under the spell of the process, the strange thrill of it. And she had a longing, hardly admitted to herself, to see or hear or speak to Laidislaw again. He had been killed on the Somme. He had left her so suddenly, without a goodbye, that sometimes she felt he could not really be dead. It only took encouragement for her to begin to believe that this feeling was itself proof that the spirit world existed, and was very close, perhaps reachable.

The first medium she encountered was, according to Laura, an obvious charlatan: Madame Fatima was a swarthy woman with lank, greasy hair and large hooped earrings, who arrived dressed in shapeless flowing robes of multi-coloured silk, and proceeded to set up a table, covered with a velvet cloth, and to arrange the room and the lighting to her requirements. She had an 'assistant' with her, a pale young man who never spoke and carried an enormous suit-case, from which she removed various items of equipment.

Violet found the whole experience, conducted in near darkness, exciting but unnerving. She was glad when Laura and George said afterwards that the woman deserved her money as a showman, but that it was all humbug, and laughed about the spirit trumpet that had appeared bobbing in mid-air and sounded a rather squeaky note, and the 'apparition' resembling a bedsheet draped over a hatstand.

But there was one medium who appealed strongly to Violet because he seemed so ordinary, did his work in a matter-of-fact way and in plain light. He was a small man with a Yorkshire accent, and a rather stiff gait – he said he had a wooden leg, souvenir of the first battle of Ypres. His suit was cheap and rather worn, which suggested he wasn't making huge sums of money from his gift, and he had a pale, seamed face full of suffering, and melancholy dark eyes. He used no special equipment, just asked that they should sit round a table with their hands flat on it and their fingers touching those of the people next to them. Then he would sit in silence, his eyes sometimes bent on the table, sometimes staring into empty air, and after a time, he would begin giving the messages from those beyond.

It was not until the second time that Mr Fletcher looked at her, and said, 'There's a young man in khaki standing behind you.'

Violet flinched violently. She stared at the medium, her eyes widening, her heart beating uncomfortably fast.

Fletcher was staring over her right shoulder, and it was almost the hardest thing she had ever done not to turn and look. 'He's a handsome, fair man, who says he was killed in the war. Do you have any idea who he might be?'

Violet's mouth was dry. At the second attempt, she managed to say, 'I think so.'

Fletcher nodded, not looking at her. 'I feel a great deal of love coming from him towards you. A great deal, indeed.' He seemed to be listening. 'He says – he wants me to tell you that he loved you with all his heart and soul, and hoped to make his life with you, if he could have done.'

Violet felt the tears burning her eyes, and wanted to say something, to send a message back, but she was incapable of speaking.

'He says—' Fletcher was continuing.

But Violet could not contain herself any longer. She turned to look behind her, breaking contact with her neighbours. There was nothing there.

'You won't be able to see him,' Fletcher said gently. 'There's no point in trying to look. I explained that before.'

'I'm sorry,' Violet said, feeling foolish.

'I'm afraid you've broken the contact,' said Fletcher.

'In that case, let's stop and have some tea,' Laura Verney said. 'It makes my arms ache sitting like this. We can resume later.'

They all got up, flexing their arms. The tea-tray was sent for, and conversation rose, as people stood around in twos and threes. Fletcher was talking to a couple across the room who had lost their son. Violet stood with Laura, George, and Angela Draycott. 'A young man in khaki, who was killed in the war,' George said, amused. 'I should think he'd be able to say that in any drawing-room in the land and get a response. Anything can count as "fair" except downright black hair. He wasn't taking any risks.'

'I think it's strange how all the spirits say the same thing – that they love you and they're happy,' said Angela, joining in the scepticism, though she was as wide-eyed and ready to believe as anyone when that was the order of the day.

'He didn't say he was happy,' Violet pointed out. She so wanted it to be true.

'I don't know why we should expect the spirits to say

343

anything brilliant,' Laura said good-humouredly, 'when most of them were just as dull as us in their lifetimes.'

'Yes,' said George. 'I must say that if I were contacting you from beyond, darling, I can't think what else I'd want to tell you except that I love you.'

'We're upsetting Violet,' Angela said. 'And, after all, there might be something in it. Mr Fletcher isn't at all like that awful Madame Fatima.'

'Of course,' Laura said, 'one must keep an open mind. Did you feel anything, Violet darling?'

'I – I'm not sure,' Violet began.

At that moment, Fletcher came over, tea-cup in his hand, looking so mundane, like a draper's clerk, rather than a converser with departed spirits. 'I'm sorry you broke the contact just then, ma'am,' he said to Violet. 'It was a nice strong flow. But perhaps we can get him back later. I didn't tell you the last thing he said, just before you turned round.'

'Oh, was there more?' Laura asked, with a glance at her husband.

'Did he say he was happy where he was?' George prompted, straight-faced.

Fletcher did not seem put out. Perhaps he was used to mockery. He only looked at Violet. 'No, he didn't say that. He said to tell you, "Show them the pictures." Does that make any sense to you?'

In the silence that followed, Violet felt herself whiten. Though she was looking into Fletcher's dark eyes, she caught the surprised glance between Laura and her husband. This was no vague, generally applicable message of love and happiness. Octavian Laidislaw had been a painter of genius, whose promising career had been interrupted by the call-up. At the Front he had done a great deal of what he believed important work, sketching and painting his fellow soldiers and the scenes of their lives in the trenches. A portfolio of these pictures had been sent to Violet after his death by his commanding officer, who had known he had no close relatives.

344

'Show them the pictures?' she said, in a husk of a voice. 'He said that? But show who?'

Fletcher shook his head. 'That's all he said before you broke the contact. Does it make sense to you?'

'Yes,' she said. Yes, it made sense. Show them – the public. Show everyone. He would have been one of the greatest and most famous painters in the world if he had not died. He had been cheated of his fame. She must give it to him. It was up to her. 'Yes, I understand it,' she said.

Since then, she had not had another message, though the Verneys had had him back several times. Violet kept going, longing for something else from Laidislaw, for just a word, a sign that he was there and watching over her. But there was nothing.

Meanwhile, with the help of the Verneys, she was planning an exhibition of Laidislaw's work for later that summer. She hadn't told her mother and brother yet, partly because she wasn't sure they would approve of reviving the whole Laidislaw question, but mostly because she didn't want to have to tell them why she was doing it.

Polly was riding up the track they called the Ridgeway, between hedges thick and fragrant with may, and ditches afroth with lacy kex. She was aware that she was looking her best in a new habit of plain black serge, made up at Makepeace's, whose severity of colour and cut showed up not only her fair prettiness but Vesper's conker-bright coat. Vesper was dancing along with her usual dislike of keeping more than one foot on the ground at a time, and Polly was sitting her bounces with consummate ease. In fact, they weren't difficult to sit, but someone who wasn't a natural horseman wouldn't know that, and the former Lieutenant – now Captain – Holford was not a natural horseman, so he was bound to admire her skill. He looked good, however, riding at her side on Jessie's Hotspur, and though she acknowledged that anyone could have ridden Hotspur because he was so well schooled and kind, still Holford sat nicely and looked extremely elegant, and very handsome.

In fact, she thought, he was more handsome than ever, for he was lean and tanned from soldiering in France, and now had a most interesting and distinguished scar on his forehead. He had had it for some weeks, so it had healed to the point where it was an acceptable thin pink line in the brownness of his smooth skin. With it, he looked a real soldier, she thought, as well as an officer and a gentleman, in his shiny boots and well-fitting uniform. He had seen action: he had been in the April offensive. She didn't ask him for the details: it was enough to know that he had done his bit.

And this leave, unlike the last one, he had come straight to Yorkshire. He was staying in York, at the Station Hotel, ready to devote the whole of his time to her. 'You don't have to see your parents?' she had asked casually.

'I saw them last time,' he said. 'That was duty – this is pleasure. I think I deserve some pleasure after – well, all that.' He dismissed his ordeal modestly.

It was fortunate that Eileen Cornleigh's current favourite beau was also at home, so that they could act as each other's chaperones. Teddy would not allow Polly to go anywhere alone with a man, but with Eileen and Frank Billington they could go to the New Picture House in Coney Street, which was grand and modern and had a thousand tip-up seats of crimson velvet, and see Theda Bara in *Salome*. They could go to the Spirit of 1918 dance in the Assembly Rooms. They could go to a tennis party at the Chubbs' place, Bootham Park, and to a garden party at Rawcliffe Manor, which Lady Grey was giving in aid of the Red Cross.

But though Eileen was Polly's best friend, and Frank Billington was very nice, today was what she had looked forward to, because she had invited Holford out riding, and Daddy didn't mind her riding alone with a man, so she didn't have to have Eileen and Frank along. Horses, it

346

seemed, were chaperones in their own right. And it was nice to do something at which she was better than David Holford, who played tennis brilliantly, had seen all the new moving pictures, danced like an angel, knew the latest tunes, and in company, like at the Greys', seemed to be able to say exactly the right thing to everyone and was the object of attention and admiration.

'It's good to be alone together,' he said, as if he had been reading her thoughts, as they picked their way across the beck – at least, sensible Hotspur picked his way across it. Vesper decided it was probably a snake, and stopped, boggled at it, tried to paw it to death with a forehoof, then jumped it in a huge bound, though it was only a trickle about two feet wide. 'I don't know how you cope with all that,' he added, when Vesper had joined him again, shaking her head with a series of triumphant snorts at peril overcome.

'It's not as bad as it looks,' Polly said. 'She's a dreadful actress, really. What were you saying about being alone?'

'How nice it was,' he said obligingly. 'Of course, one respects your father for taking such good care of you. My parents are very impressed – all the girls I know at home go everywhere these days. It's the war, of course,' he added vaguely. 'But my father thinks things have gone too far, and girls are too rackety by half. He says he wouldn't like to see a daughter of his wandering about London on her own. He thinks the old-fashioned way you're guarded is much more ladylike.'

'I'm glad he approves,' Polly said doubtfully, not sure about the 'old-fashioned' part, and wondering what Mr Holford senior's opinion had to do with anything. 'But it's rather a bore sometimes.'

'Well, we're alone now,' Holford said, 'and I mean to make the most of it. Is there somewhere we can go where we can tie the horses up and just sit and talk? I don't feel I can express myself properly on a horse, nice though this one is.'

Polly's heart beat a little faster. What did he want to

express himself about? Was he going to propose to her? Did he mean – terrible, lovely thought! – to *kiss* her? Perhaps if she found a secluded enough spot, he would. Of course, there was always the danger of someone passing by, and the thing was that *everyone* within a radius of ten miles knew who Polly was, so if she was seen it was *bound* to get back to Daddy. But perhaps it would be worth getting into trouble for a kiss. She had never yet been kissed by a man. Eileen had been kissed by Frank Billington and, understandably, was inclined to crow about it – though Eileen and Frank were practically engaged, and Frank was a local boy they had known all their lives. To be kissed by a London man like David Holford would be a *very* different proposition.

'I'll find somewhere,' she said. And then, unable to wait until then for a hint, she said, 'What did you want to talk about?'

'Oh, you, of course,' he said. 'And me. You and me.'

'Well, that's nice,' she said, feeling fluttery inside. He was so handsome and sophisticated. Frank Billington was like a stuttering idiot beside him.

'It's the nicest subject in the world,' he said. After a moment, he asked, 'Does your father own all this land?'

'"As far as the eye can see", you mean? Well, pretty much. Actually, the Morlands owned even more in my grandfather's time, but my uncle ran the estate down, and Daddy's been building it up again.'

'So it's pretty substantial now?'

'Yes, one of the biggest in these parts. Daddy's sort of the squire, though it makes him laugh when anyone calls him that. He's the Master of Morland Place – that's the title he likes. It's what Morlands have always been called.'

'But if you inherit it all, what will you be called? The Mistress of Morland Place?'

'Oh, I shan't inherit the estate,' Polly said.

'Really?' He looked at her sharply.

'The land will go to my brother,' she said. But then, seeing

348

that he seemed worried for her, she added, 'I shall have my own fortune. Daddy's going to leave me the drapery business and workshops and the city property – what's called the Makepeace inheritance, because Grandfather inherited from Mrs Makepeace.'

'That sounds like a lot.'

'Oh, it is. With the department stores in Leeds and Manchester, it's nearly half Daddy's fortune.'

'He's promised you those too, has he?'

'Well, not exactly, but the stores are called Makepeace's as well, so it would make sense. It isn't something we've talked about, really, but I've always sort of assumed they'd be mine. But even without them, the rest of it is a real fortune, so you needn't worry about me. I shall be jolly rich.'

He smiled. 'I'm glad to hear it. But I wasn't really worried. I knew your father would always take care of you – he loves you so much. Of course, when you talk about inheriting the businesses, I imagine what will really happen is that your father will give you a capital sum in their place.'

'Oh, no,' Polly said firmly. 'It's going to be *my* business, and I'm going to prove how well I can run it. Daddy jokes that I'll double the turnover in three years, and I mean to show him it's no joke. Not,' she added, her smile disappearing, 'that I'd be able to show him, because of course he'd have to be dead for me to inherit. How horrid! I don't want to think about that. I'd sooner not *have* the Makepeace inheritance, and have Daddy live for ever.'

'There's no need to be upset,' Holford said. 'Surely your father will make it over to you when you marry, won't he? As your dowry?'

'Oh, I hadn't thought of that. Yes, I suppose he will. That would be much better.' She shook her head, like a horse shaking away a fly. 'Anyway, let's talk about something else. I don't know how we got stuck on such a dull subject.' It had struck her that the discussion of inheritances was very far from romantic, and not likely to lead to being kissed.

They had reached Ten Torn Gap, and as she turned Vesper through it, the mare began to dance on the spot, wanting to dash off. 'Are you ready for a canter?' Polly asked. 'Because I'm going to have to let her go. Ready?'

'Ready,' said Holford, and the two horses leaped forward, out over the open fields, neck and neck. Polly laughed with pleasure at the speed, everything flying out of her head but the joy of the moment. Holford urged Hotspur to keep up with her, smiling at her golden beauty and his private thoughts.

CHAPTER SIXTEEN

The April offensive may have petered out, but that did not make things any quieter for Emma and Unit 8. The Germans had been held up, but the fighting continued. Reinforcements went up, the wounded and dead came down. The situation was complicated by the constant trickle of refugees and the soaring temperatures; and the line was now so close to them they suffered almost constant night air-raids.

Their camp, right beside the main road, was deemed to be too much of a target after it was hit twice in successive nights (fortunately without casualties), so the unit was moved to the garden of a monastery on the other side of the town. The warm weather made it no great hardship to be under canvas. The old monks were still in residence, and had been tending the garden up until the FANY's arrival, so it was very beautiful, and peaceful after the continuous racket of the Arques road.

The arrival of women in uniform must have been a shock to the brothers, who were already disturbed by the coming of the war, the noise of military activities all around them, and now the air-raids. The FANY tried to keep themselves as much as possible out of the way of the old men. Emma did come face to face with one of them, one evening when she had been taking a late and much-needed bath. Probably he had thought they were all asleep – or perhaps he had simply forgotten they were there. What seemed to shock him

351

most was the sight of her short hair, which she was rubbing with a towel as she made her way back to her tent. She flung the towel over her head and scuttled away, and was very sorry to learn a few days later that he had died during one of the noisier air-raids – presumably of shock, since they were told he had not been ill. Emma only hoped she had not contributed to his decline.

It was rare for anyone to have time to bathe, or sleep in their own tent, for the work was constant. Much of it now was the result of the bombings. On the 18th of May there was a particularly severe air-raid, and they were called out by the French authorities to help with the civilian wounded. The sky was lit up as bright as day by the shelling along the Front, and the noise of the guns was deafening. Bombs were exploding everywhere, the air was full of dust and flying glass, while debris and collapsing buildings blocked the roads. A bomb had fallen in a main street in the town, causing terrible damage and dozens of casualties, mostly women and children and old people. One woman had died with her baby in her arms, the baby also dead, both with their eyes wide open – presumably the concussion had killed them. An old man and woman were found in a damaged house with their arms round each other. The woman was dead from a severed artery, but the old man did not understand that he must let her go, still wanting to shield her with his body.

When they had transported the wounded to the hospital and the dead to the mortuary, and were hoping their night's work might be over, they were called to another emergency. An arms depot on the Arques road had been hit – the explosion had been so huge, they had heard it earlier even through the racket of the raid. Approaching it up the long, straight road was hazardous, for the road itself was a target. The dump was now a huge crater, but flares were still shooting up into the sky, and explosions were still going off as the heat spread to previously untouched boxes of ammunition.

It was the most frightening thing Emma had ever done. Going out in an air-raid was bad enough, but approaching the dump, knowing that a box of bullets might suddenly go off, flying in all directions, or a stash of grenades explode in front of her, took all her nerve. Yet the madness of the night shielded her from the paralysis of fear. There was nothing to be done but one's duty, and though her mouth was dry with apprehension, her limbs did not shake. Oddly, her one thought was that she was glad she had tied Benson up in her tent and not let him come out with her, though she hoped someone would find him and take care of him if they were all blown up here. The dump had been attended by Chinese labourers, most of whom were dead or had been blown to such shreds they had completely disappeared, but there were plenty of wounded with horrific injuries to be brought out, and some miraculously unhurt, but in a state of shock.

That was the worst air-raid of the month, but for the rest of May there was no peace or rest for Unit 8. At one point a large hospital in the town was struck, and Emma and Armstrong found themselves helping to dig people out from the ruins. The floors had collapsed and several patients, still in their beds, had fallen straight through to the basement, where their shock must have been compounded by finding themselves in the mortuary there.

Later in the month, they heard that a number of medals had been recommended for Unit 8 for their actions on the 18th. It caused much speculation in the mess hut, for sixteen Military Medals and two Croix de Guerre had been mooted.

'They'll never let us have all those,' Hutchinson said. 'Not eighteen medals for one small unit like ours.'

'We'll see,' said Norma Lowson. 'They wouldn't have put the names in without details. It's up to the proposers to fight for them, and I don't suppose they'd have put them in in the first place – not for women – if they hadn't meant to back them all the way.'

Lowson proved right. All eighteen were allowed, and a special ceremony of presentation was to take place as soon as the action had quietened down enough to allow it. Emma was almost more amused than proud that she was to receive a Military Medal. It would delight her friends back home, of course. She wrote to Molly and Vera about it. Molly wrote back saying she ought to have the MM engraved after her name on Benson's disc. Vera replied that what she was most pleased about was that it represented recognition from the army and the government, who had always been so dismissive of women's abilities. But to Emma, in the exhaustion of the moment, the medal seemed curiously irrelevant to what she was doing. The last two months felt more like two years.

It was bad luck on the weary British divisions sent to the Champagne district to rest that it was there that the third, and most ferocious, German thrust had been planned. Bertie was not alone in being unhappy with the general position: the bulk of the troops and the artillery were crammed together between the north bank of the Aisne and the scarp of the Chemin des Dames plateau. The danger was that if the Germans broke through on their flanks they would be trapped by the river and unable to make a quick retreat. It was discussed at one of the meetings of battalion-commanders-and-above at Corps HQ. Bertie learned that the corps commander, General Gordon, had raised the matter with the French Sixth Army commander, General Duchêne, and suggested moving back onto the south bank. But Duchêne had not absorbed the new philosophy of 'elastic defence' and was horrified at the idea of yielding a single metre of French soil unless forced to. He refused point blank, and scotched any further argument by sticking his nose in the air and declaring, '*J'ai dit*.'

However, everything was so quiet that it didn't seem as though Duchêne's refusal to see sense would have any practical consequences. Bertie's battalion was out of the line on the 26th of May, a Sunday, and as it had been a glorious day, everyone was in very mellow mood. Some of the men were actually enjoying short strolls around the neighbourhood – it was rare for Tommies to look upon walking as a pleasure – while others were enjoying a glass of beer at the tables outside the *estaminet*. One small but cheerful group was leaning over the gate of the farm at the end of the village street, where the elderly farmer had a moderately pretty single daughter. A concert had been planned for the evening, and everyone was looking forward to it. In the comfortable house that was serving him as headquarters, Bertie was pleasantly anticipating a roast duck for dinner, and a hand or two of bridge later, when he had done his duty and shown his face at the concert.

The calm was interrupted in the late afternoon when he was summoned urgently to Brigade Headquarters. The brigadier informed him that a raiding party that morning had taken a German prisoner who, after long interrogation, had revealed that the Germans were planning to attack in great force that very night.

'It could be a plant, of course, with the intention of provoking a "wind-up", but we can't take any chances,' said the brigadier. 'I want you to parade your men in full battle order as soon as you get back. I may have to send you into the front line. I know you're all tired, but it can't be helped.'

They discussed tactics and looked at maps, then Bertie drove back to his own HQ to give his orders. It was not just wind-up, as it happened. At about one in the morning the German bombardment started, guns and trench mortars firing a mixture of gas shells and high explosive. Had it not been for the warning of the captured German, the effect would have been even more shattering, after the utter peace of the previous weeks. The German artillery had ranged the Allied guns so perfectly that they were never able to fire a shot in reply: they were all destroyed within the first few minutes. The barrage then went on to cut up the wire and the front-line defences, while the gas added to the confusion. The enemy infantry advanced in great force at 3.40 a.m., and there was nothing for the Allies but to fall back, fighting as they went. Those who did not fall back quickly enough were soon overwhelmed. There were too few bridges to allow those on the north bank of the river to retreat in time, and many thousands were taken prisoner.

Bertie was glad that there had not been time to send his battalion over the river. At least they had a fighting chance; and weary though they were, they now had experience of this kind of warfare. The numbers of Germans pouring over seemed unprecedented, an unstoppable multitude. But one thing that Bertie had learned since the beginning of March was that to try to stop them too soon was futile. You had to let the countryside absorb the thrust, and make your stand on a line you had some hope of defending. So he marched his men back, gathering fleeing stragglers as he went, until he reached the railway, and set up a new line there.

The fighting was fierce, but his men were hardened, and the newcomers who had been sent to bring his numbers up were steadied by them, and keen to prove themselves. Nevertheless, they had to yield ten miles the first day – the biggest advance the Germans had ever made in a single day. A week later the line had sagged twenty miles, and Bertie's battalion was back on the river Marne, where it had fought so bitterly almost four years ago, at the beginning of the war.

But here, once again, the German advance ran out of steam. Exhaustion and the length of its supply line weakened it, and crossing the river was too much for it. At Chateau Thierry, on the Marne, barely sixty miles from Paris, the retreating British were reinforced by some American units, coming into the fight for the first time, and the line held. It seemed as though the emergency was over. Bertie's battalion came out of the line on the 3rd of June, exhausted, battle-weary, bloodied but unbowed, and marched back to billets in a village called Bochage, for a more than well-earned rest.

The new strategy of elastic defence had worked. The lines had bent but not broken; the power of the German thrust had been absorbed until it expended itself. All this had been at the cost of giving considerable ground, which never pleased the French. There had also been many thousands of casualties, huge numbers of whom were prisoners – the first large body of British soldiers to be captured in the whole four years of war. And the Germans were shelling Paris, which was worrying because there were important armaments factories in the Paris region that the Allies could not afford to lose.

At a war cabinet meeting in early June, the possibility was considered that if the French 'cracked' – and no-one, after 1917, could rule that out – the whole BEF might have to withdraw from France. Plans ought to be put in place for the evacuation, in case it should become necessary. And still valuable shipping was being sunk daily by German U-boats, which meant ever tighter rationing back home. The mood in England was sombre.

It was less so in France, where the weary soldiers came out of the line in the knowledge that, although the Germans had heavily outnumbered them, they had still been stopped. The British Army remained unbeaten. Now reinforcements were being sent out from England. And best of all, the Americans had at last joined the fight. At the end of May they had attacked the German salient around the village of Cantigny in the French Somme sector, and had driven the enemy back more than a mile. At Chateau Thierry, American artillery was still pounding the German line, and on the 1st of June the American 2nd Division initiated a counter-attack there at Belleau Wood, across the crucial main road to Paris.

Evidence so far was that the Sammies were bonny fighters, with enough spirit to counterbalance their inexperience. The word coming down from Belleau Wood was that 'The Yanks are knocking hell out of the Boche, and the only problem is getting them to stop.'

Emma had seen some Doughboys, which was what they liked to call themselves, though they were always Sammies to the British, and Yankees to the French. One day in early June, she had had to pull her ambulance off the road to let a large body of soldiers go through up the main road from St Omer. They had attracted her attention, blunted to the movements of soldiers around her, by the swift springiness – one might almost have said swagger – of their gait. Intrigued, she had rested her elbow on the lowered window of her cab and leaned out to watch them.

They seemed taller than ordinary men, and so strong, so well fed, so vibrantly healthy they were like minor deities from another realm. *Poilus* always seemed to be short, squat men, and the Tommies she was used to were thin, cave-chested and undersized. The uniforms of these demigods were so clean and new and smart, they looked like a battalion of officers. But, most of all, it was their spirit that attracted her attention. They were eager for the fray, looking around them with excited interest like boys on an outing.

Nearby, a couple of Tommies who had pulled a small lorry off the road, and were leaning against it, having a smoke, shouted, 'Go it, Sammy!' and 'They're waiting for yer, Sammy!' It was then that Emma realised, with a sensation of warmth in the pit of her stomach, that here at last were the long-promised Americans, marching up to the Front. They were so physically big they filled the road and seemed like thousands instead of hundreds. She found herself grinning like an idiot, and the next minute she was waving, too. Benson stuck his head out alongside hers and barked, wagging his tail frantically in response to her mood; and the Sammies turned their heads and looked at her, interested to see a woman in uniform, amused by her dog. They waved back as they passed, and smiled their big white smiles, so full of healthy teeth.

When they had passed the road seemed suddenly empty and grey. But she drove off towards St Omer feeling very much cheered. Such magnificent and un-used-up soldiers must surely make the difference. Surely now the tide was about to turn.

Lennie was given his leave in early June, and took his travel warrant for Morland Place, eager to get back to them all, having missed his last leave. He decided to walk from the station, for the sheer pleasure of seeing the rich green country-side, untouched by shell; the whole, straight, tall trees; the wild flowers in the hedge, the peacefully grazing animals in the meadows and the strong, thrusting crops that would not be trampled and spoilt. Not one dead, bloated horse or gaping, ruined cottage the whole way. His heart rose until he found he was whistling as he walked.

When he came in sight of Morland Place he stopped, remembering the family's losses, and tried to go on in a more sober manner, until at last he was admitted into the great hall by the magnificently unchanging Sawry, put down his kit-bag, and saw Henrietta come in from the other side.

'Lennie! My dear boy!' she said, hurrying towards him. He saw the weary suffering in her face, and wished, as he received her embrace, that there was anything he could do to ease it. As it was, he couldn't even find his tongue.

Henrietta, stepping back to look at him, seemed to under-stand, and did the talking for him. 'You come at a good time. The house is quiet and you can have plenty of time to settle in before being bothered by lots of people. I imagine you'd like a bath first of all – or are you hungry?'

'A bath would be wonderful,' he admitted.

'Then that's what you shall have. I'll send Brown to you.' Brown was Teddy's valet.

Lennie had never been valeted in his life. 'Oh! No, really—'

Henrietta reached up a hand to touch his hair – he had removed his cap – and said, 'Not immediately, dear, but in a while, just to trim your hair. I don't know who did it for you last, but he must have been working in the dark. Don't worry, Brown's not a talker.' The fingers lingered down and brushed his cheek briefly, and his heart shivered. She would never touch her sons' cheeks like that again. 'I'm glad to see you safely home again,' she said. He nodded, his throat tight. She had called it home. Oh, he wished it might be! He was longing to see Polly – but not like this. He must be clean.

Hot water, and plenty of it, Henrietta sent up, and towels warm from the airing-cupboard. He soaped and wallowed and scrubbed to his heart's content. Brown came slipping in – a thin, elderly man and, as Henrietta had said, no talker. By then Lennie was so relaxed he not only let him cut his hair but submitted without fuss to being shaved. Brown was so good at it that Lennie realised for the first time what a luxury it could be. He emerged from the valet's hands feeling like a new man.

His first meeting with Polly was a disappointment – though perhaps as he had wanted it so much and thought about it so often, it was almost bound to be. She was cool and distant with him, received his gift of a lace-edged handkerchief politely rather than gladly, and seemed to have nothing much to say to him. Things were better the next day when she agreed to go for a ride with him, but though he could not put his finger on quite what it was, he felt he could not get close to her. It was as if she was behind a pane of glass. A small smoulder of resentment established itself in a corner of his mind, with the conviction that it was that chap again, that damned smooth Londoner, who was occupying her mind. He hadn't liked the look of the fellow when he saw him, and he was sure that he would end by breaking her heart. But there seemed no way he could raise the subject with Polly.

Everything else about being back at Morland Place was wonderful. Everyone was very pleased about his promotion to captain, which had come after the Lys offensive, and wanted to hear about his experiences – though, like every other soldier, he toned them down for civilians and females. It was only to Jessie, who had been out there and nursed, and knew, that he told everything. Trapped into relative immobility by her size, she needed distracting, while he was tireder than he was willing to admit, and needed rest. So when Polly was off doing things without him (as she too often was), he tended to migrate to wherever Jessie was.

On the sofa, or the bench in the rose garden, or under the chestnut tree by the ponds, slumped in a chair beside her, or stretched on the grass at her feet, with Rug snoring beside him, he could talk with complete openness. He did not, out of his innate tactfulness, ask her about her situation, but somehow she found she could tell him everything, too: her pain and disappointment at being forced to leave France, the long agony of not being able to be with Bertie, the guilt and sadness she felt about Maud's death, the ongoing worry about the scandal in the family. Chewing a stem of grass, he listened and nodded and understood, and at the end of it told her that he thought she would find one day that none of the bad stuff mattered a button, and that if she could just get through it for a little while, everything would turn out all right.

'Being with the person you love, that counts a whole heap. It's the only thing that really matters, in the end,' he concluded.

She looked down at him, at his nice, ordinary face, firmed now into proper manhood by his experiences in the war, and thought how lucky the girl would be whom he loved truly. 'Poor Lennie,' she said, 'won't Polly notice you?

I'm sorry. But she's very young, you know – too young to settle on one thing or another. She does like you.'

'But I don't want her to like me,' Lennie said mournfully. 'I want her to love me.'

Maria came back from Hammersmith while Lennie was there, looking worn and pale from her sojourn in the dark flat with her mother and cousin. Her mother's fractious demands, her cousin's well-meaning dullness, being confined indoors, the noise and dirt of London, all had taken their toll. Then there was the housework, which she had had to do in the absence of a decent maid – all the useful girls were going into munitions or the services, and good maids were becoming impossible to find or, if found, to keep. That, and the constant fetching and carrying her mother required, had frayed her nerves, while the endless queuing at shops, the sheer struggle of rationing, made putting food on the table an exhausting task.

But hardest to bear was the tedium of sitting at her mother's side as she lay in bed or on the sofa, listening to the thin, querulous voice complaining ceaselessly, like the trickle of a mountain stream. Even when she wasn't talking, Mrs Stanhope required Maria to be there. If Maria thought she had fallen asleep and went off to do something, a minute later there would be the anxious, hurt summons. 'I only closed my eyes for an instant. Is it too much to be allowed to enjoy my only daughter's company once in a while?' Maria's unused brain fretted her into a fever; the long hours of sitting gave her intolerable fidgets in her legs. The only variation was the occasional game of cards in the evening, three-handed whist if her mother was feeling 'strong enough', or piquet with Cousin Sonia if she wasn't.

But added to these ills was something she had not even begun to suspect before she came away. As it slowly dawned on her, it shocked her. She was missing Morland Place for a very particular reason, which had nothing to do with the comfort and freedom of her life there. Realising what it was made her feel that she must be a very bad woman, and Maria was a person who did not like to think ill of herself.

After what seemed to her like years of imprisonment, she managed to find a maid who, if not very bright, was at least honest, and no more than usually lazy. Maria rearranged some things in the flat, devised a routine within the maid's capabilities, instructed the girl in her duties, and gently but firmly extricated herself from her mother's toils. When Mrs Stanhope became tearful, she told her that she was invited to Morland Place for as long as she cared to stay. 'I have to go back, but if you want to be with me, why don't you come too? The fresh air would do you good.'

'Travel all that way?' Mrs Stanhope protested. 'The doctor says I have a toxic heart. Any exertion could kill me. *You* know I can hardly get off the sofa some days. It would be quite beyond me to get to the station, let alone sit all day in a train.'

'Uncle Teddy would send his motor-car for you,' Maria said. 'You wouldn't need to exert yourself at all.'

'I detest motor-cars,' Mrs Stanhope said huffily. 'What I need is proper nursing.'

'Then you should go into a nursing home,' Maria said.

'I don't want to go into a nursing home. I want to stay here in my own home and have my daughter nurse me.'

'I'm not a nurse,' Maria said. 'I'm certainly not qualified to deal with a toxic heart.'

Mrs Stanhope was stymied, and retreated into hurt dignity. 'I wonder sometimes what I brought you into the world for.'

'Would you like to come to Morland Place with me?' Maria pressed the point.

'No. I shall stay here,' said Mrs Stanhope. 'You can go. Why should I care about such an unnatural daughter? And if I die I hope you'll be able to live with yourself.'

Maria went to pack her bag, but with a sore heart.

★   ★   ★

Helen met her at York station in her own little car. 'How have things been without me?' Maria asked. She sat beside Helen in a tense, hunched way – like a cold bird on a twig, Helen thought. Rug, sent to the back seat to make room for her, thought what she needed most was a cold wet nose in the palm of her hand, and kindly provided one.

'Oh, you were missed,' Helen said. 'I'm afraid there's heaps to do in the steward's room. Jessie did a bit and I tried to help, but I've been away a lot, and Jessie gets uncomfortable if she sits or stands for long at a time.'

'Was I missed in any other way?' Maria asked, perhaps a little grimly. While it was nice to know oneself useful, it didn't do much to warm the heart.

'I can only speak for myself, and say *I* missed you, when I was there. And I'm sure Martin will babble with joy when he sees you.'

Maria couldn't help smiling at the thought of her small son. He was very much the property of the nursery, where parents were not encouraged to interfere, but he had a special smile that he reserved for his mother's visits, and there was something about the automatic way he stretched out his arms to her when he saw her . . . 'Has anything happened while I was away?' she asked.

'Cousin Lennie's come home on leave. Poor chap is awfully lovelorn about Polly, but she's enjoying flaunting her power over him, the minx, and hardly passes the time of day with him. Oh, and Father Palgrave has started having nightmares again.'

Maria felt her cheeks grow hot. She scratched Rug's strategically placed head, and said in as casual a manner as possible, 'I wonder what's brought that on?'

'I couldn't say, not being an expert, but it's obvious he hasn't been happy these past few weeks. What Uncle Teddy calls "off his feed". Mopes, picks at his dinner, spends his evenings in his room instead of with the family. I suppose,' she added, watching the traffic for the chance to turn right onto the track home, 'there's something on his mind, but with a man who's been through what he's been through, it's hard to guess what it might be.'

Maria felt suddenly strangely happy. Her shoulders relaxed. She looked out of the window at the burgeoning land with pleasure. 'It's good to be back,' she said. 'I hadn't realised how much this place has come to mean to me.'

'Must be quite a contrast with Hammersmith.' Helen bumped the car carefully onto the track and glanced at her companion. 'Perhaps you can talk to Father Palgrave and find out what's troubling him. You and he always seem to get on so well together.'

'I'll certainly try,' Maria said, feeling a surge of affection towards her sister-in-law. 'What about you? How are you coping?'

Helen's face grew bleak. 'Not well,' she admitted. 'But we have to go on. For the children, and the family, and the country. It's when the war ends that I'm afraid of. When I have nothing of national importance to do, and all there will be for me to think about is what I've lost.'

'Oh, Helen, I'm sorry,' Maria said, with a burst of passionate sympathy, not unmixed with guilt.

'You're in the same boat,' Helen said, unconsciously turning the screw. 'And you only had a few days with poor Frank. At least I had years with Jack.' Rug jerked his head up sharply at the sound of the name, and looked intently at Helen. She said, 'No, poor old boy, he's not here.'

'But that must only make you miss him more,' Maria said. 'For me – to be honest, I can hardly remember any more what it was like to be with Frank. I mean, I remember it as a fact, but I can't remember how it *felt*.'

Helen was silent a moment. 'You shouldn't feel guilty about that. Life moves on. You're too young to shut yourself away for ever. If the opportunity arises, you owe it to yourself to live again. It's what Frank would want for you.'

'Thank you. You're a great comfort,' Maria said.

'I can't think how,' Helen said, with a short laugh. 'And I'm afraid I shall be removing my fabled comfort from you almost immediately. I have to go up to the factory tomorrow and collect a machine for the park in Joyce Green.'

'I shall miss you,' Maria said.

'I'll be back,' said Helen.

That night Maria couldn't sleep. There was too much going through her mind, an endless succession of heavy thoughts rolling by in a way that made her think of a cinematic film she had seen of tanks going down a road. The heavy image was probably also partly induced by the roast goose she had consumed at dinner, which, while delicious, was probably rather a shock to the system after the rationing cooking in Hammersmith. She decided in the end to go down to the kitchen and warm some milk on the stove, in the hope of soothing either her mind or her body sufficiently to sleep.

As she was returning to her room, she saw a light at the end of the passage, which she realised was coming from the day nursery. Her heart leaped into her throat, but she pushed it down and told herself that it was the act of any responsible adult to go and see. Someone might have left a candle unattended. When she reached the open nursery door, she saw that the light was in fact coming from the room beyond, through its open door, and was too steady to be a candle. The lamp in the schoolroom had been lit. She went forward, her heart beating fast.

Palgrave was there, sitting at his desk. He was fully dressed, writing fast, with a lock of hair falling over his forehead in a way that made her fingers long to brush it back for him. As she appeared in the doorway he started, then stood up, a blush spreading through his pale face.

'I'm sorry if I startled you,' she said.

'No – no, not at all.'

'I saw the light, so— You haven't been to bed? Are you ill?'

366

'No, I'm quite well.'

'But you're troubled. Helen told me you'd been having nightmares again.'

'Only twice. And not really bad ones.'

She stepped forward, towards him, and put down her candle on the edge of his desk to free her hands. 'Won't you tell me what's troubling you? You and I always talk about everything. Perhaps I can help you.'

'I think you're the only person who could help me, but I don't know – I'm not sure . . . I haven't always told you *quite* everything, you see.'

'Oh?' A horrible thought suddenly struck her. Was he *married*? Separated from his wife and had never told anyone? But, no, that was foolish. He was the most honest man she knew. 'If there are confidences you may not break, I understand,' she said, hoping that was not it.

'It's not confidences, exactly – more not being sure of how you would think – feel – how you might react . . . Oh, God,' he groaned, 'I'm making such a mess of this!'

She took another step closer. She felt confidence warming her – his eyes told her she was not mistaken. Why hadn't hers told him? 'You can say anything to me,' she said. 'Anything in the world. I won't be shocked.'

'You might be,' he said uncertainly. 'But – nothing ventured is nothing gained. I was writing to you, you see.' He gestured towards the paper on the desk, covered with his fine, cramped hand.

'Writing to *me*?'

'That's the feeble sort of person I am, writing so that I don't have to tell you face to face. I've been worrying and worrying about whether to say anything at all. Hence the nightmares.' Suddenly, it was as if a dam had burst. 'Oh, Maria!' He took both her hands in his. 'I can't help it, I love you! I think I've loved you since the first day I came here, but it took your going away for all these weeks to make me see it. Now you're back and – and it may be too soon, it probably *is* too soon, and you'll hate me for speaking, when poor Frank— It's not even two years yet! If it's too soon, forgive me! But if there's any chance that one day you might feel the same about me, I'll wait. I promise you I'll wait and never press you. And if I'm completely wrong and you can't care for me, I swear I'll never mention this again, and no-one will ever know. That is, if you—'

She freed one of her hands, but only to lay the fingers lightly on his lips to stop him babbling. 'It's all right,' she said. 'All the time at Hammersmith, I was realising how much I missed you, and I was shocked at myself. It *is* too soon, but I can't help it any more than you can. And, as Helen said, life moves on. I think,' she finished hesitantly, 'that it would be an insult to the dead if we didn't cherish the life they fought to give us. Don't you think?'

'You – you're saying you love me?'

She looked up at him with shining eyes. 'Didn't I make that clear? I'm sorry.'

He was smiling now. 'It would help if you could say the words.'

'I love you,' she said. 'I love you – Denis. Like you, I think it's been coming on for a long time. I'm glad you love me too! I would have felt so awful if it was just me.'

He closed his eyes and drew her against him, and they held each other for a long time, like people whom some disaster has just passed by. Then he released her just enough to look at her again. 'Helen's a wise woman,' he said. 'And it's not disloyal to Frank. It's what he would have wanted.'

'That's what Helen said. But I can't help feeling guilty. Happy, in love – but guilty.'

'You won't be taking anything away from him. What you had with him was unique, and nothing touches that.'

'I know. Don't worry. I'll get over it – the guilt, I mean. But you really love me? Really, really?'

'More than I can possibly find words to tell you. Will you marry me? Would you mind that?' She freed herself from him, and looked concerned again, biting her lip, and his heart sank. 'What is it? Shouldn't I have asked you?'

'Of course you should. And I will marry you – there's nothing I want more! But when I said it was too soon . . . The family would be so shocked.'

'Yes, I suppose they would.' He frowned, considering. 'And we couldn't be married and continue to live here.'

She shuddered. 'No, absolutely not. I wouldn't want to. I want to live with you and Martin in a house of our own, like other people.'

'You will never be quite like other people, my brilliant beloved! But that's what I want, too. I will have to look for a living – you won't mind being a priest's wife?'

'I'll be any sort of wife, as long as I'm your wife. But don't do it yet,' she pleaded. 'The family needs you even more than I do. Uncle Teddy and Mother-in-law and all the children – I can't take you away from them, especially not now, with Robbie dying and Jack being killed, and the war and everything. It would be too hard. I'm afraid we must wait.'

'Until the end of the war?' he said doubtfully.

'Who knows when that will be? I've heard them say it might go on four or five more years. I don't think I could wait that long.'

'I don't, myself, think it will be more than another two, now the Americans have come in. Perhaps even by the end of next year they'll be down to the mopping up.'

She placed her hands back in his. 'Let's wait and see. When things get better, and it won't seem like such a betrayal – perhaps next year . . .'

'I think I could wait that long,' he said. 'If I must.'

'Until then,' she said slowly – this part was harder, 'we must keep our feelings for each other a secret.'

'Yes,' he said, with a sigh. 'I do see that. But it will be hard.'

She nodded. With her hands in his, alone with him in the

369

security of the night, she knew how hard it would be to see him every day and say nothing, show nothing. 'We have to be patient.'

'Being a priest teaches you patience, if nothing else. You'll let me know when you think the time is right?'

'You'll know it too, or you're not the man I think you are.'

He smiled. 'I shall like having you for my wife. You have such a wonderful brain.'

She looked up at him in a way that made him feel breathless. 'Is that all?'

'Not quite,' he said, and kissed her.

She closed her eyes in bliss as the flood of feelings she had forgotten could exist rushed through her. In the corner of her mind that never seemed to sleep, she thought she heard a ghost sigh, but it was not an unhappy sigh. This was not a betrayal. Everything would be all right.

It was Lennie's last night. Helen was still away but due back tomorrow. She had delivered the aeroplane but had gone to Wiltshire, to check on the house and talk to the people at the factory about more missions, before coming back to Morland Place. Uncle Teddy had talked about having guests in for Lennie's last night, but he had begged him not to, saying that he wanted to enjoy being in the bosom of the family before having to go back to France. This had touched Teddy, who had told him that he was certainly part of the family and, as far as he was concerned, always would be. 'You mustn't think of this as somewhere you only come to on leave. This is your home, if you care to make it so, and for as long as you want.' Lennie could not help glancing at Polly as he said that, and she pretended not to notice, turning her head a little, which only had the effect of revealing her enchanting profile to him.

Polly was confused. She liked Lennie, and the more she was with him, the more she enjoyed his company. But he was not handsome, and not *exciting* like Holford

370

– though it had to be admitted that he had done exciting things, like that time he had jumped right over an occupied German trench and rescued a wounded colleague and been awarded the Military Medal. If only he had Holford's *air* and *sophistication*. On the other hand, she was not sure – could never be sure – what Holford really thought about her, and he was not a faithful correspondent like Lennie. It was unfortunate that dependability and faithfulness were not as interesting as enigma, and that Holford was wanted by so many other girls, which put Polly on her mettle.

But it *was* Lennie's last night, so she ought to be nice to him. After all, he was going back to the Front, and anything might happen. In the realisation of the *anything*, she turned her face back to him and smiled; and that evening she let him sit by her, and talked to him, and rediscovered what fun he could be.

It was while they were sitting in the drawing-room that the telephone rang, and after a pause Sawry entered to say to Henrietta, 'A telephone call for you, madam.'

Henrietta looked surprised. 'Can't you take it for me?'

'It's a long-distance call, madam, and for you personally. They put it through only after the person requested is on the line.'

Henrietta got up reluctantly. 'Whoever can it be? Why would anyone telephone *me*, and at this time of night?'

'It isn't *very* late, Mother,' Jessie pointed out.

'Well, it isn't daytime,' Henrietta retorted, and followed Sawry out. The telephone was too far away for anyone in the drawing-room to hear anything that was said, but a short while later Henrietta reappeared, walking unsteadily and being supported by Sawry. She seemed unable to speak. There were tears on her cheeks, and she looked round the room as if seeking someone she couldn't see there.

Jessie got to her feet more nimbly than anyone would have thought possible and crossed the room to her. She took her mother's hands, which were like ice. 'What is it? What's happened?' *Someone's dead*, she thought.

Henrietta focused on her face with a look of relief as if it was her she had been seeking all along, but still the tears flowed, and it took time for her to assemble any words. 'It's Jack,' she said at last. 'He's alive.'

Eventually all was told. It had been Helen on the telephone. When she had got back to the factory she had found a telephone message and a telegram waiting for her. The CO of Jack's squad had sent telegrams to her at the factory and at her house – he had not known she was at Morland Place. And the telephone message was from her father's old friend Hugh Trenchard, who had received the news via the Royal Air Force from the Red Cross, and had telephoned the factory as being the place most likely to know where she was.

Jack was alive, and in a prisoner-of-war camp in Germany. He was uninjured, and now that his name was on the official lists, Helen would be able to write to him, and he to her.

Helen's first priority was to tell them the good news at Morland Place, and she had felt it should be his mother who received the news. It was fortunate that Sawry had been on hand, hovering nearby because he knew how much his mistress feared electric shocks from the instrument. He had been able to catch Henrietta as she gave a little inarticulate cry and her legs gave way under her.

The news was received by the family with quiet, almost bewildered joy. Lennie, in his delight, found himself holding Polly's hand, and she did not seem to object. Teddy, unusually for him, had no words at all, only shook his head with wonder, and wiped and wiped at his leaking eyes. After a while, Henrietta caught Father Palgrave's eye, and they went together to the chapel to give their thanks where they felt it was most due. Jessie went with them, and Maria held the others back, feeling the two women who had loved Jack best should have their moment with God alone.

When, in the chapel, Palgrave was helping Jessie to her feet afterwards, a look of consternation crossed her face, and she doubled up with sudden pain.

'What is it?' Henrietta asked, taking her arm.

Jessie met her eyes. 'I think – I think this might be my time.'

Henrietta put her arm round her daughter and said to the priest, 'I have her. Go and get help. We'll need someone strong to carry her up to bed.'

'I can walk,' Jessie protested, then proved herself wrong by having to sit down.

'It was the shock brought it on,' Henrietta said. Then, 'It's not too early. Don't be afraid.'

'I am, a little,' Jessie admitted. 'But, oh, Mother, Jack's alive! He's alive!'

'It's a night of miracles,' Henrietta said.

BOOK THREE

Endings

Poppies whose roots are in men's veins
Drop, and are ever dropping;
But mine in my ear is safe,
Just a little white with the dust.

Break of Day in the Trenches, Isaac Rosenberg

CHAPTER SEVENTEEN

'Do you think we ought to send for the doctor?' Nanny Emma said quietly to Henrietta.

Jessie heard her, from that place where she was, out of time, out of the world. She did not know how long it had been, even what day it was. Once the pain had been inside her. Now she was inside the pain. It was all there was. No more Jessie, just this vast ache and struggle.

But she heard the words. She opened her eyes, but couldn't see anyone. Everything was blurred, as if she was under water. Was this death approaching? Am I dying? she wondered. She heard her own voice, tiny and far off, say it. 'Am I dying?'

Her mother was there, a cool hand on her brow, a cool cloth wiping the sweat from her eyes so that she could see again the beloved face bending over her, smiling. 'No, you're not dying,' she said. 'It's taking rather a long time, that's all.'

Jessie tried to read the truth behind the smile, but she was too tired to think. The effort was beyond her. The pain was continuous now, no ebbs and flows.

'I think we'll just get Dr Hasty to have a look at you,' Henrietta said. Behind her, Nanny Emma went at once out of the room. Henrietta bathed Jessie's face with cool water that smelled of lavender.

Jessie met her eyes, struggling to think of what she wanted to say. 'Tell Bertie,' she said at last.

Henrietta nodded. 'We've already sent a telegram.'

That wasn't what she meant. 'Tell Bertie,' she began again. Weak tears slipped out to join the sweat on her cheeks because she couldn't remember what she wanted to say.

An unknown quantity of time later, she opened her eyes wildly. Her mother was still there. 'Jack?' she said.

Henrietta bent over her. Jessie could see the strain in her face now. 'Jack's alive,' she said. 'He's a prisoner of war.'

Jessie sighed with relief. 'I thought I'd dreamed it.'

'His squadron leader's telegram promised a letter with more detail, and Uncle Teddy's contacting the Red Cross. But there's no doubt about it.'

'So glad,' Jessie said. The pain intensified. 'Mama!' she cried weakly. 'I can't. It's too hard.' She felt as though she were fading out of life, further and further from everyone she loved, down and deep into the universe of pain, falling, fading . . .

Henrietta's hand gripped hers hard, hard enough to hurt. 'You can. You will. *My* Jessie would never give up. She would fight! My Jessie *will* come through.'

Jessie gasped. For a moment she was right there, in her room again. Everything was vivid as though lit with strong sunshine, every outline standing out like stark relief, and her mother close to her, looking old and tired, but so, so dear. 'Oh, Mama, I'm sorry,' she whispered.

The hand gripped tighter. 'Don't leave me, Jess.' And it was not just a command, it was a plea. *I can't lose you, too.*

But Jessie couldn't hear her.

She came back slowly from a place of profound distance, as though drifting up through dark water from the depths of the ocean. She felt that some great change had happened in the time she had been away, something of irreversible importance. But how long had it been? It felt like centuries. Would the world even exist any more? The thought came to her that she was, indeed, dead, in which case centuries might well have passed. The darkness in which she floated was warm and comfortable, and there was no pain. She had no sensation at all. She had no body. Yes, this was death all right. And it was nothing to be afraid of. She felt comforted. She wished everyone might know that. But the living must fear death, or they would not struggle to stay alive.

She didn't want to leave this dark place, but the drifting was taking her towards the surface, to a place where two states met. She felt that she would break through the surface at some point, and she didn't want to. She wanted to stay here and be comforted; but the drift seemed outside her control. Up, slowly up, towards . . . change. A new state. It was coming, coming closer . . .

She heard a cry, piercing the darkness. Had she cried out? No, it was not her – but it was very personal to her. A cry she *must* heed, whether she wanted to or not. The surface was rushing towards her now. There was light beyond it. She didn't want – she didn't want—

She was through. She woke, opened her eyes, became aware simultaneously of the pain in the lower half of her body and the crying of a baby. She looked around, bewildered. She was in a bed, in a room. It was daylight. It was her own room. She was alive – her sensations told her that, but the pain most of all. And there was Nanny Emma, moving about on the other side of the room, with her back to her. Jessie could make no sense of it. Her brain seemed clouded and bemused, and with no sense of time elapsed. 'Did we win the war?' she asked. It seemed important to know. But the words came out as a blurred croak from her dry throat.

Nanny Emma turned with a small glad sound, and hurried over to her. 'You're awake,' she said, and cupped a loving hand round Jessie's cheek. 'My precious toad, what a fright you gave us! But you're back now.' Her voice, with its Norfolk burr, was comfortable and familiar. She took in Jessie's confused frown, and said, 'Dr Hasty gave you sleepy-stuff, my lamb. You've been sleepin' like the dead – twenty hours, it's been.' Jessie croaked again, and Nanny Emma said, 'Here, let me give you some water. You'll need to drink a lot of water now,' she added instructively, 'to get your milk going.'

She lifted Jessie's head and put a cup to her lips, and Jessie drank gratefully, the words slowly filtering through the confusion of her brain. *Milk? But this was water. What milk?*

A small sound from across the room drove the last cobwebs away, because it was definitely the sound of a living thing. There was another person in the room. Milk? As the sound was repeated, her breasts ached, and she realised it was the same cry she had heard before, though it had been magnified when she was in the darkness. She looked into Nanny Emma's face with dawning realisation, wondering joy, apprehension. 'Did I have a baby?' she asked, and, 'Is it all right?'

Nanny Emma smiled, the best smile Jessie had ever seen on a human being. 'You had a boy, my chick, a fine, big boy, and he's the sweetest, mos' perfect thing you ever saw. Would you like to hold him? Let me see if I can sit you up.'

Jessie found herself as weak as string. Sitting up made her feel dizzy, and woke the pain of her lower half into new variations. But when she had settled the pillows, Nanny Emma went across to the crib in the corner (the ancient carved-oak one that all new babies in the house used – Helen's Barbara had been its last occupant) and lifted out the white bundle. For a moment, before Nanny Emma folded the whole thing in a shawl, Jessie saw tiny red feet kicking out of one end of the bundle; and those feet made her feel almost faint with love. She had felt them so often on the inside of her, beating impatiently against her flesh. Her baby! She had done it! She had carried him to term and given birth to him! She had given him life! Without her volition her arms reached out hungrily. The seconds

380

it took Nanny Emma to cross the room were too long. She wanted him *now!*

She had him. Nanny Emma laid him in her arms; she felt the divine weight, looked into the tiny face. He was trying to open his eyes, trying to look at her, but one eye and then the other kept closing, so that he looked as though he was squinting against a bright light. But she felt, with a surge of such love it was almost unendurable, that he knew it was her: he had wanted her as much as she had wanted him, and now he was with her again, he was content.

She looked up at Nanny Emma. She had no idea how she looked just then, and Nanny Emma thought it was a great shame that first look should be wasted on her. It was Bertie who ought to have seen it. She said, 'Mr Bertie's on his way home. He telegraphed to say he was coming right away. He might be here today, or tomorrow, dependin' on the trains.'

Jessie smiled her ravishing smile in thanks. To see Bertie again, so soon – she was so lucky! But her eyes were drawn ineluctably back to her tiny son's face. She gazed and gazed, and felt she could never have enough of simply looking at him.

Bertie sat by Jessie's bed, her hand in his, and he felt he could never have enough of simply looking at her, being in the same room with her, touching her. It had been a hard struggle, he was told, and at the end Hasty had had to help the baby out. But there did not seem to be any lasting damage. The next couple of weeks would be uncomfortable for Jessie, she would have pain and feel very debilitated, but she would heal and her native vigour would restore her. And the baby seemed a perfect specimen, and none the worse for his difficult entry into the world.

'He *is* beautiful, isn't he?' Jessie said a dozen times.

And a dozen times, Bertie answered, with complete sincerity, 'He's the most beautiful baby I've ever seen.'

Jessie had thought she could feel no greater rapture than holding her son for the first time, but in fact the sight of Bertie holding him for the first time brought even deeper feelings. *I have done this for him*, she thought, as she saw the expression on his face, and she felt huge pride and even greater humility. *God is very good*, she thought. It seemed in that moment that she had been forgiven for the sin of what they had done in France nine months ago. Such joy and completeness could not come unforgiven.

After the twelfth time he said the baby was the most beautiful he had ever seen, she thought painfully of Maud, who had had to die for her to be this happy, and of little Richard, who must once have been the most beautiful baby in the world to Bertie. And so she said, 'Would you like to call him Richard?'

He looked up, moved by her generosity. But Richard had been himself, and no other little boy would ever replace him. 'Thank you, but no,' he said – to Jessie's relief, which she hoped she concealed. 'Richard was named after Maud's father,' he went on, 'so it wouldn't be appropriate.'

'My father was called Jerome, but I don't want to call him that. He doesn't look like a Jerome.'

'He doesn't look like a Peregrine, either,' said Bertie with a sudden grin. His father had been Sir Peregrine Parke. 'And I'm damned if I'll call the poor little blighter Perceval after his father.' He had always hated his first name.

'So, what then? Let me hold him again.' The baby was passed back, like something delicious, and he opened one eye to see where he was, squinted at her, and made a gurgling sound. 'I'm sure he knows me,' she said.

'He'd be an ungrateful hound if he didn't,' Bertie said, 'considering all he owes you. Would you like to give him a Morland name?'

'Edward is the most traditional Morland name,' she said. 'And Uncle Teddy would think it a great compliment.'

He heard the reluctance in her voice. 'But he doesn't

look like an Edward, somehow. And if it was shortened to Ned . . .'

Jessie saw the point. People would think he was named after her first husband. 'It might seem guilty,' she said. 'The other traditional Morland name is Thomas.'

'Thomas. Yes, I like that,' Bertie said. 'There's something solid and trustworthy about Thomas.'

'And handsome and debonair,' Jessie said.

'And intelligent and energetic.'

'And thoughtful and kind.'

'And lucky. The sort of man who makes a success of everything he touches. And is loved by his colleagues and underlings alike.'

'But never forgets his tenderness towards his mother.'

'And his loyalty towards his father.'

Jessie laughed and looked down at the baby. 'Oh, Thomas, what a lot we are putting onto your shoulders! Doomed to be a paragon in every way. How can you ever live up to it?'

'Obviously he mustn't be expected to,' Bertie said. 'We'll have to provide him with some siblings to take the weight off him.'

'Easy for you to say, when you're not sitting on a nest of hedgehogs.'

'Oh, darling, I'm sorry. Is it very bad?'

'You'll never know how bad,' she said, with perfect truth.

'Does that mean you don't want any more children?' he asked anxiously.

'Of course not. Of course Thomas must have a brother and a sister. Just not quite yet!'

Bertie grinned. 'I imagine it's hard to get enthusiastic about the process when one's sitting on hedgehogs. But do you notice we seemed to have named the baby? Are you happy with that?'

'Thomas he is,' Jessie said. 'It seems right. He *looks* like Thomas somehow.'

'Does he? Let me see. Let me have him for a bit.'

And so the happy hours passed, handing the baby back and forth, and talking pleasant nonsense.

When it was time for Bertie to go back, he said, 'You mustn't worry about me. We're right out of the line for the present, re-forming and retraining. And the line is reasonably quiet. The Germans are licking their wounds, and the Americans and the Australians seem to be taking up the slack for the time being.'

'Does that mean you might be able to visit again?' she asked, not daring to hope.

'I think it might. Probably we won't be back in action until the autumn. There's bound to be a big push in September or October, and perhaps we'll have the Germans on the run by then. There's a lot of feeling around now that the war might be over next year.'

'Oh, please, God!'

'But for now we're well back behind the line, and I shan't have anyone shooting at me for several weeks at least, more likely a couple of months. Besides, what's being a colonel for, if it doesn't mean you can slip off for a few days now and then on essential business?'

'Thomas and me being essential business?'

He lifted her hand to his lips. 'I can't think of anything essentialer.'

Mid-June, Violet thought, was the perfect time for the exhibition – the height of the Season, when London was still full, but also when it had been going on long enough for people to want a new sensation. Things seemed to have quietened down at the Front: apart from the Americans' ongoing attack at Belleau Wood, and the Australians' harrying of the enemy near Amiens – a series of bloody raids and ambushes that they, with their usual irony, called 'peaceful penetration' – there was only routine activity in the lines. As a result, officers were being given their leave, which meant many would be in London, and their families would be in a receptive mood. There had been no Zeppelin raids since that bad one on the 19th of May. And the weather was perfect, warm, bright and clear, recalling that golden summer of 1914 before the world had begun to fall to pieces.

Laura and George Verney did most of the actual work, though Violet was involved at every stage in the planning, and when it came to the hanging, she showed a taste in arrangement that surprised her friends. A smallish gallery in Piccadilly had been hired, staff engaged, food and champagne ordered, and invitations were sent out. Violet chose them herself, large, stiff cards with a gold deckled edge and heavy black printing, for she knew that they must stand out from the multitude that fell through the letterboxes of the *ton* every day. Their very expensiveness must guarantee that the exhibition would be worth attending. George contacted the various newspapers and important critics, hoping to secure their attendance and reviews, and placed advertisements in the newspapers and magazines. Much thought went into the title of the exhibition, and they decided in the end to call it 'The Artist in the Trenches'. And Violet, of course, wrote the cheques for the various expenses.

It was inevitable that the exhibition should rekindle the gossip about Violet and Laidislaw, and there were those who declared it in bad taste of Lady Holkam to parade her disgraceful connection with the artist in this way. Even if the pictures themselves were worth exhibiting, she should have let someone else do the showing. Laura had begged Violet not to tell anyone what had prompted her to it, feeling that a spirit message from the next world would not go down well in certain circles; but even without that, it was a sensational decision to many people. It seemed likely, however, that more would be provoked by curiosity to see the pictures than would refuse on principle to go near them.

Besides – many said – all *that* was a long time ago, and such things happened in wartime. It was really rather more romantic, in hindsight, than disgusting. The important thing was that the Holkams were still together and no lasting scandal had ensued. On the whole, one really would rather like to see what it was all about, and the Verney set had been assiduous in circulating hints that the pictures were quite outstanding, and that anyone with a son or husband at the Front really owed it to *them* to see them.

Acceptances started to come in, in a trickle and then a flood. Violet received one or two curious looks when the exhibition was mentioned, but the mood of the *ton* was now mostly of pleased anticipation. One thing, everyone said: with Violet Holkam, you could be sure of good refreshments – first-rate champagne and plenty of it.

Oliver was the first to confront Violet with a negative response. He called round one evening as she was about to go up and dress, having himself just arrived back from Sidcup and found the invitation waiting for him.

'Are you *quite* demented?' he enquired, with controlled anger. 'Is it a passing insanity, or will we have to hire a keeper for you? I only ask so that we can arrange our lives round your antics. It will be time-consuming, I imagine.'

'Oliver, don't make such a fuss,' Violet said, sounding calm, though feeling pinched inside. 'There's nothing mad about it. The pictures are extraordinary, and the world ought to see them.'

'And the world ought to be given another chance to gossip about you and Laidislaw, I suppose? You don't think enough was said on that subject two years ago? Have you missed the slights and insults and impertinent remarks so much you want to experience them again?'

'It won't be like that,' she said, holding firm. 'People have forgotten. The one or two sticklers who care about it won't come, and that will be that. It's my duty to show the pictures, and if duty involves some – inconvenience, one ought not to mind it.'

'Inconvenience? You think it's merely an inconvenience to shock and distress our mother?'

'She's – she's not *really* upset, is she?' The dent appeared in Violet's armour. 'I thought she would understand. She's seen the pictures. She knows how wonderful they are.'

'You *knew* she would be upset,' Oliver said gravely. 'That's why you didn't tell her about it in person, just sent her an invitation through the post. That wasn't well done of you, Vi.'

Violet blushed. 'I meant to bring it myself – yours too. They got posted with the others by mistake.'

'But you didn't say a word to either of us. You could have told us what you were planning any time these – what would it be? – four weeks.'

Violet looked down at her hands. 'I suppose I *did* know you might be upset. I didn't want anything to spoil the exhibition. I was going to have it whatever you and Mother might say, so I didn't want to have to quarrel with you, and leave a bad taste.'

'Well, now you've had the quarrel anyway,' Oliver said. He looked down at his sister's bent head, and felt love and exasperation and worry for her, and for his mother, sweep away anger. 'It's such a bad time, Vi. Mum's tired to death with her war work and her operating lists, and on top of that she's worried about Thomas. And now this. It's too bad of you. Why couldn't you wait until after the war to show the damned pictures? It can't make any difference to Laidislaw now.' She looked up at that, and he saw the hurt in her eyes, and was sorry he'd said that last bit. But it was true, dammit! 'Our duty is to the living,' he finished. Then, 'What does Holkam say about it?'

'I haven't told him yet,' Violet admitted.

Oliver stared, and shook his head disbelievingly. 'You are a strange girl. Anyone would think you'd never say boo to a goose, and then you go and do something outrageous like this and pull the house down on your head. Is there any chance you'll change your mind? Cancel it? Back down, like a good girl?'

'No,' Violet said, and met his eyes steadily. 'I'm going to do this. It's – something I have to do.'

He sighed. 'Then we'll just have to make sure it's a roaring success, so that people forget the other side of it.'

'You don't mean that you'll come?' Violet asked, hope dawning.

'Of course I'll come. Family is family, after all. I expect Mum will as well, once she's got over the shock. And Kit Westhoven's going to be home on leave. If I make him come with me, that will ensure all manner of fashionable young women turn up. He's the flapper's delight, bless him. Bon for the ladies, as they say.'

Violet's eyes filled with tears of gratitude. 'Oh, Oliver, you *are* good to me!'

'No mush, old girl,' he warned. 'I'm still angry with you, but I can't let you down. I'll come and coo over your pictures, and if anyone says a word to me about you and Laidislaw, I'll lay them out. But I recommend you write to Holkam before someone else tells him the glad tidings. He won't take kindly to hearing about it second-hand.'

Violet didn't think he would take kindly to hearing about it first-hand, either, but she knew Oliver was right. She wrote a detailed letter to her husband that very night. He was at the Front, a staff officer and one of General Haig's 'young men'. She told him that the Verneys were nominally responsible for the exhibition, which would seem quite natural, since Laidislaw had been their friend and *protégé*, and that her name was not appearing on the invitations or advertisements (though inevitably it would appear in the programmes as the owner of most of the works, but she did not mention that).

But she knew the mere mention of Laidislaw's name would be like putting a match to a bonfire, and so it proved. She received a telegram by return, forbidding her to go ahead with the exhibition, which was followed in short order by a letter that she flinched to read. In places his pen had stabbed right through the paper in his agitation. He wrote that *of course* everyone would know she was behind it, and that he refused to allow her to drag his family name back into the mud from which he had at such pains rescued it. He told her she must cancel at once, and forbade her to spend a penny of his money on any of the arrangements.

She wrote back to say that she had spent only her own money (and as she had plenty of that, she was to a great extent outside his power) and that since it was Laura and George 'giving' the exhibition, she was not in a position to cancel it. He telegraphed again, forbidding her to visit or in any way associate herself with it; and she wrote in reply, saying that, as the Prince of Wales was going to be at the opening with her cousin Eddie, she certainly must be there, or it would be seen as a frightful snub to His Royal Highness. At that point, Holkam retired defeated, merely telling her loftily in his next letter that as he evidently could not prevent her being at the opening, he hoped she would behave in a discreet and proper manner, leave as soon as possible after the prince, and not go near the place on any subsequent day. He said that he would not be coming to the opening as he could not get away from France, being heavily engaged in Versailles with discussions about the future conduct of the war.

If the last part was meant to put her in her place, it missed its mark: the relief that he would not be in London made her feel light-hearted. Besides, for the time being the exhibition seemed much more real to Violet than the war. The master stroke, of the Prince of Wales and Lord Vibart attending the opening, she guessed was down to Oliver's efforts to redeem her 'show', though she did not suppose he would ever admit it. It certainly put the seal on the exhibition's success. Everyone now meant to be there, and there would be newspaper journalists and photographers from all the illustrateds to report on what a glittering occasion it was. Violet had been wondering who to ask to escort her when she had word from Freddie that he would be home on leave. Sir Frederick Copthall had been her escort ever since she came out, a pleasant, undemanding bachelor who knew absolutely everyone and was welcome in any drawing-room. It was the perfect finishing touch that she would be able to go into that room on his comfortably familiar arm – for, despite her defiant mien, she did rather dread the looks and comments she might encounter.

But when the time came, she was too overwhelmed with emotion to notice any looks, or take in the nuances of any comments addressed to her. At the gallery there was a canopy over the pavement where the red carpet was already laid for the royal entrance. There were crowds out in the street – so large that policemen had been stationed to keep the road clear – spotting celebrities and waiting for the prince to arrive. An excited murmur arose as Violet stepped out of her motor – she had been in the illustrateds often enough for her face to be well known – and she walked up the red carpet with Freddie in an explosion of light from the photographers' flash-guns.

Inside there was already a glittering crowd of women in diamonds and long gowns, older men in evening dress, and officers in uniform. Their faces were indistinct to her, and she smiled without hearing anything they said. Waitresses handed glasses of champagne. The gallery's owner, a Mr Reed, thrilled beyond measure at the turn-out, which he hoped was going to make his name, greeted her and tried to press her hand. All of that faded into a background blur because there were the drawings and paintings, beautifully displayed and lit, and almost shockingly vivid. It was like, just for a moment, having Laidislaw there again, in the room with her. She felt his presence, like the warm breath from an oven when the door is opened suddenly. For an instant she remembered his face, his bright eyes, the sound of his voice, and her body thrilled and melted with its own memories. *Is this what you wanted?* she whispered to him inside her mind. There was no reply. The feeling of his presence had faded from her, and she knew he was gone; but his work was there – 'The most important part of me,' he had once said – and that would remain for ever. She closed her eyes for a second. She had done the right thing. *Goodbye, my darling*, she said inwardly.

And then she smiled, and did her official circuit of the pictures.

She was too bemused to take in much of what was going on around her, but Freddie, whose strong arm never faltered under her hand, fielded the requests for comment that were thrown at her, and said that the pictures were 'quite remark-able'.

'Give me a queer feelin',' he expanded. 'Like bein' back at the Front again. All these chaps – feel I know 'em.' It was a great deal from Freddie, who never said very much. And he added, 'Laidislaw did his bit. Died a soldier's death on the Somme. Knew what he was paintin', all right.' Violet pressed his arm in gratitude.

Later Laura came up to speak to Violet, and said that the officers were saying how full of insight the pictures were, while the ladies and civilians were saying it gave them more understanding of what it was really like for their men out there than anything else they had encountered. 'It's a success, Violet darling. Everyone loves Laddie's pictures. The papers are going to be full of him tomorrow.'

The Prince of Wales and Eddie came, and went round in the little bubble of space that always forms around royalty, and at the end of it Violet found herself curtsying to the prince and meeting a very penetrating gaze from him. 'Wonderful work,' he said. 'I've been out there myself, and I can tell you they capture the whole spirit and essence – quite shakes one up – remarkable. I shall recommend to the King that he comes and sees them.'

'Thank you, sir.'

'I do think it's very important these pictures are shown to as wide an audience as possible. I admire you for making it possible, Lady Holkam. It was very brave of you.'

Brave of me? Violet wondered, as she made a vague response. Why brave? And then she met the prince's blue eyes, and realised that he knew about her and Laidislaw. Someone had told him, or he had known about it all along – it hardly mattered – but he had come anyway, to put the seal of approval on it, and he had done that before he knew the pictures were any good. Had he done it for Eddie's sake? They were very close, after all. But the eyes gazing into hers were not only curious, quizzical – they were admiring. There was something about the whole business that he approved of.

Other people were clamouring for his attention, and the moment was over. He turned away, and she was left with an odd feeling of comfort. The prince was a very young man – younger than her – so it was odd that she should feel comforted by his approval; but then, after all, he *was* the Heir to the Throne.

Her mother had been operating at the Southport, and arrived late, after the prince had gone. She looked appallingly tired, and Violet flinched and came out of her dream to face the 'telling off' as she had been taught to in childhood. But Venetia, though she did not smile, did not scold. 'The pictures are extraordinary,' she said to her daughter. 'They deserve to be seen.'

Violet looked her gratitude. 'Thank you, Mummy,' she whispered.

Venetia was touched by the childhood name, which Violet hardly ever used. 'He was a man of great talent,' she said generously. It was on the tip of her tongue to say that had he lived, he would have been one of the great painters of the age. But had Laidislaw lived, Violet would have been ruined. She left it at that.

Oliver had come in with her, his friend Lord Westhoven at his side. Westhoven was the son of an old friend of Venetia's. He was a doctor, and he and Oliver had served together in the RAMC at the Front. Westhoven was still out there, but distance had not dented their friendship. He had no family now, and spent his leaves, at her request, with Venetia, which made it easier for him and Oliver to keep up with each other. He had an estate at Lutterworth, but it was run by agents and he rarely went there. He was tall, lean and fair-skinned, with rather unruly blond hair and blue eyes, and Violet could see why Oliver called him a 'flapper's delight'. He looked younger than his age, handsome, and somehow vulnerable. As he and Oliver turned away from her, Violet saw several young women hovering in the vicinity, ready to remind Oliver of some slight acquaintance so that they could make Westhoven's.

The next day the newspapers carried reviews of the exhibition, saying that it would be going on for two weeks, and urging their readers not to miss it. The pictures were acclaimed as everything from merely 'brilliant' to 'epoch-making' – Violet was not sure what that meant, but it was obviously a compliment. The reports were gushing not only from the society columns but from the art critics as well. Violet glowed with pleasure as she read them. Laidislaw's name, surely, was made. His work would never be forgotten, so neither would he be.

Most of the papers carried remarks about the Verneys and their circle as patrons of the arts, and several carried reproductions of Laidislaw's portrait of Laura. There were also mentions of his portrait of Violet, who was named as one of the guests, and some of the 'gossip' columns made sidelong references and veiled hints about her and Laidislaw. But on the whole, the success of the evening and the cachet conferred by the prince's presence had made it respectable to admire Laidislaw, and therefore it was not possible to criticise his relationship with Violet, or Violet herself.

The exhibition was a roaring success, and when the King and Queen decided to visit towards the end of the second week, it was plain that an extension would be needed. The owner approached Laura, who consulted with Violet, and the decision was made to keep it on until the second or possibly third week of July, depending on attendance – until the Season ended, in fact, and London emptied, in so far as it still emptied these days.

Violet was glad that Emma would have the chance to see it. She had written to say that she would be due some leave after six months of service overseas, and that it was to be granted in July. Violet longed to see her friend, and wondered how her experiences would have changed her. When Emma had written to say that she was being awarded the Military Medal, it seemed such a strange and unlikely thing in connection with pretty, lively Emma that it made her almost afraid to meet her again. But Venetia had said they ought to have a 'medal tea' for her, which put Violet at ease. The children would be able to attend, which would make it pleasant for everyone.

And to add to that, there was the wonderful news from Morland Place, that Jack was alive after all, and that Jessie had been successfully delivered of a son. It was a very happy time for Violet.

There had been talk already about the influenza that was 'going around' among the troops in France. Some called it 'Spanish flu', though there was no evidence it had come from Spain, which wasn't even in the war. Indeed, there was some idea it had started in the army camps back in America, where pig flu was common among farm workers, and been brought to France by the Sammies. But it was not politic to say so, of course, given that the same Sammies were to be Europe's saviours. Around St Omer it was called

'Flanders *grippe*'. Kit Westhoven told Oliver that some doctors did not believe it was influenza at all, but a sort of malaria, brought to France by the troops transferred there from Italy and Salonika.

At all events, for Emma it made for a busy June, which otherwise might have been quiet. There was a definite lull on the Front, which some attributed to the Germans' suffering from the flu as well; but in the second half of the month, a number of the Unit 8 women went down with it and had to take to their beds. Muriel Thompson was one, and since Hutchinson was on leave, Norma Lowson had to take charge, and those like Emma who had somehow escaped infection had to do the work of two or three. By the time she headed for London for her leave, she was more than ready for it.

She was disappointed not to have heard from Wentworth before she left. She had written to him to say she was going on leave, but had had no reply. Of course, the letter might have gone astray – such things happened, though remarkably rarely, considering the volume of post going back and forth across France. She hoped at least it was only that, and not that he was wounded or ill. She remembered he had said he was due leave in July, and had been thinking they might meet in England – just in a friendly way, of course. It was good, when one was doing a man's job, to have a male friend to remind one there was a difference. Armstrong had been seeing Captain Savile regularly, and since she had caught the *grippe*, he had been visiting her daily in the local hospital. Of course, it was different for them because there was definitely a romance building between them.

Emma and Benson set off on the 1st of July, cadging a lift to the station from an RASC driver, to catch the eight-fifteen train. A train came in at a quarter to nine, but she was informed that it was actually the night train from Paris, which should have arrived at two a.m., and that as her warrant was for the eight-fifteen, she was not allowed to get on anything else, even though there was room. It was frustrating to have to stand around in the station, with the precious hours of her leave ticking away, while various trains passed through that she was not allowed to board. At last, at around four o'clock, it was announced that the eight-fifteen had been cancelled and had never left Paris, and that warrants would be deemed valid for the next train to come through.

By that time she had missed the afternoon boat, and would face the problem, when she reached Calais, of trying to get her warrant changed for another crossing. She felt like weeping as she got into a compartment with some officers, who all looked as gloomy as she felt. No, not quite all – one, at least, seemed impervious to despair. He was an RAF officer, but from his accent as he made a polite remark about Benson, he was obviously American. They got chatting, using Benson's history as the excuse, and the man, whose name was Esmond, told her he had been so eager to get into the war that as soon as he had been old enough he had got himself across to England and joined the RFC. 'Best thing I ever did. What a fine bunch of fellows they are! And what do you do? You're not a nurse, I can see that, and that's not a WAAC uniform.'

It turned out that he had never seen a FANY before, which was not surprising, since there were only about four hundred of them in all, whereas there were nine thousand WAACs. He was fascinated by her job, and told her that back home in Arizona his mother drove the family truck and had made all his sisters learn to drive, saying that a woman needed to know how to do everything and couldn't depend on a man being around. 'She has the real pioneer spirit. There's a family story that her grandma once killed an Indian with a shovel.' Emma laughed, and he added, 'We always thought, back home, that English girls were delicate – kinda mimsy, you know? It's good to know you have as much spunk as our girls.'

396

They got on so well that Benson was soon lying half across his lap, snoozing contentedly. They discussed their leave plans, and when Emma said that hers was likely to be spent in the transport office at the dock trying to change her passage, he said, 'Hey, there's no need for that.' He lowered his voice. 'Don't want the others to hear, but when the old eight-fifteen was so late that I knew I'd miss the afternoon boat, I made some phone calls. It seems there's a hospital ship going across at midnight, and I'm going to wangle myself onto it. I'll get you on too, if you like. Can't make it more than two, though, so keep it low.'

Emma felt she had nothing to lose so agreed, though she wasn't sure how the wangle was going to work, and said so.

'Sheer cheek,' said Esmond, and dropped a solemn wink. 'You watch.'

When the train got in they hurried through the evening light to the docks. Emma's part was to stand around in the background while Esmond chatted, without apparent purpose, to a series of uniformed officials. Whatever he did, it worked. Eventually he came to her with a look of triumph and said, 'We're on. Come on, this way. I had to tell them you were my fiancée. I hope you don't mind. And you're going home to see your mother, who's having an operation tomorrow, so you've got to get there before she goes under.'

'I'm glad you told me,' Emma said. They had to go aboard at once, and stay on deck, as was the arrangement with their secret benefactor, which meant a long, boring wait, and no chance of anything to eat. Emma had had nothing since the garlic-sausage sandwich she had bought at St Omer station at lunchtime. However, nothing seemed beyond Esmond, who left her alone for a while and returned with a pack of chocolate, which he said he had bought from the ship's engineer officer. Emma accepted it gratefully, though she shared her half with Benson, who must have been hungry too.

The crossing was smooth and uneventful, and by the time they arrived at Victoria in the early hours they had been talking for so long that Emma felt she knew every-thing about him. She was a little worried that his interest was more than that of a good Samaritan, and that he might want to see her again, but as they got off the train he said he had a girl in Wokingham he couldn't wait to see, and asked her if she had somewhere to go. 'Can't leave you stranded here. Where were you headed for, on leave?'

'I'm to stay with a friend in London,' she said. 'I can get a taxi – it isn't far.'

'But will you be able to rouse them at this hour?'

'Oh, one of the servants will let me in,' she said, without thinking.

He smiled. 'I should have guessed. I suppose you're quite a swanky girl, despite the uniform?'

'Very swanky,' Emma laughed.

'Heaps of money and servants galore?'

'Galore and more.'

'Well, good luck to you!' he said agreeably, shaking her hand warmly. 'You kept me from going crazy with boredom, and I do thank you.' He caressed Benson's head roughly, said, 'Take care of the little feller,' threw her an ironic salute, and was gone.

He seemed to take all the energy in the world with him, and she instantly flagged, feeling the lack of sleep and lack of food, on top of the last three strenuous months of constant work. But she hadn't much further to go. There was a cab waiting at the rank, and within minutes she was in St James's Square, where orders had been left to take care of her what-ever time she arrived. She had a large helping of eggs and toast, a quick wash, and tumbled into a clean, delicious bed to sleep, leaving instructions to wake her after four hours, by which time, she calculated, Violet should be up and the house in full working order.

She woke to the news, spread over all the papers, that there had been two terrible explosions in a munitions factory at

Chilwell in Nottingham, Britain's largest shell-filling factory. More than a hundred and thirty workers, mostly women, had been killed, with scores more seriously injured. It brought it home to her, as she took breakfast with Violet (and simultaneously tried to prevent Benson from attacking the Pekingeses, whom he regarded as deadly rivals for Emma's affections), that nowhere was safe from the war.

There was also news of the spread of the influenza, which was now affecting the coal-mining districts of Northumberland and Durham, to the detriment of the nation's coal supply. When Venetia called in, on her way to the New Hospital, she brought the news that the cabinet secretary had told her the first sea lord had told *him* that the influenza was so rife in the Royal Navy that many destroyers were laid up in dock, unable to go to sea for lack of hands.

'It spreads like fire in a confined environment like a battleship,' Venetia said. 'Once one sailor gets it, they all do. The consequences are serious. Wemyss said that the loss of several merchant ships recently can be attributed directly to the influenza. And it's beginning to take hold here in London.'

'But only in the poor areas, surely?' Violet said.

'Not at all. I've been called to several cases in Mayfair, and I've heard of them in Westminster and Chelsea.' Venetia no longer conducted a practice, but old friends and former patients still tended to call for her when they were particularly worried. 'I can only tell them what they ought to know already – that there's no treatment for influenza except nursing. This is an odd variant,' she added, frowning. 'There seem to be several forms. The one I've seen most of is marked by high temperature, muscular pains, general collapse and severe debilitation. It's unpleasant, but the victim recovers in two weeks or so. Just lately, though, I've started to see something else in the hospitals, a significant number of cases marked by haemorrhage from the mucus membranes, the lungs and internal organs. In that form it's rapidly fatal.'

'I don't entirely understand,' Violet said. Growing up with a doctor for a mother, she ought to have been familiar with the terms, but she had always unconsciously blocked out the medical talk in the house as boring and distasteful.

Emma translated: 'Haemorrhage is bleeding. Bleeding from the nose, Cousin Venetia?'

'Nose and ears. Throat. Eyes, even. The lungs fill with blood and fluid. The patients cough blood, can't breathe, rapidly sink and die. And post-mortem examination shows similar destruction of the liver, pancreas, kidneys, stomach. It's as if their blood itself is attacking their body. Sometimes it's only a matter of hours between the first symptom and death. They get sick in the morning and die in the afternoon.'

'But that's horrible,' Violet said, looking very uncomfortable. 'Can't anything be done?'

'I've told you, there's no treatment,' Venetia said. 'The only thing is not to catch it in the first place. I'm telling you about it, Violet, because I believe you should think again about extending your exhibition. If the numbers of infections go on increasing as they are doing, I expect public gatherings will be closed down anyway, but you don't want to be responsible for any spread. I think you should take the children out of London.'

'Oh dear,' Emma said. 'Do you really think that's necessary? I've been so looking forward to my stay.'

'It's up to you, Emma,' Venetia said. 'You're an independent woman now. You can make up your own mind. But Violet is responsible for her children.'

'If I go down, will you come too?' Violet asked her mother.

'I can't possibly leave London at the moment.'

'And Oliver will stay, I suppose?'

'Oliver is going to move into his quarters at St Mary's. He doesn't want to risk importing the infection to his patients.'

Violet sighed. 'I had better go, I suppose. But you'll come with me, won't you, Emma?'

Emma swallowed her disappointment. 'Yes, I'll come. But where do you mean to go?'

Violet had been thinking automatically of Brancaster, Holkam's estate in Lincolnshire; but now suddenly she had an idea that impressed her with its brilliance. 'Why don't we go to Shawes?' This was her mother's small estate in Yorkshire, whose boundaries ran with those of Morland Place. 'Then you can see the Morland Place people as well. Won't you like that?'

'Oh, yes,' Emma said, cheering considerably. 'That would be wonderful. I long to see them.'

Venetia looked approving. 'And if I get a moment, I might come down to Yorkshire myself later.' It depended, though she didn't say so, on the news from Thomas. Things were growing very tense in Russia, and she was seriously worried for his safety. If he agreed to get out, she might feel able to leave the capital. 'It will take a day or two to have things got ready down there.'

'And I'll need time to arrange everything here,' Violet said. 'Shall we say we'll go down on Friday?'

'That will give me a chance to see the exhibition,' Emma said. 'It would be such a shame to miss it.'

'Yes, but Violet, you will speak to the Verneys about closing it?' Venetia said.

Violet sighed. 'I suppose so. I'll suggest we close it on Saturday, if you really think it's necessary.'

'I recommend it,' Venetia said. 'I think you'll find in any case that people are starting to go out of London.'

Violet merely nodded. She didn't yet believe it would get as bad as that. But it was hard to go against her mother's advice, and she comforted herself that the show had done what it was meant to do in bringing Laidislaw's name before the public. Everyone had heard of him now.

Perhaps she could put the exhibition on again some other time, next year, or when the war ended, or – a good thought occurred to her – in some other place. Laidislaw had wanted to take his portrait of her to New York. Now the Americans were in the war, wouldn't they be interested in his pictures of life in the trenches? She decided to talk to Laura and George about taking the exhibition to New York when the war was over. It would be something to look forward to.

CHAPTER EIGHTEEN

Now that the situation had been pointed out to her, Violet did notice that there seemed a falling-off of numbers at the gallery. She liked to call in there every day, even if she didn't stay for long. It was like visiting Laidislaw. Though she never again got that oven-breath sense of his presence, his memory was there in the bold, confident lines of his work, and it comforted her.

She spoke to Laura about closing the show on Saturday. Laura thought attendance was falling too, but had attributed it to the July weather: dry and bright, which meant, in London, brassy.

'I think those who can are going out of Town,' Laura concluded. 'I haven't many engagements after this week, and I shan't mind cancelling them. The exhibition's been a huge success, but it does rather tie one. I'll speak to Reed, and get George to put a notice in the newspapers.'

Emma had spent the day seeing other friends, having luncheon with Molly, and meeting Vera Polk for tea. That evening Violet's last engagement was to a dinner at the Vibarts', and she telephoned Sarah Vibart to say that Emma Weston was staying with her, and asked if she could bring her.

'Of course,' Sarah said, in her quick, hospitable way. 'As a matter of fact, someone else is bringing an extra man, so it works out very well.'

Emma was pleased to be dining out in style for the first time in six months, and hastened to have her trunk, stored in Violet's attic, brought down so that she could find an evening gown. She was startled to discover that nothing fitted. It was lucky that Violet's maid was good with the needle (her own maid had been let go when she went to France) and that there was a gown with sufficient material in the seams for it to be altered. Violet's maid was also, fortunately, skilled with hair, for Emma's hasty cut was looking very peculiar now. Sanders had to cut quite a lot off to get it even, and apologised as she snipped, assuming Emma must want to grow it again. But Emma was liking it short, especially as it had developed a wholly unexpected curl. When Sanders had finished, she looked, according to the maid, 'like a little dark angel, miss'. Sanders borrowed from Violet a pair of diamond clips which she fastened in the feathery curls to make the finish more sophisticated, and Emma was very pleased with it, and felt she'd never want to have long hair again.

It was wonderful to go out, silken and scented, carried in a large, silent motor-car to a grand house, which, if the blackout rules prevented it from being brilliantly lit outside as in the old days, still sported a canopy and uniformed footmen at the door. The extra man, Emma discovered as they went into the drawing-room to be received by their hostess, was Angus Knoydart, whose father had been an intimate of the Talybonts.

'How's the arm?' she asked at once, as they shook hands.

'As good as new,' he said. 'It was only a scratch.'

She looked at him curiously, remembering the paralysingly shy young man who had courted her in Scotland an age ago. This Knoydart, though still prone to uncomfortable blushes through his fair, transparent face, was quietly confident, and had no difficulty in chatting to her. In fact, she noticed, he was more comfortable with her than with any other of the young ladies in the room; and after a while she decided that it was because she had served in France and they hadn't, so they didn't understand what it was like out there. This notion seemed to be confirmed when she discovered that she had collected a 'court' around her of young men home on leave, eager to talk about the things civilians did not understand, swapping the names of places and people and events familiar to them all. It was 'old so-and-so' and 'good old such-a-place' and 'Remember when that Hun bomb fell on the supply depot and the whole road was a river of jam?' After a bit Sarah was forced to break up the happy group and disperse its members so that other guests need not stand around in silence. Knoydart managed not to be detached, but when dinner was announced he was asked to take Emma in anyway.

She enjoyed the evening, and talking to Knoydart was a pleasure. He had enough to say about himself, with encouragement, for he had done well in the war, and had recently been promoted to major – a quick climbing of the ladder that he attributed modestly to the wartime losses among officers. She privately put it down to his being intelligent and conscientious – and probably brave as well.

On her other side was another soldier home on leave: Algy, the brother of an old friend, Lavinia Maitland. He was unexacting company, when etiquette required her to turn that way. They talked mostly about food, the contrast between Sarah's dinner and the plentiful but rough army fare, and they described to each other particularly good or bad meals they had had in France. They also talked about Peter Hargrave, on whom she had had a crush back in the days of her come-out, and who had been killed at Passchendaele, which led to a rather melancholy recital of what had happened to the rest of their 'set' from before the war. When Sarah turned back to her other side, Emma was quite relieved to follow suit and get Angus Knoydart again.

After dinner, in the drawing-room, the previously absent Eddie joined them, having been released from Court duties at last, and he made the announcement that the dinner party had been arranged to celebrate: Sarah was expecting their first child. It was happy news indeed.

At the end of the evening, Emma took her leave of Knoydart, who asked tentatively if he might call on her again before his leave ended, and she was half sorry to have to tell him that they were going out of Town on Friday and were engaged until then. 'Perhaps we'll meet in France,' she said.

He brightened. 'Yes, I believe I owe you a dinner. The next time I'm near St Omer, I shan't forget.'

'I'll look forward to it,' she said, shaking his hand.

The following morning she went with Violet to the gallery to see the exhibition. She thought the pictures brilliant, but found the effect of them gathered together rather troubling. It was all too real, too vivid. She had seen these same Tommies so many times, but too often when she met them they were wounded, in pain, and the terrible ruin of their bodies was brought freshly before her mental eye as she looked at them smoking, shaving, eating, playing cards, doing the normal things they did every day in ignorance of what was coming. The pictures had been executed before the costly campaign on the Somme. How many of them, she wondered, were still alive?

At one point she was obliged to turn away, hiding her face as she took out her handkerchief and blew her nose. While she was thus engaged, a familiar voice behind her said, 'I know exactly how you feel.'

She whipped round, dabbing her wet eyes hastily, to see Captain Wentworth, of all people, standing there, smiling in a rather sidelong way. 'It's good to see that the efficient and mechanically minded Trooper Weston is still a creature of emotion underneath,' he said.

'Wentworth!'

'The same,' he admitted. 'Though I must say I hardly recognised you without Benson at heel.'

'Is that the only way you can tell me apart – my dog?'

'From the back, I should have said,' he retreated hastily; and then laughed. 'I realise, now, that didn't sound much like a compliment.'

'Oh, bother compliments,' Emma said. 'Ours isn't that sort of friendship. What are you doing here?'

'Looking for you,' Wentworth said, taking her analysis on the chin. 'I only got your letter saying you were going on leave just as I was about to. Very muddy and torn, it was, so I assumed it had done a detour or three. I got to London late yesterday, and presented myself at St James's Square this morning, only to be told you were here. So here I am. I hope Benson is all right? You didn't leave him behind in France? The poor creature will pine to death.'

'Still solely concerned about the dog,' she informed an invisible presence beside her. 'Yes, Benson is very well and, no, I didn't leave him behind in France. He's at Violet's house. It would have been cruelty to bring him here.'

'No taste in paintings?' he said sympathetically.

'Fool!' she laughed. 'Too many feet. I'm glad it was only that my letter went astray. I was worried you might have been hurt. Or ill with this influenza.'

'Right as a trivet,' he said. 'There is an awful lot of it about, though. Ten chaps in my company are down with it.'

'Cousin Venetia says there is a very bad variant of it, which causes internal haemorrhage.'

'We haven't seen any of that,' Wentworth said. 'Just the fever-and-pains-in-the-legs sort. Nasty enough, though – leaves you feeling utterly exhausted for weeks afterwards, I'm told. But I'm all right, and I can see you are. You're looking extremely bonny. Now, let me take you round and tell you about the pictures.'

'Have you seen them already?' she said, in surprise. 'I thought you'd only just got here.'

'I have. But to an expert on art, the first glance tells all there is to know. Are you an expert on art?'

'Not at all.'

'Thank God for that,' he said, taking her arm. 'Then I can say anything I like, and you won't know the difference.'

She had been right round once, but happily went round again with him; and he didn't harrow her feelings by being facetious about them, as she was afraid for just a moment he might, but was as reverent as the subject required, while putting the trench-life aspect of the subjects into context for her with a pleasantly light touch. She felt she understood them better for his commentary, and told him so.

He said, 'I'm glad to do anything that pleases you,' and then there was a little awkward moment when they couldn't quite meet each other's eyes. Wentworth cleared his throat. 'So what do you do now?' he asked.

'Violet and I are going to luncheon with friends,' she said, half regretfully, 'and to the theatre tonight. And tomorrow we go down to the country.'

'Oh,' he said.

'I'm sorry.' They looked at each other. 'What are you doing with your leave?'

'I've some family to visit,' he said lightly. 'And friends in London from the old days.'

'I'm sorry we won't be able to meet again. It seems a waste when we're on leave at the same time.' An idea came to her. 'When do you go back?'

'On the seventeenth. Wednesday.'

'I go back on the Sunday, the fourteenth. But suppose I come back to Town a day early? I could see you on the Saturday afternoon. We could go for a walk or something. If you're not already engaged.'

He brightened. 'I haven't any definite plans at all. I'd like that very much. And perhaps we could have dinner afterwards.' He grinned. 'At least you won't have to find two friends to chaperone you.'

* * *

408

Violet loved her children, but drew the line at travelling long distances in their company. She sent them off, with the nursery servants and luggage, in two motor-cars, while she and Emma and the dogs took the train. It sped northwards through a landscape little changed by the war, though there were a great many more allotments, and neat oblongs of vegetables seemed to be growing in every garden and every open space in the towns and villages they passed through. The sun shone down hard from a bleached sky onto fields of pale gold, studded with scarlet poppies and deep-blue cornflowers, and fields of green where brown cows and white sheep grazed, while in the distance the land rose in soft folds to hazy mauve-blue hills.

Emma did not even open the magazine Violet's punctilious manners had provided for her. She could not have enough of gazing out of the window at this glorious, untouched land. The trees in particular seemed extravagant, almost operatic in their height and blowsy greenness. Benson sat on her lap with his paws up on the narrow ledge and looked out of the window too, as if he had never seen such a thing. Probably, she reflected, he hadn't. Almost certainly he had been born on or near the army camp at Calais, in a land ravaged by the passage of military men and machines. 'This will be your home when the war's over,' she informed him.

By the time they reached Shawes, it had been made comfortable and the children were settled in. The peace and quiet of the country was astounding after France and then London. The weather remained perfect, the children ran about from dawn to dusk getting brown and dusty and scratched and enjoying every minute, and Emma had nothing to do but enjoy herself. It was wonderful to renew her acquaintance with Morland Place, to receive the motherly hugs of Henrietta and the fatherly kindness of Teddy, to see Jessie again, and to wonder at her baby, Thomas. At almost three weeks old, he had shed the crumpled appearance of birth and was, she thought, quite nice-looking, so she was able in good conscience to agree with Jessie that he was the most beautiful baby who had ever lived.

Nanny Emma had warned Emma that Jessie had had a hard time of it, but she would have known that anyway from Jessie's tired face, and the fact that she was still spending the mornings in bed, though she came downstairs to the sofa in the afternoons. Once Emma was there, Jessie took to having a short walk with her in the gardens each day, moving slowly and carefully as though afraid she might break something, and sitting down as soon as a bench or seat offered itself. It was so different from the energetic Jessie of old. But she was happy, that much was obvious. Jessie didn't talk much about Bertie, and not at all about the events prior to their marriage, but when she did mention him in passing, her face lit in a way that Emma found both touching and painful, because it made her think of Fenniman.

He was obviously on Jessie's mind too, because she said once, 'You ought to have had your time with him, as I've had mine with Bertie. It wasn't fair, Emma. I'm so sorry.'

Emma had only shrugged, as if to say, *War isn't fair* – which they both knew. And though Emma envied Jessie, she pitied her, too. Life couldn't do anything more to Emma, but Jessie had so much to lose. Bertie was still out there. Both those pieces of knowledge lay between them, unspoken as they sat through the hot afternoons, in the scent of roses and lavender, and the gentle droning of bees.

When she wasn't sitting with Jessie, Emma liked to go riding with Polly. Jessie was glad to have her exercise Hotspur, and Polly was full of eager questions about her life in France, wishing she was older so that she could do something of the sort. Benson tried to come with them on the rides at first, but he couldn't keep up, and it was a cruelty to watch him try, labouring along with his sides going like a bellows and his tongue flapping like a loose tie. Emma had to shut him up somewhere before she left and instruct someone to release him only when she had been gone long enough. Jessie volunteered for the job, and had the little dog with her in Emma's absence. The house pack was rather too boisterous for him, but he got on well with Rug, and the two mongrels often joined Jessie in the rose garden for a quiet afternoon's snooze.

It was such a pleasant week that Emma was sorry to have to leave. Violet and the children were staying on, and Uncle Teddy offered Emma a maid to accompany her on the train back to London. He still didn't like the idea of young women going anywhere alone, which struck Emma as kind but rather absurd when she had been driving an ambulance alone in a war zone. She refused the offer, and assured Teddy, when he quizzed her anxiously, that she would be perfectly all right with Benson.

'Where will you be staying, my dear?' he asked. 'Violet's house is closed up, isn't it?'

'I'll be with Cousin Venetia,' Emma assured him.

'I'm glad to hear it,' Teddy said, his face clearing. He had half feared she would go to an hotel. All this running around alone just wasn't respectable for unmarried girls, though he knew they were doing wonderful work and taking great risks out in France.

Emma knew what he was thinking, and laid a hand fondly on his arm. 'You needn't worry. I shall be quite safe in Manchester Square.'

She had luncheon on the train, and Wentworth was waiting for her at the barrier when the train got in at half past two. They had a long and very pleasant walk in the Park with Benson, and then he left her at Manchester Square to bathe and change, promising to pick her up later for dinner. Lady Overton was not there, but had left a message begging her to make herself comfortable and saying she hoped to see her before she went out. But when Emma was dressing, a servant knocked and said that her ladyship had telephoned to say she was delayed in a meeting and would not be home.

411

Benson was so worn out from the walk and the journey, on top of a strenuous week keeping up his end of things with the Morland Place dogs, that he hardly looked up when she left him curled up on the end of her bed.

Wentworth took her to the Ritz. They had just been seated when their attention was called to a nearby table where some old friends of Emma's, the Westerhams, were dining with Algy and Lavinia Maitland, Algy's fiancée Peta Ogilvy, and Peta's brother Bobbie. It was not possible to resist the urgent request to join forces, so they all ate together, and afterwards went on to a place George Westerham knew, where there was dancing. It was a very pleasant evening, but Emma and Wentworth had no time for private talk, not even in the taxi going home, since the Maitlands were going the same way and offered to share a cab. Wentworth rolled his eyes amusingly behind Algy's back, but behaved very properly, shook her hand goodbye at the steps of the Overton house and said he hoped to see her in France.

As she climbed the stairs to bed (Lady Overton was still not back, so she went straight up), Emma reflected that they had, after all, had plenty of time for talk during the afternoon's walk; and that perhaps it was best they had not had an intimate dinner *à deux*, since that might only have encouraged Wentworth. It would not be kind to let him think there could ever be anything but friendship between them.

In Ekaterinburg the weather was bright and hot, so hot that at noon the brazen sun reduced the town to immobility, and the summer dust settled in the wide, empty main street until the afternoon traffic should start up again. In the enervating heat, the tension of the situation seemed to Thomas even more unbearable. It was a town of rumour, suspicion, unnamed fears, shifting alliances as unreliable as quicksand. Who to trust? What, amid the mass of misinformation and political lie, to believe? Much of his day and night was spent within sight of that hateful palisade behind which the woman he loved endured the privation and fear of captivity with courage and grace.

The political set-up was complicated. To begin with there was the local soviet, and the Red Guard, each with its own command structure. Both were more extreme and revolutionary than the regional soviet. The Red Guard wanted to kill the ex-Tsar, and soon. The local soviet would have liked to kill the whole family and have done with it. But the regional soviet had direct links with Moscow, and was playing a longer game, in line with Lenin's international plans, which for the time being included preserving the lives of the Romanovs. The regional chairman, Beloborodov, communicated by telegraph with Sverdlov and with Lenin himself. Thomas had made friends with all the telegraph operators in the town, and they were never unwilling to chat about the exciting messages they were handling.

At present, the regional soviet had authority over the rest, but who knew how long that would last? For one thing, the Red Guard had the military power, and could literally force the issue if they tired of talking. For another, the counter-revolution in the country was building, and a large army of the so-called Whites was fighting its way towards Ekaterinburg, spearheaded by two divisions of crack Czech troops, driving the Reds back day by day. It was only a matter of time before they would reach Ekaterinburg. When that happened, while the Red Army was fighting to hold the front door, the civilian Communists would almost certainly be fleeing from the back door, and what would happen to the Romanovs in the confusion?

The situation was further complicated by the large presence of the Cheka, the Russian secret service, which was not entirely admitted to exist, though everyone knew of it and feared it. In Ekaterinburg the Cheka was very visible, living in style in the Hotel America, where in Room 3 they held regular meetings of the top Communists in the town. Some of the regional soviet members were known to be also

413

members of the Cheka; others might have been members, without its being known.

And then, as well as the official British, German and French embassies, and the various consulates of smaller countries, the town seemed to be a magnet for the secret services of half the world. Thomas knew most of them, especially the British, French, Swiss and American agents, and there was no barrier to the information that passed between them. More surprising, perhaps, was that the large German intelligence presence in the town was equally forthcoming. An impressive contingent had arrived openly in late May, had been welcomed by the Ural regional council, and was living visibly and comfortably in a luxurious railway train on a siding at the main station.

Despite the fact that Britain and Germany were at war with each other, Thomas had had no difficulty in ingratiating himself with the Germans. He had a particularly good source, a minor operator called Max Richter, who shared a mistress with a Cheka officer called Kanevtsev – though this fact was unknown to Kanevtsev. Max was always willing to share with Thomas anything his wily Zenobia garnered, because they had the same concern about the imperial family's safety.

In this fevered and overcrowded atmosphere, rumours bred like flies. New plots seemed to spring up every day and wither in the searing heat. Obviously many were nothing but hearsay and wishful thinking, but there was no doubt that the German government was planning something to get the Romanovs away; while in Moscow Count Mirbach, the German ambassador to the Bolshevik government, kept up official pressure for the safety and ultimate release of Alexandra and the children.

One plot Thomas heard of was to make Tsarevitch Alexei a puppet ruler in Russia under the regency of Alexandra's brother Ernst, the Grand Duke of Hesse, a high-ranking officer in the German Army. Part of Germany's war plan

414

was to extend her empire by making a string of puppet monarchies in conquered states right across Europe. While Thomas's heart approved any plan that would get the family out safely, his intellect protested at such a disgraceful design, and he was glad when, after a while, he heard no more about it.

The important thing, however, was that for the moment Lenin wanted to preserve the family to use them as bargaining counters, which allowed everyone else time to get together a credible rescue plan. As long as Lenin was of that mind – and as long as he kept control of the Urals area – the Romanovs were safe.

Safe, however, was a relative term. In the Ipatiev house, behind the wooden palisade, conditions were near intolerable. The rooms were stifling, for the windows were nailed shut, and requests to have even one opened were refused. The family's servants had been further reduced in number, so that now, besides Dr Botkin, there was only one maid and one man, a cook and kitchen boy. Their food ration had been reduced to a minimum; likewise their exercise, for where in the spring they had been allowed outside for an hour a day, now in blazing summer they were down to ten minutes.

This, like everything else inside the house, was directed by the whim of the house commandant, Alexander Avdeyev, an ill-educated, bullying braggart, who liked to drink. Under him, the guards inside became increasingly insolent. They had started pilfering from the family, and when Avdeyev did nothing to check them – telling Nicholas, when he complained, to hold his tongue – they stole wholesale: not just valuables, but napkins, handkerchiefs, shirts, shoes, which they sold as souvenirs. The family were not allowed to use the lavatory without asking permission, and were accompanied there and back by guards, which was especially upsetting for the girls. The guards scrawled obscene pictures and words on the walls they must pass, pointed

415

them out to the grand duchesses and made crude suggestions. Thomas wondered how long it would be before they went beyond words to actions.

The boy Alexei continued ill, in his latest haemophiliac crisis. Bedridden and in constant pain, he suffered terribly from the heat. Alexandra, who had heart disease as well as arthritis, was likewise frequently bedridden. For the others, boredom and fear were the hardest things to bear. The physical privations of their reduced situation worried them less than perhaps their guards hoped they would, for they had always lived very simply in the private quarters of their luxurious palaces. But the hopelessness, the worry about what was to come, and the everyday fear of what the guards might do wore them down.

Dr Deverenko went in daily to see Alexei, and from him Thomas received news, and was able sometimes to pass verbal messages – he dared not write anything down. He fretted in his helplessness. Preston, the ambassador, made regular representations to the soviet, and was always assured the family was in good health and in no danger. He told Thomas that he had to tread carefully, not to irritate the authorities, but during June a small improvement was made, in that some local nuns were allowed to take in eggs and milk daily to augment the family's diet. But Avdeyev was an incalculable hazard. He was inviting his friends in to view the imperial prisoners like exhibits at a zoo, and his bouts of drunkenness were increasing in frequency and violence.

In late June, rumours began to circulate Russia that the ex-Tsar had been murdered or executed. Berzin, the commander of the Red Guard, alarmed by the rumours, sent an urgent telegram to Lenin. Lenin's immediate reply ordered Berzin to take the entire family into his protection, and warned him he would answer with his life if any harm were to come to them. Berzin consulted with Beloborodov, and on the 4th of July Avdeyev was dismissed and the entire guard in the Ipatiev house was changed.

The new commandant was a very different sort of man. Yankel Yurovsky was about forty, strongly built with black hair cut *en brosse* and a black moustache in a square, thoughtful face. He was an educated and well-read man, the regional commissar for justice, and a member of the Cheka. He had begun life as a watch-maker, then opened a photographic shop in Ekaterinburg and, when the war began, trained at the army medical school. To the relief of those watching, Yurovsky quickly improved things in the house, and tightened security. The previous guard were now used to patrol the perimeter and were not allowed into the house on any pretext. Inside the house Yurovsky placed his own picked men, who were from the Lettish division, mostly men from the Baltic provinces, but including Hungarians and Austrians. The Letts were known as fearsome fighters, but were also famous for their discipline.

Thomas met Yurovsky – who showed immediately that he knew who Thomas was and why he was there – and felt much happier about matters inside the house. Yurovsky was plainly honest, conscientious and kindly, and would allow nothing to happen to those in his charge. Part of the cost, however, was that it would be much harder now to rescue the family without the connivance of the regional soviet and the Cheka, for the new guards were incorruptible, and Yurovsky inspected everything twice daily and had had a second machine-gun post set up on the roof. This might have been in response to the ever nearer approach of the White Army – it looked as though it could not be more than a couple of weeks before they reached Ekaterinburg – but it did not help the rescuers.

Meanwhile, Goloshchokin, senior commissar in the Urals regional soviet, was summoned to Moscow for talks with Sverdlov and Lenin himself. It did not take much imagination to suppose they were going to talk about the Romanovs.

And on the 4th of July, just as things inside the Ipatiev

house were changing for the better, they suddenly got much worse in Moscow. On that day, the All-Russian Congress of Soviets was held in the Bolshoi Theatre. Delegates came from soviets all over Russia, and it was their first chance to express publicly, to the central party, their violent anger about the shameful treaty of Brest-Litovsk, and their equally violent hatred of the Germans.

The meeting erupted. The Left Social Revolutionaries were the most vocal. They led the protests condemning the treaty and damning all Germans to hell, shaking their fists at Count Mirbach, who was listening impassively from the gallery. Two days later, two of them walked into the German embassy and shot Count Mirbach dead.

The delicate balance between Germany and Russia, which Lenin had been trying to maintain, was ruptured. It was the perfect excuse for the Germans to demand to be allowed to send a battalion to Moscow, with the threat of full invasion if it were denied. Lenin was now in violent confrontation with those on his left *and* those on his right. He had to appease Germany, since he could not afford a renewal of war, and Alexandra and the children were still useful pawns to him in that regard. On the other hand, the White Army was within days of Ekaterinburg, and the extremists of the local soviets and Red Guard were unlikely to be happy about preserving the lives of a hated German princess and her children. The closer the Whites got, the more openly the Reds talked about executing the whole lot, Tsar, Tsaritsa and family, and be done with it for good.

At this tense moment, Goloshchokin arrived back from Moscow, on Sunday the 14th of July, and immediately went into a meeting with Beloborodov and Yurovsky in Room 3 at Cheka Headquarters. The meeting went on through the night, and caused intense speculation among the intelligence communities, because it was assumed that Goloshchokin had brought new orders from Moscow concerning the Romanovs.

It seemed unbearably sinister to Thomas. Was it orders for an execution? Had Lenin decided they were more trouble than they were worth? He could not sit still, far less listen to the politely expressed anxieties of Preston. He was out far too early on the Monday morning, walking in the white early sun, lingering helplessly past the palisade – stared at, as always, by the guards. Some eyed him with revolutionary scorn for the Englishman who was also a lord; some with the natural friendliness of the Russian peasant when sober; others, in the memory that he had sometimes given them cigarettes, with sympathy for his distress.

As soon as it was late enough, Thomas started going round the various cafés where he was accustomed to find agents from other services. Everyone had the same questions as him, and no-one seemed to have any answers. He could have had all the speculation he wanted for the price of a cup of coffee or a glass of *kvass*, but it was facts he needed. In the middle of the morning, when he had drunk more coffee than was good for his digestion, and was sitting in the latest café wondering where to go next, Max came in. As soon as he saw Thomas, he hurried over, so eager to tell his news that he began before he had even sat down.

'Zenoshka was with Kanevtsev last night!' he cried. 'She was there all night. She came straight to me when she left him to tell me about the meeting. You know about the meeting?'

'Everyone in Ekaterinburg knows about the meeting,' Thomas said. 'Sit down, don't look so excited.'

Max sat, and lit a cigarette with hands that shook slightly. He remembered his manners and offered one to Thomas, dropping his lighter in the process with a clatter, and giving vent to some highly German curses.

'For God's sake,' Thomas protested, 'do you want everyone looking at us?'

'It's too late to worry about that,' Max said. 'Everyone knows who we are. Listen to me – this is more important.

Kanevtsev left Zenoshka early this morning. He was called to Room Three. She took a long time dressing, hoping to hear something more, and she was right, canny thing. He came back while she was still fiddling about and told her that they have decided to execute Nicholas.'

Thomas felt his stomach drop away. 'Good God! Are you sure?'

'True as I'm sitting here. They know they're going to have to evacuate any day when the Whites get here, and Goloshchokin's got orders from Moscow that the Empress and the children have to be saved at all costs. Beloborodov said the Red Guard would never stand for evacuating the whole family, and the regional council would be bound to side with them. In the end they decided to throw Nicholas as a sop to the Reds to keep them happy while they get the others away. Goloshchokin says the idea is to get the women right out of Russia as soon as it can be arranged.'

The relief Thomas felt at those words fought with the sick dread at the thought of Nicholas's fate. The Tsar, who had been so kind to him, had advanced him in his career – the father of his beloved Olga – the Tsar was to be sacrificed.

Max went on, 'Zenoshka says old Kanevtsev was wet-eyed about Nicholas. Who would have thought a man who looks like him could cry? Amazingly sentimental, the Russians. Of course, there's lots of them still in the Cheka who served in it in imperial days. I suppose they feel something for Bloody Nicholas – for the office, if not the man. Regicide is a big step, whichever way you look at it.'

'When is it going to happen?' Thomas asked faintly.

'Zenoshka says they're going to summon him to Headquarters later today and try him before a committee, headed by Beloborodov. They'll find him guilty, of course, and execute him tomorrow.'

'Try him for what?'

'Being emperor, if you want the truth. But they'll put something down on paper – the usual "oppression of the people" stuff. What does it matter? He had enough people executed in his time.' He studied Thomas's face, and said, more gently, 'I know you have a fondness for the old man. I'm sorry for it. But, you know, he's ready to die. There's no future for him anywhere, and I believe he's long resigned himself.'

'Yes,' Thomas said. It was true, in a way. He remembered the strange stillness and indifference with which the Tsar had abdicated eighteen months ago. He must have known then that death was the logical end of the events he had put in train. But the Tsar was also Nicholas the man, husband and father, and he loved his family more than anything on earth. No man who loved like that could ever be ready to leave them, especially when he would know their futures were anything but secure.

But there was nothing he could do to save Nicholas. He must concentrate on what he *could* do. He put his pity aside. 'Where will they take the family?'

'To Perm, to begin with,' said Max. It was the next main city to the west, the natural place to which the Red Army would retreat in its battle with the Whites. 'After that – I don't know. Maybe Moscow. But Lenin's facing trouble there. It might not be a safe place now.' Max looked suddenly troubled. 'God knows where *will* be safe. Nowhere in Russia, perhaps. It'll take time to find somewhere outside the country that will accept them. There's nothing in the world would make Lenin send them to Germany at the moment, though he had to pretend to consider it. It'll have to be a neutral place – and a secret one.'

They discussed this aspect for a while, until Max jumped up and said he had other people to see, and dashed off to spread the news in his circle. Later that day, Thomas met the Danish vice-consul, Ree, who told him he had spoken to Beloborodov himself, and confirmed that Perm was the destination. 'They will all be going there themselves, the regional soviet and the Cheka.'

Thomas was glad to get an official confirmation, and reported what he knew to Preston, who had heard the same things from the British agents. Preston was upset about the ex-Tsar's fate. 'It's a bad business, but there's nothing we can do. It's a matter for the Russians alone. But I'm glad they're saving the women.'

'The women? What about the boy?'

Preston looked grave. 'I'm afraid they'll probably shoot him, too. The male heir, you see.'

'But he's a child! They can't try him for anything,' Thomas protested.

'Of course not. He can't be officially executed. They'll do it unofficially, but they'll do it.' He shook his head. 'Poor little wretch. From what Deverenko says, it will be something of a merciful release for him. There's some doubt he could survive much longer anyway.'

Thomas felt sick at the thought of shooting the helpless boy, but he had no doubt the extreme Bolsheviks in the town were capable of it.

'What will you do?' Preston asked. 'You're welcome to stay here as long as you wish. I don't know if you have had any orders,' he added delicately, not wishing to enquire directly, 'but perhaps you will want to go to Perm yourself?'

'Yes,' said Thomas. 'My duty will be to stay with the women. I shall try to get myself on the same train with them. I hear that a German secret-service delegation will be going, and I shall try to get them to take me with them.'

Preston said, wonderingly, 'What a queer sort of set-up that is. But everything is strange here, these days.'

Tactfully, he said no more about it, and Thomas went out again to meet the German agents and persuade them to take him along. In fact, he was not sure his orders would be to go with the women. His official duty had been to the Tsar, and once the Tsar was dead, that might mean the end of it. He might perhaps be expected to go home. But he was not intending to go home. Through the rest of the day he made his plans, packed necessities, organised for money to be available in Perm, wrote letters and made certain delicate arrangements. He was glad to have something to do to take his mind off what was to happen to Nicholas – not to the Tsar, but to the man he knew, kindly, honest, loving of his family – and the crippled boy, whose only fault was to be born male into the wrong family.

Nicholas Romanov was summoned to Cheka Headquarters that afternoon, to appear before Beloborodov and others of the Urals Regional Committee. Thomas, from across the road, saw him depart in a car, and later return, but none of his sources seemed to know exactly what had transpired during the meeting or, if they knew, were unwilling to say. Later that evening there was talk that there had been a 'trial', but no-one had any details either of proceedings or outcome. But the next morning, the 16th, just at the time the family had breakfast, the car was back, containing two Red Guards and Chairman Beloborodov, and Nicholas came out and was driven away. This time Thomas did not see him return. All day his imagination troubled him with images of the deed, and with wondering what they would do to Alexei, *how* they would do it. There would be Red Guards willing enough to perform the act, he knew. Politics of that sort never had any difficulty in seeing the symbol rather than the living flesh.

That evening, he met again with Max in a drinking-tavern he frequented, and was told that Nicholas had been driven out of town that morning to a military exercise area in the woods, known locally as the Four Brothers. There Beloborodov had read him his sentence, and he had been shot by a firing squad of Red Guard who had been waiting there for them.

'Is it true?' Thomas asked. 'Is he really dead?'

'True as my nose,' Max said. 'Kanevtsev went round to

Zenoshka's apartment this afternoon and told her about it. Weeping like a bucket, he was. Said the Tsar died well, like a soldier, calmly and without struggle. Poor devil.'

'And the boy?'

Max shook his head. 'I can't find out anything, but a guard I know says he's not in the house – only the women and the servants. So I suppose they've done for him, too. They're moving the women tomorrow. If you're going, Thomas, my friend, you had better get your arrangements in order.' He looked at him curiously. 'It's a dangerous game you're playing. Once you leave here you move into uncharted seas.'

'It's uncharted for all of us,' Thomas said. 'What do you think the Whites are going to say to you, Max, when they take Ekaterinburg?'

'I shan't wait around to find out. Those Czech storm troopers hate us Germans worse than the Reds. This country is going to the dogs, my friend. I think the time is fast approaching to get out. I have a nice little escape route set up through Denmark. I hope you have something of the sort?'

'Oh, don't worry about me,' Thomas said. 'I shall be all right.'

'I *don't* worry about you,' Max said, with a slightly drunken chuckle – it had been a long day for them all. 'I've always known that an English lord is the most impossible fellow in the world to kill. English lords and cockroaches. Stamp them down, they just keep getting up again. You may go to ground, but you'll pop up again somewhere after the war – and when you do, *kamerad*, I shall damn well buy you a drink!'

'I'll hold you to that,' Thomas said, shaking the hard hand.

They moved Alexandra and the four girls out of the house during the night to a railway train with the blinds drawn down. None of the servants went with them, not even Dr Botkin. Their trunks were taken on board during the early hours of the morning.

Also during the night, Thomas left the home of Sir Thomas Preston for the last time and went with his small amount of luggage to the apartment of the estimable Zenoshka. There Max met him, and in the course of an hour, with their help, he was transformed into Paul Seichel, a Swiss doctor who was to be part of the Red Cross mission concerned with the welfare of prisoners of war: this was the German intelligence group's cover. He shaved off his moustache, Zenoshka cut and dyed his hair and parted it differently, and he assumed a pair of gold-rimmed spectacles with plain glass lenses. Surveying himself in the looking-glass afterwards was rather unnerving, for the small changes had made him look not at all like himself. More importantly, they had made him look acceptably like the photograph of the rather nondescript man on the false Swiss passport he had acquired during the day, along with the civilian clothes that would replace his uniform. Like a snake shedding its skin, he thought, looking at it lying across Zenoshka's bed. That gave him a queer feeling too. But he had chosen to be Swiss because they were neutral, and no-one disliked them. In the shifting world of revolution and international alliance, it was safer than being English or even German, but it meant he was laying himself open to the charge of desertion – and if he were to fall foul of any of the various groups of Reds, he might now be shot as a spy. The cosy situation that had existed in Ekaterinburg, where intelligence agents were all known to each other and accepted by the officials, could not be relied on anywhere else – and would probably not prevail in Ekaterinburg much longer, as the White Army approached.

His transformation complete, Thomas embraced his friends and thanked them. Zenoshka pressed something into his hand, 'For good luck. God bless you, Thomas Ivanovitch,' and Max slapped his shoulder heartily, to prove he was not close to tears, and said, 'Be careful, my friend! I want that drink after the war.'

Thomas went out into the blackness of the early hours, and made his way like a cat along the empty streets to the railway station. The other passengers were going on board, officials from the regional soviet, inner party members, and the group from the German secret service. Thomas slipped in with them, unremarked and unremarkable, and thus found himself closer to his beloved object than he had been in months, though unable to see or speak to her. So Olga was without whatever comfort it might have been to know he was near. He thought what their state of mind must be, Alexandra and the girls, knowing Nicholas and Alexei were dead, not knowing what was to become of them, and his heart bled. But it was as well, for the moment, that they didn't know he was there. He was on delicate ground, and must not draw attention to himself. It would be no comfort for Olga if he got himself killed before he was able to do what he now believed was essential. Diplomatic means were not going to save the women, and Lenin's protection would end as soon as their usefulness as pawns did. And Lenin's writ did not run throughout Russia. If Thomas was to save the woman he loved, there would have to be an escape. How in the world he was to effect it, and how they were to get out of Russia, he could not begin to imagine, but opportunity might present itself.

When he was settled in, a nervous time of waiting began. The train was being loaded with a good part of the massive bullion reserve from the banks, which was being evacuated for safety ahead of the White Army, and the task went on all night and into the morning. Thomas saw the economy of the method: the bullion would have to be moved anyway, and the fact of this being a 'treasure train' would excuse its being heavily guarded without mention having to be made of the Romanov women. But he wished they could be on their way. He was afraid that the local soviet and Red Guard would think better of allowing the women to go; and he was afraid of being discovered as an impostor and thrown off

426

the train. Once they were in Perm, no-one would know him and he could be Dr Seichel with impunity.

As he waited, he suddenly remembered the small object Zenoshka had pressed on him, which he had stowed in his pocket, and took it out to examine it. It was a medal of St Nino, a favourite saint with Russian women. She was particularly invoked by people who were in trouble with the authorities, or were being persecuted by kings and their representatives. It seemed appropriate. Thomas smiled and put the medal into his waistcoat pocket, where it would be safe.

CHAPTER NINETEEN

One of the matters with which Venetia was busy in London in July was a project close to her heart. She had been planning it for some time, and now the realisation of some assets, which had been bound up in the probate of her husband's estate, allowed her to go ahead with it.

Some years before, her old friend Mark Darroway had been running a free dispensary for the poor in the basement and ground floor of a house in Dean Street. The lease had fallen in, and the St James and St Ann Benevolent Dispensary had been going to close, so Venetia had secretly bought it, given it in trust to the neighbourhood, and paid to have the first floor turned into an operating theatre and anteroom for minor operations. Now she wanted to finish the job, by turning the top floor into a proper operating theatre, where full anaesthetics could be given, and the first floor into a ward for pre- and post-operative stay.

To do so, she had to involve Mark directly in the planning and medical decisions, which meant revealing her identity as the 'secret benefactor'. She called on him in his rather chaotic home in Soho Square, a tall, shabby house always overflowing with family and friends, and sad people looking for help, medical, financial or emotional. Mark provided the first, and Katherine, his plump, comfortable wife, the last; the middle item, Venetia knew, too often came out of Mark's meagre purse. He was a good doctor, but he gave too much of his time to free cases ever to be rich – she was afraid sometimes he was not even comfortably off. He grew thinner and greyer and more stooped every time she saw him, but his dark eyes still sparked with life, and he never seemed too tired to be interrupted.

He received her with pleasure. 'I can't think when you were last in my house.'

'I can't think either. The war has made us all so busy,' Venetia apologised.

'You must come to dinner. Do – won't you? Katherine loves to show off her cooking.'

'I would love to. The first evening I have free—' Venetia began.

Mark laughed. 'Ah, in that case I shall be waiting for the war to end. I know your schedules! I can't think how you cram so many things into one life, Venetia, my dear. You make me look like a sloth by comparison.'

'Nonsensical flattery – and don't think I shall reciprocate by stroking your fur! You get enough thanks from the poor wretches whose lives you transform. And if this flu epidemic hasn't deprived you of all sleep for days I shall be surprised.'

Numbers of victims had risen steadily, and deaths likewise. The schools had been closed early for the summer to try to stop the infection spreading. Many cinemas and theatres had also closed, restaurants were having a thin time of it, and church congregations were noticeably down. On her way over, Venetia had seen a number of people in the streets wearing masks over their noses and mouths, and she had heard anecdotally that such masks were much in evidence on the buses and tubes.

'There isn't much work in it,' Mark said. 'There's nothing we can do, even if they call us out.'

'Yes, but call us they do, and we have to go.'

'I just tell them to go to bed and sweat it out,' Mark said. 'Mostly that's what they do anyway. But I know you're busy,' he changed the subject, 'so tell me what I can do for you.'

'Just for once, it's the other way round,' Venetia said. 'But first I have to make a confession – or perhaps it's more in the way of a revelation. I'm not quite sure how to put it.'

'Jump in and spit it out,' Mark advised sensibly.

'Very well. I am your anonymous benefactor,' she said.

'You're certainly always—' He was puzzled only for a second, and then his face cleared and a positively youthful grin spread across it. 'St James and St Ann! I've always half suspected it was you! Who else would know so exactly what was wanted? That was just like you! Always looking to help others.'

'That's a fine thing, coming from you!' Venetia retorted.

'But why did you keep it a secret? Didn't want to be thanked, I suppose,' he answered himself. 'More to the point, why are you telling me now?'

She told him of her plan, and how the money to do it had at last become available. 'I want it to be Beauty's memorial,' she said. 'It will be his money entirely, and I shall put it into a trust fund, not only to build the thing but to endow it fully, so that the running costs will be guaranteed. I should like it to be called the John Winchmore Hospital. Do you think St James and St Ann would mind?'

'I think they would understand,' Mark said. 'And the John Winchmore has a good ring to it.'

'And you, of course, must be the director, and chief medical officer,' Venetia said. 'I want you to have a free hand to run it just as you like, and spend the money as you see fit. I want the poor to have the kind of facility the rich can pay for, with the standard of care and particularly the attention to hygiene that I've always tried to promote, and I know no-one could run it better than you.'

For the first time he looked doubtful. 'It's a great honour . . .' he began.

She looked alarmed. 'You're not going to turn me down?'

'Venetia, my dear, this is something close to my heart – something I want as much as you do. You know that.

But I'm not a young man any more. I'm sixty-nine. With the best will in the world, by the time the building work is done I'll be in my seventies.'

'And what then?' she said impatiently. 'You'll give up medicine and spend your days in a rocking-chair by the fire? I don't think so. For one thing, you'd drive Katherine mad.'

'She's a very patient woman,' he mentioned.

'Are you going to retire?' she demanded.

'Not in the foreseeable future. Any more than you are.'

'Well, then.'

'But the future isn't foreseeable. I'm well enough now, but who knows what old-man's illness I might get?'

'Oh, Mark, you could step out of your front door tomorrow and be run down by a cab! I'm not asking you to sign a twenty-year contract. Don't be so poor-spirited! Take on the directorship and do it for as long as you are able, that's all I ask. And when, one day in the future, you feel too tired for it, we'll find someone to take your place. Your grandson Nicholas, perhaps. He's a very promising young fellow.'

'How do you know Nick?'

'I came across him the other day at the London, and he flattered me most agreeably – almost flirted with me. He seems to know just how to get on with old ladies, and tact is a great asset in a position like that.'

He sighed, but it was with a smile. 'Very well. I shall throw myself into your project with you, and we'll see who tires first.'

'Excellent man! Now let's get down to the good part – planning the building and alterations,' Venetia said, with relish. 'Have you some paper?'

'I'll fetch some. And we'd better have Katherine in on it. I never embark on anything without availing myself of her first-rate brain.'

'Good idea. Some of her first-rate coffee wouldn't come amiss, either. I have an hour before I'm due at the New.'

'You have a list?'

'Yes, and a most interesting case among them – a deformity of the uterus I've never come across before.'

Before either of them knew it, they were deep in the most satisfying medical talk, and it was fortunate that Katherine came in ten minutes later of her own accord to see if they would like some coffee or the John Winchmore wouldn't have been discussed at all that day.

It was later that day, the 19th, when she returned home from the New Hospital for Women, and had just gone upstairs to change her clothes, that she received a caller. She descended again at once without changing, for the visitor who had been shown into her private parlour was Colonel Frederick Browning, her contact with the intelligence service. The plan they had been working on all through the winter to rescue the Romanovs from Tobolsk had been thwarted at the last minute by the decision to move the family to Ekaterinburg.

She hurried to him, wondering if there was a new plan or if one of the others she had heard of vaguely had worked, but her first sight of his grave face told her it was not good news.

'What is it?' she said. 'What's happened?'

He did not waste time with preamble. 'We've intercepted a wireless transmission from a broadcasting station near Tsarskoye Selo. The Emperor has been shot in a military execution.'

Venetia felt the shock like a blow, and her hands gripped together. 'Is it true? There have been so many rumours.'

'We're confident this one's true. It was an official broadcast, sanctioned by the Central Executive in Moscow. He was shot on Tuesday by order of the local soviet, because of the danger of his being captured by the Czechs, but Central approved the action beforehand. We've had separate confirmation from Switzerland. British military intelligence had it from an impeccable source, Prince Max of Baden,

432

He gave the same date, the sixteenth, and emphasised that it was a military execution, not an assassination. And Copenhagen believes it. King Christian is planning a memorial service.'

Venetia nodded slowly in acceptance. Prince Max was a very high-ranking German general. And Denmark had close family connections with the Romanovs. 'And the King?' she asked. 'Court mourning?'

'He's holding off for a day or two,' Browning said. 'We're not giving it to the newspapers yet, so you mustn't repeat it to anyone. But you can take it as fact.'

Venetia nodded assent. She knew that the King would dislike taking any firm decision surrounding the Romanovs, even to putting on mourning for the Tsar, which would be necessary as soon as the death was publicly announced. Delaying, dithering, had become the chosen mode in dealing with the situation. 'What is to happen to the family, the Empress and the children?'

'They've been moved by train to Perm, about two hundred miles away, out of the path of the advancing Czechs,' Browning said. 'They're to be kept in a place of safety – it seems Lenin's still hoping to use them. There are Russians in German hands he'd like to have back. Assuming, of course, that he holds on to power. There seems to be some doubt about that. But he's a ruthless operator. One would be foolish to bet against him.' He looked at her curiously. 'I suppose you'll be hearing from your son about it soon.'

'I hope so,' she said, wondering as she said it what Thomas would do.

'I hope he will use his common sense and get out now. Things are very tense in Moscow. They're worried about a possible German invasion. All the diplomatic community has packed up and left, apart from Lockhart.' Sir Bruce Lockhart was the British consul-general in Moscow. 'He's playing a lonely game – and a dangerous one – but we get vital information from him. We've heard from another source that Trotsky is on the brink of banning all British and French officers from travelling, because of their "counter-revolutionary tendencies". And the tension is bound to spill over into the rest of the country. With the Whites closing in on Ekaterinburg, the local Reds there may start getting jumpy and locking people up.'

'Oh, God,' Venetia said involuntarily. If Thomas were arrested, there would be no getting him out. With the Tsar dead, his duty there was over; but she knew that it was not Nicholas who had held him there all these years – or not entirely. She could write to him, she could telegraph him, but she would not alter his decision in any way, and she was horribly afraid that he would follow the Romanov family to Perm. She thought of that sinister suggestion about English officers being counter-revolutionaries: it was the Bolshevik equivalent to 'shoot on sight'. Until now an English officer had been the safest person in Russia, but was that now to change? There was nothing for it but to wait to hear from her son. Her only comfort was that a move to Perm was in the right direction – closer to home.

Bertie did manage to visit again. He had been awarded a bar to his DSO for his actions in bringing his men out under fire from the front line in March, and had come to London towards the end of July for the presentation, after which he had snatched some glorious days at Morland Place with Jessie and his now much improved son. Young Thomas Parke was opening his eyes properly, and seemed to be trying to recognise faces. 'He's a remarkably *good* baby,' Jessie told the doting father. 'He seems to be determined not to be any trouble to anyone now he's here. As if he knows he caused enough trouble for a lifetime before his arrival.'

'What a harsh woman you are!' Bertie said. 'None of it was his fault.'

'I know,' Jessie said. 'But I have to try to maintain a tough, practical attitude towards him, or I shall melt into a warm pool of besottedness. I love him so much – just to look at him turns me into the sort of dribbling, sentimental idiot I've always despised.'

'No-one will ever mistake you for a weak and feeble woman,' Bertie promised her. 'You can gush a little if you want to.'

She let go. 'Oh, Bertie, he *is* the most perfect creature that ever lived, isn't he?'

'Apart from myself at the same age, absolutely the most perfect,' Bertie agreed.

'I used to think babies ugly things, and not a patch on foals or puppies or kittens. I always thought animals did it much better than humans. But now—'

He caught her hand and kissed it. 'You needn't keep apologising. There's no foolish thing you can say about our son that I haven't said myself.'

'Our son. How I love those words!'

'Our son,' he said again, to please her. And then, 'Our eldest.'

She smiled assent to the proposition, but Bertie had seen the shadow enter her eyes. This was only a respite, as neither of them could forget for long. Until the war was over, they could not be confident that they would have a life together. They must treasure every moment for what it was, and not look too far ahead.

He tucked her hand through his arm, and they walked on companionably up the slope towards the Monument.

'I shall be glad when I can ride again,' Jessie said, when she found herself puffing. She was dreadfully out of condition, after almost six weeks of sitting and lying and taking invalidish walks around the gardens.

Bertie winced inwardly. 'I'm amazed you can contemplate it,' he said.

She laughed. 'Well, perhaps I will start off side-saddle! But I miss Hotspur so much, and I've been confined to the house for so long. Just think, if I were up to it now, you and I could have gone off somewhere and had a wonderful gallop.'

'Next time,' he said.

'Yes, it won't be long now. Dr Hasty is probably being over-cautious – but I feel like being cautious myself, so I don't blame him . . . I want a dog, too,' she resumed after a moment. 'I miss having that shadow behind me.' Helen was home, so Rug was not in attendance on her. 'It's such a long time since Brach died. I think I'll ask Uncle Teddy for a pup, next time there's a litter. Morland Place doesn't seem right with no dog of my own. It'll be nice for Thomas to grow up with dogs, too.'

'Where do I come into all this?' Bertie asked. 'You seem to be settling it that you and Thomas are going to be living here.'

Jessie looked embarrassed. 'Oh! Well, we are, of course, for the time being. Until the war's over. I didn't mean . . .'

'I know you didn't. I was teasing. But, as the subject has come up, do you think it would be tempting Fate to talk about where we might live after the war, always assuming . . . et cetera?'

'Oh, Bertie!'

'The thing is, you see, that, fine land though Beaumont is, I was born and bred in Yorkshire, and whenever I come back here, it feels like home. And I've never found a buyer for the Red House. It's a convalescent hospital at the moment, of course, but they'll close that down after the war. And the land is only leased out. I could get it back easily enough. The house would need some work done on it, but if you didn't like it we could pull it down and build a new one.'

'Grandiose plans!' Jessie said. 'How on earth could you afford to do that?'

'Oh, I'm quite wealthy, in a quiet way, and selling Beaumont will release the capital.'

'But what about your beautiful cattle?'

'I can bring them up to Yorkshire. The Red House has lots of good grazing land. And you could bring your horse-breeding enterprise over there too.'

'You'd want me to go on with that?'

'Did you think you were going to live in idleness for the rest of your life?'

She thought of how Ned had wanted just that, how he had hated her independence, and thanked God for Bertie all over again. 'We could breed horses together,' she said. 'Even if the army doesn't need so many, there'll be other markets. The railways need them. And people will always want private hacks and hunters. Polo ponies, too.'

'Just so. And I thought, after the war,' he went on, 'it might be fun to try breeding racehorses. Yorkshire's the county for racing, after all, and your family did well enough out of it in the old days.'

'It's your family too. Your mother was a Morland.'

'I never forget it,' he said. They reached the Monument and stopped, standing with their backs to it to look around the green and burgeoning land stretching before them. 'God, it's good to be back,' he said softly.

Jessie drew herself close and rested her head against his arm, almost as if she were cold. She loved him so much, and the thought that he might not have come back, the fear that the worst could still happen, was always too near the surface, threatening the time they had with each other. Determined not to think like that, she cast about for a different topic, and said, 'Did I tell you Helen has had a letter from Jack?'

'No, you didn't. A proper letter? She must be so relieved.'

Since they had heard in June that Jack was a prisoner of war, the only communication they had received was a printed postcard, similar to a field postcard, which the Red Cross issued and the German camp commandants preferred, since there was no need to censor them.

'Yes, a proper letter, though it didn't say much. I suppose

there isn't much they're allowed to say. He's in a camp called Holzminden, which Uncle Teddy says is near Hanover – not that that means much to me. I could hardly get to grips with France when I was at school, let alone Germany.'

'Well, it's fairly far north, on a level with Holland, and about in the middle, counting left to right.'

'Oh. How clearly you put it. I can imagine it now. But it'll be cold there in winter, I suppose?'

'Very.'

'Poor Jack. Anyway, he said that he was quite well, and being treated properly – though I suppose they have to say that or the censors wouldn't pass the letter. He said there are lots of other airmen there, and that they're keeping themselves busy. I wonder what that means?'

'Probably that they're trying to escape,' Bertie said. 'Poor devils, it must be hell to be locked up like that.'

'But at least he's alive,' said Jessie. 'Helen would sooner have it that way.'

'Yes, sorry. I was forgetting poor Robert.'

'And Frank. But, you know, I've been wondering . . .' She hesitated.

'Yes?'

She had been wondering if there wasn't a special kind of friendship developing between Maria and Father Palgrave. It wasn't anything she could put her finger on, except a sort of atmosphere between them, and the way sometimes they would finish each other's sentences. Of course, that might come from working together so much. And if Maria *were* falling in love again, who was she to criticise? But she remembered that men didn't like talk of that sort, so she said, 'Oh, nothing, really. Helen's sending a parcel out to Jack with all sorts of things, food and clothing and books. Do you think he'll get it? Or will it go to line some German jailer's house?'

'I think the Red Cross is pretty good about getting the parcels out to the camps,' Bertie said, 'but what happens after that must depend on the individual commandants.

Talking of Germans and prisoners, by the way, what happened about the prisoners of war you were supposed to be getting to help on the land?'

'Oh, they're coming next week. There's a camp being built along by Leeman's Road – it used to be the old internment camp, in fact, at the beginning of the war, and they're just redoing it, putting up stronger wire and better huts. There's been quite a lot of protest about it, but Uncle Teddy is adamant that we need it, and he simply argues to people that it's better to have them working for their keep than sitting about doing nothing. He's got it down to such a fine art he can shut anyone up in about half an hour now.'

'I can imagine it.'

'It's always the women who think the Huns will escape and murder them in their beds. Why it's always in their beds, I don't know. Does that make it worse? Uncle Teddy says these particular prisoners are the especially trustworthy ones.'

'I dare say most of them are glad to be here, rather than fighting at the Front or starving back home. It isn't much fun for anyone in Germany, these days. They're probably perfectly decent boys who loved their mothers and didn't want to fight in the first place.'

'That's what Uncle Teddy says. I'm sure he wouldn't expose us to them if there were any danger. And I must say we can use them. What with hedging and ditching that's been left because there was no-one to do it, and the harvests coming up, we need all the hands we can get. Or should I say, we need all the *Hans* we can get. I say, that's very nearly a joke.'

'You *are* feeling better,' Bertie said.

'I'm feeling hungry.'

'God bless your appetite! Let's walk gently back down the hill and see if tea is ready.'

On the 24th of July, Ekaterinburg was surrounded, and on the 25th it finally fell to the Whites. News of this was telegraphed to England the next day, when there also arrived an official telegram for the Foreign Office from Lockhart in Moscow, which had inexplicably been delayed, confirming the execution of the Tsar on the 16th, and the removal of the family from Ekaterinburg by railway on the 17th.

Two days later Venetia, to her great relief, received a letter from Thomas, which had had a remarkably quick passage considering it had come out on a roundabout route via Finland. In it he described the events in Ekaterinburg, the journey to Perm, and his new persona as Dr Paul Seichel: 'I am sorry to put off the uniform but I will be safer as a Swiss, and it will help me get out when the time comes.'

The mention of getting out made her heart rise, but the rest of the letter gave no indication that that was likely to be soon.

On arrival at Perm the family was taken to the Excise Office where they now live in upstairs rooms. They are guarded by senior members of the regional soviet, not the Red Guard, who apparently are not trusted. I have taken rooms in a building opposite, above a pawn shop. So far I have not been able to see them. Their presence is meant to be a secret so access to them is strictly controlled. Party members only are allowed near them, even to bringing their food. But the ground floor of the Excise Office is much used so I don't despair. Local feeling is not hostile to them so I may have help if I devise a plan. And the German presence watches over them carefully, so I think they are safe for now.

At the end of the letter he promised to write again when he had something to tell, but added, 'Do not try to write to me. It might be dangerous. Wait for my letter, and believe nothing I have not told you.'

On the 29th, at her request, Browning visited her and she showed him the letter, which he read with attention.

440

'This accords with what we hear from the White Russian military inside Ekaterinburg. Locals say the Emperor was shot on the sixteenth and the family was removed under guard in a sealed train on the seventeenth. Our own intelligence men who were with the White Army have been making enquiries. They say the cleaners who went to the Ipatiev house to collect their wages a couple of days afterwards were told everyone had been sent to Perm. But your son's letter puts it beyond doubt. However,' he looked grave, 'I have to tell you that Ekaterinburg is seething with rumour and counter-rumour. Some are saying the whole family was massacred inside the house and then secretly buried.'

'What nonsense is this?' Venetia protested.

He shrugged. 'It's the sort of thing that's said, particularly by excitable, uneducated people who love a bit of drama, the bloodier the better. Apparently *someone* was shot in the house, in a sort of semi-basement room. There's blood and bullet holes, and widespread talk of shots being heard. Our intelligence suggests it was probably the family servants, including Dr Botkin, who haven't been seen since the seventeenth. It will take time to find out more.'

'But you have all the evidence you need to refute the rumour,' Venetia said.

'Yes,' said Browning, thoughtfully. 'But for the time being we're holding this back. Moscow wants to keep the whereabouts of the family secret, and we feel it's in their best interest. The extreme Reds would like to kill the Empress, and probably the children too, so the fewer people who know where they are the better. There's still a good chance of getting them out, either through a German rescue plot or by Lenin exchanging them. But Lenin would have to keep the exchange secret from half of his own cabinet, and obviously a German plot would have to be secret, so we'll keep this under the rose for the time being.'

* * *

As July turned to August, the story of the Romanov Massacre grew and spread, beyond the intelligence services and into the public domain. It was such a tellable story – which fed into the general public's desire for sensation – that, like a flood, it gathered up sticks and stones in its passage until it became almost solid. More detail was added all the time: how the family was told they were going on a journey and were brought down in the middle of the night, how chairs were brought for the Tsaritsa and the crippled boy, how twelve guards entered and opened fire, how some of the girls were not killed outright and were bayoneted repeatedly by the guards until they were dead. Then details began to be added about the disposal of the bodies, how they were taken out to the woods, drenched in acid and then burned.

It was hard for Venetia to read and hear this sort of thing and keep silent, but she saw the necessity. Browning told her that the White military authority had made a preliminary enquiry, and their officer, Captain Malinovsky, had concluded that the semi-basement room, and the site in the woods where burned clothing fragments and jewels had been found, had been prepared deliberately to simulate the massacre of the family. 'Rather like flinging a piece of meat at a pack of pursuing dogs,' Browning said. 'No doubt the Reds hope it will hold up the Whites, and take some of the urgency out of their pursuit. The interesting thing is that it looks as though the Whites are going to reject Malinovsky's report and back the massacre story.'

'But why?' Venetia said. 'He's their own man, isn't he?'

'Yes,' said Browning, almost apologetically, 'but, you see, it rather suits them to have it believed that the Romanovs were massacred, the more brutally the better. It gives a rallying point to their cause – martyrs for the faithful to adore. Live Romanovs are a much trickier proposition, less sympathetic and infinitely more awkward to deal with. This way they've got a terrific story to seize the imagination and they can mobilise anti-Red hatred with it.'

Venetia looked at him carefully. 'So both sides want them believed dead?'

Browning's apology turned to sadness. 'Not only both sides in Russia. All those relatives who might be called on to take them in would be quite glad to know it wasn't going to be asked of them.'

'The King?' she said. 'He's surely not inclined to believe this nonsense?'

'Well, we haven't shown him all the evidence, only the Tsarskoye broadcast and Lockhart's telegram. It's possible for someone who doesn't want to believe to discount *them* as Moscow Central propaganda. I think,' said Browning carefully, 'that he would sooner mourn them. It's a much purer emotion.'

Venetia knew at first-hand how ambivalent the King's attitude had always been to the Tsar. In the week after the report of the Tsar's execution he had ordered Court mourning and expressed a deep sorrow at the fate of his cousin. But 'poor Nicky' was much more sympathetic dead than alive; and it was certainly easier to think of the rest of the family as dead and past their suffering than in the hands of brutal Reds, needing rescue and possible asylum.

Venetia had worries of her own. She had been visited by a senior officer from the Horse Guards who enquired in a delicate way if she knew where her son was. Thomas had been officially recalled from his duty in Russia once Lockhart's telegram had confirmed the Tsar's execution: it was no part of the British Army's duty to maintain a liaison with the German Tsaritsa or her children. But the British ambassador in Ekaterinburg had telegraphed to say that Colonel Lord Overton had disappeared some time before the White Army had taken the town. Now Horse Guards did not know whether he was dead, or absent without leave.

'We hesitate to lay any charge approaching desertion on an officer of such seniority and impeccable record,' the envoy said, eyeing her curiously and sympathetically. 'If you have no knowledge of how he may be contacted, we may be forced to conclude that the worst has happened and post him as missing.'

Venetia did not have to simulate the tears that sprang to her eyes. Her son was in a place of grave danger, from which he might not be able to extricate himself. In a sense he *was* missing, and that he might be killed was a distinct possibility.

'I'm sorry, ma'am,' said the envoy, embarrassed by his part in distressing a great lady.

She waved away his apology. 'No,' she said. 'You must do your duty. Post him as missing. And if he is not found, or heard of – if the Reds do not say they've got him . . .'

Later, when Oliver came in, he found her, not weeping, but with evidence of tears on her face. 'Thomas?' he asked, sitting down beside her.

'They're going to post him as missing.'

'You know where he is, don't you?' he said abruptly. She nodded. 'Oh, Mum!'

She pulled his handkerchief out of his pocket, her own being already wet and useless, then dried her face and blew her nose. 'He does what he feels he must,' she said. 'Like you.'

'I don't make you cry,' Oliver pointed out.

She managed a watery smile. 'You don't remember. I've cried over you many times.'

'Tears of laughter, perhaps,' he said. 'Thomas was always your favourite. You never took me seriously.'

Venetia felt guilty. She took his hand, and said sincerely, 'Darling, I'm very proud of you. And very glad to have you with me through these dark times.' He still looked at her with the eyes of the second son, who can never catch up, having lost the first race of life; so she changed the subject. 'I want to consult you about the building alterations in Dean Street. Do you think it would be practicable to put in a glass roof to the operating theatre?'

Oliver gave a shout of laughter. 'What a terrible, crashing

444

change of gears, Mother dear! Remind me never to let you behind the wheel of any car I care for.'

'That's something I mean to do when the war's over,' she said. 'Learn to drive.'

'Over my dead body,' Oliver said. 'Which, if you do get behind the wheel, will probably be the case.'

The offensives in France during July had mostly been undertaken by the French and Americans at Verdun and the Australians and Americans at Chateau Thierry, while the British forces, exhausted from the efforts of the spring offensive, had been holding the north of the line while they rested, retrained, remanned and re-equipped.

For Emma's unit, August was therefore a quiet month with no more than routine duties. Because of the prevailing lull, it was decided by the authorities that the time had come to hand out the medals awarded to the FANYs of Unit 8 for their brave actions on the night of the arms-depot explosion. The ceremony was held in the Second Army headquarters, and the GOC, General Sir Herbert Plumer, himself pinned the ribbons on the tunics of the sixteen Military Medal winners. Emma was proud of hers, but even greater than the honour of it was the knowledge that they were showing the way for women of the future, proving to men that they could step outside the traditional roles of wife- and motherhood. As Vera had written to her, 'You are showing that womanhood has no fixed horizon, and men are now accepting that.'

After the ceremony, the general invited them all to a medal tea, and proved a good host, a very genial and merry man, with a surprisingly accurate knowledge of the FANY's life and duties. His aides were delightful young men, and took away from the stewards the role of pouring out and handing round, so that it became very cosy and jolly – 'Just like a nursery tea,' Armstrong told the general innocently, making him laugh.

'I hope you had better nursery teas than me,' he replied. 'Bread and butter and plain biscuits were all I was ever given.'

The medal tea was certainly better than that, and Emma had to restrain herself from snatching and gobbling, because such dainty fare didn't come their way much in wartime. There was bread and butter, and it really was butter, which made it very popular, for the margarine that was practically universal back home was creeping into military rations as well. There were sandwiches too – actually cucumber sandwiches, for which the cucumbers had been sent from the family home in Northamptonshire of one of the young aides.

'Very well-travelled cucumbers,' the general remarked. 'You can't get them over here.'

'Not even for ready money,' said the aide, which made everyone laugh.

There were also egg sandwiches – they and the cucumber sandwiches were made with margarine, but no-one let that spoil the pleasure – and Gentleman's Relish sandwiches, which were a particular favourite of the general. There was fruit cake and Madeira cake, jam tarts and rock cakes, shortcake biscuits and ginger snaps. Altogether it was an excellent tea, the highlight of the year so far, as Emma said to the general when they made their farewells.

'It's the highlight of mine, too, m'dear,' he said, shaking her hand heartily. 'These boys of mine are fine chaps, but they don't flirt so prettily with me as you ladies.'

Also at the beginning of August there was a joint services dance, held in an enormous aeroplane hangar outside St Omer. Unit 8 was much in demand to ferry people to the event and, of course, to stay on and be the dancing partners of the men, so hungry for female company. There were two excellent bands, so they could spell each other and keep the music going non-stop, and they played all the latest jazz and dance tunes, as well as some more traditional waltzes and country dances.

446

Emma was very pleased that Captain Wentworth and one or two others from the 37th were able to make it. 'I'm also glad,' Emma said, as she worked her way up a country dance set with Wentworth, 'that we're all in uniform. It gives a pleasing kind of equality to everything – no-one eyeing anyone else's gown with a critical eye. Anyone could be anyone.'

'Dear me, how modern and Communistic of you, Trooper,' Wentworth said.

'Rot, it's not Communistic,' she protested. 'All these women are working very hard out here, and deserve to be treated equally, that's all.'

'Which, of course, is why FANYs only dance with officers, and leave the other ranks to the WAACs and VADs.'

'If you're not careful I shall chuck you and go and find myself a corporal,' Emma warned.

'You shan't,' he said, tightening his grip of her hand. 'What – do some honest WAAC out of her best chance? As it happens, I agree with you about the uniform, but for a different reason.'

'What reason?' she asked suspiciously.

'The symmetry of it. All khaki, with just a dash of airforce and a hint of navy blue. There's something terribly messy about civilian dances, with all those women in gowns of different colours and styles. I think there should be just one style of evening dress for women, as there is for men, so that these events could have a tidier appearance. More aesthetically pleasing, don't you know?' He waved a hand languidly around the room.

She couldn't help laughing. 'You're such a fool!'

'I'm a fool for you,' he said, and when she looked uncertain how to take that, he added innocently, 'I only play the fool for you. I'm quite serious when I talk to other people.' The music ended. 'Thank goodness – I'm melting with all this exertion in such heat. Will you come out for a breath of air? I heard there were some ices somewhere – we could have a look on the way and see if we can spot them.'

'All right, just for a minute,' said Emma, who was hot too. Whatever the asymmetrical properties of evening gowns, they would at least have been cooler to dance in than uniform serge.

There were no ices – or if there had been, they were all gone by now – but Wentworth secured two glasses of lemonade, and they took them out through a small door and onto the concrete apron outside. The floodlights were not on, of course – there were still air-raids – and the moon was not up, so it was very dark outside after the bright lights within. But once their eyes had adjusted, they could see an immense heaven dusted with stars.

'It's one of the few good things about the war,' Emma said. 'I grew up in London, so I hardly ever saw the stars. They really are quite magnificent when there's no outside light to compete with them.'

'Beautiful,' he agreed. 'Sometimes up on the line when there's a quiet night, I go out for a smoke and to look at them. Of course, there aren't many quiet nights. You can usually depend on some idiot deciding to send over a shell or two, just to keep everyone on their toes.'

'Horribly thoughtless,' she said. 'It's the thing that makes one quite long for the end of the war. I wish I knew about stars. Do you know many of the names?'

'A few. My father taught me when I was a nipper. That's the easiest one to spot, over there – the Plough. You see? That, that, that and that, and then those three in a curve.'

'I don't see which you mean,' Emma said, staring up.

'Look,' he said, and came up close behind her, putting his head next to hers and reaching over her shoulder to point, so that his arm was in line with her eyes. 'See it now?'

'It doesn't look much like a plough,' Emma said.

He put his free hand on her waist to steady himself. His cheek was actually touching hers now. But his voice was matter-of-fact. '*That's* the handle, you see, and *that's* supposed

448

to be the ploughshare. How can you not see it's a plough? Where were you brought up?'

'I told you, in London,' she said. She turned her face a little to look at him as she said it, forgetting how close he was. Somehow – she didn't know how it had happened – they were facing each other, both his arms were round her, their lips were touching – they were kissing.

She broke away, and he let her go, his arms falling to his sides. 'I'm sorry,' he said. 'I didn't mean to take liberties with you.'

'Liberties, phooh! What an expression!' she said, trying to sound light. 'I was just surprised, that's all.'

He held her gaze. 'No, you weren't. Not really. You know how I feel about you. You've known for a long time.'

'I – I suppose I have,' she said.

'Your voice sounds sad. I know you're going to reject me. Oh, Emma, I can't help it, I love you. You're the most splendid girl I've ever met. I know about your fiancé, and I'm very, very sorry, and I know you're not ready to love anyone again, not yet. But I'll wait. I'll wait for as long as I have to.'

'Oh, Wentworth, I—'

'No, listen, please. I don't *mind* waiting. You don't have to feel any – *responsibility* about me. I won't be a nuisance or bother you or get all spoony and embarrass you in public.' She was struggling not to smile now. There was just something about him that always made her feel more light-hearted. 'All I ask is that you let me see you, as a friend, and one day, in the future, if you feel ready to – to feel differently, well, we'll take it from there.' He looked at her eagerly. 'What do you say?'

'You look like Benson when he thinks I'm going out without him.'

'I *feel* like Benson thinking you're going out without me. You're not going to cut me off, are you? Say you won't. Say you'll let me come and talk nonsense to you whenever I can get away.'

'Now that's an offer a girl couldn't refuse,' she said. 'There isn't enough nonsense in the world.'

'Then you shall have all mine. Nonsense, rubbish and balderdash unlimited.'

'But no dying duck in a thunderstorm?'

'No avian species of any sort, in any adverse weather conditions whatever,' he promised.

'I thought avian meant to do with bees?'

'That's apian, you idiot.'

'I thought that was to do with monkeys.'

He laughed. 'Now I know you're roasting me.'

'Perhaps just the tiniest bit. One can do that with one's friends.' She smiled at him, comfortable again. She wasn't ready to love anyone else, not yet, but she didn't want to let Wentworth go. He made her happy, and she didn't want him to take himself out of her life. To laugh together like this was the perfect antidote to war.

Another couple loomed up out of the darkness, and stopped abruptly as they saw Emma and Wentworth.

'Oh, excuse me,' a male voice said. 'We were just going back in.'

Emma recognised the voice. It was Captain Savile. An instant later she saw that he had his arm round Armstrong's waist, and when they came closer still, she could see from Armstrong's ruffled hair and swollen lips that they had been doing a great deal more kissing than her and Wentworth.

Armstrong didn't seem at all put out at being discovered. 'Oh, hello, Westie. Hello, Wentworth,' she said absently, out of a dream she was living in.

It was Savile who looked embarrassed. He cleared his throat. 'I – um – we—'

'No need to mention it, old chap,' Wentworth said genially. 'It's what starry nights were made for.'

'We're engaged,' Armstrong blurted. 'Roger asked me to marry him, and I said yes.'

450

'How wonderful!' Emma cried. 'Congratulations! I'm so happy for you both.'

'And I. Congratulations, old man.' Wentworth shook Savile's hand.

He smiled back, looking a little dazed. 'I'm afraid we won't be able to get married until the war's over,' he said, 'but Dorothy says she'll wait.' Emma almost asked who Dorothy was, but restrained herself in time. 'I'm the luckiest man alive,' he finish.

They all went in together, and Armstrong (Dorothy!) and Savile (Roger!) danced together for the rest of the evening, and always seemed to be doing the waltz even when the music wasn't.

Much later, when Emma was lying in her flea-bag, with Benson contented under her hand, she thought of the engaged couple and their radiant happiness, and she cried a little, for herself and Fenniman and the happiness they had had, which had been cut short. She hoped Armstrong would have better luck. Only as she was drifting off to sleep did she let herself think about Wentworth. She thought about that kiss, and how she hadn't recoiled from it, though a few weeks ago she wouldn't have thought she could ever bear to be kissed by anyone who wasn't Fenniman. The sad truth was that he was fading from her, and she hated herself for being so shallow and fickle. But he was dead, and she was twenty-two, and sometimes she felt so alive she could almost have jumped out of her skin with sheer energy. She had loved him as much as a woman could love a man, but time – life – was hurrying her away from him. It made her want to cry, but it also made her want to know what would happen next.

CHAPTER TWENTY

Polly was out on a hot August day riding Vesper. Kai, her young hound, was bearing them company: as it was too hot to gallop, he was able to keep up without too much exertion. Polly's old hound, Bell, had died the month before, but Teddy's best bitch Helle had just whelped, and Polly was thinking about asking her father for one of the pups. Jessie was having one, and it would be fun for the pair to grow up together. She was thinking mostly about dogs as Vesper idled along on a loose rein, the long grasses brushing her belly, her blonde forelock keeping the flies out of her eyes. Just for once the mare was content to walk rather than dance, blowing the dust and flies out of her nostrils with tremendous snorts, and the occasional sneeze made her round summer sides bounce like a drumskin. It was too hot for her even to want to snatch at the grass, as normally she would have done if the reins told her her mistress was inattentive.

Polly didn't see the man until she was almost up to him. He was working on the overgrown hawthorn hedge that rimmed the field. Kai ran up to him and stood a little back, tail working uncertainly at one end and nose interestedly at the other. Vesper, who had been daydreaming, flung her head up as she suddenly spotted him, and performed an entirely unnecessary gavotte, which Polly checked easily as the man turned to see who was approaching.

'Did I startle your horse?' he said.

She knew now who he was, of course – one of the German prisoners, hedging and ditching for the Bellerbys at White House Farm. She felt a little thrill run down her spine at the knowledge – her first real live Hun soldier! He had paused in his work, laid down his tools and was standing looking at her. His lean face was very brown, and his eyes, in startling contrast, were blue as summer skies. His fair hair, cut very short, was bleached on top and at the front, and his sleeves, rolled up to the elbow, revealed bare brown forearms, long and strong and glittering with golden hairs. He regarded her with friendly interest, and his long, mobile mouth looked equally ready for humour or conversation.

She wondered if she would have known he was German if she hadn't known, so to speak, and decided that perhaps she would have. But though she was trying, she couldn't feel afraid of him. Germans had committed all sorts of atrocities in France and Belgium – bayoneting babies and raping nuns and so on – but all she could feel coming from this man was friendliness and . . . and *something*, she couldn't quite decide what it was, but something that made her want to stay and talk to him. A readiness for laughter, perhaps – which, when you thought that he was German *and* a prisoner of war, was not at all what one would have expected.

'It is very nice that your dog does not bark at me, as so many dogs do,' he said.

'It's the breed,' Polly explained automatically. 'They can't bark.'

'Like wolves?' he suggested.

'They were bred from wolves originally,' she said. 'That's how the breed was started.'

'I did not know you had wolves in England,' he said.

'We don't now, but my ancestors had to keep wolf-watch on the sheep in the olden days, right in these very fields,' Polly said. 'You speak English awfully well,' she added curiously.

453

'I learned it in school, and I visited England some times before the war. So you know who I am?'

'I know who you're *not*, because I know everyone round here. And I knew the Bellerbys had a—' She stopped, because it seemed somehow as rude to say the word 'prisoner' in front of this man as it would have been to draw attention to some physical defect – like saying 'a man with a big nose' or 'a man with a hare lip'.

He seemed to understand her problem. 'A prisoner of war?' he said easily. 'But I know what I am. You need not mind to say it. I am Erich Kuppel, by the way, if you prefer to have a name.'

'Kuppel,' she repeated.

'It means dome, or cupola – like the one on St Paul's Cathedral.'

'You know St Paul's?' she said, in sudden vague suspicion. Was he a spy like the ones she had read about, who pretended to be English and sent back information to Germany about targets for bombing?

'As I said, I visited in England very much before the war. I was four weeks in London in 1912, to study architecture. St Paul's Cathedral is almost a miracle. Do you like Wren's work?'

She knew nothing about Wren, and nearly nothing about architecture, beyond what must naturally filter into the mind of a person who lived in a mediaeval house. But she remembered something else she had heard. 'The house next to ours – Shawes – was built by Vanbrugh. It's supposed to be his best work. They call it "Vanbrugh's little gem".'

'I like Vanbrugh too,' he said, 'though he is not the master like Wren. Once in a while there is an exceptional genius, so much outside the normal you believe he must be God-touched. Wren is one. Mozart another. Do you like Mozart?'

'I've played some,' she said vaguely. She had been taught piano, as all female Morlands were. But the conversation was taking a line uninteresting to her. She liked the personal rather than the impersonal. 'I'm surprised they let you work without – without being watched.'

'But why? I have been a prisoner now since 1915. If I wished to escape I should have done it long ago. But I have no wish to escape. If I go back to Germany they will put me again into a uniform and send me to the Front to kill English people. I do not wish to kill English people. I love England. I was happy here before the war.'

'But don't you want to go home?' she asked, lengthening the rein so that Vesper could rub her itchy nose against her knee.

'After the war,' he said. 'Of course I wish to see my home again, but not if it means killing people. I am not an assassin.'

'What are you, then? I mean, what did you do in Germany before the war?'

'My father owns land, like your father.' Ah, so he knew who she was! 'I suppose you might say I am a farmer.'

'You're doing a nice job on that hedge,' Polly remarked, feeling strangely better about him now she knew he was a landowner's son – of her class, so to speak.

'Thank you,' he said, bowing in a way that was entirely un-English, but rather touched her all the same. 'It is not the first hedge I have cut. My father believes a gentleman should know how to do *all* the jobs he asks other people to do for him. So I had to learn about farming from the time I could walk. Also to groom and shoe my own horse, clean my own boots, wash my own shirts, cook my own food.' He smiled, a wide and curling smile that quickened Polly's breath. 'I am a most useful man to know in a prisoner-of-war camp!'

She felt herself smiling back at him. 'Where did the architecture fit in?'

'My father wished to make alterations to the castle – to our house, I should say. So I must study architecture – and building too. I can build a wall, if your father wishes. Also carpentry I can do, when the winter comes and there is no more field work. If the war still goes on.'

She had not missed the slip of the tongue over the castle and was intrigued, both that he came from a family that owned a castle, and that he wanted to hide it. Did not want to seem to be boasting, perhaps? 'Where is your house?' she asked.

'Near Göttingen. Do you know Germany?'

She shook her head. 'I have a cousin in a prisoner-of-war camp.'

'I'm sorry.'

'It's near Hanover.'

'Yes, I know Hanover. Göttingen is not so very far from there.' He looked to see if she wanted to know more, and said, 'They breed very fine horses around Hanover.'

Vesper, growing bored, tore a mouthful of grass, and Polly checked her. 'My cousin won't see any horses inside a prison camp,' she said resentfully, feeling a prickle of tears.

'The war, I think, will not last much longer,' he said gently. 'And then your cousin will come home to England.'

'And you will go home to Germany,' she said.

He did not answer. Kai was lying down in the long grass, enjoying the shade of it, his yellow eyes half closed, unworried by the stranger. Vesper, resigned to not eating, eased herself from foot to foot, flicking her ears against the flies, swishing her tail regularly against one flank and then the other. The man took a step closer, and put his hand to Vesper's face, flat to her forehead, and she sighed and turned her head to rub her eye against it, at her most cat-like and trusting.

'You like horses,' she said, not as a question.

'It is what I miss most, I think,' he said softly. 'I love to see your horses here. I wish I might work with them. Even with the mules,' he smiled suddenly, 'but the Mr Banks of the mules did not wish me to work on his farm.'

No, Polly thought, old Ezra would not take kindly to a Hun at Woodhouse. And she felt ashamed at even thinking

456

the word in the presence of this man, and found herself blushing.

Kuppel moved quietly but quickly backwards, perhaps taking her blush as an objection to his closeness. Vesper gave herself a tremendous shake from nose to tail, making her tack snap and ring, and Kai took the movement as a cue, and got to his feet.

'I'd better go,' Polly said. 'Vesper's being eaten by flies.'

'Vesper. A pretty name,' said Kuppel. 'And the hound?'

'Kai,' said Polly. 'It's a traditional hound name in our family.'

'So,' he said. 'Thank you for the conversation. I have enjoyed it very much. And for not being frightened of me.'

'Why should I be frightened of you?' she said. She had been going to add, 'They wouldn't have let you out alone if you were dangerous,' but decided just in time that it was better not said.

'No reason, indeed,' he said, and stood back, with a nod, as if to let her pass. He was not in her path, as it happened, but it made it seem as though the ending of the encounter was in his control rather than hers, and though she did not think of it in so many words, she understood wordlessly that, for a prisoner, such things must be important. She nodded in return, gathered the reins and, suddenly self-conscious, pushed Vesper straight into a canter. Vesper, after a long stand, was not at all unwilling. Kai bounded after them. Polly turned Vesper at the far hedge and cantered up the field to where the gate was open and passed through. At any other time and before any other audience she would probably have jumped Vesper over the hedge, just to show she could, but though she was sure Erich Kuppel was watching her, she did not wish him, for some reason, to think she was showing off.

Bertie's battalion was back in the line on the 8th of August when a new offensive was launched at Amiens. The Allies had learned a great deal from the surprise of the German offensives of the spring, and the attack was marked by meticulous preparation and sprung on the Germans out of silence and secrecy. Moreover, the troops involved – the Canadians and Australians, who had a formidable fighting reputation, and Rawlinson's Fourth Army, which was by now battle-hardened and experienced – were trained to a peak of professionalism. Wireless was beginning to replace the vulnerable surface telephone lines for battle communication. The air force combined its traditional reconnaissance role with newly learned skills in ground attack. There was almost a superfluity of tanks available, including a new class of light 'Whippet' tank, ready to follow up, with the cavalry, any breakthrough. And the infantry was fighting in the new self-reliant units, each with its own bombers and machine-gunners, which could act and react more promptly and flexibly than the large masses of willing amateurs who had marched into the withering gunfire in this area two years before.

Labour corps moved behind the first wave, repairing the roads so that the traffic could be kept flowing, and mule teams brought up ammunition to keep the advancing troops supplied. And advance they did – seven miles into German territory by the end of the first day, twelve by the end of the fourth. It was a glorious feeling for the men involved to be going forward, and at such a rate, after the stasis of so many years, and the reverses of the spring. Thousands of prisoners were taken, and hundreds of guns.

The five days passed rapidly for Bertie, so that afterwards all he could recall was a series of odd images, like photographs taken almost at random and displayed on the wall of his memory: a team of artillery horses, still harnessed together, trotting all alone down the road towards the rear (they came upon the dismounted gun and the dead gunners later, hit by a shell when they were unlimbering); a tank coming up from a dip filled with morning fog, rising slowly out of the whiteness like Leviathan from the depths; a tall Australian, wounded, walking back, holding his bloody arm against his chest, his face a shocked blank, but his rangy body swinging along with a steady countryman's stride, eating up the miles; a German ammunition train, hit by a shell and burning – a black framework filled with pale gold fire, the sparks of exploding bullets like shooting stars; a cat, presumably gone wild, hunting mice in the morning half-light at the edge of a cornfield, miraculously untouched by the passage and repassage of armies; the exact colour of a clump of poppies growing out of a crumbling, chalky bank beside the road at the top of a rise, their scarlet silk dresses cut out against a cornflower sky; the spur, blindingly silver in the strong sunshine, on the dusty boot of a trooper's severed leg sticking up from a ditch as they passed.

On the 20th of August, the French Tenth Army attacked on the river Oise and drove the Germans back three miles. Further north, the Third Army, under Byng, threw off a surprise German attack, and the next day advanced in company with the New Zealanders, and by the 29th had retaken Bapaume. On Sunday the 1st of September the Australians took Péronne in storming style, and on the same day, just to the north of Péronne, Lennie's battalion took Bouchavesnes in a very hard-fought action, which covered three thousand yards of open ground and resulted in a fine bag of guns and prisoners, though at heavy cost to the battalion. Lennie was wounded again, this time in the arm, but wrote home that it was not considered serious enough to be a 'Blighty touch', and that he had been sent to a military hospital at Calais until he could go back to his unit.

Meanwhile, the Fourth Army had been moving steadily forward. On the 22nd, Bertie's battalion was among those liberating the town of Albert, so central to the memories of all who had fought in the battles of the Somme. It was an important prize, as far as morale went, but there was little left of it on the ground. Albert was marked on the map, but had pretty much ceased to exist. Its population had long gone; there was hardly even a cellar left intact in the asymmetrical heaps of brick and rubble, twisted metal and hoops of barbed wire lining either side of what had once been the main street. The fine basilica, with its tall tower and golden Virgin holding up her Son towards heaven, was gone, like all the lesser buildings. Bertie could only tell when he had reached the town square by the wider space between ruins, and identified the larger heap to one side as all that was left of the basilica. It was a sobering moment in the advance. He had to comfort himself with the thought that at least Amiens had been saved and, apart from a dint or two, was largely intact.

Bertie had returned to the world that for him was hard reality, but for Jessie was shadow and fear. She resumed the now familiar routine of waiting from letter to letter, trying in between to keep her mind a blank as to what might be happening. Against the grinding background of anxiety, it was hardly surprising that her milk soon dried up, and young Thomas Parke had to be found a wet-nurse. Henrietta discovered, through her charitable connections, a girl, Rachel, who had recently had a baby by a soldier whose death at the Front meant she could never marry him. Jessie was glad to be able to put a little money into her pocket, and to give her the comfort of knowing she was not universally despised.

Nanny Emma accepted her with her usual calm, caring only to know that the girl was healthy and clean. Ethel was the only person who objected – she was back at Morland Place now, though whether by her own desire to return or her mother's to have her gone it was impossible to know. She was largely recovered, and only had occasional fits of weeping, usually prompted by the sight of her poor fatherless children when they were brought down to the drawing-room before bedtime. She accepted Jessie and her child, if sometimes rather aloofly, but her jealousies were reawoken by the arrival of Rachel, whose moral failings she felt she could openly object to, where she had been prevented from objecting to Jessie's.

She claimed that the presence of a girl 'like that' would pollute the nursery and endanger her own precious children, managing to imply along the way that Jessie's boy was too far gone in turpitude to suffer likewise. Henrietta was finally forced to tell her that Rachel was to stay, and that if she, Ethel, was so worried for her children she had better take them away to her mother's house. Ethel knew very well that her mother would never agree to a permanent removal. Fortunately it did not seem to occur to her that Uncle Teddy would never agree to losing them either.

So the row dissolved and Rachel stayed, and Ethel returned to the solace she had discovered during her absence from Morland Place, and which, had she known it, she shared with Violet. There was a medium in York with a growing reputation among the respectable ladies who had lost someone (which was almost everyone) and who found too little comfort in the Established Church (which was a growing number). Mrs Hardwicke, who sat as Madame Rowena, had very good results in getting messages through for those who attended, and her insistence that the proceedings were kept absolutely secret gave her clients a frisson that helped them through the dreary days of bereavement and, also, ensured that her fame spread much more quickly than it would have had she advertised. Though Violet was still at Shawes, Ethel never met her at Madame Rowena's. Violet was very careful not to attend a seance where there was any likelihood she would be recognised by anyone outside her set. She had had enough of exposure in the newspapers to last her a lifetime, and went quietly back to London every couple of weeks to see Mr Fletcher privately in a small house in Clapham where he rented rooms.

Ethel was always better-tempered after one of her trips

into York to 'see a friend' – as she described it vaguely, out of the conviction that Morland Place would not approve of dabblings in what was forbidden by the Church. Fortunately no-one was sufficiently interested in knowing the identity of the friend who had such a good effect on Ethel, though all in their own ways noticed it.

By August, Jessie was riding again, rather gingerly at first, and always carefully, for if Bertie survived she hoped they would be able to have more children together. Her reunion with Hotspur was a huge delight to them both, and he carried her with such gaiety and care that it made her almost tearful sometimes, especially when he turned his head to check that she really was there in the saddle, as though he could hardly believe it after so many long months. Together they rambled over the estate, revisiting favourite places and checking on the progress of the year as they had used to.

It was enough occupation for the first week or so. But as the exercise and fresh air strengthened her, she started to take an interest in the stable at Twelvetrees again. She did not do any of the physical work to begin with, but before long she could not resist getting more involved, strapping a horse one day and lungeing a yearling another. This, together with her continuous and growing delight in her small son, kept her from fretting herself to fiddle-strings.

And Violet was always soothing company: they were such old friends that it was entirely possible to visit her at Shawes and just sit without talking. Once in a while she took Thomas with her, as Violet seemed particularly to enjoy holding him. Her own little Octavian was two now, and far beyond that stage; but it was not only that. Jessie saw that Thomas was important to Violet in some additional way. Once, holding him, she looked up at Jessie and said, 'I told you that you would have a child, one day. And look, how perfect!' It was good to be back on the old terms with Violet, with no more shadows between them.

Uncle Teddy told her she could have one of Helle's whelps,

and she picked out a nice brindled dog-pup that she decided to call Bran. It would be some weeks yet before he could leave his mother and start his training, but it was never too soon to get him used to her, and she often slipped off to the kennel and sat in the straw by Helle, picking up the fat, woolly bundle, letting him climb on her lap and chew her fingers.

She took Uncle Teddy's kindness in letting her have one of his precious pups as a sign that he had forgiven her for conceiving Thomas outside marriage, and for marrying Bertie. In a strange way, she felt that Jack's letter from the prison camp had wrought the change. Trying to understand his thoughts, she decided that seeing the letter had made him accept at last that if Ned had been alive somewhere he would surely have found a way to write home. No letter from Ned meant no Ned. At last, after all this agonising time, he had let his son go, and accepted, as Jessie had done long since, that she was a widow, and that in marrying Bertie she had not dishonoured Ned's memory.

For some time she told herself that this idea was just her imagination, but one day Maria confided to her that Uncle Teddy had told her he was not going to pursue any more enquiries about Ned. 'He told me to get all the papers together and put them in a box, and when I'd done that, he took it away. I don't know what he did with it. I think he may have put it into one of the storage attics – I know he went up there that day, but he didn't tell me what for. And he hasn't mentioned him since.' Maria eyed her curiously. 'I suppose it must be to do with you and Bertie.'

'Why do you think so?' Jessie said, trying not to sound uncomfortable.

'The logic of the thing,' Maria said, in her brisk way. 'If he keeps maintaining Ned is alive, that makes you a bigamist.' The word shocked Jessie, and she stared, never having thought of it that way before. Maria went on, 'Either he had to give up Ned, or give up you, and I suppose, much as he loves Ned, it was easier to let him go, since he's not here and you are.'

Jessie turned her face away wryly. 'You never try to sugar the pill, do you? You just say things straight out, however painful.'

'That's what—' Maria had been about to say, *That's what Denis says*, and stopped herself in time. 'It's always better to face up to the truth,' she said instead.

Venetia never had any difficulty in filling her time, but she was glad now of extra things to keep her mind from Thomas as she waited anxiously for another letter. The flu epidemic seemed to be dying down, and she was not being called out so much on that account, but the building plans for Dean Street were a great help, and in the absence of Violet in Yorkshire, she went once or twice down to visit Oliver's 'zoo' in Sidcup. The men made it plain they enjoyed her visits, even though, as she pointed out to Oliver, she was not young or pretty.

'But they have brains, too,' he reminded her, 'and you stimulate them.'

The cinema equipment she had donated had been set up in a spare hut, and on one occasion while she was there she sat in on a showing. She had never been to the cinema, and had only seen moving pictures once before, long ago, when Queen Victoria had had one taken of her and her family walking about on the terrace. There had been great improvements in technique since then, she noted: the movements were not so jerky and the film did not flicker quite so much. The men enjoyed several comic films, but the one that interested Venetia most was a newsreel taken in France. One of the things it showed was the presentation of medals to the FANY Unit 8 by General Plumer, and there in the middle of the row was Emma, smiling, as pretty as ever despite the uniform; and soon afterwards there was another shot of the FANYs, posing by one of their ambulances, and there was Emma again with her little dog in her arms. The FANYs walked about a bit and spoke among themselves – it was strange to see the mouths moving with no sound coming out – and then Emma got up into the driving seat, still with the dog in her arms, and put her hands on the wheel as if she was going to drive off. The following caption said, 'Off to help another wounded Tommy!'

There were now many official government camera operators in France, and in letters home soldiers often spoke of being 'cinema'ed'. The rest of the newsreel showed tanks rolling through a town, troops marching up a road, and some dashing artillerymen galloping their horses with the guns bumping and leaping behind.

Oliver, almost despite himself, was becoming quite involved in the Dean Street plans, suggesting improvements here and alterations there. 'Might as well make it as good as it can be,' he said, when Venetia commented on his interest.

'It isn't that. I know you, my son, and there's something behind this. You might as well tell me.'

'Well,' Oliver said, 'I've been thinking that this war isn't going to last for ever, all appearances to the contrary, and that once I'm out of uniform I shall have to find something to do. I don't want to go into general practice. What I'd really like to do is continue with plastics, but I'm not sure the big hospitals will want to make room for a plastics unit. It's rather looked down on, you know.'

'I do,' Venetia confirmed. In the medical profession there still prevailed a tough-minded, masculine attitude that a scar or deformity was something to be put up with, unless it impaired a vital function. As it was unmanly to think about one's appearance, so a doctor who tried to improve appearances was himself somehow unmanly. She had heard the few plastics specialists who existed referred to dismissively as 'face doctors', and when essential plastics repairs, such as to cleft palates or hare lips, were performed at the big

465

hospitals, they came under the ear, nose and throat department and had to take their turn with tonsillectomies.

'Even after I find myself consulting rooms, I shall still need somewhere to operate,' Oliver continued. 'Of course there are private clinics, but one would have to take pot luck on their availability, and the facilities do vary so. What I'd really like is somewhere properly designed that I could depend on for regular lists – a place I could call home,' he added, with a smile.

'My dear, of course we could come to some arrangement at Dean Street,' Venetia said. 'I'm delighted to know that you have an ambition of that sort. I was afraid you would just drift from one thing to another. It's good to see you passionate about it.'

Oliver's face was alight. 'I know an excellent anaesthetist – David Tenby, you remember him? – who would pass gas for me. I wrote to him recently and he was very keen. Of course, to pay for all the free work I'd have to do some "beauty" work too, but I don't see why rich people shouldn't use their money to have a mole or a birthmark removed, instead of spending it on fur coats or diamond earrings. And if I'm going to get them used to having such things done in a proper, sterile environment, I'm going to have to have a clinic they feel comfortable in.'

'You shall make it as luxurious as you please,' Venetia said. 'But you'll never get the rich to have operations anywhere but in their own homes.'

'Oh, I think things will change after the war. Medicine and surgical techniques have moved on so much. Perhaps the older generation and the aristocracy will object, but the rest of the paying public will soon get used to the idea.'

'I hope you're right,' Venetia said. 'Will Kit come in with you? He has expressed an interest in plastics.'

'As soon as he's out of uniform, he'll be going home to Lutterworth to evict his stepmother and get the estate in order,' Oliver said. 'Then he'll get married and start breeding

466

a flock of little Westhovens. He has his duty to the title, you know.'

'Has he mentioned anyone?'

'A female, you mean? No, but with his looks and name, he won't have to search very hard,' said Oliver. 'The VADs are all over him.' His mind jumped back to Dean Street. 'I say, I've just thought – it will be awfully appropriate to have the John Winchmore specialise in facial reconstruction.'

Venetia smiled, catching his drift. 'Because your father's nickname was Beauty, you mean?'

'Perhaps we ought to call it the Beauty Clinic and have done with it,' Oliver said.

Venetia had a letter from Thomas at last towards the end of September, by which time her anxiety was acute. On the 30th of August an assassination attempt had been made on Lenin: he had been shot twice at point-blank range and for some time hovered between life and death. His supporters unleashed a series of bloody reprisals, with thousands of people all over Russia being arrested and summarily executed. With the Whites still advancing on two fronts, and Lenin temporarily out of the game, the various factions of the left fell to squabbling violently among themselves. In such an atmosphere, the safety of the Romanov women, and of those who were interested in them, must hang by a thread.

But Thomas wrote to say that he was well, and that the women were all still alive and well, but very depressed. He referred to them by initial – S for the Tsaritsa (from her nickname, Sunny, so as not to confuse her with Anastasia) and the girls as OTMA, which was how they had used to sign themselves when sending a joint letter or present. It was an extra precaution that proved to her he was worried about the security of writing at all.

'S health poor after they were moved to a basement for safety. A managed to escape but was recaptured. B says her mental health now quite frail. All moved to local convent,

467

safer in current political situation, and better conditions, but harder to get near them.'

B was Bauer, who, Venetia knew from previous letters, was one of the German intelligence agents watching the family on behalf of the German government.

'B says Moscow bargaining for exchange, perhaps with Liebknecht, but all must be done in greatest secrecy. Exchange best option, but B working on rescue plan in case it fails.'

It was hard not to be able to write back and ask questions, but Venetia realised it was much safer if the supposed Swiss doctor did not receive letters in code from an English aristocrat. She spoke to Browning, however, about the exchange he had mentioned, and Browning confirmed that intelligence had heard the same via intercepted telegraph messages between Riezler, Count Mirbach's successor in Moscow, and the German satellite government in occupied Kiev. 'Karl Liebknecht is a leading German revolutionary, currently in prison in Berlin. He's a lifelong friend and disciple of Lenin's, and Lenin would dearly like to have him released and sent to Russia. But Radek – the Russian equivalent of our foreign secretary – is dickering for some other Reds as well, as a more equal exchange for five women. Lenin has to tread carefully, though. Negotiating with the Germans would be unpopular, and there's hardly anyone in his own government he can trust to know about it. The women's survival depends on no-one knowing where they are. Your son is wise to be cautious.'

A few days later, Venetia was working in her laboratory when she received a visitor. The maid who came up to inform her said that a lady, heavily veiled, had called but would not give her name. Venetia's mind immediately jumped to the thought of a letter or message from Thomas. She said cautiously, 'How do you know it's a lady?'

The maid looked blank for a moment, this not being a question within her normal range of thought, but at last she said, 'The way she speaks, my lady. And her clothes. I'm sure she's quite high-up, my lady.'

'Very well, I'll see her.' Given the heavy veiling, it had better be up here, she thought. 'Show her to my private parlour. And let no-one disturb us unless I ring – no-one at all, do you understand?'

'Yes, my lady.'

The private parlour was part of a small suite of laboratory, office and sitting-room on the first floor at the back of the house, where Venetia conducted her research and had received tuberculosis sufferers via a separate staircase to the garden so that the servants need not come into contact with them. The sitting-room was small but comfortable, cosy in winter but cool, if rather dark, in the summer when there was no fire lit. When Venetia had washed her hands and taken off the protective smock she wore when working in the laboratory, she went through, just as the lady was being shown in from the corridor. She wore a fawn cloth coat and a hat with a heavy veil that entirely hid her face. But yes, Venetia saw at once from the bearing, and the quality of the cloth, that she *was* a lady – the maid's unconscious instinct had been unerring.

As soon as they were alone, she said, 'You wished to see me?'

The lady threw back her veil, and Venetia saw that it was Princess Victoria of Hesse. 'Dear Lady Overton – Venetia – forgive me for troubling you, and for this cloak-and-dagger approach, but I don't know whom to trust.'

Venetia could see that she was genuinely afraid, and from the shadows under her eyes that she had been worried for a long time. 'My dear,' she said, taking her hands, 'there's no need to apologise. Sit down, and tell me how I may help.'

Victoria was thirteen years younger than her, the daughter of Queen Victoria's second daughter Alice and Grand Duke Louis of Hesse. Princess Alice had died when Victoria was fifteen, and after that she and her siblings had spent a great deal of time in England, under the special care of Queen

Victoria, so Venetia had known her well from that time. At twenty Victoria had married a cousin on her father's side, Prince Louis of Battenberg, who by that time had become a naturalised British subject and was an officer in the Royal Navy. They had settled down in England, first at Chichester and then Walton-on-Thames, and Victoria had spent some years in Malta when her husband was stationed there. But at the outbreak of war he had been forced to resign from the navy because of his German origins, which might have caused embarrassment, and they had been living since then at Kent House on the Isle of Wight. In 1917 Louis, in common with other members of the royal family, had changed the Battenberg name to the more English-sounding Mountbatten, and at the same time the King had created him Marquess of Milford Haven.

Now the marchioness sat down in the armchair opposite Venetia, clasping her thin hands together and leaning forward with tension in every line of her body. She had inherited her mother's great beauty, which, now that she was in her fifties, stood her in good stead, but she looked tired and drawn.

'Venetia, do you know anything about Alicky and the children?'

Venetia hesitated. It was vital to keep the secret, and the more people who knew it, the greater the likelihood of spillage. But Victoria was Alexandra's sister and, more than that, as the eldest child she had become mother to all her siblings when her own mother died. She had once said to Venetia, 'My childhood ended when Mama died.' She had always been very close to Alexandra – Alicky – who had spent a lot of time in England in her childhood, and in young womanhood had often stayed at Victoria's house at Walton-on-Thames when the court was at Windsor. Venetia could imagine the desperate anxiety she must be feeling about her little sister and the children, and she had to weigh the virtues of relieving it against the dangers of widening the circle of knowledge.

Victoria's keen eyes were surveying her as she hesitated. 'I see that you do know something. I think I should show you this. It arrived two days ago.' She took out the familiar buff envelope of a telegram, which she passed to Venetia, saying abruptly, 'Read it, please.'

Venetia unfolded it reluctantly, fearing trouble. It was addressed to the Marchioness of Milford Haven and had come from Stockholm, in neutral Sweden, and was signed 'Crown Princess Sweden' – another cousin.

ERNIE NOW TELEGRAPHS THAT HE HAS HEARD FROM TWO TRUSTWORTHY SOURCES THAT ALIX AND ALL THE CHILDREN ARE ALIVE.

Ernie, of course, was the brother of Victoria and Alexandra, Grand Duke Ernst of Hesse, who, as a federal sovereign and a high-ranking army officer, had access to the most elevated sources of intelligence in Germany. Venetia looked up, and Victoria met her eyes with urgency. 'Ernie would not be careless about such a subject as this. He says "two trustworthy sources". I want to believe it – oh, so much! – but only last week the King told me that he believed Alicky and the whole family were killed – butchered – at Ekaterinburg. You may imagine what I have been going through – and now this! The hope is too painful to bear if it is to prove false. What am I to believe? Venetia, have pity on me! Tell me what you know.'

'It is utterly imperative that the secret is kept,' Venetia said slowly.

'Yes, yes,' Victoria said impatiently. 'I will not tell anyone.'

'I cannot ask for your word. I must trust to your good sense. Their safety depends on their whereabouts, even their existence, being kept the deadliest secret.'

Victoria's eyes lit. 'Then it's true! Alicky and the children are alive!'

'I have it from my son that she and the girls were moved from Ekaterinburg at the time the Emperor was executed.

I heard from him in a letter a week ago that they were alive and well, but it had been some time in transit. Your telegram is fresher news than mine.'

'Alicky and the girls? What about Alexei?'

'I have no information about him,' Venetia said sadly. 'He does not seem to be with them. It may be that he was executed at the same time as his father.' She saw the distress in Victoria's expression as she said the words. 'Nicky' was only the emperor to her, but to Victoria he was her precious sister's husband, her brother-in-law. And Alexei, her nephew . . . 'Or it may be that he died of natural causes about that time, or on the journey. He had been very ill, you know. The strain might have been too much for him, or the jolting of the train might have brought on an incident.'

Victoria digested this in silence, perhaps weighing the deaths against the hopes of life. 'Where are they?' she asked at length, abruptly.

Venetia said, 'It is better if you do not know. Not only their lives, but my son's, depend on their remaining hidden.'

Victoria did not seem to resent being kept out of the secret, as Venetia had feared she might. She said thoughtfully, 'Is that why Cousin Georgie – why the King doesn't know?'

Venetia hesitated again. 'I think it is a great deal easier for him to believe they are all dead,' she said carefully.

For the first time there was a touch of bitterness on the marchioness's face. 'Yes, otherwise he might have to decide to do something. Why didn't they get them out right at the beginning? What is going to happen to them now?'

'I can tell you in confidence that efforts are being made, on more than one front, to bring them out. I cannot tell you more.'

Victoria examined her face, looking resigned now. 'No, I suppose you can't. Poor Venetia – you must be worried about Thomas, too. Well, I will not torment you. You will let me know anything you hear that you *can* pass on?'

'Of course – at once.'

The marchioness rose. 'I will pray for Thomas when I pray for the others. I hope we shall both experience the same joy very soon.' She extended her hand, and Venetia pressed it. It was very cold. 'What a bad business this has been. Poor Nicky – I don't believe he deserved such an end. As for Alexei . . .'

'But what sort of life could he have looked forward to?' Venetia said gently.

'My uncle Leopold had the disease, and though he died young, he lived to marry and father a child,' she said. She lowered the veil over her face. 'It's the uncertainty that's the worst part – waiting and hoping and not knowing,' she said, from behind it. 'Do you believe we shall see them again?'

'Yes,' said Venetia. 'I do believe that.' But she said it more for her visitor's sake than because she felt it with great conviction. As everything in Russia disintegrated into violence and chaos, the Romanov women were increasingly isolated. They were valuable to Lenin as bargaining counters with Germany, but it occurred to her, with a cold touch of dread, that if Germany were to lose the war – *when* Germany lost the war – that value would be lost too.

CHAPTER TWENTY-ONE

At the end of September the Allied big push began. For the first time in the war attacks went in almost simultaneously all along the line. On the 26th, the Americans and the French struck the first blow between Rheims and the river Meuse; on the 27th the Third Army attacked at Cambrai; on the 28th the Second Army attached at Ypres, aided by the Belgians; and on the 29th the Fourth Army went in at St Quentin, together with the French First Army, in an attempt to take the old Hindenburg Line. The Germans fought fiercely, but as they were in action all the way from the Meuse to the sea, they had no opportunity to concentrate their forces. The Allies' advantage in numbers was not very great, but their organisation was by now much better, and German morale was flagging. Everywhere the enemy was forced back. Slowly and painfully at first, but with increasing speed and confidence, the Allied armies advanced.

Now the men were fighting a kind of war they had never fought before: out in the open, without the comfort and routine of the trench, seeking cover from the countryside itself. They were fighting over territory they had never seen before, often with nothing to aid them but very inadequate maps, advancing across canals and rivers, through farms and villages and small towns that had hitherto been German territory. It was still-populated country, and one of the difficulties was to attack the Germans without harming civilians. The weather was turning autumnal, and morning fogs, often mixed with smoke, had them stumbling forward in a grey and featureless world. Large repositionings and the moving up of artillery and tanks had to be done under cover of darkness, made all the more difficult by the unknown nature of the terrain.

But forward they went, never back, fighting, moving up, regrouping, holding on, advancing again; it was a tribute to the refinement of the organisation behind the lines that the fighting men, who were never to be found in the same place for more than a day or two at a time, were kept supplied with food, arms, ammunition, and even their letters and parcels from home.

At home, in contrast to the gloom during the spring, the mood was buoyant and hopeful. With the enemy falling back and the Americans fully engaged in the war, it seemed it must be only a matter of time before victory would be won and the war ended. That wonderful day, which four months ago had seemed hopelessly far off, was now almost within reach. With the easing of one tension, another resurfaced, and that autumn was marred by strikes and industrial unrest. The newspapers were full of violent invective against the unpatriotic strikers. Teddy had to make frequent and prolonged trips to Manchester to sort matters out and keep production going.

Violet had gone back to London, taking the children with her, leaving Jessie with time on her hands and attention to spare, and at once she began to notice a difference in Polly. She was the only one at Morland Place who did so. Teddy was often in Manchester; Helen was away a great deal, delivering aeroplanes, and visiting her mother, who was not adapting well to widowhood. Ethel was also very little at home, out seeing her friends every day, and often dining from home; Alice never noticed anything very much, and Maria and Henrietta were fully occupied with their own concerns.

Besides, Polly spent much of her time on horseback, taking her out of everyone's orbit. Jessie rode up to Twelvetrees every day, and while the weather was fine, she stayed out as long as it was light, riding about the estate and over the moors. On her outings she saw Polly at a distance from time to time, and wondered where she was going and what she was doing.

She started wondering quite idly, but the mystery seemed to deepen. She didn't meet her at the farms, and Polly didn't come to Twelvetrees, though she used to be a frequent visitor. Furthermore, through casual enquiry she discovered that Polly was not going to her Red Cross meetings. Jessie drove herself into York one day and called at Makepeace's for some strong thread, and Mrs Lowe, the manager, politely enquired after Miss Morland's health as they hadn't had the pleasure of seeing her for some weeks. Jessie was surprised, for the one thing Polly had applied herself to in her otherwise pleasure-bent life was learning the business that would one day be hers.

With her curiosity aroused, Jessie began to notice the difference in Polly at home. She was quiet, did not join in conversations, showed no interest in her food, seemed a little thinner in the face, less animated. Jessie studied her covertly, and the only reason she did not put the problem to her mother was that Polly seemed more pensive than unhappy. Jessie would have put it down to being in love, had Polly ever taken her loves that way. But she had always worn them lightly, even frivolously, playing off one suitor against another, enjoying being the centre of attention.

Of her recent interests, faithful Lennie was at the Front, having recovered from his wound in time to be in the first wave at Cambrai, and her latest 'crush', Captain Holford, was likewise engaged in the fighting, near Armentières. Jessie believed Polly wrote to both of them, but she had never been 'moony' about either. Jessie didn't think it could be one of them.

Yet it did look like love. One evening, as she sat sewing (it was amazing how much less she hated the task, now she was making things for Thomas), she watched Polly under her eyelashes. She was supposed to be reading a book at the far end of the drawing-room, but Jessie noticed that she never turned a page. She was in another world altogether, and if her thoughts were not unhappy, they were not completely happy, either. After a bit Polly put down her book, went to the piano and began playing quietly. That in itself was surprising: Polly played quite well, but she was lazy about practising, and always had to be begged and cajoled to perform, unless there were visitors she wanted to impress. What was even more surprising was *what* she was playing: not one of her well-known 'pieces', which she could do without thinking and largely without music, but a Beethoven sonata, difficult and outside her normal repertoire. And she was actually *working* at it, going back over the notes when she stumbled, repeating difficult fingerings until she got them right.

She was playing so quietly no-one else had noticed what she was doing. Jessie returned her gaze to her baby-shirt. Polly working at playing the piano? It certainly looked like love; and for once in her life Polly was not sure of a return. But who could it be? Jessie tried to think who was home on leave – though any of the local boys would surely have succumbed to Polly without a struggle. One of the officers at the camp, perhaps? The only clue was that the beloved object must like music, and Beethoven in particular. Nothing else, she thought, would have got Polly to practise a difficult piece like that.

In the middle of October, Bertie's battalion came out of the line to rest, and Jessie had a proper letter from him, solid food after the scribbled scraps and field postcards that kept her going in between whiles.

As we advance we have the satisfaction of liberating whole communities who have been virtual prisoners since the summer of 1914. I must say it is a relief to find the villages hardly at all damaged. The enemy have left behind a heavy crop of German street names and notices, the latter full of Achtungs and Verbotens, which give you a flavour of their particular kind of occupation. They were not comfortable lodgers! But they seem to have treated the natives fairly and mostly paid for what they took. Said natives are delighted to see us all the same, and cheer and wave and shout, 'Victoire' and 'Libération'. I dare say they would bring out wine and spirits to toast us, if there were any left. Instead, <u>we</u> have to give <u>them</u> our rations, and the passion they feel for a tin of British Army ration bully tells you how short commons have been on that side of the line. The prisoners we are taking are all extremely fed up, sick of the war, and want nothing but to go home. I hope, though, that you people at home are not wildly optimistic about a quick end. There is still a lot of hard fighting in the Germans, and there is a long way to go before they are back within their own borders. I believe it is only by actually occupying German soil that we shall be able to bring them to accept unconditional terms, without which we can't have a lasting peace. So don't expect an end to it all this year, my dearest love. Most of us believe it will be next summer at the soonest.

The best part of another year, she thought, before there would be an end to the agony of waiting. 'Hard fighting' – the words had sprung from the page at her. But there was nothing she could do about any of it except keep busy, and hope.

At least the October weather was fine, cold in the mornings but warm enough in the middle of the day to be pleasant. She had been out for a morning gallop on Marston Moor one day, and it was so agreeable she was riding back the long way round Healaugh. She was surprised to see Polly's mare, Vesper, at a distance, standing in a field, her reins hitched over a dead branch of a tree growing up in the hedge (they were shockingly neglected, she noted with her countrywoman's eye). The mare looked as though she had been there for some time, for she was standing quietly, munching peacefully at the grass growing near her feet.

Jessie altered her direction to go over and find out what Polly was doing – she couldn't see her, but reason said she must be nearby. Jessie had been riding across the fields but now went down onto the track that passed that particular hedge. It bent sharply and went down a dip, and for a time she was out of sight of the place and the horse. When she came back up from the dip, Vesper was gone. She pulled Hotspur up, and stood in the stirrups to survey the fields. She could not see Vesper or Polly anywhere, but after a few minutes, the golden mare and her slender rider appeared from behind a stand of trees, cantering up towards Long Marston – too far off to be hailed.

Jessie sent Hotspur on again. She might as well stay on the track now, she decided, and take the left turn towards Hutton Grange. Her mother would like it if she called in on Mrs Hutton, whose son had fallen that spring at Cambrai. She still wondered idly what it was Polly had been doing that necessitated dismounting, but as she trotted Hotspur down the track she couldn't see anything out of the ordinary. There wasn't a cottage where she might have called, or anyone she might have stopped to talk to. In fact, the only person in sight was a man slowly and methodically cutting the hedge, whom she identified after a glance as the German prisoner of war that the Bellerbys at White House had taken on.

He had been offered to the Bankses at Woodhouse, but old Ezra had practically foamed at the mouth at the very thought. Mrs Bellerby had told Jessie, with an air of astonishment, that the chap was 'very nice for a German', always polite, kept his room clean, and helped about the yard, pumping water and feeding the chickens and so on when he had done his day's work. She claimed that it 'gave her the creeps' to have him around, but it was said with a lack of conviction. It was a fact that the prisoner had been promoted from sleeping in the barn to sleeping in the little room between the kitchen and the churn-room, which had been empty since the cowman had been called up eighteen months ago. Bare as a monk's cell, it was, but a proper room, with a proper iron bedstead and under the farmhouse roof.

Jessie had never seen the prisoner before, but she knew Mrs Bellerby was using him for hedging and ditching, so it couldn't be anyone else. She slowed Hotspur to a walk so that she could get a look at him, and he stopped his work and flattened himself courteously in the hedge as she passed. She got a brief impression of sun-bleached hair and brown arms, but he bowed his head, either from humility or in greeting, so she did not really see his face.

Jessie stopped to talk to Mrs Hutton, and arrived home to find Polly already there, rubbing down Vesper in the stable. Jessie led Hotspur into the next stall, and the black and the chestnut touched noses and snorted greetings, while Kai appeared from nowhere and presented Jessie with a half-chewed old body-brush by way of a welcome present.

'I saw you in the fields,' Jessie said, 'but by the time I got to where you were, you'd gone.'

'Did you?' Polly said indifferently, disappearing behind Vesper's bulk to brush her nearside flank.

'Well, to be exact, I saw Vesper,' Jessie said. 'What did you dismount for?'

'Dropped my whip,' Polly said.

'Oh. It looked as if Vesper had been standing for some time.'

'Well, I couldn't find it at first,' Polly said. She straightened up and regarded Jessie across Vesper's back – a strangely hard sort of look. But she said, 'You must be tired. Why don't you go on in? I'll rub him down for you. I've just about finished Vesper.'

'I'm not an invalid any more,' Jessie said. 'I can strap my own horse.'

'Oh, go on,' Polly urged. 'If you hurry, you might catch Nanny Emma giving Thomas his bath. I don't mind doing him.'

Polly had pulled just the right string. It was hours since Jessie had last seen her son. 'Well, if you're sure – thank you, Polly dear.'

Polly had been in love many times before. In fact, from the time she was eleven and conceived an entirely inappropriate passion for a fat, red-faced game-keeper she had seen at the market in York one day, there had never been a time, that she could remember, when there hadn't been some particular male object in her mind. They never lasted long, those early crushes, no more than a week or so, and by the time she was sixteen and being noticed by boys of her own age and class, she recognised them for what they were: mere puppy gambollings, the way the heart practised for the real thing.

In the last year or two her interests had become more realistic. Lennie had been, on and off, a serious prospect, David Holford even more so. But now she knew that these latter preferences had been as unimportant as the early ones, mere childish fancies. Now she knew what real love was, and it was so different she wondered anyone could ever mistake the one for the other.

He was so infinitely more worth loving. She saw now the shallowness of mere good looks and charm. Of course he had those – in abundance – but he also had a mind: real learning, an education in all important subjects, a knowledge and appreciation of the arts – music, painting, architecture, literature. Added to that, his long years of imprisonment had given him a thoughtfulness that she found utterly addictive. He had awoken in her a desire to think about things properly, to learn, question, consider and understand.

She thought about him *all the time*. His image was imprinted on her mind: his face, the strong lines of his body, his voice, the way his lips moved when he spoke, his graceful, powerful movements. Away from him, she yearned only to get back to him; with him, she experienced a joy so intense and yet so quiet and satisfying it was like food or sleep to her – a necessity of life.

Nothing else interested her. When she couldn't be with him, she couldn't bear to be with other people. She avoided the family, didn't go to see friends, cut her hospital visits, Red Cross meetings and Makepeace's. The only thing that stopped her from spending every moment of every day near him was the need for secrecy. For she was not too far gone to know it would strike horror into the minds of her family, if her feelings were discovered. It was anguish to think that what she so valued was thoughtlessly hated by all around her, but so it was. And her father, despite his tolerant phrases about them being nice boys who hadn't wanted to go to war, was no different. He had had doubts about Holford, the son of a millionaire banker, being good enough for her: what would he think about a German prisoner, a hated Hun? His fury made her shudder to imagine; that he would be disgusted with her made her both miserable and angry.

So she was circumspect. She rationed her time with him, and spent the rest of her days riding alone, visiting the places where she had seen him, remembering every chance and engineered encounter. Every hedge he had laid was precious to her. The ditches he had trimmed were beautiful. She rode past the back of White House Farm just so that she could look at the small high window in the blank wall that was *his* window.

She loved him with the hopeless passion of a Juliet, even while her vigorous, healthy young spirit could not quite believe that it *was* hopeless. If only they knew him they would see at once how superior he was. None of the locals whom her father might one day consider as a match for her came close to him. She imagined scenarios in which her father might come to appreciate him, Daddy might meet him and get into conversation with him, discovering his education might offer him work at the house – cataloguing books or restoring paintings. She was sure he could do those things as perfectly as laying hedges. Or he might take over Maria's secretarial work. Eventually Daddy would find him indispensable and begin to think of him as a son. Or he might save Daddy's life . . . A bolting horse . . . A maddened bull . . . A runaway motor-car . . .

She drifted through the days in a dream of love.

The influenza that had struck in June and July came back in October. The mysterious and lethal plague that was generally called 'Spanish flu' or 'Spanish Lady' had seemed to have done its work and passed on; but in the second week of October there were reports from a training camp in Northumberland that a new batch of recruits from the West Country had brought it with them, or at least had gone down with it as soon as they arrived. It was in all the York newspapers: the previous outbreak had hit the north-east badly, and it was alarming that it had struck there again. By the passing of another week, there were several hundred cases in the camp, and a score of the lads had died.

It was rife on the Western Front, too, and once again London was badly hit. The disease seemed to have taken on a new and more severe form, and the death rate was much higher than in the summer. Previously healthy people were struck so suddenly they fell down in the street and were dead within hours. Whole streets were emptied; sometimes everyone in a single house would die, leaving no-one to alert the authorities. Undertakers ran out of coffins, and funerals were continuous, day and night, to fit them all in. In just two weeks in London there were eighteen thousand deaths, and there seemed no logic to it: the young and strong fell as easily as the old and frail; the rich of Chelsea suffered as much as the poor of Stepney.

Once again theatres, cinemas and churches were deserted, and those who had to use public transport covered their noses and mouths and eyed fellow travellers with suspicion. Newspapers were full of advertisements for patent cures and prophylactics; chemists' shops stayed open all night for sales of camphor and wintergreen, gauze masks, throat lozenges and carbolic sprays. Doctors hurried from house to house, while their assistants made up endless batches of whatever nostrum they were famed for, knowing it did no good. Nothing did any good, except to go to bed and stay there until the disease passed, one way or the other.

On the 20th of October it reached Morland land. The commanding officer of the camp up by the Monument sent a note to say that five newly arrived recruits, eighteen and nineteen years old, had been seized suddenly with the influenza, adding courteously that he thought it wise there should be as little contact between the camp and the house as possible until the disease had passed.

Henrietta agreed. In a few more days, a third of the battalion was down with it, and there had been four deaths. She cancelled the regular tea-party and the officers' dinner, and in Teddy's absence took the decision to declare the camp out of bounds. But already the flu was all around the neighbourhood, and she was being called to visit Morland pensioners and estate workers who had succumbed. It was unreasonable to suppose the house would be immune, take what precautions they might. She told the servants who came in daily that they must either stay for the time being, or keep away, promising to pay their wages either way. And she recommended plenty of fresh air for everyone who could get out of doors, especially the children. Father Palgrave was too busy, in any case, ministering to the estate and village sick to give lessons. The older children were let out to enjoy a glorious holiday, free of supervision, romping about the fields all day, taking a packet of food with them and not coming home until tea-time.

Teddy, telephoning from Manchester, decreed that Polly must stay out too, and not be allowed to go sick-visiting, or to York or the camp. Henrietta told him Polly seemed to be doing that already, adding that she had Alice and Maria to help her with the visiting and did not need Polly anyway. She had forbidden Jessie to expose herself, either, because she was still not strong.

But one of the maids, who had been walking out with a soldier from the camp, went down with the fever; and then another fell sick. Henrietta turned the guest wing into an isolation ward, and left her estate sick-visiting to concentrate on her own household. There was only so much one person could do, after all. She prayed briefly in the chapel every morning, and mentioned, humbly, to God that if He was planning to take someone from the house, perhaps He might spare those she loved and take her, because she was old and tired and surely had fulfilled her life's purpose. Of course, she added, it must be as He willed. And in the silence that followed her thoughts, she received no indication that God was considering her request.

Polly sat on the top of a grassy bank above a lane on the edge of the moor, her knees drawn up, her arms wrapped around them. Her hat was off, and the autumn sunshine, though thin, was warm on the crown of her head. The sloping field, which faced sunwards, was rabbity, and Kai had left her to hunt promising smells. Vesper, hitched to a gate-post further down the lane, was dozing, resting her chin on the top bar. She had grown accustomed to these prolonged stops. Besides, the only browse within reach

485

was bracken, which she did not eat, so there was nothing else for her to do.

The bank was held out of the lane by a stone retaining wall, which Kuppel was engaged in mending. His fingers were white with stone-dust, and there was a red tear on the back of one hand from a jagged piece of flint. He had sucked it philosophically when he had done it, and it was not bleeding, but Polly felt an anguish about it that she knew was foolish and disproportionate, but she could not help it. He must not be hurt! She adored every part of him, from the crown of his barley-fair head to the tip of the heavy boots, lane-dusty, which covered what she was sure were aristocratic feet that would dance with spirit and elegance.

They had been talking ever since she arrived, and a natural pause had ensued. She was perfectly happy just to sit and watch him work, marvelling at how he could turn his hand to anything, for he was making a neat and thorough job of the wall, and she knew walling was skilled work. But being worshipped silently did not suit him for long. Kuppel liked to talk; and Polly was happy to oblige. He had a way of drawing her out, which was so different from the boys who had hitherto adored her. They were clumsy and tongue-tied, had no topic except where they had seen her last and where they hoped to see her next. But even Holford, who was far more sophisticated, was shallow in comparison. She had regarded him as magnificently grown-up compared with local boys, because he knew about London and shows and rag-time, but Erich Kuppel had shown her what real learning was.

They talked together about everything: music, books, horses, the countryside, people and customs, politics, the war. Polly had discovered through him the depth of her ignorance, but he never made her feel it was a fault in her. Rather, he made it seem like a wonderful gift that she had a fresh, uncluttered mind into which the treasures of the world might be poured. When she talked he listened seriously to what she said, and never belittled her opinions, so that, in order to merit the courtesy, she began to think more deeply before she gave them, and found herself discovering ideas she hadn't known she had.

But she was a girl in love, and she liked best to have him talk about himself. She was interested in everything about him, from his views on politics and religion, to his favourite colour (blue) and whether he liked potatoes better boiled or roasted (roasted, but at home they also had them a different way, sliced and baked in milk with onions and herbs, with a little nutmeg grated over the top. Polly determined to find some way to suggest, without revealing the source of the recipe, that Mrs Stark do them like that).

He told her about his home, and the countryside around it, and about hunting: she was intrigued that they had fox-hunting there as well, though they also hunted deer and boar. He described his favourite rides, and remembered his horses for her, from his first pony to his last hunter. He had learned to ride on a fat pony named Klaus, who had always been referred to as Kloß. Kuppel was hard put to it to explain why the name was appropriate, and after some description on both parts, they decided that it translated as dumpling. He had never eaten a dumpling in England so the word was not known to him. Polly thought that sad, and described the delectable dumplings that floated like fluffy clouds on Mrs Stark's stews; and, by contrast, told how Lennie had told her they called army dumplings 'cobble-stones'. The conversation drifted on to Yorkshire pudding, which he had tasted and thought a great invention, and with a spare part of her brain Polly marvelled at how they could talk about food, a subject she would never have broached with any of her admirers as being too worldly and base. But it didn't matter what she talked about with Erich Kuppel. It was all interesting, and she was not the least afraid he would censure her for anything she said.

From there they somehow got onto the topic of trees

– she could never remember afterwards the precise order of links in the delicate chains of conversation they constructed between them – and he admired the deciduous woodland that abounded in Yorkshire, compared with the largely coniferous forest at home. 'They are magnificent in their way,' he said, of his own. 'Dark and – *bedrohen*?'

'Brooding,' she suggested, because it was the word often used. He accepted it.

'But beautiful, too, especially in winter, when it snows. And one always loves what is familiar, is it not so? But your woods are better for riding through.'

'But you do ride at home, through the woods?'

'Yes, of course,' he said, 'but it must be a different experience here, with the variety, and the openness. One day I would so like to ride in an English point-to-point. That must be the best of riding, better even than hunting when the fox takes his own line, not one chosen to be interesting for the riders.'

'After the war,' she said thoughtlessly, 'you must try it.'

She saw the shadow come instantly to his eyes. 'When the war ends I shall be sent home,' he said, with an air of finality.

'You must long to see your family again,' she said falteringly. 'But afterwards – later on – you'll come back?'

'They will not let us come back. You don't understand, I think, how much we are hated,' he said. 'You, with your generous heart, see only another human being, but that is not how the rest of your country – perhaps the rest of the world – sees us. It will be many, many years before we are not hated any more. Perhaps never,' he added quietly.

She could not bear the thought of him being hated. He was so good, so wonderful, talented, intelligent, kind. When she was with him and talking to him, she shut out from the front of her mind the fact that he was a prisoner – though it was always there, embedded in the back of her mind like a thorn.

And as if he had heard her thought, he said, 'It is foolish, but I forget sometimes I am a prisoner. It feels so natural to be here, working in the sunshine, talking to you. Talking to you is so easy, so much like freedom. But I should not forget.'

You should! Polly cried in her heart. Aloud, she said, 'That's not who you are.'

He put down the stone he was holding and straightened to look at her, and he looked a long time, as though debating what he might say to her. She hated it that she had made him sad, and wished the last few exchanges unsaid; but a new maturity in her told her that unsaying them would not change the facts, and the sadness of that was bitter.

At last he squinted up at the sky, and said, 'I have no watch, but I think it must be time you should go home. They will be expecting you.'

Words deserted her, and obediently to his, she half stood and scrambled down the bank. The grass was slippery-dry and she slid the last foot. He put out his hands automatically and caught hers, and the slide turned into a jump as she sprang down from the wall into the lane. She landed lightly in a spurt of dust, and looked up at him, and the world seemed to stop. His hard, dry hands were holding hers; he was so close she could feel the warmth of his body, smell the good sharpness of his clean sweat over the fresh-bread smell of his skin. The neck of his shirt was undone, and the skin in the hollow of his throat looked so tender it broke her heart. She could see the delicate points of glitter on his face that were the hairs of his beard growing since the morning's shave; the smooth, gold-brown of his skin above the beard-line was as delicious as butterscotch. The silvery front hair above his brow stood up in spikes where he had pushed his hand through it when wiping the sweat away. His eyes were blue, so blue, like skies, like cornflowers. He was so familiar to her in that moment, as the universe held its breath and the world hung motionless upon events, that it was in a strange way like looking at herself, as though there were no difference between them. She felt her hands in his, almost believed she could feel his heart beating through them. In that instant he was not outside her, not separate from her – he *was* her.

'I love you,' she said. She had not known she was going to say it until she heard the words on the air, but they seemed utterly profound, as though conveying a truth beyond any measure of doubt.

He said, 'No,' but that was not what was in his face. In the terrible, wonderful silence she yearned towards him and knew he would kiss her. She knew the moment had come, the imagined one, that would change her whole life, pivoting it on the axis of their joined lips to take an entirely new and breathtaking direction.

There was no kiss. He said, 'You must not.'

'But I do! I do love you. You *know* it's true. And you love me, too.' He didn't answer. 'You do. Say it. Oh, say you love me!' She leaned towards him urgently.

'Yes,' he said, in a sort of sigh, as though it hurt him to admit, 'I love you. How could I not? You are so lovely, so perfect, so – everything a man could want. I love you with all my heart.' She lifted her face, trembling like a rain-drummed leaf, but his hands hardened on hers, holding her back. 'It cannot be. You must see that.'

'No,' she protested, 'I don't see it.' But the tears in her eyes belied her words.

'I must not love you. Above all, you must not love me,' he said. 'You must never speak of this. They would come for me, and kill me, if they thought I had so much as breathed on you. You forget how much I am hated.'

'No-one hates you!' she cried in anguish.

'All hate me but you. I am the enemy,' he said, and a hardness came into his voice. 'I am "bloody Hun". I am "*sale Boche*". I am abhuman – a foul beast who kills and destroys and rapes and tortures.'

She was crying now. 'You've never done any of those things.'

'It doesn't matter, *herzliebste*. It is what I represent. To everyone who has lost a son, or a brother, or a father – to them, I am the man who killed what they loved. You know that this is true. Come, Miss Morland, use the brain inside that so beautiful head. It would break your father's heart if you were to care for me. What do you think he would say if he could see you now?' He saw her flinch as she imagined it. She almost paled. 'What would he do?' He pressed the lesson home. 'Would he strike me down?'

She shook her head, but it was not in denial. 'I love you,' she said. The tears ran over her cheeks. 'You are all I care about in the world. I don't care that you are a prisoner. I don't care what anyone says.'

'Then I must care for you,' he said gently. 'You should go now, Miss Morland—'

'Polly!' she begged.

'You must go now, Polly, and we must not meet again. It is not wise. These times we have had together I shall never, never forget. But you must not come to me again.'

If he had not said it in those particular words – if he had said, *You must not visit me again*, she might have been able to bear it. But when he said, *You must not come to me*, she saw it for what it was, this coming to him: the meeting of their two minds, their two souls, which she could not give up, because it was more important than life.

She straightened, and he saw her grow older under his very eyes. 'Don't say that,' she said. 'I must see you. I'll be careful. Don't send me away.'

He looked stricken. 'Send you away? How can I do that? Oh, my dear, *nothing* is in my power. There is nothing I can do about *anything*.'

She saw his lips were trembling, realised that his pain was as great as hers, and that the danger he was in outweighed anything she might suffer. She had to be sensible, for him.

491

She had to be strong, because his strength was wrapped round in barbed wire that would tear him whichever way he moved.

'I'll be careful,' she said again. He dropped her hands, defeated. She loved him more than ever, though she would not have thought that possible. Love surged up in her like the force of life. 'I won't let anyone see us. I have to see you, talk to you, while I can.'

He bowed his head, yielding, though his face was troubled. He reached her hat for her, and she put it on. She looked up at him from under it, and he thought his heart would rip in two. 'I love you,' she said. 'Say you love me, and then I'll go.'

'I love you,' he said.

'Polly,' she prompted.

'I love you, Polly.' At last he smiled. 'Such an absurd small name for such a golden creature! Though I never see you again, I swear I will love you always.'

He walked back with her to Vesper, and threw her up into the saddle. Kai had long gone home. She gathered the reins and looked down at him, and he stared at her as though he was memorising her face, as though he was to die tomorrow and they would never see each other again. Then he stepped aside to clear the lane for her. Vesper leaped into movement, fresh after her long stand, and Polly had no opportunity to look back at the tall figure in the lane before the bend of the track took her out of sight.

She arrived home to find a crisis. Four more servants had fallen ill with the flu since breakfast, making eight altogether, and her stepmother Alice, coming in to luncheon, had suddenly staggered, reached out a hand to the door-frame to steady herself, and collapsed silently to the floor. She was now in bed in her own room, being tended by Jessie – there was too much to do for her to be excused any more. Luncheon was delayed, which was just as well, as Maria had not returned from her morning sick-visiting; and when she did arrive, it was clear that she was getting the fever too. She begged Polly to take over her secretarial duties, and dragged herself to the steward's room for long enough to instruct her in the most important matters pending, then had to be almost carried up to her bed.

Polly was alone in the steward's room trying to make sense of the work when Father Palgrave got back from visiting the army camp, where the chaplain had gone down with the flu, leaving no-one to give last rites to two soldiers who were dying. Seeing Polly in charge, he instantly leaped to the right conclusion. 'Maria's sick!' he cried.

'After lunch,' Polly said. 'She'd just come in when she complained of a headache and pains in her legs—'

'Oh, God!' he cried. Polly, freshly sensitive to such things, looked at his stricken face and thought, *Why, he loves her,* and immediately thought what a good idea that was, and how well they would suit. 'I should never have gone to the camp,' he said wildly.

'I don't see how that made any difference. You wouldn't have been with her anyway, and you couldn't have stopped her catching it.'

'I may have brought back the sickness,' he said.

'She may have, too. She's been sick-visiting,' Polly said. 'Why don't you go up and see her?'

He was gone almost before she finished the sentence.

Dr Hasty came, because the Morlands were such good customers of his, not because there was anything he could do. Polly telephoned her father in Leeds, where he was at the other department store, to tell him about Alice.

'I'll come home tomorrow. You stay out of the house,' he instructed her. 'Stay in the fresh air.'

'There are too many people sick, now, Daddy,' she said. 'I have to help.' It was something she could not have said even yesterday. Today had changed things. Today she understood responsibilities.

'No. Keep away from anyone sick,' he said. 'Tell your aunt to hire trained nurses if she has to, but you stay away from it.'

She didn't, of course. Trained nurses were not to be had in the middle of a war and an influenza epidemic. Aunt Hen could not do everything, even with the help of Jessie and Ethel – Helen was away. The fact that even Ethel was pulling her weight proved how serious the situation was, but then in the afternoon a message came from Cornleigh Villa that both her parents were sick, and her eighteen-year-old sister Eileen was coping alone, so Ethel had to leave them at Morland Place and hurry to help her.

Teddy got home the next morning, and by then even he could see that there was no alternative to Polly's helping, with half the household sick. It was going through the servants' hall with impartial thoroughness: ten of them were down with it now, and had to be nursed by those left standing. But all other concerns fled from his mind when he discovered how sick Alice was.

His questioning produced the information that she had not felt well the previous morning, but had gone out anyway to do her duty, not wishing to 'make a fuss'. It was like her, he thought, torn between love and wrath. He hung tenderly over her bed, gently bathing her hot face with cool water, while her elderly maid, Sweetlove, hovered in the background, trying not to weep. She knew how lethal this influenza was, and if her mistress died, how would she get another position, at her age?

Alice looked feebly at Teddy, and her hand crept across the counterpane until he noticed the movement and took hold of it. Its grasp was frighteningly weak. 'I'm glad you're back,' she said. 'I was afraid I wouldn't see you again.'

'Bosh and nonsense,' he said. 'You'll shake this off in no time. You've always been healthy – never had a day's illness in your life.'

'That's right,' she said, and managed a smile before her

eyes drooped closed. Teddy sat with her, wishing there were anything he could do other than bathe her face. Hasty had left her medicine, but he could not see that it made any difference.

The fever mounted and she moved restlessly, her eyes rolling back and forth behind half-open lids. She frowned and muttered a little. Leaning close, he made out the words, 'Don't go. Not that ship.'

Henrietta came in, and said, 'How is she?'

Teddy looked up, and his expression told her what he could not find the words for. She hesitated to burden him further, but there was no hiding-place in this world of war and sickness. 'I'll sit with her for a while if you like,' she said.

'I don't want to leave her,' Teddy said.

Henrietta felt she was stabbing him in the heart with the words, as she said, 'It's got into the nursery. James is sick.'

Father Palgrave had never seen Maria's room before and took in nothing now but that it was small and modest. It was one of the old 'bachelor rooms', he knew, where her late husband Frank had slept when he was at home. He didn't want to think about Frank. He hurried to her bedside, and Maria looked at him with such relief that Tomlinson, who was sitting with her, hastily removed herself and went to the other side of the room to fiddle with bowls and bottles.

'I hoped you'd come,' Maria croaked.

'As soon as I heard.'

'I'm so sorry.'

'Sorry for what?'

'It's too stupid to be ill,' she said. 'You mustn't mind me. I know you're busy.'

'Nothing is more important to me than you,' he said, taking her hand and pressing it, trying to infuse some of his own vigour into her. 'I wish I could be ill instead of you.'

'No, you've had enough,' she said feebly. 'You mustn't get sick.' She closed her eyes a moment.

'What is it?'

'Hurts,' she said.

He lifted her hand to his lips, clasped it in both his, laid his mouth close to her ear to say, 'Maria, you mustn't leave me. I can't – I can't manage without you.'

Her eyes opened a little, shiny with fever like those of a stuffed animal. 'I'm sorry,' she whispered.

'We shouldn't have waited to get married. As soon as you're well, we'll do it. I don't care about anything else.' He knew he was babbling, but he felt out of control. 'Promise me you'll get better.'

'I'll try.' She moaned again, softly, then said, in a confused, clotted voice, 'Don't tell Mama. She worries.'

She seemed to be unconscious now. Tomlinson came back and he looked at her wildly. 'Is there *nothing* we can do?'

'Only pray,' Tomlinson said. It didn't seem odd that *she* should be saying that to *him*.

In the evening Helen telephoned to say that she had gone from her latest job to London because she had had a telegram to say Molly was ill with the flu, and her mother was not able to nurse her by herself. Sawry brought Jessie to the telephone as Henrietta was up in the guest quarters with the sick maids, so it was Jessie who told her that Alice had died that afternoon, burned up by the fever in a matter of hours.

'Oh, God, I'm so sorry,' Helen exclaimed. 'How is Uncle Teddy taking it?'

'I don't think he really grasps it yet,' Jessie said. 'And there's more: Maria's ill, and little James and Roberta have both come down with it.'

'It's reached the nursery?'

'Basil and Barbara are both perfectly all right,' Jessie said, but her voice was hollow with the 'so far' she could not say aloud. She was riven with anxiety for Thomas. If she lost him – oh, God, if she lost him . . . 'The other children seem to be all right, and we've moved the sick ones into the schoolroom to keep them apart.'

Now Helen was torn. 'I should come,' she said. 'I ought to help you with the nursing. Perhaps I should take my children away – you must have more than enough to do. If I came down and took them to Mother's – but I can't leave her alone with Molly. She goes completely to pieces, and the servants are too old. Oh God, what should I do? Should I send someone for them?'

'I don't see it will help to take them to your mother's house,' Jessie said, 'when there's sickness there, too. We all have to take our chances, it seems to me. There's no logic in why one person gets it and not another. I keep watching my mother, but she seems all right, and she's been with more sick people than anyone. Your sister needs you. The nursery maids can take care of your children until you can come back.'

'You'll watch them?' Helen said, in agony. 'If anything happened to them . . .'

'Of course I will,' Jessie said.

'I'm glad you were a nurse.'

'It doesn't seem to help,' Jessie said wearily.

At the end of a week, Henrietta insisted that Polly go out and get some fresh air. 'You're looking too pale and peaked,' she said. 'You've been a wonderful help, but it won't do anyone any good if you get ill.'

'I can't leave you to do it all,' Polly said. She was more shocked than she would have imagined by her stepmother's death; and desperately sorry for her father, who was taking it hard. One of the maids, Ellen, had also died; the others were recovering. Maria had hovered between life and death for some days, but she seemed now to be over the worst of it; and in the schoolroom, James and Roberta were out of danger, according to Dr Hasty, but languishing and weak with the typical enervation that followed influenza.

497

'There isn't so much to do now,' Henrietta said, though that was untrue: convalescents required more actual nursing than the critically ill, for whom nothing could be done. 'And I'm not alone. Go and have a good long ride. It will refresh you, and you'll be more help to me than if you get pulled down.'

So Polly went, feeling like a bird let out of its cage. Vesper had hardly been out in a week, and was very fresh, reverting to her old bad habits of bucking and shying so that for the first fifteen minutes it was all Polly could do to stay on and keep her in hand. The weather had changed: the golden October had gone, and it was cold and blustery with gusts of rain. The leaves, which had hung on past their time, had been stripped from the trees in a few good nights of wind and rain, and winter was obviously round the corner. What work would they give him over winter? she wondered. There was ploughing. Could he drive a tractor? Harrowing. There was stock work. He would be good with sheep, she thought, gentle and patient. She hoped that, whatever work he had, it would be solitary. If she had to see him surrounded by other people, she wouldn't be able to talk to him. After a week of fasting, she was hungry for him – for talk, yes, but to feast her eyes on him more than anything. *I have to see him*, she thought. *I have to be near him.*

She rode about the fields and tracks where she thought he might be, then widened her search. Vesper settled down, and wanted to gallop everywhere, which enabled her to cover the ground quickly, but she sulked and bucked when forced to change direction. Polly quartered the country belonging to White House, and rode twice past the farmyard, in case he should be working there, but she could not find him. A stone entered her heart. Was he sick? How could she not have thought of that before? Had he caught the influenza? Was he even now lying in that tiny cold room behind the kitchen? Would they nurse him, a hated Hun, as they nursed their own, or just leave him, not caring if he died?

She rode back to the farm again, hesitated, then dismounted, tied Vesper to the yard gate, and walked towards the house, her mouth dry, feeling frightened, bold, foolish, hopeful, anxious. The yard dog barked in a bored fashion, not bothering to leave his warm kennel on this cold day for someone he could see at a glance was not an egg-thief. No-one came out, and she went up to the farmhouse door, hesitated again, then rapped on it.

Mrs Bellerby answered it, grey and harassed, wiping her hands on a cloth, but managed a smile when she saw Polly. 'Eh, Miss Polly, what a treat to see you! Come in, do. Though you'll find me at sixes and sevens, with a load o' washing and nowhere to dry it. I hate a wet Monday! And my girl Millie's not come in this morning. I dare say I s'l get a note later that she's down with this wretched flu. It's fit to break your heart. How is the maister? I'm sorry to my heart about Mrs Morland. She was a fine lady, as kind as a summer day. And the poor mistress has her hands full, by what I hear.' Henrietta was always called 'the mistress' by the tenants and servants, while Alice had been Mrs Morland, a distinction neither of them had ever minded. 'How many is it she's got sick up the House? And that poor Ellen Bingley dying – just a lass, she was. I know her ma very well, poor thing. It's shocking. I wish I could come up the House and help, but I've more to do now and fewer to do it, and if I had six hands it'd hardly help me. I never thought to hear maself say it, but I miss that German prisoner, indeed I do.'

Polly felt cold with shock. 'Miss him?'

'Ay, you may look surprised, but he did more about the place than anyone realised, mucked out the hens, swept the yard, pumped water, dug the taties, pulled cabbages, knocked a nail in when 't was needed – and now I've to do all that maself as well as everything else, so it's no wonder if I say I miss him, and I don't care who hears me say it. German or not, he was a right Christian.'

'But why do you miss him? What's happened to him?'

Polly felt most peculiar, cold about the lips, as though she was going to faint. 'Is he – is he ill?' she heard herself saying.

'Nay, Miss Polly, he's gone. The supervisor from up the prison camp came and fetched him away. Real sudden it was – and I wasn't best pleased, as you can imagine, but he said I wasn't a special case and there was another farm that needed him more, and he was being . . . re-lo-cated, was the word he used. Which means he's not coming back. And me with nothing but old Percy, besides our Rosie and our Stephen, because our Christopher's nearly eighteen now and he'll be called up before you know it. What am I supposed to do? That's what I want to know. And if they give me another one, he'll never be as good.'

'But where has he gone?'

'Where's who gone?'

'The – the German prisoner,' Polly said faintly, hating calling him that.

'Oh, him! Well, like I said, Captain Standish, the supervisor, said he was wanted on another farm. He didn't say which one, or where, but it stands to reason it isn't anywhere near here or I'd have heard about it – and I'd have made a fuss, too, you can bank on that, for there's no-one round here needed him more than me! Why, Miss Polly, you're looking quite pale. I hope you're not going down with this wretched flu. Won't you sit down, and let me make you a cup o' tea?'

'No, no, thank you, I must go,' Polly said. 'I can't leave Vesper standing in this wind.' She had to get away quickly, before she betrayed herself. He was gone! Gone, she didn't know where, and she'd had no chance to say goodbye. He might be anywhere. He might be in a place where they hated Germans and treated him horribly. He might get hurt, or sick, and they wouldn't look after him. He might die, and she wouldn't know! It came to her, like a sickening blow, that she might never see him again. She said something, she never knew what, then stumbled out to retrieve her horse and ride blindly away.

500

Mrs Bellerby went back to her work, thinking that poor Miss Polly didn't look at all the thing, and hoping she wasn't coming down with this awful flu. Maybe it was just shock with her stepmother dying and all. It was not until some time later that she realised Miss Polly was so far from being herself she hadn't even said what she had come calling for in the first place. But if it was important, Mary Bellerby told herself comfortably, they'd surely send again.

CHAPTER TWENTY-TWO

The Germans fought fiercely, but having come out from behind their magnificent fortifications they proved vulnerable. Moreover, a hundred thousand had been taken prisoner since the beginning of August, besides the dead and wounded, and it was impossible to replace those men, while there were a million and a half American soldiers now in France, and more arriving all the time. The German general Ludendorff had been wise to try to beat the Allies before the Americans entered the war, but his Spring Offensive had failed. Now the German Army was being forced back. Also, according to intelligence sources, Germany was starving under the blockade, and there was serious unrest back home, strikes and riots.

Through October, as the Allies advanced, the German coalition crumbled. On the 30th of October the Turkish Army, driven out of Damascus by Allenby at the beginning of the month and in full retreat ever since, capitulated. The Serbian Army evacuated Salonika, and Bulgaria withdrew her troops from Greek territory. Austria was conducting peace talks with Italy at Padua, and on the 31st Hungary and Bosnia declared their independence from the Habsburg empire.

By the beginning of November rumours that an armistice was being discussed were rife all along the Front. For the Tommies fighting there it caused an unbearable tension, for it would be intolerable to catch a packet so late in the game, just when the end was in sight. But the Germans in the field were not 'taking it easy', and still seemed to have a bottomless supply of hardware. Shells fell like raindrops, machine-guns spat an endless hail of death and maiming, and every mile north and east was won at a cost of grim harrowing.

Bertie now found himself fighting his way back along the route of the long retreat in 1914, seeing familiar names on the map – Avesnes, Le Quesnoy, Bavay, Maubeuge. They were struggling towards the ugly, black and tortured coal-mining area around Mons, where the war had begun for him more than four years ago. There was a grim satis-faction in the symmetry, as well as a sour irony. One of the handful of men who had been with him since the begin-ning, 'Windy' Gayle – who had recovered from the wound taken in the March offensive, and whom he had promoted to sergeant – was hit by a shell as they advanced along a sunken road on the 5th of November and blown to pieces. It shocked Bertie when he was told, and made him angry, too. He wrote home to Jessie:

Four years in France, and killed in the enemy's death throes! How I wish the Hun would chuck it before thousands more good men are lost. All our chaps have the wind up, and who can blame them? For myself, with every day that passes I grow more certain that I must be for it. I see Cooper looking at me sidelong, and I look at him the same way, each of us wondering if the other might be a magnet for ill-luck that the other will suffer for. To die *now*, like poor Gayle, having survived so much, would be pitiful. What good can this last-minute resistance do? We hear there are armistice talks: what is there to talk about? Stop fighting first, and talk afterwards! The prisoners we take are so glad to be out of it they almost welcome capture, and talk of nothing but peace and going home. Why cannot their generals stop throwing their lives away, and surrender?

Jessie, for her part, hardly dared breathe, hardly dared think about him, in case anything she did or thought upset the delicate equilibrium of Fate. Days passed, and still the war went on. What were the generals *doing*?

With a house full of sickness and mourning, Polly had her share of tasks, but Henrietta insisted that she get some fresh air every day, so every day she rode out on Vesper, looking for Erich Kuppel. It was all she could do. She dared not ask officially, for any such enquiry would be bound to get back to her father. All she could do was to scour the countryside and try to find out, through casual conversation, whether any farm had lately taken on a German prisoner.

She rode further and further afield, and as she searched, she brooded silently on what had happened. Was it chance that he had been removed so suddenly, or malice on someone's part? Had someone seen her, or guessed, and told the authorities? Did Jessie know? She had seen her – or, rather, had seen Vesper – one day. But Jessie was fully occupied with nursing and worrying about Bertie and little Thomas, and behaved no differently towards Polly than she had before. And if it was her father who had required Kuppel to be removed, he would surely have spoken to Polly about it. But he was away a good deal, and on his short appearances at home he shut himself up in the steward's room and hardly seemed to notice her when he passed her in the house. He was in mourning for his wife, worried about his factories, and hardly spoke to anyone, not even Maria, who was the only one allowed into the steward's room when he was there.

The frustration of not knowing *why* was added to the misery of being parted from him. Perhaps for ever? She did not want to think it, but as the days passed and she could not find him, the dread began to settle on her that she would never see him again. She remembered what he had said about Germans being hated for years, if not for ever, and began to wonder whether, in fact, it was he who had asked to be moved in order to save her. This was the most miserable idea of all.

She even rode past the prisoner-of-war camp, hoping she might see him within the compound. Once, when a prisoner was standing near the wire, she called out to him, asking if he knew Erich Kuppel. The man looked blank, probably because he did not speak English. She called out the name again, several times, with increasing urgency, and another man came to join him, but both only shook their heads, whether because they did not understand or they did not know, she couldn't tell. Then she saw a guard looking at her, and had to ride away before too much attention was attracted.

Loneliness and misery were her companions, and as October turned to November came hopelessness. She searched whenever she went out on horseback, but not any more because she thought she might find him. She kept searching because to give up would be to betray him. His image was bright in her mind, the sound of his voice, his warm, living strength; and longing for him invested her dreams, so that night after night she searched through a ruined landscape for something lost or destroyed by the passage of war, something she never found.

Emma's unit was busy again, though without the added distraction of the bombings, now that the Germans had been pushed back. The Allied advance came at considerable cost in wounded men, and the constant stream gave them work enough to keep them busy. But their labours were cheered by the second stream, of German prisoners of war, whose large numbers told their own story.

There were rumours that Marshal Foch and the British

admiral Sir Rosslyn Wemyss were already deep in negotiations with German delegates for a ceasefire. The addition of circumstantial detail made it seem likely this was more than just a rumour: that the meeting was taking place in a railway carriage in a siding in the Compiègne forest, a dining car specially adapted for meetings across a table. Unsuitably to the mood of the moment, the weather had turned, and the October sunshine had given way to heavy grey skies, dank cold, and rain.

One morning in early November Emma received a letter from England in a hand unknown to her – a rather spidery, old-fashioned hand – but the postmark made her jump, for it was the town in Kent near which Fenniman's childhood home, Linton Hall, was situated. The envelope was intriguingly bulky, but the mail arrived just as the convoy was leaving and she could only stuff it into her pocket as she ran for her ambulance. She found time to read it at last while waiting for the ambulance train to come in, sitting in her cab with Benson on her knee, a tin mug of tea warming her hands and a bacon sandwich torturing Benson's delicate olfactory senses.

It was from Fenniman's father's housekeeper.

Linton Hall
Thursday
Dear Miss Emma Weston,
I make bold to write to you, and hope you will forgive the liberty, to let you know that Mr Cedric's father, my master Brigadier Fenniman, passed away on Monday last, of a Heart Attack. The Brigadier was very frail since Mr Cedric's death, and his passing was not unexpected, though still a great shock to Harrup and me, who have been with him these fifty years and more. I'm afraid my late master was not quite generous in his dealings with you, but I am sure you will understand, dear Miss Weston, that he was so set in his ways,

due to his age, that he found it hard to accept anyone he had not known for a long time. I believe he would have come to value you as his daughter-in-law if Providence had seen fit to allow Mr Cedric to live to make you his wife. I know that you loved Mr Cedric as much as we did, and I pitied you from my heart, I really did, when he Fell. I wished I could have written to you then, but I could not go against my master's wishes. However, I take leave, dear Miss Weston, to send to you now, per package, your letters to Mr Cedric, which I found in his kit, which was sent home after his death. The trunk was in the Brigadier's room and neither Harrup nor me was allowed to touch it, but after his Passing we had to look into everything for the lawyers, and Harrup agrees with me that they did ought to be sent to you, and we felt you would like to have them. I end this letter, dear Miss Weston, taking the liberty of hoping you are Well, and assuring you that I remain always,

Your humble obedient Servant,
Kitty Eagan

The bundle of letters, the envelopes addressed in her own hand, was held together with a piece of string. It was a small enough bundle, for their engagement had been short, and the sight of it brought it home to her, with the usual sharp pain, that he really was gone. There was a stain on the corner of one envelope, a rusty mark that might have been mud or tea but she feared might just as easily have been blood.

She untied the string and spread them out on her lap, looking at his name written in her own hand. His warm hand had received and opened them; his living eyes had scanned the words. Had they been the best she could write? Had she put enough love into them? Her memory of what she had said in them was completely gone, and she was strangely reluctant to re-read them. It would be like violating his privacy. The finality of death came home to her: there was nothing she could do now to change what she had written, or what he had thought about it. He was in his grave; he was one of The Dead, that unknowable, unreachable company.

She stared at the envelopes dry-eyed, wishing Mrs Eagan had not been so kind. For what was she to do with them? Impossible either to keep them or throw them away. His letters to her were in a box in her kit, but she had not looked at them since she had come to France. Somehow, now she had seen what war was like, she did not think they would have any power to comfort her.

The bell rang from the station office, warning that the train was approaching. She shuffled the envelopes hastily together, dropped one, stooped to pick it up, and saw there was something written on the back.

> The fog is in No Man's Land.
> Gunfire like a false dawn runs along the line,
> Sullen orange bleeding into grey.
> But the thought of you is lovely, clean and clear,
> A rose in a ruined land.
> I hold you safe in my thoughts.
> Life has no fear but the fear of losing you.
>
> The fog is in No Man's Land.
> Droplets like false diamonds hang along the wire,
> Sullen grey on unremitting grey.
> But the thought of you is jewel-bright and dear,
> A finch in a winter garden.
> I hold you close in my heart.
> Death has no sorrow but of leaving you.

She had always known what he meant to her; now, as absolutely, she knew what she had meant to him. The sudden intimacy of reading his words hit her like a physical blow. It was as if he had spoken to her with his living voice. Vividly his face was in her mind, as she had not been able to conjure it for months, real, looking down at her and laughing as he had in life. Her sense of loss was sickening; her mind reeled and plunged. She sat rigid, her throat aching, her spirit a howling wilderness of longing for him. *Fenniman!*

The train could be heard now, but she couldn't move. Only when Benson whined and nudged her was she jerked back into reality. Her hands shook as she pushed the envelopes into her coat pocket; her legs felt weak. As quickly as it had come, his bright image had faded, and inwardly she cried out and reached after it, knowing it was no use, knowing that she would not be able to bring it back.

The train came steaming and grunting into the depot, and work took over all but a tiny corner of her mind. And there, in a whiteness of shock, she wondered about the poem. Had he written it that last morning? Was it in his breast pocket when he was hit? (That rusty stain . . .) The life they should have had together had ended that day, but her lover had reached out from beyond death, and it made her feel as though that unlived life was still going on somewhere, like a train that had been turned by the points onto another, parallel, line. Somewhere Fenniman lived and they were together, as they had been meant to be, in some place she did not know and could not reach.

The whole day she felt lost and alone, out of her place, a ghost in the real world. In the mess that evening she could not join in the cheerful chatter; and when she got up to go to bed, rather earlier than her usual time, Armstrong said, 'I hope you aren't going down with the flu, Westie.'

'You're very pale and strange-looking,' Bullock agreed, looking across at her. 'Did something happen today? You look as though you'd seen a ghost.'

'It's nothing,' she said. 'I'm just tired.'

She went to bed, with Benson pressed warm and solid against her side under her hand, reassuring. It was a long time before she could sleep, and then she dreamed of being

509

lost in London, walking and walking down streets of identical houses, trying to find a tube station, which would be her only way of getting home. Every time she turned a corner she thought the station would be there, but found only another identical street.

She woke unrefreshed, weary from having walked all night. Outside there was a cold, windless day, seamless grey of sky, with a prickle of rain that was hardly rain: such blankness it was almost as if the real weather had been cancelled and this was what was underneath. She washed and dressed, took Benson out, standing patiently in the dank morning while he found exactly the right bush for his requirements, then went heavily to the mess-hut for breakfast. She felt the atmosphere as soon as she entered, and caught the looks that were thrown at her.

Hutchinson came towards her, looking grave. 'Westie—'

'What is it?' she heard herself ask. Her voice sounded far away. In the weariness of strain and broken sleep, she felt nothing, no fear or apprehension, though Hutchinson's expression was weighted with bad news.

'Westie, I'm so sorry,' Hutchinson said. 'We've just heard – a message came in. I know what good friends you were. It's Wentworth.'

She tried to react to the words, but everything inside her was numb, as though her whole body had been given novocaine. 'What's happened?' she heard herself ask.

'He was leading his company against a German position near Avesnes. They got into a sunken lane, but a Gerry machine-gunner pinpointed it and opened fire. Seven of them were hit, including him. They got him back to the aid station, but they couldn't do anything for him. He died soon afterwards.'

The failing German fortunes, though welcome to Thomas as an Englishman and a soldier, only increased the danger to the Romanov women. The anxiety in the small circle of

510

intelligence agents in Perm was noticeably increasing, while the Cheka, who guarded the women, were growing ever more secretive, excluding even top Bolsheviks in the town from their counsels. The White Army was still approaching, the Red Army still falling back. The tensions between the various layers of the revolution were hovering on the brink of hostility and, according to the German agents, the exchange talks between Moscow and Germany had stalled.

The news came at the beginning of November that the Kaiser had offered to abdicate in favour of his son, and though he immediately retracted the offer, it was a sign of how desperate things were growing in his empire. The German Navy had mutinied, and there were mobs on the streets of Berlin, Cologne and Hamburg demanding an end to the war. Red revolution was in the air, Communist agitators were everywhere, openly vocal, and red flags were flying on civic buildings in many cities. The value to Lenin of the Romanov women as pawns was diminishing daily. If Germany was defeated – and it now looked to be only a matter of time – Lenin would not need to appease her to keep her from attacking Russia.

Thomas felt increasingly helpless, while his own position grew more precarious. He was almost sure that some in the Cheka knew who he really was, and that they were held off from exposing him, or even executing him, only by the residual respect they had for England and the success of her armies at the Front – or perhaps by their contempt for and dislike of the local soviets, who would certainly have wanted his blood if they had known who he was. Relations between the British and Bolshevik governments were confused. There was still a British diplomatic presence in Moscow, but who knew how long that would last? When the Reds turned and rent each other, which seemed likely to happen at any moment, the bloodbath might well overwhelm all foreigners on Russian soil, regardless of their origins.

And there was nothing Thomas could do to get the Romanov women away. Their imprisonment in the convent might have been more humane and tolerable to them than their incarceration in a cellar in the town, but it made it harder to get to them. All he and Bauer, and the others who had an interest in them, could do was to wait and watch for an opportunity. They had, however, been able to pass messages occasionally through the nuns, who were naturally drawn to humanitarian pity for their 'guests'; and Bauer, as a physician, had been able to visit at irregular intervals.

From him Thomas had the few precious scraps of news about them, which were all that kept him going. Anastasia, it seemed, had been badly affected by her failed attempt to escape, and had retreated into strangeness. Pretty, sunny Marie, who had been known affectionately back in the old days in Tsarskoye Selo as 'plump little bow-wow', had grown thin and sad, her looks gone, her eyes hollow. She had been the late Tsar's favourite. Tatiana was probably the best placed, for her strong religious beliefs and love of religious forms allowed her to escape the horrors of reality by spending most of her day in prayer, meditation, and reading the religious texts the nuns were glad to lend. The Tsaritsa's health was very fragile: she was confined to bed, weak and in constant pain, consumed with mourning for her husband and son, resigned to death. Yet, deprived of the various medicines, drugs and copious draughts of strong coffee she had taken in the days before the revolution, she was probably in a calmer state of mind than she had been for many years.

It was Olga, Thomas felt, who would be bearing the main brunt, intelligent enough to understand fully the situation they were in, without the dampening effects of madness, illness or religion. Her faith was strong, but she set less store by ceremony than her sister or mother, and as the eldest daughter she felt responsible for the younger ones, while being incapable of affecting their welfare in any way.

When the news came, by Bauer's secret wireless link, that

the Kaiser had abdicated on the 9th of November and Germany had been declared a republic, Thomas feared the worst. The war must end now, very soon, but already the Romanov women were reduced in status, no longer the blood relatives of a powerful ruler but the abandoned remains of a past regime. He was in an agony of suspense, but the Cheka did not order their execution, or throw them to the local soviet. Lenin still wanted them alive: that was what Bauer heard from the German ambassador in Moscow. It was believed he was preserving them for a possible show trial, to be held at a time that would most serve his purposes. Such a trial would result in a death sentence, that was obvious, but they were to be kept alive for the time being and, whatever the reason behind it, Thomas could only be glad of the respite.

In England, the news seemed to come pell-mell in the early days of November: after years of grind and a spring of retreat, uncertainty and depression, there were advances and victories now one after the other: Turkey and Austria collapsed in the east, Germany fell back and failed in the west. It had been driven out of the seemingly unbreakable Hindenburg Line. At Ypres the Allies had advanced in one day to what in 1917 they had struggled for three bitter months to reach: Passchendaele was taken, and they swept on to Roulers, the 1917 objective that had evaded them. The indefatigable Americans were flattening all in their path in the Argonne. Valenciennes was taken. Suddenly it began to dawn on a war-weary nation, accustomed to hearing that there would be victory 'next year', that the end must only be weeks, perhaps days away.

At Morland Place, Jessie helped her mother nurse the influenza victims. Some of the earliest infected were convalescing now, but there were three in a critical state in the 'isolation ward': another maid, and two from the village, a Morland pensioner who had no-one to nurse him, and a boy of fifteen whose mother could not cope. In the school-room – the 'children's ward' – James and Roberta had been joined by the five-year-old son of one of the laundresses; she had no-one to leave him with while she was out working. It seemed to Jessie ironic that it had taken until now for Morland Place to turn into a hospital.

The nursing was time-consuming but not arduous to one who had nursed at the Front, and she soon got into the rhythm of it. Because it came more easily to her than to anyone else in the house, she undertook the lion's share of the work, and persuaded her mother to excuse Polly as much as possible. Polly, she thought, was looking peaked and unwell, certainly paler and thinner in the face than she had been in the summer.

Henrietta, who placed great emphasis on everyone's eating well, was too tired and preoccupied to notice that Polly ate very little at mealtimes. With half of the household staff in bed, she had to help Mrs Stark in the kitchen and oversee the essential housework. The remaining servants did their bit manfully, though it hurt her to see Sawry – who was not getting any younger – doing fires and lamps and boots like the most junior of footmen. It was a relief that Teddy was away again, for without him lower standards could prevail. Helen was still away nursing her sister and Ethel nursing her parents, and in the depleted household, meals were informal affairs. The four of them left – Henrietta, Polly, Jessie and Father Palgrave – often ate quickly and in preoccupied silence as if each was alone at the table.

Henrietta discovered a dozen times a day how much she missed Alice, who had been a quiet presence in the background to whom she could always spill out her worries. She discovered, too, how much Alice had done, things like mending, dusting the delicate ornaments and picking and arranging flowers, which Henrietta had not noticed at the time, but noticed now they were left undone. But when

Jessie asked if Polly could be relieved of nursing cares, Henrietta agreed without hesitation. Polly was not a born nurse in any case, and had her office duties which, with Maria sick, no-one else could do.

Into this atmosphere the war sounded only a distant note. Jessie received a letter from Bertie, written on the 8th of November:

We are fighting alongside the Canadians now, which engenders a wonderful kind of confidence. Together we constitute a sort of flying-column pursing the fleeing Germans, who are running so fast it's hard to keep up with them. We sometimes enter a town within hours of their leaving it, and it is amazing how quickly the population can change flags from German eagles to Union Jacks! Everywhere we go there is huge celebration – in one town the mayor handed out cigars to our men as they passed, though I think they'd have preferred Wild Woodbines. As resistance crumbles, we have to seek out the Hun positions, and they surrender quickly. But still the fight goes on and we are suffering casualties. I have to report that Cooper was hit yesterday. A nest of machine-gunners, hiding in a wood, opened up as we were going up to clear them out, and in the resulting hail, a bullet took a piece out of his calf and broke his leg. It was his first serious wound of the war and, thank God, it is not life-threatening, but he is out of it now. There was the most comic mixture of relief and annoyance on his face when he realised he would be going home before the end. When he had gone I had the most curious thought: that perhaps he had intercepted the bullet that was meant to kill me. He was standing beside me when he was hit. Has he saved my life? Will I therefore survive this ghastly war? It *must* end soon, surely? Damn these negotiators, these circumlocutory, heartless old men, for every extra man who falls while they ponder and talk, talk, talk. Oh God, for peace! To stop the madness for ever, and come home!

Bertie was within striking distance of Mons early in the morning of the 11th of November. The Canadians were up ahead of them, and were to enter the town at around four in the morning and secure it, after which Bertie's battalion, together with the 5th Lancers, were to pass through them and try to catch up with and engage the Germans. He was waiting beside the road for the signal to come through from the Canadians, missing Cooper as the fresh-faced but rather clumsy lad who had replaced him as his servant brought him his tea. Cooper would have scrounged or wangled him coffee from somewhere. He supposed he would have to do without coffee, even *ersatz*, until the war was over.

The morning was cold and damp, the sky so low it would be hard to know when dawn arrived. He warmed his fingers on the tin mug, watching his breath smoke up and blend with the foggy air. The lad, Higgins, had brought him an army biscuit as well, which he looked at with disfavour, but he could hardly expect a boy new to the trade to find anything better in a place like this – an empty field between villages – when they had advanced so fast yesterday their luggage had not caught up with them. He felt he could hardly be bothered to try to crunch the flinty thing, but he would be hungry later if he did not eat it. He could put it in his pocket, but experience suggested that, once they had started moving, he would forget it.

With an effort he broke it, then noticed a skinny mongrel dog hovering near him, shivering either with cold or fear or both. It had the hopeful but frightened eyes of a family pet abandoned and gone wild. There was always someone worse off than yourself, he reflected, with early-morning profundity, and squatted down to call to it. The creature crept closer, tail slotted into the groove between its legs, plainly

516

fearing a blow or kick, and he held out the smaller half of the biscuit. He had to extend his arm fully before the wretched thing would come close enough to snatch the morsel from his fingers, back off a few feet and crunch it up with eager relish. 'How hungry do you have to be,' he said aloud, 'to enjoy hardtack so much?' The animal flattened its ears ingratiatingly, eyeing the hand that held the remainder.

But Bertie saw his adjutant, 'Dickie' Dixon, coming up with a message, so he straightened up, throwing the biscuit to the dog, who snatched it and galloped out of the way of Dixon's approaching feet.

'Are the Canucks in?' he asked, dusting his fingers on his trouser leg, and taking a sip of tea.

'It's not that, sir,' Dixon said. He looked oddly unsettled, and Bertie wondered if it was bad news from home. 'It's a message from Divisional HQ. It seems that Marshal Foch and the Germans signed the armistice agreement at five this morning. There's to be a ceasefire everywhere at eleven. All hostilities are to stop at eleven a.m.'

There seemed to be a silence, a stillness, in which every detail of the scene imprinted itself on his mind in a way he knew he would never forget. He saw the exact texture of the cobbles of the road, shiny with damp, the way the mist was catching in the bare tops of the trees growing out of the hedge opposite, the mild green of an empty and flattened cigarette packet in the rough grass at the roadside, the drops of condensation forming on the edge of Dixon's cap-peak and the red roughness of his skin from this morning's cold-water shave. *Where were you when the war ended?* One day people might ask that, and he would know, he would remember. But *What did you feel when you heard?* they might ask. And the answer was, Why, nothing. Nothing at all.

'The war's over?' he said aloud.

'It's over, sir. It's over.' Dixon sounded bewildered. The muscles of his cheeks, the skin around his eyes, seemed taut, as though he were holding back something, some tremendous emotion. After a moment he went on, 'Do you know, sir, what the first thing I thought was? "I've got a future ahead of me!"'

A future. It came to Bertie slowly, like water seeping. He had believed for so long he would not survive the war that life after it had been a storybook thing, imagined but unreal. Now it seemed he was to see it, after all. 'You have, Dickie,' he said. 'And so have I, by God!' Even as he said it, he half expected to hear the scream of a last, fated shell coming down to get him. But the gunfire was all in the far distance, like a rumbling of summer thunder, and the only extraneous sound nearby was the yarking of a crow hidden somewhere in the mist.

'I wonder what it'll be like, sir,' Dixon said.

'Not like it was before,' Bertie said, 'that's for sure.' That world was gone. Whatever it was they went back to, it would not be the England they had left in 1914.

A signals clerk trotted up. 'Message, sir, from Colonel Hilton, CEF. Mons is secure, sir.'

The Canadian Expeditionary Force. Technically, they were still at war. 'Who else knows this, Dickie?'

'Well, sir, the signalling officer and the clerks do. I came straight to you.'

'We'd better keep it to ourselves for now. I'll parade the men later and tell them, but we must advance at least to Mons. Orders are orders.'

'Yes, sir,' Dixon said, but an irrepressible grin broke through. 'It'll be more comfortable in Mons than out here.'

'Go and tell the signals unit to keep it quiet, and give the order to move off.'

It was around nine o'clock by the time they reached Mons. The Lancers had gone by, posting past them to cross the town ahead of them, but there was no possibility of the West Herts getting through easily. The streets were full of Canadian soldiers and French civilians in heavenly holiday mood, and

518

the battalion was soon surrounded by women, children and old men, beaming and cheering, waving flags, pressing gifts on them, biscuits, apples, cigarettes, even cognac and cigars, though how they had kept them from the Germans Bertie couldn't imagine.

Everywhere he could see tall Canadians with girls hanging on their arms. One had a length of sausage in one hand, which he was chewing between kissing the girls impartially; another had a chrysanthemum stuck behind his ear and a fat cigar between his lips. As the West Herts struggled against the flow past a convent, the nuns were bringing out saucepans of coffee and bottles of wine. There were all the makings of a fine party and a vast communal headache. Bertie remembered the last time he had seen Mons, choked with retreating soldiers, and fleeing civilians loaded with their most portable belongings, when the cry on every side was 'The Germans are coming!' They could not get through the narrow streets then either. Nothing and everything had changed.

Nevertheless, he kept his officers and NCOs up to the mark, the battalion moving forward, though it took them a ridiculous amount of time to get through the centre. There was open ground to the north of the town, along the canal, which he well remembered, and he ordered a halt there, and had the men form up so they could do a roll call. The Lancers came clattering by, going back into the town, and their officer reported that the Germans were out of touch. 'You've heard the news? There's no chance of catching the Huns before eleven anyway, and we can't engage them afterwards, so there seemed no point in going on.'

They would have to wait here, then, for further orders, Bertie thought. Well, there were some warehouses and empty factories that would make shelter for the men for the time being, and he could set up headquarters in a hotel in the town. His entire battalion, he could see by the excited faces and eager chatter, had heard the news by now, but still it fell to him to make it official. Someone found him a box to

519

stand on, and he got up on it, to be greeted by an anonymous yell from the back somewhere of 'Good old 'Yde Park!'
and a great cheer from the men. The company commanders
were smiling even as they officially deplored this breach of
discipline. The happiness coming off the assembled men was
like the heat of a city that dissipates a fog. He half expected
to see the clouds part above them and the sunshine pour
through.

He held up his hand and got silence, and said, 'Men, I
have to tell you what I imagine every one of you knows by
now. The armistice has been signed, and all hostilities will
cease at eleven a.m. – in fifteen minutes' time.'

It was amazing how much noise five hundred men could
make when they all roared at the same moment. He felt
himself almost lifted off his feet by the gale of joy. In the
pause at the end of the first cheer, as they drew breath for
another, he added in their own language, 'War napoo! Unless
we are very unlucky, we shall all see Blighty again. We won,
lads – we won!'

He had to let the ensuing roar play itself out, for there
was no possible way to halt it prematurely. When they
quietened down again, he said, 'I know I don't have to
remind you that we are still under orders, and I trust you
to show the civilians of this town that the British Army
conducts itself just as well in the best of times as it does in
the worst. We're going to bivouac here for the time being,
until we get further orders from Brigade HQ. But I can
promise you some sort of celebration tonight, so I think
when you've done your fatigues you can start working on
a sing-song.'

He dismissed the parade, and was at once surrounded by
officers wanting instructions. There would be much to do,
to settle the men in and make them comfortable, set up
kitchens and latrines, report to HQ where they were, bring
up the baggage, find a suitable hotel for his office and billets
for the officers; and if they were here for any length of time,

there would be the task of keeping the men busy. At the moment they were too happy about the war ending to wonder what would happen next, but Bertie anticipated there would be plenty of toil and trouble ahead for the commanding officers before they saw home again. He was still giving orders when a cacophony of church bells broke out all over the town, signalling that eleven o'clock had struck, and it was over, over, it was really over at last.

He found time that afternoon to write to Jessie.

My dearest love, the armistice is already four hours old. I wish I could have been with you when 11 o'clock struck. The relief is impossible to describe. It's hard to take in that here really is the end to it all. No more slaughter, no more maiming, no more mud and blood, no more disembowelled horses, blasted trees, gutted villages, ruined landscapes. No more of those hopeless dawns, crouching in sodden trenches with the rain chilling the spirit, waiting to go over the top. No more of that unendurable screaming of shells. All I can think of is that suddenly there is silence – mile upon beautiful mile of it, all along the front line from Switzerland to the sea. In my mind I see an endless succession of gloriously silent guns. Germany is utterly defeated, the war is over, and I shall be coming home to you.

At eleven o'clock Lennie's battalion was advancing in drenching rain on a town through which, according to a cavalry scouting party, the Germans had only just passed. If they could catch them up before they reached the town beyond, they could capture them, and everyone was looking forward to a lively scrap and a near-bloodless victory. Quite a few of the men had not long been out and had never seen the enemy at close quarters, and with the rumours of a cease-fire flying about, many of them were hoping for a good show before it was over. It would be jolly hard luck to have to go home and say you had not had a fight at all.

As his company marched into the precincts of the town he was aware of some kind of disturbance up ahead, and for a moment his blood quickened as he thought perhaps the Germans were still there, after all. But there was no gunfire, only a mixed clamour of voices. And then something began to be shouted, coming nearer as it passed from person to person. A noise above him made him look up, and he saw a man leaning out of a window. The man shouted, waving his arms, with a wine bottle in one hand, 'Cheer up, Tommee, an armistice 'as been signed. Ze war is over! Peeace! Peeace!'

It was extraordinary to Lennie afterwards to remember how little effect the news had on his men or on him. At first they were too tired to take it in, having been marching hard for several days, while the relentless rain made it difficult for hearts to lift even to such news. And when they did take it in, there was no enthusiasm. The orders to follow up the Germans were countermanded and they were halted in the town, and it seemed really just a pity to have been made to stop when they had the Germans cold. There was a sense of anticlimax and emptiness, as no-one quite knew what was to happen next.

However, a hot meal and a double rum ration did a great deal to revive spirits, and when the rain stopped in the afternoon, the battalion bands came out and marched about playing popular tunes, and the order came that the men could 'slack off' for the rest of the day. By evening the streets were full of citizens and soldiers happily fraternising, dancing, singing, firing off Very lights and flares, cheering and laughing until they were hoarse.

Lennie and his fellow officers and leading citizens were entertained to dinner in the town hall by the brigadier and the civic council, with plenty of wine and a great many speeches in two languages. Lennie was sitting next to a very fat woman who had put on a puce satin evening dress cut very low. At first, in the dank atmosphere of the long-unheated hall, her exposed flesh was an acre of bluish duck skin; later, when food and drink and the presence of so many people warmed it up, it ran with sweat. She kept toasting Lennie with very moist eyes and he was afraid at every moment that she was going to kiss him, a peril that rather distracted him from the speeches. On his other side was an elderly town clerk with very few teeth, in a rusty suit that smelled overpoweringly of mothballs, who talked to him incomprehensibly in French whenever Lennie turned that way, clutching at his arm with a hand like a claw and fixing his face with mournful brown eyes and specks of spittle.

Lennie, who was normally abstemious, drank a very great deal that night, and began to feel quite detached from the surroundings and the events. He tried to feel glad about the armistice, but managed only to conquer his disappointment at not having a last crack at the Hun. They had won, which was the good thing. But now it was over, all he could think about was the friends with whom he had joined up at the very beginning, in August 1914, and who were all dead. Captain Lennox Manning, MM, was the only one who had come through, and it made him want to cry. 'I've been right through it, from the very beginning,' he informed the fat woman. 'Four years and three months. The whole darned war. Think of that!' The woman, who was inexplicably blurred, said something in French, and raised her glass to him again. As she swam in his vision, he thought she must be very drunk to move about like that; and then he thought perhaps it was him who was drunk. 'The only one left,' he informed her, feeling tears welling in his eyes. 'Granny Ruth will be so proud of me.'

'*Pauvre petit*,' the woman said, leaning forward and baptising him with a splash of wine from her accidentally tilted glass. 'Leetle Tommee.'

And at that point Lennie thought it would be a good idea to rest his head on the tablecloth, because it felt far too heavy to stay up.

Jessie was in the 'isolation ward', bathing the face and neck of the old man, who was muttering and restless with high fever. The fifteen-year-old boy had died yesterday, making the third death in the house from the influenza. She tried to keep herself cheerful with the thought that no more of the children had become ill, and that little Thomas, whom she did not allow herself to approach closely while she was sick-nursing, was, according to Nanny Emma, 'fit and bonny as an eel'. And Maria was recovering, though desperately weak. Father Palgrave's visits to her bedside were so frequent and prolonged and his anxiety over her so pronounced that she felt certain there was a special feeling between them, and she was glad for Maria's sake, though she wondered how Uncle Teddy would like it. He did not take kindly to defection – but perhaps she and Bertie had set a precedent, and he would not mind so much. Frank had only been his nephew, not his adopted son.

Her thoughts were wandering along these familiar paths, as they tended to while she was occupied with the routines of nursing, when suddenly the house-bell began to ring violently. She jumped up in alarm, put down the bowl and ran to the door. Her first thought was Zeppelins – but there had been no raids anywhere for months. Was it a fire? She sniffed for the smell of smoke. Something was going on downstairs, a general noise of disturbance and voices. She hurried along the passage, and at the junction found her mother, who had come out from Maria's room.

They met each other's eyes blankly. 'What is it?' Henrietta said.

'I don't know,' Jessie said, and they hurried down the back stairs together. In the lobby at the bottom they found

Sawry, pulling on the bell-rope like a madman, his eyes popping, sweat beading his face.

'Sawry, stop, stop!' Henrietta cried.

'What is it? What's the matter?' Jessie shouted above the noise.

He turned to them, but kept on pulling the rope. 'It's over,' he shouted. 'It's over.' One of the maids came running in from the hall, wiping her hands on her apron. He grabbed her arm, shoved the rope into her hand. 'Ring it!' he ordered her. 'Pull! It's over.' He ran past his mistress into the hall, and there was a mill of servants there, all looking bemused, including Mrs Stark, who was weeping. Sawry grabbed her by both hands, and capered, dragging her round with him.

'He's gone mad,' Henrietta said. 'Oh dear, what can we do? We must send for Dr Hasty.'

Sawry recollected himself at last, dropped Mrs Stark's hands, and presented himself to his mistress, looking a sketch with his hair awry, his collar burst, his waistcoat undone and his face red. 'I beg your pardon, madam,' he said, in an approximation of his normal manner, though his voice shook. 'I forgot myself. A boy came up from the village, madam. It's over! The war's over! They signed an armistice this morning. All weapons to be laid down at eleven o'clock.'

Jessie looked at her mother, and read in her eyes what so many women would feel at this moment, no joy, no relief, just a terrible sorrow. Cold in the clay of France lay two of her sons, and a nephew who had grown up in her nursery was dead and lost, his body never to be found. It was victory, then, but a price had been paid. Thousand upon thousand in the mud lay the Fallen, each one of them king of some woman's heart.

Jessie took her mother's cold hands, and sought some gladness for her. 'Jack will come home,' she said.

Henrietta nodded. *And Bertie*, she thought, but her tongue was dry in her mouth and she could not speak. She wanted to be glad for Jessie's sake, for all their sakes, but there was nothing but weariness in her. Her boys, her lovely boys! Tears came belatedly to her eyes, and she saw them mirrored in Jessie's before the two women clasped each other close, while in the background the servants chattered excitedly and the house-bell rang on, joined at a distance by the first of the church carillons.

Emma was in the station yard that morning with the convoy, waiting for the hospital train, when suddenly the church bells in the town started ringing, first one and then another, with a ragged, unmusical ding-dong that was more like a tocsin than a peal of joy. She thought at first it must be an air-raid warning. But the Germans were far away and on the run. Benson started to bark out of the window. She saw several people run across the yard to the dispatching office. Curious, she got down from her cab. Daniels, a new girl, came round from her ambulance looking frightened. 'What is it?'

'I don't know,' Emma said. 'We'd better find out.'

More and more bells were joining in, and there was a distant splurge of sound like a lot of people cheering. Another person came running across the yard, a young girl in a black dress and blue apron, whom Emma recognised as the waitress from the Trois Oiseaux just outside the depot gates. She looked around as if for help, and came across to Emma and Daniels, her face completely out of control, as though all her muscles and nerves had forgotten what they were for. She looked at them wildly, her mouth open as she searched for English words and failed to find them. Then she cried, '*La guerre – finie! Toute finie!*' And then she burst into tears.

'I wonder if it's true,' Daniels said.

'I suppose it is,' Emma said. 'Listen to those bells.' They stared at each other blankly for an instant. Emma didn't want to look inside herself, afraid of what she might find. She didn't want to feel anything, not now, not yet. It was almost with relief that she heard the sound of the train shuffling over the last points, coming into the siding. 'Well, we've got work to do,' she said. 'I expect we'll hear all about it later.'

CHAPTER TWENTY-THREE

London erupted with joy. At eleven o'clock a crash of victorious gunfire made anyone who had been in France jump, and those who had been at the Front duck; but then the reassuring 'all clear' sounded from the plinth of Nelson's column, and went on sounding. Immediately, as though by magic, the streets filled with hundreds, then thousands of men and women. Schools were let out, and children began running and shrieking between them, breaking the early mood of bemusement, giving licence finally to let go of wartime discipline, quietness and economy. Office workers flooded out, customers in shops put down their purchases and the assistants left with them. The steady November drizzle was forgotten. In the sudden realisation of joy, it might have been blazing sunshine for all anyone noticed. Nobody cared that it was not, in fact, the end of the war, only a cease-fire. What mattered was that the fighting was over and nobody else would have to die.

Maroons were let off from the roofs of police and fire stations, factories blasted on their sirens, the tugs and ships on the Thames and every railway train at every siding sounded their hooters in an orgy of raucous sound. Flags appeared from nowhere, then whistles, rattles, bugles – anything that would make a noise. 'God Save the King' was sung for the first of a thousand times, followed by any other popular song that came to mind. The soldiers home on leave dashed out to join the fun or, if wounded, poured from hospitals and convalescent homes in their 'blues' to bellow 'Good-bye-ee', 'Pack Up Your Troubles', 'When This Lousy War Is Over', and other less civilised ditties from the Front. Old men put on their rows of medals from the Boer and Crimean campaigns before shuffling out to join the crowd; anyone displaying a wound stripe was a hero, and anyone in nurse's uniform was cheered to the echo.

The crowds slowly converged, as though drawn by an irresistible force, on Trafalgar Square, the Mall and Buckingham Palace. Official cars in Whitehall and Parliament Square could barely move: Winston Churchill, trying to drive from the Admiralty to Downing Street, performed the journey at snail's pace with twenty revellers sitting and standing on the roof of his motor. The Mall filled from side to side, and as more and more people packed in, edging down towards the Palace, distributaries of the flood went up lampposts and trees and Queen Victoria's statue and were even squeezed up the palace railings. When the King and Queen came out on the balcony, with Princess Mary in VAD uniform, a roar went up as from a single throat, and went on and on, pounding down the Mall like a tidal wave, bearing up the suppressed emotion of four and a half years of privation and suffering, fear and death, released at last in a composite bellow of joy.

Virtually no work was done that day. Shopkeepers could not keep their assistants behind the counters, traffic could not move, factories and offices closed. The tube trains were packed, and one woman was heard to shriek from the middle of a press of bodies, "'Ere's one jam as ain't rationed, any'ow!'

As the early dusk fell, a new delight awaited Londoners, for the streetlamps came on fully for the first time in years. A determined effort had been made during the day to clean off the black shading that had partially obscured them. Theatres and cinemas were lit up, and hotels and clubs had all their lights on and the blinds up, adding to the brightness of the streets. And when the face of Big Ben was suddenly illuminated, another roar went up. The long, long dark was over. For some little children, who could not remember the time before blackout, the lines of sparkling lamps gleaming through the fog were like a fairyland.

Violet had given in to the pleas of her older children and her own curiosity and walked with them to the Mall to watch the King and Queen and Princess Mary drive down in an open carriage, then went across the park to see Big Ben and hear it strike. Everyone was very kind, despite their boisterousness, and willing soldiers lifted the children up on their shoulders to see the King go past; but at Parliament Square she decided it was getting too rough for them, and sent them home with their nurse while she, not wishing for so flat an ending to the outing, decided to visit her mother.

Taxis were having difficulty in getting through, but buses were moving, if slowly, and on the impulse of the moment she climbed aboard one, mounted the stairs and was borne in stately fashion up Haymarket and Regent Street to Oxford Circus, then along Oxford Street. The view of the crowds could not be bettered and she was so engaged by the new perspective and astonished by the sheer volume of humanity and its riotous joy that she almost forgot to get off. She belatedly recognised Baker Street and managed to descend the stairs, where the conductor refused her proffered half-crown out of sheer holiday spirit – 'No charge today, mum! Got no change, any'ow!' – so she never discovered how much the journey should have cost.

It hadn't occurred to her that her mother would be out, but so she was. However, Oliver was at home, and greeted her with delight. 'I'm so glad you came! I thought I was going to be left alone to celebrate. I don't know where Mum is – she had a list this morning and I suppose you can't expect surgery to wait, but she ought to have been home by now. I was thinking we ought to go to the Ritz for lunch.'

'London's packed with people behaving like mad things,' Violet said. 'It reminds me of that day in August 1914 when a huge crowd gathered in front of the Palace to cheer because war had just been declared.'

'I remember,' Oliver said, and, suddenly serious, 'Hard to think that most of the men in that crowd are dead now.'

Violet nodded. She thought of Laidislaw, and of the young men she had danced with, Kit Dawnay, Peter Hargrave, Tim Beaufort, John French . . . They would never dance again, never come home. 'How can they be happy?' she said. 'How can any of us be happy?'

'Because we're alive. We owe it to them to be happy. We survived because of them.'

A maid came in just then with a telephone message from Venetia: she had been waylaid by the hospital directors, who had more or less kidnapped her for a victory luncheon with the benefactors and other senior surgeons, so she would not be home until some time in the afternoon. So Violet and Oliver went to the Ritz, where they found a crowd of acquaintances so determined to celebrate that there was no choice but to join as a party. It was all very exhilarating. Violet found herself next to Dickie Damerel, who was home on hospital leave and delighted with the thought that perhaps now he would not need to go back. Oliver, she noted, was deep in conversation with Lady Verena Felbrigg, who was in VAD uniform, as she had just come off duty at the Royal Free, but looked extremely fetching in it.

The party looked like going on for the rest of the day, but when she had finished luncheon Violet wanted a change of scene, caught Oliver's eye and dragged him away to walk the few yards down Piccadilly to call on Eddie and Sarah Vibart. At once they were subsumed into their celebrations. The Prince of Wales and some of his friends were coming later and they would have dinner and find some dancing. Violet and Oliver had to send messages home and have evening clothes brought over, for Eddie refused to let them go now they had arrived. So, for the rest of the afternoon they chatted to friends and drank champagne, and leaned out of the windows to watch the crowds milling slowly down Piccadilly. It was wonderful to see the streetlamps come on, and to know there would be no more Zeppelin raids, no more fateful telegrams from the War Office – and perhaps, one day soon, no more rationing.

In St Omer, there was also dancing. The French people were wild with joy. As they had paid the highest price of the war, not just in deaths and mutilations but the destruction of vast swathes of their country, so now their euphoria was correspondingly great. The streets were quickly decked with bunting, some of it very faded and torn after four and a half years out of use. The bells rang constantly, and there were services of thanksgiving, not just in the churches but impromptu on street corners, in public squares, in factory canteens and hospital wards. Wherever civic dignitaries could assemble an audience, there were grand speeches and solemn thanks and the promise of memorials and monuments. The FANY drove that afternoon with flags on their ambulances, French, British, Belgian and American, and as darkness fell they marvelled at the sight of the town lit up, and at the feeling of going out in bright moonlight without stopping to wonder if there would be an air-raid. 'No more bombers' moons,' Bullock said. 'Just moons.'

The restaurants, cafés and bars were full, and overflowed into the streets, and before long someone would turn up with a squeeze-box and someone else with a fiddle, and there would be dancing, right there on the cobbles under the lamps. Old people circled together, silent in almost intolerable relief, soldiers jigged about madly with WAACs and VADs, and French girls made do with the French boys who were too young to have been called up yet, and therefore had all their eyes and limbs, even if their self-esteem had been damaged by the fact that they would never now see action.

Lowson and Hutchinson could not wait to organise a dance of their own, and Emma could not be so churlish as to refuse to join in the celebrations, though she felt only numbness. She could not be glad, except with a detached rationality, about the end of the war. She could not feel, or think, or smile. She did not want to go home. Here in France was the only reality she could recognise, the only place she still had a purpose. But she stitched on a smile and went to the dance, drank the wine that suddenly flowed copiously from previously hidden reserves, danced with the men who, behind their delighted grins and exuberant joy, seemed only marginally less bewildered than she felt.

The one thing that pierced her numbness on the evening of the dance was the announcement made by Armstrong and Captain Savile that they were going to get married next week, unable to wait any longer. The FANYs clustered round them, and when Emma took her turn to embrace her friend, Armstrong caught her hand and said, 'Westie, I want you to be my bridesmaid. Please say you will. Roger and I both want it so much!'

'Of course I will,' Emma said. 'I'm honoured to be asked.'

Savile leaned forward to kiss her cheek and said, 'Thank you, my dear. The honour is ours.'

Tears prickled Emma's eyes, but she blinked them back. She had not cried for Wentworth, and she was damned if she would cry now out of sentiment. She was glad for Armstrong's good fortune, and was sure they would suit and be very happy.

And the wedding was a joyful occasion in which the whole unit joined, even Benson, who followed the bride and brides-maid down the aisle, wearing a huge bow of white ribbon to which the wedding ring was attached, to be delivered to the groom. Emma danced at the wedding feast whole-heartedly; but a few days after that, when she was asked if she would like to move to Poperinghe, she accepted at once, even though Armstrong and Bullock, her particular friends, would not be going.

Ambulances and drivers were needed at Pop, as everyone called it, for a number of reasons. It was a primary route for soldiers going home to Blighty, and for wounded coming back from the northern part of the line. There were hospitals to evacuate and parties of nurses, doctors and officers to move to various locations. But there were also work parties being formed for the enormous task of clearing up, which was already starting – removing shells, unexploded bombs, cordite, wire and all the other war debris – and there were always accidents, some of them horrific, requiring ambulance transport.

The conditions in the work camps were less than ideal, given that winter was coming on in the foggy, swampy region of Ypres, and the Spanish flu was still claiming victims, so a constant stream of the sick swelled that of the wounded. And there were, as the weeks went on, returning refugees, many of them old or ill; and before long, returning prisoners of war, who had been turned out of German prisons in Belgium, and survived on what the Belgians – themselves close to starvation – had spared them. Many were sick, too, after months or years of incarceration in poor conditions with inadequate food.

Emma was glad to go to Poperinghe, glad to be needed, glad to be kept constantly busy. She was relieved also to be in a new place with people she did not know – for the Pop unit was taken from various sources, and only two others went from Unit 8, girls with whom she was not particularly intimate. She wondered whether Hutchinson had offered to send her for that reason, guessing she wanted to be left alone. But it was only a passing, idle fancy. Mostly she didn't think at all, just did her difficult, exhausting job in the ravaged, desolate land.

She had a letter, sent on from St Omer, from Lord

Knoydart, hoping to come and visit her, which she did not answer. But when she did finally receive a visitor, it was one she was not expecting, but was very glad to see, whose presence broke through the film of ice she had allowed to form over herself. It was Violet's friend Freddie Copthall, and he swept down on her with unexpected firmness and took her off to luncheon in a hotel restaurant.

Freddie was so nice and undemanding, and she knew him so well from home, that there was no strain in being with him. He chatted to her without requiring much in the way of answers, telling her that he had been with Haig at his temporary GHQ when the armistice had 'come off'. 'It was a train, you know, in a siding at Cambrai – not very promisin' as far as jolliness went, but these top-brass chappies do themselves all right, so there was a bottle or two of this and that on board.'

'What were you doing there?' Emma asked.

'Oh, Haig was havin' a meetin' with his army commanders, and I'd been told off to go along with General Byng. Did I tell you I'd been moved to Byng's staff?'

'No, I didn't know that. That's rather an honour, isn't it?'

Freddie looked alarmed at the idea of a compliment. 'Lord, no! They just chose me because I had a stiff nanny. Know which fork to use and so on. Staff have to dine an awful lot, you know. Helps to have chaps with decent table manners, that's all.'

Emma found herself laughing, and it felt both painful and good. 'Freddie! That must be nonsense!'

'Fact,' he assured her. 'Felt they could spare me from the fightin' troops, because I'm such a dud. Found my *métier* at last, doin' the polite to the general's dinner guests.'

'Oh, Freddie!'

'Anyway, they were discussin' what to do next, Haig givin' his orders for us to advance across the German frontier. That's our new Front: thirty-two miles wide, from Verviers to Houffalize. Odd,' he added reflectively, 'how it don't matter any more sayin' where we're goin'. Got used to secrecy.'

'We got used to a lot of things that we'll have to get un-used to,' Emma commented.

'Feel sorry for the chaps, you know – the ordinary soldiers. They've been thinkin' as soon as the war was over, they'd be off home – that very minute.' He shook his head. 'Haig was talkin' about the importance of keepin' the troops amused – said the best fighters could be the hardest to deal with when it was quiet. So it sounds as if it'll be a good long while yet for most of 'em.'

'And as long as they're out here, we'll be here,' Emma said, not without satisfaction.

'Saw you on the cinema, by the way, gettin' your medal,' Freddie said. 'Jolly well done! Frightfully proud to know an MM.' Emma shrugged modestly. 'They had the camera chappies out for Haig's conference, too – sent all the generals off afterwards to get themselves cinema'ed. Made poor old Plumer go first. My chap Byng and the rest of 'em chaffin' him and tryin' to make him laugh, actin' like a lot of schoolboys. Might be in one of the pictures myself,' he added thoughtfully, 'standin' behind Byng in the group.'

'I shall look out for you if ever I see the film,' Emma said. 'Imagine, both of us being film stars!'

He laughed heartily at the thought. 'Fancy a spot of cheese to finish off with?' he asked, as the waiter bustled past. '*Garçon!* French cheese ain't much to write home about – not a patch on ours – but it does to fill a hole. Saw Holkam at Cambrai, of course.'

'I was wondering whether you did,' Emma said.

'Oh, yes, hoverin' about at Haig's shoulder like a fright-fully superior butler,' Freddie said, the closest she had ever come to hearing him say anything unkind about anyone. 'He'll be in the picture all right. Very much the man of the hour. That's something Violet's got used to that she'll have to get un-used to – bein' at home without him,' he added. 'Wonder how she'll like havin' him around again.'

Emma didn't answer. Yes, the end of the war was going to throw up a great many things that had been decently buried for four years.

Freddie tacked off on another course. 'Haig was hintin' at some more medals comin' the way of the FANY, by the by. He's no end impressed by you females. Made a very pretty speech about not bein' able to win the victory without the help of all the women, and so on. So you may end up with another gong to put beside your MM.'

'Surely not,' Emma protested.

'True as a gun.' Freddie poured the last of the wine into their glasses. 'One thing about bein' on the staff,' he said with satisfaction, 'you get all the griffin!'

The terms of the armistice signed on the morning of the 11th of November were that the German Army must withdraw, within fifteen days, from all the territories it had occupied in France, Belgium and Luxembourg, and from Alsace-Lorraine, which had been ceded to Germany by the French after the defeat of the Franco-Prussian War. As a further safeguard, during the subsequent sixteen days they were to withdraw from all that part of Germany between the river Rhine and the French border, and were to yield three Rhine bridgeheads to the Allies, at Cologne, Koblenz and Mainz. Mainz was to be held by the French, Koblenz by the Americans, and Cologne by the British. General Plumer was to command the British part of the army of occupation, which was to be called the British Army of the Rhine.

A week after the armistice, Jessie received a letter from Bertie to tell her that his division was to be transferred wholesale to the army of occupation, and that they were under orders at any moment to entrain for Cologne.

Instead of coming home to you, I shall be travelling two hundred miles in the wrong direction! It is very hard, when I had hoped so much to be seeing you within a few weeks, holding you in my arms and renewing acquaintance with young Thomas. It is hard on the men, too, the married ones and those with families. As you can imagine they are extremely fed up, and there is a great deal of muttering. I have to try to put it across to them as an honour – which it is, for there are some units they would not risk sending, but the West Herts have always acquitted themselves well. Comfort yourself, my very dearest, with the knowledge that we shall be well fed and cared for and have light duties, and no-one will be shooting at us! I am trying to look forward to it. I have never been to Germany, and hope to do some sight-seeing. Travel, they say, expands the mind. Some of our fellows do see it that way – the unmarried ones, those who came out lately and are disappointed not to have seen more of the war. They'd as soon go on to Germany as back to the boredom of life at home. Darling, I shall be desperately sorry not to be with you at Christmas. But think what a triumph it is – that most German of rivers, the Rhine, guarded by Tommy Atkins, and the British flag flying over Cologne town hall! It is the greatest expression of our victory, and I shall eat my Christmas dinner in the heart of the Kaiser's territory with all the pride that my men deserve.

After the euphoria of armistice came the anger against the Germans who had started it all. Newspapers were full of demands to 'make the Germans pay', and in the House there were calls for German war criminals to be handed over for prosecution. A general election had been called for the 14th of December, and some of the politicians began courting popular opinion by pandering to the upsurge of hatred. Lloyd George, who had at first been conciliatory, now began calling for the Kaiser and the German military leaders to stand trial, and for all German citizens in Britain to be expelled. Some newspapers, knowing hatred sold copies, fanned the flames, particularly the *Daily Mail* and *The Times*, Lord Northcliffe's organs. For the first time in history, women would be voting, and it was women who had the most cause to hate the Germans, who had stolen their husbands, sons and lovers, and condemned thousands to a life of spinsterhood.

It was also useful for the government to deflect anger onto the Germans, for there was a lot of discontent about the slow rate of demobilisation and the way it was being handled. For the government, in so far as it could spare attention from the election, the priority was to get the right men back into work, so those with essential jobs, like coal miners, were to be released first, regardless of length of service. Furthermore, it made sense in the national interest to release the men who had most recently joined up: having only just left a job, they could be slotted back into it more easily than a man who had been away for years and become institutionalised.

But as it was quite likely that job had originally belonged to the man who had volunteered in 1914, it seemed he was being punished twice for his patriotism, by being kept in uniform and losing his job into the bargain. To the soldiers themselves, the only proper way to organise demobilisation was by length of service, with the longest-serving at the top of the list. In fact, many commanding officers charged with the job ignored the government's instructions and released the men by this rule.

Difficulties multiplied with the slow rate of release: those still in uniform expected to be allowed to 'slack off' now the war was over, and in the absence of anything useful for them to do, they resented being kept to the old routines, parades and fatigues and spit-and-polish, and marching with full kit 'like pack animals'. But if the men couldn't go home, the officers had to maintain discipline, and acts of disobedience had to be punished lest they turn into full-blown mutiny. The government was terrified of Bolshevism spreading from Russia, and tended to see any troop protest as being ideologically motivated. It ordered commanding officers to stamp down hard on any examples of dissent.

After the election, when Lloyd George and the coalition were returned with a majority of 262, the new secretary of state for war, Winston Churchill, turned his attention at last to the problem, and ordered a speeding-up of demobilisation. He said that military needs should be considered as well as industrial. The army must retain large numbers of soldiers for the time being, and essential industry must have its manpower back, but the oldest and longest-serving and those who had suffered most must be let go as soon as possible.

This change of emphasis took time to filter through, and officers were glad to have Christmas parties to plan and pantomimes, concerts and revues to rehearse to keep the men occupied through December. They dreaded the anticlimax that would inevitably follow in January. There were even, mad as it seemed, new men and officers still being sent out. The army machine ground small, but it ground exceeding slow, and was very hard to throw into reverse.

Bertie heard and read about all these things, and felt glad at least to be in Cologne, where the men had a purpose, and the novelty of the place, the people and the situation kept their minds busy.

One day at the end of November, Emma was on her way to collect some medical personnel from a camp when she saw an American mobile canteen at the side of the road. She was a little early, and it was cold, and as it was a long time since her breakfast she decided to have a cup of coffee and a bun to warm herself up. She chatted to the volunteer worker, Amy Beck, a very cheerful young woman with wiry fair hair like an Airedale terrier's. Suddenly the conversation flagged and failed. Amy was staring at something in astonishment. Emma turned too, and saw the most extraordinary collection of men coming down the road.

They were formed up like soldiers, but they were shuffling rather than marching. Instead of one mass of khaki or blue, they were dressed in a motley variety of every uniform used by the Allies since 1914, even down to the red cap and trousers of the original *poilu*. There were Tommies and Doughboys mixed up together with Frenchmen, and even a few Italians in grey-green, and a sprinkling of men in prisoner-of-war drabs, which gave the clue to their identity.

An NCO in charge of them paused in a friendly way to explain that they were prisoners who had been turned out of various camps by their captors, and had made their way somehow to the borders. The different groups had been gathered together and eventually brought by train to Poperinghe, and were now being marched to a repatriation camp.

'They look in a pitiful state,' Emma said quietly, as the column straggled past. They were thin and hollow-cheeked, some had bandages round old wounds, and some limped badly or were supported by others.

'That's right, miss,' the NCO said. 'Most of 'em are half starved. Well, I suppose you couldn't expect the Gerries to feed 'em when they couldn't feed their own sojers. All the same . . .' He sniffed, as if uneasy about offering any excuse for German frightfulness. 'Hun bastards,' he concluded. 'Pardon my French.'

Amy, ever practical, said, 'We have some bars of chocolate under the counter, Sergeant, that we've been keeping for a special occasion. Would you allow us to give it to them?'

'Well, that's right kind of you, miss,' said the sergeant. 'A little bit wouldn't 'urt, though some of 'em is so starved they might chuck it up again.'

Amy pulled out the bars eagerly, and Emma helped her break them up, and then with the pieces on two tea-trays they ran alongside the column offering them to the men. There were smiles and feeble jokes in acknowledgement, and Emma understood that it was seeing a woman again, and the simple act of kindness, that pleased them as much as the chocolate itself. Emma was approaching a man in khaki with RAF wings on his tunic when he halted, disconcerting the man behind him, then stepped out of line to say, 'Emma? Emma, it's me, it's Jack.'

She stared, and then was ashamed that she had not known him, and blushed. She held out her hands, and he took them, but held her away. 'I'd hug you, but I'm lousy,' he said. 'You're looking well!'

'And you look—' He was too thin, his eyes were shadowed and his cheeks were seamed under a bristling of stubble, but in comparison with some of the others he was bonny. 'How are you?'

'Not so bad, considering,' he said. 'I've got some bad sores, and my hair's coming out in clumps, but I think my mother would still recognise me.'

'But how did you get here?'

'Woke up one morning and found our guards had simply scarpered. Left the doors unlocked and hopped it. So we let ourselves out. Afraid it was a trick at first, but we soon heard about the armistice. So then it was a matter of getting home. Had to walk most of the way. People fed us when they could, though they didn't have much themselves.'

'Do they know at home?' Emma asked.

'We were given field postcards yesterday at a camp in Holland. I don't know how long that will take to get there.'

'Sorry, miss.' The column had passed now, and the soldier guarding the rear was waiting impatiently, sympathetic but nervous about discharging his duty. 'Got to get on.'

'I'll write to them,' Emma said. 'When will you get home?'

'I don't know,' Jack said, moving on obediently, looking

back at her over his shoulder. 'Soon, I hope. It was good to see you. That uniform suits you.'

Venetia's pleasure over the armistice was muted by her concern for Thomas. Even the prospect of voting in a general election for the first time in her life could not thrill her beside the worry for his situation. But two weeks into December she had another coded letter from him, which relieved the anxiety for a time. It was dated the end of November.

Siberian forces approaching, Bolsheviks evacuating important units westwards. B says they are to move SOTMA tomorrow, by army truck to Perm II station, then by rail to Glazov. Cheka still to guard them as Red Army not trusted. We shall follow. This must be our chance. Talk is that they will be taken to Moscow in spring where it will be impossible to rescue them. In Glazov or on the journey we will strike. Pray for us. I am well.

As always, there was nothing for her to do but wait. She turned her mind instead to contemplate the satisfaction of knowing that her godson Jack was safe. Helen had called on her way through London to tell her the news: Molly was sufficiently recovered now to be left with their mother.

'It was such a long process getting him back, poor Jack,' she told Venetia. 'When they got to Poperinghe they thought they would be put straight on a train to Calais, but instead they were sent to a repatriation camp nearby. They were told it would only be a forty-eight-hour stay, but even so, any delay would break your heart in a situation like that.'

'I suppose they had to clean them up,' Venetia said.

'Yes, that's what it was,' Helen said. 'They bathed them, cut their hair, deloused them and gave them clean clothes.

And they fed them. Some of them were so far gone in starvation the food made them really ill. It's dreadful to think of.'

'You have to go slowly at first. But you can't expect hungry men to hold back when it's put in front of them.'

'Then they all saw the medical officer,' Helen went on. 'Jack wasn't too badly off, compared with some of them. He's suffering from skin irritation caused by the lice – of course, having been in the RAF he hadn't been exposed to them before he was captured, so he hadn't become inured. And he has septic sores on his chest and down his legs.' She stopped abruptly at the thought of her Jack suffering from such things.

'They'll heal,' Venetia said comfortingly, 'as soon as he has a proper diet again and his body restores itself. How was he treated in the PoW camp?'

'I haven't heard anything about that. He wrote to me from the camp in France to tell me what I've told you. After the two days, they crossed to Dover, and then had another disappointment: instead of being put on a train to Victoria, they were taken up to Dover Castle for a further medical examination. But he was able to telephone briefly to say they were only keeping him one night. The medical officer apparently said he did not want to keep anyone who had been through so much from going home, and asked if he could be sure of getting proper medical treatment there. Jack said his sister was a trained nurse, and that clinched it.'

'So he's going to Morland Place?'

'Yes, and I'm meeting him there. Well, he'll want to see the children, and there are better facilities than at Downsview House.'

'I'm sure you're right. The rest of the family will want to see him, too.'

Helen smiled suddenly. 'It would be cruelty to make his mother wait any longer.'

'Quite,' Venetia said. 'And what happens then? Is he completely free?'

'He has twenty-one days' leave,' Helen said, 'and then he has to go back to his depot to receive his discharge papers, and that will finally be that. He'll be a civilian again, and I shall have him completely at my mercy.' She glanced at the clock. 'I mustn't miss my train.'

Venetia stood up. 'Of course. I won't keep you. Thank you for coming and telling me. I shall hope to hear the rest of the story one day, when you and he have time to visit me again. I'm so glad, my dear, that you and the children will have him home for Christmas.'

'Yes, it is a blessing,' Helen said. 'And only a few weeks ago we were talking about the war lasting another year.'

Molly wrote to Emma to tell her about the rest of Jack's journey, just as Helen had told it to Venetia.

He's now at Morland Place, and he and Helen are staying there for Christmas because it would be simply mean to go away when he's the only bit of cheer they have, poor things, what with Bertie in Cologne, and Lennie in Amiens, with no hope of getting out before January or February, not to mention the three who won't be coming home at all. I believe you will be having Christmas in France, and I hope you will manage to have a little pleasure. I hear that the FANY is wonderfully companionable, and I envy you. It must be nice to have close friends of that sort around one. My work has been rather solitary. I don't know what you mean to do after the war, but when you come back to London I hope you will consider a plan I have just thought of – that we should get a flat together! I certainly mean to go on working, and I know my mother would feel better about my living away from home if I shared with another girl. As you have lost your fiancé and I mean

545

never to marry, we ought to suit very well. Now *do* think about it. I'm sure we could have lots of fun as two gay 'bachelors'!

Emma had not yet thought about 'after the war', though she knew in the back of her mind that sooner or later her work with the FANY would be over and she would have to go home and face life. The idea of going back to the old round of idleness appalled her. The whole purpose of social life to the unmarried girl was to find a husband, and she had no interest in that any more. She had not thought about 'getting a job', but it was certainly better than doing nothing, and sharing a home with another girl was better than living alone. The alternative was to live with Violet. But Lord Holkam would be coming home, and she did not wish to be *de trop*. Besides, as a sort of 'lady companion' to Violet, she would inevitably be pulled back into the social round that would give her mind too little to do. Living with Molly would be fun. Molly was lively and original, and together they could make other friends of a similar mind.

She sighed as she put the letter by, and Benson, who had been dozing on her feet (she was reading the letter in bed), looked up and flattened his ears ingratiatingly at her. 'I know she likes dogs,' Emma said, 'so you'll be all right. Two girls living in a flat, and having jobs. What a strange sort of world we'll be going back to, Benson. Nothing will ever be the same again.' The new world facing her seemed just then too daunting, too strange and uncharted. She turned her mind instead to contemplate the time she still had left as a FANY, and hoped it would be months rather than weeks, despite the cold and terrible conditions.

Venetia, Oliver, Violet and the children were going to Ravensworth for Christmas, to spend it with Venetia's sister Olivia and her husband. But just before Christmas, the plastics unit at Sidcup gave a party for their special friends, and

Violet and Venetia were both invited. Freddie Copthall was home, so Oliver asked him to escort his sister. Holkam was in Paris with the peace conference, and Kit Westhoven would not be having leave until after Christmas. There was still a great deal of ongoing medical work in France, and as his contract did not expire until June, he would certainly not be returning to civilian life before then.

It was a delightful party, with the patients who couldn't go home determined to make the most of the occasion. There was a cinema show, and a pantomime acted by the more mobile patients and made all the more ridiculous by their terrible deformities and strange pedicles, which they played up for all they were worth, because to be laughed at on their own instigation was infinitely better than to be pitied. There was a very great deal of food and drink, and the party ended with dancing, doctors, nurses, guests and patients all mixing together regardless of social position.

Venetia was intrigued to see that Oliver had invited Verena Felbrigg and that he danced with her several times. Venetia knew Verena's mother, Lady Roughton, and thought Verena a nice, sensible girl. She had joined the VAD two years ago when her elder brother Victor had been killed on the Somme, and had only been waiting to be old enough to go and nurse in France – twenty-three was the minimum age, and she was only twenty-two. Her father, the earl, was with Allenby in Egypt. There was another brother, now the heir, at Eton, Venetia remembered, and a younger sister in the schoolroom. As Oliver had never shown any serious attention to any female apart from Jessie, Venetia drew comfort from this new turn of events, and hoped it was a sign that he was ready to settle down at last. It helped a little to take her mind off Thomas, and keep her from wondering where he would be spending Christmas.

She was looking forward to going to Ravensworth, where Olivia and Charlie lived in a small house on the edge of the Southport ducal estate, their childhood home. They would certainly be asked up to the Big House while they were there. Given the armistice, there would probably be a lively party of celebration. As Freddie had no family, she asked Olivia if she could bring him too, for Violet's sake. And before they left Sidcup, she heard Verena Felbrigg saying to Oliver that the Southports had invited her and her mother from Boxing Day for a Saturday-to-Monday, which was all very satisfactory. It was a pity, she reflected, that there was no hunting yet. Verena had the kind of figure that suggested she'd be good on horseback, and there was nothing like the hunting field for fostering romance.

The Morlands' sick were recovering. Ethel's parents were rather pulled by the disease, but after six weeks were well enough to be glad about the armistice and to start planning Christmas festivities. Ethel had come back to Morland Place, where all but two of the maids were back at work, and only Maria was still struggling to regain normal health, looking shrunken, pale and weak. In the circumstances, Denis Palgrave had said nothing more about their getting married – she was clearly not up to it – and their love was still their secret. When she was completely well, they would discuss it again, he thought, and he would approach Mr Morland about his situation. For the moment he was glad to leave things as they were. Maria was being well looked after, and little Martin was happy in the nursery. He wondered if he could have afforded the care they both needed if they had already been living in a house of their own.

James had fully recovered, and though Roberta still had a lingering cough, it did not seem to trouble her greatly. With James back to normal, Teddy began to come out of his shell. He was far from his old cheerful self, but at least he was showing interest in local matters. The one that seemed to take his imagination was the suggestion that a local fund should be got up for a war memorial. Helen, who had no delivery jobs now, had taken over some of Maria's office work, fitting it in between being with Jack and the children, and it was to her that he talked about the memorial, saying that though there would doubtless be many of them in future, he wanted theirs to be the first and best.

It was Helen who had the idea that the Monument might be put to good use. It was a grandiose memorial started by Teddy's brother George, which his bankruptcy and death had left unfinished. It stood on the top of a rise up by what had been the mares' fields, not far from where the army camp now stood. 'It would save a lot of time and money to adapt it, rather than building from scratch,' she said to Teddy, 'and it's in the most wonderful position.'

Teddy saw the point. It would be far bigger and grander that way. He could have the pinnacle finished off in gold leaf, as the original plans had intended: you'd be able to see it for miles around, glinting in the sun. Why shouldn't it be on Morland land? The family had given enough to the war, hadn't they? The Monument had been started as a memorial to George's son, killed in a shooting accident. If Teddy finished it, it would have the names of all the local fallen engraved on it, but to him it would be a memorial to his son Ned. It still hurt him bitterly that Ned had no grave, that he would never know where his poor bones lay.

Discussion of the idea took up many evenings, along with plans for the Christmas celebrations. Henrietta was glad to see Teddy interested in something again, though it could never distract him entirely from thoughts of Alice, especially in the evenings when her empty chair, which no-one quite cared to take over, reproached them from the fireside. It would be nice to have a full house for Christmas, she thought, with Ethel back, Jack and Helen staying on, and Helen's mother and sister coming to stay for it, at Teddy's invitation.

She wished Polly didn't look so peaked and unhappy, though. She wished she knew what was wrong with her, but Polly was masterly at evading subjects she didn't like, and

549

the people who pressed them. There had been a letter from Captain Holford, Henrietta knew, saying his unit was transferring to the Army of the Rhine, so he would not be in England for Christmas. Perhaps that was what was upsetting Polly – that or Lennie's absence. Or perhaps she was just growing up too fast. Eighteen was a difficult age for a girl, the more so in wartime, when the normal things girls did were suspended. It had been a hard year for all of them, she thought, with a sigh, turning the heel of the stocking she was knitting quite automatically. It was khaki, and who would wear it now, after all?

Jessie, sitting nearby and embroidering, laboriously, on a bib for Thomas, looked up at the sigh. She had her new hound pup sleeping against her feet, and a half-finished letter to Bertie in the leather case by her side for when she got tired of sewing. She looked, Henrietta thought, happy and peaceful; a proper matron, with her baby upstairs in the nursery and her husband who would, now, be coming home to her. It had been a hard year, but there had been good things in it, too. Bertie would come home; and if there were ghosts in the corners of the room, of Frank, Robbie and Ned, who never would, they were quiet ghosts now. They had given their lives willingly for what they loved, and should be at peace.

Jessie sensed her mother's thoughts. 'They're here too,' she said, 'watching us. They'll never be far away from us.'

Henrietta nodded. 'I was just thinking that. But if you and Maria and Ethel have let them go, I should too.'

'You gave most of all,' Jessie said. 'More than anyone else. You were their mother.'

550

CHAPTER TWENTY-FOUR

The Spanish influenza went on through the winter, claiming victims in every part of the country and every walk of life. It was still rife among the men at the Front, and rampaged through the demobilisation camps – particularly hard on those who had survived everything the enemy could hurl at them only to succumb to a disease. One such victim was the airman Leefe Robinson, famous for being the first man to shoot down a Zeppelin. He had been at the same prison camp as Jack. He fell sick soon after being repatriated and died at his sister's home on the last day of the year.

Jack fell silent when he was told. He would never talk much about Holzminden, except to say what trumps the other chaps had been. When the family asked if he had been mistreated, he said no. There had been a lot of shouting, and being woken in the middle of the night for pointless roll calls, and being put in solitary confinement for minor breaches of rules that changed without warning. The commandant had been quite potty, he told them, a vulgar little man given to uncontrolled rages, particularly when he was laughed at – which was often, since to laugh at their captors was one of the ways in which the prisoners kept up their spirits.

Another way was to try to escape. In July there had been an audacious mass escape from his camp: twenty-nine officers had got out through a tunnel before it had collapsed on the thirtieth man. Ten had made it back to England, and were later decorated by the King; the other nineteen had been caught and returned to camp, after a local farmer had raised the alarm because they had trampled his field of rye. Jack had not been involved in the escape, for the tunnel had been started in November 1917 and he had only arrived at the camp in April 1918, but he had helped with such things as disposing of earth and sewing escape clothes. Those re-captured had been put into solitary confinement and subjected to constant petty annoyances, like being woken several times a night to be counted, but there had been no serious reprisals, no beatings or executions. Conditions in the camp had been grim and there had never been enough food, he said, but, no, they hadn't been mistreated. It hadn't been a bad place, on the whole. He was sure there were far worse.

As 1918 turned into 1919, Jack remained at Morland Place, for his ulcers had not healed, causing Henrietta and Helen great concern. Jessie said it would be a long process: his general condition had been poor, and until his body was strong again it would be slow to heal itself. But he seemed content to stay where he was, doing little but pottering about the grounds with the adoring Rug, who could never bear to be out of his sight. He read a lot – he had developed a voracious appetite for books – went for gentle walks with Helen and renewed acquaintance with his children.

Helen admitted there was no point in thinking about going home to Wiltshire. There, they would be subject to rationing – it was important to fatten Jack up – and she would have no help with nursing him and tending the children. It was better all round that they should stay at Morland Place until he was completely well. Then he would have to consider what to do next. She thought his best option would be to approach his old friend Tom Sopwith for a job. If successful, they would probably have to move to Surrey, so it was possible they would never go back to Downsview House. Helen contemplated this fate without undue sadness.

She loved their little home, but things had changed so much that perhaps it had served its purpose.

The winter weather was hard, and both Jack and Polly caught bad colds, which frightened the household, who feared it was influenza. Both retired to bed and seemed content to be there. Polly, usually so active and impatient of constraint, went so willingly that Teddy was convinced the Spanish Lady had got her. He hung around her room, neglecting his work, in agony that she, too, would be taken away from him. Jessie tried to reassure him, as soon as Polly developed the streaming eyes and nose of the normal cold, that these were not symptoms of the Spanish flu, but she could not make much of a dent in his fear.

Polly did not hear or heed the agonised whispered conversations about her. When the wretchedness of the cold passed, she went on feeling languid and had no urge to get up. Her room was cosy, with a big fire throwing a rosy light over her familiar furniture and childhood possessions. She was content to lie there and watch the flames, to be fed at intervals and to think of nothing. She wished she might be a child again. The state of grown-upness, to which she had aspired for so long, was painful, and promised nothing but sadness. Erich Kuppel was lost to her. To send the German prisoners back had been a priority of the government, and they were all gone now. A lifetime without him stretched before her, and her only comfort was to lie watching the flames and revisiting her memories of him. As long as she stayed there, she would not have to make any decisions about the future.

Bertie wrote that he was expecting to be in Cologne at least until June; but he got leave in early February. He travelled through atrocious conditions to get home. The snow was down, not only in Germany, which expected it every year, but in England, where heavy falls, coming infrequently, could never be wholly prepared for. Jessie knew how bad the travel would be and how long it would take him. She was in terror that he would catch a cold, which would turn to flu or pneumonia. That was what had killed her father, and she knew Bertie's robustness had been impaired by four and a half years of war.

But when he arrived at last she could see that, though he was tired, cold and heartily glad to be done with travelling, he was in better case than she had seen him for years. The reason was soon apparent: he had been enjoying himself in Cologne.

'Of course I'm well,' he answered her question. 'Light duties, no-one shooting at me, unbroken sleep in a proper bed! How could I not be well?'

'I can see you've put on weight,' Jessie said approvingly. He had been far too thin the last time she had seen him. 'They must be feeding you well.'

'The army has always fed us well. But I'm not doing anything to work it off. No more marching for me. I have a horse again, and a car and driver. I couldn't count the miles and miles of France I've covered on my own two feet, but Germany hardly knows the kiss of my shoe leather.'

Jessie smiled. 'It's good to see you so cheerful.'

He took her hands and kissed her. 'I would sooner be at home with you,' he said, 'but as the army still owns me, I might as well try to enjoy it. Cologne is a handsome city. The cathedral is magnificent, there are art galleries and museums, and wonderful old buildings. And the opera is a very big thing over there. I think we could go to a different one every week if we wanted to.'

'But aren't the people – well, hostile towards you?'

'You can't expect them to be enthusiastic about our presence, but I must say they're always polite. They seem anxious to please us. They serve us with a smile in the shops, and the men say they're very honest about changing French or English money. I think they're just glad the war is over. It was the military and political class who promoted it.

The ordinary people never wanted to fight us in the first place.'

'I suppose they've lost sons and husbands too,' Jessie said grudgingly, unwilling to think well of any German after five years of hating them.

'And they've suffered much worse shortages than back here,' Bertie said. 'I think one of the reasons they don't mind the occupation is that the army is spending money and bringing in supplies.' He smiled suddenly. 'I wrote to you that Cooper was back with me, didn't I?'

'Yes. He must have been furious not to be demobbed,' Jessie said.

'No, darling, he's a regular soldier. The army's his life – though he was cross not to have had some Blighty time. But he was very sniffy about having anything to do with Huns, until he realised the wonderful new wangling opportunities it presented. The local people need *everything*, and Cooper's ready to supply them, as well as ferreting out whatever we officers want. He hasn't been so busy since he was back in barracks in 1914 with his own trading empire. That man will go far,' he laughed, 'as long as he can keep out of gaol!'

Emma was still at Poperinghe, in what was called an 'outpost' of Unit 8. Driving conditions in the Ypres area were atrocious, the roads pocked with shell holes. With the larger holes, on a dry day, it was possible to get down and drive out again in first gear, but on wet days the vehicle would simply sink in, burrowing itself further with every turn of the wheels. And when the holes were filled with water, there was nothing but previous experience to distinguish between a shallow, crossable dip and a deep pit. Then there were the exposed stretches where the mud and slush caused the wheels to skid, so that the ambulances performed an uneasy waltz back and forth across the road, with the driver praying they would not meet something coming the other way or end up in the ditch.

The surroundings were desolate, lakes of brown and greasy water, abandoned guns, barbed wire, ammunition boxes and shell cases, burned and wrecked tanks sinking slowly into the morass like dying prehistoric beasts, no house intact, the tortured trees nothing but splinter-headed stumps, no blade or leaf of greenery anywhere. It was impossible to imagine the tidy farms, fertile fields, peacefully grazing cattle and miles of fruit trees in blossom the area had once boasted. The only thing that could raise the spirits was the knowledge, to be repeated to oneself every hour or so, that the Germans were beaten and gone, and that there was no danger now of being fired on.

As well as her normal work, Emma was detailed to take parties of nurses, doctors, military men and visiting politicians on guided tours of the battlefields. The military excursions were the most lively, as old battles were revisited and disagreements arose as to who had done what at which particular spot. The arguments grew heated when it came to the question of whether what had happened *should* have happened. 'Why didn't you advance when you were ordered?'; 'You were told to take that position by nine o'clock'; 'You didn't send up the reserves I asked for'; 'Why did you ignore my request for more ammunition?' The nurses, by contrast, usually began the tour in high spirits, because any outing was a welcome break with routine, and ended very sober and reflective, having seen how appalling it really was.

One military outing stopped in the middle of the day up at Tyne Cot, near Passchendaele, on the ridge that encircled the Ypres basin. Here there was a military cemetery, which was being enlarged by bringing in the dead from smaller burial grounds in the area: the intention was to make it a memorial to the dead and missing. The place got its name from the German pillboxes that had been there earlier in the war, which the Northumberland Fusiliers had said resembled typical Tyneside cottages. From Tyne Cot there was a fine view over most of the old Ypres Salient, right down to the shattered remains of the city, and the military gentlemen had brought with them a picnic luncheon, over which they refought the various campaigns in which they had been involved.

Emma got tired of listening to them, and took Benson for a walk down the road that wound along the ridge from Langemaark to Passchendaele. It was peaceful being with Benson, for the world to him contained no past or future, no hopes or regrets, no sorrow over the ruin of the land: to him, the Ypres Salient was simply a collection of smells, some that were interesting and some that were not. She was waiting for him to finish investigating a hole under a large tussock of grass, when a military motor passed her, halted and backed up level with her. Next to the driver, well bundled up in his greatcoat against the cold, was Angus Knoydart.

'Emma! Well met! I recognised your coat as we passed. What are you doing here?' He looked around for a motor. 'Not stranded? Do you need a lift?'

She came across to him. 'No, I'm just stretching my legs. The car is back there. I've brought a party of brass on a sightseeing trip, and they're just having their sandwiches and refighting Second Ypres.'

'Lord! I'd have thought once was enough,' he said. 'I'd heard about these trips. Didn't know they'd roped you in on it.'

'Oh, it makes a change from the other stuff, evacuating hospitals and transporting PoWs. So you're still here?'

'Not for much longer, thank the Lord,' he said. 'My unit's standing down next month, so I hope to be out of it all and a free man by the first of April.'

'And what will you do when you're a civilian again?'

'I haven't absolutely decided yet. Of course there's the estate, which needs attention, but I'm not sure I want to shut myself up there permanently. I've got used to having company and plenty to do. I was rather thinking of finding something down south – a business, perhaps. Of course, I shall have to look into the state of my investments, which will keep me in London for a while.' He seemed pleased with the idea, and perhaps his pleasure was not unconnected with his next question. 'What about you? You must be coming to the end of your service?'

'They're looking to disband our unit in the spring,' Emma said, stuffing her hands into her pockets. There was a cold wind along the top of the ridge here; but it was so comfortable talking to an old friend, especially one so easy to get along with as Knoydart, that she had no desire to cut the conversation short. 'But I've heard unofficially that there's likely to be work out here at least until June. If there is, I shall volunteer for it. I'm not ready to go home yet.'

'I'd have thought anyone working with the wounded would have had more than enough.'

'But I'm not sure what I'll be going back to.'

He nodded. 'It must be hard to adjust, when you'd expected to be married by now. But you're a wonderful girl, and one day you'll find someone else.'

I already had, she thought, but she didn't say it. 'The one thing I'm not going to do,' she said instead, firmly, 'is waste my life parading myself like a prize cow on the marriage market. I must have something to do, not just go from party to party, following the Season.'

'I quite agree,' he said. 'I enjoy society as much as the next man, but I've got used to being busy. One must do something.'

'*You're* all right,' Emma said. 'You can take up your seat in the Lords. There'll be plenty for Parliament to do, rebuilding everything.'

His eyes lit as the idea came to him. '*You* could stand for the Lower House. You could become an MP!'

'I'm too young.'

'No, no, I read about it somewhere. The vote was only

for women over thirty, but the Qualification Act allows them to stand for Parliament at any age after twenty-one. I remember there was a polemic in the newspaper about the anomaly.'

'Are you sure? But, anyway, I really hadn't thought of a political career.'

'Your father was an MP. You have the background, and your name would carry weight.'

She shook her head, but the idea was intriguing, and one always needed meaty things to think about while driving. She was sure Vera would thoroughly approve of the whole idea. She would be sure to know what to do, and be eager to help her: she'd probably write her speeches for her! 'I'm not sure,' Emma said, 'whether I'd like it. It might be rather dull.'

'Never that!' he said. 'Think what fun we could have, you in the Lower House and me in the Upper! We could join forces and start a campaign.'

'A campaign for what?'

'Oh, we'll think of something,' he said airily. His driver coughed, and he said, 'Yes, all right, Simpson. Emma, I have to go – but let's keep in touch when you get back to Blighty.'

'Write and give me your direction when you know where you'll be,' she said, and gave him her hand. And then she smiled. 'Though I suppose I could always contact you through the House of Lords!'

Polly had a letter from Captain Holford, which she took away to her room to read. She was up and about now, having no excuse to remain bed-ridden, but a fire was kept in all day on Teddy's orders, in case she should feel the need at any point to lie down and rest. He was still nervous about her, and was quite glad that she did not seem to want to racket about on horseback in this terrible weather.

She sat in the chair by her fireside, with Kai and her new dog, Silka, across her feet, and opened her letter. It began with the news that Holford was going to be demobilised at the end of February.

As soon as I'm free of the army, I shall be in a position to join my father in the business, which of course will be mine one day. But before I settle to that, there is something else I have set my heart on, and I think you know what it is. I mean to come down to Yorkshire and propose to you in person as you deserve, but I feel I ought to set the record straight at the earliest opportunity. I could not speak before because I did not know when I would be free, and I hope you did not think my silence meant I was indifferent. Now I am in a position to lay everything before you fair and square, and so, dear Miss Morland, will you marry me? I shall tell you when I come to see you all about your myriad personal charms, so please take that as read for the moment, and let me tell you instead what my plans are. First, to be married as soon as possible. St Margaret's, Westminster, I think. Then a honeymoon. With Germany defeated the world is our oyster again. We shall go to America. The long sea-voyage will be a chance for us to be alone together, and then we shall have all the excitements of New York. I mean to expand my father's business in the New World, so I shall have some affairs to attend to, but there will be plenty of shopping and sight-seeing for you to do while I'm engaged. When we tire of New York we can go on to Boston and Washington, which I hear are well worth visiting. We could take two to three months about it altogether. When we get back to England, we'll take a country house for the summer, which will give us time to look for a suitable house in London. A permanent country place can wait until next year.

You will have time now to plan your wedding dress and make out your guest list. I have, of course, told my parents about my intentions, and my mother is very happy to organise the wedding. It will be more convenient for her to make the arrangements, seeing she is in London, but of course your own people will want to be involved. As soon as I am back I think we should arrange for my people to meet yours – perhaps a Saturday-to-Monday at our place or yours. All these details shall be ironed out, my dear Polly, as soon as you write back to tell me you accept, because frankly, I cannot wait until March to hear it from your own perfect lips. Write soon and relieve my anxiety.

As Polly read the letter, she thought how excited she would have been to receive it only a few months ago. Her first proper proposal – that was, from a grown-up man, not an infatuated boy with no present hope of fulfilling the matter. And it was Holford, whom every girl in York had wanted, the handsome, sophisticated, charming Holford, who carried such an air of the wider world about him. She would have been so gratified, thinking of the other girls' envy that he had picked her.

But any pleasure she might have had in the compliment had no weight against her sadness. And was it even a compliment? He spoke of anxiety, but there was no hint in his letter that he had any doubt of being accepted. He had planned everything without asking her opinion, the wedding, the honeymoon, the life afterwards. St Margaret's, Westminster, where all the top people got married, would have been a social triumph; but it would break her father's heart if she were not married in the chapel at Morland Place. A girl was married from her own home – that was the tradition.

Holford wanted to take her away from it all. His vision of their life together did not include Morland Place. She saw now, from her new perspective, that he was not like her: his interests were quite different from hers. A house in

London, a place in the country (probably in Surrey, like his parents'), everything revolving round his father's business, which would one day be his. A Town life, with a little bit of carefully manicured country thrown in merely for social purposes: *his* life. But Polly belonged to the land she had grown up on, something Holford would never understand. She couldn't marry any man who wanted to remove her from what gave her life.

In that moment, staring into the fire, with Silka's body across her feet and Kai snoring gently as he toasted his belly, she thought that she would never be able to do it. And that meant she could never marry, for the chance of finding a man who wanted to live at Morland Place with his in-laws was very small.

The odd thing was that, as she thought it, the feeling that accompanied the decision was relief. She would never get married. She knew it with the certainty of eighteen; and that was good because she didn't want to. The man she loved was lost to her for ever and she would never love again, and marriage without that perfect love was not to be contemplated. She was Polly Morland of Morland Place, now, and for ever.

It was in March that Denis Palgrave finally made official his desire to marry Maria. She was sufficiently restored to health to begin to feel the awkwardness of the situation. As strength slowly returned to her, she wanted to be with him properly, and she hated any shadow of subterfuge. He insisted, however, on speaking to Teddy alone, saying it was something best settled between men. Teddy was, as it were, *in loco parentis* to Maria: he wanted to ask him for her hand in form.

So one day, when the children were having their dinner, he went down to the steward's room. At a raise of his eyebrow, Maria excused herself and slipped out, leaving a slightly surprised Teddy waiting to know what he wanted.

Palgrave clasped his hands behind his back, cleared his throat, and said, 'I have something I wish to ask you, sir, or tell you, but first of all I would like to say how happy I have been here, and how grateful I am to you for taking me on, when few would have given me the chance. You have been kindness itself, and I shall never forget it.'

'Good God,' Teddy said. 'What is all this? Never forget it? Are you leaving? What have we done wrong? If there's any little thing I can change—?'

'No, sir, no, sir,' Palgrave said hastily. 'It's nothing like that. The fact of the matter is – oh, this is difficult! Well, I had better just come out with it. Maria and I have fallen in love, and I want your permission to marry her.'

Teddy stared blankly for a moment, then pleasure spread slowly across his face. 'You and Maria? I never thought – of course, you do spend a lot of time together. And you're both so bookish. And little Martin's already fond of you. You ought to suit very well, very well indeed. I give you my blessing with all my heart, my dear fellow!' He frowned. 'But we shall have to think about the arrangements. The priest's room is a bachelor room – designed that way, of course. It won't do for a couple.'

Palgrave interrupted as soon as he could, though he felt a cad for it. 'Sir, Maria and I both feel it would be too awkward to go on living here as a married couple.'

Now Teddy looked taken aback. Half his pleasure in the news was the thought of securing the two of them from ever leaving. He hated people to leave. 'Nonsense,' he said. 'A house this size has room for everyone. Any arrangement you want can be accommodated.'

'Maria wants a home of her own,' he said awkwardly. 'She wants to bring up her own child. I don't want to leave your service, sir, but Maria's wishes must come first.'

'A home of her own, eh?' Teddy's mind was already searching for a way round the problem. 'What about the gatehouse? That's empty at the moment.' He read the priest's face and went on quickly, 'Too small and too gloomy. Not the right place to bring up a child. Though you could leave Martin here in the nursery. No, of course, Maria wants him to herself. Well, well, women have their little fancies. Now, look here, you must just leave this to me. I'll find you somewhere, don't fret.'

'Sir, I shall have to leave your service,' he said anxiously, 'and try to find something else. A salaried position, if not a living, so that I can keep a wife and child.'

'But you've got a salaried position here. What's the point in finding another? You must stay! We've just got used to you. Now, don't worry!' His lifted his hands placatingly as Palgrave tried to speak. 'You shall have your house and Maria shall have her home, but it shall be near enough for you to come in by day, so that you can tutor the children and serve the chapel. And that way Martin can still grow up with his cousins. You wouldn't want to take him away from them, now would you?' he concluded beguilingly.

'No, of course not, but—'

'And any other little ones you and Maria may have,' Teddy continued, 'you'll want them to be part of the Morland Place family. There are one or two nice cottages I can think of, and if they don't suit, there are plenty of houses in the town. It can all be arranged, my dear chap, with no trouble. It's not the time to go looking for a position, believe me. You'd end up a schoolmaster, and you couldn't support a wife and child properly on that. And we can't do without you. Stay here, and I'll find you a house. Now, are you happy with that?'

It would have taken a more determined man than Palgrave to deny Teddy, and in truth Palgrave didn't want to deny him. He didn't want to leave his cure at Morland Place, and this way, it seemed to him, he and Maria would have the best of all worlds.

'If Maria is happy, I am,' he said. 'I must put it to her first, but—'

564

'Yes, of course. Maria shall have her choice and be satisfied, I promise you.'

'You are very generous, sir, and I shall be glad not to leave my post.'

'Good, good. We'll call it settled. And then,' he added, with relish, 'there'll be a wedding. You'll get married in the chapel here, of course? We'll have the fellow from the village in – always liked him – unless you have some friend you'd rather have do it? Oh, this will be prime!' He rubbed his hands. 'A wedding in the house! Weddings are the best of all celebrations. The women shall have new dresses and that will make them chirp like birds, and Mrs Stark likes nothing better than making wedding cakes. I think you've hit on the very thing to make the house buzz again! It's just what we need to cheer us up after this terrible war and the influenza and everything.'

Palgrave went off to find Maria, hoping the compromise would go down all right with her; amused at the thought that Uncle Teddy was probably now convinced the whole thing had been his idea.

Six months had passed since Thomas had been posted missing in August. Now in March the War Office wrote to Venetia again, to say that in the absence of any information as to the whereabouts of Colonel Lord Overton, or of any contact with him, it was obliged to assume he was dead and to post him 'believed killed'.

'This is a mess,' Oliver said. 'You'll have to make him come home now.'

'But I don't know where he is,' Venetia said. 'I haven't heard from him since the beginning of December.'

And in January Colonel Browning had come to tell her gravely that they had 'lost track' of the Romanovs. The women had been moved from Perm, but then had 'disappeared'; no further news of them could be gleaned from any of the sources. She had wondered even then if Browning were telling her everything. She was in a small circle within the intelligence circle, privileged to received information denied to others. But was there yet another circle within that, from which she was excluded? Nothing seemed more likely. The thing about secret-service work was that you never knew for sure when you had got to the heart of things. Did Browning really know more that he couldn't tell her? But surely, *surely*, if he knew where Thomas was, he would tell her at least that he was alive?

She stared at her younger son bleakly and said, 'Oh, Oliver, I think he *may* be dead.'

Oliver was silent. There was no comfort he could offer his mother. She knew far more about the situation than him. 'What happens,' he said at last, 'if he is assumed dead?'

'The lawyers will have to be told. I believe in the case of someone being missing, a period of seven years has to elapse before they're legally declared dead. Then the title and the estate will pass to you.'

'But I don't want them!' he cried.

'Nevertheless,' Venetia said, 'that is what will happen.'

'Can't we keep it secret?'

'Darling, not possibly. The War Office will include him in the list they send to *The Times*. It's bound to get out. In fact, we'll be lucky if it doesn't make a newspaper splash. The Earl of Overton missing in Russia? They do so love anything about people being murdered by Bolsheviks.'

Oliver blenched. 'Don't say that.'

'I have to face it as a probability. I haven't heard from him. And he hasn't drawn any money since December.'

'I never asked you, because I felt you wouldn't want to tell me, but how did he get hold of his money?'

'I arranged for a sum to be deposited for him to draw under a false name. He had an identity as a Swiss doctor.'

'Good Lord! How very – cloak and dagger!'

'You would have to know eventually, anyway. When you take over the estate—'

'Don't say "when",' Oliver objected. 'I tell you, I don't want the estate. It's Thomas's, and I don't believe he's dead. He'll pop up somewhere. Not even the Reds would be mad enough to kill him.'

Venetia shook her head sadly. 'They operate by rules of their own now, which are hardly rules at all. If he gets in their way, they'll kill him without a second thought.'

Oliver sat down beside her. 'Well,' he said, 'if you're determined to believe he's dead, and I'm to be forced to become the earl, you had better tell me everything. All the details, right from the beginning. I think I deserve it.'

'Yes,' Venetia said wretchedly, 'I suppose you ought to know.'

It was work enough for the lawyers when there was an orderly transition of title and estate, but the fact that the incumbent was only 'missing believed killed' made the process even longer-winded. Temporary arrangements had to be put in place while enquiries were pursued, but the solicitor confessed he had little idea *how* enquiries were to be made inside Red Russia in its present state of turmoil.

Oliver didn't care how long it took. Apart from remaining convinced Thomas was alive – or, rather, not being convinced he was dead – he was discovering, now that it looked likely, how much he had never wanted to be earl. He had his own plans. His term of contract with the army expired at the end of February, but the work at Sidcup would be going on for some time yet, and he had been re-engaged on a short contract as a civilian doctor. Kit Westhoven would be finished at the end of June, and when he came back, Oliver meant to talk to him about setting up somewhere together. But if Kit didn't want to, he would do it alone.

It did occur to him that the money from the earldom would be useful, but there was too much else involved with being earl that he didn't want, and he was afraid that once he got sucked in, he would never get out again. And aside from all that, he had loved his brother. They had been very close in childhood, and though they had led their later lives apart, he didn't want him to be dead. So he went on stubbornly believing, and prayed nightly for good news.

Venetia mourned her son the more bitterly for the element of doubt that would always hang about the loss. She appreciated better than ever how Jessie must have suffered when Ned was declared missing. Jessie was coming to London for a visit in April, to stay with Violet for Easter. All her fears and uncertainties were resolved now, and Venetia was glad. Her own, she supposed, would never end.

It was a week before Easter, and Venetia was returning home from visiting Lady Sarah Vibart. The Vibarts' new baby, born in February, rejoiced in the suitably regal names of George Albert Edward Victor. He had been christened in the Chapel Royal, and the Prince of Wales had stood sponsor, which boded well for his future career. And Eddie was proving a touchingly fond father.

As she trod up the steps to her house, a shadow detached itself from the gloom of next-door's railings and flitted towards her. She turned with a jump, fearing she was going to be attacked and robbed – such things had become sadly commonplace during the blackout years – but the figure halted and raised its hands defensively.

'No, lady. No, lady. No hurt you,' he said, in a thick accent. It was a bearded man, tanned of skin, wearing baggy, ill-fitting trousers and a heavy pea-jacket, with a cap pulled down over his eyes, and a kit-bag slung on his shoulder. He looked dirty and rough, his nails were black, and his nervous grin revealed several missing teeth.

'What do you want?' she asked sharply, mentally calculating the distance to the front door. She edged up another step to give herself some advantage.

'Got message,' the man said. He was standing quite still, and now he dropped his hands to his sides as if further to demonstrate his disinclination to attack.

568

'A message for me?' Her heart quickened. If there was to be a message from Thomas, this was just how it might arrive. The man, now she inspected him, was probably a seaman – the beard and the dark skin suggested it. 'Give it to me.'

'You Lady O-ver-toon?' he said, in a way that suggested he had had trouble learning it.

'I am Lady Overton. Give me the message.' She held out her hand.

'Man say you give me money for message. Five pound.'

'Yes, I will give you five pounds. Give me the message.'

A disconcerted look passed over his face. He had not expected her to agree so readily; now he wished he had asked for ten. But he regarded the firmness of her face and thought better of renegotiation. He shrugged and took out from his pocket a folded square of paper.

Venetia was trembling inside, but her hand was surgeon-steady as she took it. Apart from the messenger's, Thomas's hand must have been the last to touch it. It was almost like touching him. It was stiff writing-paper with a linen finish, unlike any paper that had been available in England for years, and it was slightly grubby from transit, but otherwise undamaged. She unfolded it.

Her heart was beating so hard that for a moment she could not focus on the writing. It was in capital letters, in pencil, soft pencil that made thick, dark marks on the white surface. When her tumbling senses stilled enough to make it out, she read: 'I AM SAFE IN A SECRET PLACE. BE AT PEACE. ALL IS WELL.'

She drew a long breath, of hope mixed with disappointment. Was that all? Why was it written in capitals? Was that even his writing? Yet who else would send her secret messages? She wanted so much for it to be from Thomas, her first-born, her dear son; but there was so little here to hold on to.

'Five pound?' the man urged.

'Yes,' she said heavily, and began to feel for her bag. 'The man who gave you this, what did he look like?'

The man shrugged. 'Big coat, hat, not see much. Very cold.' He mimed huddling down into a big coat, pulling his hat over his eyes.

'Where did you meet him?'

He looked wary. 'Not to say. Secret. Quick, quick, give me money. Maybe someone come.'

She took out a five-pound note. The man's fingers fastened on it but she did not release her end. She looked into his eyes. 'He's my son. *Please*. Where was it?'

Something changed in his eyes. There was, perhaps, sympathy, a warmth of humanity, that had not been there before. He seemed to contemplate some decision; then, without letting go of the banknote, he reached his other hand into an inside pocket and drew something out, which he offered to her. 'Send this for you,' he said, and a little shrug told her he had been meaning to keep it.

He laid it in her palm. It was a religious medal, such as Catholics and Orthodox Christians wore round their necks or carried in their pockets. Silver, with the raised likeness of a saint – cheap and poorly executed so that it was not possible even to tell which saint it was.

Her fingers on the banknote must have relaxed, for a little tug pulled it from her and he pocketed it with amazing swiftness and melted into the dusk. On the back of his kit-bag she could see the stencilled word 'Mitsui' as he swung round the corner.

Venetia trod slowly up the steps, feeling cold and slightly sick, as though she had had a shock. But her mind was working. Mitsui? She had heard of the Mitsui company – in fact, she rather suspected she had shares in it. She must check with her man of business: he had got their money out of Germany when the war began and reinvested it in neutral places, and she thought Mitsui – trading, mining and banking, one of the oldest private banking companies in Japan – might have been one of them. And Japan had been one of the destinations mooted for the Romanovs, when there had still been hope of getting them out. There were docks in Tokyo – no doubt Mitsui had berths there – with regular routes to Vladivostok. Was he, then, in Tokyo, her lost son?

All is well. Did that mean he had got them out, the women – or some, or at least one of them? If they had all been lost, surely he would have come home? He would have told the sailor not to reveal where he was. The Reds would hunt them down if they got any clue of their whereabouts. Their safety depended on no-one's ever finding them.

On the other hand, those capitals might have been anyone's, and the message was so general as to be meaningless. Would not Thomas have written in his own hand, and told her something more than 'I am safe'? Had the sailor met someone who had been involved in passing one of the other messages, been told that Lady Overton was good for cash in exchange for a note, and concocted one? And the silver medal: Thomas had never worn or carried anything like that, but they were freely available in shops all over Russia – including, one supposed, at Vladivostok docks. Five English pounds was a high price for a cheap silver medal and a folded sheet of writing-paper. If it was a trick, it had turned a good profit.

She went into her house, locking the strange little interlude deep inside her. Whether it were a true message or not, Thomas must remain dead so that no-one would look for him. She felt the shape of the medal in her palm, and wondered, as perhaps she would wonder for the rest of her life, if he had sent it to her in the absence of anything else to hand, to convey to her his love and comfort. The alternative was that he was dead, tumbled into an unmarked grave in the endless forests of Russia. All she had to cling to was the hope that she would receive another message one day. But she was an old woman: she longed to see him, but she knew the odds were that they would never meet again.

★   ★   ★

Jessie had been taking a walk in Green Park while Violet had a fitting. The weather was just mild enough, after a cold start to spring, to make walking pleasant, and it had been good to see the flowering shrubs beginning to bud, and the trees getting their leaves. Now she was stepping along Piccadilly on her way back to Violet's house. She was enjoying her holiday, though she missed little Thomas more than she would have expected. Violet had begged for her company, and promised her entertainment, parties, the latest shows – all the things she did not get in Yorkshire. It was a nice way to pass a few weeks while she waited for Bertie to come home.

She was approaching the Ritz when she had to stop to allow a woman to push a wheelchair across the pavement in front of her to the hotel entrance. The woman was tall, handsome, perhaps about Jessie's own age, wearing a very well-cut navy coat and dress and a hat whose width and flatness pronounced it to be this year's. There was something in her carriage and the way she pushed the chair that made Jessie think she had been a nurse. One of those many girls from good families who had become VADs, she thought, as one recognising a sisterhood.

The man in the chair looked older, in his forties or fifties, with grey hair, cut very short. The little of his face Jessie could see – it was turned away from her – was hospital pale. He was wearing a dark overcoat, and the tartan rug over his lap did not disguise from the professional eye that he had lost both legs. It was a common enough sight, these days, but she felt a pang of pity. It must be such a hard thing for a man to come to terms with.

All this passed through her mind in the few seconds it took for the chair to be wheeled from the kerb to the door. The woman, turning the chair to back through the door, laid a hand tenderly on the man's shoulder, and he turned his face up to smile at her; then, as the chair swung round, he looked straight at Jessie.

Her heart seemed to stop. The huge shock clutched at

572

the pit of her stomach and the hairs on her neck stood up. It was Ned. She knew she was staring unbecomingly but could not help it. The doorman hastened to the woman's aid and the couple passed on into the hotel, but Jessie stood where she was on the pavement, struck rigid, her mouth dry.

It couldn't have been Ned. Of course it wasn't Ned. Ned was dead. Besides, the man in the chair was much older. Ned would have been thirty-three if he had lived, and that man looked ten or fifteen years older than that. His pale face was deeply lined, his eyes pouched, his hair silver at the temples. And he had looked straight at her without the slightest flicker of recognition.

And yet – and yet . . . Something in her had jumped in recognition, and it wasn't because he resembled Ned as she had known him. A man coming up behind walked round her, lifting his hat but saying in a very testy voice, '*Excuse me!*' which made her realise she could not stand there like someone struck by lightning, blocking the pavement.

She began to move on, and then, on a mad impulse, turned and went into the hotel. The couple had disappeared from view. She went up to the reception desk, where a small, elderly man in hotel uniform came to her at once with an eager smile. Men who had jobs, these days, had to look after them.

'*Yes*, madam, *can* I help you?'

It would be foolish, having come this far, not to ask, at least. But she felt herself blushing with shame as she said, 'A lady came in just now, pushing a wheelchair. I saw them from a distance and thought I recognised them, but I can't quite place . . .'

The man did not need her to justify her curiosity. 'Yes, of *course*, madam! They are staying at the hotel. Mr and Mrs Smith – Mr John Smith.' As Jessie looked blank, he added, 'Mrs Smith was a Miss Linscott before she married, daughter of Sir Gerald Linscott, the MP.'

It really would be too ill-bred to push it any further, so she said, 'Ah, yes, that must be why I recognise her.'

'Would you care to leave a message, madam?' the eager one asked, his hand drifting towards the notepaper on the desk.

'Oh, no, thank you – the acquaintance was quite slight,' Jessie said. She stitched on a conspiratorial smile. 'It was idle curiosity on my part. Quite unforgivable.'

'Oh, not at *all*, madam,' he said. '*Most* understandable. Is there anything else I can assist you with?'

'Thank you, no,' Jessie said, turning away. It wasn't Ned, of course it wasn't. How could it possibly have been, anyway? He was dead these four years. She felt she had made a fool of herself, and decided to stop and have a cup of coffee, to make amends to the hotel, as it were. She went into the Palm Court, where she sat down at a table in the furthest corner. There was only one other guest there, an elderly man on the far side who had nodded off over his teapot and newspaper. The waiter came to her at once, a man in his fifties with friendly eyes and a fatherly face. She liked the look of him, and when he brought her coffee, she smiled as she thanked him.

Seemingly encouraged, he said, 'Excuse me, madam, but I couldn't help overhearing you asking about Mr and Mrs Smith.' He paused, to see if she would rebuke his impertinence.

Jessie felt her stomach churning, though she wasn't sure why. Her hands felt cold. She heard herself saying, 'Do you know them?' She was committed now to hearing what she suddenly felt she didn't want to know. It wasn't just ill-bred – it might even be dangerous.

'Oh, yes, madam. I've known Mrs Smith – Miss Linscott as was – since a child. Her father, Sir Gerald, always stayed here when he came up, and he often brought Miss Linscott with him. A very pretty, pleasing child she was. They had a party here for her coming-out – that would be in, oh, nineteen ten, I think it was.'

'And Mr Smith?' she asked, as casually as she could.

'That's a very sad story, madam, very touching,' the waiter said, and paused to see if she wanted to hear it.

There were no other customers, no-one in earshot – even the man on the desk was at the far end with his back to them, bent over a ledger. Her curiosity was piqued, and no-one would ever know she had given in to it. 'Do tell me, if you please.'

The waiter was plainly glad to oblige. 'Well, madam, Miss Linscott was engaged to a very nice gentleman before the war, but when the war broke out he went into the Royal Flying Corps and, to cut a long story short, he was shot down before they could get married.'

'How sad,' Jessie said.

'Yes, madam. But like many another brave young lady she decided to serve her country by joining the VAD, and she nursed right through the war.'

'I guessed she was a nurse,' Jessie said. 'How did she meet Mr Smith?'

'Well, madam, at the armistice, the Germans were anxious to get rid of all their sick PoWs as soon as possible, and they evacuated a whole lot from a prison hospital in Holland and dumped them in the hospital in Belgium where Miss Linscott was nursing.'

'And Mr Smith was one of them?'

'You've guessed it, madam – though Mr Smith isn't his real name.'

Jessie felt her stomach twist again. 'Oh?'

'Or I should say,' the waiter corrected himself, 'that no-one knows what his real name is.' He took up the coffee pot and refilled her cup. 'When he was captured he was badly wounded. Head and legs. The Gerry doctors had to take the legs off to save his life. And when he came round, he'd lost his memory completely.'

'Wouldn't there have been an identity disc?' Jessie asked faintly.

'There can't have been, madam, because they'd no idea who he was. Put him down as John Smith, and he was in different prison hospitals the whole of the war. When Miss Linscott found him he was in a poor way. The Gerries didn't have much to spare by the end, and the hospital cases were all half starved, she says. But she nursed him back to health, and then, having buried her heart, as they say, when she lost her fiancé, she decided she couldn't do better than to dedicate her life to a man who'd lost everything serving his country.'

'It's a touching story,' Jessie said with difficulty. 'And he still has no idea who he is?'

'Not the faintest memory of anything at all, madam. Can't even remember which battle he was captured in. But Miss Linscott says she knew right away he must have been a gentleman before the war.'

'I wonder his people didn't make enquiries about him,' Jessie said.

'Well, if they did, madam, they wouldn't get any answers, would they? Being as he hadn't got a name. Gerry didn't even know he was an officer. And, frankly, their records weren't up to much. Ever so many prisoners of war weren't on any list at all. You hear every day of men coming back from PoW camps that their families thought were dead all along.'

'So she married him,' Jessie said, more to herself than to the waiter.

But he answered, 'In February, down at Sir Gerald's place in Sussex. I saw the photographs in the *Tatler* – very nice. And now she's brought him up to visit the limb hospital at Roehampton to see if they can fit him with artificial legs.' He glanced round. 'Excuse me, madam, while I attend to these ladies.'

Two women, carrying small dogs, had come into the Palm Court, and he went to seat them and take their order.

Jessie drank her coffee, her thoughts in turmoil. She had

seen young faces seamed with pain often enough while she was nursing: suffering could easily age a man ten years. And Ned's batman had told them Ned had had a head wound and been hit by shrapnel in both legs. But there must have been many thousands of men with leg wounds, and hundreds at least who had lost their memory from head injuries or shell shock.

She remembered the blank look he had given her, without spark of recognition. She remembered his companion, the sensible nurse's hands gripping the handles of the chair, the brisk, efficient walk, the pretty, careworn face. She remembered the tender touch on the man's shoulder, and the smile that had passed between them. Whoever he was, he was in good hands now, and a broken-hearted young woman had found a man to love and a new meaning for her life.

She finished her coffee without tasting it, put the cup down in the saucer, stared into its empty depths. To find out more – even to ask the questions – risked everything. The ugly word 'bigamy' squatted in a corner of her mind like a spider. She saw Morland Place, her mother and Uncle Teddy. She saw Bertie and her own little Thomas. She had more than half a suspicion that she was pregnant again. She was only waiting for Bertie to come home in June to begin her new life, her real life. The world before the war was impossibly far off now, like a child's tale, or a dream of a distant land. Nothing in it was real any more.

Ned was dead. They had all – even Uncle Teddy – laid his memory to rest at last. And John Smith, whoever he was, had a new life, a new family, and the love of a good woman. He had suffered enough for his country. Let him have a little peace.

The waiter finished serving the two women, and came back to her. 'Will there be anything else, madam?'

Jessie started, and then looked up. 'No, nothing, thank you,' she said. 'Nothing at all.'